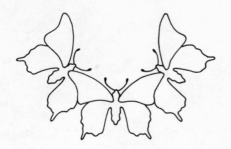

TRIPLETS

TRIPLETS

A NOVEL BY
Joyce Rebeta-Burditt

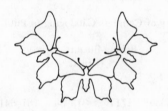

Delacorte Press/Seymour Lawrence

Published by
Delacorte Press/Seymour Lawrence
1 Dag Hammarskjold Plaza
New York, N.Y. 10017

Manufactured in the United States of America

First printing

Designed by Richard Oriolo

Library of Congress Cataloging in Publication Data

Rebeta-Burditt, Joyce
Triplets.

I. Title.
PS3568.E27T7   813'.54   81–5418
ISBN 0–440–08943–3   AACR2

FOR MY FAMILY

TRIPLETS

TRIPLETS

CHAPTER 1

Cleveland— 1977

"Your pa was a saint!" Kate Gallagher Dunn squared her small jaw and awaited a response from the handsome man and two attractive women sitting opposite her. Suddenly she trembled, and tears came to her eyes.

Alarmed, Julie leaned forward. "Pa didn't have a long illness, Ma. That's a blessing."

"He didn't suffer," John added. "That's a blessing, too."

"Some blessing," Jill murmured. "Trust Catholics to wring a blessing out of a man dropping dead in his prime!"

It was that most desolate of moments following a funeral. The secondary relatives had departed en masse, like extras in an epic, exhausted by the rituals of Mass, graveside benediction, and comforting words delivered in hushed tones over a dessert and coffee buffet at the home of the widow. Only the immediate family remained, sipping cold coffee and wondering what next, always a dilemma for those with no prior experience at being immediate family.

"You're not the one to speak of blessings," Kate snapped at Jill. "A woman who comes to her father's funeral and announces she's getting a divorce!"

"I didn't announce, Ma," Jill protested. "You asked why I came alone, and I told you. That's all."

"Well, it's a good thing your father didn't live to hear it. The shock would have killed him." Kate snapped her fingers. "Like that!"

"Every word of the eulogy was true," John said quickly, his preemptive tone indicating the right to speak for them all. "As Father Shaughnessy said, 'He was a man for all seasons, a man of his times, a man of the spirit, a man of the world.' . . . May I have Pa's overcoat, Ma?"

"His overcoat?" Kate was puzzled. "I should think you'd want his watch or his sword. You'd look so dashing wearing Pa's Knights of Columbus sword, John."

"I don't belong to the Knights, and I can't wear a sword to the office. What I'd like is Pa's coat."

"John's practical, like Pa." Julie smiled at her mother. "Besides, I'm the eldest, and I'd dearly love Pa's watch. I'll treasure it, Ma."

"Jill's the oldest, and she should have Pa's watch." Kate glared at Jill. "But she loses everything. Remember my garnet earrings?"

"The dog ate your earrings, that was twelve years ago, and I'm not the oldest." Jill shifted her rapidly numbing posterior, wiggling for a width of sofa without a lumpy protrusion.

"You're the one that hound followed home, and you must be the oldest." Kate frowned. "Aren't you?"

"No, Ma." Jill wondered how a woman who could rattle off the names of every saint in the liturgical calendar *and* their areas of expertise—martyr, virgin, bishop, prophet, tool-and-die maker— could forget the order in which she'd given birth, even to triplets. "Julie was first, then John, twenty-one minutes later, then me, nine minutes after that."

"Then, who was the breech?" Kate's eyes darted from one to the other, like Miss Marple hot on the trail of the culprit.

"Julie was first, and she was the breech," Jill replied.

"Ha! That's where I get confused. Being breech isn't like Julie. It's definitely something Jill would do." Kate shook her finger in the direction of Jill's nose. "You're involved with another man. Don't deny it!"

"I'll see what's keeping Candy in the kitchen." John leaped to his feet and hurried toward the kitchen. "Candy? Honey?"

"There. You've embarrassed your brother." Kate folded her arms, glaring at Jill. "I hope you're satisfied."

"I didn't bring up the subject, Ma," Jill said unhappily.

"Wasn't it a lovely funeral?" Julie said brightly. "The Mass, the music . . ."

"It was a mistake to have only desserts," Kate decided. "Next time I'll have sandwiches, maybe hot casseroles."

"The desserts were lovely." Julie was sincere. "The cakes, the tortes, that eight-layer—"

"Pah!" Kate interrupted. "It looked like a Pillsbury Bake-Off in here."

"But, the Knights of Columbus guard was impressive," Julie resumed, brightness undimmed.

2

"Pa cut such a splendid figure in his Knights uniform. Most men don't look manly in plumes. Pa . . . Pa . . ." Kate's lower lip trembled.

Julie blanched. "Perhaps Steve will reconsider the divorce," she said loudly. "He's always been such a reasonable man. Don't you think, Ma? Ma?"

"The divorce isn't Steve's idea," Jill said firmly. "It's a mutual decision."

"How can you possibly want to divorce Steve?" Julie asked. "He stood by you through your . . . uh . . . troubles. Not many men would do that."

"Steve was wonderful." Jill squirmed, uncomfortable with more than lumps in the sofa.

"I'll never forget the night Steve called and said you'd tried to kill yourself," Kate reminisced. "I was at your house in ten minutes. There you were, dripping blood and screaming like a banshee . . . and, that adorable little Daisy. Ah, it broke my heart."

Jill felt a familiar lurch of her stomach, like the beginning of morning sickness. "More coffee, Ma?"

"And your house! What a mess! Dishes unwashed, beds unmade—"

"Tea? Brandy? A muzzle?"

"Steve had you stashed in the hospital and was home again before I could get to the vacuuming." Kate shook her head.

"It doesn't seem right to expect a man to bear with the worst and then deprive him of the better," Julie clucked. "I could never do that to Fred."

"What makes you so certain your husband would bear with the worst?" Jill asked, wondering if Pa was somewhere in Heaven, livid at having lost center stage at his own funeral. "Go right upstairs now, interrupt Fred's phone call, and say, 'Fred darling, if some snowy night I should eat two pounds of Hershey's Kisses, then slash my wrists, would you hie me off to the loony bin? And having done that, would you then spend the next few months bringing me "worthwhile" reading and referring to my nervous breakdown as "a marvelous opportunity to stop smoking"?' "

"It's like you to make fun of Steve for having more concern for your welfare than you do," Kate said tartly.

"I wasn't making fun, Ma," Jill began, then stopped. She supposed she was, just a little, and she supposed she shouldn't, not at all. That belonged in the past, along with the . . . uh . . . troubles.

"You're still seeing a therapist, aren't you?" Julie asked.

"Well, yes. . . ."

3

"Good, that's sensible, considering . . . uh . . . What does he say about your divorce?"

"Well." Jill hesitated. If she told them the truth, that Dr. Kerry disapproved, they'd only pounce on his opinion. Jill didn't need such an impossibly stacked deck. Her slip-sliding stomach had been agreeing with Kerry for weeks. "If my life is to be the topic under discussion, perhaps you'd like to hear about my new job?"

"Job?" Kate looked dubious. "You've never worked."

"I do now." Jill smiled. "Starting next week I'll be reading scripts for Marshall Productions."

"Reading?" Kate asked "Somebody's paying you to *read*? What kind of a job is that?"

"It's a fine job for Jill." Julie was pleased. "It isn't too taxing."

"It's something I can do and my boss, Dan Carmichael—"

"Aha!" Kate's finger was poised for shaking. "He's the boyfriend!"

"Dan Carmichael is a happily married man," Jill said sharply. "He's well respected in his business, and I'm lucky to be working with him."

"If you're determined to go through with the divorce, I should think you'd move back to Cleveland," Kate said. "Los Angeles is no place to raise a young daughter. It's wall-to-wall nudists playing volleyball with everything jiggling. I saw it on the Channel Ten News."

"Everyone in my neighborhood wears clothes, Ma." Jill smiled. "And I'd never take Daisy that far from her father. At twelve every girl's poppa is Prince Charming."

"Poor Daisy." Kate sighed. "Torn between mother and father."

"We're not tearing Daisy, Ma." Jill twitched; the backs of her knees felt warm and prickly. "There's no hint of a need for her to choose sides, no sly little digs or bedroom secrets. . . ."

"Lucky for you!" Kate snorted. "Well, all I can say is . . . is . . ." Whatever Kate was going to say was lost as her eyes drifted to a gold-framed picture of Pa, taken the night he was elected president of the Kiwanis.

Julie glanced nervously at Jill. "If Jill's about to become a working mother, she'll have to get organized." Julie paused, then raised her voice. "Won't she, Ma?"

There was no response from Kate.

"Won't she, Ma?" It was close to a shriek. "Ma!"

"What?" Kate shook herself out of her drift.

"Jill will get organized."

4

"And my roses will bloom for Christmas," Kate scoffed.

"Organization isn't that difficult." Julie smiled her relief. "All she needs is a schedule." Julie glanced at Jill. "What's wrong? What are you doing?"

"Scratching."

"Why?"

"I'm itching."

"Why?"

"I don't know!" Jill dug at the backs of knees that were burning hot and as lumpy as Kate's sofa.

"Change your brand of pantyhose," Julie advised. "Or your soap. Or your body lotion."

"It's hives, not an allergy, Julie, and I don't use body lotion. It makes me feel hermetically sealed."

"You never had hives when you were married," Kate said sagely. "Or when you weren't working."

"Julie works." Jill scratched furiously. "She doesn't have hives."

"*I* have a schedule." Julie smiled. "With a schedule there's no reason for anxiety. It's simple. Just get a large bulletin board and glue on seven rows of manila envelopes, one row for each day of the week."

"Is there any ice in that bucket, Ma?" Jill pointed.

Kate looked. "Melted. There's none in the kitchen, either. Next time I won't have fruit punch. I'll have brandy Alexanders and to hell with the bluenose cousins."

"Under each major envelope you glue as many subenvelopes as your activities require," Julie continued. "For instance, under *Home* I have all domestic duties—washing, ironing, cleaning, cooking, et cetera—listed in rotating order. Under *Work* I have a schedule of the classes I teach, with subenvelopes for class assignments, preparation time, testing periods, project-planning, research, et cetera. Under *Children* I list Morgan and Kendrick, with subenvelopes for their music lessons, dental and doctor appointments, work and play. Then there's *Community* and *Church,* both with—"

"Sounds very efficient," Jill interrupted. "But I'd make a note to buy the bulletin board and then lose the note."

"You can't possibly manage without Steve," Kate said flatly. "What if you go crazy again?"

"I'll take a cab to the loony bin, Ma, or one of those tour buses so I can see movie stars' homes on the way." Jill shuddered. Kate's question had pounded through her recent nightmares and was one Dr. Kerry asked frequently, usually while recommending that she increase her weekly appointments from once a week to at least twice.

"I wish you'd move back to Cleveland," Kate said wistfully. "Julie, too. Chicago is so far away."

"John lives in Cleveland, Ma," Julie said cheerfully. "That should be a great comfort."

"I wish. . . ." Kate's gaze drifted to a picture of Pa taken the night he was elected president of the Junior Chamber of Commerce. "I wish you were all babies again, and Pa . . . Pa . . ."

The tears came before Julie could divert Kate with a shouted question. They flowed unchecked down Kate's cheeks, filling the fine lines around her nose and running, unnoticed, into her partly opened mouth.

"Weren't the flowers beauti . . ." Julie trailed off. It was too late. "I'd better see what's keeping Fred." Julie's leap was a ladylike version of John's. In ten seconds she was halfway up the stairs, calling, "Fred? Honey?"

For endless minutes Jill sat opposite her mother, longing to do more than keep silent company to Kate's wordless grief. But what could she say? All the comforting words had been said. The echoes of them draped the room like paper festoons left after a party. Jill sighed, wishing she possessed Julie's ability to move ever forward in an orderly manner or John's effective pragmatism, his facility for removing himself from situations he'd correctly analyzed as having nothing to do with him. No runners in circles, they.

They are the movers and shakers. I, the movee and shook-up.

Kate wept on, her mute grief more disturbing than wails would have been.

Slowly Jill rose from the couch and walked to the sideboard, where the brandy was kept. She poured a small amount into a cranberry glass and offered it to Kate. When Kate failed to respond, Jill wrapped Kate's fingers securely around the stem.

"Drink this, Ma," Jill said softly, and sat on the couch close to Kate. She waited until Kate had taken a sip, then reached for her hand and gently began stroking it. It was all she could think to do. They sat side by side for what seemed like a very long time, Kate sipping and Jill stroking in long, smooth rhythms interspersed with soft pats.

Neither had spoken when Candy, who epitomized her name with taffy hair, strawberry lips and a delicious figure, emerged from the kitchen drying her hands on a towel. "All spic and span," she chirped, then noticed Kate's tears. "Oh, Mother Dunn."

Candy knelt on the floor next to Kate. "You go ahead and cry. Get it all out of your system."

"A daughter's divorce is not something you get out of your system," Kate snapped. "A daughter's divorce is a knife in her mother's heart."

"Divorce!" Jill dropped Kate's hand. "I thought you were crying about Pa!"

"Pa wouldn't want me to cry," Kate asserted. "Pa would want me to carry on. I am carrying on, not crying."

"Who's crying? Ma, are you crying?" John asked from the doorway. He saw the tears glistening on Kate's cheeks. "I'll go find Julie and Fred."

"What is this with everyone running off to find someone else?" Kate demanded. "You're too old to play hide and seek. Sit."

John sat. "I filled out Pa's insurance forms for you, Ma. I'll put them in the mail at the office tomorrow."

Candy smiled sympathetically at Jill. "You must feel just terrible about your divorce."

"I don't think I'm allowed," Jill said ruefully.

"Uh . . ." John cleared his throat. "I've been thinking about joining the Knights of Columbus."

"That's wonderful, John!" Kate exclaimed. "Your father would like that."

"And maybe the Kiwanis and Junior Chamber," John added. "Businessmen should. The contacts you make can be invaluable."

"Your father used to say that," Kate said approvingly.

"I'm asking for a transfer to our new computer division. If I get the transfer, it means a promotion, so . . . I thought . . ." John's hands gripped the well-worn arms of his father's easy chair. "Where's Pa's coat?"

"In the hall closet," Kate told him. "Where else would it be?"

"Thanks, Ma." John catapulted from the chair and disappeared down the hallway.

"Coat?" Candy asked.

"John wants Pa's coat," Kate shrugged. "The watch keeps perfect time, and the sword could slice stucco, but he wants the coat."

"You mean the coat Pa wore for seventeen years?" Candy was baffled. "It's older than both our daughters put together."

Kate bristled. "Pa's coat was custom-tailored, very expensive. Besides, Pa didn't like changes. Look at the furniture." Kate scanned the living room. "Colonial would look good in here, maybe prints on the chairs and the sofa in velvet."

"Ma!" A glowing Julie walked into the room followed by a tall, sandy-haired man upholstered in tweed. "Fred's had excellent news. I know it'll cheer you up. It did me."

"You're moving back to Cleveland!" Kate's eyes gleamed.

"No, Mother Dunn." Fred paled at the thought. "I've just spoken to Dean Harvey on the phone, and he informs me that I've been appointed chairman of the biochem department."

"That really makes my day." Kate set her glass on the coffee table. "Light maple tables would look nice with Colonial. I'm tired of all this dark oak."

"Though this appointment is an honor, it's hardly a surprise." Fred chuckled, a sound like a billy goat strangling. "As far back as Choate, then later at Princeton, I was preparing for—" Fred glanced at the assembled Dunns, none of whom seemed to be listening. "I may as well be on Easter Island, talking to the statues."

Julie squeezed his arm. "I'm so very proud of you, Fred."

Fred gazed at her fondly. "Of course, Julie, your responsibilities as faculty wife will increase commensurately."

"It's just another envelope on the bulletin board, Fred." Julie smiled adoringly. "Minor adjustments here and there."

"Maybe earth tones," Kate mused, turning to Jill. "What would you think of beige and brown with just a touch of rust?"

"For what, Ma?" Jill blinked.

"It's a good thing you have a job reading." Kate glared. "No one would pay you to listen."

"Jill has a job?" Candy was astonished.

"I'll be reading scripts for Marshall Productions," Jill told her.

"Like for television?" Candy asked, blue eyes sparkling.

"Yes."

"That's *wonderful!*" Candy was impressed. "You'll know before anyone else what's going to happen on television shows."

"Possibly. I'm not certain. I haven't started the job yet."

"If you find out what's going to happen on *Goldfarb's Girls*, please let me know. It's my favorite show!"

"Cross my heart." Jill smiled. "I'll send Mailgrams."

Candy sighed. "I don't know how those Goldfarb's Girls do it, always chasing crooks and never a hair out of place. And their figures —oh, my! If I hadn't had two children . . . well, John would kill me if I went braless."

"Braless!" Julie clucked disapproval. "And you wonder why we don't let our children watch television."

"The vast wasteland grows ever more bleak," Fred intoned. "A soporific for the illiterate masses."

"Come again?" Candy frowned.

Pompous ass, Jill thought, hoping Candy's feelings hadn't been hurt. She glanced in Candy's direction, then stifled a gasp.

John had quietly entered the room and was standing alone off to one side. Wrapped in Pa's overcoat, which he'd buttoned to the neck, he was the shadow-ghost of Pa, an image modified only by time and a subtle difference, a certain . . .

Pa was not a saint. Pa was . . . dark corners.

Jill stared, then looked around her, expecting an equally strong collective reaction. Everyone seemed occupied, oblivious to John. John himself appeared preoccupied, hands jammed deep in coat pockets, eyes on the floor and lips moving, as though he was debating himself or rehearsing a speech.

An overwhelming urgency compelled Jill toward Kate, who had wandered to the windows and was lost in contemplation of the draperies.

"Ma." Jill nudged her, convinced that Kate would see in John what she saw, would experience the same urgency to talk about Pa, *now,* before it was too late.

Too late?

"Ma." This nudge was more of a poke. "Look at John."

Kate looked, a long, heart-stopping moment. "John's right. The coat fits." She shook a fistful of drape under Jill's nose. "Print or plain?"

"Ma, don't you see . . ."

"Jill," John called, "may I see you and Julie in the kitchen?"

"Certainly." Julie smiled her faculty-tea how-may-I-serve-you? smile. She followed John to the kitchen as Jill trotted after them.

"As you know," John began, "I'm negotiating for a transfer to our computer division."

"Solid move," Julie said approvingly. "Computers are undeniably the future."

"Yes, well," John continued, "my preliminary interview is tomor-

9

row. I've filled out the necessary forms, background, personal data, and I . . . I've taken the liberty of . . . of . . ." John straightened, took a deep breath, and regarded them levelly. "I've listed myself as a single birth, with the two of you as my twin sisters."

"Why?" Jill demanded, astonished. "How can you do that?"

"Now, wait. Let me explain." John frowned. "This is a conservative corporation looking for employees who will fit their conservative corporate image, not people whose background is singular and bizarre. . . ."

"Who's bizarre?" Jill asked. "I don't understand how being one of triplets can—"

"I understand," Julie interrupted. "Believe me, Jill, on those rare occasions when I've mentioned the circumstances of our birth, well, between the raised eyebrows and the snide remarks . . ."

"It's freakish," John stated flatly. "And I can't afford it."

"Afford? How can you not afford the truth?" Jill protested. "There's nothing freakish about us. You make it sound like we're joined at the hip."

"You are not a businessperson, Jill." John's tone was patronizing. "You wouldn't understand."

"But—"

John placed a placating hand on her arm. "I've made myself a year older, Jilsy. Haven't you always wanted an older brother?"

"Never." Jill shook her head.

"Well, I have." Julie kissed John's cheek. "Your little deception is safe with me, dear."

"Then, it's settled." John rocked on his heels, pleased. Then a slight, puzzled frown creased his forehead as he pulled an object from Pa's coat pocket. "What's this?"

They gathered around him, one on each side.

"Why, it's an old picture of Pa," Julie said. "It must have been taken on the steps of a museum or library. See the stone gargoyles in the background."

"Pa never wore caps." John's frown deepened.

"He must have at one time." Julie smiled. "It's there in the picture."

John shivered, then thrust the picture at Jill. "Give this to Ma."

Abruptly he linked arms with Julie, and together they left the kitchen.

Jill looked after them, then at the photograph. Obviously it had

10

been taken when Pa was John's age, perhaps younger. The edges were yellowed, and it was faded.

Still, it was Pa—Pa's face, Pa's eyes and hair beneath a cap. Pa never wore caps.

Jill looked from the picture in her hand to the closed kitchen door. The photograph was a shadow-ghost of Pa in the same way Johnny . . . a shadow-ghost. . . .

Idly Jill turned the picture over. On the back of Pa's picture, written in Pa's hand, was a name—Joseph.

Jill returned to the living room, the picture secreted in her pocket. She'd keep it to herself . . . because . . . because . . .

Dark corners.

"Johnny, guess what?" Candy was saying. "Jill has a job."

"She has?" John was surprised.

Candy jiggled John's elbow like a little girl tugging at her daddy's sleeve. "If I had a job . . ."

"You have a job, sweetheart, taking care of the kids." John smiled benevolently. "Don't worry about money. My transfer will mean a substantial raise."

"If you say so, but—"

"My God!" John exclaimed, looking at his watch. "We'll never get Fred and Julie to the airport on time."

"Airport?" Kate quavered.

"I've calculated the time." Fred remained calm. "We have precisely—"

"Bagley Road is closed for repairs, Fred," John informed him. "We'll have to take a detour."

"Oh, no!" Fred had the look of a man betrayed. "I'll get our coats." He ran for the closet.

"What will I do at five o'clock?" Kate blurted, bewildered by the sudden activity.

"I'll call you often, Ma." Julie hugged Kate fiercely, her face distraught. "You call me, too. Oh, Ma!"

"I always start Pa's dinner at five o'clock." Kate's voice was high and strained. "Thirty-four years. Five on the dot."

"Bye, Ma." Julie turned quickly and fled out the door, closely followed by Fred.

"Candy, hurry," John urged from the doorway. "I'll call you tomorrow, Ma."

"My heart is pounding." Kate's hand flew to her chest. "My heart

11

is leaping!" The front door slammed with a crack like a rifle shot. Kate went dead white. "I'm having a heart attack!"

"Ma!" Jill rushed to her. "Don't. Please. Lie down. Here." Panicked, Jill eased Kate onto the sofa. Kate's body felt stiff, almost cold.

"I'm going to die on this ratty old sofa," Kate moaned. "No deathbed. No loved ones. No priest! Mother of God, where are my children!"

Jill hovered above her. "Please don't die, Ma. What can I do?"

With both hands clutching her chest Kate opened eyes fiery with exasperation. "Anyone with half a brain would have called an ambulance by now."

"Right." Jill dashed for the phone.

Kate raised herself on one elbow. "Tell them Bagley Road is closed. Tell them they should come by way of Brookpark. . . . Jill . . . listen to your mother . . . Jill?"

CHAPTER 2

Los Angeles—1980

"Damn!"

Jill Dunn Kenyon glanced nervously at the floor indicator in the interminably rising elevator and kicked the nearest wall.

"Damn, I could go into menopause on this elevator!"

She was late, by her watch almost an hour, and inching upward in this Sunset Boulevard elevator, designed with Muzak and mirrors to resemble a piano bar, made her feel strangled and furious.

"Now! Now! Now!" Jill demanded through clenched teeth while Mr. Muzak, that old smoothie, assured her, "You Light Up My Life."

Being late was her own fault, a fact that only heightened her anger. She was a fool for scheduling a supposedly therapeutic appointment with Dr. Kerry for a time that overlapped with her very first programing meeting in the very first week of her new job. She kicked the wall again, deriving as much satisfaction from the ache in her toe as from the solid *thud* it produced.

She'd left Dr. Kerry's office at a dead run, then driven recklessly, careening around corners with fingers crossed on the wheel and one eye on the sky, searching for fire copters. According to radio bulletins, the Santa Anas, those maverick winds that blow in off the desert like a belch from a blast furnace, had fanned three separate fires in tinder-dry Los Angeles.

The elevator lurched and shuddered. Jill clutched the wall, her heart accelerating into a full, flying flamenco. She felt a familiar itching begin on the backs of her knees. "Damn Dr. Kerry! Talk, talk, talk, and I still have the hives!"

Still, when Kerry wasn't asking breathless questions about the men in her life, or how she felt about leaving the security of a small movie production company for "the larger arena of a television network," there was a technique or two he'd taught her which actually helped. For instance, deep breathing.

What the hell! I'll try it.

She gave up trying to punt the elevator, closed her eyes, and as the elevator doors slithered silently open, inhaled deeply to a count of six.

"Jill Kenyon!"

Jill's eyes popped open. A foot away two men in the hall were staring at her.

"Oh, hi." Jill pulled her what-a-pleasant-surprise smile out of her pocket and stepped off the elevator.

"So nice to see you again." The shorter man smiled. "My client here just sold a show to your boss, Dan Carmichael."

"Wonderful," Jill said, peering closely at him. He obviously recognized her, but from where?

His name! His name!

She tried a quick series of mental connections, mental associations —short, elf-faced, bald, ears like sugarbowl handles—but the only name that flashed through her mind was Elmer Fudd.

"You'll love the show," he enthused. "It's like *Three's Company*, only instead of two girls and a man living together, it's two men and a girl. Innovative, huh? Hey, have you and Howard met?"

Jill held her breath. *Have we?*

"We haven't met." The taller man smiled. "I'm Howard Lawler."

"Hello." Jill shook hands, determined to remember his name. She pictured him as carrying a briefcase and backing away from an attack by an infant.

Howard Lawler. Coward Lawyer. Howard Lawler. Got it.

"Jill is the new director of movies and miniseries," Fudd explained. "She'll be Carmichael's right-hand man . . . er . . . woman . . . er . . . person." He arched an eyebrow at Lawler. "They work *closely* together."

The tall one smiled, neglecting to release Jill's hand. "I see."

See what?

"Well, good luck with your project." Jill tugged her hand loose and backed away. "It was nice meeting you . . . uh . . ." *Noel Coward . . . Leslie Howard . . . Howard Coward . . . shit! Gone already. God!*

"My pleasure," whoever it was said as Fuddy nodded, grinning like a Kewpie doll.

Jill turned, stumbled, and dropped her purse. Behind her the men stepped into the elevator.

"Attractive woman," one said. "Who's she fucking?"

14

The other man laughed, a nasty, humorless sound. "Are you kidding? Why do you think Carmichael hired—" The rest was lost in the closing of elevator doors.

Creeps!

Jill scooped up her purse and ran. She steamed down the hall past the mailroom, and several secretaries who didn't seem surprised to see her making like O.J. in the gray-flannel halls.

Stop! Running through the halls is not the corporate way.

She slowed to a more dignified pace, then pictured Dan glowering at his watch as the meeting began without her. She ran faster.

Seconds later she arrived, red-faced, panting, and perspiring, at the door of her outer office. An attractive thirtyish lady at the secretary's desk looked up smiling.

"Hi. I'm Polly Pritzer, and you must be . . . Oh, dear . . . are you all right?"

"Fine, wonderful, I'm dying. Oh, God." Jill sank into a chair.

Polly hurried around the desk. "Is there anything I can do?"

"No," Jill gasped. "I'll be all right in a minute. Are you my permanent secretary? Please say you are. I've had three in five days. One went to lunch, got married, and never came back."

"I'm permanent, if it works out," Polly said. "At the moment I'm temporarily assigned to this office."

"That's something we may have in common." Jill was breathing more easily now. "I feel like Alice, tumbling head-over-rabbit into Wonderland."

"An apt description of UBC," Polly grinned. "Your boss, Dan Carmichael—"

"Dan!" Jill leaped to her feet. "I'm late for a meeting!"

"Whoa, whoa." Polly held out a restraining arm. "Carmichael called ten minutes ago. He said you are to catch your breath first— *then* proceed to the meeting. They won't be discussing movies for at least an hour." Polly opened eyes that danced with amusement. "Carmichael seemed very certain that you'd need time to catch your breath."

"I worked for Dan at Marshall Productions. In nearly two years I had a total of nine days when I didn't need to catch my breath." Jill shrugged. "Dan says that being organized would ruin my style. What style, I'd like to know?"

"Carmichael must know, or you wouldn't be here." Polly smiled.

"Then I wish he'd explain it to my family." Jill sighed. "When I

15

called my mother to tell her about this job, she said, *'Now you'll have to get organized!'* "

"Not 'congratulations'?" Polly frowned.

"My sister sent me a sample schedule printed on graph paper in four colors. Reading it made me dizzy."

"*Still* no congratulations?" Polly's frown deepened.

"My brother sent me flowers with a business card announcing his latest promotion. I'm sure *that* was meant as congratulations." Jill didn't sound sure at all.

"However it was meant, just relax," Polly advised. "Carmichael is on your side, and—"

The phone rang, startling Jill.

"Jill Kenyon's office," Polly answered smoothly. "Just a moment." She covered the receiver with her hand. "It's your daughter."

"Something's wrong!" Jill reached for the phone, yelling, "Daisy, what's wrong?"

"Cramps and a headache are bad enough, Mom." Daisy's voice was debilitated, un-Daisy-like. "I don't need shrieking in my ear."

"Oh, you poor thing." Jill sympathized. "Are you at home?"

"That's why I called, Mom." Daisy sighed. "You made me cross my heart."

"It's a prudent agreement, Daisy. If you ever go home from school sick, and I don't know about it—"

"I know, Mom." Daisy recited in a patient monotone, "The big earthquake will strike and you'll be at school, digging through the rubble—"

"Don't scoff, Daisy. It could happen." Jill frowned at the phone. "Do you have aspirin, honey, a heating pad, tea—"

"I have everything I need, Mom. May I go lie down now?"

"Sure, honey, and listen. I'll bring pizza tonight. Maybe a salad?"

"Mo-om!"

"Okay, okay. You don't want to hear about dinner now. I understand. You just go to bed, and I'll be home as soon as I can." Jill said quickly, "Call me if it gets worse."

"Don't worry, Mom. It's only cramps, not the plague." Daisy sighed with the relief of one who's done her duty and can now do as she pleases. "Bye."

"Daisy! Daisy!" Jill called, but Daisy was gone. "Rats! I wanted to tell her to take a hot bath. That usually helps."

"Lately I jog," Polly told her.

16

"You what?"

"When I have cramps, I jog."

"Wonderful." Jill groaned. "I need to be surrounded by stoics. I couldn't jog if I was being chased by hired assassins."

"Take your phone messages with you." Polly stuffed several slips of paper into Jill's pocket. "When your meeting is over you can show me where everything is. I think your filing system was based on the *I Ching*."

"Wish me luck." Jill waved at Polly and stepped into the hallway leading to the massive double doors that separated UBC's top executives from the contamination of its messy masses.

Come the revolution, everyone will have double doors!

Jill paused at the door to the conference room, crossed her fingers, then opened the door and entered, eyes wide.

The conference room was just as Dan had described it, only infinitely larger and more intimidating, as were the executives sitting around the polished mahogany table, some twenty-six in all.

Fifty-two eyes turned toward Jill as she slunk through the door. They followed her mortified progress as she rounded the mile-long table, heading for the empty chair next to Dan's. The chair beckoned her, glimmering miragelike in the hazy distance.

An eternity later Jill slipped into the seat next to Dan's. She leaned toward him, guilt compelling her to excuse herself. "Sorry I'm late. Out of gas. Freeway."

Carmichael glanced at her; by the glint of his eye, both wise and amused. "Bullshit. Shrink appointment. Relax."

Jill grinned, far from relaxed, but on firmer footing. UBC might be foreign and frightening terrain, but Dan was territory as familiar and comfortable as her backyard. She should have known better than to fib to him. She should have known better than to think he'd buy it.

"If everyone who had more important things to do—and may do them elsewhere in the future—is in her seat, we'll continue the meeting," Dale Neiman said in a silky purr. Jill felt him looking at her and scrunched down in her seat, leaning instinctively toward Dan, as one with a chill would lean toward a fire.

Yesterday Dan had briefly introduced her to Neiman, whom he'd later characterized as "Senior Vice-President and Chief of Mediocrity, a man whose delusion of adequacy is exceeded only by his delusions of sexual attractiveness to women."

And indeed Neiman had clasped Jill's hand in his sweaty little paw, then fixed her with a look intended to be soulful, but which had slurped over her, pegging him as a sticky cross between a lascivious wimp and a wet-eyed weasel. When she'd asked Dan how Neiman had become senior vice-president of everything that wasn't nailed down, Dan had replied that Neiman had been at UBC since its inception and knew where the bodies were buried . . . had himself planted a few. "Welcome to the 'larger arena,' " Dan had winked.

"Next on the agenda is *Man from Quasar,*" Neiman hummed, peering down the length of the table. "Ken?"

At the far end of the table an extremely tall, painfully thin young man, himself new to the company, twitched and flushed, an unfortunate combination that gave him the look of a nervous flamingo. "In this week's episode"—his voice cracked—"the Man from Quasar falls into a volcano that is actually the underground headquarters of the archvillain, Crench." Ken gulped, glancing at Neiman.

"Sounds like *Goldfinger,*" Neiman said, with a sly little smile.

Ken opened his mouth to speak, but only a gurgle came out. He tried again, voice cracking: "Quasar encounters an army of monsters whom Crench has constructed from parts of animals and people he's trapped in his volcano."

"Sounds like *Island of Dr. Moreau,*" Neiman cooed at the trembling newcomer. "Ah well, continue. I'll suffer through."

Now that everyone's attention was focused on the unfortunate Ken, Jill allowed herself surreptitious peeps and glances the length and width of the conference table. Again, Dan's wry descriptions provided a running mental commentary on what she saw around her. Though twenty-six separate bodies occupied the plush club chairs, the executives in them were divided into two easily distinguishable groups.

On one side sat the L.A. people, mostly tan, mostly trim, casually sprawled in poses copied from *Using Body Language to Intimidate the Shit out of Anyone, Anytime,* staring with mellow superiority at their New York counterparts, whom they viewed as uncreative, uptight assholes who spent their days in bureaucratic nondecision and the strict avoidance of any thought, word, or deed that would put their precious corporate tushies on the line.

Opposite them resided the New York people, gray-suited, with complexions to match, sitting stiffly with legs crossed and sphincters compressed to the jugular, staring with contempt at those they called the "L.A. whackos," who would, unless constantly restrained, drive

UBC into bankruptcy with "creative" ideas that cost millions and were usually so dreadful that airing them was out of the question and watching them in company screening rooms was commonly thought to cause stroke, cancer, and the loss of body hair.

At the head of the table sat UBC's recently appointed president, Teddy Lawrence, whose hiring had been accomplished under circumstances so unusual that no background briefing from Dan was necessary. Along with the rest of the country Jill had read it in the newspapers.

Lawrence was not a career network executive. Lawrence was an astronaut.

During the heyday of America's space program he'd been selected as NASA's first man on Mars and begun the rigorous training designed to place him on that planet's surface within a projected five years.

However, the following five years saw the first space program failures and escalating Vietnam involvement, unforeseen factors leading to massive NASA budget cuts, and diminished interest in the conquest of space. While all but the obsessively star-struck admitted that the program had been unofficially scrapped, NASA hung on to Man on Mars, its dwindling budget, and Lawrence, who continued to train.

Then, in a series of events still shrouded in mystery, Lawrence had checked into the Mayo Clinic for unspecified treatment of an undisclosed ailment. There he'd met Henry Gregg, UBC's elderly chairman, who maintained a suite at the Mayo. Ten days later Lawrence resigned from NASA, and UBC had a new leader.

Having been dubbed by Gregg as "the greatest television mind of our time," Lawrence arrived at UBC amid pomp, circumstance, skepticism and envy . . . in short, a reception akin to that accorded Julius Caesar on the Ides of March. Lawrence had taken no notice. Like Santa Claus, he went straight to his work.

Now, a scant two months later, Lawrence was securely ensconced and referring to those who hissed and scratched across the Great Divide of his conference table, as "My Team."

Though Lawrence sat at the head of the table, he was turned away from it, apparently oblivious to everything except a huge freestanding blackboard placed to his left. On the blackboard was written the entire prime-time schedule of all four networks in columns divided into nights of the week and time periods. With his long, thin face propped up in one hand, Lawrence stared entranced, as though the board was the Rosetta Stone and he a wandering metaphysician determined to decipher its secret.

"At the end of this episode there's a really neat explosion," Ken said, trying for a big finish, "with heads and manes, arms and tails flying everywhere."

Neiman made a face. "Sounds like something I wouldn't want to see on an empty stomach. Any girls in this episode?"

Ken glanced at the report in his hands. "Uh . . . no."

"Forget the girls," Lawrence said, his eyes on the board. "Just tell them to make the hero likable. In the last episode I rooted for the archvillain, Crench." Lawrence rose from his chair, walked to the board, and picked up an eraser. There was a collective intake of breath as Lawrence erased something, his body blocking the table's view of the board. No one exhaled. What was he doing? Whose show was he canceling? Whose job was on the line? They waited endless seconds. The only sound in the room was that of chalk against blackboard as Lawrence filled the empty space. With what? Whose show? Whose possible promotion? Some of the New York people appeared to be turning blue.

Lawrence turned and noticed everyone staring at him.

"The jerk who wrote this board misspelled *Freak People*." He shrugged. "I fixed it."

A strong, stale breeze blew through the room, as everyone exhaled at once. One of the New York people sputtered, choking, and was pounded on the back by the man sitting next to him.

"What the hell's the matter with you people?" Lawrence seemed genuinely puzzled. There was silence.

From the middle of the table the mellifluous voice of a born FM announcer said, "There's nothing wrong, sir. I'm sure I speak for everyone when I say there's unanimous support for the position you've taken on correct spelling."

The voice was that of L. B. Fontaine, late of CBS, NBC, ABC, PBS, now of UBC, and determined to stay. Behind his back, he was referred to as "Syco" Fontaine.

"And we will continue to support that position," Fontaine added, but Lawrence was already lost in the board.

"Have we finished *Man from Quasar*?" Neiman asked.

"Not quite," Ken replied, sounding as though he wished they had.

20

"Uh . . . the star of the show hasn't reported to work for three days. He says his back hurts, but the producers told me—"

"Shit!" Neiman barked. "You were droning on about exploding volcanoes, and the star of the show is . . . you imbecile! Of all the— What the hell do you want?" His secretary, Shirley, had materialized at his elbow and was trying to thrust a message into his hands. "This better be important." Neiman snatched the message from her, scanned it, and announced, "Laurel Canyon is on fire. Does anyone care?"

"Jesus Christ! My house!" Ken leaped to his feet and ran to the door. He was gone before the report he'd been holding fluttered to the floor.

"Now, what the hell are we going to do about *Man from Quasar?*" Neiman demanded. "We don't even know what the goddamned producers told him."

"I have an idea, darling." It was Angela Kent, according to Dan's briefing, the Vice-President of Casting and reigning Mother Superior of UBC, a lady whose legendary attributes included a knack for well-timed swooning. When crossed, which seldom happened, Angela would shriek "I'm going, I'm going!" and fall to the floor in a faint or a fit, only God and Angela knew. The paramedics summoned on each occasion would arrive, sirens screaming and oxygen tanks at the ready, to be rewarded eventually by Angela's fluttering eyelids and a "Thank you, darlings. I thought I was GONE." Angela would then return to whatever dispute her going had interrupted, seemingly energized, a benefit not shared by those she confronted, who usually allowed her to have her own way rather than risk a repeat performance. Angela was always going, but Angela never went.

Now she was peeping coyly at Neiman from behind the raven wings of her Ann Miller hairdo. "I think we should recast the hero of *Quasar* with a real star like Jim Arness."

"Isn't Arness, well, a little long in the tooth?" Neiman frowned.

"He's *my* age." Angela glared, then began fanning herself furiously. "Is anyone else warm? It's suddenly stifling in here."

Neiman blinked rapidly. "Arness is a wonderful idea, Angela. Call his agent. You're brilliant."

"Thank you, darling." Angela beamed, and ceased fanning.

"Next on the agenda— What do you want now?" Neiman scowled at Shirley, who'd arrived with another message. Reluctantly Neiman read it out loud: "Point Dume is on fire."

Fontaine leaped to his feet and ran to the door. "My house! My house!"

"What's wrong with this place?" Neiman demanded. "Everything's burning down. This would never happen in New York." His eyes gleamed. "Point Dume! What a wonderful name for the underground headquarters of Crench. I'll call the *Man from Quasar* people!"

"Wait, Dale!" one of the gray New York people called out to him. "Before we take a break, I think we should discuss the bomb threat."

"What bomb threat?" Neiman's face went from purple to fish-belly white.

The gray man raised his hand in a calming gesture. "Now, now, don't get excited. We've kept it under wraps for a couple of weeks, but now"—he shrugged—"the legal department has received its third message, a cut-and-paste job with phrases cut from *The New York Times* and glued to the back of a guava jelly label—"

"What the hell does the guy want?" Neiman yelled.

"He's threatened to blow up UBC unless we take *Freak People* off the air," the gray man explained.

"Has anyone notified the police?" Dan asked.

"Goddammit, no!" Neiman shouted. "That's all we'd need. We'd have news people swarming all over us, including our own."

"Hire him," said a voice, accompanied by a soft giggle.

"What?" Neiman, along with the rest of the table, stared at Zippy de Franco, a dreamy-eyed, blond young man slouched in a chair on the L.A. side.

"Hire him." Zippy repeated both suggestion and giggle. "Give this Mad Bomber guy a job. He's obviously some kind of anti-establishment radical, so bring him into the establishment. People don't blow up systems that get them their goodies."

"That's the *worst* goddamned idea—" Neiman began.

"Highly creative," Lawrence interjected, his eyes glued to the board. "*My* kind of idea."

"And one that certainly merits further discussion," Neiman agreed quickly. "*Now* what the hell is it?" Once again Shirley was at his elbow, holding another message slip. "If anything else is on fire, I don't want to hear about it, unless it's this building." He glanced at the message. "Oh, shit! The guy who plays Crench has just been arrested for beating up his lover." He reread the message. "*Lover!* An L.A.P.D. motorcycle cop! Christ, wait'll this hits the papers!"

Neiman ran for the door. "I'll call the producer! I'll invoke the morals clause! I'll . . . why does everything happen to me!" The door slammed behind him.

Chairs scraped against burnt-orange shag carpeting as people rose, stretched, and began gathering in tight, cliquey circles to discuss the Mad Bomber, Crench's unfortunate predilections, and the ramifications of both.

Jill lit a cigarette and sat back in her chair. Dan had disappeared in the first wave of rising and stretching, and she certainly wasn't about to join one of the groups without him.

Zippy de Franco slipped into the seat next to hers.

"Hi. I'm Zippy de Franco, and you're Carmichael's girl. Want some *zoom* pills?" He held out a small bottle, half-full of round, brown lumps. "Guarana root. An organic high."

"Uh . . . no, thanks," Jill said, wondering if this was a standard network introduction.

Zippy leaned closer and whispered. "Maybe you're into the white stuff, you know. . . ." He sniffed elaborately.

"God *no!*" Jill leaned away.

"Just trying to be friendly." Zippy looked genuinely crestfallen.

Jill stared at him, wishing Dan's network briefing had extended to the etiquette involved in declining hard drugs. "Thanks for the offer, Zippy, but I'm one of those people who's allergic to everything. Even aspirins. Even vitamins. Once I went into shock from a placebo. Sorry."

"That's cool." Zippy slipped the bottle into his pocket and got up. "Too bad, though. Goin' through life straight's a bummer. Big B."

Jill watched as Zippy jittered his way across the room, joining a small, tight circle which automatically opened to accept him.

Jill wondered if her explanation had been plausible, or more to the point, socially acceptable. Plausible or not, it was true. Her reaction to drugs of any kind was so unpredictable that even during her days in the psychiatric ward her doctor had prescribed only vitamins, and then watched carefully for adverse reactions.

"Something screwed-up in your chemistry," the doctor had said, and Jill nodded, not in the least surprised. Like being breech, it seemed like something she would do.

Jill sighed, wishing she possessed the nerve required for a solo foray into the larger arena. This was much like the first day at a new school, with the cliques, the chatter, the backs turned in exclusion, only in this arena there wasn't even the solace of a jungle gym to climb.

She reached in her pocket, grateful for the messages foresighted Polly had stuffed in her pocket. Reading them would give her something to do. She picked one at random.

Just like a lottery. And the winner is:

Nick Anders.

Oh, my God! I forgot to call him. He'll be hurt. He'll be wounded. When I call him he'll accuse me of causing his writer's block, his nasal congestion and his dog's distemper. But call him I will. Besides being impossible, Nick is cute, cuddly, warm, and a gorgeous lover. What's a little irascibility now and then?

I'll call him for a date, Jill decided, wondering if a suggestion that they meet in his four-poster might sound a trifle blatant.

She reached for another message.

And the winner is:

Carl Foster, M.D.

Ah, his usual morning-after-the-night-before call—ten solid minutes of "You were wonderful, wonderful," even on the morning when I fell sound asleep in the middle of his lovemaking. Well, he's kind, intelligent, gallant, and doesn't blame me for anything. Or maybe he does, and I just haven't noticed.

Jill returned the slip to her pocket, remembering Dr. Kerry's assessment of her love affairs: "You are not ready for commitment, hence your propensity for lovers you don't love."

Kerry could *hence* all he wanted. She did love Nick and Carl, both of them, equally. *That* was the problem. Her love life would have only one solution—bigamy—and wouldn't Daisy love writing "Dear Mom" letters to the Big House, where Jill would be serving one-to-five with time off for behavior that could only be good with both men on the opposite side of the bars.

Jill pulled out the final two slips and shuffled. There would be no further lovers in this deck. Who but an imbecile would draw to a full house?

And the winner:

Steve.

An ex-husband isn't a lover. He's more like joker's wild. Wonder what he wants?

Jill unrolled the last crumpled roll of paper.

And the final winner is:

Mother.

Mother!

24

Okay, I'll call her. I'll call Mother and Steve and Carl and Nick and then run like hell home to Daisy and my old chenille bathrobe and the stories I invent about my childhood to make Daisy laugh. I'll lock the door and bolt it and string wolfbane and garlic from the rafters. . . .

"Where's Carolyn McCaffery?" It was Lawrence, leaning toward her with a look so intense, Jill wondered if a schedule had magically appeared on her face.

"I . . . uh . . ." Jill tried to remember what Dan had told her about Carolyn McCaffery. He'd said it would interest her particularly because . . . because . . . oh, yes. "Carolyn's in labor, Mr. Lawrence."

He was astonished. "Labor? Labor, like in giving-birth labor?"

"That's what I've heard." Under the table Jill's knees knocked. She held her breath, wishing she'd forayed into the larger arena. No clique could be worse than this unplanned, unwanted conversation with *the boss.*

Lawrence's eyes popped. "Do you mean that when Carolyn gave her report in yesterday's meeting, she was *pregnant?*"

"She must have been. I don't know. I wasn't here yesterday."

"You weren't giving birth, were you?" Lawrence's eyes narrowed.

"No, I don't do that anymore. I mean, I'm new here. Today's my first—"

"So, when will Carolyn be back?" Lawrence asked, peering at her as though she should know.

"Uh . . . well . . ." What could she say? Six weeks? Six months? For all she knew, Carolyn McCaffery would climb off the delivery table, tuck her baby under her arm, and race back to give Lawrence's report, as God, and Lawrence, intended. "Uh . . . soon?"

"Hope so," Lawrence said, and returned to enraptured study of his board.

Rats! My first conversation with Lawrence and I wasn't even coherent.

"I've seen you looking happier, kid."

Jill whirled to find Dan returned to his chair, a welcome apparition.

"Dan!" She clutched at his arm. "Where have you been?"

Dan looked startled, then grinned. "It's nice to be missed, but calm down. Somebody rattle your cage while I was gone?"

"No, yes, oh, rats, Dan." Jill tried two deep breaths. "I talked to—" She gestured toward Lawrence. "Or rather he talked to me, and I didn't acquit myself very well. I was so nervous. . . ."

"Relax, Jill." Dan's voice was discreetly low, but very firm. "Remember what I told you when I asked you to leave Marshall Productions and work for me here?"

"Vaguely."

"Then, I'll say it again. Your first month is for listening and learning the business. That's *all*. You won't make any mistakes I can't cover. Knowing you, and I do, you won't make any mistakes at all."

"But I sounded like a fool with Lawrence and felt like one, too."

Dan glanced at Lawrence. "Don't worry about him. He's not of this world. Just relax and enjoy."

"Enjoy!" Jill flushed, realizing she'd raised her voice. "On my way in this morning I ran into an agent whose name I should have known. I went blank. I have such a problem with names, Dan. . . ."

"I didn't hire you for your ability to remember names, Jill." Dan smiled. "I know what you can do. You've got creative judgment and good instincts. Give yourself time. In six months *I'll* be working for *you!*"

"Never!" The thought made Jill smile, and the smile was the automatic relaxation Dan had intended it to be. "I could be here twenty years and not understand how a television network operates."

"Who says UBC is a television network?" Dan chuckled. "I hear the board of directors is trying to reincorporate as a charitable institution."

"You don't like UBC?" Jill was surprised.

"Until recently, I've liked it very much. A television network can be exciting and vital, even when it isn't in first place. In fact, sometimes it's that insane race for the top that . . . Well, I've spent thirteen years of my life in network television. Whenever I've changed jobs it's been for something better and it's been my choice. I'm not about to lose my optimism now."

The door opened, and Neiman hurried in, followed by Shirley, who was scribbling notes on a pad.

"Everything's under control," Neiman announced. "Crench has been bailed out, and if Arness is available,"—he glanced at Angela, who preened—"we'll make him an offer."

"What about the adverse publicity?" Dan asked. "The L.A.P.D. lover?"

"A mistake, all a mistake," Neiman interrupted. "It seems our star was stopped on a minor traffic charge by an officer, a total stranger to him, who mistook his friendly cooperation for something more . . . uh . . . personal." Neiman fixed the table with a baleful stare.

"That's the story, and anyone who says otherwise can look for a job selling shoes. Got it?"

Everyone at the table nodded, except Dan, who rather elaborately turned his back.

"Next on the agenda—movies!" Neiman barked.

"Jill Kenyon has a project she'd like to discuss," Dan said.

Jill's eyes flew wide open. "Dan, no!" she hissed.

Dan leaned closer and whispered. "I'm not giving you time to get nervous. Go ahead, get your feet wet. Your idea is a natural for Lawrence. Can't miss. Trust me."

"Oh, my . . . well. . . ." Jill began inauspiciously, fervently wishing she was somewhere safe, like the underground headquarters of Crench. "The project is a book—*Man Plus*, by Frederick Pohl, and it concerns the triumph of the human spirit—"

"*Screw* the triumph of the human spirit," Neiman snapped. "What is it *about*?"

Good point!

Jill took a deep breath.

"It's about an astronaut who undergoes a radical physical metamorphosis designed to enable him to live without support systems on Mars."

"*What!*" The sound emerging from Lawrence's mouth was a roar in a wind tunnel, a deafening howl that bounced off the walls.

"Oh, my God!" Dan breathed, his arm protectively circling the back of Jill's chair. "What in hell. . . ."

"Is this some stupid, fucking *joke!*" Lawrence's long, thin, Afghan-hound face was dead white, except for a flaming red circle beneath each cheekbone. He beat his fists on the table in a rhythm that pounded out his shouting. "Never" . . . *bam* . . . "as long as I goddamn live" . . . *bam* . . . "will a fucking movie" . . . *bam* . . ." be fucking made" . . . *bam* . . . "about fucking Mars" . . . *bam*. . . ."

CHAPTER 3

"Back so soon?" Polly looked up from where she sat on the floor, cross-legged and surrounded by a Himalaya of files. "The meeting can't be over yet."

"The meeting is most definitely over, Polly. It ended when Lawrence flung a marble ashtray through the conference room window." Shoulders slumped, Jill trudged into her office.

"That's terrible!" Polly struggled to her feet and followed Jill. "Are you all right?"

"It could have been worse. It could have been me going through the window."

"*You?*" Polly's eyes bulged. "Whatever did you do?"

"I was discussing a project Dan and I were certain Lawrence would love. Slight miscalculation, huh?"

"A man of Lawrence's background should have better control," Polly said tartly.

"Reminded me of home." Jill smiled. "A man of mercurial temperament is my emotional equivalent of Mom's apple pie."

"How peculiar. Then you aren't terribly upset."

"Sure I am. Dan is in Dale Neiman's office right now, getting chewed out for an idea that was mine to begin with. I've certainly made Dan look bad."

The view from Jill's window was a scene from Dante's *Inferno*. Flecks of ash from fires miles away swirled past while the sun poured gold through layers of smoke, producing a sky the color of nicotine stain. "Dan's probably trying to think of a kind way to fire me, Polly. After what's happened, I couldn't blame him."

"Ah, but I could." Dan stood in the doorway, his smiling lips and troubled eyes transmitting a mixed message. "What happened was my fault."

Polly moved toward the door. "Back to the files." She closed the door behind her.

"*Man Plus* was my idea, Dan, so if Neiman is furious at you—"

"Neiman's a thermometer, Jill. Lawrence runs a fever, Neiman gets hot. He thinks it's his job. Neiman's not your problem." Dan sat on the edge of an oatmeal-colored couch opposite Jill's desk. "Your problem is a boss who forgot that men don't honeymoon with ex-wives."

"Which means?" Jill sat on the couch next to Dan.

"I should have suspected Lawrence would be bitter over NASA's failure to land him on Mars. But he's seemed so immersed in television, so oblivious to anything else, it didn't occur to me."

"Me either, Dan, and it should have. No one likes having a major disappointment waved in his face." Jill lit a cigarette. "I know what I read in the papers, but I still don't understand how Lawrence came to be president of UBC."

"*Variety* called it 'Henry Gregg's stroke of genius.' They were half-right. Our venerable chairman's been senile since North Korea crossed the thirty-eighth parallel. For the past twenty years his participation in UBC life has consisted of an annual speech at the affiliates' banquet and drafting memos to various programing chiefs demanding the return of *The Ed Sullivan Show*. Most UBC executives had forgotten Gregg was still UBC chairman, so empowered."

"Enter Lawrence—"

"On a gurney, so the story goes. What a meeting of minds that must have been." Dan laughed. "Gregg, with his Zurich rejuvenation specialist pumping him full of goat glands—"

"Goat whats?"

"*And* something called primate placenta. Wait'll you see him, Jill. Gregg could pass for one of the bodies Neiman's buried." Dan stretched, finally ready to unwind. "So this irresistible, albeit embalmed-looking force meets Lawrence, who was if not immovable, then certainly grounded. They talk, and Gregg discovers 'the greatest television mind of our time.'"

"An astronaut? How?"

"That's the best part." Dan laughed. "For the past twelve years Lawrence's reduced-budget space-training has amounted to one hour a day spent in a weightless environment, floating upside down sucking Tang through a tube. For the remaining twenty-three hours he watched television. Lawrence impressed Gregg simply by naming every show aired on television since 1968, along with plots, characters, casts, and spin-offs."

"*That's* why Gregg calls Lawrence the greatest television mind of our time?"

"The goat glands don't keep him logical, Jill, just vertical." Dan pulled a slip of paper from an inside pocket. "Gossip out, business in. First, there's a departmental report due. I'll write it tonight, you'll look it over tomorrow, and from then on we'll do the report together. Second, you are to hire an assistant."

"I can't!" Jill blurted out.

Dan blinked, startled by her vehemence. "Why not?"

"I've never hired anyone before."

"Oh, is that all?" Dan grinned. "I thought it might be a religious conviction."

"May as well be." Jill wiggled apprehensively. "What if you don't like the person I hire?"

"I won't take him dancing." He handed a slip of paper to her. "Your predecessor compiled a list of applicants. Just interview these people and make a decision."

"Decision-making isn't my strong point, Dan, even when I know what I'm doing."

"There, there, Mother Courage, you'll be fine. Just trust your instincts. I do." Dan rose, his time for unwinding over. "Everything's a mystery the first time. After that it's just part of your résumé. Any questions?"

"Just one. How's Nancy?"

Dan shot her his quick sidelong glance, the one Jill had dubbed the "Carmichael cutaway." "My wife is feeling neglected, thank you. I suggest she go out more with friends. She suggests I be home more with her. It's the eternal triangle, Jill, a man, his wife, and his job."

Then he was through the door and gone, taking his troubled eyes. The smile had been for Jill, and that he left with her.

Jill studied the list of applicants. All but one were recent graduates of prestigious universities where they'd acquired degrees in Communication and/or Film. Two bore the same surnames as prominent television producers, one, that of a powerful agent, and a fourth, that of a renowned studio mogul. All were male. Evidently Jill's predecessor had favored male media majors with industry ties, Young Turks in training. The unconnected and Turkettes need not apply.

"You have an admirer," Polly announced as she burst through the door carrying an octagonal terrarium, which she placed on Jill's desk. "Here's the card."

While Jill read the card Polly rotated the terrarium, admiring it from all sides. "Nice. Very nice. I love ivy and African violets."

"From the guy who loves you," Jill read. "I'm in trouble."

"Why?"

Jill showed her the card. "It's unsigned. This could be from a holistic physician named Carl, or a writer of promise named Nick, or perhaps my ex-husband, Steve, ordered it four years ago, and the traffic being what it is on the Santa Monica freeway, it's only just arrived."

Polly was impressed. "Carl, Nick, and Steve are *all* 'the guy who loves you.' "

"I have an overly complicated life." Jill groaned. "Disaster is what I deserve."

"Give me the card," Polly directed. She held it lightly between tapered fingertips. Her eyes were closed, and she breathed rhythmically. Long seconds passed before she opened her eyes and smiled. "The man who sent this card has long white hands and dry skin."

"Carl!" Jill exclaimed. "I should have known. Nick would have sent wildflowers tumbling out of a jar, and Steve sends flowers only to those whose temperature has reached one hundred and three. I'll call and thank him." She reached for the phone, then swung to face Polly. "How did you do that?"

Polly examined her fingernails. "Um, sometimes I pick up vibrations."

"You're psychic!" Jill stared.

"And sometimes I don't pick up anything at all."

"But, how—"

The phone rang. Polly quickly reached for it as Jill watched, thoroughly intrigued. She'd always pictured psychics as dreamy-eyed visionaries draped in bangles, not crisp, sandy-haired ladies in beige shirtdresses.

Polly punched the hold button. "It's your ex-husband."

Jill was awed. "You picked up his vibration?"

"He told me." Polly frowned.

"Of course." Feeling foolish, Jill picked up the phone. "Hello, Steve."

"Felicitations." His low voice rumbled through the phone. "How's the new job? Settled in yet?"

31

"It's nice of you to ask." Jill was pleased. "I'm not sure whether I'm settling in or sinking fast."

"Now, Jill." Steve's tone was his all too familiar *Father Knows Best*. "There you go again, allowing anxiety to overwhelm you before you begin. If you'd only learn to—"

"I know, Steve." Jill's teeth ground in automatic reflex. "Take one thing at a time, don't speak to strangers, look both ways before crossing, think positively . . ."

Stop! He can't help it!

With a mighty effort Jill clamped her lips together, remembering Dr. Kerry's assessment of Steve in the days before they'd deliberately torn asunder what God had impulsively glued together: "Your husband's basic attitude is and always will be parental, a common personality development in those orphaned in early childhood and forced to 'mommy' and 'daddy' themselves."

Let him play daddy. It's the best he can do.

Jill forced her pleasantest voice. "And how's your job?"

"Fine," Steve replied.

Jill smiled. Steve was always "fine." On the day his law office in Cleveland had burned to the ground, Steve was "fine." No need to become emotional, not with adequate insurance. With Steve, losses were either covered or cut.

"I've hired a new associate, Ron Blume, and put him in charge of actresses." Steve chuckled.

"Canny." Jill laughed. "No more midnight phone calls from weeping clients."

"A hazard of show-biz law," Steve agreed. "Fortunately Blume seems attuned to the chronically distraught, which means I can return to shuffling papers, not egos. Now, about Daisy."

"She's sicker!" Jill leaped to her feet.

"Calm down." Steve shouted his standard admonition. "Daisy's fine. She just called me to ask permission to stay overnight at Karen Seymour's house."

"You're kidding. A few hours ago Daisy called me, dying with cramps, and now she's ready for a slumber party."

"Daisy recovers from her ailments, Jill. She doesn't nurse them along."

Unlike some people you think you know.

"I see, Steve." Jill's voice was cold. "Daisy called you to ask permission to do something she knew I wouldn't allow."

"Daisy isn't sneaking behind your back, Jill. She told me she called you first but you were in a meeting."

"All right. So Daisy had no ulterior motives," Jill conceded. "Let's just say I'd rather she didn't go out tonight. After all, she did come home sick from school."

There was a long pause, then, "Try not to be too protective of Daisy, Jill. She's a responsible girl. She knows how she feels."

Steve can't help it! I can't stand it!

"Thank you for explaining Daisy, Steve. After fifteen years as her mother she's a total mystery to me."

"I didn't mean—"

"Sure you did."

"You sound frayed, Jill. Try to get more rest. You know how your nerves—"

"Steve." Jill warned, her "pleasant" voice twisting into a growl.

"Okay, okay." Steve sighed. "I'm only thinking of what's best for you."

"I know what's best for me, Steve, and it's all the things you predicted would be my ruination. I eat cold pizza for breakfast, go for walks after midnight, watch *The Late Late Show*—"

"I'll call you this weekend," Steve interrupted. "Good-bye."

"Damn!" Jill scowled at the dead phone in her hand. "Would you die if you didn't have the last word?"

Jill jumped. Polly stood just inside the door holding a stack of scripts with multicolored covers. "Dan Carmichael sent these. They all seem to be marked 'Rush.' "

"Rush it will be. I may get one or two read before, uh"—she consulted the list of applicants—"Alex Friedman, male but unconnected, arrives."

"Your first interview?"

"Yes, and I haven't the slightest idea of how to go about it."

"Ask incredibly personal questions in an incredibly impersonal voice," Polly advised. "It's called the corporate interview."

"Sounds more like the third degree."

Suddenly the office door flew open, and a trumpet blasted "Ta-da."

"Ack!" Polly flung the scripts in the air, and Jill jumped to her feet, heart racing, as a rotund man in blue leotards bounded into the room.

"Hello, Ms. Kenyon, well, hello, Ms. Kenyon," he sang, to the tune of "Hello Dolly," *"Alex Friedman's asking for a job! He's got talent,*

Ms. Kenyon. He's got heart, Ms. Kenyon. He's still growing, he'll be glowing, he'll be growing strong. . . ."

Jill eased herself into her chair, trying to look like a person who takes the unexpected in stride, while Polly stared with unconcealed irritation at the bright-blue creature who continued his falsetto squeal while pirouetting around the room. *"Don't forget, Ms. Kenyon. You won't regret, Ms. Kenyon, . . ."* He whirled into an end table, bounced and whirled on.

The act finally ended when the shrieking man threw himself on his knees before Jill, blasted another *Ta-daaaaa* on his trumpet, and presented his card.

"Live and Lively Messages," Jill read, then looked down at the kneeling figure. "You're not Alex Friedman?"

"Gracious, no." The man looked horrified. "I'm an announcement."

"Oh, I see." She didn't, not quite. "Well . . . uh . . . thank you. That was very . . . uh . . . entertaining."

"You're welcome." The man glanced over his shoulder at the open door.

"Perhaps you'd like to get up?" Jill suggested.

"This Friedman guy's supposed to be right behind me," he said petulantly.

"I'm sure Mr. Friedman wouldn't expect you to kneel on my carpet until he arrives," Jill assured him. "Perhaps he's caught in traffic—"

"Nah, he was right behind me in the hall. Hell, that's his problem. I did my number. I ain't getting paid to wear calluses on my knees." With a rolling motion he rose to his feet, brushing at his blue spandex knees. "All I need is a run in my leotards! Cheez, what a day!"

"Thanks again," Jill called as he went out the door.

For a second Jill and Polly stared blankly at one another, then simultaneously burst into laughter.

"I hope Lawrence doesn't see him." Jill giggled. "UBC will have a show starring an overweight elf who sounds like a banjo in heat."

"An Emmy-winner for sure." Polly smiled. "I'll just stroll down the hall and see if I can find Mr. Friedman."

"No need," said a voice from the doorway. "Mr. Friedman has found you."

He stood in the open doorway, one hand resting lightly on the frame, the other, gracefully, on his hip. It was a pose Jill recognized from old Errol Flynn movies.

Having made his first impression, whatever it was meant to be, he undraped himself from the doorway and walked into the room.

"I'm Alexander Friedman," he announced. "Call me Lexy."

His hand surrounded Jill's, and he pumped so enthusiastically that Jill's head bobbed up and down. She was startled to see the poseur in the doorway turn into a puckish young man with forthright brown eyes and a Peck's Bad Boy smile.

Twenty or thirty? Hard to tell.

"I was just down the hall, checking things out," he said, as though excusing himself for coming late to class. "Did you like my announcement?"

"I won't forget your name." Jill smiled.

"That's the idea." Friedman looked pleased.

"Excuse me, the files," Polly murmured, and was gone before Jill could properly introduce her to Friedman. "Thanks, Polly," Jill called after her.

As the door closed behind Polly Jill turned her attention to Friedman, who was staring at her so intently she automatically checked to see if any buttons had come undone.

"Hey, 'scuse me for staring," he said, without a trace of apology in his voice, "but it's not often I meet a lady with emerald-green eyes. Man, have I got a weakness for emerald-green eyes! They just put me away! I see green eyes and I . . . am . . . gone." His arms spun windmills as he flopped into the nearest chair, then slumped, motionless, his head to one side.

Jill laughed out loud. The dramatic rendering of "I . . . am . . . gone" had all the spontaneous energy of that moment in the circus when the clown leaps out of the ring and into a patron's lap. Jill had always adored circuses, been particularly partial to clowns.

"Stop beating around the bush." Jill grinned at him. "Do you like green eyes or don't you?"

Alex shrugged and he was Peter Pan momentarily subdued but certain of his right to fly. "I know I get carried away sometimes, but, man, when I'm into something, I'm into it, all the way. You're that way yourself. I can tell."

How? Perhaps, like Steve's mommy/daddy, it shows in my face.

"Getting carried away has caused me no end of trouble," Jill admitted.

35

"Yeah," he whispered confidentially, "but I'll bet you've had some hot, happy times."

Jill's early-warning system flashed red. Quickly she averted her gaze to the ceiling.

Careful! You're life could plummet from overly complicated straight into chaotic. This is one juicy man.

"It's like this green-eyed thing," Friedman continued. "I'm so whacked out by them, I tried to talk my wife into green contacts. She said I'd have to be a fucking magician to get her to stick pieces of plastic in her eyes."

Safe, on a technicality.

Jill resumed eye contact. "You're married?"

"Six months next week. Man, I dig it. There's always someone to talk to, and you don't have to go out to get laid."

And Dan thinks he's pragmatic. Wait'll he meets this guy!

Jill was trying to think of an incredibly personal question when Friedman leaned forward, gripping her wrist. "Hire me now. In ten minutes I'll take a load off your back."

"What load?"

"The little shit your time is too important to fuck with—reports, requisitions, reading scripts by unknowns, dealing with secretaries. I'm *great* with secretaries."

"In what way?" Jill asked, anticipating an incredibly personal answer.

"Not what you think." He grinned. "Or at least not unless they're happily married or know the name of the game. I am simply the world's greatest schmooze."

"Wonderful!" Jill heard the sarcasm in her voice and saw Friedman's eyes darken in response.

"Hey, don't knock schmoozing. You zig a little, zag a little, stroke a little, let the other guy win the preliminary while you hold out for the main event. That way you get what you want without making the other guy so angry he comes after your balls. It's the way of the world. Am I wrong?"

Jill thought about it. He wasn't subtle, but he wasn't wrong.

"I'm not knocking schmoozing," she told him. "I'm just not good at it. My boss says he'd love to play poker with me. My face gives it all away."

"That's why you need me," Friedman said earnestly. "I give nothing away."

"What do you do besides schmooze?" Jill asked.

"Well"—he beamed at her, a smile that could light up Chicago— "I made films in college, both directed and produced. After college I worked in New York for Morris Productions, a hole-in-the-wall outfit run by three gay fuck-ups who could never pay the rent. We did one film while I was there—a porno with giraffes and a water buffalo. From there I went to Marcus Productions. We made two movies, one about a stunt man who steals cars on the side and the other, a flick that had no script, no stars, no story line, but a dynamite ending with a fire and a race riot. It got kinda out of hand in the shooting. Man, don't ever hire Teamsters as extras. Those suckers love to bust heads!" He took a deep breath. "And, I worked for the Ohio Film Commission for three months. Fucking near died of boredom! Man, when I lose my hair, my teeth, and my balls, I'll go back to Ohio to die. What a fucking elephant graveyard!"

"I'm from Ohio, and I love it." Jill couldn't resist a shot at the world's greatest schmooze.

Friedman's face went red, then white, then an attractive shade of gray. "Oh, Christ, have I blown it! I have stuck my foot in my mouth, clear down my throat, and straight out my ass!" He threw back his head and laughed. "Holy shit! And I wanted this job so bad I could taste it." He shook with nervous mirth, then quieted down. "Well, I said it, and I meant it. Ohio may be home to you, but I'd rather crawl into an alley off Broadway and snuggle up to a wino than ever go back. That's the way I feel."

"Liking Ohio is not a job requirement." Jill reached for a cigarette, thinking she could do worse than to hire someone who said what he felt.

Friedman slipped a lighter out of his pocket and lit Jill's cigarette.

"Cigarette?" Jill offered.

"Don't smoke." He put his lighter away. "UBC has some good shows in the works."

"How do you know?"

"I saw a report. It was lying on somebody's desk, down the hall. I just took a peek."

For the next several minutes he regaled her with his opinion of at least a dozen projects, emphasizing his points with forefinger stabbing the air.

"That was some peek." Jill whistled, impressed.

Friedman tapped his forehead. "Photographic memory."

37

"Photographic?" Jill quavered. "Names, too?"

"Of course."

Eureka!

"An ability to remember names is important to you?" Friedman asked, his expression telling her he already knew.

"It's an interesting talent." Jill tried for noncommittal. Her poker-loser's face cracked, and she smiled broadly. "Well—"

There was a rap on the door, and Dan Carmichael's face appeared in the doorway. "Oh, excuse me. I thought you were alone."

Friedman was already on his feet, right hand extended. "It's a pleasure to meet you, Mr. Carmichael."

Dan glanced quizzically at Jill. He had no choice but to enter.

"This is Alexander Friedman," Jill explained. "He's applying for the assistant's position.

"Call me Lexy," Alex said, shaking Dan's hand. "It's a real pleasure to meet the man who predicted the rise of cable television when everyone else thought it was a pipe dream. Your speech to NATAS was ahead of its time."

"That was three years ago!" Dan exclaimed.

"You don't soon forget a speech that combines vision with practical application." Alex shook his head admiringly. "No one else was talking all-news-and-sports nets then."

"I'm sure there were others, Friedman," Dan said, but he smiled.

"It's as you said then, sir"—Alex gazed at the ceiling as though words had appeared there—" 'network television must rise to the challenge of this new and viable competitor with programing of such quality that it will compel viewer attention.' "

"My God, you remember my exact words!" Dan was astonished.

"Doesn't everyone?" Alex seemed equally amazed.

"Hardly," Dan said, but pleasure had smoothed his face, and he looked ten years younger than he had when he entered the room. "Good luck to you, Friedman."

"Call me Lexy." Friedman pumped Dan's hand again.

"May I see you outside for a moment?" Jill asked Dan.

Dan glanced from Friedman to Jill. "Sure."

In the outer office Polly peeped around her barricade of files, then withdrew, buried again.

Jill got right to it. "I'd like to hire Alexander Friedman."

"That was quick." Dan executed a perfect cutaway.

"He's got the right background and some abilities I think would be . . . uh . . . useful," Jill explained.

"What's the hurry? If he wants this job tonight, he'll want it in the morning. Why not sleep on it?"

"Sleeping on decisions tends to confuse me," Jill said earnestly. "I begin to see both sides of the question and debate myself into a muddle."

"Is there room in your muddle for two?" Dan's question was light, his tone was not.

"What's wrong, Dan?"

"Nothing." He shrugged, then tried for a chuckle. "I always thought the phrase 'television is Fantasyland' meant the shows and not the network. I'm an old dog, kiddo, with little taste for some of the new tricks."

"Can I help?" Jill asked, resisting a sudden urge to put her arms around him.

Dan/friend, got it?

Got it.

"You already have." Dan smiled. "For the past week when I've walked into your office, I've seen the face of a friend. And someone I respect. That's a lot."

"Thank you." Jill was pleased. "You wanted to see me about something?"

"It's about those scripts I sent you. I hate to throw a 'Rush' at you first thing, but if you can, read and evaluate them before morning. Your predecessor was somewhat lax." He paused. "Actually the son of a bitch spent all his time trying to hustle up a job at what he called a 'real network.'"

"Consider them done."

"Terrific." Dan smiled. "Now, about Friedman. I told you to trust your instincts. If he's what you want . . ."

"Thanks, Dan." She watched as he left her office, his stride less jaunty than usual and his shoulders just a bit stooped.

"Polly?" Jill peered over the barricade. "Yoo-hoo."

Polly popped up, a file folder in each hand. "You rang, master?"

"Polly . . . uh . . . I don't mean to put you on the spot, but did you by any chance pick up a . . . uh . . . vibration from Friedman? I mean, just in passing maybe?"

Polly shook her head disapprovingly. "A snap judgment of a person's vibration isn't fair. It would be like breaking into a psychiatrist's office to get the goods on a guy you're dating." Her eyes gleamed. "Come to think of it, that's a wonderful idea."

"Friedman has a photographic memory, Polly. He remembers *names.*"

"If you like him, don't ask my opinion." Polly wrinkled her nose. "Sometimes I have an instinct; sometimes I don't. Besides, I have a natural bias against men who wear their hair the way Jane Fonda did in *Klute.*"

Jill laughed. "Friedman isn't gay, if that's what you're thinking. He's married, *and* he cheats on his wife."

"Don't just stand there." Polly waved her folders. "Hire him. UBC needs more macho men."

"Macho? You mean UBC is . . ."

"Piggy heaven." Polly laughed at Jill's surprised look. "Yes, I know Carmichael isn't. He's the exception, and you are fortunate. Stick around. You'll see."

"Perhaps you're being cynical."

"Perhaps I have reason."

"Well." Jill sighed. "I've been told I have the extravagant impulses of a romantic. A touch of cynicism might toughen me up."

"Remain a romantic," Polly advised. "Cynics begin their days with stewed prunes."

"Words to live by." Jill smiled and opened the door to her office, where she found Alex, comfortably at home, sitting at her desk, leafing through her pile of scripts. "Find anything you like, Alex?"

"Mostly garbage," Alex said confidently. "Your life will be easier when I'm screening this shit for you."

Jill ignored the implication of *fait accompli.* "Tell me, Alex, how did you know about Dan's NATAS speech? I've never heard about it, and I've known him for—" She suddenly realized. "You checked him out!"

"Of course. I like to know exactly what I'm getting into." Alex's confident grin faded. "Is that wrong?"

"It's . . . it's . . ." Jill couldn't put her finger on exactly what it was, outside of smart strategy. Perhaps too smart. . . .

"Oh, fuck!" Alex threw himself face forward on Jill's desk, his arms over his head. "I blew it again! I was just trying to make a good impression, show you that I'm enthusiastic, that I'd work my ass off for you, that you'd never regret hiring me. Never!" He unburied his head and looked straight at Jill, who was astonished to see tears in his eyes. "If there's one thing I am, it's *loyal!*" He reburied his head. "But I blew it. I didn't know when to stop. So *kill* me. I did my best.

I didn't even mention that my wife and I are just in from New York, down to our last fifty bucks, and have no place to sleep. I don't mind for myself. I can take shit, but, man, I think Nina's pregnant. If anything happens to Nina because I blew the only fucking job I ever fucking wanted, I'll kill myself! I went to a shrink once, and he told me I'm capable of suicide, so you know—"

"Stop!" Jill shouted, panting as though she'd run the three-minute mile. "I was just about to tell you, you're hired."

"No shit!" Friedman leaped to his feet.

"No shit." Exhausted, Jill sank into a chair.

Friedman bounded straight into the air, spun twice before hitting the ground, then danced around the room shadow-boxing the Abbey Rents furniture. "Hey, hey, hey. Wait'll I tell Nina! We are gonna boogie tonight!" He froze in midair, dukes up. "When do I start?"

"Uh . . . tomorrow. Nine o'clock." They hadn't discussed his salary, his office, the location of the men's room, or who's on first.

I've never hired anyone before. Dan!

"Nine o'clock. You got it!" He threw his arms around Jill, hugging her so fiercely she heard her ribs creak. "I love you, lady!" He aimed a warm, moist kiss at her face that grazed her nose before landing full on her mouth. He released her slightly, then, just as she'd gasped a needed breath, pulled her to him again. "Don't ever try to hold me down," he whispered, his brown eyes a flat, dull gray.

"I was planning to tie you to a chair and make you work with a muzzle." Jill used the last of her breath.

He went almost limp, then released her, the shadow of a frown on his face. "Hey, don't mind me. I get a little intense when I'm happy, and, son of a bitch, am I happy! Christ!"

"If it's all right with you, we'll talk salary tomorrow," Jill suggested, mentally crossing her fingers.

"No sweat." His eyes danced amber again. "Hey, for you I'd work free!"

"You *are* intense, aren't you?"

She walked him to the door, for a moment afraid he'd grab her again. She braced herself, but he stood quietly, one hand on the doorknob. "All bullshit aside, I do thank you. This means a lot to me." He leaned over and, very gently, kissed her on the cheek.

"Sure thing, Alex. See you tomorrow."

He was gone, tossing an ain't-we-got-fun! wink over his shoulder as he hopped through the door.

41

Jill stood behind the closed door, motionless in the sudden stillness of her office.

Who was that masked man?

Beats me.

Thank God he's not volatile.

Gotcha.

She lit a cigarette, then strolled into the outer office. Polly emerged from her snowbank of paper, hair tumbling into her eyes.

"I think I just hired a cast of characters, Polly. Now I hope I like the play."

CHAPTER 4

"Why can't I stay overnight at Karen's?" Daisy greeted her.

"Pizza's hot, Daisy. Put the salad in bowls."

Daisy carried the salad to the kitchen, her face set in what Jill called "Daisy's downtrodden look."

She set the table in silence, then sat down. Jill was determined to respond to nothing less than civil, and Daisy determined not to respond at all.

As usual Jill caved in first. "Cramps better?"

Daisy nodded yes and went on munching.

Jill tried again. "How was your English test? Should have been a snap. You studied hard enough."

Daisy shrugged.

Jill switched to a less personal approach. "Have you been watching the news? Are the fires out yet?"

Daisy shrugged again.

"Do you think the Middle East will see peace in our lifetime?" Jill's voice was raised. "Oh, I give up."

"I still don't know why I can't stay at Karen's," Daisy complained.

"You didn't feel well today. It's a school night. You need your rest."

"I feel fine now. My homework is caught up. I slept for two hours this afternoon."

Ah, she's going to nail me with logic.

"Let me put it this way, Daisy. You can't stay overnight at Karen's house because I say so."

"That's no reason."

"I'm the mother, and you're the kid. That's reason enough."

"Kid!" Daisy was indignant. "This is no kid you're talking to. I'm a 34C."

"And stop wearing my bras. You're stretching them out!"

"Why is it," Daisy asked, "that everytime I want to do something you turn . . . motherly?"

"Because that's what I am, Daisy."

"Oh?" Daisy wound up, preparing to let her have it. "How many mothers work until eight or nine every night, tiptoe in after midnight a couple of times a week, and—"

"Look here," Jill interrupted. "A new job can be very demanding. It takes time to break in, to familiarize—wait! Why do I always end up defending my life to you?"

Daisy popped a pepperoni circle into her mouth. "Beats me. I've got enough on my mind without worrying about a middle-aged lady."

"Oh, thanks. And I'd just convinced myself that thirty-five is the first flush of my prime." Jill pushed her chair away from the table and carried her plate to the sink. "I'll try not to bore you with my middle-aged problems."

"You could tell me about your boyfriends. That would be interesting." Daisy's green eyes sparkled as she assumed a listening position.

"What boyfriends?" Jill demanded, wondering if it was too late for Daisy to spend the night with Karen.

"The guys you go out with. The reason you come home after midnight." Daisy waited, then grew impatient. "You know, the guys who call you all the time. There's the one with the James Bond voice who thinks he's so suave." Daisy cocked her head to one side and affected a deep, throaty voice. "Is your mother free, my dear?" She giggled. "Free! Someday I'm going to say, 'No, she's not free, sir, but she sure is reasonable.' We'll see how suave he is. Then"—she grinned mischievously—"there's the one who runs all his sentences together, like spending more than two seconds on the phone with a kid would give him a case of the crud. Those boyfriends."

"They're just friend-type friends, Daisy." Jill wondered if Daisy would like to stay over at Karen's for a year or two. "Not boyfriends."

"It's all right, Mom," Daisy said with a twinkle. "You've been divorced three years. It's okay to date."

"Thank you, Dear Abby Kenyon."

"Don't go getting all miffed." Daisy rinsed her plate in the sink. "I don't know why you're so mysterious about your social life, anyway. I wouldn't freak if these guys came over. Most of the kids I know have divorced parents who date. Alice Wilson's mother has sleep-overs."

"She has what?"

"Dates who sleep over." Daisy dug into the cookie jar. "Alice said she used to hate it when she woke up in the morning to find some clown in the bathroom using her toothbrush, but her mother told her you have to kiss a lot of frogs before you find a prince, and she'd rather kiss them at home than stay out all night and leave Alice alone. That made sense to Alice. She hated waking up in the middle of the night with spooky noises all over the house and nobody there, not even a dog. Anyway, now Alice's mother has a steady boyfriend, and Alice says it's almost like being a family again. Want a peanut-butter wafer?"

"Thanks." Jill had no intention of allowing herself to be placed in the frog-kissing category with Alice Wilson's mother and her flopovers. "Uh, Daisy, the reason you haven't met the men I date is because . . . uh—"

"Yes." Daisy leaned forward attentively.

"—because I'm not dating anyone who's important to me. It's just casual dating, not like . . . you know . . ."

"Meaningful relationships?"

"You could say that." Jill wished lockjaw on whoever had first uttered that phrase. "I'm more involved in my work than anything else. The few dates I do have are . . . uh . . ."

"They keep you from going totally buggy." Daisy nodded. "I understand."

Good for you. I just got lost. You can't be talking about sex!

Jill cleared her throat. "I know that being the child of divorced parents isn't easy."

"How would you know?" Daisy asked reasonably. "Your parents were together till death did them part."

"I can imagine, can't I?"

Can I? Can I really?

"Maybe." Daisy was dubious.

"The point is, I'm aware that your father and I have made life more difficult for you, and I feel guilty about it."

Daisy made a lemon-sucking face, her habitual response to Jill's frequent references to guilt. "Being divorced is easier than getting divorced, you know. Remember the night Dad called you all those names, and you threw his new suit in the shower, and he chased you around the house yelling he'd teach you to behave like a lady if he had to break your neck, and you threw the second-best lamp—"

"I remember. I remember."

I will never mention guilt again.

"*That* was difficult. We had a lot of nights like that before the divorce." Daisy sighed. She stretched, arms over head, then bent over gracefully, placing her hands on the floor, one beside each instep. Upside down with her head between her legs, Daisy looked Jill straight in the eye. "I couldn't have taken much more of that."

"Neither could I," Jill agreed.

Daisy arched right side up again. "So all things considered, the divorce was probably an improvement. Want another cookie?"

"No, thanks."

Daisy searched through the cookie jar, acting as though it contained fifty-seven varieties instead of just peanut-butter wafers. Being suddenly busy was one of the signals she used to indicate the end of a conversation.

"I wish you'd told me how you felt about the divorce sooner, Daisy." In her relief Jill ignored the signal. "You wouldn't have heard so much about guilt."

"I knew you'd say that. I just *knew* it!" Daisy pursed her lips and gazed heavenward, with a look of restrained exasperation, so reminiscent of Steve that Jill was tempted to laugh. "I only meant that it was better to put the marriage out of its misery, Mom, not that it's okay you let it get miserable. I don't know why adults can't keep the promises they make."

"I'm sorry, Daisy. There are some things I can't explain to you and that's why I feel so guil—"

"Mom!" Daisy interrupted "the word." "You and dad aren't all that bad. Neither of you gives me the crazies often enough to interfere with my schoolwork or keep me awake."

"Wonderful!" Jill tried not to be insulted by the compliment. "Parents who make you crazy, only part of the time, are devoutly to be wished."

"You could be worse. Like Maybelle Smith's parents. They're divorced, too. When Maybelle's dad showed up on weekends to take her out, he and her mom would have terrible fights. Maybelle started getting headaches in her right eye—migraines, I think they're called. So Maybelle's doctor told her parents they'd have to mend their fences or Maybelle might spend her whole life lying in a dark room with cold cloths on her head. They didn't want that, so they went to a divorced persons' workshop up near San Francisco, at one of those places where everyone walks around nude. They were gone for a week, and when they got back, they told Maybelle they'd worked through their hostility and gotten in touch with their bisexuality."

"Bisexuality?" *I don't believe that word came out of your mouth!*

"That's not the worst part. Maybelle's parents were so thrilled not to be just ordinary, dull, divorced people, they joined a bisexual group at the Sexual Freedom Now Institute and were part of an article on alternative life-stylers in *Los Angeles Magazine.*"

"God, Daisy! They didn't give their real names, did they?"

Daisy nodded. "In letters four inches high. In a couple of weeks they're supposed to be on Henry Sitzbach's *Six O'Clock See It Now News,* discussing their sexuality in front of the whole world. Now Maybelle has headaches in both eyes and thinks she'll just die."

"How can they do that to poor Maybelle?" Jill asked.

"Oh," Daisy shrugged. "They think they're very hip and with it. You know how dumb 'with-it' middle-aged people can be."

"I'm beginning to."

"Mickey Angelo's father comes over drunk and tries to beat up his mother. The police have a special code number for their house."

"Daisy!" Jill was appalled. "Don't you know any normal people?"

"Not grown-ups," Daisy said solemnly. "The kids are okay, though."

"How can the kids be okay?" Jill was upset. "They're lives are so . . . unconventional."

"I try not to judge my friends by their parents. And I didn't think you'd get all tweaked out of shape hearing about it. I was just trying to say that you and Dad aren't so bad. In fact, sometimes I think you have definite potential."

"What kind of potential?" Jill was suspicious. Daisy's compliments often came barbed and booby-trapped.

"Well," Daisy mused, "you and Dad are better friends than when you were married, and you say there's no one important in your life, and Dad doesn't even date, and according to Dr. Joyce Brothers, the rate of remarriage among divorced couples is—"

"Zero, as far as I'm concerned," Jill said quickly, dismayed at Daisy's idea of "potential."

"Dr. Joyce Brothers says that divorce often provides a couple with an opportunity to relate in new ways."

"I should hope so," Jill agreed. "Throwing lamps does not make me feel like a nice person."

"So, if you and Dad are relating better—"

"We're relating from separate houses, Daisy. When we're ten miles apart, the furniture doesn't get broken."

"But Dr. Joyce Brothers says that it's possible for couples to start over."

"Stop!" Jill ordered. "Stop reading Dr. Joyce Brothers. Stop fantasizing, at least about your father and me. Don't you have any ongoing teenager-type problems?"

"Parents are the most ongoing problem teenagers have!" Daisy slammed the refrigerator door. "Boy, just try to talk to you. The littlest thing gets a big overreaction."

"Okay. So maybe I overreacted," Jill admitted. "But if I didn't care what you think, I wouldn't react at all."

"I'm going to call Lenny," Daisy announced, heading for her room.

"All right." It was Jill's turn to be relieved. "Wait! Who's Lenny?"

"A guy in my English class," Daisy called back. "He's asked me out."

"That's nice." Jill stacked their plates in the dishwasher next to their breakfast bowls. Then, struck by a disquieting thought, she walked down the hall toward Daisy's room. "Daisy, dear, are Lenny's parents into anything . . . unusual?"

"They're *normal.*" Daisy slammed her door.

Thank God!

Jill finished in the kitchen, then took her briefcase to the bedroom. She put it on the middle of the bed, found the television remote-control box, and automatically punched UBC. The television set came alive with a grating sound of static. The picture, when it came into focus, was *Please stand by.*

Rats.

Jill turned the sound low, stretched out on the bed, and opened the briefcase. Her sister Julie's sample schedule lay on top, a silent admonition. Jill tossed it to one side, then, with a sigh, retrieved and reread it.

Why am I doing this?

Dr. Kerry would mumble of a more than sibling rivalry, a compulsion to identify while simultaneously establishing an identity separate from womb-mates (his own mordant term). He'd hold forth on the subject of multiple-birthers (worse yet), an area in which he had no experience but an abundance of opinions.

Julie's schedule would have overawed a West Point commandant. It was a diary of duties, a compendium of obligations to be met and crossed off, a minute-to-minute commitment of time, requiring a sprinter's speed and the endurance of a marathoner.

Where is the time for fun? Spontaneity? Kicking cans in the park? Daydreaming? Reading? Where, indeed, is sex?

Sex wasn't on the schedule. At first Jill assumed that Julie was naturally too reticent to list sex, but bathing was on the schedule, along with feminine hygiene and depilation, so . . .

If I were married to Fred, sex wouldn't be part of my schedule, either. But where is the fun?

Shaking her head, Jill set the schedule aside. As a youngster Julie's life had been crammed with activities that increased in number and scope as she grew: the Young Ladies' Sodality, Girl Scouts, Student Council, Choir, English Club, History Club, Future Teachers of America, Candy Stripers, on and on.

Jill remembered one moment in particular—a late winter afternoon in the bedroom they'd shared, Julie running in from one activity to change clothes for another. Jill had been lying on her bed, reading one of the Brontës.

"How can you pass time so *aimlessly*?" Julie had demanded, pulling her sweater over her head.

"Reading is fun," Jill had replied.

"Fun!" Julie shuddered. "But you're not *accomplishing* anything!"

Accomplishment! Julie's definition of fun.

And Johnny's?

Whatever the fabric of his fun, it was a cloth he'd been careful to cut away from home. Once past the restrictions of childhood John's standard reply to Kate's "Where have you been?" was "Hanging out, Ma, just hanging out."

Though Jill had often seen John in her fantasies as a spirited participant in the adolescent adventures she knew would have been hers had she been male and allowed to leave the house with her destination unspecified and no phone number "to call in case your mother needs you," she'd known in her heart that John indeed was just "hanging out."

Hanging out/hiding out.

The Johnny who'd once sung songs of his own composition in a clear, expressive tenor that floated from his throat, a honeyed gift, his birthright, had gone stony silent in his fifteenth year.

"Ah, just listen to that." Kate had sighed with pleasure one night as they lingered over after-dinner tea, chatting, save for Pa, who sat

49

at the table as silent and isolated as a prisoner in self-imposed solitary confinement. Above them, in the bedroom, John sang of promises and sighs. "It's a pleasure of Heaven we have in our house."

"Johnny should take voice lessons," Julie had remarked. "Sister Mary George said so. She told the whole class he's gifted."

"That he is," Kate agreed. "It runs in the family, you know. Your Pa has a lovely voice, and his broth—"

"Kate!" Pa's voice was sharp, a shot, a blow, a slamming door. Kate's face had gone white, dead white. She held her breath.

Pa's questions demanded answering, and answering required breath. Kate breathed.

"Johnny's singing," Kate whispered. "You've heard him sing before."

"Never!" Pa bellowed. "I'll have no son of mine singing."

Pa's chair had crashed to the floor behind him as he exploded from the table, but not before it glanced off the sideboard, smashing Kate's heirloom soup tureen. What Pa wouldn't have, ceased to exist. Johnny never sang again.

Do you sing now, Johnny? When you sang, you were a butterfly. Is it safer to be an empty cocoon?

Jill sighed and stretched on the bed, glad for work to turn her mind from questions without answers.

In the next two hours she read four scripts, two about people with incurable diseases, one about a doctor trying to cure an incurable disease, and the last about a doctor *with* an incurable disease trying to save his marriage.

She tossed the last one on the pile and rubbed her burning eyes, then her forehead, where a headache was beginning to throb.

Wonderful. I'm developing symptoms!

While Jill was hunting through the remaining scripts, looking for one whose main character didn't have a suspicious cough, the door-bell rang.

Rats!

Jill rolled off the bed, shouting in the direction of Daisy's room, "I'll get it!"

"You're darned right!" Daisy shouted back.

It was one of their rules: Daisy was never to open the door late at night. It was a sensible rule, and one which had often kept Jill on the porch, pounding on the door and trying to convince her skeptical daughter that she was indeed Mom, who'd forgotten her house key —not L.A.'s latest rapist-killer, invariably a native of Omaha who'd moved to L.A., where rapist-killers are accorded proper publicity, not left to languish on back pages, cheek-by-jowl with real-estate ads.

Cautiously Jill opened the door.

"Whistling Christ!" Patti Gerard bubbled with laughter. "You open the door like a scared old lady."

"I was afraid you might be a native of Omaha. Come in."

The invitation was unnecessary. Patti was already in, striking a model's pose under the living room's Tiffany lamp.

"Have you ever seen anything so fabulous?" Patti demanded.

"Never," Jill replied as expected. "Do you mean your dress, your makeup, your hair, or your shoes?"

"The dress, the dress." Patti held up a fistful of skirt. "I found this fabulous dress in a Thai restaurant on Fairfax. The daughter of the old Thai couple who run the restaurant designed it. Two hours ago she was wearing it."

"Wonderful." Jill yawned. "Right now on Fairfax a Thai refugee is running around naked, screaming about crazy Americans."

"I'm going to make this girl a star," Patti enthused, "and she's going to make me a fortune. I've signed her to a contract. For the next year she'll design and make dresses exclusively for my boutique. When I'm ready to open my own shop, I'll take her with me."

"It is a beautiful dress." Jill admitted.

"I'll make it to Rodeo Drive if it kills me." Patti spread her arms expansively. "Which brings me to you."

"I don't want to make it to Rodeo Drive, Patti. Parking lot attendants mash your car if it isn't a Mercedes."

"That's not what I mean. Have you read *Dress for Success*?" Patti inspected Jill's khakis and shirt. "I didn't think so. You are dressed for impending doom."

"Patti! Give me a break. I am neat, clean, and comfortable. I hate wearing clothes that feel like they're wearing me."

Patti pulled a notebook from her large leather purse. "Here's what we'll do. First, a facial at Elizabeth Arden. Then, we'll have your hair done at Jon Peters—"

"I like my hair—"

"It looks like you cut it yourself," Patti snickered. Jill blushed. "You *didn't*!"

"Just the bangs. . . ."

"I don't want to hear about it." Patti groaned. "You haven't changed since the day I met you."

Jill laughed. "Sure I have, Patti. When we first met, I hadn't

51

brushed my hair in six days. Between the rats in my hair and my nuthouse pallor—"

"That's the past," Patti said quickly. "Let's talk about something else."

"I didn't know you were still touchy about it,"

"I'm not touchy," Patti said impatiently. "I just don't want to talk about it. Outside of you and the hospital staff in Cleveland, no one knows I've been anywhere other than La Costa. I'm not like you, Jill, telling the world."

"I don't tell the world," Jill objected. "Just friends, people I know well enough to trust and confide in."

"You're Little Mary Sunshine, thinking your friends will always be your friends." Patti almost sneered. "Listen, kid, people can turn. When they do, and they want to destroy you, they'll use any weapon they can. I'll be damned if I'll be the one who hands them the gun."

"That's paranoid," Jill snapped, then reconsidered. "Forgive me, Patti, but I can't feel as you do. I have to feel that my friends are my friends, that they'll continue to care about me just the way I am. Carl knows, Nick knows—"

"Telling lovers! That's crazy!"

"We must be cured, Patti. I call you paranoid, and you call me crazy, and neither of us hits the other." Jill laughed, then suddenly confided, "I told Dan Carmichael."

"Your boss? Oh, Jill."

"I felt I should. His wife was having problems, nothing major, just a moping around the house, run-of-the-mill depression. I thought I might help. Dan says I did. I even showed him the scars on my wrists."

"I would *never* do that," Patti asserted, "with Dan or anyone else. As far as I'm concerned, that was another life. Maybe it didn't even happen."

"Don't say that," Jill said sharply. "What you were in the past is an important part of what you are now. When you first arrived from Cleveland to stay with me, you were so frightened you couldn't go to the mailbox. Now look at you—confident, successful, and so gorgeous I feel like the 'before' picture whenever I stand next to you. You have a right to be proud of your accomplishments, the more so because of what you've gone through."

"How's Carl in bed?" Patti asked.

All right, Patti. That's more than a hint. I'll back off.

"I've had worse than Carl." Jill grinned. "How's that for ambiguous?"

"I've got one who'd put you away." Patti's eyes glowed. "Best mouth in the world and the second-best lay. If that isn't enough, he's married, which means he doesn't demand too much of my time, and he's not too bright, which means there's no danger of falling in love."

"Can't argue with perfection." Jill laughed.

"He has a hideaway for romantic trysts," Patti went on, "a fabulous place above Sunset with sparkling Burgundy always on ice and a stereo that oozes Mantovani."

Jill listened, trying to keep a straight face.

"Go ahead, laugh. He has money, not taste." Patti grinned. "You'd love his little retreat, Persian rugs on the walls, mirrors on the ceiling, and outside, a secluded deck and hot tub with a view overlooking the All-American Burger. And the bedroom! You wouldn't believe it!"

"Red-velvet and gilt? Whips and chains?"

"Worse. On the dresser in his clandestine hideaway, the idiot has a family portrait, a wife who looks like Eva Braun and kids—God knows their gender—you'd swear they're orangutans!"

Jill laughed. "You must have turned off like that!"

"Me?" Patti giggled. "Never! I just turned the Swiss Family Hideous to the wall, grabbed him and got what I'd come for. Your turn." Patti settled back. "What's Carl like?"

"Well, let's see." Jill smiled. Comparing lovers was their oldest tradition. In the psychiatric ward Patti had crawled in under the piano where Jill lay curled in a fetal ball, introduced herself as though at a garden party, and then gone on to graphically describe her affair with a Cleveland meteorologist who'd screwed her, high above Cleveland, in a weather balloon. Jill hadn't responded, hadn't even blinked, but the next morning woke up laughing. In her first deliberate, conscious act in weeks she'd gone searching for Patti to babble the story of her affair with an ear, nose, and throat man who'd blown out her sinuses and read her his novel-in-progress (he fancied himself the Joseph Wambaugh of medicine) as literary foreplay to his lovemaking, which he did as ineptly as he wrote and practiced medicine. They'd laughed that morning, and it was then Jill knew she'd get well. "Let's see. I would say that making love with Carl is like jumping into a pile of dry leaves. He's all dry and rustly, with little things that poke you here and there."

Patti laughed. "Why do you bother? With him or that other guy, what's-his-name, the writer?"

"Nick can be bliss when he's in the right mood." Jill knew she sounded defensive.

"So, you wait for right moods and jump into dead leaves. Fabulous!" Patti tucked her notebook into her purse.

"Everyone needs someone, Patti, and nothing comforts like skin." Jill sighed. "I can't imagine hurting and having no one to hold me."

"Sounds like you miss being married." Patti observed. "Too bad Steve turned out to be a bastard."

"Steve's a good guy, Patti. It's just that he has a need to play daddy while my need is to rebel against anything remotely resembling authority. Our marriage was cut off at the impasse."

"Time to go." Patti smiled. "Before you get to the part where the failure of your marriage was all your fault."

"Well, whose was it?" Jill asked. "You have to see Steve's point of view."

"No, I don't," Patti said decisively. "And if you want to saddle yourself with the thankless chore of *understanding* the men in your life, it's your grief."

"Nick and Carl are nice guys—"

"They should be," Patti interrupted. "You pamper them enough."

"The pampering is mutual, Patti."

"*Never!* From women it's expected. From men it's a favor, and you'd damn well better be grateful. Men! Fuck 'em, forget 'em, and rotate 'em like tires." Patti stepped onto the porch.

"Words to live by." Jill laughed. The Patti reflected in moonlight was a softer Patti, a less than tough cookie, a lady with eyes like bruised sapphires and a full, rosy mouth.

"Whistling Christ! I almost forgot. How's Daisy?"

Jill smiled. "Tonight she told me she has enough on her mind without worrying about a middle-aged lady."

"That sounds like Daisy, and she sounds just fine. I'll call you tomorrow." Patti waved.

"Wait!" Jill stepped onto the porch. "Who's the first best, Patti?"

"First best what?"

"You said your guy was the world's second-best lay. Who's the first best?"

Patti's laughter could be heard in the next block. "The next one, Jill. Always the next one. Gives me hope on bad days."

54

Jill waited until Patti was safely in her car, then turned off the porch light and closed the door.

In the bedroom she kicked off her shoes, wiggled out of her clothes, slipped into a man's striped nightshirt, and flopped into bed. The television flickered. Jill turned up the sound and live coverage of the fire, an inferno that leaped from hill to hill, incinerating ground cover and exploding trees.

The UBC man-on-the-spot attempted to interview a homeowner hosing down his roof and got hosed down for his intrusion. Evidently the homeowner had neither time nor inclination to "tell the good folks out there what it feels like to see your home go up in smoke."

The announcer made no mention of which fires were out and which were spreading. For all the audience knew, the fire might be outside their windows, eating the begonias.

Jill peeked through the shutters. No fire. She picked up a script and read three pages before starting to doze. With "The Star-Spangled Banner" playing lullaby, she fell asleep, one final thought skidding through her mind.

I forgot to call Mother. Rats!

CHAPTER 5

Jill handed the folder to Dan, then sat quietly, waiting for his reaction. Finally Dan looked up.

"Impressed?" Jill asked.

"I certainly am," Dan affirmed. "Friedman's been working here for all of ten minutes. Where did he get all this confidential information?"

"He seems to have a penchant for . . . uh . . . checking things out," Jill explained. "But isn't it well done?"

"It is." Dan returned the folder to Jill. "The entire research department couldn't do better if you gave them a month."

"Man, I can't tell you what that means to me!" Alex was decorating the doorway with his swashbuckler's pose. "Thank you."

"Good job, Alex." Dan said approvingly. "Your report indicates a real talent for scheduling."

"No shit! You really think so?" Alex glowed.

For a moment Jill wondered if Alex would throw his arms around Dan and whirl him, but he settled instead for a vigorous pumping of Dan's hand. "I really appreciate that, sir."

"Quite all right. Quite all right." Dan finally pulled loose and turned to Jill. "Will you stop by my office before lunch?"

"I'll be there," Jill promised.

"And welcome to the shop, Alex." Dan moved quickly toward the door as Alex reached, once again, for his hand. "I think you're going to run rings around us all."

Then Dan was gone, leaving Jill smiling after him while beside her Alex twittered and twitched, the perpetual-motion machine.

"Man, that really meant something coming from Dan," Alex bubbled. "It did mean something, didn't it, Jill?"

"Certainly. Dan's not stingy with compliments, but he doesn't spread them around, either. If he says you have talent, he means it."

"Shit, I've always had talent," Alex proclaimed. "The only problem is trying to get someone to fucking recognize it." He reached across Jill's desk, picked up a paperweight, and shook it, causing snow to fall on a miniature skyline. "Man, from now on this is the closest I plan to come to winter. My wife feels the same way."

"How is . . . uh . . ."

"Nina."

"You said she might be pregnant."

"Hope not. I'm not ready for that." Alex tossed the paperweight onto the desk. "I sent her out first thing this morning to make the round of agents."

"Agents?"

Alex preened and reached for his wallet. "Man, I got the world's most beautiful wife. She's a model. Here, look at this."

"Gorgeous," Jill said softly. From her picture Nina Friedman was indeed beautiful, platinum-haired, doe-eyed, with a wholesome all-American smile that was also mysteriously sultry.

Alex tapped the picture with his forefinger. "Man, if she was three inches taller, she'd be Cheryl Tiegs. Wish I could take her somewhere and get three more vertebrae shoved in her back. I could live with having a famous wife."

"Most men couldn't." Jill was impressed. "I give you credit."

"Hey, a million bucks is a million bucks! I wouldn't mind taking money from a woman. Women have been soaking men since Adam and Eve."

"Oh." Jill reeled with Alex's split-second transition from liberated husband to chauvinistic Scrooge. "Well, about your report. It's—"

"Think Lawrence will like it?" Alex interrupted.

"Why wouldn't he? It's good enough to send him into orbit, which is more than NASA could do."

"If Lawrence likes it, I'm in!" Excitedly Alex hopped backward, narrowly missing Polly, who'd quietly entered the room.

"Your office is ready, Alex," Polly told him.

"Dynamite! Where is it?"

"502. Next to Fontaine's office."

Jill frowned. "There's nothing next to Fontaine's except the men's room."

"Alex's office is *between* Fontaine's office and the men's room," Polly explained.

"But that's a supply closet!" Jill was incredulous. "You can't put Alex in a supply closet."

"I'm not putting Alex anywhere," Polly said sharply. "Whoever makes these decisions assigned him the only available space."

"Who *does* make these decisions?" Jill reached for the phone. "I'll call."

"Nehemiah Holmes." Alex supplied the information. "Office management. Been with UBC fourteen years. Son's a drag queen."

"Whomever." Polly scowled at Alex. "If you want another office, you'll have to put it in writing."

"I'll live with it. For now." Alex blessed Jill with a dazzling smile. "I'm just happy to be working here."

"You must be thrilled beyond sanity if you're willing to work in a space that isn't the size of a decent burial plot. Well, go get settled. I'll see you later."

"Lunch?"

"Sure." Jill glanced at her calendar. "No. Sorry. I already have a lunch date."

"Mañana." Alex followed Polly to the door.

"Alex! Wait!" Jill had an idea. "Has Nina ever done any dress modeling in department stores or boutiques?"

"That's how she started . . . Saks, Marshall Field. Why?"

"I have a friend who manages an exclusive boutique. She may be in need of a model. I'll give you her number for Nina."

With one bound Alex was at her side. Jill flinched, expecting a bear hug, but Alex stood quietly. "Think your friend would hire Nina?"

"Don't get excited, Alex. It's only a thought."

"Wow! You're terrific!" Alex swung Jill off her feet, whirling her in long, looping circles.

"Alex, Alex, it's okay." Jill held on for her life. "Alex, put me down! Alex!"

Jill spun through the air, wondering how she'd explain cracked ribs to Daisy. . . . *Mommy was attacked by a whirling dervish, dear. He didn't mean to break Mommy's bones, but dervishes whirl, and that's what they do.*

"Alex!" Polly called from the doorway. "Alex! Alex! Your temporary secretary is here."

"Yeah?" With a gesture that resembled a bow Alex lowered Jill to the ground. "Redhead?"

"Quite possibly." Polly smiled sweetly. "Who knows what color his hair was before he went bald."

"A male secretary?" Alex frowned, then smiled. "This might be a kick. I'll go get acquainted."

"You do that." Polly stepped aside.

"My God!" Jill was sitting on the couch, breathing hard. "Remind me to send Alex a telegram if his wife gets the job. It's dangerous to be in the same room with him and good news."

Polly straightened a pile of already straight scripts. "I think his behavior's appalling."

"Alex is ebullient, Polly." Jill smiled. "He walks around in a charged field. Energy begets energy. We'll never be bored."

"Worn out is more like it, Jill. Genies don't always return to their bottles on cue," Polly warned. "By the way, a Dr. Kerry called. He wants to change your Wednesday appointment to next Thursday."

"Wednesday, Thursday, what's the difference?" Jill asked, once again scanning Alex's report. "We've been working on the same case of hives for three years."

"Why so long?"

"Conflict of interests. Kerry insists on knowing why I itch. I just want to stop itching . . . say Polly, I could do a compatibility graph to accompany Alex's report. See?" Jill drew an arrow across Alex's page. "This show could be teamed with this one . . ."

A few minutes later the paper in front of Jill was covered with arrows, lines, and circles. Two cigarettes burned in her ashtray, and she was humming under her breath. Polly tiptoed out of the office.

An hour later Jill pressed her buzzer, and Polly reappeared.

"Will you clip these together, type, copy, et cetera?" Jill asked. "What's next?"

"A Marshall Bellarmine called about a so-called zookeeper project," Polly replied. "He was screaming."

"Dan told me about that one." Jill grinned. "Seems that Bellarmine, who produces movies, wants to sell us a wonderful story about a zookeeper in love with a gorilla. He says it's a metaphor for our times."

"Beg pardon?" Polly blinked.

"My sentiments exactly, but then, I've never claimed to be an intellectual. I read Buckley for the jokes." She looked at her watch. "Time to see Dan before lunch. I'll be back at two. If anyone wants to know where I am, you haven't the foggiest. If Daisy needs to reach me, I'll be at this number." She handed a slip of paper to Polly. "Lunch and romance, hopefully in that order. I'm starved."

"So am I, but lately more for romance." Polly sighed. "Bring back a doggy bag."

Jill found Dan looking out the windows of his comfortably furnished office. Genuine oil paintings, the corporate stamp of status and tenure, covered his walls and his couch was brightened by pillows needlepointed in purples and blues.

"Marshall Bellarmine called about the zookeeper project," Jill announced. "Polly said he was screaming."

"He's been screaming for fifty-seven years. Some bellow their way to the top."

"Bellarmine's the top?"

"For Bellarmine, getting elected president would be a step down. Look at this."

Jill joined him at the window. Outside a ragged-looking man of indeterminate age paced the sidewalk, carrying a red-lettered sign: UBC SUCKS!

"Ah, a critic," Jill said. "Who is he?"

"Our resident picket," Dan told her. "He's been with UBC longer than most of the executives. The personnel department is afraid he'll claim retirement benefits."

"He has the look of a man who's spent most of his life in an institution," Jill observed. "Do you suppose he has anything to do with the bomb threats?"

"The police are keeping an eye on him." With one smooth motion Dan pulled the cord that closed the draperies. "That's enough of the view overlooking lunatics and smog."

"Your plants are flourishing." Jill gestured approvingly.

"They are supposed to indicate an atmosphere that supports life. UBC should be sued for false advertising." Dan sat at his desk. The shadows beneath his eyes shone a deeper gray than his hair, which waved away from his face, imparting a father-confessor look Jill found irresistible.

DAN/FRIEND.
GOT IT?
GOT IT.

"You wanted to see me?" She had never seen him so preoccupied. Whatever was on his mind ran through his conversations, discernible but indecipherable, like a subtext in a foreign language.

"I want you to give the departmental report in the meeting this afternoon." Dan was direct. "You had a bad initial experience. I think it's important that you get right back on the horse."

"No problem." Jill grinned at his look of surprise. "The horse didn't bite. He just ran away with himself."

"You're not afraid of Lawrence, are you?" He regarded her thoughtfully.

"Please. The man is a saint." Jill smiled.

"Obviously we go to different churches." Dan shook his head. "Well, that's it. Nothing else on my mind."

"Bullshit," Jill said quickly. "I know better than that, Dan. You said we're friends. It goes two ways, you know. I can be a good listener."

"I'll have to work it out on my own, Jill. . . ."

"Nancy?"

His face remained blank for a moment, then he nodded, slowly. "She's in therapy. She says it's helping, but . . . last night when I arrived home, I found her sitting in the dark. She told me that after listening to herself in therapy, she's decided she's a shallow, boring woman who deserves having to pay someone to listen to her. She was laughing when she said it, but . . ." He picked up a letter opener and toyed with it, running his finger lightly over the sharp edge. "Nancy isn't boring and shallow. She never was . . . ever! She's . . . unhappy."

"Why, Dan?" Jill asked softly.

"That's what I ask myself, usually on my way home from work late at night. What does that tell you, kid?" He jabbed the end of his thumb with the opener. A small spot of blood appeared. Dan stood up, shrugging his shoulders in a deliberate release of tension. "Lunch?"

"I have an appointment. Thanks."

"I'll ask Alex." Dan smiled. "I can introduce him to the cuisine in the commissary, which will net him an immediate introduction to the nurse in the infirmary. That constitutes the grand tour and baptism by blue-plate special. See you later."

Jill resisted an impulse to go after him, knowing it was comfort for herself she sought, along with her desire to comfort him. Instead she walked slowly in the opposite direction, toward the elevators.

Ten minutes later Jill was running up the stairs of Carl's apartment building. She rapped on his door, two knocks, one knock, two—not a signal exactly, just her own pet knock.

He opened the door with a flourish. "Sweetheart!"

"I have forty minutes," Jill announced. "What in God's name is that smell?"

"Why do you always begin by telling me when you have to leave?" Carl was aggrieved. "Your clock-watching does not enhance the experience."

Jill sniffed, wrinkling her nose. "Are you boiling somebody's gall bladder?"

"It's a special treat." The pain in his voice was unmistakable. "Poached salmon with bay leaves. I'm sorry you find the aroma offensive."

"Oh, no," Jill amended quickly. "Now that I know what it is, it smells . . . divine."

Jill followed Carl as he led the way to the kitchen. He removed the lid from a steaming soup kettle and inhaled deeply, his conventionally handsome face blissful. "Your treat."

Jill waved away the steam and peered inside. At the bottom of the kettle was a blob that might once have been salmon, bouncing slightly in seven quarts of rapidly boiling water.

"How long has this been . . . uh . . . poaching?"

"Since this morning, when I left for hospital rounds." He slipped his arms around Jill and pulled her close. "I've been thinking about you since I woke up this morning." He licked her earlobe, then gave it a quick little nip. "I have a salad in the refrigerator. Another special treat."

"Wonderful." Jill wished he would nip at her earlobe again.

"I thought we could eat Oriental-style." He gestured at the dining area, where he had carefully set two formal places, complete with napkins and a rose, in a vase, on the floor. "Romantic, isn't it?"

"You're going to spoil me with all these special treats." Jill wondered if she was supposed to crouch, squat, or merely sprawl on the white linoleum floor.

Lying down would be nice. That's why I came.

"My girl could use some spoiling." He kissed her cheek. "And this way I don't have to disturb my work."

The kitchen table was stacked high with books and papers, notes, and manila envelopes, all heaped around an ancient typewriter.

"I'm doing a paper for the *Journal.*" Carl removed a bottle of wine from the refrigerator, set a corkscrew in place, and began a twisting motion. "It's called 'The Challenge of Holistic Medicine.' As Atwater

Simone said in his unparalleled 'Holistic Approach—Folk or Fact?':
'The segmentation of human beings into body parts has made sick
people sicker, and has never made anyone well.' " He stopped twisting and stood for a moment, as though savoring the thought. "Brilliant, isn't it? So simple. So true." With some difficulty he resumed
twisting. "This corkscrew doesn't want to—"

"May I try?" Jill offered.

"No, sweetheart. I can manage. You get the salad."

Carl's refrigerator contained the bachelor's staples, a stick of butter on a saucer and month-old English muffins. There were two
covered bowls.

"Which bowl?" Jill didn't want to blunder into, God forbid, a medical specimen.

"Blue." Carl's face flushed with exertion as he twisted the corkscrew harder and faster.

Jill pried up the blue bowl's lid. Inside was something left over
from the special-effects department of whatever studio had made
The Green Slime.

"You doused it with salad dressing before you left for hospital
rounds," Jill guessed.

"I know how much you like blue cheese . . . whoops!" Carl lifted
the corkscrew and frowned into the bottle. "The cork seems to have
. . . uh . . . splintered and fallen in. Ah, well, a little cork never hurt
good wine."

Jill looked from the slime in the bowl to the bottle in Carl's hand
to the rapidly boiling pot on the stove.

"Last one in bed is a rotten egg!"

"Jill!" Carl was shocked. "How can you be so crass? I have feelings,
tender feelings for you, feelings that go far beyond the limited time
we spend together—even more limited now that you have that ridiculous job. Television! Opiate of the masses! Mind rot!" He waved the
corkscrew in the air. "If our relationship means nothing more to you
than fleeting physical moments—"

"Twenty-two minutes, Carl."

"I'll turn down the bedspread." Carl ran past Jill into the bedroom.

Jill threw the bowl into the sink, dropped the bottle of wine into
the wastebasket, switched off the fire under the pot, and followed
Carl into the bedroom. He was carefully folding a green chenille
bedspread.

"I treat people, not diseases," he was saying, "whole human beings, not parts." He opened the closet and removed a garment bag, unzipped it, and slipped the bedspread inside.

"My father treated parts." Carl shrugged out of his sweater and folded it neatly. "He'd come home from the hospital and say to my mother, 'I had a ruptured spleen today,' or 'I did a gall bladder' or '*My* diabetic had cardiac arrest.' No names, no faces. Just parts. My father called me 'Son,' never Carl. Just 'Son.' A part of himself."

He stepped out of his trousers, reaching in the closet for a pants hanger. Long since undressed, Jill watched from the middle of his bed while Carl lined up his pants creases with infinite care.

If it wasn't for his holistic lovemaking, which certainly treats all of my parts, I'd be better off in the commissary, risking ptomaine with Alex and Dan.

"Medicine must treat the entire being." Carl stuffed mahogany shoe trees into his shoes. "When physicians become open and honest, sharing and caring . . ." He sat on the edge of the bed and reached for Jill.

Finally!

The sheets made a rustling sound. Jill smiled. He moved closer. More rustling. Jill tried to swallow the laughter bubbling in her chest.

"What's funny?" His mouth was an eighth of an inch from her lips.

"The sheets." She giggled. "They sound like a pile of dry leaves."

"I hadn't noticed." Carl was peeved. He shifted his weight, pulling the sheets with him.

Rustle, rustle was all Jill heard.

"Oh, God," she burbled, overcome with giggles. She buried her head in the pillow, trying to control her laughter.

"Nerves," Carl said softly. "You've been working too hard." Gently he began rubbing her back. "Breathe slowly through your mouth."

She did, and two minutes later, giggling gone, she wrapped her arms around Carl's neck, melting into him like butter into hot toast.

Fifteen minutes later Jill was scooping her pile of clothes from the floor and running for the shower. "You were wonderful . . . wonderful," Carl called after her.

She tossed her watch onto the counter and jumped into the shower, emerging four minutes later, clean, dripping, and soothed. After a cursory blotting with one of Carl's oversized towels she dressed quickly, then feeling like someone who'd been caught in the rain, she returned to the bedroom, where Carl was removing the bedspread from the garment bag.

"We have so much in common, Jill." He shook out the spread. Jill paused in her search for her shoes.

What? Outside of lunch and romance, neither of us has ever understood a word the other has said.

"Carl." Jill strapped her shoes. "Next week I'll bring sandwiches?"

"I wanted today to be special," he said gloomily. "That's why I cooked."

"It wasn't your fault, dear. I appreciate the thought."

He followed her into the living room. "I think it's time we extended our relationship, Jill."

"To what?" It sounded like he wanted to add on a room.

"To a more meaningful relationship, one with caring and sharing and—"

"What an interesting thought," Jill interrupted. "Call me tonight. We'll talk about it."

She opened the door and leaned up to kiss him. He scowled. "Your job isn't good for you, Jill. It's dulling your sensibilities."

"Tonight." She aimed at his face and kissed air as he turned away.

"Listen to me, Jill. Your job is causing great stress, anxiety, fatigue, depression."

Jill gave up trying to kiss him. "Bye." She ran down the stairs.

Carl leaned over the railing and shouted. "Depression causes cancer."

Jill continued to run.

"You don't have to get cancer, Jill. You can marry me!"

Jill skidded and stopped, tripping over her feet in the process. She *couldn't* have heard what she'd heard. She looked back at Carl, who was hanging so far over the railing she was afraid he might tumble into the stairwell below.

"Think about it, Jill," he called.

"I will." She waved and ran on.

Confused, she pulled into traffic. What had brought that on? Carl had never mentioned marriage. Come to think of it, he had never mentioned seeing her more than once a week. Until today he'd seemed content with their casual arrangement. Until . . . her new job. Her new and demanding job. Her new, demanding, and intriguing job in a field he disapproved of.

She considered the choice Carl had presented: Marriage to him and health, or her job and the certainty of cancer.

In the name of love a curse has been placed on your head.

Love? More likely fear, a fear of loss in Carl, who considered her to be part of his whole. To lose her would be amputation—perhaps little finger, perhaps vital organ . . . perhaps. . . .

Polly looked up from the salad she was eating at her desk. "How was lunch?"

Jill's empty stomach gurgled. "If you happen to be in the commissary, I'd appreciate a ham-on-rye."

"I'd give a week's salary for a lunch like that." Polly bit a carrot in two. "Here's your report."

Jill scanned the pages. "Not bad. Reads well. My part and Alex's complement one another."

"That's what I thought." Polly handed Jill a folder. "An index of your files, phone calls to return, and your schedule for the remainder of the day."

"You're a whiz, Polly." Jill was delighted. "Oh, my God, look what I've done!"

"What?" Polly looked over her shoulder.

"I have a date tonight with Nick." Jill groaned. "I never have dinner and romance on a day when I've had lunch and romance."

"Why?"

"One man a day is a hobby." Jill grinned. "Two is a profession."

"I'd say two is almost adequate."

"I'd better call Nick before he begins planning dinner. I can just see it now, Polly—Nick's candlelit loft and another fine kettle of fish!"

Nick's phone was answered by his recorded message, self-consciously cute and replete with obscure literary allusions. Jill waited for the end of the recording, waited and waited while Nick's voice rolled on, confiding wittily phrased innermost thoughts to absolute strangers.

Finally her ears were blasted by a long, piercing *beep*, and she spoke her message. "Sorry. Can't make it tonight. Love, Jill."

She hung up, aware of voices other than Polly's in her outer office. They increased in volume as she read Polly's file index.

Curious, Jill punched her buzzer.

"Who's out there?" she asked when Polly appeared.

"Alex Friedman and Zippy de Franco have found each other!" Polly snickered. "Alex is doing all the talking. Surprise! Surprise!"

Jill stretched and got up. "I want Alex to read his part of the report in our meeting. It will be his introduction to UBC and UBC's introduction to Alex."

"Alex doesn't need introducing," Polly said. "While you were at lunch he was up and down the halls, ringing more doorbells than an Avon lady on speed."

Jill arrived in the outer office just as Alex was chewing the last of a cookie. "Hi."

Zippy giggled. "Hi, Jill. How they hanging?"

"Hello, Zippy." Jill decided to think of Zippy as quaint.

"Got to go now. Almost time for the meeting." Zippy lurched lopsidedly to his feet. "See you through the double doors."

Not to mention the looking glass.

"Zippy's a dynamite guy," Alex said loudly, in the direction of Zippy's departing back. "Sharp *sharp!*"

"Uh, yes. Let's talk about the report."

"Dan loved it, *loved it.*" Alex followed her into the office. "When you impress an old pro, that's something. Isn't that something, huh?"

"Sure is. Have you read my addition to the report?"

"Yeah." Alex flopped full-length on the couch.

"Don't get so excited. Your blood pressure will go up." Jill's empty stomach gurgled. "Do you have any more cookies?"

"Nah, they were Zippy's. I could go for more myself, but Zippy said I could have only one. Weird cat, that Zippy. Checked him out. He comes off like the Young Turk of all time, but there's something mushy 'round them edges. I'll check him with another source. Ain't nothing you can't get a handle on if you know where to grab."

"Sounds like a personal problem," Dan said from the doorway. "Interoffice grabbing can lead to big trouble."

"Not if you're good at it." Alex grinned.

"May I see you outside for a moment, Jill?" Dan asked.

"Sure." Alex leaped off the couch. "What's going on?"

"Nothing important." Dan told him. "Just business left over from before you were hired."

"Oh." Obviously disappointed, Alex took the report from Jill's desk and returned to the couch. "Man, I just love my report!"

"I can have it enlarged if you like." Jill teased. "You can hang the pages wall-to-wall in your closet."

"Holy shit! What an idea! Do it!" His cup of enthusiasm overflowed, splashing a startled Jill.

"Back in a minute, Alex," Jill said, wishing she'd kept her mouth shut.

Once in the outer office Dan asked her to walk down the hall with him. "We'll take the scenic route past the mailroom." They walked, Dan silent, Jill wondering.

"I read your part of the report." Dan squeezed her arm. "It's fine. In fact, it's a doozy."

"I'm pleased if you are." She was, to the tips of her shoes.

"Alex wanted to know which part of the report I liked better, his or yours." Dan sounded annoyed. "He's a gloryhound, Jill."

"He's young, Dan, eager . . ."

"And, his emphasis is wrong." He glanced at her, frowning. "You know how the commissary is at lunchtime with people from all over the company coming and going. Well, Alex knew every one of them, not personally of course, but who they were, their positions in the company, backgrounds, even what are commonly referred to as skeletons in the closet. I didn't know half the details Alex told me, and I'm supposed to be the old honcho around here."

"You've probably heard all the gossip and never paid much attention. What passes over your head sticks between Alex's ears."

"It's not the gossip, Jill." Dan was specific. "It's the energy expended in the wrong direction."

"Energy he has," Jill agreed. "Alex spills more than you and I drink."

"I'll give Alex a fair shake, Jill," Dan promised. "But, for Christ's sake, tell him to stop the running commentaries on everyone who comes through the door. He sounds like a walking CIA file."

"I will, Dan. He'll be wonderful. You'll see."

Their conversation had brought them full circle. They entered the outer office, arm in arm.

"Meeting time. The three of us should go in together. I'll introduce Hot Stuff"—Dan grinned—"get him off to a good start."

Alex was where they'd left him, sitting on the couch.

"Rise and shine, Alex," Jill said, patting him on the shoulder. "Time for the meeting."

"Call me Lexy." Alex stared straight ahead.

"What the hell's wrong with him?" Dan bent over for a closer look. "You all right, Alex?"

"Call me Lexy." Alex's eyes were fixed at some invisible point just over Dan's head.

"What's going on here?" Dan demanded. Then, with a look of dismayed realization: "Has Zippy de Franco been here?"

"Just a few minutes ago. Why?"

"Did Zippy give Alex anything to swallow, snort, smoke, sniff, or shoot?" Dan asked angrily.

"Just cookies," Jill replied. "Chocolate chip."

"The chips aren't chocolate, Jill. They're hashish." Dan's fist slammed the edge of Jill's desk. "That goddamned de Franco!"

"What do we do now?" Jill felt a warm, prickly itching begin at the backs of her knees.

"Damned if I know," Dan said. "Grab Alex! He's falling over!"

Jill lunged for Alex, grabbing him just as he slid over the edge of the couch. She propped him up. "Stay, Alex."

"Call me Lexy." He smiled the cherubic smile of a two-year-old drifting off to sleepy-bye.

"I could kill Zippy de Franco." Dan paced the carpet.

"It's all my fault," Jill moaned. She wanted to run to the ladies' room, pull off her jeans, scratch with something hard and sharp, and . . .

Dan whirled. "How is it your fault, Jill? I didn't tell you about Zippy, that half-assed. . . . Trust Neiman to hire some flaky. . . ."

"Here you are." Polly ran in, breathless. "I've been up and down the halls looking for you." She glanced from Jill to Dan. "You already know about Alex."

"Call me Lexy," Alex crooned.

"Will you stay with Alex, Polly?" Jill asked. "Just watch him, make sure he doesn't fall off the couch or wander away?"

"I charge extra for baby-sitting," Polly said. "Okay, okay, I'll look after the lad."

"I feel terrible about this." Jill groaned, stabbing at her legs.

"Feel terrible later," Dan instructed. "We're late."

Dan gripped Jill's elbow and propelled her out of the room. As they reached the hall she dropped her letter opener. She tugged at Dan, wanting to stop and retrieve it, but he pulled her along. Jill tried to scratch as she ran, but couldn't. Dan was flying.

Rats, she silently screamed, as Dan opened the double doors and pushed her through.

CHAPTER 6

"Where's your new guy . . . uh . . . Friedman?" Neiman asked as Dan and Jill pulled their chairs up to the conference table.

"He was going down from Jerusalem into Jericho and fell among thieves," Dan responded blandly.

"What the hell does that mean?" Neiman challenged.

Dan turned his back on Neiman. "Did you bring both copies of the report?" he asked Jill.

"Right here, Dan . . . uh . . . oh, God!" While Jill struggled to control the half of her that was visible above the table, beneath the mahogany she was rubbing her legs together wildly like a demented cricket. "Excuse me, Dan I need . . . coffee."

She twitched to her feet and hurried toward the kitchenette, a small, efficiently organized space just off the conference room.

A sleepy-eyed young man lounged against the counter, reading *People* magazine.

"Ice cubes," Jill gasped hoarsely. She reached for the refrigerator door, but the young man intercepted before she could touch the handle.

"*My* job, miss. You look like you could use a drink."

"No drink." Jill hopped up and down. "Just the ice."

He removed a tray from the freezer and slowly, very slowly squeezed the release handle. "Lawrence here yet?"

"Not yet. Mr. Lawrence is late."

He tossed the ice into a glass. "I'd better keep a lookout. Lawrence likes his Tang made fresh. Scotch? Perrier?"

Jill whisked the glass out of his hand, shook out the cubes, sat on the floor, hoisted the legs of her jeans and slammed the ice against the backs of her legs. "Ahhhh."

He stared at her. "You work here?"

No, I just come here to put ice on my legs.

"I'm in Programing."

"You!" he snorted. "Goddamn affirmative action! Boy, this is one lousy time to be white and male. I can't get my foot in the . . . goddamn! Lawrence's here! Time to reconstitute."

He reached for the Tang and a beaker as Jill scrambled to her feet.

Lawrence was already enthroned in his chair and staring at the board when Jill slipped into her seat. Everyone else was properly in place except Angela Kent whose chair was occupied by L. B. "Syco" Fontaine.

"I have several announcements," Lawrence said.

He rose from his chair and walked to the board, where he stood stroking the frame gently as one would an old, faithful dog. Finally, he faced the chronically tense executives.

"This is not a scheduling board. This is a vertical crap table." His eyes darted from one startled executive to the next, defying disagreement. There was none. "During the week to come," Lawrence continued, "a computerized scheduling system will be installed. The system will provide an instantaneous compilation of data correlated from Programing, Research, Program Practices, Business Affairs, and all other pertinent areas of operation. I will program the system. Any questions?"

Dumbfounded stares greeted the question. No one knew what to ask. Even if they had, Lawrence's ominous demeanor precluded the asking.

"Uh . . . sir . . . allow me to express my support for technology." There was no mistaking the mellifluous tones of L. B. Fontaine. "And, of course, my admiration for your grasp of it. I think I can speak for us all when I say—"

"Where the hell's the producer of *Harris the Magnificent*?" Lawrence barked. "I want to meet with him now."

"I'll go find him." The unquenchable Fontaine leaped from his chair, heading for the door at a dead run.

Lawrence glowered at the slamming door, then rubbed his chin thoughtfully, musing aloud, "What we need is a show that deals with life."

Neiman sighed. "Life is a highly promotable concept, sir, and one we should certainly discuss, but—"

"As I see it"—Lawrence ignored Neiman—"in television, as in life, symbols are important. Think of the eagle. Think of the flag."

71

He paused, allowing the assemblage to think of the eagle, think of the flag. "These symbols bring to mind pride, tradition, a noble heritage. They are symbols to salute. Now, think of the UBC symbol."

Twenty-six executives stared at one another, faces registering panic. Who knew the symbol?

"UBC doesn't have a symbol," Lawrence said, to a collective sigh of relief, "an oversight I plan to rectify. I have instructed Research to delve into UBC's origins and report back to me with recommendations for a symbol which will reflect the tradition of this network. Now"—Lawrence turned away from the table—"for my final announcement: Zippy de Franco has been promoted to Vice-President and Special Assistant to the President. It's time we had innovative thinkers in effective positions."

A general gasp circled the conference table, and every eye turned to Zippy, who blinked, giggled softly, and said "Oh, wow!"

The questions would come later, in the halls, the offices, the men's room, the bar across the street, the parking lot, and everyone's bedroom: "Why him? Why not me? What the hell is a special assistant? How will this affect me?" At the moment there was nothing anyone could say, no reaction possible beyond a shocked and silent sucking of air.

Lawrence ignored the consternation around him. "Movies. What's going on in the movie department?"

"Car . . . Car . . . Car . . . michael," Neiman sputtered, choking on Lawrence's final announcement.

"Jill," Dan whispered.

Jill nodded imperceptibly and removed the report from its folder. At first she was shaky, nonplused by the strained, tinny sound of her voice, but gradually grew more confident, warming to her material. Ten minutes later she closed the folder, quite pleased with herself.

Lawrence swung around in his chair and looked directly at Jill. "Interesting report. Good job. Yours?"

"The graph is mine," Jill replied. "The first half of the report was written by the new man in our department, Alexander Friedman."

"Where is this Friedman?" Lawrence asked.

"Uh . . . writing another report," Jill vamped, "equally brilliant."

"Tell him to come to meetings," Lawrence ordered. "We need all the brilliance we can get."

"Certainly. . . ."

The door crashed open and Fontaine burst into the room, dragging behind him a red-faced, grunting man.

"What the hell is going on?" the man shouted. "Our meeting isn't until three o'clock. Why have I been dragged here bodily by this *dolt?*"

Neiman jerked to his feet, ran around the table, and brushed Fontaine aside. "So glad you could make it, Jim. Sorry about the confusion. Sit down. Coffee? Tea? Chivas Regal?"

Somewhat mollified, Jim allowed himself to be guided to a chair opposite Lawrence.

"I think you know everyone on our staff." Neiman beamed at Jim, his best "make nice" smile. "So, how's the family?"

Jim opened his mouth to reply.

"Harris the Magnificent is a jerk," Lawrence snarled.

Jim's mouth snapped shut, his eyes burning with anger. When he spoke, his voice was calm, almost emotionless, the voice of a man who knows he might leave this meeting unemployed. "You want Harris to be more likable?"

"Yeah, he's an asshole."

"You got it. I'll make him a mensch."

"How?"

"Easy." Jim leaned back in his chair, his face puckered with creative effort. "We'll give him a crippled mother, an orphaned brother, a mangy dog, a talking bird, a fucking goat if we can find a cute one. We'll throw him into situations where he's the champion of the underdog. We'll give him a sense of humor. We'll give him endearing flaws. If we have to, we'll give him leukemia. Every week he fights for his life."

"Don't identify the disease," Lawrence cautioned. "Too much reality makes audiences nervous."

"I hear ya. Anything else?" Jim inquired.

"What about girls?" Neiman asked slyly.

"For you or for Harris?" Jim quipped, and everyone laughed on cue. "You want tits, you got tits."

"That's it." Lawrence dismissed him. "Thanks for coming."

Quickly Neiman rose from his seat, took Jim's elbow, and guided him toward the door. "Thank you, Jim, thank you." Neiman bowed him out. "Do say hello to . . . uh . . . the wife."

"I'll do th—" The door slammed in Jim's face.

Lawrence swung back to the board. "Either that son of a bitch makes Harris likable, or I'll cancel the fucking show. Anybody got a pastrami sandwich?"

Several people patted their pockets for possible pastrami caches.

"I'll get you a sandwich, sir," Fontaine offered. "I'll go to the commissary. No, their sandwiches are inedible. I'll go to a deli . . . in Beverly Hills. No." He clasped his hands together in anguish. "L.A. pastrami stinks. I'll have to go to New York."

The door flew open, and Angela Kent swept into the room. "Sorry I'm late, darlings," she said breezily, "but the doctor wouldn't let me go without additional tests. He said major surgery may be required, but I . . . Why are you sitting in my chair?" she glared at Fontaine.

He looked up at her fearfully. "Uh . . . I just thought . . ."

"Oaf!" Angela leaned over, rapping Fontaine smartly between the eyes with the rape whistle she wore around her neck. "Cretin!"

"Ouch!" Fontaine whimpered, holding the bridge of his nose. "Ow."

"Well?" Angela was poised, whistle ready.

"I'm moving, I'm moving." He slithered out of the chair, circled Angela warily, and retired to the sofa in the corner, where he continued to whimper as both eyes turned black and blue.

"Where's McCaffery?" Lawrence asked. "I want to hear about limited series."

"Uh . . . uh . . . uh . . ." Neiman waffled fearfully.

"Well?" Lawrence's cheeks grew dangerously pink.

"Well . . . uh . . . it's a boy," Neiman quivered.

"What is?" Pink deepened to red.

"Carolyn McCaffery isn't here because she's given birth to a baby boy," Neiman stammered, then dove under the table.

"Wonderful!" Lawrence shouted. "A baby! A boy! A birth! Isn't that wonderful . . . wonderful . . . wonderful!"

Twenty-six heads bobbed up and down. *Wonderful! Wonderful!*

A transcendental smile transformed Lawrence's face. "Birth," he reflected. "So often, the beginning of life."

Neiman's face appeared over the edge of the table. He blinked like a man emerging from a bomb shelter and blushed, embarrassed at having been the sole victim of a false Lawrence alarm.

Lawrence watched as Neiman inched his way into his chair. "Perhaps you should see Angela's doctor, Dale. Your nerves seem to be getting the better of you."

Jill covered her mouth with her hand, forcibly repressing a laugh. She looked up to see Polly open the door and peer in.

"Who the hell are you?" Lawrence demanded.

"Polly Pritzer." Polly was unfazed. "I have a message for Jill Kenyon."

Lawrence flushed, upset at having his inner sanctum invaded. "This had better involve a death in the family."

"Close, sir," Polly said.

Jill leaped to her feet, heart frozen in her chest. "Mother!"

Thirty seconds later Jill and Polly were trotting down the hall together. "What's wrong, Polly? What did my mother say?"

"It was your brother who called, not your mother. I was out of the office when he called, taking Alex to the men's room. Just to the door," she explained at Jill's look. "Once I got him in, he refused to come out. He was singing 'I've Got To Be Me!' to the mirror."

"The message, Polly, the message!" Jill was frantic.

"The switchboard operator said the message was urgent, but what it was, she didn't say. . . ."

"It's my mother. I just know it's my mother." Jill groaned. "I should have called. I forgot. No, I didn't forget. I put it off. Polly . . . do you think . . . do you pick up any vibrations . . . about . . . I mean . . ."

"It's definitely your mother," Polly said. "That much I know. But I'm not certain how serious it might be. Try not to worry."

"Please try to get my brother on the phone. I'll call my mother's house."

"Sure thing." Polly picked up the phone as Jill flew into her office. Alex was sitting behind her desk, his hands folded, staring straight ahead with a smile Jill remembered from pictures of saints blessed with the Beatific Vision, or Daisy, as a baby, with gas.

"Excuse me, Alex," she said. "I need to use the phone."

"I like this chair," he said, his lips pursed in a pout.

"You may sit in my chair later," Jill promised. "Right now I need my desk."

"I like this desk," Alex purred.

"It's a wonderful desk," Jill agreed. "May I use it for a moment?"

"Mine!" Alex bleated, covering the desk protectively with both arms. He sounded exactly like Daisy when she was two and certain everyone else's possessions were hers. Jill looked at Alex helplessly, wishing she could simply pick him up, as she had Daisy, tuck him under her arm, and carry him off to his room. She was pondering the problem when Polly stuck her head through the door.

"Your brother just left his office. I missed him by ten minutes."

"Damn!" Jill said. She looked at her wrist where her watch was supposed to be but saw only freckles and a fine white line. "My watch! I left it at Carl's! Rats!"

"There's a three-hour time difference between L.A. and Cleveland," Polly said. "Do you want me to call your brother's home?"

"Wait twenty minutes, Polly. It'll take him a while to get through traffic."

"Any luck in reaching your mother?" Polly asked.

Jill pointed at Alex. "Alex won't move away from the phone. Whatever that stoned-out de Franco slipped him has regressed him to an infantile stage."

"Are you sure? That may be the real Alex Friedman you're seeing. Wait." Polly had an idea. She leaned over Alex, tapping his shoulder to get his attention. "Alex, if you'll sit on this nice comfy couch, I'll let you play with the pretty Rolodex."

"Neato!" Alex snatched the Rolodex from Polly and bounced on the couch, spinning Rolodex cards like a pinwheel. Within seconds he was wall-eyed, then mesmerized, then stuporous. He promptly fell asleep with his hands cradling his cheek.

"Thanks, Polly." Jill grinned. "Some day you'll make someone a wonderful mother."

"First I have to make someone," Polly said, looking grim.

Jill picked up the phone, gave her mother's number to the operator, and waited. After a few moments the operator informed her that there was no answer at that number—did she want to call later?

"Please keep trying." Jill hung up. "What'll I do, Polly? John doesn't answer, my mother doesn't answer, and the message says it's urgent."

"Perhaps the operator misunderstood. Perhaps your brother just called to chat."

"*Him?*" Jill said, with the look of one who's been told John Paul Number Two is on the line. "My brother doesn't call me to chat. Oh, he's great at small talk, but he saves it for the Kiwanis, the Knights, the Jaycees. He used to call, but, well . . . I had been having problems, wasn't exactly coherent part of the time, then I was . . . away. Then came the divorce. Then he called one summer night, and a man who wasn't Steve answered my phone. Johnny hasn't called since, not to chat. He's a good guy, Polly, and he cares about me. It's just that when he thinks of me at all, he pictures a little black sheep leading

76

herself down various paths overgrown with primroses and shudders at the thought of hearing about the next step on the way."

"So, he only calls when something's gone wrong in Cleveland." Polly sniffed.

"He can't cope with behavior he sees as erratic, Polly. I can't fault him for. . . . Oh, God, I just know that something is terribly wrong with my mother. She's dying. She's dead."

"Sit in your chair," Polly commanded. "Close your eyes, breathe through your mouth and relax. I'll find your mother."

Shaking, Jill complied. Soon the only sounds in the room were Alex's gentle snoring, her own regular breathing and equally regular breathing from Polly.

Gradually Jill's shaking subsided. She felt herself unearthed, unfettered, floating through a prism, where she dissolved and re-formed into diverse selves, Jills of many colors, rippling through beneficent vapors, drifting, drifting . . .

"What the hell's going on here?"

Jill's eyes flew open to the sight of Dan Carmichael rooted to the spot in the doorway and staring from herself to snoring Alex to Polly, who apparently was deep in a trance.

"Uh . . . Alex is sleeping off his cookie, and Polly's trying to find my mother," Jill explained.

Dan blinked at Polly. "Has she looked under the couch?"

"Sometimes Polly senses things, Dan. She picks up vibrations . . . uh . . . prescience-wise . . . um . . ." Jill foundered in embarrassment.

"Oh, great. Just when I was beginning to think of your office as the last bastion of sanity in this . . . this . . . madhouse!"

"What's wrong, Dan?" Jill frowned at Dan's obvious agitation.

Dan took up the pacing where Jill had left off. "I don't mind that the chairman of the board is senile. He's roughly four hundred years old, and he's earned it. I don't mind that the new president is a displaced Buck Rogers. I've worked with chief executive officers equally strange and less bright. I don't even mind a vice-presidency for a kid who should be in a drug rehab program. A Special Assistant, whatever *that* is, doesn't intrude on my territory. *But* after you left the meeting, Lawrence announced that UBC is abandoning all documentaries, something we did well and could point to with pride, in favor of what he terms 'hotsy-totsy television.'"

"Hotsy who?"

77

"Totsy. You remember her. Lovely girl. Used to twirl tassels in Long Beach." Dan kicked the desk in a surprising and uncharacteristic display of temper. "Shit, Jill, the Man in the Moon thinks we're about to become an industry powerhouse. He's, quote, 'pledged himself and UBC to ratings and financial superiority,' unquote. Damn the torpedoes, full schlock ahead!"

"Maybe it'll get better," Jill said soothingly.

"Sure." Dan smiled. "NASA will be allocated a massive increase in budget, and the Man in the Moon will suit up and blast off."

Jill's laugh was cut short by Polly's exclamation: "Your mother's in a large room with many machines!"

"My God! Intensive Care!" Jill cried.

"Your mother?" Dan asked. "What can I do to help?"

"I don't know!" Jill snatched the phone from its cradle. "I'll have to go home, see her, find out—" She looked at the phone in her hand. "Who am I calling?"

"I'll call hospitals in Cleveland," Polly volunteered.

"Dan! How can I go home now? I just started here!" Jill groaned, realizing that flying home to familial responsibility meant flying away from employment responsibility.

Money-duty. Blood-duty. Guilt-booty. Tutti-frutti!

"What choice have you got?" Dan asked reasonably. "If the situation should turn out for the worst, you'd never forgive yourself."

"But you're already working too hard, Dan, too many hours! I can't—"

"You must," he interrupted, gesturing at Alex. "The Boy Wonder and I will hold down the fort."

"But—"

"Say hello to Cleveland for me. I spent a month there one weekend." Dan tugged at Alex, finally hauling him to his feet. "C'mon, sonny, you can sleep it off in my office."

Alex leaned on Dan's shoulder, making an instinctive nuzzling motion toward his neck. "Stop that," Dan ordered. "Affectionate, isn't he?"

"None dare call it horny," Polly said from the doorway. "Jill, your brother's on the line."

Jill picked up the phone, waving good-bye to Dan, who was foxtrotting Alex out the door. "Johnny!"

"Jill, how are you?"

"How's Mother?" Jill countered anxiously.

"The doctor is running tests, Jill. We don't know yet." He sounded calm. "I'm sure there's nothing to worry about. There never is."

"But how does she *feel*?" Jill persisted.

"Same as always. She thinks she's dying."

"*Is* she?"

"Has she yet?"

"*Johnny!*"

"Well, *has* she?"

"No." Jill had to admit that Kate remained very much among the alive and kicking, the screaming and yelling.

"Ma won't die this time either, Jill." John sounded certain. "I stopped at the hospital after work. A dying woman does not ask her son to bring eyebrow tweezers."

"Ma would," Jill insisted. "She'd be afraid the undertaker wouldn't pluck and people at the funeral would say she let herself go."

"You're overreacting, as usual."

"I'm coming home." Jill announced, all vacillation over.

"That's cra . . . not necessary." John's tone fell between exasperated and soothing. "What can happen if you wait in L.A. for news?"

"I'll tell you what'll happen, Johnny. The time I don't come is the time you'll call to tell me that Dr. Keriakan has just pulled the sheet over Ma's pug nose. I've had nightmares about that."

"There's no need for nightmares, no need for undue alarm."

"*Undue!* If you're not going to be alarmed when your mother's in Intensive Care, then when—"

"I wish we could talk longer," John interrupted, "but we were just on our way out the door. The Knights of Columbus are having a spaghetti dinner at St. Monica's Hall, and Candy and I are—"

Jill cut him off. "You'd better hurry before all the garlic bread is gone. I'll see you in Cleveland."

"That's up to you, Jill." John sighed. "It's a long, expensive trip for no reason."

"I hope," Jill said fervently. She hung up, torn between wanting to hug her triplet and strangle him. She propped her aching head in her hands. "Ohhh."

"Bad news?" Polly inquired.

"No. Yes. Oh, shit, who knows? I won't know until I get to Cleveland. With Johnny there's never cause for alarm."

79

A few minutes later Jill was on her way to the elevator, carrying her bulging briefcase and Polly's good wishes.

The elevator door slid open. Inside, Zippy de Franco was alone and humming Mr. Muzak's disco rendition of "Don't Cry For Me, Argentina."

"Hi, Jill. How they hanging?" The elevator doors slid shut. "Do you . . . ?" He did an unmistakable bump and grind.

"Beg pardon?" Jill frowned, uncertain as to whether he was inquiring about sex, dancing, or possibly a slipped disk.

"You're divorced, right?"

"Yes, I am."

"Well then, do you"—he bumped again—"with guys?"

Jill didn't know whether to laugh ambiguously, wink noncommittally, pretend she'd gone deaf, or kick him where his were hanging. "No, Zippy. I don't."

"Lesbian, huh? Hey, that's cool. Different strokes." He resumed humming, then, "If you change your mind, you know where I hang out."

"Sure." She didn't, but she wasn't about to ask. Zippy de Franco probably hung out in the Batcave.

"Mon-u-men-tal stuff going down." Zippy giggled. "Now that I got the franchise, I'm going to follow through. UBC is on the move. Going *up*! Hotsy-totsy TV! Stand back and watch our dust!"

The elevator doors opened. Jill stood back as Zippy zoomed into the lobby. He flashed through the crowd of businessmen and shoppers with the skill of a broken-field runner, zigzagging so successfully that he bumped only one or two demographically undesirable old ladies.

Jill watched him go, thinking that a UBC on the move might be exciting. So far the only dust visible at UBC had been the kind that regularly disappeared up Zippy de Franco's nose.

CHAPTER 7

"It's not that I don't want to go to Dad's," Daisy was saying. "It's just that I had plans for the weekend."

Jill packed hurriedly, remembering that September in Cleveland could be hot, cold, sticky, crisp, rainy, humid, or sunny—sometimes all in the course of one day.

She added a ski sweater to a suitcase that included a green, gauzy dress, tennis shoes, black pumps, tweed jacket, striped blouse, T-shirt, wool suit, cotton skirt . . . She paused, considering her closet. "Where's my tank top? My thermal underwear?"

"Everytime I have my heart set on something, something dumb happens," Daisy complained. "Nobody asks me what *I* want to do. Nobody cares about *my* plans."

Jill rifled through her closet, selecting, rejecting. She settled on her best dress, a basic black that could go to any function dressed up or dressed down, with or without pearls, with or without a scarf—if need be, with or without Jill. She folded it, then shivered, shuddered, and threw it on the floor of the closet. She couldn't take the perfect funeral dress to Cleveland!

Expecting the worst is my nature: preparing for it is not.

"Lenny has tickets for Alice Cooper," Daisy continued. "It's Alice's first L.A. concert in ages, and who knows when he'll be back? Mother?"

Jill was in the bathroom, gathering jars and bottles.

"Mother!" Daisy's eyes shot green sparks. "Just how soon do you think Alice Cooper will be back?"

"How would I know, Daisy? He never calls. He never writes."

"Why does it have to be this week, Mom? Couldn't Grandma's liver fall out *after* the concert?"

"It's not her liver, Daisy. Please get my makeup case, dear." Jill didn't want to argue. If the plane crashed, Daisy's final memory would be of Jill screaming at her. She'd be unalterably warped, grow up to God knows what perversions . . . perhaps sharing Zippy's dust in the Batcave.

"I hate life." Daisy handed Jill the makeup case.

"Tell me what the problem is, Daisy." Jill conjured up her Mommy-can-fix voice.

"Lenny has tickets for Alice Cooper, and now I can't go."

"Why not?" Jill cushioned her cosmetic jars with rolled-up pantyhose. "Lenny can pick you up at Dad's house."

Daisy flopped on the bed. "I haven't told Lenny I'm divorced. He's always talking about his family like they're the Waltons, only kosher, and from the way he talks . . . I'm not ready to tell him yet, Mom."

Jill reached out to stroke Daisy's hair, but Daisy pulled away. "You really like this Lenny, don't you, honey?"

"He's just a guy." Daisy's mumble wasn't very convincing. "I mean Lenny's okay. He isn't always doing backflips like the dumb jocks who think muscles impress girls or giving girls nougies to show that he likes them. Lenny talks to me, like a person. And he can fix anything, toasters, lamps, his friends' cars. He's a wizard at stuff like that."

"I'm impressed." Jill smiled, hoping her show of enthusiasm would cheer Daisy.

"He can be nerdy, too. Last week I told him that someday I'd like an insect collection like the one in biology lab. So yesterday while I was doing my homework the doorbell rang, and when I answered it, there was no one there . . . just a package on the porch. The card on the package said 'To help start your insect collection.' Inside were a Snail Jail and a Roach Motel. Really!"

Jill laughed. "Now I *am* impressed. Hang on to this one, Daisy. A guy who can make you laugh is better than one who brings you diamonds. Rarer, too."

"I thought it was kind of dumb." Daisy squinted at Jill. "You really think it was funny?"

"Very. And I can't believe that a guy with a good sense of humor is going to like you less because your parents are divorced."

"Lenny's very conservative, Mom. He's always talking about the druggies, the loadies, and the freaks. He thinks Alice Wilson's mother, with her sleep-overs, is messing Alice up. He says that people without anchors go floating away like helium balloons, and Alice

Wilson's mother is no anchor. She's more like a millstone." Daisy shrugged. "That's what Lenny says."

"You're afraid Lenny will think you're the type who floats away?"

Daisy avoided Jill's eyes. "Lenny's the only person I know who uses the term *broken home.* No one says that anymore. Everyone's home is broken."

"Or bent out of shape," Jill agreed. She sat on the bed next to Daisy. "You have two choices, honey. Call Lenny, tell him the truth, and trust he likes you well enough to overlook your . . . uh . . . broken home, or tell him you'll be away for a few days and will have to miss the concert. I'm sorry that my problem has caused you a problem— or rather, your grandmother's problem."

"It's not your fault." Daisy attempted a good-sport smile. "Or Grandma's, either. She can't help it if her body is beginning to go. It must be scary to get old and know that the next knock on the door may be the Grim Reaper."

"Daisy! You're giving me chills!"

Daisy sat up, hands planted on hips. "Well, it's true. You're born, you get old, and you die. That's it."

With that she was gone, leaving Jill with the impression that her life had just flashed past like an express train.

It must be wonderful to be at an age when being born seems like yesterday morning and dying is off in the misty reaches of time.

She folded a half-slip, placed it neatly in the suitcase, then glanced at the clock and gasped. No time for folding, no time for neat! She pulled her underwear drawer from the dresser and upended it over her suitcase, then sat on the case and bounced until she heard the latch click.

Just time for a shower.

As Jill ran for the bathroom the phone rang. She reversed direction in mid-step, tripped, lunged across the bed, kicked her own shin, and sprawled, phone in hand.

"Damn!" she shouted into the phone. "What is it?"

"Hi, honey." It was Nick Anders. "You sound like your house is on fire and you're running around trying to save the Picassos."

"Listen carefully, Nick." Jill hunkered over the phone like a quarterback with fourth down and goal to go. "I wish I had time to talk, but I don't. My mother is sick. I'll call you from Cleveland."

"Cleveland!" He wailed. "You can't go to Cleveland now. I've written nine pages and I can't continue until you've read them."

"And I will, the second I get back," Jill promised. "Meet my plane. I'll read them on the people-mover."

"By the time you get back I'll have writer's block." Nick's voice was shrill. "You can't imagine what it's like to pour your soul into your art, to strive for truth and beauty in this city of Philistines. There are people in this town who have never heard of Kierkegaard."

"Shocking."

Who, What, or Where The Hell Is Kierkegaard?

"Listen Nick. I'll give you my mother's address. You can send your script to—"

"Script!" Nick fairly dripped disgust. "I'm talking about my novel."

"Novel!" Jill exclaimed. "What about the script Lorimar is paying you to write? Isn't it overdue?"

"A TV movie with car crashes—pap! I can crank that out with one hand."

"Then crank. They'll never hire you again if you don't deliver on time."

"Dealing with the execrable blunts my instincts for art." Nick was scornful. "I am not accustomed to whoring."

"Whore! Whore! It pays the rent."

"Jill!"

"Listen, Nick . . . dear. You owe everyone in town. Now I personally love your way with words but even if you finish your novel, how many people will read a book that contains a three hundred page dream sequence with no punctuation?"

"Joycean in the scope—"

"Incomprehensible in the reading—"

"Philistine!"

"I'll call you from Cleveland." Jill hung up. "Damn!"

In a shower so quick she washed only her front, Jill wondered why her phone conversations with Nick invariably ended with swearing and hanging up. "A rocky romance" the fan magazines would call it. Rocky, stormy, turbulent, tempestuous . . .

Ah, if only it was that exciting. If only Nick was actually larger than life instead of only larger than Carl.

Jill carried her suitcase to the hall, calling, "Daisy, time to go."

There was no response. She found Daisy in her room, bouncing on her bulging suitcase.

"Lenny's going to pick me up at Dad's." Daisy's delighted smile lit up the room.

"That's wonderful, Daisy. I knew that if you just told him the truth. . . ."

"I told Lenny that I'm spending a few days at our summer home and he should pick me up there."

"Summer home! In Encino? Eight miles away from where we live!" Jill shook her head. "He believed that?"

Daisy clumped past Jill, bending under the weight of her suitcase. "It's not an actual lie, Mom. Look at it this way—I live here most of the time, but I do spend time at Dad's too—lots more during my summer vacation. So, Dad's house *could* be considered my summer home."

"Perhaps *you* could consider—"

"That's just what I'm doing," Daisy asserted. "What I told Lenny is mostly the truth. This way, I'll get to see Alice Cooper and Lenny will get to hear about the divorce when he's ready."

"Daisy, have you ever heard the expression *building a house of cards?*" Jill asked. "And of how that house is likely to come tumbling down?"

"I'm not building anything, Mom. I'm just . . . remodeling a little." With that, Daisy flounced out the door, leaving Jill to turn off the lights, lock up, and wonder how she'd produced a daughter with self-confidence rivaled only by Kissinger's.

Jill piled the suitcases into the car, and they were off, soon cruising the heavily trafficked Ventura Freeway.

"I'm going to ask Dad if I can see a lawyer," Daisy announced.

"Divorcing us?" Jill inquired. "You already have a winter home and summer estate, both in the San Fernando Valley. What more could you possibly want?"

"You know I want to change my name," Daisy said. "You promised I could do it when I'm sixteen."

"You aren't sixteen yet." Jill marveled at Daisy's knack for pushing pet obsessions at times when she already felt pushed to the limit.

"I'll be sixteen in just a few months, and you know how long legal arrangements take. If I wait much longer, I'll be your age before it's done—too old to care what my name is."

"True." Jill wondered how Daisy would like walking to her summer home. "At my age, it's all I can do to keep myself clean."

"If I tell Dad you said it's okay with you, he can start legal proceedings," Daisy pressed.

Jill smiled in the darkness. Despite an urge to abandon Daisy at the side of the road, Jill had to admire her tenacity. "You may not tell your father any such thing. I like the name Daisy. I should. I picked it."

"I *hate* it!" Daisy said vehemently. "Ever since first grade, when the kids used to come up, pull my fingers, and say 'Loves me, loves me not.' How could you give me such a dumb name?"

"I didn't think it was dumb. I thought it was lovely and romantic and feminine. Daisy was the heroine of *The Great Gatsby*. At the time you were born, I had an F. Scott Fitzgerald view of the world and a high opinion of romantic love."

"Boy, that's even dumber," Daisy scoffed.

"I was nineteen, Daisy, and not nearly as jaded as you seem to be now. Perhaps not quite ready for motherhood, either." Jill glanced in the direction of an ominously silent Daisy "I loved and wanted you, honey. Make no mistake about that. I yearned for you in my heart, but at nineteen there's a difference between fantasizing a daughter named after a Fitzgerald heroine and the reality of having a child. Not many teenagers handle it well."

"Then why did you have me?" Daisy asked impatiently. There was a long pause, then, "Mo-om. Was I an *accident*?"

"Only in the timing, Daisy." Jill winced. Daisy never asked "important" questions when there was time to talk, only when bathtubs were overflowing, pipes bursting, divorce papers being signed, and planes taking off. "Your father and I wanted children, honey, but neither of us expected to be parents before our first wedding anniversary." Jill smiled, remembering their first anniversary, an early dinner rushed through to get home to the fascinating creature gurgling in her yellow bassinet.

"You could have used the birth control pill." Daisy pointed out.

"If we had, where would you be?" Jill grinned at her. "Besides, at the time I thought birth control was wrong."

"That's the dumbest yet."

"If you've recently graduated from twelve years of parochial school, it isn't dumb, Daisy. It's written in rock. I'm not the only female raised in the Catholic tradition who thought I was trading my soul for my first Enovid prescription. That's the way it was then, and the theory hasn't changed, just the practice. Now it's take the Pill, cross your fingers, and hope God's judgments are less grumpy than the Pope's." Jill sighed, wishing morning sickness on the College of Cardinals.

Daisy pounced on Jill's distraction. "So then, changing my name is all right with you? I can tell Dad?"

"Sure. No. Wait! Please, Daisy. I've got so much on my mind." Jill pulled into Steve's driveway. "Talk to your father. If he agrees, I will."

"I *hate* it when parents do that! 'Ask your mother.' 'Ask your father.' I'll never do that to my kids."

"I'll remind you of that in twenty years." Jill was wrestling Daisy's suitcase from the car trunk to the driveway when Steve came out of the house, waving at them both.

"Hi," he called, glancing at his watch. "You're going to miss your plane."

"Don't say that," Jill begged. "I had a few delays in leaving the house."

"Her phone just never stops ringing," Daisy said brightly.

"I see. I'll leave you two alone to say good-bye." Looking rather disgruntled, Steve hoisted Daisy's suitcase and walked off toward the house, listing beneath the weight of Daisy's teenage necessities.

"Why did you say that?" Jill demanded. "What my phone does is none of your father's business."

"Don't be mad," Daisy whispered intensely. "I just want Dad to know you're popular. If he thinks no one else wants you, he won't, either. Men pursue women who are in demand. I read that in *Seventeen*."

"Your father and I are *not* going to reconcile, Daisy." Jill began, then remembered Steve's warning about missing the plane. She hugged Daisy fiercely. "I *hate* this. I hate having to say we'll talk later, but I have absolutely no choice. And I *hate* having no choice!"

"Are you mad at me, Mom?" Daisy asked plaintively.

"No. No. No. Not with you." Jill hugged her again.

Steve approached them, all signs of disgruntlement gone. "You'd better go, Jill. I'll look after the princess."

"Thanks, Steve." Jill smiled with relief at Steve's sensitivity. No arguments before flights, thank God. "I appreciate your looking after Daisy on such short notice. Truly."

"My pleasure," he said sincerely.

Jill got into the car. Steve leaned halfway through the window, gingerly patting the hand nearest him on the steering wheel. "Try not to tie yourself in knots."

"I'll try."

"You know how you overreact." His brow furrowed. "You won't be of much help to your mother if you fall apart yourself."

"I won't fall apart, Steve." Jill started the engine, vowing not to fall apart, at least until she got the goddamn car out of Steve's goddamn driveway.

"Drive very carefully," Steve called. "Don't take any risks. If you miss this plane, there's another. It's not life and death, Jill, no matter what you think."

"Okay, okay." Jill waved, and backed up.

"And tell your mother I miss her," Steve shouted, having the final word as was his practice, his habit, his way of life—at least with her.

Jill backed out, watching Steve walk toward the house, hand in hand with Daisy. Daisy was already chattering, most likely about changing her name. Or perhaps she was coaching Steve on the behavior required at that golden moment when Lenny would arrive on his doorstep, tickets for Alice Cooper in one hand and conservative views in the other.

Jill pulled onto the freeway, pondering Daisy's equivocal attraction to such an apparently conventional boy. In comparison, the home lives of her other friends ranged from the mildly nonconforming to the ostentatiously aberrant. Daisy not only took these diverse lifestyles in her own stolid stride but seemed to find them inherently interesting. Yet here she was, caring enough to feel insecure and feeling insecure enough to lie to the most traditional person she knew.

Perhaps to Daisy, Lenny was exotic, as divergent from the mainstream of her teenage life as Jill's own teenage next-door neighbor had been, a black-jacketed "greaser" she sometimes glimpsed zooming out of his driveway on his huge and ominous Harley. As different, and as fascinating, in an entirely opposite way.

It could be that Daisy's living the flip side of my own adolescence.

It was a conceit that disturbed her. There had to be some happy medium between growing up as Cleveland tumbled blissfully unaware into the sixties and growing up in the eighties in Los Angeles, where the smell of success could outstench the pollution and today's lunatic fringe become tomorrow's establishment.

Still, the eighties have also arrived in Cleveland, and the city my mother persists in calling Lost Angeles can no longer be the sole harbinger of flash-frozen change.

Jill pulled into the sprawling LAX parking complex, wondering if the home she was flying to would in any way resemble the home she remembered.

She longed to go home, ached to go home, but to the home where a radiantly healthy Ma and a Pa in the best of moods would meet her with open arms, where an unrestrained Johnny ran whooping at Indian games in the backyard, where Julie chased butterflies, laughing . . . *that* home.

Would the Los Angeles she returned to be the Los Angeles she was about to depart from? More to the point, would the Daisy she hugged upon her return be her own unique and familiar Daisy or some stranger with a new personality to match her new name.

Jill parked, and staggering beneath her wardrobe for all seasons, made her burdened way toward the terminal, wondering if she would ever learn to think of change in terms of possible gains instead of only losses to mourn.

CHAPTER 8

Cleveland's Hopkins Airport had undergone massive changes. In the past five years it had come to resemble O'Hare, a perhaps conscious, albeit unmalicious bamboozle perpetrated by city fathers anxious to cheer travelers whose trips to their city had invariably begun with "Dammit, I have to go to Cleveland."

As Jill rode the escalator to the baggage level she was jarred by the sight of a jagged heap of metal, brilliantly floodlit, in a small courtyard just outside a mammoth window.

"What's that?" she inquired of an elderly man on the descending step ahead of her.

"The new abstract sculpture," he sneered. "I wouldn't hit a dog in the ass with it."

"Oh." Jill wondered what could have inspired the airport committee to commission a sculpture that so perfectly duplicated a wrecked fuselage.

A half hour later, Jill was driving a bright red Pinto down Brookpark Road, now in its seventeenth year of reconstruction.

The exact location of Presbyterian General Hospital was hazy in Jill's memory, but she did remember it as being within walking distance of the Rialto Theater, where as a child she'd been repeatedly dazzled by Disney. While the airport, with its changes, had been an unfamiliar portal, the familiar ruts of Brookpark Road provided a reassuring status quo.

As a youngster, Jill had negotiated these potholes daily to and from Our Lady of Perpetual Hope School. Later she'd bumped her way over them to Steve's office for frequent lunches during the honeymoon days of their marriage. Still later an uncharacteristically spontaneous "Let's go for a ride" from Steve to a then-pregnant Jill had begun as a fifteen-minute jaunt and ended, sixty-eight potholes later, in a maternity ward with Daisy on the way.

As she approached Socha's Sohio her hands turned the steering wheel, automatically taking a shortcut she'd forgotten she knew. She smiled and, firmly grounded now, drove on, surprisingly excited by shadowy glimpses of familiar landmarks.

Home is always home, even when it's the place you spend most of your life trying to escape.

Jill swung left at the fork, taking the branch that went through the Italian district around St. Rocco's, the Bohemian district around St. Prokop's, the Greek district around St. Theodosius', and the red-light district around five bucks a thrill.

She slowed, straining through the darkness for the glow of the Rialto neon. It appeared on her right, an emblazoned marquee announcing that this palace of her childhood fantasies was currently presenting *Pussycats in Bondage* and *Devil Women from Hell.*

"No!" Jill involuntarily exclaimed. It was a personal affront, this warping of an innocent playground.

The sign over the hospital parking lot had two letters missing and half the lights gone. As Jill drove into the lot she was greeted by "Freedom Now" scrawled in red paint on one wall. She parked, hoping the message hadn't been written by a patient with reason to flee.

Jill went through the door marked "Emergency Only," then down a short narrow corridor to the nurses' station. The nurse behind the desk didn't look up as she approached.

"Excuse me," Jill began, "I'd like to—"

"If you're in labor, you'll have to go 'round to the Allyn Street entrance." The nurse continued to study her crossword puzzle.

"I am not in labor," Jill responded, thinking that if she was, she would prefer to give birth in a more hospitable atmosphere, like the lobby of the Rialto. "If you'll just direct me to ICU."

"Oh?" The nurse turned her puzzle book upside down. "Do you have chest pains, nausea, vomiting, dizziness, numbness"—she suddenly yawned with her mouth wide open—"pain in your left arm? 'Scuse me, but the night shift's a killer. I got three kids at home, two preschool, and if you think it's easy to sleep during the day with kids running around the house—"

"Please," Jill interrupted. "My mother's in intensive care."

Indignation flickered in the nurse's eyes. "You're not a patient," she accused. "Visiting hours are over."

"But I just came in from Los Angeles," Jill protested.

"Sorry. Rules are rules, and ICU personnel adhere strictly to

91

them," the nurse said with a sniff. "Visitors cause stress, and stress is the primary reason we lose people."

"My mother will suffer considerably more stress if she thinks I didn't care enough to come."

The nurse looked disgusted. "So who's talking about patients? We lost three nurses last month. Quit, just like that!"

"But . . ."

The nurse picked up her pen and resumed frowning over her puzzle, totally oblivious to Jill, who waited, trying to think of a way to reengage her. UBC life had demonstrated the value of converting antagonists into allies, of offering something deemed to be of value —as Zippy's Mad Bomber idea had obviously been to Lawrence—in return for favors and practical support.

"Thanks for your help," Jill said pleasantly. "I'll be going now, but I do feel bad about the hospital's bequest."

"Wait. What bequest?"

Jill shrugged casually, taking a step toward the door. "My mother's physician told me that she's recently stricken a sizable bequest to Presbyterian General from her will and only I could change her mind. Well, if she's still with us in the morning, I'll certainly try—"

The nurse was on her feet and leaning over the counter. "I'm sure there's something we can do. I mean, you've come all the way from Los Angeles. . . ."

"Rules are rules." Jill moved closer to the door. From behind her she heard quick crepe-soled footsteps, then felt a hand on her shoulder.

"Rules are meant to protect, not to be arbitrary." The nurse smiled stickily at Jill. "What did you say your mother's name is?"

"Dunn. You've heard of the Shaker Heights Dunns. Steel, coke, pig iron, smelting."

"Smelting. Certainly. Everyone's heard of the Dunns. Go right up. Six West."

"How kind of you." Jill beamed.

"My pleasure," the nurse responded. "If this hospital doesn't get some money soon, well . . . Maybe they'll finally hire a security guard for Emergency. You wouldn't believe what walks in off the streets. Most nights I sit here terrified." She raised her voice as Jill stepped into the elevator and punched six. "Just last night a loony with a knife came in and threatened to kill me unless he got—"

The doors slid shut on a bemused Jill, who would never know what the man with the knife was so crazy to get. If it was medical attention, the poor guy was shit out of luck.

The doors slid open, and Jill stepped out into a corridor where institutional green paint blistered over cracked plaster walls. The carpeting was thin in spots, revealing patches of cement. Instead of the usual antiseptic smell, there was a heavy, sweet mustiness, such as might be found in houses boarded up after an epidemic.

At the far end of the corridor was a white neon sign embellished with a red arrow. Beneath this sign a man dressed in something long and black leaned against a wall, smoking a cigarette.

A doctor? A patient? A pervert from the Rialto? She moved closer. "Johnny!" she cried, breaking into a run.

She threw herself at the tall figure, clasping her arms behind him in a fierce and delighted hug.

"Careful, careful, my cigarette," he cautioned, hugging her gently with one arm.

Jill buried her face against his lapels and continued to hug, marveling at how little he'd changed. He was tall and still so slim she could feel the outline of his ribs through his tightly buttoned coat—the coat his father had worn with such a fine indifference, as though protection from adverse elements could be of only slight concern to one in control of his fate.

Jill held him at arm's length, gazing up into eyes a deeper emerald than her own. "How do you do it, you Black Irish devil! You're more gorgeous than ever, and you still look nineteen!"

The faint line between his eyebrows deepened as he scowled down at her, uncomfortable, as usual, with compliments. Simply to tell Johnny that he looked healthy was to invite a swift change of subject. He looked more than healthy. With thick, softly curling hair the color of India ink, fair skin blushed with rose, and green-aquamarine eyes to which slight myopia imparted a perpetually questing look, he resembled a hero of old, one who in another age would have worn armor with grace but now seemed intent upon shrinking as far as possible into the recesses of a twenty-year-old coat.

"I'm so happy to see you, Johnny, so happy to be home." Jill smiled. At that moment she was wholeheartedly, singlemindedly, blissfully happy to be standing in a corridor that looked like a flophouse foyer, smiling up at the brother who'd shared the moment of conception and, for nine months, an unparalleled Eden, who'd been closer than any husband or lover, closer than anyone except, of course, Julie.

93

Is Julie here?

She flung her arms around Johnny again, buying one final serene moment. As the coat's tweedy texture scraped her nose and cheek she was overwhelmed with a mystical sense that while her arms enthusiastically enfolded her brother, her father's arms were tenderly enfolding her. It was a sensation beyond comfort, and she dissolved into it, thinking that while familiar streets may point the way home, the essence of homecoming lay in the first welcoming embrace of blood kin.

John moved restlessly, as though anxious to extricate himself.

"Thank God you've come," John said.

Jill backed away, chilled. "Why? Is she . . . Johnny?"

"She's . . . uh . . ." He ran long fingers through raven hair and gestured toward the doors that stood sentinel over the secrets of Intensive Care.

"It's all right, Johnny," Jill said soothingly, looking at his pale, tight face. "I'll go in now and see Ma."

He didn't respond. Johnny distraught was Johnny gone mute, a silence that slammed the door on distress. She'd seen him like this before.

A picture fell out of her memory, then went up in smoke, leaving only wisps of an image—a very small Johnny lying sprawled on a cold gray floor, eyes wide and fingers on lips, saying not a word.

"Don't worry." Jill squeezed his shoulder, then inhaled deeply before turning the doorknob.

The revolution is closer—the dying have double doors.

The room Jill stepped into was jammed floor-to-ceiling with the latest in medical hardware. The rest of Presbyterian General might be dilapidated enough to embarrass a slumlord, but the inside of Intensive Care looked like Mission Control.

Several nurses sat behind a long, walled panel, closely observing closed-circuit monitors that made actual face-to-face contact with patients virtually obsolete. Muted hums and soft, burping beeps emanated from some of the machines, while others whirred and spat a continuous roll of electrocardiogram tape. Periodically a nurse would rip off a length of tape, glancing at it with the practiced eye of a stockbroker following the Dow.

A nurse caught sight of Jill and hastily rose from her chair.

"Visiting hours are over," she said in a loud whisper.

"I've already gone through that downstairs," Jill told her.

"Oh? *Oh.* You're Mrs. Dunn's daughter!"

Jill nodded.

The nurse winked conspiratorially. "Mrs. Elliot called from Emergency. We're all so excited. We had no idea your mother was so wealth—well disposed toward Pres Gen."

"How is my mother?" Jill's concern brought her voice above the prescribed whisper.

"Shhh," The nurse cautioned, then shrugged, evidently less interested in Kate's health than in her wealth—well-disposition. "Her vital signs are excellent. Look for yourself." The nurse pointed toward Mission Control. "Monitor Seven."

Jill looked. Monitor Seven's screen was black, with a white zigzag line across the top, a squiggly line in the middle, and pulsating dots at the bottom. All it lacked to qualify as a really great video game was a little ball bounding back and forth.

"That's very impressive, but what the hell does it mean?" Jill demanded. "I don't want to see a machine. I want to see my mother."

"*Shhh.* There's no reason to raise your voice. I'll explain the readout." The nurse smiled proudly. "Our monitors provide a complete clinical picture."

"I don't care about clinical pictures. When I see my mother, I'll ask her how she feels and she'll tell me."

"All patients ever want to talk about is how they *feel*." The nurse grinned. "If you want to know how they *are*, you look at the readout."

"*Where is my mother?*" Jill asked loudly.

The nurse blanched. "Round the corner and jog to the right. It's the bed with all the after-hours patients gathered around it."

As Jill rounded the corner she heard the "clinical picture" nurse say to one of her colleagues, "This better be one hell of a bequest. ICU looks like the Lost Tribes of Israel is having a picnic back there."

The short hall opened into a spacious room that reeked of Lysol and held a dozen or so beds with screens placed between them. Jill walked quickly, eyes straight ahead, avoiding the sight of those unprivate beds. Beneath the Lysol was the pungent aroma of death.

As she approached the windows Jill heard the voice that had penetrated the bars of her crib, the wicker sides of her bassinet, and, quite possibly, the walls of the womb prior to birth.

"I am a dying woman, and what's the last thing I'll see in this

95

world? I am going to God with eyes that have closed on *Pussycats in Bondage!*"

"Mother Dunn." It was Fred's best authoritarian voice. "Rest assured, you are going nowhere. Your vital signs are excellent. . . ."

"Don't talk to me about vital signs!" Kate declared. "They told Uncle Dimmy his vital signs were perfect, and he passed away in the middle of a sentence."

If Jill had known how to go about girding her loins, she would have done it, but the closest she'd ever come to a demonstration was watching Nick struggle into spandex briefs three sizes too small. So, she simply stuck her head around the curtain and said, "Hello. How are you, Mother?"

"Make them move my bed away from the dirty movie," Kate greeted her.

"Jill! I'm so glad you're here!" Julie wrapped her in a warm, back-patting hug, then gave her a kiss on the cheek and a quick appraisal with cool, green eyes accustomed to instant evaluation. "You look tired."

"It's her hair," Kate shouted. "Women over thirty shouldn't wear long hair." She snatched an aluminum water pitcher from the bedside table and waved it before Jill's face. "See how messy you look?"

Obediently Jill looked, seeing an aluminum-distorted reflection with both eyes sliding to one side of a nose that covered half her face.

"I could audition for the lead in a horror movie." Jill agreed. "Hello, Fred."

Fred nodded in Jill's direction.

"How are you, Jim?" Jill smiled at a short, round man who was sitting on a chair pulled close to Kate's bed. "I haven't seen you since Ma—" She was about to say "since Ma's last illness," but stopped herself, feeling it imprudent to remind Kate that all Dunn family reunions occurred around her various sickbeds. "—since last year."

"I'm fine, Jill," Jim said, with a worried smile.

"That's good to hear." Jill had been pleased the first time Kate had introduced her to "my friend Jim Anderson," a retired electrician she'd found wandering through Fazio's produce section, lost in the profound confusion of recent widowerhood. Behind Kate's back they called Jim "Ma's steady," Julie with some disapproval, John with apparent indifference, and Jill with gratitude that fate had provided Kate with a companion.

"What has Dr. Keriakan found out?" Jill asked.

"Nothing," Kate snapped.

"Nothing?"

"He's still trying to decide which end of the stethoscope goes in his ears," Kate said angrily.

"Please, Ma," Julie pleaded. "Keriakan is a fine doctor. He took good care of Pa."

Kate sat bolt upright. "Your father *died!*"

"Let's talk about you, Ma," Jill said hastily. "Someone in the emergency room must have told you something."

"It's my heart." Kate sank into her pillows, eyes closed and one hand fluttering weakly on her chest. She held the pose for a moment, then opened one eye. "Jim, tell her it's my heart."

"It's her heart." Jim complied. "One moment it was fine, the next it was banging and thumping in her chest. I saw it."

"You've had it before, Ma," Jill pointed out. "Dr. Keriakan has assured you it signifies nothing."

"Nothing to *him.*" Kate was furious. "It's not *his* heart blowing up like a bagpipe, pressing on *his* stomach, *his* lungs, *his* liver—"

"Your heart's not enlarged, Ma," Jill said calmly, wondering how Kate had come to think of her heart as roughly the size of a boneless rolled turkey.

"Probably not," Jim agreed, "but *Prevention* magazine says that banging and thumping can be tachycardia, and tachycardia is . . . Wait, I have the article right here." From an inside pocket of his mackintosh he produced a well-worn magazine.

"I'm sure the article is very enlightening." There was an edge to Fred's voice. "But as unorthodox as this may seem, I find the diagnosis of the attending physician preferable to that of a magazine."

Kate was sitting upright again, this time waving both fists in the air. "How can you get a diagnosis from an attending physician who won't attend? Where is Keriakan?" Angrily she turned to Jill. "Why haven't you made them move my bed? You don't care where I die."

"I do care. . . . I mean, you're not going to die. . . . I'll go talk to the nurse." Thankful for reason to escape, Jill scooted around the screen, nearly colliding with a nurse carrying a tray.

"Ooops." Jill pulled up short. "Excuse me."

"Dr. Keriakan has prescribed medication for your mother." The nurse appeared to be aggrieved, as though face-to-face contact with an actual patient was a chore akin to grave-robbing.

"What kind of medication?" Jill asked worriedly.

"Nerve medication," the nurse explained sourly. "Your mother's yelling is making the other patients nervous. This'll quiet her down."

"Why wouldn't Ma be upset?" Jill demanded. "She's been here for hours, her doctor hasn't arrived, no one will tell her what's wrong—"

"Dr. Keriakan is on his way, and he's specifically ordered this medication to calm her. We simply cannot have patients shouting in Intensive Care."

Jill frowned. "Ma's not disturbing anyone."

"Think not?" The nurse was indignant. "One of our patients is, has been comatose for days, prognosis terminal, no chance for recovery. Your mother started shouting, his EEG needle jumped a mile, and now he's over in the corner asking for soup."

"Soup? Ma should send him a bill."

"He will not live," the nurse hissed through clenched teeth. "His vital signs are terrible."

From behind Jill the sound of Kate's voice thundered, "Get me away from this window. It's an occasion of sin. Where the hell is Keriakan?"

"I'm going to medicate her before she does any more damage." The nurse brushed past Jill.

Jill followed the nurse around the screen as Julie was pleading, "Please, Ma, you'll make your heart leap again."

"Here we are, Mrs. Dunn," the nurse said perkily, "nice medicine for you."

"For me?" Kate was as pleased as though someone had just announced the arrival of flowers.

The nurse handed her a pill cup. "You'll feel so much better, dear. Down the hatch."

"Wait!" Jim stopped Kate, who was eagerly reaching for the pill cup. "What are you giving her, nurse?"

"A happy pill," the nurse chirped. "Here we go."

Fred cleared his throat. "Miss, I'm sure you're acting upon doctor's instructions. However, will you kindly be more specific than 'happy pill'?"

"Centrax." The nurse shot him a look that could level the Grand Canyon.

"Which is?" Fred was not easily leveled.

"Tranquilizer," the nurse snapped.

"Hold on." Jim reached under his chair, producing a thick dog-eared book. "I'll look it up."

The nurse glimpsed the title. "Lay people are not supposed to have copies of *The Physicians' Desk Reference*."

"And patients are not supposed to be medicated for the benefit of hospital routine," Jill told her.

"Maybe you think it's good for your mother to get herself all worked up like this," the nurse said sarcastically.

"We could wait for Dr. Keriakan to arrive," Julie suggested. "I'm sure we'll all feel better after we've talked to him personally."

"*You'll* feel better!" Kate shouted. "*Your* heart isn't leaping out of your chest! Where's Keriakan? Why is a filthy movie shining in my window?"

"On the other hand," Fred said thoughtfully, "perhaps the medication is a good idea. You could take a nice nap."

"*You* try to sleep in a room full of dying people!" Kate cried. "You close your eyes, they take you to the morgue."

"That's *not* true, Mrs. Dunn." The nurse shoved the pill cup at her. "Take this."

"Wait!" Jim ordered. "I've got it. 'Centrax,' " he read, " 'Adverse reactions include dizziness, weakness, drowsiness, ataxia, headaches, confusion, tremor—' "

"Keriakan's trying to *kill* me!" Kate pulled the sheet over her mouth and glared at the nurse. "Get away from me!"

"—vivid dreams, palpitations, diaphoresis . . ." Jim continued.

"The next time I'm dying, I'll go to another hospital," Kate screamed.

The nurse leaned over Kate. "Have you ever been placed in restraints?"

Jill clamped a firm hand on the nurse's shoulder. "You are *not* placing anyone in restraints. Is that clear?"

"Fred, *do* something," Julie begged.

"Listen to reason, Mrs. Dunn." The nurse reached for the sheet covering Kate's mouth.

"*Awk.*" Kate whimpered and pulled the sheet over her head.

"Don't be childish." The nurse tugged at the sheet, Jill tugged at the nurse, Julie reached for Fred, and everyone shouted at once in a babble that sounded like a tent revival.

Unnoticed in the fray, a tall, burly figure stepped around the screen. "What's going on here?"

"Dr. Keriakan!" the nurse shouted, and everyone fell silent.

Kate peered over the sheet, flashing her best Garbo smile. "How nice of you to come, Doctor."

Ignoring everyone but Kate, Keriakan sat on the edge of the bed. "How are you, my dear?"

"You tell me." Kate batted her lashes.

Keriakan patted Kate's hand, blessing her with a smile that never quite reached his eyes. "We'll find out, won't we?"

"Doctor?" the nurse said hesitantly.

"Yes?" Keriakan noticed the pill cup. "What's that?"

"It's the Centrax you prescribed."

"Thank God." He popped the pill in his mouth. "The man who discovers the cure for migraine will win the Nobel prize." He glared at the nurse. "Fetch Mrs. Dunn's medication."

"But—"

"Thank you." He dismissed her.

"If we can discuss—" Fred began.

"We'll discuss when we have the results of the tests," Keriakan countered.

Kate fixed him with a mournful stare. "You're expecting something serious."

"Not at all." He patted her hand faster. "I'm expecting only good news."

"For you maybe. Your heart isn't leaping out of your chest." Kate's voice was rising. "Well, aren't you going to examine me? I don't pay doctors for chitchat."

Keriakan sighed, rose from the bed, and turned to the family. "If you'll all leave the room for a few moments . . ."

"Of course." Fred couldn't wait.

"Don't go home," Kate called anxiously.

"We'll be right outside, Ma," Jill promised.

As they filed out Jill heard Kate whisper to Jim, "Don't worry. I won't take any Centrax until I see what happens to Keriakan."

Jill walked into the crumbling corridor, scanning the hallway for John.

"Ma doesn't seem to be seriously ill," Julie observed.

"She's healthier than all of us put together," Fred humphed. "Where's your brother?"

"Where *is* Johnny?" Julie turned to Jill. "He wouldn't have just gone home, would he?"

"I find it highly inappropriate that a son-in-law exhibit greater concern than a son," Fred fumed.

"Johnny's extremely worried about Ma," Jill snapped angrily, thinking that *exhibit* was an excellent description of Fred's formally arranged concern.

"Then why isn't he here?" Fred turned his back, ignoring the scoring point.

For the same reason we all whistle past graveyards, you ass: denial, psychological shield of the terrified.

"Here he is," Julie announced, pointing down the hall to where John was emerging from the elevator. The coat flapped behind him as he approached.

"Johnny, where were you?" Jill called.

"Calling the office," John replied briskly. "I'm responsible for purchasing a new line of computer systems to be delivered on an impossibly tight schedule. . . ."

"I know just what you mean!" Julie's eyes lit up at the word *schedule.* "It can be difficult to juggle and juxtapose, but the key to a successful schedule is absolute adherence, no deviation, no robbing of Peter to pay Paul. But isn't that the point, Johnny—doing what needs to be done in an orderly manner. For instance—"

"Dr. Keriakan is with Ma," Jill interrupted, growing impatient, perhaps from boredom, perhaps from envy at Julie's gift for organization. "He's examining her now."

"How is Ma?" John's question was casual, but he stiffened, as though expecting a blow.

Tell me you're worried, Johnny. No one will hit you if you say how you feel.

Abruptly the double doors swung open, and Keriakan walked into the hall, holding his head and mumbling.

Alarmed, Jim plucked at his arm. "Tell me! What's wrong!"

"God, what a pain!" Keriakan groaned.

"That's no way to speak about Mrs. Dunn." Jim was offended.

"Migraine," Keriakan moaned. "Nothing helps. I shoot Cafergot. It could be water. Medical science! Pah!"

"What about Ma?" Jill reminded him.

Keriakan stood for a moment, swaying, eyes closed. When he opened them, his lips were curved in his Ben Casey smile. "Mrs. Dunn will be fine. Why don't you join her, Mr. Anderson. She's waiting for you."

"Certainly, certainly." Jim sprinted through the door.

Keriakan waited until the double doors were safely shut, then turned to the family.

"Your mother's illness is an attention-seeking device," he said flatly. "It's a very common problem among self-centered older women who are also nervous wrecks."

"But her heart! All that leaping!" Julie was confused.

"I have been practicing medicine for twenty-three years," Keriakan said, "and not once has a patient's heart leaped out of his chest. There are no hearts flopping around on my waiting-room floor." He pressed his hands to his forehead.

"Dr. Keriakan." John's confusion was equal to Julie's. "Are you telling us that Ma is falsifying symptoms for attention?"

"No, no, no," Keriakan shook his head. "She has symptoms. She has rapid heartbeat. She gets herself all worked up over nothing and *boom, boom, boom,* it's off and running like Pimlico. But it means nothing. Nothing. She'll live for a thousand years, long after I've died of migraine."

"I'm sure Ma's symptoms frighten her," Jill pointed out. "I don't think its fair to dismiss them as an attention-getting device."

"I am being blunt for a reason. I want you all to know that your mother is as healthy as the proverbial pony and will continue having these symptoms." He glanced up and down the corridor. "Why aren't there ever chairs in these places? Do you know what happens when I walk out of Intensive Care to tell some woman who's standing up that her husband just died? She faints, that's what. Then, either I catch her and risk throwing my back out, or she knocks her head on the floor and I'm checking for concussions in the hall. They should at least provide chairs for new widows."

"What can we do for Ma?" Jill dragged Keriakan back to the point. "There must be something."

"Certainly," he said cheerfully, "ignore her."

"Dr. Keriakan!" Julie, John, and Jill exclaimed simultaneously.

"Please." He fended them off with upraised hand. "I know whereof I speak. Years ago my own mother suffered from similar symptoms. She'd call me shrieking that she was having a heart attack. I'd drop everything and run like the rescue squad. At first it was once a week, then twice, then every day, then four times a day. . . . My practice was suffering, my marriage disintegrating. I was shooting Cafergot like a junkie. And my mother had become a chronic invalid."

"What did you do?" John asked.

"First, I acknowledged the symptoms. Then I prescribed placebos and a regime. Worked like a charm." Keriakan puffed, pleased with himself. "I can do the same for your mother. I'll prescribe three colors of pills, all sugar, to be taken on a schedule so complex she has to write it down. I'll give her an intricate diet, along with stern instructions to walk two miles a day regardless of the weather."

"Isn't that . . . well . . . deceitful?" John asked, looking at his shoes. "It sounds like a trick and I don't like—"

"Mr. Dunn," Keriakan interrupted, "the placebos are harmless. The diet, which is primarily fresh vegetables and fruit, would benefit anyone. Your mother will drink lots of water, take brisk walks around the block, swinging her arms to 'out with the bad air, in with the good.' I only wish I had the time to be as healthy as she will."

"It sounds rather sensible to me," Julie remarked.

"You're certain there's nothing seriously wrong with Ma?" Jill persisted.

"Cross my heart," Keriakan said, and he did.

"Well, then, that's settled." Fred rubbed his hands together in a satisfied gesture. "Julie and I will return to Chicago."

"When will you give Ma the results of her tests and tell her about the regime?" Jill asked Keriakan.

"Tomorrow morning. You'd all better be here. Selling the regime to the patient works best when the family is standing around the bed oohing and aahing over the 'cure.' Positive reinforcement and a regime. Works every time." With that he unceremoniously lumbered away.

"Julie and I can't be here in the morning," Fred objected. "We have a flight to catch."

"I have an early meeting," John added. "It's crucial."

"I'll ask Keriakan what time he's coming in," Jill volunteered. "If it's early enough . . . I'll catch him."

"We'll be with Mother," Julie called after Jill, who was racing down the corridor.

"Doctor, doctor." Jill reached his side, breathless.

Keriakan gestured at the elevator doors. "A watched pot."

"What time will you be here tomorrow? My brother and sister have plans—"

"Seven thirty." The elevator doors slid open. "That way my migraine will be gone by noon."

"That's early enough. We'll be here." Jill smiled. "Is your mother still following the regime?"

Keriakan held the elevator doors with one hand. "I'm afraid not. Six months ago she called my office, complaining as usual, so I had the pharmacy send another pound of placebos. The delivery boy found her dead on the floor."

"That's terrible!" Jill was shocked.

"People die. That's life." He shrugged. "Believe me, Miss Dunn, I did what was best. If I allowed myself to think otherwise, I'd be a basket case. It was her time, that's all. Good night."

"Oh, dear," Jill said to the closed elevator doors. Slowly she walked down the hall, her momentary optimism concerning Kate's condition descending in the elevator along with Keriakan.

Oh, shit, Jill said to herself as she rounded the screen protecting the critically ill in Intensive Care from Mother, whose problem, according to Keriakan, lay in being critically well.

"What's the matter?" Kate looked frightened. "I know. You've talked to the doctor, and he gave you bad news."

Jill could have kicked herself for carrying her oh-shit! face around the screen. "No, Ma. Dr. Keriakan expects your tests to be negative."

Kate's eyes narrowed. "Are you saying there's nothing wrong with me?"

"Of course not, Ma." John came to Jill's assistance. "Dr. Keriakan feels that whatever you have is . . . fixable."

"We'd best leave, Mother Dunn. You need your rest," Fred said solicitously with a private let's-get-out-of-here look at Julie.

"We've tired you enough," Julie agreed.

"When will you be back?" Kate demanded.

Everyone looked at Jill. "Dr. Keriakan will be here at seven thirty," Jill said. "So will we."

"Our plane leaves at nine thirty," Fred said approvingly. "Plenty of time."

"And my meeting's at nine." John was pleased. "I'll have time to hear the good news, then get to the office."

"Plane? Meeting?" Kate's voice receded like a wave at low tide.

Julie kissed Kate on the cheek. "Sleep well, Ma. We'll be here first thing in the morning to hear wonderful news."

"Where are you going?" Kate asked querulously.

"Dinner, Ma," Jill explained. "We haven't eaten yet and—"

"You haven't eaten?" Kate seized the opportunity to give orders. "Then, go straight to my house. The freezer is full of food, all wrapped and labeled. There's ham from Easter and turkey from

Christmas. Eight minutes in the microwave, and you're eating. There's three-bean salad from the potluck last summer at St. Monica's, and cake from—"

"We'll find everything." John interrupted the inventory.

"You *are* going to my house?" Kate asked suspiciously.

"A splendid idea, Mother Dunn." Fred leaned over, giving Kate a desultory peck. "I can't wait for dinner."

With Fred's kiss as the signal they all descended on Kate, lips puckered.

"Sleep well, Ma," Jill whispered, and hugged Kate.

Kate returned the hug. "You try to sleep with filth blinking in your eyes. Even Sodom didn't advertise in neon."

"I think I'll stay a while longer." Jim settled himself into his chair with the air of one about to spend the night.

"See you in the morning, Ma." John smiled.

"Use the good dishes," Kate called after them. "And clean up the kitchen when you're through. Remember, Jill washes, Julie dries, and John puts away."

"Yes, Ma." Julie nodded.

"And Fred?"

"Yes, Mother Dunn?" Fred smiled, prepared to give advice.

"You sweep." Kate's voice carried around the screen and beyond.

At Mission Control the full complement of nurses was lined up, staring at them.

"I don't care about your mother's plans for this hospital," one of them said. "Special privileges cause nothing but disruption."

"Whoops." Jill nudged John. "I forgot something. Wait for me at the elevator."

Jill retraced her steps, rounding the screen to find Kate and Jim in a tender embrace. "Oh, my God, excuse me!"

"Ack!" Kate immediately disengaged and fell back on her pillow, both hands clutching her chest.

"I'm sorry." Jill wiggled with embarrassment. "I didn't mean to interrupt—"

"You interrupted nothing," Kate said coldly while Jim stared at the ceiling. "There was nothing to interrupt."

"Of course," Jill quickly agreed, desperate to be gone. "I just had to tell you . . . If the nurses say anything about remembering the hospital in your will, go along with it."

"What?"

"If they seem to think you're wealthy, don't enlighten them."

"What?"

"If anyone mentions the bequest, just smile."

"Bequest."

"Or smelting. If anyone mentions smelting, you're the original Cheshire Cat."

Kate popped up, all embarrassment gone. "You've gone crazy." She turned to Jim. "I knew it! It's not enough my heart is leaping, my daughter's gone nuts! I told her not to divorce Steve. That man was all that stood between her and insanity. Did she listen to me? Does she ever—"

"Kate, dear." Jim patted her hand. "I think Jill's trying to tell you that the nurses are under the impression you're wealthy and plan to leave money to the hospital."

"Why would anyone think that?" Kate frowned.

"You'll get better service, Ma," Jill said.

"I will?" Kate brightened.

"Top drawer."

"In that case, I'm Mrs. Gotrocks herself."

"Wonderful, Ma. See you in the morning." Jill all but ran out of the room.

She scurried toward the elevator, wondering why these things never happened to John or Julie. They would never walk in a room and catch mother necking. Or fabricate the story that led to the walking in. Or have heard the ultimate fate of Keriakan's mother.

Bitter fruit: Legacy of bad seeds.

"Something wrong?" John asked as she joined them at the elevator.

"No." Jill decided to keep her sour harvest to herself. Why shock Julie with tales of geriatric affection, infuriate John with fictional smelting fortunes, and upset them all with the end result of Keriakan's regime?

"Are you staying at Mother's house?" Jill asked Julie.

"We're at the airport hotel," Fred answered for her. "Your mother's house is too far out of the way." Of what, he didn't confide.

Jill shivered, suddenly chilled, and reluctant to be alone. "How about a cup of coffee?"

"I need a hot bath and bed." Julie yawned as they entered the elevator.

John shook his head. "Sorry, Jill. I've got to get a jump on my computer orders. We'll meet here at seven fifteen."

In the lobby Julie half-kissed, half-yawned against Jill's cheek. "Night."

Jill left the hospital on legs that felt like she'd walked from Los Angeles. She drove to Kate's house, bouncing between the pervasive fatigue that is jet lag and the insalubrious sensations that always marked her reunions with John and Julie. Whatever the time, place, or precipitating event, Jill invariably felt herself the twisted apex of an otherwise perfect triangle.

Outside of the expected "How's Daisy?" John and Julie seldom asked questions about her life. It was as though they were afraid that single probe would fling open Pandora's box, loosing an outpouring of bats to screech and nest in their hair.

In the darkness of Kate's driveway Jill groped for the key to Kate's door. She let herself in, then felt her way down the hall to the living room, where she reached for the switch and flipped on the light.

She blinked in the sudden brightness, then gazed around, feeling like an unwelcome intruder in the familiar room. Jill shivered, bone-cold and edgy in the midnight house.

She turned the thermostat to seventy-five, laid her briefcase on the table, and reached for the phone.

When the direct dial beeps had subsided, there was a noise like someone picking up and dropping a phone, then Steve saying, "Oh, shit, hello."

"Is that any way to talk to the only wife you've ever owned?" Jill grinned at the receiver.

"You're in Cleveland! How's your mother?"

Jill decided to tell Steve the whole story, particularly the part about Keriakan's mother dropping dead. She *had* to tell someone. "The doctor says she'll be fine, Steve, but I'm worried because—"

"That's the trouble with you," he interrupted. "Any molehill you encounter is immediately transformed into a mountain. If the doctor says she's fine, then she's fine. You should try not to overreact."

"I should?" The anxiety she'd felt, kept to herself, and was about to confide froze in her throat. "Is there anything else *I should* do?"

"Don't be that way." Steve sighed his own particular sigh, overly long, like a slow leak.

"What way?" Jill was icy.

"If I don't jump in and overreact right along with you, you freeze me out," Steve complained.

"You didn't give me a chance to tell you why I'm worried. You always leap from the fact that I'm worried to your opinion that I shouldn't be, without ever waiting to hear why. That's what went wrong with our marriage."

There was a long, frosty silence, then, "What went wrong with our marriage, Jill, was your penchant for strange bedfellows."

"And you think that was our only problem!" Jill shouted into the phone. "You're the good guy, and I'm the creep. Well, let me tell you, buster, the day they make you a saint, I'll be right there throwing flowers. At your fucking righteous head!"

She slammed the receiver into the cradle.

Aw, shit. If my marriage was a western, I'd be Black Bart.

She stood up, feeling each vertebra creak and unfold. Purse and briefcase in hand, she started for the stairs leading to the second-floor bedroom. She was halfway up and straining to see past shadows that obscured the end of the hall when she shivered, changed her mind, and returned to the living room.

She sat in a chair opposite the cavernous fireplace, which had always reminded her of the cave of an unloved animal.

A line from the Bible came to her mind: *Comfort me with apples.*

Jill hoped Kate had apples. She felt in dire need of comforting, specific comforting, the comforting obtainable from another's hands, another's mouth, but she was alone in this large, nervous house, fully two thousand miles from anyone eager to hold her. And being held was the only comforting that had ever made sense.

There'd better be apples. Apples will have to do.

Or voices.

She reached for the phone.

"My typewriter's hot!" Nick answered the phone ebulliently. "I've got to get back to the muse."

"I thought *I* was your muse," Jill said wistfully.

"You are, babe, you are. Just wait'll you get back." He laughed. "I'll show you how a writer heats up his muse. Till then, I'm rolling up the pages. Ciao."

Jill dialed Carl's number and waited for the connection, trying to think of a greeting that would make him laugh.

"Dr. Foster's exchange," a nasal voice answered.

"Oh, shit," Jill blurted out, not the greeting she'd planned.

"Same to you, sicko," the service exclaimed and disconnected.

Jill held the receiver in her hand, reluctant to hang up, casting about in her mind for someone else to call. The silence in Kate's house was palpable, frightening, containing more shadows than the upstairs hall.

Kate's rooms were alive with memories scattered like ephemeral bric-a-brac. To walk through the house was to risk knocking them over, a shattering beyond all repair. To sit in the silence was to invite echoes, the sounds of voices and occasions past.

It was Jill's experience that she could no more pluck a specific memory from the air within Kate's walls than she could lie down to sleep, and choose the subject of her dreams. Both were random by nature, wantonly so, by some mysterious, malevolent design. The pleasantest day could end in chilly sweat at a nightmare so disruptive, she would waken and lie staring at the ceiling until dawn. The search for a happy memory, the quintessential family moment, could loose an avalanche, each stone a separate and barbed memory thundering down on her head.

Dan Carmichael is still awake.

Jill rolled the idea around in her mind. She longed to hear his voice, his sincere questions about her mother, his laughter at her description of the futuristic Intensive Care Unit hidden in the heart of crumbling Pres Gen.

Comfort taken from Dan is grand theft.

Jill picked up her briefcase, tucked her purse under her arm, and climbed the stairs, resolute and whistling.

Entering the room she'd shared with Julie, she flicked the light switch, hoping to keep both shadows and memories at bay.

She kicked off her shoes and lay down on the fluffy coverlet, fully dressed and rigid on her childhood bed. She turned on her side, trying to relax, but failed, and, sighing, stretched out on her back again.

"Damn!" she complained to the picture opposite her, a cute black kitten chasing a ball of red yarn. She opened her briefcase. So be it. Let sleep be elusive. She'd work on next week's update and read a script or two.

The script she pulled from her briefcase had a yellow cover. Jill smiled. She'd never yet read a yellow-covered script that hadn't put her to sleep, a phenomenon she'd confided to Dan, who'd accused her of superstition beyond even Irish genes. "God saves me from superstition," he'd smiled, crossing himself.

Dan.

She flipped the script open and was halfway through the description of the hero, a standard television purveyor of irresistible machismo and deathless derring-do, when an image, a face, popped out of her memory. She sat up, startled, wondering if the script had triggered this flashback or if it was one of the memories lurking within Kate's walls.

Jill looked at the title page of the script: *The Adventures of Peter Blackmore.*

That's it. Peter Blakely. I haven't thought of him in years.

She settled against the pillows, allowing the face of Peter Blakely to float and dance over her head. She remembered the time, oh, years ago, when they'd checked their romance into the Sheraton Motel on Brookpark Road, unaware it was swarming with convening Moose, or Elk, or some such group imbued with an instinctual desire to socialize wearing red fezzes.

Their own instinctual desires had nearly been thwarted by a desk clerk who'd informed them that the only room available was a studio, a glorified closet really. Would they take it? Of course. Their weekly three-hour rendezvous required little space and less elegance. The essentials they brought with them—abundant energy and mutual heat.

Peter couldn't still be single, not after all these years. He's too juicy.

Jill reached for the phone and dialed a number that had popped out of her memory along with his face.

If a lady answers, I'll hang up. And curse.

"Hello." The deep voice was definitely no lady.

"Demolished any beds lately?" Jill smiled, keeping her voice light.

Ten minutes later Jill was in Kate's shower, hot water cascading down her back. It would take Peter another twenty minutes to get there, thirty if her directions were as bad as she thought.

She stepped out of the shower, pulling Kate's old chenille robe around her. She had plenty of time to repair her makeup, find two glasses and the brandy Kate sipped to ward off cardiac arrest, then air out the bedroom, which smelled of old schoolbooks, birthday notes from maiden aunts, and the ineffable ashy aroma of chronic frustration, the signature fragrance of adolescent virginity.

Jill flew down the steps to the kitchen. Unlike Peter Blackmore of television adventures, her Peter would require no stunt man. In the morning she would need ice for lips swollen by the best kisser in Cuyahoga County, maybe the state, possibly the world.

"Comfort me with apples," she whispered under her breath.

CHAPTER 9

The sound of a ringing telephone insinuated itself into Jill's dream that she, John, and Julie were trapped in the underground headquarters of Crench. They stood back-to-back-to-back inside an ever-shrinking circle of advancing nine-foot toads, each with Dale Neiman's face. To the left of the terrified triplets a man wearing a space suit wildly humped a scheduling board which was fetchingly attired in black panties and bra. To their right Alexander Friedman combed his hair with a ringing telephone, shouting cheerfully, "Hey, man, don't you just love me in bangs?"

As the toads advanced Jill and Julie screamed with fright and clung to John, who unbuttoned his coat and wrapped one side around each sister, enclosing the three of them in its voluminous folds. With her lips pressed against John's neck Jill murmured, "Dan . . . Dan . . . Dan . . ."

"Honey . . . honey . . . hey!" Someone was shaking her. "Wake up, honey. I can't answer this phone."

Jill moaned, trying to fight her way out of the nightmare. Her flailing arms found Peter as he shook her again.

"Hello." She was reeling with confusion, suspended between the shadows of her nightmare and the dawn-glow of her childhood room. "Who is this . . . ? John!"

"I've been ringing for two solid minutes." John sounded weary, but not really annoyed.

"I'm still half-asleep, Johnny. What's wrong? Ma?"

"Ma's fine," John replied quickly. "I mean, I haven't heard anything to the contrary, so I'm assuming she's fine. I'm calling to ask if we can meet for breakfast at Marco's Coffee Shop, near my office."

"I suppose so." She leaned over and gave Peter a quick good-morning kiss. He'd been gently rubbing her back, and now, with the best devilish smile east of Chicago, he began gently rubbing her front.

"I'm sorry to ask you this," John went on, "but I've been at the office all night. The brass has decided that our inventory of microcomputer components has to be completed yesterday."

"You sound harried," Jill sympathized. "I'll be there as soon as I can."

"Fred and Julie will meet us when they've finished packing for their flight home. We'll discuss what to do about Mother, then go straight to the hospital."

"See you in an hour." Jill hung up, wishing that "what to do about Mother" didn't have to be jammed into the odd corner of everyone's life.

"Good news?" Peter mumbled. He'd worked his way beneath Jill's wrapped sheet and was nuzzling the places he'd been rubbing.

"Stop, Peter," Jill insisted, poking the bulge under the sheets that most resembled a head. Stopping Peter was not something she wanted to do. In fact, if the legendary Good Fairy had appeared at that moment bearing one, and only one, wish, fame would be out of the running and fortune not a consideration. Jill's wish would be for a month locked in this room with Peter, without phones, without interruptions, with only the distractions that she and Peter would invent.

Just Peter and me and, occasionally, room service!

"Stop, Peter." Jill tried again.

Peter's response was muffled against her hip. Jill looked at tenacious Peter, weakening, then at the clock, and pulled her legs off the bed. She stood, trying to smile at him.

"If this was L.A. and all I had planned was going to work, I'd call in sick."

"You would?" He was skeptical.

Jill rolled her eyes. "For you, I would call in dead."

Peter laughed, as she knew he would. "But this isn't L.A. and it isn't work. It's Cleveland and a family conclave to discuss my mother, the demon of intensive care."

"And if you don't go, you'll feel guilty." Peter supplied what he knew was coming next.

"Of course."

"Ah." His smile was rueful. "I remember you. You're the lady who makes love like there's no tomorrow and feels guilty every kiss of the way."

112

Jill tied Kate's bathrobe around her. "Not true. I feel guilty before and after . . . never during."

Peter smiled, stretching his long, lean frame against the softness of Kate's pillows. "You mean that everything's okay when you pull up the sheets?"

"More than okay." Jill nodded.

Peter got out of bed. Jill watched him walk toward her, hoping he'd kiss her, and to hell with the time.

He did kiss her, on the cheek. "You were born to make love. Too bad the way you were raised fucked you up."

"What kind of a kiss was that?" Jill didn't want to think about the way she'd been raised or the fact that she'd just spent the night making love in a room where she'd slept alone during all those burdensome virginal nights . . . including the night before her wedding.

On that night Kate had bustled into her room, determination squaring her jaw. "It's time for me to tell you about sex," she'd said. Before Jill could recover from her embarrassment sufficiently to tell Kate she'd read a book on the subject, Kate had said "Douche after" and immediately departed, leaving Jill shaking her head with amusement but not particularly surprised that Kate's primary interest in the act of love would be how to clean up the mess.

"Okay, lady, you said you were in a hurry." Peter was behind her, pushing her toward the bathroom. "Shower time."

"I'll go first," Jill said, glancing at the clock. "I have to get out of here."

"Honey, I can't shower after you leave, then calmly let myself out of your mother's house. The neighbors will think I've made off with the flatware. Let's go."

"Not together!" Jill was taken aback.

"Sure, you've showered with—" Peter began to laugh. "You haven't." He shook his head, kissed her tender, puffy lips, and swept her off her feet. "Catholic girls!"

In the bathroom, Jill was uncomfortable standing on the cold tile floor, uncomfortable waiting while Peter made sure the water would neither scald nor freeze, uncomfortable fetching the towels from her mother's overstocked and painfully tidy linen closet, uncomfortable removing her robe. But once in the shower with Peter her discomfort vanished. She washed his back, and he soaped her front, and they rinsed off, hugging under the full, steady stream of warm water.

"It's like kissing under a waterfall, isn't it?" Jill gurgled up at him.

"Just like the movies." He grinned, pulled her very close, and kissed her again, this time moving her carefully backward until her back was pressed against the shower stall. "Now, I'm going to show you something," he said.

More minutes later than she could afford, Jill stepped out of the shower. "Has anyone ever drowned doing that?"

"If they have, it didn't make the papers."

Now that Jill was out of the shower, she was shivering slightly.

"Cold?" Peter asked, wrapping her in a towel.

"Not really." Jill avoided his eyes. "I think I've found something else I like best during."

He kissed the end of her nose. "How can you still feel guilty? I understand about before, but now you aren't married."

"I have a wonderful life." Jill shrugged. "When I was married, I didn't feel married. Now I'm divorced, and I don't feel divorced."

"That's the Jill I remember." Peter was amused. He hesitated, then shrugged. "Actually, you're the Jill I couldn't forget."

With one shoe on her foot and the other in her hand Jill hobbled toward Peter. "What do you suppose might have happened if I hadn't moved away?"

"I wouldn't have married Crazy Camille." Peter stuffed his wallet and keys into one pocket, and his tie into another.

"Married? You!" Jill was surprised. "The last great American bachelor! When? Crazy *who*?"

"*Was* married, Jill. We had three glorious months." Peter said. "Three glorious months out of a four-year marriage is the reason I'm not married anymore."

"What happened?" Jill asked.

"Next time," Peter promised. "If I leave you curious, you'll call me."

Peter walked her to the garish Pinto parked in the driveway. "I'm parked down the street. Call me if you can break free for dinner tonight."

She watched him walk away before getting into the car. "A true rarity," she mused. "A man I like waking up with."

She pulled into traffic, wondering why her mental list of friends and lovers invariably placed friends in Column A and lovers in Column B.

Lovers should be friends, the best and closest of friends—and so seldom are.

114

She glanced at the dashboard clock, wondering what she'd say to John and Julie. Since she was the one who was insisting on the need for a contingency plan, she thought it best to have one in mind. She wouldn't tell them about Keriakan's mother, not yet, but she did want to broach the subject of shared responsibility for Ma, if not at this juncture, then at some point in the future, when *Kate* and *responsibility* would be synonymous terms.

Jill wondered if there would ever come a time when she would be so uncertain of Daisy's love that she would feel the need to test it with repeated emergency calls for ongoing medical crises.

She thought of Kate in Intensive Care, with Jim at her side and her heart visibly pounding in the glow of the porno movie marquee.

Mother's not wrong. Nothing gathers her children faster than those calls from Intensive Care. Fact is, nothing else gathers us . . . period.

She thought about that for a moment, a plan beginning to form in her mind.

She found them in a back booth, Julie and Fred staring into coffee aswirl with rainbows.

"The coffee is greasy," Julie announced by way of greeting. "What happened to you?"

"I got here as fast as I could." Jill sat down. "Good morning, John. Hello, Fred."

Fred nodded his hello, and John waved without looking up from his work. His briefcase was open, and charts, brochures, and forms all but covered the table. John scribbled madly, alternating between red and black pens.

"I didn't mean 'What happened—why are you late?' " Julie amended. "I meant 'What happened? Your hair is wet.' "

Fred scowled, trying to look out a greasy window. "It can't be raining. We didn't bring an umbrella."

"You look exhausted, John." Jill slid closer to him in the booth. "My hair is wet because I just got out of the shower."

"Oh." Julie continued to stare at Jill. "You aren't wearing makeup."

"Sometimes I don't," Jill told her. "I'd love some coffee."

"Your lips are puffy," Julie observed. "The circles under your eyes are darker than John's."

"One hundred and ninety-four separate components would give

115

anyone circles." John glanced at Jill. "I hope you weren't up all night worrying about Ma."

"I can't say I was." Jill squirmed, wishing the subject of her looks would die a quick death. "Are there menus?"

"The sky's growing darker. There may be a storm," Fred said gloomily. "Perhaps I should call the airport."

"Our flight won't be delayed, will it, Fred?" Julie asked anxiously. "If I miss my afternoon classes, I'll have to reschedule my Flaubert lecture, which will mean rescheduling Dante and backing Milton up until midterm, unless I schedule an additional lecture which would conflict with Father Norton's youth group and—"

"The weather will be perfect." Jill interrupted Julie's domino theorizing. "I heard it on the radio."

"Positive?" Julie asked.

"Absolutely." Jill crossed her fingers behind her back.

"Good." Julie relaxed. She glanced around the coffee shop. "We should order soon. Dr. Keriakan will be waiting for us."

At the counter a waitress poured coffee for a line of truckers who wolfed, slurped, and gobbled as though they were afraid their cargoes might leave without them. Jill waved at the waitress. With a smile that said "Howdy," the waitress returned the wave.

"I want buttered toast, not a new best friend." Jill sighed.

"What's that on your neck?" Julie asked, staring anew at Jill.

"What?" Jill touched the side of her neck, knowing before she did so what was there. "I scraped myself shaving."

Julie's eyes narrowed, and Jill marveled at how much her sister sometimes resembled Kate.

"Your clothes look like you slept in them," Julie persisted.

"I fell asleep without unpacking my suitcase," Jill said. "Do they have doughnuts?"

"I thought you said you were awake all night." Julie was not about to be distracted from her cross-examination.

"I didn't say that." Jill searched her mind for a change of subject. This was almost as much fun as being guilty of murder and having breakfast with Colombo.

"When did we stop looking alike?" she asked Julie.

"When you grew three inches and she dyed her hair brown," John answered for his sister. He finished one form, threw it in the briefcase, and reached for another form and a brochure. "Did you know that there are voice computers that feature communication in conversational tones?" he informed them. "We should get Mother one for her birthday, programed to say 'Yes, Mother, you're right' every ten seconds. It would calm her right down."

"It would backfire," Jill was certain. "Within two weeks she'd change her will, leaving the smelting fortune to a pile of nuts and bolts."

"Your mother does not have a fortune," Fred said, but there was a question in his eyes. "I'll see what's keeping the waitress."

Jill watched Fred as he marched across the restaurant like Patton en route to Palermo, his purposeful strides fueled by imagined masculine forcefulness.

"Why do you look so depleted if you got a good night's sleep?" Julie continued her probing.

"Jet lag." Jill pulled an irrefutable explanation out of thin air. "Why did you dye your hair brown, Julie? It's been so long, I've forgotten."

"I've almost forgotten, too." This time, it was Julie who was squirming uncomfortably in her chair. "To the best of my recollection I decided that flaming red hair was too . . . singular."

"Singular? I haven't heard that word since Sister Mary Martha told us that 'the Devil sets snares for those who make themselves singular,' way back in the good old days at Our Lady of Perpetual Collections." Jill laughed. "I think you would have made a great nun."

"And I think you spent the night with a man!" Julie snapped. "That's what I think."

Jill bit her tongue. She should have known better than to tease Julie, who had packed away her sense of humor along with her much sighed-over travel posters on the day she'd married Fred.

"And furthermore"—Julie spat out the words—"I think that willfully throwing away your marriage was foolish."

"That's your opinion, but it's my business," Jill asserted. "And I fail to see that it's any of yours."

"You're my sister." Julie had her own irrefutable explanation. "I worry about what's going to happen to you."

"Oh, eventually I'll throw myself in front of a train," Jill said, then shrugged at Julie's shocked look. "It worked for Anna Karenina."

"That's your problem, Jill. You don't take anything seriously." Julie sighed and shook her head. "You're thirty-five years old, you have an impressionable teenage daughter, and you flit from man to man."

"Flit? Who says I flit?" Jill demanded.

"Mother told me," Julie said, then, "Now, don't roll your eyes that way. She worries about you, too." Julie lowered her voice confidentially. "I'm sure it isn't too late to reconcile with Steve. Just apologize to him and promise there won't be any further . . . indiscretions."

"I can't do that." Jill understood that Julie's intentions, as always, were good, even if her method of expressing concern had a certain bull-in-the-china-shop quality. But, then, who could expect finesse from a woman who would deliberately dye her hair mousy brown?

"You cannot go on this way." Julie was adamant. "You are pursuing an impulsive way of life that would be detrimental to anyone, but particularly to a woman with a nervous system as precariously balanced as yours."

"Catch me." Jill grinned. "I'm about to fall off my nervous system."

"All right." Julie gave up. "Don't listen. But you can't get away with this forever."

"You think I'm getting away with something," Jill said, beginning to understand.

"If you have no concern for yourself, then you must consider Daisy."

"What about Daisy?" Jill asked angrily.

"The things you expose her to—" Julie shrugged, as though the rest was self-explanatory.

Jill took a deep breath. "Whatever you know of my life comes from embroidered tales of Ma's. Just so you'll have it straight from the source, I expose my daughter to a mother who loves her, who cares about what she thinks, and encourages her to be independent so she can build her life based on her own values, not on some antiquated system of warped, inhibiting beliefs—"

"Are you talking about the Church?" Julie interrupted.

"I most certainly am."

"Added to everything else, your daughter is growing up without the bulwark of the Catholic Church."

"Some terrific bulwark!" Jill was incensed. "It's dynamite if you're a man. If you're a woman, you're a second-class citizen unless of course you can pull off the trick of being *both* virgin and mother, in which case you're in like Flynn."

"That's blasphemy!" Julie covered her ears.

"That's the truth!" Jill shouted.

John slammed the lid of his briefcase. "What the hell are you two yelling about? I'm trying to concentrate."

"Women can't be priests!" Jill shouted.

"You want to be a priest?" John blinked. "I thought you liked television."

"I . . . do. . . . I . . ." Jill lowered her voice, feeling foolish. "Julie's also upset because I'm divorced and I date."

"Why shouldn't she date?" John asked Julie. "She's been divorced for three years."

"Hark." Jill grinned. "Do I hear a voice of sanity?"

"You know better than that," Julie said to John, her face registering patient disappointment. "We weren't raised to believe that marriages can be dissolved like sugar in water. Do you feel your marriage to Candy is dissolvable?"

"No," John responded instinctively. "It's forever."

"See?" Triumphantly Julie turned to Jill.

"I don't see anything except that you think you're irrevocably hogtied to Fred, and John feels he's permanently attached to Candy."

"Hogtied!" Julie exclaimed. "No wonder your life is chaotic. You walk away from your responsibilities and then rationalize irresponsibility as just another point of view—"

"Ah, your mother wears army boots!" Jill threw her pack of cigarettes on the table. She'd had enough of the Grand Inquisition and catalogue of sins.

"Jill, you must listen," Julie said earnestly. "Nothing will work unless you think of life as a schedule—"

"Oh, God!" Jill began to laugh and, ignoring Julie's obvious resentment, continued to laugh in high, squealing whoops as Fred approached the table.

John buried his head in his hands. "The lines on the forms are blurring," he moaned. "One hundred and ninety-four components are running together in my mind—except for the voice computer. That's a grabber."

Fred looked dejected. "The waitress says she can't take care of us until she serves the guys who keep the big rigs rolling." He glowered at the uproarious Jill. "I take it you've come to an equitable solution concerning the problem of Mother Dunn."

"We haven't even discussed it." Jill was chagrined.

"Too late now." John consulted his watch. "We should be at the hospital oohing and aaahing for Keriakan. Let's take separate cars."

"But what about next time?" Jill asked as John rose from the table. "What about the time when Ma *will* be in serious condition. We aren't prepared—"

"We'll cross that bridge, et cetera." John stuffed papers into his briefcase.

"I shall not leave a tip." Fred shored up his dilapidated masculine forcefulness. "Come, Julie."

But Julie continued to sit, staring into space and fingering a napkin.

"Come, Julie," Fred repeated, then turned to Jill. "What's wrong with Julie?"

"I owe her an apology," Jill whispered. "I said something I shouldn't."

"Undoubtedly," Fred concurred. He walked away, following John, who had paused at the counter to pay for the coffee.

Jill leaned closer to Julie. "I didn't mean to offend you," she said, knowing in her heart it was true.

"I'm only concerned about what you're doing to yourself." Julie didn't look up from the napkin she was shredding. "I fear that with the problems you've had in the past, such an . . . unstructured . . . life-style could lead to collapse."

She looked at Jill with eyes that were no longer cool and appraising, but more like the eyes of the carrot-haired three-year-old who's shared a playpen with her livelier sister and brother, watching timidly from the corner for the moment when she might be invited into their play. "That can happen, you know. One crack and the most solid foundation can crumble until you find yourself standing in the ruins of your life. And you're so ver— volatile, Jill."

Jill smiled. "I laugh when I'm happy, cry when I'm sad, yell when I'm angry, and bitch when I'm disappointed. Perhaps to you that's volatile."

"I'm not the wholly stuffy person you think I am." Julie said with an endearing wistfulness.

"Oh." Jill grinned, hoping for a smile in return. "You're about to confess you've seduced a student."

"No! Never!" Julie was shocked.

Jill placed a friendly hand on her arm. "I am teasing you. Teasing is something I do only with people I love. It's a form of humor which indicates closeness. Got it?"

"I suppose so, but it's so hard sometimes."

"Teasing?"

"Being." Julie sighed. "Just being is hard." She shook herself. "That's why I'd feel so much better if I knew your life was as settled and solid as mine . . . that you had someone perfectly dependable to turn to as I have."

"You mean Fred?"

"Of course I mean Fred." Julie scanned Jill's face for the hint of a snicker, a flicker of sarcasm.

Carefully Jill composed her face. "Fred is your rock and your staff, as I'm sure you are his."

"I don't know what I'd do without Fred." Julie stared into space, the napkin a snowfall in her lap. "I'd . . . Well, we'd best go. The men are waiting."

She rose abruptly and walked away from Jill, her brown hair the exact shade of her coat and her purse and her gloves and her shoes and her . . .

Outside, Fred stood beside their rental car, pointedly staring at his watch and tapping his wing tips. "John's already gone," he called. "We'll take separate cars."

Jill started the Pinto and pulled into traffic, thinking that she'd always expected the judgment she'd seen in Julie's eyes, only from a source higher up and not until ten minutes after Gabriel's fortissimo Taps, blown on mankind's final, frenetic fandango.

If Julie only knew that she lives in a world where divorced mothers have sleep-overs, where fun couples discuss their sexuality on the Six O'Clock See It Now News, *where any number of assorted and consorting adults with foundations as cracked as San Andreas still somehow continue to function, spinning through the funnels of fractured lives.*

Of course, Julie's response to such revelations would be to point a Cassandra finger and warn of risks piled too high. And, indeed, most of the people Jill knew seemed to be involved in an emotional pyramid scheme where the buy-in was risk and the pay-off excitement, where each additional gamble only boosted stakes higher.

Jill knew her desire to inform Julie about these existential speculators had sprung from a desire for vindication, an impulse to say, "See, Julie, I'm not so bad."

Jill turned into the parking lot of Pres Gen, wondering when, outside her family, she'd last heard the terms *right* and *wrong*. During her days at Our Lady of Perpetual Guilt everyone and everything had been one or the other. It had been a system perhaps narrow in scope and limited in perspective, but it simplified life, made choices unambiguous, and delivered certainties, rewards for the righteous, damnation for the evil.

Now everyone spoke of psychological motivation and sociological circumstances, of environments that bred sociopaths as mindlessly as bacteria in a petri dish.

To add to the mix, there were the games people played because others had played games with them, and psychological battering, which was, as closely as Jill could determine, what Cinderella had suffered with the abuse of her stepsisters and what they in turn had suffered from her, because every day of their lives began with a chipper good-morning from a ravishing creature who looked better in soot than they did in silk—and if that isn't psychological abuse, what the hell is?

Add to that the good guys who are good, so the psycho-theory goes, because of a neurotic need to conform, and the mix becomes mush, clear choices impossible, and the concepts of right and wrong, artifacts in a museum without visiting days.

We've fallen on imperspicuous times, when not only is nothing as it seems—nothing is as it was five minutes ago.

The television preachers who bellow that the end is near, Armageddon is *now,* Christ is packing His suitcase for a return appearance, might well know whereof they speak when they warn that there's hardly a minute left to receive salvation and kiss the loved ones good-bye. Of course, their message becomes murky when they follow such exhortations with requests for love-offerings to build a nifty temple in Tuscaloosa, but, then, nothing's perfect, and a temple-in-progress might be just the thing to stay that terrible swift sword.

Love-offerings won't save us. In politics, big bucks can result in a winner, but in this case massive donations supporting God would seem to be highly ineffective. No one sends a nickel to Mammon, and lately he looks like a shoo-in.

Jill entered the hospital elevator, pushing the button to the floor where the ICU sat, like a bionic Jewish Mother, monitoring the vital signs of patients who would never say thank you or even call.

As Jill stepped out of the elevator she saw Julie, John, and Fred standing in the hall.

"Dr. Keriakan is with Mother now," John informed her. "We're supposed to wait here."

122

"What happened to the idea of the whole family oohing and aahing at bedside while he explains the regime?" Jill asked.

"We were all ready, just waiting for you," Julie explained. "Then the head nurse came out and said she didn't care what the nurses on the late shift did—she wasn't going to allow us to barge through her ward like the Flying Wallendas. She told Keriakan she'd cut off his privileges if he let us in."

"That's ridiculous!" Jill exclaimed. "A nurse cannot rescind a doctor's staff privileges."

"I don't think that's what she meant," John said dryly. "She called him Poopsie, and he called her Toots."

"Oh, well. . . ." Jill joined them in leaning against the wall. "City hall you can fight, but threaten a man's nookie—"

"Jill!" Julie was horrified.

The double doors swung open, and the burly figure of Keriakan lumbered into the hall.

"You may see your mother now." Both hands were pressed to his temples. "Migraines! All I can see are flashing spots and wavy lines. Someday I'll walk out a window."

"I'm sorry you're not well, doctor," Jill said sympathetically. "Did Mother respond positively when you told her about the regime?"

"The regime is wonderful," Keriakan said. "However, there's no accounting for people."

"You told Mother Dunn that her tests were perfect?" Fred asked.

"I showed her the readout and gave her a cardiogram suitable for framing." Keriakan massaged his forehead. "More than that no man can do."

"She must be very relieved." John smiled.

"*Relieved* isn't the word," Keriakan agreed.

John extended his hand to Keriakan. "I'd like to shake your hand, doctor."

"Please don't." Keriakan backed away. "Shaking, patting on the back, even a little jiggle—they all cause shooting pains."

"Then, we'll just thank you and go in to see Mother." Julie shared John's pleasure.

"Only for a moment," Fred cautioned. "We must make our plane."

Fred was reaching for the door when Keriakan said, "Wait, just a moment. Before you go in—"

"There's something wrong with Mother's heart?" Jill was anxious.

"Your mother has a heart like a herd of Arabian horses. Her readout should be in a textbook, it's so good." He closed his eyes, continuing to message. "There's just one, little thing . . ."

"What?" Three voices harmonized.

"She appears to be in a coma." Keriakan sighed.

"What!" they shouted in unison. The shout was followed by a cacophony, a babble of questions.

"Please, please." Keriakan attempted to calm them. "Let me explain."

"Everyone be quiet!" John shouted them down. "The doctor is going to explain."

"Thank you," Keriakan said to the ensuing silence. "Now, where was I?"

"You were telling us that our perfectly healthy mother is in a coma," Jill reminded him.

"Oh, yes." He was silent for a moment, obviously composing himself. When he spoke, he was wearing the Ben Casey smile.

"Your mother is a three percenter. That means she is among the three percent of all patients who experience an adverse reaction to good news."

"That's impossible!" Fred announced flatly.

"It's possible when there are psychological elements, as there are with Mrs. Dunn," Keriakan declared. "Usually, acknowledging and prescribing a regimen will result in a happy, cured patient. Occasionally, the opposite is true. The patient goes into a decline."

"Why?" Jill asked.

Keriakan shrugged. "Some people get more out of being sick than they do out of being well."

"How ridiculous!" was Fred's opinion.

"How sad!" was Jill's. "What can we do?"

"Nothing," Keriakan replied. "Either she'll come out of it or she won't. It's up to Mrs. Dunn herself."

Fred cleared his throat. "To recapitulate—there's nothing wrong with Mother Dunn."

"Outside of the coma, not a thing." Keriakan nodded.

"That's wonderful news." Fred beamed. "Julie, let's go."

"Wait!" Jill commanded. "You're not going to leave me with Ma in a coma."

"Fred, dear," Julie said quietly, "I would like to see Mother before we go."

"But if she's in a coma—" Fred began.

"I feel guilty about leaving," Julie told him, then turned to Jill. "I wish there was something I could do."

"There is." Jill was blunt. "Feel guilty enough to stay."

"We should see Mother," John decided. "Perhaps we can talk to her, bring her out of this."

"I'll be in the physicians' lounge with a cold compress," Keriakan informed them. "If she comes out of it, call me."

A few moments later they were gathered, like a circle of nervous crows, around Kate's bed. In the chair next to the window Jim slept, mouth wide open, snoring gently.

"Are you sure she's breathing?" Julie whispered, staring at an apparently comatose Kate.

"Certainly, dear," Fred said reassuringly. "If she stopped breathing, the monitor would alert the staff."

"I'm not sure three men with machine guns could alert this staff," Jill said, wondering if migraines could be catching. She rubbed the back of her neck where it felt like a centipede had taken up tap-dancing.

"She's not moving," John observed.

"You don't get around much in a coma," Jill said, sinking into the chair opposite Jim's. She leaned her elbows on Kate's bed, noticing how peaceful and calm Kate looked. There was even the hint of a smile on her face, as though she'd finally found a dream worth having.

"Ma?" Jill called softly, thinking how pretty Kate's face could be when it was empty of tension and temperament. "We're here to talk about your birthday party."

"Her what?" John strained to hear.

Jill shook her head at John, warning him to be silent.

"We're planning a party for your birthday in February, Ma, a big family gathering.

"I doubt we could attend such a function—" Fred began.

John, who'd caught on, poked him.

"We've decided to tell you so you can invite friends." Jill waited, hoping for a response that didn't come. "We need your advice on the menu, Ma. No one plans a party better than you."

They waited, hovering and expectant, but the only sound was Kate's even breathing.

Jill rested her head on the bed. Arranging a party for Kate had been her contingency plan. Before the detour of her convoluted

125

debate with Julie she had decided to approach her brother and sister with the idea of positive reinforcement for Ma, a gathering predicated on celebration, health, and sheer fun.

Jill moved her cheek against the coolness of Kate's sheets, wondering if it might be too late for parties, too late for health, too late for anything except illness, hospitals, and portents of death.

In a world of unsung heroes and publicized villains, where there's time for winning the battles but not for preventing the war, Jill couldn't fault herself for failing to think of a party for Mother sooner. She couldn't, but she did, and she would, forever, if Kate continued to decline.

"Your idea didn't work, Jill." Fred gestured toward Kate's unconscious form.

"Are you sure?" Jill whispered. "Ma looks wildly enthusiastic to me!"

Everyone whispered at one another, but continued to stare at Kate, who neither twitched, nor moved, nor gave any indication of life.

"What's going on?" Jim suddenly woke up and leaped to his feet. "Where's Kate?"

"It's all right, Jim." Jill said quietly. "Ma's here, in her bed."

"Oh . . . oh." His eyes darted around as he tried to get his bearings. "I was dreaming," he decided, and sat down again, sighing. "I dreamed that the mighty Kong was making off with Kate."

"Whatever for?" Fred asked.

"You should have heard her screaming," Jim went on. "Is there any change in her condition?"

"None," John said. "And, according to Keriakan, there's nothing any of us can do."

"He's wrong!" Jim's eyes flashed. "According to *Astounding Health,* kelp is the answer."

"Kelp?" Jill was confounded. "You mean seaweed?"

Jim nodded. "And megadoses of B-15. As soon as old man Bailey opens the doors of his health-food store this morning, I'll get what she needs."

"I'm sure if vitamins were the answer, the doctor would have told us," Fred said.

"They don't want people to know," Jim whispered. "They deal in mumbo-jumbo and we pay big bills."

Julie looked worried. "But—"

126

"Vitamins aren't going to hurt Mother," Jill pointed out. "And if by some chance Jim can convince her to wake up and take them—"

"That would be the end of her coma!" John exclaimed.

"Exactly."

"Allow us to wish you the very best of luck, Jim." Fred shook Jim's hand. "And do let us know if it works." Fred placed a firm guiding hand beneath Julie's elbow. "We must be leaving," he informed Jill.

"Oh, my God, so must I." John glanced at his watch.

Her brother, sister, and Fred busied themselves with the mechanics of leaving while Jill watched, chewing the inside of her mouth.

If I had a nine-o'clock flight to Chicago, or a meeting in an office across town, would I be leaving now?

She couldn't be absolutely sure, but some instinct told her that the flight would be taking off, and the meeting would go on, without her, and Lawrence would be issuing his instructions to her empty chair.

"I'll call from Chicago," Julie promised, and hugged her. "Take care of yourself."

"What? And break a lifelong tradition?" Jill exclaimed in mock horror, then, noticing Julie's guilty face, she added, "Have a good trip."

"Oh, I will." Julie was cheerful. "I love flying." She lowered her voice. "It's Fred who's white-knuckles all the way!"

John squeezed Jill's hand. "I'll call this evening."

John followed Julie around the screen. Fred was the last to approach Jill. "Some practical arrangement should be made for the payment of Mother Dunn's medical bills. I suggest you assume power of attorney."

"Making myself responsible?" Jill asked.

"It is a pragmatic solution." Fred's logic was flawless.

"I'll consider it," Jill said evasively, knowing that once they were gone, the responsibility for all decisions, major and minor, would be hers alone.

"Fine." Fred was satisfied, as well he might have been. He turned to follow John and Julie.

"Fred?" Jill called after him.

"Yes?" He paused at the screen.

"Don't worry," Jill said reassuringly. "That rumor about the general level of incompetence among airline mechanics—not true!"

Fred's eyes popped. "What rumor? What airline?"

"It's nothing." Jill shrugged. "A rumor begun by railroad interests."

"Good heavens! Where did you hear this? Has it been in the papers?"

Jill cocked her head to one side, as though she had heard a voice. "Julie's calling. You're late!"

"Good heavens!" Fred exclaimed, disappearing around the screen.

Jill stared at the screen with an undisguised malice that cheered her for ten seconds—then, sank like a stone.

"I'm leaving, too," Jim announced.

"What a surprise." Jill yawned. She reburied her head in her arms.

"But I'll be right back," Jim said quickly. "I'm bringing kelp, B-15, and whatever else old Bailey recommends to get Kate back on her feet. Would you like some dried apricots?"

Jill peeked at him through her fingers. "Will you bring me a glazed doughnut?"

Jim looked shocked. "Before I'd bring you sugar fried in fat, I'd take a gun and shoot you."

"An even better idea." Jill closed her eyes.

She heard Jim leave, and soon her own even breathing blended with Kate's. She was half-asleep, drifting off in a sea of confused and confusing thoughts, when she heard a voice.

"Where's John?"

She looked up to see her sister-in-law, Candy, holding a man's shirt and looking irate. "He told me to bring him a clean shirt."

"Hello, Candy. John's gone to the office."

"Well, here's his shirt." She waved it like a drip-dry flag. "The girls are waiting in the car."

"You missed him by two minutes." Jill wished Candy would stop glaring at her as though missing connections with John was somehow her fault.

"Now I'll have to chase all the way over to his office," Candy complained. "What's wrong with your mother?"

"Nothing. Dr. Keriakan says she's in the pink of condition."

Candy wrinkled her nose. "Then why does she look dead?"

"She's gone into a psychological decline, Candy," Jill explained.

"*My* mother wouldn't do that," Candy declared. "She hasn't got a psychological bone in her head."

"How restful that must be." Jill smiled.

"I'd better go." Candy hesitated. "Say, Jill, do you know John Travolta?"

"No." Jill shook her head. "I've never met him."

"Kate Jackson?"

"No."

"Robin Williams?"

"No."

"Henry Winkler?"

"Uh-uh."

"Aren't you working for a television network?"

"I am."

"Then why don't you know any television stars?" Candy demanded.

"Network employees don't hang out with the stars, Candy."

"Then what good is being in television?" Candy wanted to know. "You may as well work for the May Company."

Jill gestured in the direction of the shirt. "You'd better hurry. The last time I saw John, he had ring around the collar."

"Soap residue." Candy sighed. "I keep telling him to shower with Zest. He doesn't listen."

"What can you do?" Jill shrugged. "He used to put beans up his nose."

"He did?" Candy gave her a peculiar look, and was gone in a rustle of skirts.

Jill returned her attention to Kate, who slept blissfully on.

"So, tell me, Ma," Jill said softly, "is Jim a comforting kind of apple? I hope so." She sighed, and laid her head on the bed, brushing Kate's hand with her cheek. "Why do they all look so good on the tree, Ma? So fresh and full of the promise that, once you picked them, they'll fill all the empty spaces. And why do I have so many empty spaces? And why is it that lately every one of my beautiful, bountiful harvest turns to sour, green, bellyache apples? Tell me, Ma, why should that be?"

CHAPTER 10

"Please connect me with Jill Kenyon's office." Jill was in Kate's living room, update in hand and phone pressed to ear.

She'd rushed back to Kate's after Jim's return from the health-food store. His arrival had awakened her, and she'd watched, aching from having slept in a chair, as Jim, like a hoary Mary Poppins, pulled bottle after bottle from a bottomless valise. He's piled everything on Kate's bed—a mountain of vitamins, minerals, dried herbs, powdered roots, pulverized twigs, processed salts, and herb teas. The only puzzling item had been a fifth of Courvoisier brandy, but Jill remembered the brandy at Kate's house and decided that Kate had her own medical contingency plan, one that had preceded Jim and new-wave nutrition.

The phone in Jill's office continued to ring in high-pitched machine gun bursts. She wondered why Polly wasn't picking up. Placing a call to herself was strange enough—not getting an answer was stranger still.

"Ms. Kenyon doesn't seem to be answering." The operator announced the obvious.

"Her secretary should be there."

"When the cat's away . . ." The operator giggled. "Know what I mean?"

"No, I don't." Jill wondered how Polly would like being compared to a hedonistic mouse. "Perhaps we can try the message center."

"We?" The operator was testy, but the phone rang immediately.

"Message center," a young masculine voice answered.

"This is Jill Kenyon. I'm out of town on business and my office isn't answering. Did Polly Pritzer call in sick?"

"Nah. She's in Carolyn McCaffery's office. Want me to switch you down there?"

"Please." Jill was puzzled.

The phone rang yet again and was answered by yet another unfamiliar voice. "Carolyn McCaffery's office."

"This is Jill Kenyon. May I speak to Polly Pritzer?"

"Ms. Pritzer cannot be disturbed," the woman said.

"Who *is* this?" Jill felt like she'd fallen into a Fellini movie.

"I'm Marietta Palmer, Ms. McCaffery's secretary."

Jill decided to try the personal approach. "Ms. Pritzer is *my* secretary. If Ms. McCaffery was out of town and trying to reach you in another office, you'd want to be disturbed, wouldn't you?"

"She'd have my ass if I didn't."

"Then, please—"

"Well . . . okay. But if McCaffery gets steamed, she'll yell at you," Marietta warned.

"I'll try not to cry."

There was a sound like that heard in submarines immediately preceding "Dive! Dive!" Despite the volume and abrasiveness of the noise, several long seconds passed.

"McCaffery," a vibrant woman's voice finally answered.

In the background Jill heard a sound like the wails of a tormented soul. What the hell was McCaffery doing to Polly?

"Carolyn," Jill raised her voice. "This is Jill Kenyon."

"Movies and miniseries." McCaffery identified her instantly. "What can I do for you?"

"Is my secretary there?" Jill asked.

"What? Speak up!" McCaffery shouted. "I can't hear you with all this noise."

"Polly! Polly!" Jill yelled.

"Polly. Oh, that's right. She's yours. Hold on." There was a crash in Jill's ear as McCaffery dropped the phone on a hard surface.

Jill waited, picturing Carolyn McCaffery releasing Polly from the rack.

"Hello." It was Polly's voice, and, surprisingly, Polly was also shouting to make herself heard over the screaming.

"What's going on?" Jill shouted. "What's all that screeching?"

"It's gas!" Polly shouted.

"What?"

"The baby has gas!" Polly bellowed. "I've been trying to burp him."

131

"Carolyn brought her baby into the office?" Jill tried to imagine an infant within the gray-flannel walls.

"He's a wonderful baby," Polly shouted. "If only he'd burp—"

There was an abrupt cessation of the screaming. "He burped!" Polly exclaimed.

"Thank God for that!" Jill continued to shout, caught up in the rhythm of the thing.

"I'm not deaf," Polly said. Her voice had an unmistakable edge to it, as though she was angry, confused, offended, tired, or God knows.

"Are you by any chance baby-sitting?" Jill asked.

"No." Polly was definitely tense. Jill heard her say to McCaffery, "Donny seems to be falling asleep, and I don't want to wake him. I'll take this outside." Jill listened as McCaffery mumbled something, then Polly said, "Just a minute, Jill," and pressed the button that put her on hold.

Jill waited, mentally tapping her foot and scanning the update, trying to remember the reason she'd called.

Polly returned, her voice low and urgent. "Did you tell Carolyn McCaffery that I'm psychic?"

"No." Jill said truthfully. "I wouldn't do that. What the hell is going on, Polly?"

"Carolyn called me an hour ago," Polly whispered. "She asked me to give her a psychic reading. She wants to know if she's going to stay at UBC or take another network job she's been offered."

"Which network?" Jill was interested.

"Can't tell you. Professional ethics."

"All right, then." Jill was still curious. "Why is Carolyn's baby in the office?"

"Guilt. She said she couldn't leave him at home. Everyone at UBC has been in here today, cooing and clucking over Donny."

"I can imagine." Jill smiled, picturing an endless stream of strange faces hanging over the befuddled infant. "I think it's nice to bring a baby in for a day. Gives everyone a chance to be human. But I'll bet Carolyn will be relieved when tomorrow comes and all she has to deal with is limited series."

"Apparently not." Polly sounded amused. "Carolyn told me that this experience has opened her eyes to heretofore unexplored possibilities. She's going to bring Donny in every day."

"You're kidding!"

"Personally I don't see how anyone can work in an office

full of Huggies and Similac, but Carolyn's all enthused and it's her baby, so . . ."

"The men will put a quick end to that."

"I doubt it," Polly replied. "The men are all grumbling and sniping, but Lawrence spent most of the morning in McCaffery's office, hovering over Donny and kitchey-cooing. He promised Carolyn that tomorrow he'll bring Donny a moon rock."

"Moon rock? I guess Carolyn will be staying with UBC." Jill smiled. "Was she pleased with her psychic reading?"

"Actually she was more interested in other . . . uh . . ." Polly's voice hushed to a confidential whisper. "She gave me scripts to read, Jill. I'm supposed to tell her which are the hits and which are the turkeys."

"That's ridiculous, Polly! Carolyn can't expect you to predict shows."

"I can do that." Polly's voice was barely audible.

"You can?"

"Sometimes all I need is the title of a show, and I know. I've been doing it for years, just to amuse my friends."

Jill stared at the phone. "Amuse? An executive who could do that would get a million-dollar bonus."

"That's not all," Polly went on. "When a network's schedule is printed in the paper, I can predict its outcome. A hit show glows blue. A turkey glows red."

"Red? Blue? What does the UBC schedule look like?"

"A firestorm," Polly said gloomily. "Everything's red, except *Freak People,* which is a pulsing copper color. I suspect it's a bad omen."

"That's because you've seen the show." Jill giggled, struck by the thought that predicting failure for the UBC schedule was a psychic feat comparable to predicting February snowstorms in Chicago. "I shouldn't ask, but what else is going on?"

"Construction has begun on Lawrence's computer system. The halls are full of men in white overalls who've ordered us to keep all office doors closed. They're worried about dust."

"Dust?"

"The computer is sensitive to dust until it's assembled," Polly explained. "So, it's business as usual, but we're not allowed to walk in the halls without special permission."

"Sounds like Our Lady of Perpetual Boredom," Jill said. "What else?"

"Zippy de Franco hired the Mad Bomber."

"You're kidding!" Jill exclaimed.

"It's true. Zippy felt that his idea about bringing the Mad Bomber into the establishment was the reason Lawrence promoted him, so, like a brave little soldier, he went out and made good. He calls it 'actualizing the concept.'"

"I don't care if he calls it chocolate pudding," Jill objected. "Hiring an anarchist is nuts!"

"Most people around here are saying it's innovative."

"How the hell can they?"

"Because Lawrence says so."

"That's a very good reason. Have you seen the Ma— new employee?"

Polly's voice was a whisper again. "He looks like Haldeman or Ehrlichman or maybe John Dean—short hair, glasses, three-piece suit. He carries a clipboard and runs after de Franco, making copious notes. His name is Smythe Jones."

"Ethnic fella, huh?" Jill laughed. "What's his job?"

"Special Assistant to the Special Assistant, and if you think *that* hasn't got everyone crazy. . . ."

"I'll bet. What does Dan think of all this?"

"I haven't seen him today. He's trying to do ten things at once. There are problems on the rock-and-roll movie. . . ."

"What problems?" The twinge Jill was feeling could only be guilt.

"Delays in shooting, director off on a binge . . ."

"Poor Dan!"

"He needs you, Jill," Polly said softly. "What's going on in Cleveland?"

Quickly Jill filled her in on Kate and her decline.

"Have you brought in a shrink?" was Polly's first question.

"My thought exactly. Keriakan is certain Ma's coma is psychological."

"Do you know anyone there?"

"The best, Polly. Several years ago he pulled me out of a downhill run. Since this problem's been dumped in my lap, I'll have to handle it the best way I can."

"And quickly," Polly advised. "I don't mean you should run out on your mother, but you do have a job to protect."

"How's Alex?" Jill asked. "Did he survive Zippy's cookie?"

"Alex Friedman will survive Armageddon."

"He's giving you problems," Jill said, expecting the worst.

"Not Alex. He's been too busy decorating his closet."

"Decorating? How can he decorate a two-by-four closet?"

"With wall-to-wall red velvet cushions, strobe lights, and quadraphonic speakers. It looks like a disco whorehouse."

"You're exaggerating." Jill laughed.

"Come back and see for yourself."

"The minute I get Dr. Kaiser on Ma's case," Jill promised. "To quote Keriakan, 'More than that no man can do.' "

"I'll be happy to see you. Any instructions until then?"

"I'll put the update in the mail, Polly. Ask Dan to call me when he can. Oh"—she'd nearly forgotten—"I'd best speak to the interior decorator. He must feel like he's been hired and abandoned."

"A stunning idea." Polly snorted. "Hold on for the BMOC."

The buzzing sound resumed, this time like the drill of a sadistic dentist. Jill cushioned her teeth with her tongue and waited it out, wincing.

"It's your dime." There was no mistaking Alex's voice.

"It's Jill," she said, wondering if he always answered his phone that way.

"Jill! My woman of mystery!"

"You've got the wrong woman, Alex." Jill grinned at the phone.

"Not so, green eyes." He laughed. "Any woman who would go to Cleveland on purpose is a mystery to me."

Jill remembered the totality of Alex's stupor. "Did Dan tell you about my family crisis?"

"Hey, I was in your office when you decided to go, remember?" He sounded puzzled. "Are you all right, Jill? Family problems getting to you?"

"I'm handling it." Jill was beginning to feel disoriented. "So, you've fully recovered from Zippy's transcendental dessert."

"What?"

"The cookie. You were zonked silly."

"What cookie? What are you talking about?" he said, sounding as though she had him hopelessly confused with someone else. "Memory lapsing again, Jill?"

"Alex . . . I . . ." This was getting nowhere. If the incident was gone from Alex's memory, it was gone. "Have you read a script titled *The Adventures of Peter Blackmore*?"

135

"Did you have shock treatments, Jill?" He threw her a curve. "I mean, when you had your problems."

"No." She felt a familiar heat begin behind her knees. "How did you know I had prob—You checked me out!"

"How else could I have found the best fucking boss in this town!" He said it with such conviction that Jill blushed through the heat of her hives.

"About *Peter Blackmore* . . ."

"I was going to read it last night, honest to God, but then Nina and I went out to celebrate. . . . Fuck, I wanted to tell you the news in person."

"Nina's pregnant!" Jill was excited. "She had the test!"

"Hah. She's having it tomorrow or next week or sometime. There's no rush."

"What then?"

"Nina got the job with your friend Patti Gerard!" he exulted. "She starts tomorrow, modeling clothes by some Chink refugee who can't cut a dress taller than five foot two. For the first time in Nina's life being short is an advantage. Do you know what a natural blonde is going to look like modeling an Oriental line?"

"Wonderful?" Jill smiled and scratched simultaneously.

"Fucking erotic." Alex was graphically certain. "Put a sexy Western body in sexy Eastern clothes, and every dumb bastard in this country is gonna think his old lady is about to turn geisha for him. It's like I told Patti, 'Honey, you gotta play the fantasy to the hilt— shoot a layout just this side of bondage.'"

"*You* told Patti?" Jill had never known anyone who could tell Patti anything.

"That's gonna be her whole campaign," Alex said proudly. "East meets West, and the return of the sexy, docile woman. It'll ride the reactionary tide. Guys are tired of shelling out so their old ladies can look like *Vogue* at ERA meetings. A new trend's a-coming, thanks to you. You put it all together."

"Swear you won't tell anyone," Jill begged, certain she was about to become personally responsible for the defeat of the ERA. "Please, Alex, just read that script."

"It's good?"

"It could be. It's very visual and a terrific adventure. All that's missing is heat."

"Huh?"

"You know. People in personal conflict as well as jeopardy from

136

outside sources, skeletons in closets, wicked women, driven men
. . . contemporary gothic novels." She waited, but there was no
response. "Tolstoy, Alex. Natasha losing her virginity to the bad guy
and André finding out. *Soap!*"

"Gotcha." Alex sounded excited. "I'm making notes. I'll bring it up
at the meeting."

"What meeting?"

"Zippy de Franco's called a meeting. It's to be an overall discussion
of projects."

"Or a projected discussion of overalls," Jill sneered.

"You don't like Zippy."

"I don't like what he does. Well, you can't go to the meeting alone,
Alex. Call Dan in from location."

"He didn't leave a number." Alex sounded unconcerned.

"If he can't be reached by phone, go out there and get him."

"To Encino?" Alex asked, as though Encino was the land of the lost.
"But I'll miss everything that's going on here."

"Alex, the meeting is not a surprise party. There are no prizes or
balloons. Besides, it's neither fair nor reasonable to ask you to represent a department you've worked in for a matter of days."

"I don't mind," he said cheerfully.

"Have you read all the reports?"

"I've been decorating my office. . . ."

"All the scripts?"

"Wait till you see it. I put in . . ."

"The update?"

"Where is it?"

"What the hell did you think you were going to do in the meeting?" Jill asked through clenched teeth.

"Wing it?"

If the hives hadn't been spreading faster than Jill could scratch, she
would have laughed. There was something funny and rather touching about Alex's naïveté.

"Listen, Alex. Find Dan," Jill insisted. "Who knows? You may get
to him before the meeting starts, and neither of you will miss it."

"Okay. Okay. Which way is Encino?"

"Ask Polly. She'll point you in the right direction." Jill paused. If
he followed Polly's directions, Alex would stand a very good chance
of winding up in Death Valley. "Ask Dan's secretary. And tell Nina
I said congratulations."

"Oh, sure. Bye."

Jill all but tossed the phone at the cradle and ran toward Kate's kitchen, scratching with one hand and opening the freezer door with the other. She reached past the rows of freezer-wrapped bundles and grabbed a bag of ice, flopped on the floor, pulled off her jeans, and laid the entire bag across the backs of her legs.

"Ahhh," she sighed as the ice soothed the heat and tempered the hives. She rolled over and lay on her back, propping the ice bag under her legs, then folded her arms under her head and began the deep breathing Polly had taught her. She looked up.

Oh, God, even Ma's ceiling is spotless.

Jill rolled over again, pulling herself to her feet. Carrying the ice bag with her, she went to the living room and Kate's phone.

A few minutes later she was talking to a nurse.

"There's no change in Mrs. Dunn's condition," the nurse said. "Her vital signs are better than most of the staff's."

"She's still in a coma?"

"Her clinical picture is excellent," the nurse said emphatically.

"I don't care if her clinical picture's by Rembrandt," Jill said. "There is a problem!"

"Her problem is psychological." The nurse's voice was cold. "Psychological problems are outside the province of Intensive Care."

"I'm sure anything that doesn't cause your monitors to beep and go bananas just mystifies the hell out of you," Jill said angrily. "Well, I'm bringing in someone whose province it is."

"That's your prerogative," the nurse said loftily.

"Bet your ass!" Jill shouted, and hung up.

Jill returned to the kitchen, threw the leaking ice bag in the sink, and opened the ironing-board closet, where the phone book had resided on the top shelf since before Jill was born.

She opened the book to the Yellow Pages, riffling through to *Physicians.* She knew that somewhere in her memory Neil Kaiser's number lay dormant, slotted in limbo along with the numbers of pizza joints that delivered, dry cleaners who had gone out of business, and the nursery school where Daisy had made clay giraffes.

She found it, and wondered how she could have forgotten a number she'd called a thousand times; when haunted midnights panic-fueled with solitaire accelerated into demented dawns; when days that began with "Something wonderful will happen today" crashed into the late-afternoon barrier of "Nothing ever changes"; when "I'm better" was an occasional message, purposely brief, because better can be tenuous, a feeling often dispersed more quickly than the words; when "good-bye" was the final message, an explicit word delivered with another, implicit message—"It's not *my* idea to go. Help! Help!"

Jill dialed, the butterflies in her stomach beating their wings against the kind of trepidation usually reserved for phone calls to lovers.

A woman's voice answered. "Dr. Kaiser's office."

Jill hesitated, "May I speak to Dr. Kaiser, please. It's Jill Kenyon."

"Jill! How are you?" she asked effusively. "This is Mrs. Silverstone."

"Mrs. Silverstone! I thought you would have retired by now."

"Oh, gracious me." Her laugh was quivering silver. "I did retire, my dear. Dr. Kaiser gave me the loveliest going-away party *and* two tickets on a Princess cruise to Acapulco. Isn't that just like him?"

"I wouldn't know," Jill said. Her Kaiser-inspired trip had been to a mental institution. "Did you enjoy Mexico?"

"Loved it," she thrilled. "I came back to Cleveland determined to retire there. The people are so sweet and good-natured. Sensible, too. If everyone in Cleveland took a siesta every day, the city council wouldn't fight with the mayor and Lake Erie wouldn't be polluted."

"I'm sure," Jill agreed, wondering how.

"The city should build fountains at Public Square. People could tether their burros and stroll."

"That would be nice." Jill stared at the phone. "So why aren't you in Mexico, Mrs. Silverstone?"

"When I came back to sell the house, Dr. Kaiser was waiting on my doorstep." She laughed. "Such a dear man! I'm the only receptionist he's ever had, you know. He said he wanted me to return to the office. He was afraid my retirement might trigger premature senility."

"Is that possible?"

"Between you and me, Jill I think he was too late."

Jill smiled. "You sound sharp as ever, Mrs. Silverstone."

"Not really. I get all of his patients mixed up. Not that I want to remember any of *this* batch. He has a whole string of burnt-out hippies left over from the sixties. You can't imagine how depressing this waiting room is with them all sitting here in their love beads and wrinkles. You, my dear Jill, had style."

"Thank you." Jill grinned. "Is Dr. Kaiser in?"

"Oh, my gracious." The silver showered into Jill's ear. "Here I am just chatting away. As I said, I think Dr. Kaiser was too late." There was silence, and the butterflies had begun their blind, instinctive fluttering, when Mrs. Silverstone returned to the line. "I forgot to ask, Jill. Are you feeling poorly again?"

"No," Jill said quickly. "This call is about someone else. My mother has a problem, and since Dr. Kaiser is the knight in shining armor of shrinkdom . . ."

"That's very flattering." It was a new voice, a deep voice, resonant and harboring a chuckle. "This is Dr. Kaiser."

"Oh, God." Jill groaned, thinking this would be an appropriate time to die. "So how's business?" she asked. "You cure anybody this year?"

"One or two here and there," he said evenly. "How have you been?"

"Fine." Jill was breathless. "My daughter is fifteen and a normally abnormal adolescent. I'm working for the United Broadcasting Company in the programing department. . . ."

"You are?" He sounded surprised. "You never showed much inclination toward a career when I knew you."

"Yeah, well, being crazy used up all my energy."

"And your husband? How's Steve?" he asked.

"Steve is fine. We're divorced, but he's fine. Now, about my mother?"

"Divorced? How long ago?" His surprise had compounded into something approximating shock.

"Three years," Jill answered obediently.

"Well, well. Then you've recovered from the trauma," he commented.

"Certainly."

"That's interesting. What's this about your mother?"

"She seems to be in a psychological decline," Jill explained, relieved that the subject had finally shifted away from her life. She filled him in on Kate's condition, finishing with "Do you think you can help her?"

"Possibly. Of course, I have to know more about the case."

"I'm sure if you called Dr. Keriakan . . ."

"That's certainly something I will do," he said, "but what I have in mind is talking in more detail with you."

"I was hoping you'd take the case." Jill heard the plea in her voice. "I have to return to Los Angeles."

"I'm sure you do." He was soothing. "So, I suggest we meet this evening. If I can get a clear picture of what's going on with, uh, what is her name?"

"Mrs. Dunn."

"Mrs. Dunn, I might be able to help very quickly."

"Do you really think so?" Jill was overjoyed.

"Possibly. Can you be here at seven this evening?"

"Oh, yes, of course." Jill was delighted. "The same office?"

"Yes," he said. "See you at seven."

He hung up, leaving Jill hopeful and nervous, happy and apprehensive, awash with anticipation and atwitter with dread.

Conflicting emotions had always made Jill hungry. She went to Kate's kitchen where she microwave-defrosted, cooked, and devoured fried chicken labeled "June twenty-third, the only cookout John junior has invited his mother to so far this summer."

She glanced at the clock. Four hours to go.

She climbed the stairs to her old room and curled up on her bed with her scripts, much as she had curled up with her books in the days of childhood griefs and pleasures. She slipped as easily into the stories meant for television as she had into the world of the Brontë sisters, as always finding relief from the burden of herself in printed escape.

A few hours later she looked up from a note-covered script to find that she only had time to shower and dress.

She drove through the last straggles of Cleveland rush-hour traffic, taking the old surface streets she knew and avoiding the new interstate.

As she drove she tried to concentrate on anything except where she was going and the person she was about to see.

Perhaps Zippy never hired the Mad Bomber at all. Perhaps his anxiety to please Lawrence had impelled him to go out and create a Mad Bomber. Perhaps the man who looked like an accountant named Smythe Jones was in fact an accountant named Smythe Jones —or an actor from Central Casting playing an accountant who was playing a Mad Bomber named Smythe Jones. Or perhaps— This particular road had taken one turn too many. Jill decided to switch to another road before she had a head-on collision with herself.

There was the matter of Polly's psychic gift, which apparently ranged from finding lost mothers in large white rooms that turned out to be Intensive Care, to predicting hit shows and what should be scheduled where. Could Polly possibly develop a prince-detector, thereby ending frog-kissing forever?

And what of McCaffery and Baby Donny? Was she striking a blow for female liberation or taking advantage of her position, an advantage not available to secretaries and file clerks who also had children and might harbor a secret desire to have the tykes with them as they went about making a living. And the position. What was it for if not to be used to full advantage—or was that notion undemocratic, elitist, and unfeminist?

And what of Baby Donny? Is there a chapter in Spock that covers the rearing of a child at a television network? Would the raising of Donny be of interest to the Rand Corporation? Would— This road was getting lost in a maze.

And what about Alex? Had the cookie caused amnesia, or was he embarrassed at having lost control? Jill could empathize, remembering herself under the nuthouse piano, humming her tune and sitting in a puddle. At least in the nuthouse there were locks on the doors, bars on the windows, and a staff to discourage the curious from wandering through the people zoo. Alex had been very vulnerable the day of the cookie debacle. He'd also been lucky. No one had seen him, no one had known. He'd been well looked after by Polly and Dan.

And Dan. Dan. Dan in Encino with a rock-and-roll band, over budget, over schedule, overloaded with work that should have been hers to share.

And shares and ratings and Lawrence's dust-free computer system and a Zippy de Franco who could call meetings of his own. And where was Dale Neiman, and where was Alex's male secretary, he of the bald head and elegant air, and where was Dan, where in Encino—

And where the hell am I? I've done it again.

She was at an intersection, wondering how she'd gotten there. Ten minutes after seven and lost!

She turned left on a hunch and within three blocks saw a filling station that was an old familiar landmark.

She turned right at the station and from there could have found her way to the medical building blindfolded. In fact, considering how often her trips to this office had been blind flights of pure anxiety, she already had.

The medical building seemed oddly deserted—not really so odd, considering the hour. The elevator whirred and creaked just as it always had, and Jill feared plunging to a fourteen-floor death just as she always had.

The door was open, and Mrs. Silverstone's desk was empty except for a the bud vase containing one yellow rose. That, too, hadn't changed, despite Mrs. Silverstone's retirement, despite her memory, despite the aging hippies and her vision of a downtown Cleveland inhabited by sweet-tempered strollers with burros.

She glanced around the office, uncertain as how to proceed. Without Mrs. Silverstone to announce her, she had no idea of how to let Kaiser know she'd arrived.

She was moving toward the desk and Mrs. Silverstone's intercom when the door to the inner office burst open and Neil Kaiser appeared.

"Well," he said, leaning against the doorjamb. "Well, well."

Through butterflies and blindness Jill noted that he hadn't changed, not really, unless the gain of sixty pounds could be deemed significant. In some people it was, in some it wasn't, and Jill would hardly have noticed except that forty pounds of it seemed to have accumulated in the area of his face. Actually it was rather attractive in a stolid sort of way. At their last meeting he'd been thin-cheeked, like Lawrence. His thinness had given him a drawn and haggard look she'd found romantic, since she'd attributed this to overwork born of admirable dedication. But this was better. This was the man of full maturity, the promise become prime, potential realized and power settled down to stay. This was a man of substance.

"Well, well, well, well." He smiled at Jill, who continued to stare at him with eyes like green and glowing Christmas lights.

CHAPTER
11

"Well, well, well, well." Neil's record seemed to be stuck.

Jill sat in a chair in the middle of his office, trying to follow him with her eyes as he circled, intent on viewing her from all sides. Her head refused to swivel three hundred and sixty degrees, so she waited, muscles tense and nerves caught in a vise whose opposing sides were pleasure and pain—pleasure at being in a place which once had been her sole safe haven with the person who miraculously transformed her from a non-functional "thing" into a real person; pain at the loss of this place and this person, a loss doubly poignant and profound because it had not been her idea, no, nor his.

The move to California had been Steve's idea, his dream of a law office drenched in perpetual sunshine. Like a dutiful wife, she'd followed, leaving behind her therapy, her family, everything familiar and dear, buoyed only by Steve's assurances that "You'll love L.A." Stubbornly, she hadn't, didn't, never would. She loved the ocean, but that was all. When she said as much to Steve, he'd accused her of always "hating everything, so what difference does it make?"

"You look smashing" was Neil's verdict. "Your life must agree with you."

The vise squeezed tighter. Jill squirmed in the chair. "Thank you. I suppose it does."

"Nothing missing?" His arms were folded. He looked straight into her eyes as though searching for something.

"So far as I know, nothing is missing." She tried to keep her voice light.

"That's something of which we're not always aware until we're confronted with it, hmmmmm?" He turned away, breaking their gaze.

"My mother—" Jill began, hoping a quick focus on the problem that had brought her there would halt her internal somersaults.

Neil was patting his pockets, searching for something.

Jill took a deep breath and continued. "According to Dr. Keriakan, her physical condition is excellent. There was a minor heart problem years ago, but—"

Neil was removing an envelope from his pocket.

"—nothing to worry about . . . and. . . ." Jill stopped. Neil didn't seem to be listening. He was tapping the envelope on the back of his hand.

"Do you know what this is?" he asked.

"No."

"Divorce papers. I'm getting a divorce."

"You! *You!* You're getting a divorce!"

The vise clamped shut.

"My goddamned marriage didn't work out." He shrugged. "It happens."

When does it happen? You told me never to divorce Steve. "All marriages can be worked out," *you said.*

"Your children? What about them?"

"*She* gets the kids." He laughed, a short, bitter sound that burst from his throat. "Even though she's been going at it behind my back with some dumb wop who thinks he's a hotshot real-estate developer. He bought a swamp outside Willoughby and thinks he can turn it into country-club estates. Ha! The foundations will sink in the muck! Wait and see." His eyes gleamed with the anticipation of revenge.

"I'm so sorry," Jill said, wishing she could think of something more adequate. He'd always had the right words for her.

"Don't be." Neil raised his hand, perhaps embarrassed by her obvious sympathy. "I should have known this would happen. The minute I graduated med school, she quit her job and began giving birth like a Mormon. Establishing a practice wasn't hard enough. I also had to come home every night to a woman who'd given up thinking, given up growing, given up everything except mindless gestation. That and television. She ate, watched television, and gave birth six years in a row. For seven solid years the front of that woman's blouse was soaked through with milk." He shuddered. "I love the kids, every one of them. I'm glad they were born. But"— he shouted directly at Jill—"did my wife have to breast-feed?"

Jill jumped, clutching the arms of her chair. "I don't know."

145

"Did you?"

"What?"

"Breast-feed!"

"No, I didn't!" She hoped it was the right answer.

"See! See!" Neil slapped his arms to his sides and stomped around the room. "I should have known it years ago. We were mismated from the beginning! Mismatched from day one!" Neil paused, glaring at Jill. "She was neither wife nor helpmeet. She was a glandular response." He resumed stomping. "She watches soap operas. Calls them 'my stories.' My *stories*! *My God!* A master's degree in accounting and she ends up with a mind like mush!"

His stomping brought him to within a few inches of Jill's chair. He hovered over her, his hands covering hers on the armrests.

"*You!*" he roared. "You have a mind!"

"I have?" Jill knew she'd had one when she came in, but couldn't attest to its whereabouts now.

"Of course you have. A good one." Neil's face softened, relieved of its rage. "Have I ever lied to you?"

"Um. . . ." Jill struggled to reconcile the Neil Kaiser of '71 with the man whose face was a scant inch from hers. "No, you never lied to me. I believed every word you said."

"I know," Neil said, and kissed her, a kiss that fired her heart as surely as it broke faith.

Her hands remained on the armrests, and his hands were still on hers. It was a tentative kiss of the kind exchanged by adolescents more curious about kissing than interested in kissing one another.

Neil continued to kiss her. Jill desperately wished she could abandon herself to the feeling, that the almost audible ticking of her mind would quit intruding and leave her to the moment she'd lived in a thousand imaginings. This moment with Neil had been her favorite fantasy for an uncomfortable number of years—safest of all fantasies, because never for one second, even in the weeks spent under the nuthouse piano, had this fantasy moved beyond fantasy to the dangerous realm of possibility.

Now it was here, real, three-dimensional, no longer a controllable fantasy. The observer in Jill stood in the corner, taking Polaroid pictures.

Neil's mouth shifted slightly, his tongue pressing her lower lip. As her own lips parted, a tide of remembered emotion rolled in, engulfed her, and washed the silent observer out to sea.

146

Jill wiggled her fingers and tugged, freeing her hands. Eagerly she wrapped her arms around his neck, pulling him closer until he was over her, and she was stretched out full-length in the chair, arms wrapped around the magic that had transformed her, the purveyor of magic, the magician, her secret love.

He began propelling her, his lips locked to hers, in the general direction of the floor.

As Jill slithered to the floor she tried to think of herself as boneless and graceful, as a spirit wafting its ephemeral way, as a Slinky. But her head banged the backrest, and her arm caught, stuck between the seat and its cushion. Finally she landed, her passion-smoothed face creased with a wince. The *Neil, Neil, Neil,* echoing romantically through her head was replaced by a silent *ouch, ouch, ouch.*

Jill lay on the floor, Neil's lips glued to hers, her leg twisted beneath her, looking like a seductive accident victim being given mouth-to-mouth resuscitation by a passing Samaritan who had, willy-nilly, become emotionally involved.

Neil was fumbling with her skirt, or pants, or pantyhose, or something down there, perhaps even himself. It was difficult to tell with one leg and her tailbone going numb. She raised her hips to help him, a maneuver which effectively zigged her into his zag. His nose mashed her nose, and his teeth clicked hard against her teeth, nipping her upper lip as well.

Jill decided she'd better quit helping before she was permanently maimed. She relaxed as best she could, wiggling the toes on the leg with the creeping paralysis and thinking that this all would be so much easier without Neil's apparent determination to accomplish the entire act of love without removing his lips from hers.

So, she lay there, eyes tightly closed, cheeks aching from the marathon pucker, thinking she'd finally, finally discovered exactly what marriage was for. It wasn't for children. It wasn't for growing and developing as a person in concert with another human being. It wasn't even for expressing human affection. For that you can go to the pound and adopt a dog.

Marriage was for going to bed decently, with dignity and comfort, with freshly brushed teeth and freshly laundered jammies, without buckles and buttons and shoes and underwear to get in the way. It was for a turned-down bed, a turned-out light, and a tranquilly turned-on couple unhampered by the need to cope with an unfamiliar body and inappropriate furniture.

*There's a lot to be said for spontaneity, but never by anyone who's
ever tried to make love fully dressed on the floor.*

Neil continued to fumble. In the next moment Jill was grateful her
leg had gone numb, because Neil seemed to be bouncing up and
down on it. A moment after that he gave a cry that could have been
joy or completion or the result of sticking his thumb in his eye.

As Jill lay still, eyes tightly closed, lips pressed against his, and the
Wonda-Weave carpet itchy against her bare behind, she waited for
some signal that it was time to open at least one eye.

"I love you," Neil murmured against her mouth.

"My leg," Jill murmured against his.

"I have always loved you," he said out of both sides of his mouth.

"It's numb to my hip." Jill tried, unsuccessfully, to move.

He raised his head, gazing at her fondly. "How could I have let you
go?"

"Neil . . . dear, please . . ."

"You'll never walk out of my life again!"

"I'll never walk anywhere again." She groaned. *"Get off!"*

"What?" He leaped as though someone had yelled "Fire!"

"Oh, God . . . please . . . dear . . . move . . ." Jill thought it quite
possible that his leap had crushed her kneecap.

"Oh, of course." He finally realized her problem and moved to one
side.

Jill tried to move her leg. She shivered as the first blood began to
flow through blocked veins.

"That was extraordinary." Neil turned toward her with a dazzled
smile.

Like getting mugged in an alley.

"Sometimes she speaks in tongues," Neil said, gazing into the distance.

"Who?" Jill glanced around to see if anyone had come in.

"My wife. She went into a religious phase after the last child was
born. I told her six was enough, and she took up with the Holy
Rollers. Reaction formation, that's what it was. Speaking in tongues
and adultery. The woman's clearly insane."

"Ow! Ow! Ow!" Jill bellowed as pins and needles struck like instant
retribution from a cranky God.

"Sweetheart, what is it?" Neil's eyes were wide with concern.

Speechless with pain, Jill gestured at her leg. He leaned over and
began rubbing with long, firm strokes.

Oh, God. If I'd known this was going to happen, I would have shaved my legs.

"Did you say you love me?" She asked incredulously.

He stopped rubbing. "I did."

"Do you?"

"I do." He was matter of fact.

"My God!" Jill sat up, throwing her arms around his neck. "I've longed to hear you say that."

"You have?"

"Since ten minutes after I met you." She smiled at him.

He looked confused. "I wasn't sure you particularly liked me."

"Why? How could you not know?"

He shrugged. "Week after week in my office you just sat there, hardly saying a word."

"I was psychotic, dear."

"And you moved away." Accusation flattened his voice. "I missed you."

"I missed you, too." Jill snuggled into his arms. "Oh, how I've missed you."

Neil's arms tightened around her. "We don't have to miss each other anymore."

She snuggled closer, lulled by the sort of contentment she hadn't known since the days when her father had carried her to bed with piggyback rides.

"My God! The time!" Neil exclaimed. "Christ."

He leaped to his feet, tumbling Jill backward onto the carpet. "I'm late! She'll kill me!"

"Who? Who'll kill you?" Jill wondered if he'd gone daft with the joy of their reunion.

"Can you just hurry it along?" Neil handed Jill pantyhose that seemed to be beyond repair.

"I don't understand." Jill stared at her pantyhose.

"Here are your shoes, and what's this?" He held up an item that any fool would know was panties, even the fool Jill was thinking herself to be.

Neil placed a firm hand beneath her elbow and guided her swiftly toward the door.

"Wait! Neil!" Jill was bewildered. "I thought you were divorced."

"Divorcing," he said calmly. "Divorcing is not divorced."

"Obviously. Not if you're dashing home for brussels sprouts." Jill wondered how much it would cost to have him killed.

"A temporary situation," Neil said soothingly, pulling her close. "I want to come out of this divorce clean. There can't be anything for her to nail me with."

"Nail *you*? What about the hotshot real-estate developer?"

"She can deny that, Jill, and judges are notoriously biased toward women." He held her away from him, smiling gently. "We'll work this out, sweetheart. Our finding one another after all these years is more than coincidence. You must see that."

She looked into gray eyes that conveyed the old magic, recast the old spell. "You're right, Dr. Kaiser. When weren't you?"

"That's my girl." He patted her bottom, and they resumed their walk to the door. "I'll go on home, tell her I was tied up with a patient. We'll see what she says about that."

"How will you know, what with her speaking in tongues and all?" Jill remained slightly disgruntled.

"I'm doing the best I can, Jill. Divorcing isn't easy. You know that."

"Yes, I do." Jill remembered the days of her own divorce, the constant vacillation between strident rage and inchoate lamenting, the gamut run daily from "I'm free!" to "I'm dying!" So if Neil was somewhat distracted, divided, and daffy, it was only to be expected. Who should understand better than herself?

Jill squeezed his arm empathetically. He smiled at her fondly, then whooshed her through Mrs. Silverstone's domain to the door. He opened it a crack and peeped through, nervously scanning the hall.

"I'll go first," he instructed. "You count to ten—no, better make it fifty. That'll give me time to get to the parking lot. Got it?"

She nodded. "We could pull off a bank job with less planning."

"I'll call you in the morning, sweetheart, right after I call my lawyer. I want him to get this damn divorce on the road!"

He was halfway through the door when he turned, closed it, and took her in his arms again. "I hate leaving you. But once we get through my divorce, we'll never be separated again." He wrapped her in a hug, then grinned. "By God, when I cure them, they stay cured!"

She watched as he sped down the hall and punched the elevator button. Then, too impatient to wait, he opened the door next to the elevator and, without a backward glance, vaulted down the steps.

Jill sighed, dizzy with overload and in definite need of a circuit

breaker. Counting as Neil had instructed would help her to focus—
"to center herself," as Carl would have said.

She counted to twenty, slowly, exhaling on even numbers. She was
approaching what she hoped was her center when she became aware
of a strange rumbling noise. Glancing back over her shoulder, she
expected to see the Remington prints swaying in the onset of an
earthquake. But this wasn't California. This was Cleveland, and the
rumbling was emanating from the center she'd been struggling to
discover. Her stomach was growling.

*Terrific! I'm standing here counting like pom-pom pullaway and
starving to death.*

A moment later she was through the door, no longer a lunatic
counting out loud in an empty office. Now, firmly in control of herself
and her situation, she was striding purposefully toward the elevator,
her Lollipop panties in her pocket and her second-best shoes in her
hand.

An hour later she was at Kate's, the telephone clasped in her hand.
"I *know* Dr. Kerry is there. Please let me speak to him."

"I think the doctor has left for the day." The receptionist was
cool.

"No, he hasn't. It's six o'clock in Los Angeles. Dr. Kerry's in his
office filling out insurance forms and watching Henry Sitzbach on the
Channel Six See It Now News."

"If I say he's gone—"

"He isn't!" Jill insisted. "He's sitting there mumbling that he could
get higher ratings if only someone would give him a break."

"You sound upset, Mrs. Kenyon." The receptionist yawned audi-
bly.

"Upset!" Jill yelled. "In the last twenty minutes I've eaten a whole
box of Twinkies!"

"I'll see if the doctor is in," the receptionist said hastily.

Jill waited, phone gripped in one hand and purse in the other. She
desperately wanted a cigarette but at the moment couldn't seem to
loosen her grip on either phone or purse.

"Hello." He was there!

"Hello, hello . . . *oh* . . . *oh* . . . *oh* . . . Dr. Kerry!" Jill began to cry.

"What's wrong, Jill. Why are you crying?" he asked.

"Oh . . . oh . . . oh . . ." She couldn't get her breath. "My mother
. . . oh . . . and then . . ."

"Something's happened to your mother?" He jumped on it.

151

"No . . . she's . . .fi . . . fine," Jill managed to say at last. "Her coma isn't serious."

"Her what?"

"But something *has* happened, Dr. Kerry," she blurted. "It's either the best thing that ever happened, in which case I'll be moving back to Cleveland or it's the worst thing that ever happened, in which case I'm going to be crazy again. I can't afford to be crazy now. Who would pay my bills? But I'm in love, so in love, and Daisy will adore the change of seasons, especially autumn. Crimson is only a color until you've seen maple trees here in October. On the other hand, there's my job and I love it, and I've learned so much from Dan. And Dan. I'd miss him like blazes, but, then, Dan has Nancy. Why shouldn't I have Neil? I do understand how traumatic a divorce can be, but why is Neil still running home to dinner? Is it me he loves, or is he just reaching out in a difficult time? I believe what he says, and even if I don't, I believe he believes it, which is almost the same thing. I know how good he was for me, and I know I could be good for him. God knows, no one will ever love him more . . . oh . . . oh . . . oh." She was crying again. "What do you think, Dr. Kerry? What should I do?"

There was a long silence, then "Have you been drinking?"

"No!"

"Then I think you should have a stiff belt."

"Mother has a bottle of cardiac-arrest brandy," Jill told him.

"I'm not going to ask what that means." He sighed. "Get the brandy and come back to the phone. Wait. Did you call collect?"

"No, I'm paying."

Still carrying her purse, she went to the kitchen, found the brandy, and made her way back to the phone, feeling better already. Her outpouring to Kerry and the accomplishment of a simple task had calmed her considerably. She fished her lighter and cigarettes out of her purse, sat down on the floor, and picked up the phone.

"Hello," she said in a much calmer voice. "I have the brandy."

"Pour a small amount and drink it all at once." Dr. Kerry sounded like an air-traffic controller trying to guide a crippled craft to a safe belly-landing.

Jill poured as instructed. "I feel better. Maybe I can work this out by myself."

"Like hell!" Kerry was indignant. "I want to know what's going on."

"Oh." Now that she had exploded and discharged her overloaded circuits, Jill didn't want to tell him. He'd be sure to have an opinion, perhaps one she'd rather not hear.

"It's really nothing," she said casually. "Is Henry Sitzbach still doing child molesters, or has he moved on to the psychological effects of plastic surgery? Should be interesting, don't you agree?"

"Jill!" Kerry shouted, then spaced out his words: "What . . . has . . . happened . . . in . . . Cleveland?"

Rats. Jill took a sip of the brandy and a very deep breath. She told him the story, omitting only the fact that as a lover Neil would make a great short-order cook.

"Holy shit!" he said when she'd finished. He whistled through his teeth, and Jill held the phone away from her ear, wincing.

"I don't know what to say," Kerry confessed.

"And I don't know what to do," Jill said desperately.

Dr. Kerry cleared his throat, "Uh . . . why don't you come home. Perhaps the perspective of distance—"

"But isn't this just what I've always wanted?" Jill interrupted. "I've told you about my fantasies—"

"Fantasies are fantasies"—he was on firmer ground now—"and not meant to be acted out."

"But Neil did," Jill protested. "Didn't he?"

"Well . . . uh . . . you might say that."

"If Neil did, it must be all right. I mean, he was always the very best shrink— Oh, I didn't mean to imply that you're a schlump." Discussing one shrink with another made her feel like a fink. "I'm sure what Neil did is all right. Isn't it?"

"Uhhh . . . I think the actual rule is something like . . . uh . . . Once a patient, always a patient."

"But, it isn't as though Neil ever told me he loved me while I was his patient. Or proposed marriage. Or proposed *anything.*" She paused, considering the past. "Come to think of it, he never even sent me a Christmas card."

"Hold that thought," Kerry advised, "and, as I said, distance might give you more perspective—"

"Haven't you always said life is a gamble?" Jill interrupted. "And shouldn't it be, Dr.Kerry? I have friends who would call this a miracle, and here I am, ready to call it impossible. Haven't you been trying to teach me to throw off the shackles of the past and dispense with the tyranny of the shoulds? Haven't you told me that a liberated woman needn't engage in a slavish following of outdated rules?"

"Uh . . . sometimes rules are useful, Jill."

"Did you or did you not," Jill demanded, "tell me to laugh at conventionality?"

"You've done more than your share of chuckling." Dr. Kerry's voice was sharp. "And I would say that right now you're edging your way to hysteria. Now, listen to me. *Fact:* You have not seen this shrin— man in years. *Fact:* You are seeing him at a time when his judgment may be impaired by a highly traumatic personal crisis. *Fact:* You are still heavily involved in a fantasy, which may not be reality-based. *Fact:* You are seriously considering a drastic change in life-style, not only for yourself but for your daughter, based on a wholly emotional reaction to an untoward physical event."

"What untoward physical event?" she asked, puzzled.

"Getting screwed."

"Oh, that." She hadn't thought of it as untoward, but, then, it hadn't been particularly physical, either.

"Which brings me to—*Fact:* You are in a highly emotional state which requires a period of evaluation and assessment—"

"You want to put me in the hospital!" Jill exclaimed.

"Of course not. We don't put people who can get up in the morning in the hospital. That's what Valium is for, so everyone can go to work." He took a moment to collect himself. "What I mean is that you should come home and think this over."

"But—"

"That's the beauty part of miracles, Jill." His voice was soft, seductive. "If it's real, it'll be there. If it's a miracle, it won't go away. *Che sarà, sarà,* Jill. Know what I mean?"

"Not really," she said, sipping her brandy and trying to keep an open mind.

"*If* you are the love of his life"—Kerry was adamant—"and *if* he is the love of yours, then you don't have to pack up the crockery and move tomorrow. Come home. We'll discuss."

"I'll think about it," Jill promised. "I still have the problem of my mother. I'm quite concerned about her, Dr. Kerry. It's not a—"

"Call me tomorrow," he interrupted. "My beeper just went off."

"Since when do shrinks carry beepers?"

"Dinner. My wife . . ."

"Oh." Jill was about to hang up when she was afflicted with an impulse to be honest with him. "I have to see Neil again, Dr. Kerry. I can't leave Cleveland without at least that."

He sighed resignedly. "If you must see him, be aware you have very mixed feelings."

"Aware?" Jill grimaced. "Dr. Kerry, ambivalence is my life!"

"So I've noticed. Good-bye."

Jill sat on the floor sipping brandy, worn out by the wonder of it all. That morning seemed an eon ago, an event floating in some distant limbo with Daisy's vision of death.

A shower, that's what I need.

In the bathroom Kate's robe hung on the peg where she'd left it after her shower with Peter. It was like having Kate there, saying, "All right, young lady, what have you to say for yourself?"

Honest to God, Ma, I didn't plan all this!

Jill stepped into the shower, wondering if there was a special dispensation for unplanned concupiscence. Perhaps an eon in Purgatory would do it. . . .

She soaped and scrubbed, allowing the hot water to soothe her. Fifteen minutes later she was dripping on the bathmat. She heard Kate's voice say, "Wipe up the puddles," so she wiped up the puddles.

In the bedroom she stretched out on the bed and reached for a script. Concentration on work was what she needed. Thinking about Neil would do nothing but send her swinging between *It's wonderful* and *It's Awful*.

For the next twenty minutes Jill read *Two Guys from Lapland*, the stirring saga of Kierke and Sven who arrive in America with not a kronfeld in their pockets but possessed of a burning desire to make good and a secret process for flash-freezing mackerel.

Finally Jill threw the script on the floor, abandoning the Nordic Butch and Sundance as they were about to rent a warehouse from blond socialite Tiffany Van Cleef, who was accompanied by Doffy Cash, young, street-smart former stickball champion about to turn pro boxer under the tutelage of Sparky Karks, once a contender, now a— *Yuck!*

It was a few minutes past ten, too late to go to a movie, too early to go to sleep, the witching hour in reverse. The only options were television or thinking.

Thinking about Neil would make her crazy. Thinking about Kate could— *Kate!*

Jill dialed quickly.

"Hello?" Candy answered on the first ring.

"It's Jill. Have you heard anything about Mother?"

"No." Candy was munching on something. "What's she done now?"

"That's what I'm calling to ask. I was out for a while. Has the hospital called you?"

"Nope. Not a jingle."

"Well, I just thought . . ." Jill's voice trailed off.

"Don't worry," Candy said sternly. "Keriakan says she has a heart like a herd of buffalo."

"Arabian horses."

"Buffalo, horses—what's the difference? She's healthy as a cow."

"Is John there?" Candy's refusal to act as a worrying partner made John the logical alternative.

"No. The Knights of Columbus is having its annual banquet. John went in full regalia. You should see his headgear, Jill. Fourteen cockatoos died for that hat."

"Wonderful. He should wear it when he visits Ma. She'll think he's Saint Francis of Assisi and come right out of her coma."

"Poor John's been so busy." Candy sighed. "He's going straight from the Knights Hall to his office. I don't know how long he can keep up this pace. He never sleeps. . . ." She drifted away. "May I call you back? I'm watching *Man from Quasar* and he's trapped in the underground headquarters of Crench."

"With half-men–half-beasts?"

"You're watching it, too!"

"Not the longest day I live." Jill wondered if Candy would be so nonchalant if the woman in a coma was *her* mother.

"Come to dinner tomorrow," Candy said cheerful. "I'm making duck-and-prune chowder. With my recipe I get two whole quarts from one wing and a thigh."

"Sounds delicious. Good-bye, Candy."

Jill sat on the edge of the bed, rubbing her neck and worrying about Kate, hooked up to a monitor that recorded vital signs envied by those in the know.

She wanted to call Neil, but of course couldn't, even if she had his home number, which she didn't. Part of her suspected that her hour with Neil had been a hallucination brought on by stress, strain, jet lag, Twinkies, worry, fretting, a falling barometer, and a moon on the cusp. More than anyone could handle, God knows.

Jill reached for the phone.

"Hello." It was Fred.

"This is Jill."

"Your mother is better." His voice went up.

"No."

"Your mother is worse." His voice went down.

"No."

"There's much to be said for stability," Fred said evenly.

"Please, Fred. Is Julie there?"

"Julie's asleep. I sent her to bed."

"Is she ill?" *Please, God. Not another complication.*

"Just fatigued. Julie went to Father Norton's youth group after a highly exhausting day and came home done in. She had papers to grade, but I decided she was far too weary to do it tonight, so she's set the alarm clock for an hour earlier in the morning. I can't disturb her."

"Of course not," Jill agreed. "I'm just so worried about Mother."

"You have a tendency to be subjective, Jill, to forget that the prime essential in any situation is the taking of a backward step. You need to disassociate yourself emotionally in order to effect an objective solution."

"Do tell," Jill said, thinking that if Fred could be bottled and sold over the counter, America would sleep tonight.

"I suggest you get a good night's sleep and contact an attorney in the morning."

"I doubt an attorney will be necessary, Fred."

"An attorney is *imperative*," Fred asserted. "Of the *utmost* importance. I must insist you do it. If Mother Dunn should, God forbid, pass—"

"Good-bye, Fred." Jill hung up, quickly.

Jill stretched out on the bed, trying to relax. She searched for a soothing mental image, but the only pictures that floated by were Kate's face, eyes ominously shut, and Neil's eyes, alight with pride at having cured her.

She swung her legs off the bed.

In the living room, she turned on every light, then the television set.

No shadows here. Only in my head.

The Channel Four news anchorman was one of those TV clones manufactured in numbered lots by Famous Announcers School. "The Cleveland Chamber of Commerce met today to discuss the city's new image," he was saying, "its evolution from mistake on the lake to powerful industrial force."

Jill watched the accompanying film, documentary footage depicting the heart of the newly hustling city, with barges crisscrossing the Cuyahoga River, smokestacks blowing like overwrought teakettles, and an endless stream of apparently hyperthyroid Clevelanders scurrying across busy streets. The film looked vaguely familiar. Jill concentrated, searched her memory, and finally found it. The same Cleveland television station had used the same film some eight years before to support its campaign against Cleveland's industrial pollution.

Jill blinked with admiration.

It isn't often you can use the same film to prove pro and con.

The announcer droned on. Despite her anxiety, Jill was beginning to drowse when the final news item caught her attention.

"The fires that have plagued Los Angeles are finally out."

Something's going right!

He continued. "The last smoldering embers were extinguished by a deluge that has turned the City of the Angels into a virtual swamp. Numerous accidents are reported, and the threat of mudslides. . . ."

No news is good news.

The news ended and the *Tonight* show arrived. Jill nodded, finally falling asleep somewhere between a lady with a myna bird who had to be bleeped and the author of a book on peace of mind through high colonics.

Her dreams were cloudy, murky, and opaque, visions of escalating entropy in uninhabitable lands devoid of color, dimension, or hope. Then suddenly she was in a large room, not unlike the intensive care unit at Pres Gen, surrounded by surgeons whose masks muffled their voices.

"Hit and run," one surgeon said, *"of a particularly vicious kind. Luckily the authorities know the make of the car."*

"Hit and run?" Dream Jill asked weakly. "How could this happen? I was at home, at my mother's."

One of the surgeons leaned over her, "We know," he said. "It came in the house after you, broke the lock with its bumper, and roared through the door."

Dream Jill gazed at the surgeon, dumbfounded.

"It wasn't an accident," the masked figure said. "It was attempted murder. What else can you expect from a '41 Kaiser?"

"What?" Dream Jill tried to get up.

"Those Kaisers will kill you," Masked Doctor intoned. *"Lousy mileage, too."*

The ringing phone woke her. She fumbled for it, drenched with sweat.

"Hello," Jill said groggily.

"Hello," a man whispered. "Jill?"

"Who is this?" She propped herself on one elbow, still dazed by her dream.

"It's Neil."

"Neil Kaiser?" Jill was startled into sitting up straight.

"I had to talk to you, Jill, to prove that this evening wasn't a dream."

"Dreams are funny things, Neil," Jill said, wishing with all her heart that Neil hadn't chosen this moment to call. "Sometimes they tell us things—"

"I love you," he whispered, "and I've been thinking about you for hours."

"Where are you?"

"In my den at home. I know I shouldn't be calling from here, but I just had to hear your voice. I know when I fell in love with you."

"You do?" Jill asked, unable to recall a specific came-the-dawn moment. Her memory of being in love with Neil was similar to the Baltimore Catechism's definition of God—it had no beginning and, so far, was without end. "When did you fall in love with me?"

"Do you remember the night in the hospital when you were packing, determined to leave?"

"I remember," Jill said. "The nurse called you."

"I came right over," Neil said. "I got out of bed and came over."

"You were in bed at nine thirty?" She was surprised, then wished she hadn't asked. His marriage must have been more . . . robust . . . in those days.

"A psychiatrist's life is not easy, Jill." He sighed.

"I remember that night, Neil. You made me sit down and talk to you. 'One last chat for the road,' you said."

"You *do* remember." He was pleased. "What I remember is a very frightened girl telling me there was no point in getting well, no point to living, no point to life. Do you remember that girl, Jill?"

"Yes, I do," she said softly. "I haven't forgotten how it was with me then."

"And I knew if I allowed you to leave the hospital, you'd go off a bridge. Was I wrong, Jill?"

"No, you weren't, Neil. It was on my mind."

"There you sat, insisting that nothing good would ever happen for you again. You'd lost your faith, you said, your faith in yourself, your faith in the future, your faith in the power of faith. Do you remember what I said to you then?"

Jill nodded as though Neil was in the room with her. "You said, 'Borrow mine.' "

"You looked at me for the longest time, then asked me why I would lend you my faith."

"And you told me that, for the moment, you cared more about me than I did. You were right, Neil. I had no caring left."

"So we struck up a bargain," he continued. "In return for my faith you agreed to stay."

"That's when you fell in love?"

"No. It was when you went to the door and stood for a moment, your hand on the knob, then turned to me and said, 'Now that you've got me, don't you dare let me fall.' " He laughed softly. "You were so fierce about it. It was a promise to fight and a threat all at once. It stopped me cold. *You* stopped me cold. Did I ever let you fall, Jill?"

"Never," she whispered, "you never did."

"Sometimes these days I feel like I'm falling," Neil whispered. "Who heals the healer when the healer needs healing?"

Jill didn't answer. She knew it was true. Most of the truths she knew in her life she knew because Neil had taught her. He'd taught her and showed her and pulled her along when she had neither strength nor desire to go on.

"Now I need you, Jill," Neil whispered, and his need reached out to the memory of her own. "Do I have you?"

"Of course." It was the only possible answer.

"I'm happy. I'm so glad I called."

"So am I," Jill agreed, thinking about karma and miracles and things that are meant to be.

"Well, I've kept you awake long enough. May I call you tomorrow?"

"Of course."

"We'll decide when and where to meet." He hesitated. "My office is hardly . . . appropriate. Now be a good girl and tuck yourself in."

Jill tried to stifle her giggle. He heard it anyway.

"All right"—Neil chuckled tolerantly—"this isn't the first time you've laughed at me, and with any luck, it won't be the last."

"Sorry."

"Don't be. I like you the way you are. I should. I had a lot to do with it."

"True."

"And, Jill?" His voice was very low. "Have patience, please, if you can. This is a difficult time for me. Good night"

"Good night," she said, and hung up.

She lit a cigarette and leaned back, thinking about Neil and that night in the hospital. She was nine years older and perhaps a year and a half wiser, but if she was wiser at all, it was thanks to Neil.

Jill glanced at the television set, then got up and turned up the sound. It was an old movie, a very old movie. Sylvia Sidney was crying.

Jill watched, though she'd seen the movie before. During her divorce watching old movies had been the pattern of her sleepless nights. For months she'd seen more of Ruby Keeler, Joan Blondell, and Ginger Rogers than she had of her closest friends, and she'd identified and wept with them all as they sobbed their way through the Depression, lost love, and tight tap shoes.

And now she was crying, weeping with Sylvia over the loss of her lumberjack lover on the trail of the lonesome pine.

She put her hands to her face. Huge tears fell through her fingers and she wondered why some tears are hot and others tepid, why some splash while others just roll down your cheeks.

She knew it wasn't Sylvia's loss she was feeling, but her own, a sense of loss she'd felt for as long as she could remember, sometimes intensely, like a pain that took her breath away, sometimes barely noticeable, like background music, but always, like tinder with potential to ignite, ubiquitous, disturbing, and there. Like Satan, her loss had borne many names—divorce, death, moving away, a puppy that had drowned just after her eighth birthday, Daisy's first day at school, insanity, and oddly enough, sanity, too, for her sanity had left her bereft of the ignorance that passes for bliss. And the struggle for sanity, once over, had been sorely missed. It had been a battle cleanly joined with an unambiguous enemy, a fight to the death in definable terms.

The names had come and gone, but the sense of loss remained, an effect with many causes or perhaps, more fundamentally, with none.

Jill fell asleep, again as usual, before the happy ending. This time her dream took her down a river where she sat astride a log, searching the brush on the banks for signs of her lost lumberjack. Then suddenly, it was *Deliverance,* and she stood, feeling mortally threatened, surrounded by a crowd of people whose heads came to points, playing "Who's Sorry Now?" on their banjos.

The telephone woke her again. This time she reached for it, squinting in the early morning sunshine that was pouring through Kate's front window.

"Hello," she said, shaking her head. Her eyes were blurry and her mouth acid with the taste of tin.

"Hello." It was Neil. "I'm at the office."

"Already? What time is it?"

"Seven thirty."

"My, my." She smiled sleepily. "You are a wonder, charming ladies on the phone all night and still in the office early. I bet you also leap tall buildings at a single bound."

"I have to talk to you, Jill." His voice was flat and very far away.

"What is it, dear. Are you all right?"

"I'm fine." He sounded strained. "But after thinking it over, I've decided that we shouldn't see one another until after my . . . difficulties have been resolved."

"What?" Jill wasn't quite sure she was awake. "I don't understand."

"It's as I said." His voice was cold. "I don't want to give my wife any reason to nail me, so . . ."

"But I'll have to return to Los Angeles without seeing you again," Jill protested. "Last night you said—"

"That was last night. Discretion is the better part of everything, Jill. I think my wife is having me followed."

"Followed!"

"The deacon of her church is a born-again detective." Neil paused, as though expecting her to say something.

Jill would have said something if anything, even one word, had occurred to her, but her mind had gone blank as a newborn's, so she was silent.

"I knew you'd understand," Neil said quickly. "Good luck in Los Angeles. Good-bye."

For a full two minutes Jill sat with the phone in her hand and no one at the other end of the line. Finally she replaced the receiver and stood up.

Understand what? she thought, her head a throbbing switchboard of terminally tangled lines. *Am I supposed to understand the Neil Kaiser of "I want you. I love you. Stay and be mine," or his alter ego, the Neil Kaiser of "Go away. Get out of my life. I've got problems of my own. Good-bye"? Who am I supposed to choose in this multiple-choice relationship? Which is the lady and which the tiger, and which will take my own "It's wonderful"/"It's awful" by the hand and lead it out of the woods?*

The tangled lines of her thoughts converged on one synapse. Jill blinked at what felt like a pop in her head. She tried to recall the symptoms of a stroke. Other than falling down dead, she couldn't remember one.

She stared at her surroundings. The topography of Kate's living room was suddenly as unfamiliar as the dark side of the moon.

She remembered reading or hearing somewhere—or perhaps it was a thought of her own—that when cognition stalls in high gear, the mental machinery intent on self-preservation switches to instinct and habit.

It must be true. Either Neil has gone mad, or I'm on my way, but right now I need to do something positive.

Instinct moved her to the phone, guided her through dialing, and raised the receiver to her ear.

"Hello." The sleepy voice was Daisy's.

"Daisy?" Jill said, as though it was the only word she knew. "Daisy?"

"Mom? Mom, is that you?"

Something healthy in Jill's mind switched on, giving her a simple instruction—"Talk to Daisy."

"Hi, Daisy," Jill said, putting one mental foot before the other.

"Mom, it's four thirty in the morning here." Daisy was alarmed. "Is something wrong?"

"No, no, everything's coming up roses." Jill lied lightly and well. "I'm sorry to wake you, but . . . I have to go to the hospital to see Grandma in a minute, so . . ."

"How's Grandma?" Daisy asked, sounding as though she had a clothespin on her nose.

"She sends her love," Jill lied again. "You sound funny."

"I have a cold. It's in my head and chest, and my nose is all red. I look terrible."

163

"You never look terrible." Jill smiled, beginning to ease into herself, to connect with the self that was the mother of Daisy.

"I look like Miss Piggy. My eyes are all beady, my nose is all snouty, and I honk when I sneeze. And my throat is sore." Daisy sounded like a very little girl.

"I wish I was there," Jill said, and that wish was suddenly true and so overwhelming that Jill felt her arms physically ache with the need to have them around Daisy. "I'd tuck you in bed in flannel jammies and rub Vicks on your chest."

"I haven't got enough problems, you want to smear gunk on my chest," Daisy moaned.

"You always seemed to like it when you were little."

"*You* liked it," Daisy corrected. "You used to sit by the side of my bed and say 'Now, Daisy, this will make you feel better.' And then you'd rub that goo all over me. Ick! The things I do so you won't feel guilty."

"Thanks," Jill said, shaking her head, delighted to have found a Daisy who was Daisy as usual. "What else is going on?"

"Nothing," Daisy answered, in a tone that said otherwise.

"What is it, Daisy?"

"You're in Cleveland."

"I know where I am," Jill responded. "I asked you what's wrong."

"You can't do anything about it from there," Daisy said. Her resentment was clear, along with the woe.

"About what? Tell me, Daisy."

"It's too late anyway." There was the hint of tears trying to find their way through Daisy's stuffy nose.

"Tell me!" Jill demanded.

"Daddy ruined my life!" Daisy wailed. "I'm going to stay in the house and never go out, not till the day I die!"

"Uh . . . Daisy?" Jill stopped, unsure as to how one goes about calming a hysterical fifteen-year-old long distance. "Try to stop crying. It'll make your cold worse."

"Old wives' tale," Daisy snapped. "It figures."

"You can get mad at me if you think it'll help, but—"

"And don't give me permission to be mad at you. I *hate* it when you use psychology on me! You're not that good at it, you know."

"I thought I was."

"Just because you fell for that stuff, doesn't mean I will."

"I'm easily manipulated." Jill smiled at the phone. "So, what did Daddy do?"

"I've never been so embarrassed in my life. First I came down with this cold, and then my period came back. How come my period came back, Mom?"

"I don't know." Jill frowned, wondering the same thing. "And?"

"And I didn't have any of my stuff here at Dad's, so I told him I was going down to the drugstore to get what I needed. Well, Dad said he wasn't going to let me out of the house with a fever."

"Dad was right about that," Jill said firmly.

"Who cares?" Daisy was crying. "So then he said he'd go to the drugstore for me. I told him what I needed, and he hit the roof, just like that."

"I don't understand." Jill was puzzled. "Is there something you left out of the story?"

"No, that was it." Daisy insisted. "I told him to get Tampax, and he blew his cork. He said that unmarried girls don't use Tampax, they use Kotex!"

"Oh, I see," Jill said, torn between an urge to laugh at Steve and cry with Daisy. "Honey, your father is rather old-fashioned in some respects, and he doesn't know much about girls especially—" Jill's words were drowned in Daisy's weeping.

"I don't even know what he was talking about, Mom! Is it some sort of custom? On your wedding day you get a pop-up toaster and a box of Tampax?"

"Almost. At least it used to be. Well, honey, I can understand why you're upset."

"That's not all. Right in the middle of our fight the doorbell rang. It was Lenny. *And Dad asked him in!*"

"Oh, dear." Jill winced for her.

"And there I was, all crummy and yucky from crying and a cold. I didn't even have any blush on." Daisy sniffed. "How come guys feel free to drop in like that? I mean, are you supposed to spend every waking hour wearing mascara, just in case?"

"I'm sure he's seen you without."

"But not with a nose like a light bulb, in the middle of a fight with my father. And he's never even met Daddy before. There I was, introducing Lenny to a man whose Adam's apple was jumping up and down. You know how Dad looks when he's mad."

"I vaguely remember," Jill replied, trying to push the too vivid memory from her mind.

"And I could just hear Lenny thinking, 'Broken home, broken home.' I mean, I could see it on his face."

"I'll bet Dad was very nice to Lenny," Jill said, knowing Steve would be.

"Oh, *sure*," Daisy said. "He shook hands and everything. Then he stood there and glared at Lenny like Lenny was some sort of sex fiend."

"I can imagine." Jill could.

"Then, Lenny told Dad that he'd dropped by to tell me what time he'll pick me up for the Alice Cooper concert. Then Dad said I probably wouldn't be able to go, what with my cold, and I said I'd be much better by then, and Dad said a cold takes seven days if you treat it and seven days if you don't, and sitting in a crowd at the Fabulous Forum inhaling pot smoke would only make it worse!" With that, Daisy let out such a wail that the Hound of the Baskervilles would have slunk away, out-howled. "He treated me like a *baby*!"

"Oh, Daisy!" Jill didn't know what to say.

"I ran into my room, and when I came out, Lenny was gone. Daddy's ruined my life!"

"I'm so sorry. I'm sure your father didn't meant to. . . ."

"He apologized," Daisy said grimly, "but I haven't accepted."

"Dad just wasn't thinking."

"He's forty-two years old!" Daisy yelled. "He should know better!"

"We usually know better, Daisy." Jill sighed. "We don't always do better."

"I'll never be able to look Lenny in the eye again! And I was up all night coughing, and my period is back, and I've had cramps twice in two weeks, and I have to put up with this crappy Kotex. . . . None of this would have happened if you had been here." Daisy said angrily. "Why aren't you here?"

"I'm not there because . . ." Jill was stymied. She ran through the reasons in her mind. Mother, Neil, Fred's instructions to contact an attorney, Candy's plans for duck-and-prune chowder, Mother, Mother, Mother and her psychological she'll-come-out-of-it-when-she-wants-to decline. On the other side of the scale was one lone reason to go home. That reason being Daisy, it won hands down.

"I'm coming home," Jill told her. "If I have to bring Grandma attached to a monitor, I'll be there."

"You will?"

"Your cold will clear up, you'll get to see Alice Cooper, your cramps will go away, I swear."

"I can't ever see Lenny!" Daisy cried. "I'll die of embarrassment."

"You'll even see Lenny. A miracle will happen. It's karma."

"When are you coming?" Daisy asked, sounding brighter. Jill was both touched and thrilled that she could cheer Daisy by the simple act of coming home.

I make a difference to her!

"As soon as I see Grandma. I'm on my way now. I'm running. I miss you, Daisy."

"I miss you, too, Mom," Daisy said, and hung up.

Jill ran to get dressed, concentrating on Daisy, focusing on Daisy, centering on Daisy.

First she'd talk to Steve, explain to a forty-two-year-old man that modern, unmarried girls use Tampax. Then she'd stuff Daisy full of vitamin C before taking her to an internist just to make certain hers wasn't a more serious upper-respiratory infection. Then she'd make an appointment with her GYN to see why Daisy's time of the month had become twice a month. And Lenny . . . she'd have to think of something. Daisy could survive a cold and menstrual dysfunction, but embarrassment could be terminal for a fifteen-year-old.

Jill threw clothes on her body as carelessly as she'd heaped them into her suitcase. Her plan for Daisy would get better, tighter, and surer, with more angles than Pythagoras ever knew. She'd do what she'd promised Daisy. Be there.

CHAPTER 12

With her suitcases in the car and her flight confirmed Jill sped to the hospital. She was surprised to find Candy sitting on the floor outside Intensive Care, the large satchel beside her giving her the look of a bag lady waiting for a bus. Candy was so engrossed in her magazine, she failed to look up as Jill approached.

Jill stood over her, took a deep breath, and announced, "I'm going home now."

Candy stared up at her. "Want to hear your horoscope? There's a new man coming into your life."

"No thanks, Candy." Jill smiled. One more man in her life and she'd have her very own paragraph in Guinness. "Why are you sitting in the hall?"

"Keriakan asked me to wait here while he examines your mother. He'd better hurry. I'm taking a dressmaking class at the Y and I haven't finished cutting out my pattern."

The double doors opened. Jill expected to see Keriakan, but it was Jim who emerged, hair rumpled and eyes distraught. "Jill! Glad you're here. C'mon."

Jill glanced at Candy, who was oblivious to everything except her magazine, and followed Jim through the double doors.

"You've got to help me, Jill." He clutched at her arm. "I can't get through to the nurses."

"Have you tried anonymous threats?"

Jim, the literal-minded, stared at her. "I couldn't do that. Reason should prevail."

"When has it ever?" Jill took a deep breath and announced, "I'm going home now."

"They refuse to observe nature's rules," Jim complained. "It's not that they aren't *aware*. It's money, Jill. There's agribusiness, petrobusiness, and medibusiness. The medical profession is killing us."

"As we speak." Jill wondered if she'd suddenly taken to speaking Swedish; no one seemed to understand the words coming out of her mouth.

Jim tugged at her sleeve. "Kate needs minerals, B complex, certain salts," Jim explained earnestly. "I know she can't swallow pills in a coma, but everything in my valise is water-soluble."

"Wonderful." If Jim chucked the whole thing in Lake Erie, Cleveland sportsmen would be catching catfish the size of Jaws.

"I begged the head nurse to prepare an IV for Kate, natural nutrients dissolved in sterilized water. It makes so much sense, Jill. And do you know what she said?"

"Did it include the word *crazy*?"

"How did you know?" Jim was impressed. "You must talk to her, Jill."

"But if you've tried and haven't gotten anywhere . . ."

"Look, there she is." Jim pointed at the nurse known as Tootsie. "Go ahead."

"Jim, I . . ."

Jim glared at her. "You have a responsibility to your mother."

"Oh, God." Jill groaned, responding to a phrase that has compelled more reluctant people into more antipathetic action than any other in history, with the possible exception of "War Declared."

Jill shuffled towards Tootsie with all the élan of one about to make a fool of herself.

"Hello, Miss . . . uh . . ."

"Hoover." The nurse folded her arms.

Promising start. She's coiled like a rattlesnake.

"How's my mother this morning?"

"Stable."

"That's . . . uh . . . good. So, how are your monitors coming along?"

"Our monitors do not 'come along,' Miss Dunn. They are consistent in every respect," Hoover said sternly. "And I'm not about to prepare a kelp IV for your mother."

"But—"

"I get more aggravation from well-meaning family and friends than I do from the patients," she complained.

"The patients are mostly unconscious," Jill pointed out. "How aggravating can they be?"

"Hoover, Hoover." They were interrupted by the familiar pained voice of Keriakan, who was slowly making his way toward them, shambling between banks of monitors like Yogi Bear lost in a forest of blinking, beeping trees. "One more morning like this and I'm going into roofing. Good morning, Miss Dunn."

"Mrs. Kenyon," Jill corrected.

"My father was in roofing," Keriakan confided. "No patients, no paperwork, no migraines. Just blue sky overhead, fresh air, and the tools of his trade. So once in a while a bird shit on his head. Big deal. No one ever sued him for malpractice."

"Mother is suing?" Jill asked hopefully. A mother in litigation is a mother out of a coma.

"No, no one is suing." Keriakan's voice emerged as a nasal whine of chronic pain. "It's just one of those days. Everyone I admitted with one disease is coming down with another. My heart failure has come down with pneumonia. My collapsed lung doesn't think I have enough to do, he's impressing me with a stroke. Pah! Every time I shore them up here, they spring a leak there."

"You poor darling," Hoover clucked.

"How is my mother?" Jill wondered what additional symptoms Kate had developed just to aggravate Keriakan.

"That reminds me." Keriakan turned to Hoover. "Prepare the papers for Miss Dunn to sign."

"Certainly, Doctor." She smiled and departed.

"What papers?" Jill asked.

"We're transferring your mother," Keriakan explained. "She no longer meets the criteria for intensive care. Unfortunately she's been stable for more than twenty-four hours."

"Oh, dear." Jill was dismayed and beyond that frightened for Kate. "Where are you transferring her?"

"We don't have facilities for psychological problems." Keriakan shrugged. "For that you need funding, grants, psychiatrists who want to practice here. We'll find her a bed in maternity."

"Maternity! But—"

"It's the only ward outside ICU that's fully staffed. Granted, it's a little noisy sometimes, what with women in labor and babies crying, but, then, the racket might wake her up."

"If my mother comes out of her coma in the maternity ward, the shock will kill her!" Jill protested. "I can't let you do that."

"You have no choice." Keriakan was firm. "Here's Miss Hoover with the papers."

Miss Hoover handed Keriakan a form. "There's a man in the hall who says he wants to see you, Miss Dunn."

"Johnny? My brother?"

"He says he's a friend of your brother-in-law."

"Fred?" Jill was puzzled. Why would a friend of Fred's pay her a social call in the hospital?

"Sign here." Keriakan handed Jill a pen.

"I can't." Jill backed away. "I can't make a unilateral decision concerning my mother."

"You're the only family member here, Miss Dunn. You must take the responsibility."

Jill backed toward the double doors. "I have to call my brother and sister. I have to see the man in the hall. I have to go to Los Angeles."

She turned and fled through the doors, nearly tripping over Candy, who was sitting on the floor surrounded by pink gingham, thread, scissors, and pattern pieces.

Candy glanced up at Jill, her mouth full of pins. "Wha . . . Keriaka . . . Ma?"

"He wants to move Ma to maternity."

Candy's eyes grew wide and the pins fell from her mouth. "She *isn't* . . . she *can't* be . . . no wonder she went into a coma . . . Jim?"

"No, no, no. They have to move Ma out of Intensive Care, and that's where they have empty beds."

"Oh." Candy patted the floor. "You made me drop my pins."

"Look, Candy, I have to reach John. How can I—"

"Excuse me for interrupting." A tall, thin man with a complexion the color of the institutional green walls approached Jill with hand extended. "Miss Dunn. I'm Uriah Barton, of the legal clinics of Hookstratten and Barton, attorneys to the middle class."

"Hello." Jill shook the hand, thinking that if this was an ambulance chaser, he was certainly no sprinter. Kate had been in the hospital more than two days.

"You're probably wondering why I'm here," he said smoothly.

"No, I'm not. Don't take it personally." Jill leaned over Candy. "Please get John on the phone."

"I'm a friend of Fred Hildebrandt's," Barton continued. "We were roommates at Princeton."

"What a thrill, Mr. Barton. *Please*, Candy—"

"I can't reach John at the office." Candy sighed. "His secretary always says he'll call me back, but he never does. The only time he ever got on the line right away was the day I got crazy and threatened to put the cat in the microwave. Then he screamed at me. I don't understand John sometimes. He never even pets the cat."

"Just *try*," Jill begged. "It's important. It's about Ma."

"Your mother is the reason I'm here." Barton smiled. "I'm prepared to assist you."

"Terrific." Barton was beginning to sound like the Man from Glad. "You can begin by getting my brother on the phone."

"Has anyone seen my pinking shears?" Candy asked, lifting pieces of material and pattern. "My seams are unraveling."

"No faster than I am, Candy." Jill sighed.

"I have the solution." Barton produced a paper from his briefcase. "Chip . . . er, Mr. Hildebrandt suggested . . . er . . . sign here."

"What's that?" Jill eyed the legal-looking form suspiciously.

"Petition for a court order granting you power of attorney," he explained. "We must take steps to have your mother declared incompetent."

"I can't do that!" Jill backed away. "For one thing, it isn't right. For another, Ma would kill me."

"Nonsense. Your mother can't move." He radiated logic.

"Believe me, Mr. Barton, Ma would find a way."

"Miss Dunn, there you are." It was Keriakan, waving his transfer form.

"I haven't spoken to my brother and sister," Jill told him.

"No time. No time. We *must* move your mother." Keriakan pushed the paper under her nose.

"Don't sign anything without the advice of an attorney," Barton advised. "What is that document?"

"It's permission to transfer Mrs. Dunn from Intensive Care to a more appropriate floor," Keriakan explained.

"Since when is maternity appropriate for someone in a coma?" Jill asked.

"Maternity!" Barton exclaimed, then squinted at Keriakan. "This requires an explanation, doctor. We may have grounds for a suit."

"The hospital rules clearly state—" Keriakan stopped, glaring at Barton. "Who the hell are you?"

"Call John," Jill ordered Candy as Barton and Keriakan babbled at once, waving their papers beneath one another's noses.

"I paid forty dollars for this course," Candy said obstinately. "I have to be there in a hour with my pattern pinned. I'm not going to flunk cutting out."

"Good God, I'll call." Jill dug through her pockets for change. "Anybody got a dime?"

"Sure." Barton turned his back on the red-faced Keriakan and handed Jill a coin. "I'll bill you."

Jill walked toward the elevators and phone, leaving the two men arguing while Candy snipped and slashed, pinked and pinned.

After being put on hold by the operator, Jill finally talked to his secretary, who told her that John was in a meeting and could not be disturbed.

"Tell him it's an emergency."

"I will," she said sweetly.

"I mean tell him *now*."

"He can't be disturbed."

"Oh?" Jill ground her teeth. "Well, when he can be disturbed, tell him that his mother is in the maternity ward, his wife is making a dress in the hall, a strange lawyer is suing the family quack, his sister is on her way to Los Angeles, and papers are being signed declaring the whole family incompetent."

"Is there anything else?" the secretary asked cheerfully.

"Tell him I said good luck," Jill hissed. "Oh, and the next time there's a family emergency, he should call Ann Landers."

"Is that Ann with an *e*?" she inquired pleasantly.

Growling, Jill hung up, then turned to find Candy at her elbow. "What did John say?"

"He was in a meeting."

"Told you so." Candy smiled.

"Give me some change, Candy. I'm going to call Chicago and tell Machiavelli Hildebrandt what I think of his machinations. If he wants papers signed, he can damn well come to Cleveland and sign them himself."

"Just a minute." Candy searched her pockets, coming up with a handful of change. "You can't be mad at Fred. He just wants what's best for your mother."

"What's *best*?" Jill snorted. "Would being declared incompetent improve the quality of *your* life?"

"Well . . . uh . . . ." Candy held up her pattern envelope. "Do you think this pattern will make me look too bosomy?"

Jill glanced at the picture. "Dolly Parton won't lose any sleep."

173

"I'm heavy-bosomed," Candy fretted. "The sewing instructor told me."

"Hello," Jill said into the phone, then to Candy, "Oh shit, it's a machine."

"Maybe I ought to have my bosoms lifted," Candy speculated. "What do you think?"

"Why aren't they home?" Jill pounded the wall in frustration.

"If I had a job, I could save up and get them lifted," Candy said wistfully. "If it was my very own money, John couldn't complain."

"The trouble with me is that I say one thing and do another." Jill stared at her reflection in the phone. "I say I'm going home, then I stand here like my feet are glued to the floor. Why aren't I at home with Daisy, at work with Dan? Why haven't I killed that son of a bitch Neil Kaiser?" Jill yanked the receiver off the wall and began dialing. "The buck stops here. I'm going to tell Neil to take his Yo-Yo and shove it."

"Do you think it's very painful?" Candy asked.

"Is what painful?" Jill snapped. "What the hell are you talking about?"

"I'm talking about my bosom." Candy's chin quivered. "You don't have to yell."

"Dr. Kaiser's office." It was Mrs. Silverstone.

"Hold on." Jill covered the phone with her hand. "I'm sorry I yelled Candy, but if you don't know if your bosom is painful, how am I supposed to?"

"You weren't even *listening*! Nobody listens to me." Candy flounced off down the hall.

Jill shook her head and returned to the phone. "Mrs. Silverstone, this is Jill Kenyon."

"Oh, my dear, how are you?" Her silvery laughter fluttered the full range of the scale. "It seems like only yesterday we talked."

"It *was* yesterday, Mrs. Silverstone. Is Dr. Kaiser in?"

"Oh, gracious, no. You know how the dear man is. He's gone fishing."

"*Fishing?* He's gone fishing? Is that for real, Mrs. Silverstone, or is it an expression like 'cashed in his chips' or 'bought the farm'?"

She laughed. "Dr. Kaiser doesn't know anything about farming and he would never gamble. He's just off on one of his little excursions. Last time he brought me three wall-eyed pike. I breaded them with sourdough crumbs and a scant teaspoon of lemon peel. They were—"

"I'm certain they were delicious. Will you please tell Dr. Kaiser
. . . tell him . . ." Jill was stymied. She couldn't ask Mrs. Silverstone
to pass on "I love you, I hate you, let's get married, I'll kill you, you
saved me, you've done me in." "Tell him I called to say good-bye. I'm
going back to Los Angeles."

"I'll tell him, dear. Oh, by the way, he left a message for you. Now
where . . . here it is. He said he's turning your mother's case over to
Dr. Henrick Eckler—"

"Turning it over? He never took it!"

"And he wants you to think of yourself as a Significant Other in his
life."

"A who?"

"Shrink lingo. It means VIP. Isn't that sweet!" Mrs. Silverstone
waited for Jill's agreement, but Jill was silent. "If I were you, dear,
I'd deep-six Eckler. No sense of humor, and he reeks of garlic. What's
wrong with your momma?"

"She . . . uh . . . sleeps a lot. Depressed, I think."

"Happened to me once." Mrs. Silverstone sighed. "I didn't go out
of the house for six weeks. But I came out of it."

"How?" Jill asked quickly.

"I ran out of bread. I ran out of cereal. I ran out of dry milk and
Morning Thunder tea. I *had* to go out. I'm a child of the Depression,
you know. To me being hungry is the worst thing. Once I was out
of food . . . well, I had to choose between my depression and something that frightened me more." Mrs. Silverstone laughed. "Deary
me. Well, I do wish you luck with your momma. But don't call Eckler,
my dear. As Dr. Kaiser's hippies would say, 'Bummer, bummer, bad
vibes.' "

"Thanks for the advice." Jill smiled at the phone. "All of it. Good-
bye."

The worst thing. The worst thing.

For Mrs. Silverstone it had been hunger. For Jill it had been . . .
what? After all this time she still wasn't sure. She did know that at
some point her illness had become a 51 percent proposition, with the
51 percent in the deficit column. That shift in balance had surely
involved a "worst thing," even if its nature was fuzzy and its specifics
forgotten.

Jill walked down the hall to where Jim had joined the dynamic duo
of Keriakan and Barton.

"How can you stand there arguing with Kate's health ebbing
away?" Jim was saying.

175

"Ebbing?" Keriakan snapped. "Nothing is ebbing except my patience. I will not stand here and be treated like Dr. Frankenstein by some shyster—"

"Shyster! That cuts it!" Barton declared. "I'm applying for a court order restraining you from removing Mrs. Dunn from Intensive Care, and you, Keriakan, will hear from *my* attorney. I do not take kindly to slander."

"I have to go now." Candy scooped her pattern and material into her bag. "My class starts in fifteen minutes." She smiled at Jill. "Don't forget dinner. If John gets stuck at the office, you and I can eat and watch television." She waved and departed, her errand of mercy thankfully completed.

Keriakan waved his paper in Jill's face. "Your mother must be moved immediately. Sign here."

Barton elbowed him out of the way. "You see how imperative it is that you sign this petition. Your mother must be protected from this . . . person." He thrust his paper at Jill. "Sign here."

Jill looked from the scarlet-faced Keriakan to the pale, pinched Barton.

"Stuff 'em," she said, and walked through the double doors.

Jim followed her, running to catch up as Jill hurried toward Kate's section of Intensive Care.

"What will they do with your mother?"

"Nothing," Jill replied grimly. "Don't worry, Jim. I'll take care of it."

"Thatta girl." Jim patted her back. "I should have known. Your mother's always said she likes you best."

Jill skidded in midstride. "She *has*?"

Jim nodded. "She told me that in times of crisis you come through."

"She told you that?" Jill grinned.

"She said you're Johnny on the spot if you aren't in the loony bin or off with some man."

"Oh." Jill's grin faded.

"She said that some of your solutions are worse than the problems, but at least you try."

"Oh."

"She said she's seen you take an ordinary crisis and run it right into catastrophe, but you do call every week."

"Stop," Jill begged. "I can't take any more compliments."

Jill rounded the screen, nearly running into Miss Hoover, who was carrying a large plastic bag. "You're mother's personal effects," she said. "Ready for transfer to maternity."

"Wait," Jim called after her as she scooted away.

"Let her go, Jim. Mother's clothes are the least of her problems."

Jill approached the bed and looked down at Kate, who appeared to be sleeping peacefully. "Ma's lost weight."

"Her illness is caused by multiple deficiencies," Jim declared.

Whose? Jill wondered.

"Ma," she called softly, "I want you to listen to me."

She waited for some flicker of comprehension from Kate. There was none.

"I have to go home now, Ma. I've made a reservation on a flight to Los Angeles."

There was no response.

"Dr. Keriakan insists you be transferred to another section of the hospital. Your vital signs are excellent, and your tests are all negative, so he can't keep you in Intensive Care. The only space available is maternity. You know, Ma, women screaming, babies crying."

She waited. There was no movement. She took Kate's hand in hers.

"I can't allow that, Ma. If there's no reason for you to be in Intensive Care, there's less reason for you to be in maternity. I won't embarrass you by putting you in a place you don't belong."

Jill paused. The small hand in hers was utterly still.

"Daisy isn't feeling well, Ma. Besides that, she's going through one of those rare times when she needs me, if only to fight with and nag at. Remember, Ma? Remember how I argued with you when I was fifteen and you said, 'Just wait till you have children and see how crazy they make you.'"

Jill laughed, a soft, rueful sound. "You were right, Ma. Only your children can kill you. Jobs come and go. Even husbands—God knows mine went. But a child! Why is it that when Daisy is upset and I most want to help her, everything I say comes out wrong? And she ignores me a lot, as though she's afraid that by giving me an inch of her life I'll immediately demand a mile. I know adolescence is hard and she's going through what she has to go through to grow up, but sometimes it hurts, Ma. When I reach for her and she pulls away, it's a feeling like grief. Have you ever felt like a terrible mother?"

There seemed to be a flicker, the shadow of a twitch from Kate. Jill held her breath, but there was nothing more.

"Other people are doing my job at work, Ma. That isn't right. Work is important. You and Pa taught us that. I've never known anyone who worked harder than you and Pa. Please talk to me, Ma."

There was no sign that Kate had heard.

"Julie's gone back to Chicago. She couldn't miss any more classes, and of course Morgan and Kendrick needed her, too. She's worried about you, Ma. She calls night and day. And Candy was here to see you, but Dr. Keriakan wouldn't allow her in. She waited in the hall for a very long time, then left disappointed. And John's working so hard, he's been sleeping in the office. Wouldn't Pa be surprised that he's so good at his job? Wouldn't Pa be proud of John? Ma?"

Jill sighed, released Kate's hand, and sat back in the chair. Her neck was beginning to ache, and the light from the window had the blinding quality of an unshielded light bulb. Jill tried to move her chair away from the light, but it poured in, leaving Jim in the shadows. Jill peered into the corner but could see only Jim's outline. Then she heard even breathing that wasn't coming from Kate. *Wonderful. Here I'm trying to wake Ma up, and I've put Jim to sleep.*

Jill reached for her purse and a cigarette. There was no smoking allowed, but she needed a cigarette, if only to hold in her hand. She tapped it against her knee, unable to think of anything else to say. If Kate had pushable buttons, she'd have pushed them. All there was left was Kate's "worst thing."

Her voice, when it came, was strangled. "I love you, Ma, but I didn't make you sick, and I can't make you well. If I sat in this room for twelve years, I couldn't make you better. Since staying here won't make you better, leaving won't make you worse. You don't seem to be in a mood to take care of yourself, so I have only one alternative." Jill paused, hands shaking. "I'm going to put you in a home."

"Home!" Kate bellowed, and sat straight up. "Like hell you will!"

"Kate, you're awake!" Jim awoke, overjoyed.

"Did you hear what Jill said?" Kate shouted at Jim. "She said *home* to her mother!"

"Feeling better, Ma?" Jill smiled.

"If being so upset a stroke would be an improvement, then I feel wonderful. Where are your brother and sister?"

"You know where they are, Ma." Jill said. "I just told you."

Kate glared. "I was unconscious. What could I hear?"

Jill smiled and said nothing.

"Two of my children have abandoned me, and the third wants to put me in a home." Kate shouted at Jim. "I go to Mass every day, why am I cursed?"

"Oh Kate," Jim enthused. "You're just like your old self." He set the valise on the bed. "I brought vitamins, minerals, kelp—"

"Give me that." Kate snatched the valise from Jim and pulled out the bottle of brandy. "Now, where the hell is a glass?"

Jill offered the toothbrush holder. "Use this, Ma."

Kate took the blue plastic cup. "I'm not speaking to you, Jill."

"Now, Kate." Jim's tone was fond and just a bit condescending. "You don't mean that."

"Don't tell me what I mean!" Kate pushed at the sheets and swung her legs over the bed. "If you think for one minute you can tell me what to think, or feel, or do—"

"What's going on here?" It was Miss Hoover, followed by Dr. Keriakan. "Why, Mrs. Dunn! You're conscious! That's wonderful!"

"I'll never speak to my daughter again!" Kate shouted. "If she was in the street about to be hit by a car, I wouldn't yell 'Look out.'"

"Shhh, please, Mrs. Dunn," Miss Hoover begged Kate while staring at Jill as though expecting to see Lizzie Borden's ax in her hands.

"It's just as I told you," Keriakan said in a low voice to Jill. "Acknowledge the symptoms, prescribe a regime. Works every time. With some patients it just takes longer."

Jill stared at Keriakan. She might have known he would take credit for Kate's "cure."

"You are one of the great healers of our time," she told him, thereby assuring Kate a direct and perpetual hotline to Keriakan.

"Why, thank you. *Great* may be a somewhat extravagant word." He thought it over. "But, then, what other word is there?"

Miss Hoover approached Kate, leaning over the better to smile warmly into her eyes. "I'm so glad we're well enough to go home, Mrs. Dunn. I hope we won't forget our little promise to the hospital."

Kate looked confused. "I was making promises while I was unconscious?"

"The bequest, Ma." Jill said quickly.

"Oh, that." Kate waved Miss Hoover away. "I've changed my mind. I'm leaving my vast wealth to old people so they won't have to depend on their rotten children."

"But, Mrs. Dunn," Miss Hoover protested, "you've had the very best care—

179

"It was free?"

"Well, of course not, but—"

"It's *my* vast wealth." Kate glared. "You can go whistle."

Miss Hoover straightened, her face set and her lips pursed. "We need this bed," she snarled at Jill. "Please see to it that your mother is ready to leave as soon as possible." She brushed past Jill and was gone.

Keriakan looked at his watch. "I have to be getting along. I have patients who are in greater need than you, Mrs. Dunn. I see no reason to examine you now."

"Who said I'd let you?" Kate snapped. "Where the hell are my slippers. This floor is like ice."

"You don't have slippers, Ma," Jill said. "You came in as an emergency."

"Tell that person," Kate ordered Keriakan, "that I'm not surprised that a daughter who would put her mother in a home would also neglect to bring her slippers. Tell her my feet are freezing and my heart is breaking, but I'm not surprised."

"Your mother said—" Keriakan began.

"I heard, I heard." Jill sighed. She approached the bed and tried to slip her arm around Kate. Kate shrugged her off.

Daisy. Ma. Why won't anyone hug me?

"I have to go home now, Ma," Jill said.

"Ask me if I care," Kate responded, then, realizing she'd spoken to Jill, shouted at Keriakan. "Tell this stranger—"

"Family disputes!" Keriakan scowled his exasperation. "If I wanted to handle family disputes, I would have become a psychiatrist. Talk about migraines! No wonder they"—he curled his hand into the shape of a gun and stuck it in his mouth—*"bam . . . bam . . . bam."* He shook his head. "Well, Mrs. Dunn, all's well that ends well. If you have any further problems, call me."

"Good-bye, Ma," Jill said quickly, and walked around the screen, leaving Kate with Keriakan. She smiled to herself. Obviously Keriakan had meant to leave her with Kate, and she'd beaten him to the exit line.

As she walked through the double doors she saw Barton mumbling to himself and pacing in tight little circles, his face creased with frowns.

"Ah, Miss Dunn." He fell into step beside her. "I've already missed two appointments. If Fred had told me this was going to take all morning . . . Where are we going?"

"I don't know about you"—Jill saw the elevator doors opening and walked faster—"but I'm on my way to Los Angeles."

He tried to block her path. "But you haven't signed this petition."

"I've no plans to do that, Mr. Barton." Jill stepped into the elevator.

"But I promised Fred!" He shouted as the doors began to close. "Now my daughter will never be asked to make her debut at the Assembly Ball!"

The doors shut, and Jill punched the lobby button. As the elevator descended she put her cigarette in her mouth and lit it.

So, her journey to Los Angeles began, as had most of her journeys, with an impulsive decision and a broken rule.

CHAPTER 13

"Jill Kenyon's office." Polly answered the phone on the first ring.

"Polly! Thank God you're there!" Jill paced Steve's living room, dragging the phone cord behind her. "I came straight from the airport to Steve's, and Daisy isn't here! I called Steve's office, and he's out. Daisy's been sick, Polly. Where can she be? What's happened to her?"

"Calm yourself. I'll close my eyes and concentrate. You sit down and breathe."

Jill sat, thinking that you really know your life is under control when you have to be told to breathe. She was cold from the rain, tired from the trip, cramped from the plane, and claustrophobic from ten minutes spent in a house where there was a place for everything, everything in its place, and she felt like discarded furniture awaiting pickup by the Goodwill.

"You say she isn't feeling well?" Polly sounded thoughtful.

"Cold. Menstrual dysfunction. Why?" Panic pelted her like an ice shower.

"Daisy's surrounded by people," Polly said in a dreamy voice.

"Oh, God, she's in the hospital! Are the walls white?"

"The walls are white. The room has many windows—"

"I will *never* leave Daisy again," Jill vowed. "*Never*, so long as I live!"

"There are maps on the walls—"

"Maps?"

"—and a flag," Polly continued, "and three guinea pigs and a dark-haired boy. Does Daisy have auburn hair and green eyes?"

"Guinea pigs? What kind of hospital is that?"

"She's blowing her nose, smiling at the boy, and tugging at the collar of a blue cashmere sweater."

"She's in school!" Jill realized. "I'll kill her!"

"Her eyes are very bright," Polly went on. "It may be a low-grade fever, or it may be the boy. He's awfully cute."

"I don't care if he's John Travolta!" Jill was indignant. "She's not supposed to be in school when she's sick. And what's wrong with Steve, allowing her to go! Wait until the next time he tells me *I'm* irresponsible. . . . Did you say a blue cashmere sweater?"

"That's what I saw."

"Terrific. A fifteen-year-old girl who should be home in bed is in school wearing my sweater. Wait till I get my hands on her!"

"There's another problem, Jill." Polly's voice was low, intense. "While I was trying to find Daisy another image intruded. It was Dan, standing in a bright, white light. The light was suddenly extinguished. I don't like it, Jill. He hasn't been into the office today."

"Perhaps he's still in Encino with the rock-and-roll movie."

"The rock-and-roll movie is over."

"It wrapped? Already?" Jill was confused. "It couldn't have—"

"Dan shut it down at two o'clock this morning," Polly interrupted. "I don't know the details. When I got to work this morning, Alex told me about it, then went straight into Zippy de Franco's office."

"Did you ask him what happened?"

"Alex was not in an information-imparting mood," Polly said tartly.

"I'm on my way. Please stay in my office, Polly. Perhaps Dan will call in."

"I'll be here," Polly replied. "I can call McCaffery, report on her scripts by phone. She's got two turkeys, one marginal, and one about organized crime with the criminals as the heroes."

"The audience is supposed to root for people who machine-gun other people?" Jill scoffed.

"Its aura is the color of Paul Newman's eyes," Polly informed her. "A guaranteed hit!"

"Show biz!" Jill reached for her purse. "I'll be there, Polly. Keep a light in the window."

Jill ran for her car, dodging raindrops the size of marshmallows. Her drive to the office was made more exciting by a freeway jammed with skittish L.A. drivers who, unaccustomed to driving in the rain, compensated for their lack of expertise by driving faster, often sideways.

Running across the parking lot to the building, she glanced up at the conference-room windows. Heretofore open to smog, rain, and

183

the smoke from biannual fires, they were now covered with dark, heavy draperies. Jill wondered why, then remembered the new computer system. Perhaps computers, like vampires, required darkness to function.

Jill was eager to see the new computer, eager to see Polly, eager to see Electric Alex and his Energy Field, but most of all, eager to see Dan. Polly would be a comfort and Alex a battery charge, but seeing Dan was a need.

Why am I so comfortable with Dan? I'm never comfortable with men who aren't lovers.

She thought of Julie, whose luck had run to meeting a rod and staff free to marry.

Perhaps if I'd said more rosaries, perhaps if I didn't swear . . .

She ran into her office, calling, "Polly, Polly." But Polly was not at her desk, and the inner office was deserted. Both lights on her phone were lit, and her buzzer was ringing like the last call for doomsday.

Dan? Daisy? She reached for the phone just as both lights went off and the buzzing stopped.

Rats.

Polly had neatly arranged a stack of memos accumulated while she was gone. They were standard stuff, network folk keeping their names alive through interoffice communications; memos from Business Affairs announcing that, yea, verily, the deal had finally gone through on some forgotten project, research memos specifying which shows might best sell Chocks, Crest and Cold Water All to women 18–39, memos from Broadcast Standards objecting to almost everything having to do with real life, but in the spirit of détente and "don't call us the censors" offering to trade two *hells* for a *bastard,* but only in drama and only after nine P.M. when the children of America are either safely tucked in bed or hanging out in someone's basement drinking Boone's Farm Apple Wine, memos signed "Alexander T. Friedman."

As if by reading his name she'd conjured up the person, Alex appeared in the doorway.

"Hey, man, am I glad you're back," Alex leaped into the room and jiggled to her side. "Welcome! Welcome! Welcome!" He aimed a kiss at her cheek, missed by several inches, and landed on her neck where he remained. "Yummy," Alex mumbled. "Charlie or Chanel?"

"Talcum powder left over from a shower in another life." Jill pulled away from him, laughing. "What's going on?"

"Lawrence's called a meeting. Ten minutes."

"Dan's here?" Jill started for the door.

"Wait, Jill. Dan still hasn't showed."

"What happened last night? The rock-and-roll movie?"

"Heavy stuff. I know you like Carmichael, but I think maybe that dude's gone a little . . ." Alex's finger whirled a circle next to his ear. "Know what I mean?"

"No, I don't." Jill frowned. "*Tell* me."

"Yeah, well, it was like this." Alex assumed his fighter's stance, prepared to act it out. "They were shooting the fucker—"

"The movie?"

"Yeah, and Carmichael was there. So was I. It was after midnight, and they were doing the scene where the guys in the band stop their van in the street, jump out, and begin to play. See, in the story they've blown their gig. The guy who owns the club tells them their act is shit, they should get out of rock and roll, so they're trying to prove—"

"I read the script," Jill interrupted. "What *happened*?"

"Oh, yeah. Well, the director called a take five, so most of the actors went off and got stoned, and when they started the scene again"—Alex began to laugh—"these guys jump out of this van, and, man, I've never seen anything so fucking funny in my life . . . all this wild shit, mostly obscene and—"

"What about *Dan*?" Six minutes to meeting time, and she still didn't know.

"Oh, him." Alex shrugged, evidently less interested in Dan than in "wild shit." "Dan got pissed off and told the director to stop shooting. The director got pissed off and told Dan to go fuck himself, he was getting some really great footage. Then Dan said UBC wasn't about to pay for film it can't air. Then the director asked Dan who made him the guardian of American morals, and Dan said no one would have to look for this movie, they'd be able to smell it coming, and the director said he wouldn't stop shooting, and Dan said if they continued to shoot, it was their money, not UBC's. Then Dan walked off, and the film shut down. That's it."

"Poor Dan. I should have been there," Jill lamented. "What did Dan say? What's the next step? Is the movie down for good? What's Dan's plan?"

"How do I know. I don't read fucking minds."

"You didn't ask him?" Jill was astonished. She stared at Alex, who

185

was examining his fingernails. "You didn't leave with him, did you, Alex?"

Alex shook his head. "Nah. I figured Carmichael needed time to cool down, and, besides, somebody had to stay behind and schmooze these guys. They're too important in the business to let them think all UBC guys are . . . whacked out."

"What's whacked out about not paying for something you can't use, Alex?"

"Hey, what's a few feet of film you can't use? Big fucking deal. They could have reshot the scene. This isn't the fifties, Jill. Everyone uses a little. Carmichael pulled the plug because fun makes him nervous, and, babe, that ain't smart. You gotta go with the flow."

"Spare me, Alex. I'm too exhausted to flow." Jill sighed, wishing she could hear Dan's side of the story, likely a more substantive account than Alex's description of a middle-aged fogey overreacting to harmless hijinks. She reached for the phone. "Dan never overreacts. I'm calling his house."

Alex placed his hand over hers. "People have been calling his house every ten minutes all day. Face it, the man is incognito. Let sleeping dogs . . . I'll fill you in before the meeting."

"Fill me in on what?" Jill glanced at the clock. One minute and counting. *Dan.*

"I did a report, a few memos, made a few recommendations . . . like that. Time to go." Alex bounced toward the door.

"What memos? What report? About *what?*" Thirty seconds and counting. *Dan.*

"Take them with you." Alex thrust the papers into her hands. "Read them in the meeting. You'll love them. Zippy did."

"Zippy!"

"Been a big help to me Jill. Shit, you were off in Cleveland, and Dan's been whack—busy. Zippy's a dynamite guy, really plugged in."

"Plugged in, burnt out . . ."

"And that Mad Bomber guy, Smythe Jones, he's really buttoned down. A regular straight arrow, doesn't drink or smoke." Alex shook his head at that. "So maybe he got a little excited about *Freak People,* so what? He's a hell of a guy. Shit! We're late!" Alex grabbed Jill's arm and propelled her into the hall.

"Alex!" Jill panted. On the backs of her knees heat announced hives. *Dan.*

"Straighten up, Jill." Alex opened the double doors. "You're walking like Quasimodo."

"Wait!" Jill tried to scratch and run simultaneously.

"And do something about Polly," he ordered. "While you were gone I asked her to type my memos. She said she was busy. What she is, is lazy and snippy."

"What happened to your secretary?" Jill wondered if she'd have time to get ice from the kitchenette.

"He didn't work out. If I want someone who looks down his nose and corrects my grammar, I'll go back to P.S. 92. I'm interviewing." He brightened. "The chick with the biggest tits and tightest jeans gets the job."

"Jill, Jill." Polly's voice stopped them at the conference-room door.

"Oh, fuck." Alex grimaced. "Here come that uppity broad. I'll see you inside."

Alex rushed into the conference room as Polly, breathing hard, approached Jill. "I'm sorry I wasn't in your office, but Angela Kent had one of her spells. She sent her secretary to fetch me before the paramedics arrived. *How* do people find out I'm psychic?"

"It's your vibration." Jill couldn't resist. "Have you heard from Dan?"

"Nothing. He hasn't called, and I can't pick up a clue. It's a blank wall. I'll keep trying." She peered closely at Jill. "You have hives."

"This is my first meeting without Dan."

"Don't forget to breathe."

"Words to live by." Jill grinned. "Do I have any messages?"

"Dr. Kerry called. Wants you to make an appointment."

"Lunchtime tomorrow."

"Got it. Patti Gerard called."

"I'll call Patti later."

"I'll remind you. A Dr. Kaiser called."

"Neil?" Hives prickled like burrs under her skin.

"He said that the wall-eyed pike weren't biting and he wants to talk to you." Polly frowned. "If I were you, I wouldn't bite either, Jill. I don't like what I heard on the phone."

"You should have an affair with him, Polly. It's like that song, 'Torn Between Two Lovers,' only both of the lovers are him." Jill shrugged at Polly's you-should-know-better look and walked into the conference room, intent on Neil.

I love him. I hate him. I'll kill him. Marry me.

She looked up.

Oh, my God!

The newly installed computer system made Mission Control of Pres Gen look like a Tinkertoy factory. On three sides of the room, data banks the size of steel gym-lockers rose solid against the walls. Each seven-foot rectangle contained, at eye level, an inset metal wheel that whirled first clockwise, then counterclockwise. Above each wheel a shatterproof glass panel studded with rows of gauges glowed and flickered in the darkened room.

The conference room walls had been stripped of pictures and painted a flat steel-gray. The orange shag carpet had been similarly replaced by a thick wall-to-wall matting of some metallic fiber, also gray.

In the center of the room stood a horseshoe-shaped enclosure half the size of an orchestra pit. The horseshoe was freestanding, set on a base, and approximately five feet in height. The outside was black and padded with a material at once shiny and dull, like rock flecked with ore. On the inside there were three tiers of knobs, buttons, dials, and toggle switches set above a shimmering black counter which appeared to be lit from within, though the actual source of light was a row of purple globes, not unlike strobe lights, recessed into the ceiling above.

In the center of the horseshoe and attached to its base was a massive black chair, contoured to fit the human body but not just any human body. *One* human body. And he was sitting in it.

Teddy Lawrence, late of the USAF and NASA, sat facing the computer, with a microphone in his hand and a baby in his lap.

"I don't believe it," Jill breathed.

"You ain't seen nothing yet." Alex was at her elbow, whispering. "Wait'll you see him play a tune on that sucker. Lawrence claims the data banks contain everything ever known about television, including the license number of the RCA dog."

"What's the microphone for?" Jill whispered.

"Lawrence talks to it." Alex grimaced.

"Does it talk back?" Jill was awed.

"Not yet. But there's an office pool going and the bet isn't *if,* it's *when.* So far the sucker talks in symbols no one understands. Except *him.*" He pointed at Lawrence who was bent over the baby, cooing and clucking. "*He* says it speaks the language of pure mathematics. Pure bullshit, if you ask me."

"If my brother could only see this . . . this. . . ."

"Who knows what the fuck it is." Alex snorted. "Lawrence says it's a scheduling board, but to me it looks like the file cabinet that ate Toledo. Everytime someone comes up with an idea, he punches it into that fucker. The goddamned thing goes bananas for thirty seconds, then Lawrence tells us what it's decided. *It!* The rest of us might as well go home." Alex sighed. "I'll never get a VP this way."

Jill tried not to laugh. "Cheer up, Alex. Maybe the computer will take a shine to you and spit out a promotion."

"Don't let Lawrence hear you call it a computer. *He* says its name is Abelard."

"Abelard?" Jill frowned.

"I think it's an acronym, but for what I don't know."

"Is that Carolyn McCaffery's baby?"

"Yeah," Alex whispered. "Lawrence thinks his little ass is solid gold. The only time he lets the kid out of his sight is when McCaffery feeds him, and I got money says Lawrence will be doing that, too. One thing I'll say, though. The little bastard never cries when he's sitting in Lawrence's lap. And McCaffery! She can't fart without Lawrence smiling at her. If I could get knocked up, I would!"

"Alex!" Jill stifled a laugh not solely provoked by the ludicrous mental image of a pregnant Alex Friedman, but also because this room was a nerve-racking incongruity, like suddenly finding an operating room in the heart of the Polo Lounge.

"Alex, buddy!" Zippy de Franco had slithered out of nowhere and was standing behind Alex with a friendly hand on his shoulder. "Hi, Jill, how they hanging?"

"Jill just got in from Cleveland," Alex explained.

"You've been gone?" Zippy asked, then giggled softly. "A low profile won't buy you any Blue Chips."

"She had family problems." Alex went on explaining Jill's business. "This woman's all heart. Family's in trouble, she drops her job like a hot rock, and . . . Hey, Jill, I forgot to ask. Did your mother pull through?"

"Alex! Am I wearing black?" Jill stared at him, wondering if he really thought she'd be in the office oohing over Abelard if her mother had just passed away.

"Let's grab a seat," Zippy said to Alex. "This clambake's about to start."

189

As they walked toward the conference table with Jill following, Zippy asked Alex, "Hire a girl yet?"

"I'm still interviewing."

"Try Margie in Personnel." Zippy winked. "You won't do better."

"I'll write it down." Alex pulled a Gucci notebook from his breast pocket and jotted *Margie* on the cover.

"Now put four stars after it." Zippy leered.

"Four!" Alex whistled. "Christ!"

They walked off together, leaving Jill looking for a place to sit. The conference table had been pushed against one wall, squeezed in like an afterthought in the room that now belonged to Abelard. The comfortable club chairs had vanished, replaced by the kind of narrow wooden chairs Abbey Rents delivers to weddings, wakes, pyramid parties, and spontaneous left-wing demonstrations.

The chairs were jammed so closely together that the usual careful and mutually agreed-upon separation of the Los Angeles and New York contingents was impossible to maintain. The denim-clad spilled into the laps of the gray-suited, and tanned elbows jostled for tabletop space with pale manicured hands. Beneath the humming of Abelard's mechanical minions there was a rumbling of human discontent. The audible conversation, however, ran to elaborate courtesies, to "Excuse me, did I poke you in the ribs?" and "Was that your knee? So sorry."

The only women present, besides Jill, were Angela Kent, looking chicly wan, and Carolyn McCaffery, looking anxiously in the direction of her baby. They were seated, or rather squashed in, at the far end of the table.

Alex had already seated himself between Zippy and a sallow young man with spectacles, whom Jill figured to be the highly touted Smythe "Mad Bomber" Jones.

"Come sit here, my dear," Dale Neiman called to her. He was patting the empty chair next to him and smiling.

Reluctantly Jill walked toward Neiman and squeezed into the seat. In the process she jarred the gray-haired man next to her.

"Excuse me," she said, but he stared straight ahead, no doubt lost in nostalgia for the Big Apple.

"Hello, Dale." She tried to smile at him. She'd never sat between two New York people before. They smelled funny, like tabby cats.

"Well, my dear, I hear that your leader had a very expensive temper tantrum last night." Neiman's lips curled in his weasel smile.

190

"Your young man down there"—he gestured toward Alex, who was slapping his thigh in hilarity at some joke of Zippy's—"filled us in on the details."

"He did?" Jill wondered if Alex had described the scene to Neiman as he had to her, complete with "whacked-out" and circles whirled next to his ear.

"I'm sure Dan had a very good reason for doing what he did," Jill said firmly.

"And we're all waiting to hear what it is," Neiman said smoothly, "including a reporter from one of the trade publications."

"Reporter?" Jill wasn't sure why, but the word gave her a chill.

"Your boss has antagonized a very powerful studio, and the head of that studio is charging us with network interference and censorship. In print, no less. We have to answer those charges. Or rather, Carmichael does."

"Oh, dear." With all her heart Jill wished Dan would arrive to clear away this escalating confusion.

"Now, now." Neiman patted Jill's hand. "I don't want you to feel that you are in any way part of this fiasco. We at UBC are quite fond of you and feel you have a very bright future right here with us. Don't be upset."

Of course not. The sharks are circling, with my best friend as bait, but why should I worry? I'm safe here on the deck with all these nice folks and an orchestra playing "Nearer, My God, to Thee."

Lawrence leaned over Donny. "Would you like a ridey-poo?" Reaching behind him, he pushed a button. There was a whirring sound and the horseshoe-shaped console, chair and all, whooshed from the center of the room to within a few inches of the conference table.

"Christ Almighty!" Jill exclaimed. For a moment she'd thought Lawrence and Donny were about to crash into the table.

"Pneumatic," Neiman whispered, patting her arm in a fatherly gesture. "It moves on a cushion of air."

At the far end of the room Angela Kent was waving her arm for recognition. "Teddy, oh, Teddy," she called in her best Gloria Swanson voice, but Lawrence was engrossed in clucking at Donny and oblivious to everything else.

"Theodore!" she snapped, and it was Joan Crawford returned from a bitch's grave. Lawrence looked up, his attention riveted.

"Thank you, darling," Angela cooed. "Before we become bogged down in the necessary but ofttimes dreary business of discussing series episodes, I have some fantastic news for you." She smiled dazzlingly, ignoring the malevolent stares of those responsible for the "ofttimes dreary" episodes.

"Fantastic?" Lawrence's face was alive with interest.

"I have discovered a marvelous new talent," Angela gushed, "a girl named Victoria Whitney, whom I guarantee will be television's next Suzanne Somers."

Lawrence rubbed his chin thoughtfully. "I'm not sure television needs another Suzanne Somers."

"Then she'll be the next Mary Tyler Moore—I tell you, she's a *star!*" Angela waved an eight-by-ten glossy of a lovely young woman, with the word *star* scribbled across the bottom—in Polly's handwriting!

"We'll see about that," Lawrence said. He shifted Donny to a more comfortable position, then turned a dial with a black-gloved hand. The horseshoe reversed itself, slithered across the room, and swiveled, facing the computer. Lawrence pressed buttons and pushed levers, then flipped a switch. A panel in the ceiling slid open, and a four-by-six foot television screen descended, swooping down as though it had materialized from another dimension.

"Christ!" Jill exclaimed.

"There, there." Neiman's fatherly hand was patting the inside of her arm, an area in unfatherly proximity to her bosom. Jill shifted away from him, and Neiman frowned.

Lawrence picked up the bullet-shaped microphone, flicked a switch, and said, "Good afternoon, Abelard. I have a question. We're considering an actress named Victoria Whitney. What do you think?"

Now Lawrence was punching buttons, turning dials, and flipping switches at a pace that reminded Jill of silent movies, of Chaplin scurrying off double-time and the Keystone Kops chasing Fatty Arbuckle on legs that pumped so hard they blurred. It was all done with his left hand while his right encircled Donny.

The screen filled with grids and rows of symbols that appeared and were erased so quickly that there was barely time to blink before they were gone. Lights like laser beams flashed out of nowhere and zapped, crisscrossing the screen in a light-show of colors like phosphorus explosions. Jill's eyes stung and teared in the onslaught of brilliance.

She turned away from the screen, looking down the table at the mesmerized programers, whose faces danced with the reflection of pulsating lights. Suddenly there was a collective gasp.

Either an optical illusion made it appear that laser beams were hurtling toward the conference table, or Abelard's temper was akin to Lawrence's, and he (it?) was indulging in his own version of hurling ashtrays.

Chairs scattered as executives ducked, seeking an escape route under.

Then it was over, and the screen went dark. Lawrence reversed his buttons, switches, and dials. The horseshoe slithered once again to the edge of the conference table. Everyone sighed, relaxed, and made a great show of pretending nothing had happened.

"Abelard loves the idea," Lawrence announced, beaming. He bent over Donny. "Did oo-ums like that?"

Evidently oo-ums had liked it very much. Donny cooed and gurgled at Lawrence, his huge, dark eyes blinking gently.

"All right." Lawrence was all business. "We have a new star. What'll we put her in?" His eyes swept the table. "Well, I'm waiting." He waited for all of three seconds. "Abelard can't do *everything,*" he said, then smiled ominously. "Well, he could, but if Abelard does everything, why would UBC need all you high-priced talent?"

It was a good question, and everyone at the table began babbling at once in a stunning overflow of ideas.

"Man from Quasar?" Neiman suggested hopefully. "The girl has tits."

"Too small a part." Lawrence shook his head.

"We could create a show for her," Angela suggested.

"She's too new," Lawrence decided.

"She'd be great as the gorilla." Zippy giggled softly.

"What?" Jill leaned toward Neiman. "What gorilla?"

Neiman smiled chummily. "Zippy bought a wonderful Kafkaesque property about a zookeeper and a gorilla."

"Zookeeper! But Dan turned that down. How could Zippy buy it?"

"The Special Assistant to the President can do whatever he wants, wouldn't you think? As for Carmichael, he's not here."

"Kafkaesque?" Jill blinked.

"The zookeeper and the gorilla is a metaphor for one man's struggle to achieve autonomy in a faceless society," Neiman replied enigmatically, then at Jill's bewildered look, "NBC has a hit show with a monkey. We want one, too."

"I understand," Jill told him, feeling hopelessly entangled in the ropes she was supposed to be learning.

"The Natasha part in *The Adventures of Peter Blackmore!*" Alex leaped to his feet, toppling his chair.

"Brilliant! Abelard couldn't have done better!" Lawrence bestowed his highest praise upon Alex, who retrieved his toppled chair with a bend from the waist that was more of a bow.

"That young man's a comer," Neiman whispered to Jill. "The memo he wrote on *Blackmore* sold the show. Now he's come up with the perfect casting idea."

"What memo?" Jill asked.

"You don't read memos written by people who work for you? How interesting." Neiman turned away from Jill, settling his gaze on Lawrence. "Lawrence is a true visionary," he said, loud enough for Lawrence to hear.

A flushed and excited Alex waved at Lawrence, determined to hold his attention. "Sir? Sir? The producer of *Peter Blackmore* will be here in five minutes. I took the liberty of calling him."

"Good thinking," Lawrence said approvingly, then bent over Donny. "Would oo-ums like to hear a report from Mommy?" Donny gurgled. "Oo would?" Lawrence smiled at Carolyn. "Donny wants to hear Mommy."

Mommy had the look of a woman whose child has been kidnapped by the emperor of the realm. She was caught between joy at her rare good fortune and sorrow at having to share what had been hers alone. "I have a brief rundown on limited series," Carolyn said, taking a quick peek at the notes she'd spread out on the table. Jill recognized Polly's handwriting.

Jill pulled her folded memos out of her pocket and settled back to read.

A woman whose perfectly healthy mother lapses into a coma shouldn't be surprised to find a network guided by a psychic and a Rube Goldberg machine.

Alex's memo was interesting, and more than interesting . . . it was familiar. Jill was reading the ideas she'd dictated to Alex on the phone from Cleveland. Even the wording was identical. Polly was right. Alex was a young man in a hurry—too much of a hurry to even paraphrase. At the top of the *Peter Blackmore* memo was the list of executives to whom Alex had sent it—everyone who'd ever worked for UBC including three vice-presidents who'd passed away. At the bottom was Alex's signature, a flourish of letters so elaborate, John Hancock would have swooned.

How can Alex sign his name to someone else's ideas? Jill wondered. At the very least, it's thoughtless. Perhaps that's it. Perhaps his enthusiasm overwhelmed his judgment. . . . Perhaps he overlooked, forgot. . . .

Enough "perhaps." I'll ask him.

"Abelard agrees!" Lawrence's triumphant booming snapped Jill from her reverie. "*Machine Gun Killers* is a hit!" He bent over Donny. "Doesn't oo-ums have a smart mommy?"

Oo-ums gurgled happily.

"Uh . . . sir?" Carolyn's voice was tentative. "Perhaps I'd better take Donny now. He must need changing."

"*No!*" Lawrence exclaimed, then solicitously patted Donny's tiny bottom. "He's dry, Carolyn. I'll let you know when he needs you."

"All right," Carolyn agreed, but hers was not a happy face.

"Mr. Lawrence . . . sir?" It was Smythe "Mad Bomber" Jones. "If you would, sir?"

"What is it?" Lawrence scowled. "Well, speak up. There's a producer waiting outside."

"Just take a moment, sir," MB's voice was extremely polite. "If you'll consult Abelard concerning the future of *Freak People*, I'm certain you'll have conclusive proof that the show is detrimental to—"

"Bullshit!" Lawrence exploded, then glanced quickly at Donny, who seemed unperturbed by the outburst. He continued in a softer tone. "*Freak People* will remain a UBC show, Jones. And there's no reason to consult Abelard. America has already rendered its verdict. America is watching *Freak People*. To cancel this show would be to spit in the eye of the American people. Would you ask me to spit in America's eye?" Lawrence fixed MB with the look of an apoplectic eagle.

"Uh, no, sir," he said. "I wouldn't do that."

"Good, Jones, good." Lawrence relaxed, then smiled. "Besides, you owe your job to that show. If you hadn't sent that letter threatening to blow us up. . . ." He threw back his head and laughed heartily. "Ah, the passionate excesses of youth! Soon past. Very soon past." He stopped laughing. "Anything else, Jones?"

"Yes, sir, I've made some calculations, and according to my figures, we can fit three more chairs at this table if everyone tilts seven degrees to the left."

"You're kidding!" Lawrence was intrigued.

"I never kid, sir," MB replied.

"Are you sure your figures are correct?"

"I never make a mistake, sir. Ask Abelard."

"Any man who tells me he can compute as well as Abelard is a liar." Lawrence was testy.

"I never lie, sir," Jones said mildly. "I always mean what I say."

Lawrence rubbed his chin, "Well, that's interesting information, and at some point I may check it with Abelard, but we have no need for three more executives at this table. In fact, I think we could do with three less." He glowered at the assembled multitudes, who shifted and squirmed in their chairs.

"On with it," Lawrence ordered. "Bring in what's-his-name."

"Saul," Neiman whispered. "Saul Green."

The door opened and a tall, slender man walked into the room. He headed straight for Lawrence, then stopped dead as the impact of Abelard hit him. "Holy Jesus!" His eyes were the shape of the globes in the ceiling.

"It's a set. Right?" He grinned. "It's got to be a set. *Battlestar Galactica? Buck Rogers?*" He looked around the room, his grin fading. "*Star Wars? The Empire Strikes Back?* A low-budget exploitation flick aimed for the drive-in market?" His grin was gone. "If it isn't a set, what the hell is it?"

Neiman pushed a chair toward Saul Green, who sat down rather quickly.

"It's merely another research tool," Lawrence said in an offhand way.

Saul Green continued to stare, bug-eyed. "Uh . . . that's a nice baby you got there." He started to point at Donny, but his hand was shaking, so he pulled it out of the air and sat on it.

Lawrence smiled affably. "So, how are you, Paul?"

"Saul," Green said quickly, "if it's okay with you."

"Sure. We want *The Adventures of Peter Blackmore* on the air in three weeks."

"Three weeks!" Saul was astonished. "I can't get a staff together in three weeks!"

Lawrence leaned over Donny. "Isn't the nice man funny?" he cooed, then, to Saul, "it's simple. You write the script this weekend—"

"Weekend!" Saul interrupted. "No one can write a script in a weekend."

"Why not? It's only sixty, seventy pages."

"That's typing, not writing," Saul protested.

"Cast it Monday, throw some sets together, start filming on Friday. What could be simpler?"

Saul stared woefully at Lawrence. "I can't work under that kind of pressure."

"Then we'll find someone who can." Lawrence rose from his contour chair, carefully cradling Donny. "Is there any pastrami? I'd kill for a pastrami sandwich. Where's my Tang? What the fuck's going on here? Why isn't anyone around when I need them?" He bent over Donny. "We're going to the kitchen and kick ass." Donny gurgled gleefully as they walked off, disappearing through the door to the kitchen.

"What the hell?" Saul stared after him.

"Let me explain," Neiman said soothingly. He approached Saul, dropping a conciliatory arm around his shoulders. "What Mr. Lawrence means is—" Neiman stopped, glancing around the room. "Take a break. We'll reconvene in ten."

Neiman walked off with Saul. Twenty-six executives rose from the table with a sound like swarming bees.

Jill saw Alex walking out the door with Zippy.

"Wait," she called. "Alex, wait a minute."

By the time she reached them, Alex's face was clouded with impatience.

"I need to talk to you, Alex."

"We only have ten minutes." Alex frowned. "Zip and I are going to grab a hamburger. We could be here all night."

"It's important." Jill felt like Oliver Twist asking for gruel.

"Well, if it can't wait . . ." Alex shrugged, giving Zippy a "Hey, man, it's a bore, but what are you gonna do?" look.

When they arrived at her office, Polly was nowhere in sight. Both phones were ringing, with God only knew what news of disaster. Well, God would have to handle it himself.

"What's this?" Jill handed the memo to Alex.

He took it, barely glanced at the contents, and handed it back. "Pretty good, huh?"

"Alex, how could you do this? How could you sign your name to ideas that aren't yours?"

"What do you mean?" Alex looked shocked. He snatched the memo out of her hand and stared at it. "Your name isn't here! Why

197

isn't your name here?" He took a step toward her, and instinctively Jill took a step back.

"That's why I asked, Alex. I thought you could tell me."

"That son of a bitch!" Alex shouted. "That fucking asshole secretary! If he was here, I'd fire him again. I told that bastard that *your* name should go on this—" He stopped, peering closely at Jill. "You didn't think I'd ace you out, did you, Jill?"

"Well . . . uh . . ."

"Oh, shit!" He howled, waving his fist at the ceiling. "You fucking well did!"

Then he was on the move again, with Jill backing away. She ran into the corner of her desk.

"Ouch! Listen, Alex. I'm sure we can clear this up."

"Clear up!" Alex jiggled towards her. "What can we clear up if there's no trust between us?" His nose was mashed against hers. "How could you think I'd try to ace you out? I would die for you! How could you think? *How? How?*"

Jill leaned backward, aware she'd stopped breathing. *Breathe,* she commanded herself. Her hand reached behind her, in an instinctive grab-hold-of-something gesture. She picked up the phone.

"Hello," she said, and her hello went up Alex's nose. "Excuse me, Alex."

He took two steps backward, and Jill breathed again.

"Jill!" It was Patti Gerard. "Goddammit, I've been calling and calling. I'm glad you're back. Your secretary's a doll, what's her name, Polly? Kept me up to date. Your momma's a corker all right. Every night I get down on my knees and thank God I'm an orphan."

Jill half-listened while staring at Alex, who was pacing the perimeter of her carpet.

"I can't work under these conditions," Alex mumbled, eyes fixed on the shag. "My heart'll give out. I'll lose my hair."

"Are you there?" Patti asked. "Jill?"

"I'm here. I think."

"Good," Patti went on. "You won't believe what happened to me. The most incredibly gorgeous guy ran into my car at a stop light on Sunset. Just a fender-bender, nothing to squawk at, but even before the good-hands people could get to the scene, we were at his place tumbling into the sack. Well, I gotta tell you kid, looks aren't everything. I mean, honey, it was an inch long, and he didn't know what to do with it. And I told him so." She laughed merrily. "Now *he's* suing *me* for whiplash! Can you believe? When will I learn to keep my trap shut with men? I think something, it comes out my mouth."

Alex moaned at the carpet. "I finally find the one place I want to work and a boss I'd walk through walls for, and what happens? She doubts me. She hates me."

Patti's giggles cascaded through the phone. "But as the song says, 'It don't worry me.' I've got a dynamite lawyer who's also a pretty good fuck—that is, if you don't mind the type who has to talk through the whole thing. It's like going to bed with a play-by-play announcer, but he gets off on it, so—besides, I just got myself a new one. He's only twenty-four and fabulous, and I love it! I'll tell you about him later. I just called to thank you for Nina. She's a fabulous model. Fabulous."

"I can't stay under these circumstances," Alex said bleakly. "I'll write out my resignation. I'll move to Philadelphia. Remember what that shrink said? I'll shoot myself!"

"Alex!" Jill exclaimed.

"Nina's husband?" Patti asked. "Yeah, he's a fabulous guy. If I had a man that interested in my career, I'd never let go. He's even sexy. Don't you think he's sexy, Jill?"

"One of a kind," Jill mumbled.

"Gotta go," Patti said breathlessly. "Watch the baseball game on TV tonight. You'll see me sitting next to my gorgeous kid—*me*, a thirty-nine-year-old woman wearing a baseball cap and yelling 'Go, Dodger blue!' It's dumb, I know, but worth it when I get him home. Bye."

Jill stood with the phone in her hand, wondering what she could possibly say to Alex. When confronted with a flat denial, only two choices are open—believe or not.

Alex took the phone from her hand. "You don't believe in me anymore. I'm going." He started for the door, his head so low that from the rear it appeared he'd been decapitated.

"Alex, wait." Jill looked from the memo in her hand to Alex's headless torso. "I don't know what to think."

"I'm the best friend you ever had." He sniffled. "Well, here's looking at you, kid. Sayonara."

Alex charged blindly at the door, running into Polly, who was on her way in. "You hate me, too." He hissed in her face.

"I don't hate anyone," Polly told him. "I just suffer fools less gladly." She leaned around Alex, looking for Jill. "Dan's in his office."

"I'm on my way," Jill said.

"I'm going with you," Alex decided.

"No, you aren't, Alex. I'm going to see Dan alone." Jill tried to wriggle past him in the doorway.

"I may not be here when you get back." His voice was casual, but the threat hung in the air.

"Then, go. Or stay. Do what you have to do, Alex. I'm going to see Dan alone."

Jill left Alex glaring at her back and ran down the hall with Polly at her side.

"A reporter is in the office with Dan," Polly said.

Jill stopped, frowning at Polly. "Why do I feel like I'm on my way to get my heart broken? Maybe sometimes I'm psychic, too."

CHAPTER 14

The knot in Jill's stomach tightened as she slowly opened Dan's door. The only light in Dan's office was that of a small desk lamp with a jade-green shade. It glowed softly, casting shadows rather than illumination.

A man Jill had never seen before sat on Dan's couch, notebook in hand, while Dan stood near the windows, his back to the room.

"Dan?"

"Come in, Jill," he said, turning to greet her.

Jill perched on the edge of the nearest chair, for the first time uneasy in a room that had been a haven for her. She blinked in the uncertain light, groping for the person of Dan and finding only his silhouette. Her inability to see his eyes was frustrating, and it gave her the disquieting sense of a broken connection. Their ability to read one another so clearly had been based on their mutual willingness to be read. Now Dan was hiding, and Jill wondered if she'd done something to cause him to withdraw.

"Mr. Simon from the *Reporter* has a few more questions," Dan said, "and then you and I will talk. Mr. Simon, this is Jill Kenyon, the director of my department."

Mr. Simon, a thirtyish man with intelligent brown eyes, rose briefly and shook Jill's hand. "Pleased to meet you. What do you think of the way your boss shut down *Rock and Roll Love*?"

"Jill wasn't there," Dan said quickly, "nor have we discussed it. That's not a fair question, Mr. Simon."

"I get paid to ask pointed questions, Carmichael, not fair ones." Simon smiled.

"At least you're honest about it," Dan said, then, abruptly, "Can we get on with this?"

Simon's pencil was poised. "The studio claims that you, and therefore UBC, have interfered with the creative process. Is that true?"

"UBC had nothing to do with it. I made the decision unilaterally."

"Why?"

"I did it because of a personal conviction that getting stoned and unrestrained on a set isn't creative, contemporary, expressive, innovative, sophisticated, outrageous, or funny. It's sophomoric, unprofessional, and unacceptable."

"But the studio said—"

"I'm not interested in what the studio said," Dan interrupted.

"If they put enough pressure on UBC, you could lose your job," Simon said ominously.

"I stand by my decision. Next question." Dan turned his back so abruptly that Jill flinched, hoping Simon wouldn't interpret the gesture as one of contempt.

"As long as I'm here, there are some questions I'd like to ask," Simon said. "For instance, don't you feel that networks have a responsibility to upgrade the quality of television?"

There was a chuckle from Dan. "Oh, Mr. Simon, the questions you ask! And the answers we both know I'm supposed to give. Right now, I'm supposed to answer your question in the affirmative, and then you counter with 'And what are you and UBC doing to upgrade the quality of television?' and then I run through a laundry list of UBC shows guaranteed to uplift America, all coming next year, of course —and all shows specifically designed to enrich your life, contribute to your understanding, teach your children, cure your dandruff and save your soul. Then you run back to your newspaper and write up what I've said, highlighting the picture I've painted of glories to come with your own snide remarks and caustic comments."

"That's clouding the issue." Simon was obviously annoyed. "I'm in the business of reporting television news."

"You're in the business of turning witty phrases and trying to sound smart," Dan corrected. "And of telling the good folks out there what they *should* want to watch."

"That's hardly fair," Simon remarked.

"But pointed," Dan said.

"All right." Simon tapped his notebook with his pencil. "I'd like you to answer the question concerning network responsibility."

"A network's responsibility is to its board of directors, its affiliates, and its stockholders," Dan said. "It's a business like General Motors and AT&T. When the ratings go down, the stock goes down, and the business is in trouble. The business of business is business. Next question, Mr. Simon."

"But that attitude is hardly fair to the creative community," Simon said, " 'to the talented writers, producers, and directors who struggle to create and present their work in the great American art form television should be.' "

"You're assuming that creative expression is the goal, Mr. Simon. If it was, they would be writing, producing, and directing whatever they please, whenever they please, Off Broadway or Off Melrose Avenue, in basements, in churches, in each other's backyards. But they don't. There are big bucks in television, my friend, and the goal isn't art, it's a house in Bel-Air and a Mercedes. Or three. Next question."

"But where does that leave the audience?" Simon demanded.

"Where it's always left them," Dan sighed. "Sitting at home with an insatiable taste for shit."

"You don't mean that!" Simon's astonishment brought him to his feet.

"Dan!" Jill interrupted. "Perhaps Mr. Simon can come back later when you're feeling better."

"Don't do that," Dan ordered. "I don't need protection. I mean what I say. Look, Simon, you seem bright enough, and there's nothing wrong with your hearing, so listen. Creative people come to the networks to sell ideas they hope will make money. Networks buy ideas, then put on the shows they think the audience will like best so *they* can make money. The audience decides which shows will stay on by watching or not watching them. So, when I'm told that the American public hates what's on television, I say, 'Bullshit.' And, further, I say to the audience, 'If you don't like it, stop watching. Exercise your vote. Throw the rascals out.' "

"So." Simon scribbled furiously. "You don't mind if I print that a high-level network executive has stated that the audience has an insatiable taste for shit?"

"If the people say television stinks but continue to watch, what would you call it?" Dan asked. "People say they want television to better inform them, but they don't watch *CBS Reports* or *NBC White Paper*. They say they want culture, but symphonies, documentaries, opera, and the ballet end up last in the ratings. They say . . . they say . . . but what they watch is something else. The people lie. The networks lie. The creative community lies, only with better syntax

203

and jokes. Not only does the emperor have no clothes, my friend—
everyone is running around stark naked."

"Then you're saying that the system is so screwed, it can't possibly
work?" Simon stated.

"It's working right now." Dan lifted up his arms in an elaborate
shrug. "The networks make money. The creative people make
money. The audience makes the final decision. The system is what
it is. We make too much of it, perhaps because television comes into
our homes. We take it personally, surround it with a mystique, but
we seldom, if ever, simply switch it off. More people disinherit their
children than give up prime-time viewing. More people shoot their
spouses than their television sets."

Dan was quiet, and there was a quality of finality in the silence.

"Is there anything else you'd like to say?" Simon asked.

"There is one more thing. Years ago Joseph Kennedy pointed out
that business is amoral. He was right. The only sacred trust involved
is the obligation to be dollars-and-cents successful. The rest, Mr.
Simon, is bullshit."

"If that's the way you want it, Carmichael. It isn't often a man gets
to write his own obituary." Simon got to his feet, checked the creases
in his beige suede trousers, and went to the door. "You know, Carmichael, I like you, but that's something I'll keep to myself. I might
want to work here someday." He opened the door and was gone,
leaving Jill staring blankly at Dan.

Jill's formless sense of foreboding was beginning to take shape.
"Have you been fired?"

Dan shook his head no.

"Then what is it?" she pleaded. "You know that what you just said
to that reporter was, well . . . nobody says things like that, Dan. Not
publicly."

For a second he seemed to be reaching for her, then he turned
again to the windows. When he spoke, his voice was barely audible.
"Nancy's dead."

"Oh, my God!" Jill gasped. Both hands flew to her open mouth, and
she stared at his back, unable to move. "Oh, my God!"

"When I got home last night, the phone was ringing. It was the
hospital. They'd been phoning for hours. Nancy's car had gone off the
road into a ditch on her way home from a dinner party. The police
think she was sideswiped." He was silent for a moment, then continued in a voice that choked on the words. "They told me she was

alive when the paramedics brought her in, conscious on and off for nearly four hours, calling for me. But I was out chasing a rock 'n' roll movie, Jill. I couldn't be reached. Nancy was dead when I got there."

Jill was at his side. She tried to put her arms around him, tried to pull him close, tried to wipe away the tears that were streaming down his face. Dan pulled away from her. "Don't try to comfort me, Jill. I don't deserve it. I wasn't there when she needed me."

"But you didn't know! You couldn't have known." Jill tasted her own tears, ached with her need to hold him even if he couldn't allow himself to be held. To touch him seemed essential. Not to do so required prodigious effort, possible only because that was his wish.

"The person I cared about most is dead, and in the past month I've managed to get home for dinner five times. Something always came up, Jill, paperwork, meetings, screenings . . . Our last vacation was three years ago. I cut it short and flew back here because the director of a movie whose title I can't remember was threatening to quit. I kept promising we'd go away together, but we never did."

"Oh, Dan." Gently, tentatively, Jill laid a hand on his heaving shoulder, hoping he wouldn't push it away. He didn't. "I'm sure Nancy understood."

"She did understand," Dan said. His weeping was muffled against the draperies. "Nancy understood everything I told her. And God help me, I told her. I told her how important my job was, how important I was, and how much it all mattered. Nancy would sit and listen to me and say, 'Yes, dear, I know.' She bought it, Jill, every word of it. And she was proud of me, so goddamn proud. It takes a very special woman to be proud of an asshole who's gotten his priorities so fucked up he can feed his wife a line of bullshit and expect her to—" His voice broke and there was only the sound of his sobbing.

"Don't do this to yourself," Jill begged.

"Myself! Myself!" he shouted. The face he turned to her was swollen and white with rage. "My wife died in unspeakable pain in a room surrounded by strangers with no one to hold her hand. Myself! I'm sick of myself!"

"Please, Dan, let me help."

"I can't." He shook his head vehemently. "Thank you. I know that you care and I appreciate it. I just can't respond. Understand?"

"Right now, you hate yourself," Jill said bluntly. "That's why it's important for you to be around people who care about you."

"No." Dan was adamant. He began stuffing papers into his briefcase. "I can't attach myself to your kindness, Jill. I haven't earned it."

"But you have. You've been a good friend to me."

"Do you believe in God?" Dan asked abruptly.

"I . . . I . . ." Jill was surprised by the question. "I'm Catholic."

He looked up and, for a second, was Dan again. "I didn't ask what church you went to before you became embarrassed by going to church. I asked if you believe in God."

"I . . . I . . . don't know." His posing of the question confused her more than the question itself.

"At one time I knew," Dan said. "The existence of God and a soul within me were certainties for me. I'm not a religious man. I never will be. But knowing there was a God, that I had a soul, gave me a time and place and purpose in this world. But I allowed myself to forget." He closed his briefcase, meeting Jill's eyes evenly. "So now I've lost Nancy, along with the certainties that made me the man Nancy mistakenly thought I was." Dan picked up his briefcase, looking around the room in an uninterested way as though anything he'd forgotten could be easily left behind. He put his arm around Jill. "I looked in the mirror this morning, Jill. I wasn't there anymore."

Jill rested her head on his shoulder while the little girl in her silently cried. *Don't leave me, please, please, please. . . .*

"Where are you going?" the grown-up Jill asked out loud.

"I don't know," Dan hesitated. "That's not exactly true, Jill, but I'm not ready to say where I'm going. I promise I'll call before the end of the week."

"Will you be back?" she asked, already knowing the answer.

He shook his head against her hair. "I won't be back."

"I knew that." Jill tried to control her tears, but they were beyond her. "How did I know that?"

"You know a lot, cookie, even things you think you don't know." He turned her face with his hand and tilted her chin upward. "I'm running out on you, Jill. That's because I'm a bad guy."

"You're not!" Jill protested. "I won't listen to that!"

"Oh, I am. My saving grace, if I have one, is that I don't want to be." He kissed her forehead gently. "So, I'm abandoning you. But I'll keep in touch and I mean that. We'll talk. I won't be far away. I promise I'll be there if you need me."

"I'll need you." Jill was certain.

"You'll need someone," he agreed. "Walk me to the door."

They walked to the door with their arms around each other's waists.

"Stay here," Dan said. "Sit in my office for as long as you like."

"I wish there was something I could say . . . or do." Jill held him, dreading the closing of the door.

Dan smiled, the sadness in his eyes defining the burden he carried. "Say my good-byes for me, will you? Right now I couldn't abide being consoled for the loss of Nancy. The simple truth is, I gave her away."

"I'll say your good-byes," Jill promised.

"My resignation is in the top drawer on the left. Please send it to whomever."

"I will." Jill nodded. Dan opened the door. "God bless you," she whispered.

"I don't deserve that, either," Dan said. "We'll see." He slipped through the door and was gone, leaving Jill standing alone, staring at the closed door.

Jill didn't know how long she stood in the middle of the room, but gradually she became aware that her whole body was aching as though in the aftermath of a tremendous physical exertion or, more to the point, the exertion involved in forcing herself to stand still. She'd wanted to run after him, to compel his return, to assuage his loss by offering herself or whatever part of herself would best fill his need.

Instead she sat in his chair, feeling his presence, stroking its arms as though they were his. The brown leather felt warm and alive beneath her cold, clammy hands. She sat straight, both feet on the floor, stiff-backed and rigid with waiting. Her head knew that he wouldn't return, because that's what he'd told her and Dan never lied, but her body waited because his return was the demand of her heart.

"I cannot bear it. I will not," Jill said aloud, then cringed at the childish sound of it.

Nothing compounds but loss. Jill switched off Dan's jade-green lamp.

She sat in darkness, alone in a sea of loss that rolled over her, crashing in separate waves—Pa, gone quickly, his enigma intact, Neil Kaiser, torn away in mid-need, Steve, a failure of faith, and now Dan, a haven and guide as reliable, as constant as the North Star.

They'd been grenades, these losses, explosions that ripped away irreplaceable parts.

Jill placed both hands flat on Dan's desk and pushed herself out of his chair. Leaving the room was essential. Its comfort was gone. Dan had taken it with him, leaving only pain—his and hers—behind.

Jill desperately needed a painkiller. Polly. Daisy. Someone to hold, someone to hold her.

Jill left Dan's office and walked through newly alien halls, through passages dimmer and narrower than they had been two hours before.

Before going home to Daisy, she'd see Polly and be comforted. Be comforted, hugged, told it would be all right, *she* would be all right.

Polly wasn't at her desk. In her office Jill found Alex sitting in her chair shuffling through her papers.

"I can do some of this paperwork at home for you." Alex didn't look up.

"Where's Polly?" Jill asked. It was vaguely unsettling to see Alex so comfortably occupied with her responsibilities.

"I didn't know where you were, and I didn't need her, so I sent Polly home. I had to practically push her out of here, and she went grumbling all the way." His eyes flicked in Jill's direction. "Must be that time of the month."

"Maybe not, Alex." Jill was instantly angry. "Perhaps she was waiting for the person she works for to suggest she go home. Didn't you ask why she objected to leaving?"

"That's the trouble with you," he said smugly. "You haven't learned that you don't ask secretaries what they think. You *tell* them what to do."

"Oh, I see," Jill said. Since Alex was firmly ensconced in her chair, she sat on her couch. "The way you tell me what to do."

"I don't know what you mean." His face was as blank as his voice. "I've never tried to tell you what to do."

"Of course you haven't, Alex," The sharp edge of sarcasm Jill heard in her voice pleased her. Anger had always been a quick antidote to pain. "You threaten to quit when I question you—but that's not telling me I'm forbidden to ask questions. You peremptorily dismiss my secretary—but that's not telling me you have the right to make my decisions. You tell me you may not be here if I don't allow you to see Dan—but that's not coercion, is it? Alex? Well, is it?" There was a note of hysteria underlying her disdain, and she fought to hold on to the anger that would keep her tears at bay. "Well!" she shouted. "Say something."

Alex said nothing, just sat and observed Jill's trembling chin, her hands twisting in her lap. He rose from her chair, walked past her, and deliberately closed the door.

"What happened in Dan's office?" Alex asked softly.

"Don't ask me now." She shook her head, then hid her face in her hands.

"Tell me. Is Dan angry with you?"

Jill shook her head no and felt Alex's arm around her. Very gently, he pried her hands from her face. "Tell Alex what's wrong," he whispered. "I told you Dan's been whacked out, so if he did something—"

"Dan isn't whacked out!" Jill shouted and burst into hard tears.

Alex pulled her close, guiding her head to his shoulder. "Now tell me," he directed, his voice comfortingly firm.

She told him, halting over the words and choking on her tears. When she described Nancy's death, Alex whistled and said, "Poor Dan, poor guy."

She went on, ending with Dan's departure and promise to call. "Do you know what this means?" Alex said, his arm tightening around her. "Do you understand the ramifications for us?"

"What ramifications?" Jill was befuddled, exhausted with crying, and feeling as though her head had been emptied of everything except misery and mush.

"Someone has to fill his job, Jill, and that someone is going to be you." He was squeezing her, bruising her ribs. She hadn't the strength to wiggle away.

"I don't want Dan's job," she protested. "I want Dan!"

"Does Lawrence know yet, or Neiman?" Alex asked excitedly.

"No," Jill said weakly. "Dan asked me to say his good-byes"

"Great!" We have time to make plans. Here's what I want you to do—"

"Stop!" Jill's tears poured out, and she shook with violent weeping.

Alex shook his head. "You're making yourself sick, Jill. And you're not helping me, either. Pull yourself together, or they'll think you're too weak to take over, and then where will *I* be? I've been on the street, Jill. It's cold out there." He cocked his head to one side. "All this carrying on—are you sure you weren't fucking Dan?"

"Alex!" Outrage lent her strength. She pushed him away and leaped to her feet. "How could you say such a thing? Dan loved Nancy and was faithful to her. I wouldn't . . . couldn't . . ."

Her momentary surge of energy vanished, and, knees shaking, she stared at Alex, who was looking at her with a mixture of pity and disbelief.

"Okay, okay, I believe you. Whatever you say, Jill. Here, sit down before you fall on your face." He helped her to the couch, and she sat down, thinking it quite possible that she would never get up again. She turned away from Alex, wishing she had something to wipe her wet, gooey face.

"Hold on," he instructed, and was gone, returning in less than a minute with both hands full of Kleenex. "Blow," he ordered, and she blew. He mopped her face, spreading her lipstick and smearing her mascara, but Jill didn't care. She cared about nothing except the image of Dan in her mind, an image that grew transparent and faded as she reached for it. He was inexorably moving away from her, and the comfort he'd provided grew as dim as UBC's halls.

"Better?" Alex asked.

She nodded yes, not because she really felt better, but because Alex's attempts to console her, though clumsy, were so obviously well-intentioned.

"Do you have a boyfriend?" Alex asked. "Someone special?"

"No." Carl, Nick, Neil, and Peter put together did not constitute one special boyfriend. They were more like strangers in the night, or the Big Parade.

"Ah, I'm sorry." His voice actually sounded sincere. "You should have someone special in your life." He pulled her close again.

She nestled against him. He'd told a lonely truth. What she needed was not a body, but a person, a love, a commitment, the other half of herself, the completion that would make her whole and banish loneliness forever.

"You need to get laid," Alex said softly, his fingers working the buttons on her blouse.

"I don't think so." Jill moved his hand, but she didn't push him away. He'd held her, dried her tears, been her friend. The hand stroking her hair was compassionate. The hand stroking her breast was warm and alive. He was stroking her for her sake, because stroking was what she needed. He cared about her.

I can't imagine hurting without having someone to hold me.

"I'll turn down the lights," he offered. "Don't move."

Her hand touched the neck of her unbuttoned blouse. "You're married."

"This is just what you need," he assured her, switching off all the lights, except one, in the room. On his way to the door he paused, leaning over to kiss her. His mouth was gentle, his kiss tender, like the soft, salubrious touch of one with a gift for healing.

"I'm going to lock the door," he whispered. "Stay there."

"Alex, we can't," she objected. "Not in the office. Someone will come in."

"No one will come in. You've got nothing to worry about, and besides, who cares?"

"*I* care!" Jill said emphatically.

He walked slowly toward her. "You've really got me going, Jill."

"I'm sorry," she said sadly. "I didn't mean to. . . . I want to go home."

Alex closed his eyes for a second, then said with a soulful sigh, "Are you playing hard-to-get or are you honest-to-God nervous?"

"Honest-to-God nervous. I'm sorry."

"Okay. I can understand that. I don't want the new head of the movie department to be nervous." He reached for her hand. "C'mon, get up."

Alex pulled her to her feet. Jill smiled ruefully at him and turned her back, pretending to be occupied with brushing her skirt. She felt embarrassed and more than that, frustrated.

Nothing comforts like skin.

"Give me a hand." Alex was behind her.

Jill turned around. Alex was tugging at one end of the couch.

"What are you doing?" she asked, thinking that perhaps moving furniture was Alex's way of dissipating sexual tension.

"I'm moving the couch. With this sucker in front of the door you won't be too nervous to fuck."

"But, Alex," she protested, then gave up and simply watched him wrestle the brown-leather barrier to a position blocking the door. In spite of herself she was impressed.

"A little ingenuity does it," he panted, the couch firmly in place. "The Oakland Raiders couldn't get through this sucker." He sat on the couch, patting the seat beside him. "C'mon, honey, we've had this appointment since the first time I walked through your door."

"But, Alex." She was unwilling, unable to move.

Alex rose from the couch, his hand outstretched. "All right, I'll come to you."

He did. He pulled her to him. Once again there was the balm of his restorative kiss, Then another. When she was thoroughly dizzy, he swept her off her feet and carried her to the couch.

He laid her down and stretched out as best he could in the narrow space beside her.

"It's not exactly a suite at the Bel-Air," he said, kissing her nose, "but you're going to like this."

Her smile was automatic. "The quality I find most appealing in you is your quiet self-effacement."

"That's only because I haven't fucked you yet." He grinned down at her. "When I do, that's what you'll like best."

His mouth covered her laugh, and his hands roamed her body as he moved half on top of her.

"Oh, Alex," she said finally.

"Call me Lexy," he said, getting busy with buttons.

A short time later, light seconds actually, they lay quietly, breathing into each other's mouths. Alex sighed and thoughtfully removed the elbow digging into Jill's side.

"Yummy," Alex whispered. "Now, tell me that wasn't fantastic!"

It was on the tip of Jill's tongue to do just that, but she didn't. There are things you don't say to men, primary among them being "You're a lousy lover," especially when you suspect lousy is the best they can do. Besides, Jill's need had been to be held, to be comforted. That she had been. Alex couldn't be faulted for having uncomforting skin.

Jill remembered her mother's standard warning about sex—you'll hate yourself in the morning.

Morning? Why wait? I hate myself now.

Alex raised himself up on one arm and looked at his watch. "Holy shit!" he exclaimed. "What the fuck am I doing here? Nina's waiting for me at Musso and Frank's!"

Jill loosened her arms. "Don't let me stop you." She winced as he shifted his weight, rolling off her in a tumble that took him to the floor.

"Oh, Christ! I hit my tailbone. Fucking can kill you."

"And here I thought it was the cure." Jill watched as Alex creaked to his feet and laboriously pulled on his shorts. He swung from the waist, stretching his back, then shook one leg at a time. "No permanent damage. I'll be a little stiff in the morning, but, then, being stiff in the morning can be a lot of fun." He grinned at her, clearly pleased with himself. "I'll drop by and see you some morning. You'll give up Post Toasties forever." He reached for the rest of his clothes, pulling them on quickly. "Nina's gonna be pissed. And when she gets pissed, she drinks wine. And when she drinks wine, her face gets all puffy, and that fucks up her close-ups. And tomorrow morning she's got a session with your friend Patti and that gook designer. Where do you

212

go for makeup in this town?" he asked, zipping up his pants. "Nina's pretty good, but I think she could use a pro, someone who can give her eyes just a little slant."

Jill wished he would hurry, go, be gone. "Ask Patti about makeup. She'll tell Nina where to go, probably even take her."

"That Patti has drive. She's going to make it in this town. Stick close to her, Jill. She can give you pointers. Her ass ain't half-bad, either. I love women with handles." He ran his fingers through his hair. "Got a mirror?"

Jill shook her head. "No."

"It's okay," he said. "I'll stop in the men's room on the way out. Give me a hand with this couch, will you?"

"Sure," Jill said, swinging her legs to the floor; without looking at Alex, she walked to one end of the couch and leaned against it.

"You push and I'll pull." He choreographed, and she did, thinking that, unbeknownst to him, he'd just described their lovemaking.

She strained against the couch, desperate to have Alex out of the room.

As the couch slid away from the door the mental image of herself nude and moving furniture flashed through her mind. She was torn between embarrassment and laughter, realizing that this situation was not unlike the dreams which found her stark naked in a festive throng, covered with shamed goose bumps and asking for directions to the bus station.

"There!" Alex was panting from all his exertions. "Well, got to run!"

He flung both arms around her in an effervescent embrace. "You're terrific, you know that. And I'm going to have to be very careful not to fall wildly in love with you. Gain ten pounds, you need handles."

He bolted for the door, then halted. "You don't carry Kleenex. You don't carry a mirror—not very feminine."

"I don't do windows, either, Alex," Jill said, beginning to feel a chill.

"But you fuck like an angel." He grinned and was gone, leaving her shivering, uncomforted and sad in the cold empty room.

Dan . . . Dan . . . Dan.

213

CHAPTER 15

"Mom!" It was Daisy flying out the door for a fast and furious hug, Daisy with a kiss that ricocheted off Jill's cheekbone, Daisy holding her at arm's length for a two-second scrutiny, then another crushing hug. "I'm so glad you're home, Mom. What happened to your makeup? You look terrible."

With her arm around Daisy's waist Jill walked into the house. "You sure know how to cheer up an old lady, kid."

Daisy's eyes glinted mischievously. "There are lots of middle-aged people older than you, and some of them even look it."

"You have your grandmother's way with compliments," Jill laughed.

"How is Grandma?"

"Furious at me." Jill sighed, sinking wearily onto the couch.

"Then she's better. I'm glad." With an air of proprietorship Daisy settled herself in Steve's favorite chair. "But you do look awful. Why?"

Jill shot Daisy what she hoped was a scathing look. "Mothers get that way from worrying about daughters who won't stay home when they're sick. When I talked to you on the phone I got the impression you were dying."

"I felt rotten," Daisy said. "Everything was falling apart. Haven't you ever felt like everything's gone so wrong, nothing will ever go right again?"

"You're talking about my good days. So what's changed. What's improved?"

"My cramps are gone, my cold is better, Dad said I can go to the concert tomorrow night, Lenny likes Dad, Dad likes Lenny, and we went to Scandia for dinner," Daisy enumerated happily.

"Oh, my." Jill marveled, wondering why all of Daisy's clouds had silver linings while hers were stuffed with monsoons.

"So, your father's introduction to Lenny didn't ruin your life after all." Jill felt like the cavalry who'd ridden horses to death rushing to prevent a massacre, only to arrive and find the Indians and settlers dancing a do-si-do.

"Well . . . guess not." Daisy had the grace to be momentarily embarrassed. "Actually Lenny thought Dad was terrific. He said that most kids from broken homes don't have fathers who go crazy when they're sick or worry about them inhaling pot smoke at concerts. He said a father like that is a real anchor." Daisy hugged herself, smiling. "And Dad said Lenny is the first kid he's met in a long time whose good manners seem to be natural to him, instead of just an act to make an impression." She glowed with the contentment of one who's putting the pieces in place and discovering a picture. "You know, Mom, it never occurred to me that the way Lenny looks people right in the eye is unusual, maybe because that's what Dad's always done. He makes me feel like what I'm saying is really important. Haven't you noticed how Dad looks straight at you?"

"And sometimes straight through. Where is your father, the paragon?"

"Dad said he needed toothpaste and stuff. He's down at the supermarket making faces at the cantaloupes. I would have gone with him, but it's embarrassing the way he pushes the basket up and down aisles, mumbling to himself and jerking his eyebrows like Jack Nicholson."

Jill laughed. "That's the way he sorts things out, Daisy. He putters around, holding imaginary conversations with people, mostly his partners. He fires Bradford, yells at Bloom, and gets it out of his system. That way nothing regrettable comes out of his mouth."

"It's still embarrassing. Clerks ask him if there's something wrong, and the other customers turn around and stare. I feel like I should walk behind him with a sign that says, 'He's not nuts. He's just thinking.'"

"I know what you mean." Jill laughed. "When I was in the hospital with Patti Gerard, we used to make the patients who thought they were Abraham Lincoln and Jesus Christ walk ahead of us. We'd walk behind pretending to be nurses' aides."

Daisy arched her eyebrows in unconscious imitation of her father. "Tell me about the hospital, Mom. Wasn't it scary?"

"No, not at all," Jill said brightly, wishing she hadn't raised a heretofore sleeping dog subject. "Actually, I went expecting something extraordinarily horrible, and what I found was rather ordinarily sad."

"But what did you *do* there?" Daisy, as always, was curious. "I mean, I've seen movies and there are always people screaming."

"Nothing that dramatic." Jill said hastily. "I talked to my doctor, made a few ashtrays, tried not to aggravate the nurses, and watched television. That's about all." Jill stabbed her cigarette out in the ashtray, thinking that this wasn't the most comfortable conversation she'd ever had. "I'd like something cold to drink, wouldn't you?"

Jill started toward the kitchen, with Daisy right behind her. "What were the other patients like, Mom? I know Patti Gerard but, I can't believe she was ever crazy. I mean, she laughs all the time and she has the best wardrobe. Nothing bothers her."

"People change, Daisy. Sometimes several times in one day." Jill opened the refrigerator thinking of Alex and the excitement inherent in never knowing, minute to minute, which one of him would walk through the door.

"Tell me about the other patients," Daisy persisted.

"Well"—Jill handed Daisy a Pepsi—"the guy who thought he was Jesus Christ would forgive your sins for a Marlboro."

"That is crazy!"

"Don't knock it, Daisy. From him you got real compassion for a Marlboro. From the doctors we got Thorazine for three hundred a day."

"And the Abraham Lincoln guy?"

"He went around freeing the cleaning ladies and claiming his doctor was John Wilkes Booth. There were only one or two interesting people, Daisy. Mostly, everyone moped."

"But how did you know *you* belonged there. What made *you* decide—"

"That was a long time ago," Jill interrupted, "and the details are fuzzy."

"If it happened to me, I'd remember."

"You are not me, Daisy. I'm getting old, and I have trouble remembering breakfast." Jill smiled at her daughter, thinking that she wasn't as easy to distract as she had been during the golden age of motherhood, when a cookie, a wisecrack, or an order to wash her hands would do the trick.

"But we've never talked about this, and I'd like to know—"

"Where is everyone?" It was Steve, calling from the living room.

"Dad's home!" Daisy whooped, and ran off, leaving Jill thinking it ironic that Steve would turn out to be the cavalry for her that she hadn't been for Daisy. Ironic and familiar.

Someday I'll tell Daisy about the hospital, she thought. *Someday when it's the right time.* Even as she thought it she knew that it wasn't the time she lacked but the willingness to relive the emotions. An honest sharing with Daisy would necessitate going beyond wisecracks, beyond the telling of tales. With Patti it was a gentleman's agreement to go for the jokes, play down the pain, and avoid the reopening of wounds.

Jill slammed the refrigerator door, thinking that she could sum up that time in her life in just a few sentences. "I went to the hospital with slashed wrists and came home with scars. Between the coming and going, Neil Kaiser cured me. And that, darling Daisy, was that."

Jill leaned against the closed door, wondering if a cure for mental illness, like hair coloring, could fade after a period of time, and if the natural black roots of her insanity might be growing out again.

From her post in the kitchen she could hear Daisy and Steve chatting. Jill smiled at the wonder of being fifteen. Yesterday's villain, Steve, had been transformed into a hero and Daisy's life snatched from ruin, all because the thermometer read normal, cramps disappeared, and father and boyfriend had struck a common chord. Actually, when Jill thought about it, that was a lot.

"How's Kate?" Steve asked, walking into the kitchen with a bag of groceries in each arm.

"She's fine. Or at least, out of the hospital."

While she helped Steve unpack the groceries, Jill told him what she had done in Cleveland, omitting Peter and Neil, of course.

"I'm glad your mother's better. But you took an awful risk."

"What do you mean?" Jill asked, stacking green beans in the pantry.

"Just that. What would you have done if your threat to put her in a home hadn't brought her out of her coma? Allowed her to be transferred to maternity? Signed the power of attorney? Put her in a home?"

"I wouldn't have done any of those things." Jill stacked tapioca under the green beans.

"Those were your only options, Jill. And calling your mother's bluff was . . . well, she could have gone right into shock." Steve sighed, the familiar sound of patience stretched to its limit. "That's the trouble with you. You never think things through."

217

"I knew it would work out," Jill protested, much too loudly even to her ears.

"How?" Steve demanded. "How could you think that such a hare-brained scheme—"

"I just did, that's all." Jill tossed boxes of Rice Krispies into the pantry, suddenly aghast at the picture in her mind—her saying *home* to Kate and Kate dying of shock.

I almost killed my mother!

"You simply lucked out, Jill. Intuition is wonderful in moderation, but it can't be the basis of everything you do."

"Oh?" Jill felt tears, hot and about to boil over. "Do I hear the logical male taking a snipe at female intuition."

"Logic has no gender," Steve said dogmatically. "Daisy is logical."

"What?" Jill threw the box of Minute Rice she was holding to the floor.

Let him put away his own dismal groceries. Trust Steve to buy boring food.

"Let's get this straight, Steve. When I talked to Daisy from Cleveland, she said you'd ruined her life."

"What?" His supermarket face went into action.

"Don't wave your eyebrows at me, Steve. According to Daisy, you'd treated her like an irresponsible three-year-old, and she was devastated. Now I return to find that you're the man of the hour, and Daisy, the logic queen, is not only wise beyond her years, she's wise beyond mine. Either the invaders have snatched the bodies I left, or I have cornered the North American franchise on nuts."

"Among other things Daisy's decided to wait until she's eighteen to change her name," Steve said smugly. "That's exactly my point. Eventually Daisy thinks things through."

"I'm sure dinner at Scandia didn't hurt," Jill said angrily. "I'm certain she was more receptive to a point of view served between the Caesar salad and the banana soufflé."

"Dinner was a treat, Jill, a father-daughter occasion. I wasn't trying to cajole or coerce her. I'm annoyed you should think that." But he didn't look annoyed. He looked hurt.

"C'mon, Steve, isn't the idea to get what you want any way you can? For instance, if you don't want to cope with your wife, you take her off to the nuthouse."

"Not cope?" Steve's voice was raised. "All I ever did was cope."

218

"You didn't even ask me how I felt about going." Jill was furious at the memory. "You just stuffed me in the car like a bag of laundry and hauled me away."

"You were bleeding to death, dammit!" Steve was livid.

"We could have talked about it first," Jill insisted.

"Where? In the morgue?" Steve shouted. "It was too late for talking. If you had told me *before* you had an impulse to pick up the razor, I would have stopped you."

"You stopped me from doing enough things when we were married, Steve. You wouldn't let me drive the last two months I was pregnant because you were afraid I'd go into labor in the car."

"When you did, we had barely time to get to the hospital, Jill. If you had been alone, you would have given birth at a Mobil station surrounded by mechanics."

"And I had to go to bed every night right after the eleven o'clock news. I was the only person in America who didn't know what Johnny Carson looked like."

"When you stayed up late, your nerves went to hell. Look what happened. Was I wrong?"

"You wouldn't let me eat spicy food—"

"You'd bloat up like a blimp and have a stomach ache all night. And blame *me* for it."

"You made me go to the Schick Center—"

"You said you wanted to quit smoking." Steve glared. "You said you'd do anything to stop."

"And you . . . you . . ." Jill tried to think of any moment in their marriage when Steve hadn't been right. There had to be something, one day, one hour, one minute in all those years. She ran it over in her mind.

Let's see. First we said "I do," then we walked down the aisle, then I tripped over my train and ripped Steve's lapels. Rats!

"Well"—Steve sighed—"all that ended the day I moved out."

"Aha!" Jill wasn't ready to end anything, except possibly Steve. "Not quite. How many about-to-be-ex-husbands tell their about-to-be-ex-wives what divorce lawyer to hire. Huh? Tell me that?"

Steve leaned on the back of the chair. "Jill, you came to me crying, saying your lawyer was ripping you off, asking my advice."

"I was just asking your professional opinion. I didn't ask you to call my lawyer and fire him!"

"You were weeping in my office, Jill," Steve said through clenched teeth, "sitting in my client chair, wringing your hands and threatening to go insane!"

Embarrassed, Jill sat at the table and studied its surface. "Well . . . I might have been . . . exaggerating. I was somewhat distraught."

"Bananas! You were bananas! You had an impulse to slash at your wrists, then you decided you didn't want to die. You had an impulse to run off with another man, then you said you were sorry when I found out. Not just once, Jill. Twice! Once can happen to anyone. Well, maybe. But twice is a pattern. Did you expect me to wait for three? Three is *wanton!*" He turned toward her, his eyebrows and Adam's apple bobbing wildly about. "Do I look like the kind of man who'd be married to a wanton woman?" He lowered his voice to a sad, mournful sigh. "You don't think things through, Jill. You don't consider the consequences."

"Oh, Steve. What am I going to do?" Jill burst into tears. She flung her head toward the table, intending to bury her head in her arms, but struck her eye on a box of vanilla pudding instead. "Ouch!"

"Jill, what's wrong?" Steve was at her side.

"Dan Carmichael's left the company, and I'm scared!"

"What happened? Was he fired?"

"No." Jill sniffed, touched her stinging eye with one tentative finger, and told Steve the whole story. He listened intently, looking straight into her tear-filled eyes.

"I'm so sorry," Steve said finally. "Sorry for Dan and sorry about Nancy. I met her once. Quite a lady."

"She certainly was. Now Dan's gone, and I've no one to depend on, no one to—" Jill stopped, sniffling. Steve wouldn't know what she meant by a rod and a staff. To him such a person was someone who'd direct her every waking moment.

"What about that guy you just hired? Alex . . . uh . . ."

"Friedman?" Jill winced as Steve turned her head, examining her eye.

"Pretty bad scrape. It may swell." He dabbed at her eye with his handkerchief. "Friedman should be of some help."

Alex wasn't any comfort. Why would he be of any help?

"I'm sure he will . . . ow!" She pulled away from his dabbing.

"I know it hurts, Jill, but if you don't let me fix it, you might get an infection."

Jill sat still, allowing Steve to fix her eye with the same efficiency with which he fixed everything else.

"You should have called me from Cleveland, you know. I could

220

have given you legal advice. That lawyer was pushing you. So was the doctor. And you should have told me about Dan when I got home from the store. I would have realized you were upset. We wouldn't have gotten into a pointless discussion about past mistakes." Steve leaned closer and touched Jill's cheek gently. "Next time tell me. Will you?"

She nodded yes, trying to avoid the direct and steady gaze that seemed to be reading her thoughts. That he read her distress about Dan was acceptable. She'd volunteered that. What she had to protect was her unforeseen and subversive desire to be held by Steve, to be comforted, calmed, and soothed in arms that had proved reassuring through countless restless nights and endless frightening days. She had long since forfeited the right to his comfort, both de facto and de jure.

Still, as she looked into the eyes that had looked into hers over breakfast tables, Daisy's crib, anniversary dinners, and across rooms at cocktail parties, PTA meetings, and divorce court, she considered it. Longed for it.

You can't go back.

I want to—just for tonight.

Tough luck, lady.

"What's going on?" Daisy stood in the doorway, frowning at them both.

"We were having a discussion," Steve replied.

"What's wrong with your eye, Mom?" Daisy asked, suspicious. "Did anyone throw anything?"

"Of course not, Daisy." Jill was shocked. "We don't throw things. Well, not anymore. I banged my eye on a box of pudding, and your Dad was trying to help."

"I should have known," Daisy said. "As soon as the divorce papers were signed, you two turned into Eleanor and Franklin. Everybody else's parents turn into Margaret and Pierre. You two are the only ones I know who cry."

"Your mother's an emotional woman, Daisy," Steve said quickly. "Will you please get some Sporene ointment from the medicine cabinet?"

"Daisy, what did you mean—*you two*?" Jill's hand pressed her rapidly swelling eye.

"The ointment's next to the mouthwash, Daisy. Please hurry. Your mother's eye is a mess."

"I want to know what Daisy meant," Jill insisted.

Daisy looked from her mother, who wanted the question answered, to her father, who obviously didn't. "What's Sporene ointment?"

"An antiseptic." Steve sighed with relief. "I'm sure your mother has some at home."

"Uh-uh. When Mom cuts herself, she gives it a squirt of Chanel Number Five. I *never* cut myself." Daisy flounced down the hall toward the bathroom.

Jill squinted at Steve. "What did she mean—*you two*?"

"You should recognize her adolescent sense of drama. You live with it."

"I thought I lived with the logic queen. C'mon, Steve."

"Chanel Number Five?" he asked loudly.

"The alcohol kills the germs and I smell good."

"Bananas."

"Resourceful."

"Here's the ointment." Daisy handed the tube to Steve, who spread a careful fingerful around Jill's eye.

"It smells like rancid tuna fish." Jill tried to hold her breath.

"Hold still, this is just what you need."

Jill held still, trying to remember where she'd heard that before. Dan? No. She remembered. It had been Alex who'd said it, and Dan that she'd needed—or perhaps what she needed was Steve.

The tears splashed down her cheeks, bringing a rancid tuna fish taste to her mouth.

"Does your eye hurt that bad, Mom?" Daisy was all frowns and concern.

"Your mother's exhausted. She needs a good night's sleep."

Daisy's frown disappeared. "I have a wonderful idea. We can sleep here tonight. Mom won't have to drive home."

Oh, God, the kid's playing Cupid, and I'm so confused, it sounds good. If I stay here tonight and don't stay forever, it'll break Daisy's heart.

"Where's my purse?" Jill struggled to her feet. "We have to go home."

Propelled by the fear of Daisy's ongoing (and Jill's latest) fantasy, Jill hurried into the living room, with Daisy on her heels.

"But I have all my things here, Mom. I can sleep in my room, and you can sleep—"

"At home in my own bed," Jill finished quickly.

"I was going to say you could sleep with me. You don't have to get bent."

"That's not such a bad idea," Steve remarked from the doorway. "You're really done in, Jill, and your eye is damn near shut. You could go right to sleep now—"

"No! I want to go home." Jill knew she sounded like a child grown tired and cranky at a birthday party, but she didn't care. "Kiss your father good night, Daisy. I'll wait in the car."

She sat in the car, waiting for Daisy and wishing she'd asked Steve for ice. Her eye was beginning to throb.

She glanced at the clock on the dashboard. *Rats.* She hadn't had it fixed. If it wasn't for Steve's proddings and reminders about servicing and warranties, she'd never have anything fixed. Steve had a knack for making timely repairs, while Jill's propensity had always been to ignore signs of deterioration until the only option remaining was to discard old for new.

All right. I'll get the clock fixed. And on the way home I'll stop at Carl's and pick up my watch.

Daisy opened the car door, jumped in, and handed Jill a round object. "Dad sent you this."

"What the hell is it?" Jill squealed, dropping the thing in her lap. It was a blob, as ice cold and clammy as everyone's nightmare of death.

"It's an ice bag, Mom, for your eye. Are you sure you don't want to stay here tonight? You're a wreck."

"I know." Jill started the engine. "So, I can either sit here, sending up flares, or I can tow myself home."

"I'll hold the ice bag on your eye while you drive," Daisy offered.

"Just be careful. I haven't lived my life yet."

Jill backed out of the driveway, thinking how peculiar it was that though she'd already lived two or three lives, she was in essentially the same drifting boat as Daisy—waiting to live the life she wanted.

Jill turned the car radio to Daisy's favorite station and immediately felt self-consciously ancient. The golden oldies they played were songs from 1972. Daisy held the ice bag to Jill's eye and sang along with a group of young men who were evidently upset about the night Chicago died.

Aren't we all? Jill turned right onto an off ramp.

"Why are we getting off here, Mom?"

"I left my watch at a friend's house. I'm going to pick it up."

"Patti? Or a boyfriend?"

"A man who is also a friend." Jill wished she'd realized that Daisy would want an explanation. What had Steve said about not thinking things through?

"Which boyfriend is it?" Daisy pursued. "Suave or sexy?"

"He's just a friend, Daisy."

"So how come you left your watch in the house of 'just a friend'?" Daisy asked, sounding wise.

"I . . . uh . . . don't remember."

"Oh, sure." Daisy was smug. "You even sleep with your watch on. The only time you ever take it off is when you take showers. Do you take showers at 'just a friend's' houses?"

"That's enough, Daisy," Jill warned her. "I'm too tired to play Perry Mason. I've told you Dr. Foster is a friend and that's all." She pulled up in front of Carl's apartment. "Wouldn't you be upset if I implied that Lenny is more than a friend to you?"

"Yeah," Daisy agreed. "But that's me, and you're you. Face it, Mom, you're carnal."

"Daisy!" Jill reached for the hand that was holding the ice bag to her eye and pulled it away. "How can you say that?"

"That's not an insult, Mom. If a woman isn't carnal by the time she's your age, it'll never happen. Women who never become carnal get dried-up and cranky and won't let their children grow up. My psych teacher, Mr. Hahn, said so."

"That's what they're teaching in school?"

"Mr. Hahn wasn't exactly teaching," Daisy explained. "He was talking about his wife. She never got carnal, and he says she's a bitch."

"Oh, God," Jill groaned. "For this I pay taxes."

"He said we should give our parents lots of privacy if we want to get out of the house before we're thirty-eight." Daisy sighed. "Maybe I didn't give you and Dad enough privacy."

"You gave us more than enough," Jill assured her. "It's not your fault we used it for fighting. Now you wait here—"

"I want to come with you. I want to see if he looks like he sounds on the phone. From the way he goes on about getting down and getting real and being honest and open, I've been picturing Obi-Wan Kenobi."

"Picture Henry Sitzbach on the *Six O'Clock See It Now News,* only without the charisma. You'd be closer. Wait here."

"But, Mom," Daisy protested.

"Give me a break, Daisy. If I tell him you're waiting for me in the car, he'll just hand me my watch, and I'll leave. If you come in, he'll feel the need to be charming and impress you with holistic theories and, God forbid, boiled fish. Do you want to drink fruit juice and hear about being open and honest for the next two hours?"

Daisy thought it over. "I'm too young for that kind of excitement. Hurry up, Mom. I'll lock the car doors."

Jill trotted up the path, then took the stairs two at a time. The throbbing in her eye was spreading throughout her head, but she felt this the best possible time to recover the watch. Carl would have a minimum amount of time to ooh and aah over her eye, give unwanted advice, and ask about her trip. It would give him no time at all to discuss the marriage proposal Jill considered Carl's triumph of mind over matter—he'd made up his mind, and her opinion didn't matter.

She knocked at his door. The lights were on. Jill knew that Carl, even more frugal than Julie, would not have the kilowatts piling up if he were not at home. She tapped again, without response, then tried the door and was startled as it swung open under her touch. She stepped in, calling "Carl, Carl."

Still no answer. Definitely worried, Jill decided to investigate. No telling what could have happened. The L.A.P.D. was forever breaking down the doors of apartments where people lived alone, in response to complaints from the neighbors that "something smells funny." Most often the cops found that a tenant in arrears had made a midnight move, leaving no forwarding address, but plenty of garbage. But occasionally they found the tenant, bloated, blue, and, like the garbage, needing to be hauled away in a Hefty Bag.

Jill tiptoed into the apartment, shuddering with guilt over having made fun of Carl and neglecting to call.

If he's alive, I'll marry him. It's the least I can do.

There was a sound coming from the bedroom Carl used primarily as a den. She hurried down the hall and looked in.

"For Christ's sake"—she whistled softly—"this really takes the cake."

He was sprawled in his easy chair, head back, snoring lightly with the sound Jill had always thought of as his post-coital wheeze. Opposite him, in the space he'd told her was a storage area for books, wood-louvered doors framed a flickering television set. On the television set three zaftig ladies all America knew but Carl had claimed never to have seen, romped and jiggled. The son-of-a-bitch hypocrite had fallen asleep watching *Goldfarb's Girls.*

"Goddamn, I ought to dump his organic apple juice over his head and give him a holistic thrill."

Briefly she considered waking him with a shrill "Aha! Gotcha, you bastard!" but thought of Daisy in the car. She knew Carl would rise to the occasion with a defense that, if not stirring, would be wordy enough to make the *Bakke* decision simplistic by comparison. And she'd eventually accept his defense, not because of its incontrovertible truth, but because a dedicated semanticist can take you to Pittsburgh and convince you it's Bombay if that's what he chooses to do.

She hadn't time to cope with Carl's words or the energy to deal with the anger she felt at the way he'd always loaded television with contempt and, through guilt by association, heaped it on her.

"You can go screw yourself, Carl," she whispered, "because I won't. Not anymore."

She retrieved her watch from his bedroom dresser and left the apartment, locking the door behind her. She'd fix him. The next time they talked, she'd ask for her watch. Let the son of a bitch go nuts searching his apartment.

She was forced to tap on the car window twice before Daisy— who'd learned from *Baretta* that stranglers are not above disguising themselves as priests, old ladies, or mothers—would unlock the door.

"Was he upset because you ran in and ran out, Mom?"

"Actually, Daisy, I've never seen Carl quite so open and honest."

They arrived home just as a fine, misting drizzle was beginning to form small, trickling rivers on the windshield.

"Just in time," Jill said. "My luggage won't get soaked."

"The ice has all melted," Daisy shook the ice bag. "Wasn't it lucky Dad thought of it?"

"Your father lives smart. He's always said there's no such thing as luck. If there was, maybe we'd still be married." Jill was surprised at the wistfulness that had crept into her voice.

"Maybe Dad's luck is changing, Mom. Have you met his neighbor?"

"No." Jill was startled.

"Dad says I should call her Mrs. Barnstrom, but she says I should call her Susan. She brings him casseroles with zucchini and cheese."

"Older widow-type lady?" Jill asked casually.

"Divorced. No kids, blond, about a size seven—"

"I don't think we should discuss your father's friends, Daisy—"

"—teaches political science at UCLA . . . campaigns for the ERA . . . wants to go into politics someday—"

"Help me get my stuff in the house, Daisy. My suitcases will get mildewed."

"She used to be a legal secretary," Daisy said. "Dad says she has an orderly mind."

Jill jumped out of the car, slamming the door so hard the car rocked. "Take this." She handed a suitcase to Daisy.

"Dad says she gets so much done because she's well organized. He said I should use her as an example."

"Being organized is an ability that often develops with age. Your father is older than I am, and I'm certain this Mrs. Barnstrom person—"

"She's younger than you, so you'd better get with it."

"And you'd better get in the house before your sniffles turn into pneumonia and you kiss your concert good-bye," Jill snapped. "I can be twice as strict as your father, you know."

"That'll be the day." Daisy smirked, then turned, skipped a few feet, stopped, and returned to where Jill, exhausted and woeful, stared unseeing through the deepening drizzle.

"I only told you about Susan so you know you don't have forever to get back together with Dad. Don't worry, Mom. It's like *Gone With the Wind*. You'll think of something."

"I'll think about it tomorrow." Jill wished she wasn't too tired to enjoy Daisy's simple approach to complexities, her single-minded pursuit of scattered possibilities.

"Okay, Mom, just don't wait too long. Dad would kill me if he knew I told you, but he really has cried—"

"He has?"

"On your wedding anniversary—or what would have been. I reminded him of what day it was. Dad cleared his throat, harumphed, and said he'd forgotten, but there were tears in his eyes. Then he got all embarrassed and said he was allergic to the cleaning lady's furniture polish."

"Maybe he was telling the truth," Jill suggested, remembering how careful she'd been to spend her last three anniversaries in the company and, eventually, the beds of other men. *We all have our own way of crying.*

227

"I can get Susan's recipe for zucchini and cheese," Daisy offered. "I won't tell her it's for you."

"Go in the house, Daisy. I'm right behind you."

After they'd wrestled the suitcases into the house, Jill sent Daisy to shower and get ready for bed, then collapsed on her bed, thinking that this was one of those times when fatigue was a friend. She would have to think about everything tomorrow. Her head had thought its last thought for today.

Within a few minutes she was drowsing and drifting, carried along on an amiable tide, a rhythm natural before birth and elusive ever after, smiling at a half-dream, half-vision of herself, standing before a gray clapboard house at the edge of a sunlit beach. She knew she'd come home and wondered how home can be a place you've never seen. She watched herself walk up a sandy path, relaxed but eager for the inside of the house. She was about to open the door when the phone rang.

Caught in a warp between two realities, Jill tried to shake herself fully into the reality where the phone was ringing. She fumbled for the receiver.

"Jill, I know it's late, but I had to call you. . . ."

"Patti?" Jill opened her eyes, or rather the one that would open, and struggled to sit up. She groaned, feeling like the victim of one of those accidents where no one gets the license number but witnesses agree that the culprit was an old/young, man/woman driving a Chevy/unicycle. "What time is it? I was asleep."

"Oh, sorry, Jill, honest, but I just had the juiciest, most incredible, fabulous fuck since . . . since . . ."

"Yesterday?"

"I knew you'd want to hear about it—I mean, you two are practically related." Patti laughed.

Jill swung her legs over the side of the bed, then clamped a hand over her eye, certain it was about to fall in her lap. "Listen, Patti, I've had a really rough day. Can we talk about the gorgeous kid tomorrow?"

"Gor— oh, him. I sent him packing. He was wonderful, a bona fide second-best lay . . . but, oh, the life-style. After we went to the ballgame, we went to the Roxy. It was packed with freaks who looked like my worst Thorazine nightmares, and once we got in the show, it wasn't a show. It was a frontal assault by psychopaths with safety pins through their noses. Punk rock makes my teeth ache, Jill. I mean, whatever happened to rock and roll? I was into that from the start. . . . Jerry Lee Lewis, the Beatles, Morrison, Hendrix, Joplin. . . . I even freaked out at Woodstock, but this—"

"Do you think we can talk about the decline of rock and roll tomorrow, Patti? I have to see if Daisy's in bed—"

"So I went flying out of the Roxy before the end of one set, with Rog trailing behind me. Well, of course I wanted to come right home and hop into bed. I mean, that's what he's for, isn't it? But Rog wanted to stop at the Roller Palace and, honey, that was it. I haven't been on skates since fourth grade, when I skinned both knees and put my lower teeth through my lip—the plastic guy fixed that when he did my nose. There isn't a lay alive worth broken bones."

"I agree, Patti." Jill knew from experience that the only thing to do with a wound-up Patti was let her run down.

"A bruised hip once in a while isn't so bad. I don't mean on purpose. I'm not a masochist. But sometimes those ex-jocks don't know their own strength, and when they get to banging away—"

"I'm sorry your romance broke up." Jill tried to sound sympathetic.

"Oh, that's not what I called you about. After I left Rog at the Roller Palace and came home, *someone* dropped by." She was gleefully mysterious. "Guess."

"Santa Claus? Mrs. Olsen with a pound of mountain-grown?"

"Alex! The doorbell rang, and there he was! He said he'd just dropped by to thank me for being so terrific to Nina, so what could I do? I invited him in for a glass of wine, and he had a couple of joints, and one thing led to another . . . and whistling Christ, Jill, that's the juiciest man!"

"Alex?"

"The *best*!" Patti enthused. "I've finally found the first-best lay!"

"Alex Friedman?" In addition to the throbbing, her head seemed to be spinning. "Tonight?"

"He told me I fuck like an angel, and I told him he fucks like the devil himself."

"The Alex Friedman who works for me?"

"Well, of course," Patti replied. "Is there another Alex Friedman?"

"Earth isn't that big a planet." Jill groaned.

"You must be tired, Jill." Patti sounded disappointed. "I thought you'd be interested. And excited."

"There are no words to describe my feelings," Jill said, with the absolute conviction of truth.

"Well . . . okay." Patti sighed. "But, Jill, don't forget. Within your horny little grasp is someone who's married, safe, and the world's best—"

"Me!" Jill yelled. "Me!"

"Sure, that's why I called. He's perfect for you. You even work with him, Jill, and I don't mind sharing—"

"Me! How can you think— He's married! I work with him!"

"That's what I just said. He's perfect! Jill, what the hell's going on? I thought—"

"Mom!" Daisy was leaning against the doorway, bent over almost double, her face like powdered ash. "I have cramps again."

"Oh, Daisy, no. Good-bye, Patti." Jill hung up immediately. Daisy was moaning with pain.

"It's awful, Mom," Daisy whimpered.

"I know, honey." Jill put her arm around Daisy and helped her into her room. "I'll get the heating pad and aspirins, and tomorrow I'm taking you to the doctor's."

Daisy made a face. "I don't want to go to the doctor's, but I'm getting tired of this, Mom."

"I don't blame you, Daisy. Problems that go on without resolutions eventually wear people out."

Jill plied Daisy with the old standard remedies, then sat by her bed until Daisy said she could fall asleep. Jill pulled the light summer quilt to the tip of Daisy's chin, tucking her in as though she was still the Daisy of teddy bears and Dr. Dentons.

"Sleep tight, Daisy. You'll feel better in the morning." Jill brushed strands of hair away from Daisy's eyes, gently kissing the nose that was the duplicate of her own.

"I know I'll feel better," Daisy said, either believing it or echoing Jill's jerry-built optimism. "We should talk about Dad's birthday, Mom. I think we should have a party."

"Tomorrow, Daisy, when you've had some rest."

"But we have to plan something nice before Susan does. She'll ask Dad first."

"Tomorrow, honey." Jill's fingertips massaged the sides of Daisy's neck with the soft, easy strokes that had always calmed her, even in her cradle. "Sleep now."

Daisy's lashes fluttered, and she purred like a drowsy kitten. "I'm counting on you, Mom. Don't blow it."

Jill smiled. "Don't worry about Dad's birthday, honey. He might have a problem choosing between me and Susan the Perfect, but I know he'll want to spend that evening with you."

Jill turned out the light and returned to her room, where she stretched out on the bed.

Nothing compounds but loss . . . and worry.

Jill knew that her next sojourn on an amiable tide would be hours, not minutes, away. She reached for the television remote control and flipped the switch. Gradually a movie, grainy with age and jumping with slipped frames, came into focus. Jill watched for several minutes but didn't see anything or anyone familiar. It didn't matter. Jill's sole purpose in watching was to keep her mind from the whirlwind of Steve's neighbor, Daisy's dysfunction, and Alex, Patti's long-sought-after best lay.

And I thought Alex was mediocre.

Who are you trying to kid?

He was godawful!

So Jill pondered, waiting for Joan Blondell to appear. She had to appear. She was in all of these movies.

Maybe it isn't Alex. Patti thinks he's terrific. Alex thinks he's terrific. Oh, shit! On top of everything else, I'm a rotten lay!

Jill groaned, turning her head into the pillow just as Joan Blondell swung into the bar, hips three seconds ahead of her torso, and said "Howya doin', kid?" to the pug with the mug.

CHAPTER 16

"I'm fixing your breakfast, honey," Jill said through Daisy's closed bedroom door. "We have to leave for the doctor's in less than an hour."

"How did you get the appointment so fast?" Daisy yawned her way past Jill, tousled and leggy in a blue-striped nightshirt. "You didn't tell him it was an emergency, did you?"

"I told him how you felt last night and that this has been going on for a while," Jill explained, grateful that Dr. Baker, who could always resist a patient in agony, was an absolute sucker for worried mothers.

"I hope you didn't make me sound like Ali MacGraw in *Love Story.* I hate having anyone hovering and clucking over me."

"Who hovers and clucks? I don't hover and cluck."

"But you'd like to, and you would if I let you." Daisy smirked, closing the bathroom door.

In less than an hour they were juiced, egged, toasted, and on their way down Ventura Boulevard toward the doctor's office.

Jill leaned over to pat Daisy's hand. "Try not to be nervous, honey."

"I'm not nervous, Mom."

"I know that the first examination by a gynecologist can be . . . traumatic . . . but I hope you won't be apprehensive. Or embarrassed."

"I don't like going to doctors, but I'm not apprehensive. Why would I be embarrassed?"

"Well . . . you know." Jill hesitated, startled by the sudden thought that Daisy might *not* know. She swerved to the curb, parked, and turned to Daisy. "*Do* you know about . . . what Dr. Baker. . . . I mean . . . the procedure . . . ?"

Daisy rolled her eyes. "Do I look like a person who thinks she's on her way to have her tonsils checked out?"

"But the examination itself—"

"Mom." Daisy was trying to be patient. "I've had three health classes, including one for girls only. I've seen films like *The Miracle of Menstruation* and *Birth: The Natural Way.* My social-science teacher is pregnant and one of those people who believes in 'sharing the experience.' I've read your copy of *Our Bodies, Ourselves,* some of my friends have had GYN exams, and of course I've learned a lot from you."

"What have you learned from me?" Jill demanded, frantically wondering if Daisy might have overheard her conversations with Patti.

"Remember the book you gave me when I was seven, the one with the cartoon eggs and sperm?"

"With mommy and daddy faces." Jill smiled, guiding the car into the mainstream of traffic. "Silly, huh?"

"I thought it was wonderful," Daisy said enthusiastically. "Just when I was wondering where babies came from, you gave me that book. How did you know I was wondering?"

"Because I was that age when I started wondering, Daisy. And asking questions."

"Did Grandma give you a book?"

Jill laughed. "Grandma told me that when a man and woman get married, they light a candle in church. If God hears their prayer for a baby, they find one sleeping in their bed when they get home."

"What a thing to tell a little kid!" Daisy exclaimed indignantly.

"Some people can't talk about sex." Jill shrugged. "From cradle to grave the subject is taboo. At Our Lady of Perpetual Repression sex education consisted of studying the reproductive system of crayfish. My first menstrual period came as a complete surprise."

"What did Grandma say about that?"

"She said, 'Now you are a woman.' I wasn't quite eleven at the time. She told me it would happen once a month. . . . She didn't say why. . . . I should stop wrestling with my brother, and I shouldn't take a bath when I had the curse because I might get TB."

"How could she tell you that?" Daisy was incredulous.

"She believed it, Daisy. That's what her mother had told her. When there's no sex education, it's myths that get handed down."

Daisy shook her head. "If I was being raised like that, I'd go crazy."

"From your mouth to God's ear." Jill laughed, turning into the

233

parking lot. She pulled into a space and stopped the car. "Sure you're okay, honey?"

"Positive, Mom." Daisy looked impishly at her mother. "A woman takes these things in stride."

"How silly of me to forget." Jill laughed. "Let's go. You'll like Dr. Baker. If you were going to cast him in a movie, he'd be the favorite uncle who brings fuzzy bunnies and always says the right thing."

"I'd rather have a doctor I'd cast as a doctor, Mom. Lenny can bring me fuzzy bunnies."

"He's a good doctor. Honest."

While Daisy was being examined, Jill sat in the waiting room across from a young girl not older than Daisy, who was, as Kate used to say "in a family way." There was no maternal "glow" about her, no Madonna-like aura. Her ankles were swollen, her eyes shadowed with circles, and she moved restlessly, trying to find a comfortable position. She was heartbreakingly young, pale, and exhausted, and Jill found herself hoping that, for Daisy, motherhood would be in the distant future, a clear and joyful choice.

I'd better meet Lenny soon. I'm beginning to hate him already.

Finally Daisy emerged from the examining room, looking surprisingly like Daisy. Jill jumped up.

"How was it, Daisy?"

"I didn't love it a lot, but it didn't ruin my life, so you can relax, Mom." Daisy smiled at Jill's anxious look.

"Well, what did he say? What's wrong?" Jill demanded.

Daisy was casual. "He said that I shouldn't worry, it's just one of those things."

"One of *what* things?" Jill asked frantically. "Phases of the moon, an old Gypsy curse, voodoo—what?"

"He said he'd talk to you himself if you got all tweaked. Boy, has he got you pegged."

Jill rapped on the receptionist's window. A few minutes later she was sitting in the office across from Dr. Baker, who wore pleasantness like aftershave.

"That's some fine lady you have there." Baker said exactly the right thing. "You must be very proud."

"I certainly am—when I'm not tearing my hair out. What's wrong with her, doctor?"

"It's a menstrual dysfunction."

"I knew that before I got here. What's the cause? What's the cure?"

"At her age it's most likely a temporary hormonal imbalance, very common actually and usually self-correcting. Of course it could be a more permanent type of deficiency. Diet could be a factor, or stress. The pituitary is sometimes involved—"

"What is this, multiple choice?"

"Now, Mother, relax," Baker said soothingly. "I've ruled out anything serious. There are no tumors, cysts, lesions, gross pelvic abnormalities—"

"*Stop!* I don't want to hear about the horrible things it could have been!" Jill clutched the arms of the chair.

Dr. Baker regarded her thoughtfully. "How did Daisy react to your divorce?"

"Very well. In fact, she was wonderful. She told us that she knew we both loved her and the divorce was nobody's fault, just one of those things that happens in the best of families and . . . oh, dear."

"That's a rather mature reaction for a twelve-year-old, wouldn't you say?" He nodded wisely.

"I didn't react that maturely, and I was thirty-two." Jill groaned. "Maybe if I hadn't fallen apart, Daisy could have acted more her age."

"Perhaps. And perhaps Daisy's reaction would have been no different. Still there's always an emotional aftermath to divorce."

"Daisy has emotional problems?" Jill gasped.

'Now, now, I'm not saying that. I'm just saying we have to consider all the factors when treating a patient. Don't buy a problem until it's a problem, Jill. I would say you have more than enough right now. You're alone, concerned about your daughter, and . . . um . . . well . . ."

"What?" Jill couldn't have forgotten a problem. It was names she forgot and the good things. "What are you talking about?"

"Sometimes a physician is . . . um . . . reluctant to mention a . . . um . . . black eye," he said hesitantly.

"Oh, this? It's nothing." Jill shrugged it off. "I hit my face on vanilla pudding."

"Oh?"

"A box," Jill elaborated. "My eye hit the corner."

"Pudding." He nodded.

"In my ex-husband's kitchen. Steve took care of it."

"So I see."

"No, you don't. Oh, rats." Jill sighed. "Let's get back to Daisy. What can we do?"

"Just keep an eye on her for now. If this continues I can put her on birth-control pills, but I'd rather wait. These things usually straighten themselves out, given a little time."

He rose from his chair and came around the desk. "I know it's not easy to be patient when you're worried about your daughter, but try."

"And the emotional problems?" Jill asked anxiously.

"*Possible* emotional problems," he corrected. "If Daisy's having a delayed reaction to your divorce, she should get over it."

"Should? *Should* is not a comforting word, Dr. Baker," Jill frowned.

"Don't worry, but do be alert for additional symptoms."

"Additional . . . ?"

"Nightmares, insomnia, regressive behavior, you know, thumb-sucking, wetting the bed, like that . . . various manifestations of acting out . . . overeating, anorexia, promiscuity, running away from home . . ."

"Oh, my God!"

"Now, Mother, relax." He laid his uncle's hand on her shoulder and patted gently. "I didn't say any of these will happen, I just said be alert."

"Alert? I will never sleep again!"

"The *worst* thing you can do is act like there's something wrong."

"You mean I'm supposed to act like everything's normal and be alert for signs of abnormality, both at the same time?"

"Exactly." He smiled.

"Bernhardt wasn't that good an actress. Fonda would have trouble with this."

"Try not to forget that Daisy's problem will likely correct itself without intervention. So, don't overreact. And call me if anything happens."

"Call? You'll hear from me without help from Ma Bell." Jill walked to the waiting room, thinking that her life was becoming ever less like *The Waltons* and more like *They Shoot Horses, Don't They?*

Daisy looked up from the *Vogue* she'd been reading. "Finally!" she exclaimed. "I thought you two were in there having an affair."

"Daisy!"

"Well, what else could it be? Even *your* life story wouldn't take this long."

"We were just talking, Daisy." Jill wondered if Daisy's irritability was an "additional symptom." "Sometimes that takes a while."

"I've missed English, History, and Nutrition. I always have Nutrition with Lenny."

"Oh, I see. C'mon, you can have lunch with Lenny."

On the way to school Daisy bubbled with plans for Steve's birthday. "So, you ask him to dinner, Mom. And ask him where he'd like to go. Hey—maybe Dad would like it if you cooked, you know, rare roast beef and that casserole he used to like. Wouldn't that be nice, Mom?"

"Very," Jill replied, looking sideways at Daisy, whose dancing visions of old times would have been clear to a stranger. "I'll call him today, Daisy. We'll work something out."

"You don't think he'll have other plans, do you, Mom?"

"Of course not, honey," Jill replied, knowing that Steve, whatever his plans, would be with Daisy on his birthday.

"Maybe Dad could even come for breakfast and spend the day. We could go out for brunch, to that place we used to take you on Mother's Day. . . ."

"What did you dream about last night, Daisy?" Jill pulled up to the curb in front of the school.

"Dream?" Daisy looked puzzled. "I don't know. Something weird, I suppose."

"Why do you suppose?" Jill pounced on it. "Do you often have weird dreams?"

"Sure." Daisy jumped out of the car. "Doesn't everybody?"

"What did you dream?" Jill persisted. Whatever it was, she'd repeat it verbatim to Dr. Kerry, who viewed most dreams as additional symptoms.

Daisy leaned halfway out the car window. "Who can remember?" She wrinkled her nose. "Violence, sex, hard drugs, rock and roll."

"Daisy! Are you serious? You're teasing. You're not teasing. You're serious. You're not serious?"

"What I am is late." Daisy grinned. "Thanks, Mom."

"For what?"

"For seeing me through another rite of passage. I didn't think you were going to make it, but somehow you always come through."

"Well, my goodness." Jill didn't know what to say. "You're welcome, Daisy. My pleasure."

"If you need any help with the change of life, do let me know." Daisy laughed. "I'll take you to a film on the Miracle of Menopause."

She waved and ran up the steps to school, leaving Jill looking after her and thinking that whatever the problems, whatever the additional symptoms, whatever rites of passage and confusion ahead, she wouldn't trade places with any other mother, not for a minute.

As she walked into the UBC building the guard at the reception desk startled her with "Morning, Ms. Kenyon, nice day."

"Uh . . . very nice," she replied awkwardly, "uh . . . Ralph."

"Frank," he said, smiling as though his name didn't matter.

"Frank," she repeated.

I'll picture a hot dog in uniform.

"Frank, Frank," she repeated in the elevator. "Frank, Frank, Frank." She wasn't surprised she'd forgotten his name, but she was simply astonished he'd remembered hers.

"Where's Polly?" Jill asked Alex, who was sitting in her chair behind her desk.

"Where the fuck have you been?" Alex slammed down her phone.

"And a gracious good morning to you, too." Jill threw her purse on the couch.

"I was just trying to reach you at home. Where the fuck were you? Where the fuck did you get that black eye?"

"A minor accident," Jill said. "Tell me, Alex, if you couldn't say fuck, would you be able to talk?"

"Accident, my ass." He grinned. "You're into something kinky, sweetstuff, but we'll concentrate on that later. Have you heard the news?"

"What news?" Jill stood next to Alex, tapping the back of her chair.

Alex flashed a jubilant smile. "You've got Dan's job. And I've got yours."

"Oh, God," Jill groaned, leaning against the desk.

Alex jumped up and guided her into her chair. "Sit here," he ordered. "There was a top-level meeting early this morning. They decided to move us both up. At first they were pissed at Dan because of the way he just walked out, but then someone—Neiman, I heard —said it's a waste of time to be angry at a guy who's gone round the bend. He's more to be pitied."

"Dan *hasn't* gone around the bend. He made a decision."

"Walking out on a job like Dan's isn't a decision—it's mental illness. That's what everyone thinks. Except you. And if you know what's good for you, you'll keep your opinion to yourself."

"If I know what's good for me?" Jill echoed. That sounded like the airing of her opinion would be immediately followed by two hooded gangsters' nailing her kneecaps to the floor.

238

"This job will be good for you." Alex knelt next to her chair and beamed up at her in his best Peck's Bad Boy style.

"I'm not ready for this, Alex." Jill sighed. "It's like trying to do surgery after one year's pre-med. I haven't learned enough yet."

"What's to learn? You could run this fucking company right now better than the fools who are doing it. I know I could. And don't forget, angel, you got me. I'll be with you every step of the way."

"In that case my worries are over," Jill groaned.

"They should be." Alex smiled. He patted her knee gently, then began stroking it with a motion that gradually lengthened and swept halfway up her thigh.

"Don't, Alex." Jill removed his hand.

"You're right. I'll behave. People have been popping in and out of here all morning. Of all days for you to be late! Neiman's been in a dozen times to inform you of your promotion. And Carolyn McCaffery bounced by with her kid. And Fontaine. And, shit, half the staff. Even Zippy dropped in, and all there was to congratulate was your empty chair."

"Did he notice?"

"Zippy's a real power here, Jill. You've got to stop turning your nose up at him."

"I wouldn't do that, Alex. He might stuff something up it."

Alex's face twisted with frustration. "I don't understand your fucking attitudes. Carmichael flips out, and you act like your father died. You're not excited about your promotion. You don't want to schmooze the people who can help you. And you didn't even call me last night!"

"Call you? Wasn't my heartfelt thanks at the door enough?" Jill reached for a cigarette. "You're right, Alex. I should have sent you roses."

"I didn't mean that. I meant that it's important we keep in touch. My career is linked to yours and—"

"You weren't home last night, Alex." Jill cut him off abruptly, wondering if his narcissism would compel him to tell her about Patti Gerard.

He looked at her blankly. "Oh, yeah, that's right. But I called you this morning. Where the fuck were you?"

"I took my daughter to the doctor's."

"Christ! On the most important morning of your life?" He was incredulous. "Isn't there somebody you can hire to do stuff like that, a nanny or something? The head of the movie department can't be schlepping kids around like a housewife."

Jill picked up her purse. "I'll leave you to your new office, Alex." Jill stopped at the door but didn't turn around. "You're not a sensitive person, Alex. Did you know that?"

"Only schmucks have time to be sensitive, Jill, and I'm no schmuck. I'm a winner."

Jill nodded, not in agreement with his sentiments but in acknowledgment of her first unconditionally comfortable moment with him. Alex had finally defined himself, and Jill's roller-coaster ride with him was over. Though it had ended badly, with him on the bad-guy side, she was glad it was done. Though Alex might dismay her in the future, he would never confuse her again.

Jill arrived in Dan's office to find Carolyn McCaffery changing Donny on Dan's desk. Polly sat on the couch, eyes closed and breathing deeply.

"Hi, Jill," Carolyn greeted her. "Congratulations. You must be very excited about your promotion."

"So far it's a learning experience." Jill glanced at Polly. "Is she where I think she is?"

"Polly is . . . uh. . . . What happened to your eye?" Carolyn busied herself fastening the snaps on Donny's jump suit.

"A minor accident."

"I know what you mean," Carolyn said sympathetically. "I used to have them all the time when I was married to my first husband."

"It's nothing like—"

"Not another word," Carolyn interrupted. "You don't have to make up a story for me. I understand."

"But—"

"She's very good, isn't she?" Carolyn indicated Polly. "I hope you don't mind, but I asked Polly if she would try to pick up a vibration for me."

"Limited series?" Jill asked.

"Screw limited series." Carolyn was unexpectedly vehement. "Don't get me wrong, Jill. I like what I do, and I'm good at it. But that's not why I'm consulting Polly this time. My instincts have been telling me to grab Donny and run like hell."

"Why?" Jill asked. "I would think that having your baby in the office would be the best of both worlds."

"At first I thought Lawrence's fuss over Donny was rather sweet and considered a man who likes babies and isn't afraid to say so a

breed apart." Carolyn carefully wiped Donny's tiny, drooly chin.
"Then I began to get nervous in meetings when Lawrence wouldn't
allow me to check Donny's diaper and more nervous when he'd just
walk off with him. There's something wrong when a man carries a
baby around, talking corporate planning as though the baby understood every word."

"What are you going to do?"

"That's what I've asked Polly." Carolyn sat on the couch, stretching Donny across her lap. The baby lifted his head and looked around
curiously. "I like my job, but I like my baby more, and I'm not willing
to trade one for the other. If Polly can come up with a solution—"

"Oh, dear." Polly yawned, without opening her eyes.

"What is it?" Carolyn cried. "What's wrong? What do you see?"

"Middle East turmoil, continuing inflation, the Dodgers in the
toilet, Linda and Jerry split." Polly sighed. "Why do I do this? There's
nothing but trouble."

"What is she talking about?" Carolyn demanded of Jill.

"Sounds like she took a side-trip."

Polly opened her eyes and saw Jill. "Hello." She smiled.

"What is it, Polly?" Carolyn asked anxiously.

"Carolyn," Polly said softly, "is your marriage happy?"

"What?" Carolyn frowned. "Of course."

"Oh," Polly said. "It would save you some trouble if it wasn't."

"What . . . ?"

"I'll tell you all at once. Lawrence already thinks of Donny as his.
Unless there is some kind of intervention, and there might be, his
obsession will only become more pronounced. But he won't take
Donny away from you. He believes a child needs his mother."

"What a surprise! It's such a normal idea."

"Lawrence is latently normal. However he will soon pressure you
to marry him."

"*Marry!* What's my husband supposed to do? Give the bride
away?"

"Don't say that around Lawrence," Polly cautioned. "He'll love
the idea."

Carolyn's eyes flashed. "Why the hell doesn't he marry some
woman and make his own baby?"

"He can't," Polly said solemnly. "He has no balls."

"C'mon, Polly. A man who was an astronaut can't be without courage."

"Courage he has," Polly said. "But he has no balls. You see, something went wrong. Perhaps twelve years of weightlessness produces a condition NASA didn't foresee, or it could have been the continual wearing of a flight suit—who knows? But the reason for his hospitalization at the same time as the chairman of the board, well, Lawrence was undergoing necessary, unfortunate surgery."

"Christ!" Carolyn exclaimed. "No wonder he's . . . whatever he is."

"That's *his* problem," Polly continued. "Yours is that Lawrence wants a son and heir, even more so now that his hopes for immortality in space have been denied. He'll do *anything* to keep Donny!"

"Well, he's not marrying me," Carolyn declared. "And my son is not his ticket to immortality."

"You said there might be some intervention," Jill reminded Polly.

Polly nodded. "A man. But that's iffy because the man is iffy. He has more than one personality, and it depends upon which one gains control. One of his personalities could cause Lawrence to move to another location."

"Who is he?" Carolyn asked.

Polly shrugged. "He's curiously blank. But some people are." She stood up and stretched. "Ahhh, I feel like a rusty gate." She closed her eyes for a moment, then turned to Jill. "I almost forgot. There's a letter on your desk. It was delivered this morning, by messenger, from Dan."

"Dan!" Jill leaped for her desk and the gray folder that held her mail. She found the envelope and ripped it open.

"But what shall I do, Polly?" Carolyn asked. "Shall I wait for this possible intervention, resign, what?"

"I can't make that decision for you. I can only assure you that eventually the answer will come very clear."

"Shit and Shinola!" Carolyn exclaimed. "Until Lawrence arrived this wasn't a bad place to work, even with the Boys' Club." Carolyn picked up her diaper bag and settled Donny more solidly on her hip. "You'll find out, Jill. You can't go to the men's room with them, and they won't invite you into the Club. They close ranks . . . scared shitless of us, they are. . . . It's the territorial imperative, and we're—" She sighed. "I'm going on like this because Lawrence is waiting for Donny in my office, and going on gives me another few minutes alone with my son. That ought to tell me something. See you later, Jill. Good luck, and . . . well, don't take this the wrong way, but that fellow who works for you—Friedman?"

"Alex?" Jill looked up from her letter.

"I ran into him in the hall this morning, and he gushed like a grandpa over Donny. Such coos and gurgles you've never heard, all from a distance of six feet away. That man *hates* babies, Jill. Get the picture?"

Jill nodded. "In living color."

"Get rid of him," Carolyn advised.

"He's Zippy de Franco's new best friend," Jill said. "Neiman thinks he's a young Silverman."

"The Boys' Club strikes again—you're screwed." Carolyn shook her head. "See you at the meeting. I'll be the woman holding the Pampers and wearing the anxious expression."

Jill waved at her absentmindedly, her attention absorbed by the letter. "You'll never guess where Dan is," she told Polly.

"He's in a garden somewhere, I think."

"If there's a garden at the Franciscan monastery in Santa Barbara, you're right." Jill laid the letter on the desk and stared at Polly. "I'd like to say I'm surprised, but I'm not. Part of me knew he'd go somewhere like that. Much as I'll miss him, it would be wrong to wish him back."

"Is he there permanently?"

"He doesn't say. It's more of a note than a letter really. He just tells me that's where he is, and then he says, 'I hope you understand that my decision is the one I feel I must make. Again, wish me well if you can and know that I'm reachable by phone. Being summoned to the phone is not standard procedure here, but the easing of an overburdened conscience is. So, call according to your need. Trust yourself and your perceptions. If you find that hard at first, act as if. . . . Love, Dan.' "

" 'Act as if.' " Polly smiled. "I like that."

"Which perceptions should I trust, Polly?" Jill lit a cigarette and looked out the window. It was beginning to drizzle again. "Do I trust yesterday's perceptions or last week's or the perception I had this morning or the one that might strike after lunch, the perception that tells me to be fearful or the one that urges me to be brave? I have more perceptions than UBC has flop shows, and, like our schedule, they're subject to split-second change."

"Until you know, act as if," Polly advised.

Jill turned away from the window. "Time for the meeting. Hand me my lance, Sancho Panza, and point me toward the windmills."

243

CHAPTER 17

Lawrence's horseshoe slid silently across the floor. "Whee!" he said, his head close to Donny's. "Oo-ums just loves that, doesn't oo?" He scratched Donny behind the ears, much as one might a cat. "We're going to attach a pretty toy to our chair, Donsy, nice birdies or mousies. Won't that be fun?"

Donny gurgled, a reaction Lawrence read as affirmation. He smiled broadly, patting the infant's head. "Doodie."

Lawrence's gaze darted around the room, finally settling on Smythe (MB) Jones. "Make a note of that, Jones, a mobile for the control center."

"Right." Jones all but saluted.

"Now," Lawrence said, "you've all heard of Carmichael's unfortunate collapse." He waited. There was no response from those squeezed, squashed, and jammed around the conference table. He scowled. "You have heard, haven't you?"

There was veritable symphony of *yes, sirs* accompanied by the kind of vigorous head motions usually associated with bobbing for apples.

Jill sat silently, wondering what need compelled them to think of Dan's decision as a mental collapse. They seemed threatened by the idea that one of their number could walk away without a backward glance.

"However," Lawrence continued, "we are fortunate to have within the UBC family just the person who can fill Carmichael's shoes." He pointed at Jill, who was sitting, by choice not by chance, between Neiman and Alex. "Jill Kenyon. Right there. The girl with the shiner."

There was polite applause. Neiman leaned toward Jill. "You'll be wonderful, my dear. Later you'll have to tell me what I'm sure is the titillating story behind that black eye." His face contorted in a half-smile, half-leer, showing off small teeth pointed like needles.

Lawrence raised his hand to still the lingering applause. "Enough. Enough. Now for the exciting news. As the senior executive among us, Dale Neiman will make an important announcement."

"Thank you." Neiman rose to his feet. "I'm sure you all remember that the UBC research department, in conjunction, of course, with the full facilities—"

"Whee!" Lawrence chortled as the horseshoe whooshed across the floor. "Whee!" Lawrence looked up from Donny's rapt face to find everyone staring at him. "What's the matter with you people? Get on with it, Neiman."

"Certainly, sir," Neiman said with the pleasantest of smiles. The face he turned to the table was set in an icy mask.

"UBC has a new symbol, therefore, a new logo, therefore, a new image, therefore, a new overall promotional campaign." Neiman hissed the words through clenched teeth. "Mr. Lawrence and that contraption—"

"Whee!" Lawrence said, in an ominous tone.

"—and Abelard," Neiman corrected himself, "have concluded that a symbol which reflects the origins of UBC will represent us most successfully. As most of you know, UBC's roots lie in an Australian land company formed by four escapees from a penal colony who were later recaptured and returned to some Aboriginal hellhole where presumably they perished. However, in the five years the felons were at large, they managed to build the company into a semi-sizable enterprise which was then confiscated by the government and sold to the highest bidder, a New York manufacturer of saltine crackers." Neiman leafed through his stack of papers and sighed. "I seem to have extensive material concerning the manufacturer and his five lovely daughters. However, I feel that going through it at this time would be extraneous to our purpose."

"There might be a series in it," Carolyn interjected.

"I have just the man for the part of the merchant," Angela said excitedly. "David Doyle. I mean, really, how long can *Charlie's Angels* last? As for the daughters, we simply gather up all those fallen angels, and in one fell swoop—"

"Can we get back to the subject at hand?" Neiman's teeth clenched again. "We'll talk series later. Suffice it to say that saltines begat pretzels, pretzels begat corn chips, corn chips begat Cheese

245

Puffs, and so on and so on until we reach the present time, with diversification as far-reaching as Super Bread, the Maxwell Brothers Circus, off-shore oil drilling, Sylmar Plastics, and, of course, UBC. Well, that's it. Up to date." He laid his notes on the table and sat down, looking weary.

"The symbol, Neiman," Alex whispered, leaning around Jill. "What's the fucking symbol?"

"Oh, shit!" Neiman jumped to his feet. "Just building the moment." He smiled lamely, then shuffled through his notes, found an eight-by-ten glossy, and held it up for the table's appraisal. "This is our new symbol."

"What in the world is it?" Angela asked the question no one else dared to.

"It's a wombat," Neiman replied. "An Australian marsupial." He surveyed the boggled faces before him. "I think I have a headache," he said and sat down.

"It looks like a fucking rat." Alex whispered to Jill.

"Tradition! Bedrock tradition! *Roots!*" Lawrence boomed, sliding up behind Neiman. "Gimme that picture." Neiman handed it back over his shoulder.

Lawrence bounced Donny while waving the picture in the air. "Have you ever *seen* such a face? Look at it! *Look!*"

Necks creaked and craned as everyone rushed to comply, though there seemed to be considerable confusion as to which face they'd been ordered to admire—Lawrence's, Donny's, or the wombat's.

Lawrence held the picture an inch from Donny's nose. The baby cooed.

"Donny *loves* it!" Lawrence exulted. "So will America! This precious little wombat face will become as familiar as Mickey's or Minnie's, Popeye's or Richard Nixon's. Along with this dynamite darling, we have a brilliant new slogan, created by Abelard—'*UBC, Warm as a Wombat!*' Let NBC be proud, CBS be elegant, and ABC be whatever it is besides noisy—UBC will be the network with *warmth,* the network with *heart,* the network that loves *you*! Brilliant! *Brilliant!*" His cheeks glowed dangerously pink. "Well, isn't it? *Isn't it?*"

"Time to change Donny." Carolyn swooped in from his left, snatching Donny from his arms before he knew she was there. "Back in a minute!" Her voice combined perky, chipper, and desperate as she fled from the room with Lawrence shouting after her "Come back, Donny, come back!"

"If you ask my opinion, the wombat is problematical," Angela Kent began.

"You can take your fucking opinion and shove it up your ass!" Lawrence roared. His fist smashed against switches, and the horseshoe flew in the direction of Angela's chair.

"He's trying to run me down!" Angela wailed. "I'm going! I'm going!" Her arms flailed the air, her eyes rolled white, and she pitched off her chair, hitting the floor with a thud.

The room was pandemonium, with cries of "Call an ambulance!" and a scraping of chairs as people scrambled to reach Angela's prone form.

"I'll call the paramedics," Neiman suggested. "Maybe they'll have something for my headache." Holding his head, he ran from the room.

"Is that woman sick?" Lawrence demanded. "Sick people have germs, and, goddammit, we have a baby to consider. Where is Carolyn with Donsy?" He pulled a lever on his horseshoe and hopped out. "Carolyn knows Donsy gets upset when he's away from me." Lawrence followed Neiman out of the conference room.

So many people had clustered around Angela that she'd disappeared from sight. "Do you think she'll be all right?" Jill asked Alex.

"I've got ten bucks says she won't." Alex was digging into his pocket. "That's no spring chicken choking down there."

"Alex!"

"You're on." Zippy matched Alex's ten. "That old broad's going to outlive us all."

As Jill walked away she heard Zippy saying "What the fuck's wrong with Jill?"

"Forget her." Alex scowled. "Let's go down to your office. I've got a dynamite idea—"

Jill heard the double doors clang behind her as she continued down the hall to her office. She'd use this time to call Steve, to invite him to his birthday party, and tell him of her conversation with Dr. Baker.

Once on the phone she *acted as if* it was important she speak to Mr. Kenyon immediately, and, like magic, his secretary put her through. She went through her entire conversation with Dr. Baker, including the *he said*s, *then I said*s.

"You're overreacting again, Jill," Steve said. "Daisy has growing pains, that's all."

"But Dr. Baker said—"

"You told me what he said. He was discussing possibilities, *remote*

247

possibilities, not probabilities, and there wasn't one certainty in the lot."

"But Daisy's problem is—"

"Right now Daisy's biggest problem is a mother who is overly protective. You have a tendency to clutch at only the negative straws. Did you know that about yourself?"

"I'm sure if there's anything I don't know about myself, you'll find it your God-given duty to tell me." Jill winced.

Stop! He needs his mommy/daddy. He's the only mommy/daddy he's ever had.

"I'm only trying to help, Jill. Don't look too hard for symptoms that aren't there. Daisy will sense something and feel pushed." He laughed. "Not that Daisy can be pushed any more than you can. You're both obstinate as hell."

"I know." Jill smiled at the phone. "I think we're both Scarlett O'Hara, each waiting for the other to be Melanie."

"And you're still waiting for Ashley. Well"—he hurriedly changed the subject—"I've got a meeting."

"Before you go, I want to ask you to dinner on your birthday." She added quickly, "It's important to Daisy that you come."

"Set an extra place, and let me know what time to be there. I wouldn't feel a year older without Daisy singing 'Happy Birthday' off key in my ear."

"I'll tell her." Jill smiled. "Thanks, Steve."

"Don't thank me for doing what I want to do, Jill. Thank you for the invitation."

He hung up, and Jill sat back in her chair, wondering how Steve could possibly hear words like *anorexia, promiscuity, emotional problems* and *tumor* without wanting to jump out the window. She mulled it over, then erased *tumor* from the list. That was one of the dreadfuls Dr. Baker said Daisy definitely did *not* have.

She sighed. So, there was some truth after all in Steve's observations. She had clutched at that negative straw, even pushed it from "definitely not" into the "possible" column.

Still, if she overreacted, then Steve underreacted. If her reactions were muddled by overdoses of guilt, then his were equally muddled, but by what? Denial, most certainly, a refusal to admit the existence of negative straws.

She looked out the window. Rain pelted the glass, and a sheet of it hung like a curtain on the far side of Sunset.

Where's the picket? Where do the street crazies go when it rains?

"Meeting's canceled." Alex stuck his head in the door, making a face so amazingly like the wombat's that Jill burst out laughing.

Why not? The jackass is nature's clown.

"Is Angela worse?" Jill asked.

Alex shook his head. "Nah, that old broad's gonna dance on our graves. She signed one of the paramedics to a contract, says he looks like Erik Estrada."

"Then why is the meeting canceled?"

"Lawrence's running all over this fucking building looking for Donny. I'll tell you, Jill, if I was that fucking McCaffery, I'd *give* the kid to him." He lurched to her side. "Now we can get down to business." He thrust his hand down the front of her blouse. "Buy bras that fasten in front."

"For Christ's sake, Alex!" Jill twisted away from him, knocking him backward. He reeled halfway across the room, caromed off a table, and landed on the couch.

"Deliver me from fucking women!" he said, shaking his head. "First it's yes, then it's no. Makes you crazy." He looked at her, eyes sparkling. "It's this office, isn't it? You're not comfortable here. Okay, so we'll go to a motel." He struggled to his feet, coming toward her with a peculiar sideways gait. "You loved last night. Admit it."

Jill watched him closely. She'd seen Alex sparkling and reeling before. "Have you been eating Zippy's cookies?"

"Hey, shit, that meeting was fucking tense." Alex grinned. "Living life in the fast lane, you got to slow down when you can, how you can. Work hard, play hard, and beat the devil at his own fucking game. Now, c'mere."

He tried to pull Jill toward him, but she eluded his grasp and headed for the door.

"Where the fuck are you going?" Alex was befuddled.

"The meeting is over, Alex. The workday is over. I am as anxious to get home to my daughter as I know you are to get home to your wife."

"Who? Oh, fuck, I'm dizzy." Alex aimed his seat at a chair.

"Nina. Remember? Lawfully wed and all that?"

"Oh, yeah." Alex's eyes had lost some of their sparkle and were beginning to cross. "Reminds me. I'll be an hour or so late tomorrow. She's having an abortion."

"I'm sorry, for her sake."

249

"She wants me to go with her."

"God knows, in time of crisis I'd want you with me."

"That's what she said. She was scheduled for today, but, what the fuck?, you and I just got promoted, so I told her to reschedule. It's not like an abortion is a real operation, Jill. Beats hell out of me why Nina's moping around the house like some fucking brood mare. She knows this is the wrong time to have a baby. Fucking women ain't fucking rational, none of 'em."

"We should never have been given the vote, Alex."

"What the hell's the matter with you?" Alex stood up, then promptly sat down. "You've been a bitch on wheels all day."

"For no reason?"

"Shit, no," he said emphatically. "You got promoted, didn't you? You should be walking on fucking air."

"Good night, Alex."

She walked out of the office with Alex's "Fucking women!" ringing in her ears.

A light drizzle was falling by the time she reached her car and she was shivering by the time she reached home. She parked the car, ran the few feet to the porch, and shook herself like a wet dog before entering the house.

"Daisy, Daisy," she called. "Where are you?"

There was no answer—hardly surprising, since the house was rocking with music so loud, Jill wondered why the paint hadn't fallen from the walls.

She knocked on Daisy's door, trying for a rhythm different than the drummer's. Still no response, so she opened the door and went in. Daisy was lying on her bed, engrossed in a book.

She glanced up, saw Jill, jumped, and shouted something Jill couldn't hear.

Jill motioned at Daisy to wait until she turned down the music.

"You shouldn't sneak up on people like that!" Daisy said indignantly. "You scared me out of my wits!"

"I didn't sneak. I came in the house like a normal person. You're going to go deaf with the music that loud."

"I'd forgotten it was on." Daisy shrugged. "I'm reading *Wuthering Heights.*"

Jill blanched. "My God, Daisy! Don't read that!"

"Why not? It's a super story. I'm just at the part where Cathy gets married, and Heathcliff—"

"You're at an impressionable age, and girls who read *Wuthering Heights* at an impressionable age get fixated on Heathcliff."

"Fixated?" Daisy's eyes were round.

"You'll think a man has to roam the moors howling like a wolf to be interesting and beat down your door and maybe your head to show you he cares," Jill said earnestly. "You'll think a man you can't count on is romantic, Daisy. It'll ruin you for men in the real world."

"Is that what happened to you, Mom? You fell in love with Heathcliff when you were my age, and now you like crazy men?"

"Well . . . not necessarily." Jill wished she hadn't turned down the music.

"It would take a lot more than a book to make me like a certain kind of man," Daisy said, hopping off her bed. "It would take a certain kind of man."

"What kind?" Jill asked curiously.

"Not Heathcliff, for sure." Daisy plugged in her curling iron. "He's interesting but awfully grouchy. He's always shouting at Cathy, telling her what to do."

"Is Lenny more your type?"

"Lenny's a kid." Daisy plugged in her curlers. "We were talking about men."

"We were, weren't we?" Jill smiled. "Would you like a tuna fish casserole? I can put white wine in it and make it French, or diced chilies and cheese and make it Mexican. I know it's not Scandia, but . . ."

"I ate," Daisy said. "And now I have to get ready."

"Get ready for what?"

"Alice Cooper. Remember? My concert. Lenny will be here in half an hour."

"Rats."

"What's the matter, Mom?"

"Nothing." Jill tried to turn off her "motherly" voice. "I'd forgotten about it, that's all."

Daisy eyed her speculatively. "If you need someone to talk to, you can always call Patti Gerard."

"Thanks, Daisy." Jill smiled. "I think I can manage an evening alone."

While Jill was changing out of her wet clothes the phone rang.

"Jill!" It was Patti Gerard.

"Just the person I'm supposed to call."

"You are?" Patti was curious. "Why?"

"To talk about men, what else?"

"They certainly seem to be my specialty, don't they? That's why I'm calling you, Jill. I have a date tonight."

"Hold on, Patti. I'll call the newspapers. They'll want to save page one."

"I'm serious, Jill."

"C'mon, Patti. You saying you have a date is like me saying I'm going to have dinner. In fact, I probably go without dinner more evenings than you go without—"

"Jill, listen! Have you ever gone out with a guy who didn't want to fuck you?

"Sure. Once in fourth grade I—"

"Jill!" Patti shouted. "I'm serious. Take this seriously."

"All right," Jill agreed. "But the next time you change the rules, don't do it in midstream. What's up?"

"I've gone out a few times with this guy. Well, actually, he's my accountant. He's single, nice-looking, pleasant personality, reads a lot. We go out to dinner, and after dinner he takes me home. That's it, Jill."

"Sounds nice."

"What's wrong?" Patti asked desperately. "Is it him? Is it me?"

"You are serious, aren't you?" Jill frowned. "Look, Patti, I hate to admit it and blow my half of our who's-scoring-what? game but I've gone out with plenty of men who've taken me home with nothing at the end of the evening except a polite kiss at the door."

"And there's nothing wrong? They're not gay?"

"Patti," Jill sighed. "I'm from Cleveland. I went to Our Lady of Perpetual Misperceptions. I've been raised to believe that when a man asks you to dinner, it's tacky to ask if he's gay, asexual, pathologically shy, or has been wounded in a major war. It's all right to ask if he's married or hits."

"I still don't think you're taking this seriously," Patti complained.

"That's because I don't understand what's troubling you. A nice man takes you to dinner and talks. What's so awful? Does he eat with his hands?"

"Of course not. He's—"

"He's nice, isn't he, Patti?"

"Uh-huh."

"Don't worry, Patti," Jill said gently. "So are you."

"He'll be here any minute, Jill. Should I wear my green lace or the rose print or my white silk suit?"

"You're asking *me*?" Jill laughed. "According to you, I make Rosie the bag lady look like the queen of *Women's Wear Daily.*"

"You're right. What am I doing? I'll wear that fabulous new creation by my Thai designer," Patti decided. "Read *Dress for Success,* don't wear jeans to work, get a sophisticated haircut. Talk to you later."

"Good-bye, Mother." Jill laughed. "Have fun tonight."

She hung up, then looked up to see Daisy eyeing her quizzically. "Patti?"

"As prescribed."

"Oh, good." Daisy was pleased. "Then you feel better. Are you going to tell me to have a good time, too?"

The affirmative about to roll out of Jill's mouth was drowned in a clap of thunder that shook the house. Bolts of lightning, visible through the bedroom window, crackled and ripped through the sky.

"Holy Christ! You're not going out in this!"

"But, Mom, you promised! Even Dad promised! You both said I could!"

"I didn't know there was going to be a typhoon!"

"Los Angeles doesn't have typhoons, Mom. It has seasonal rains." Daisy folded her arms, digging her heels into the carpet. "Besides the concert is inside the Forum, not out in an open field."

"But you'll have to take the freeway," Jill fretted.

Daisy's eyes glinted sharp yellow points. "Lenny got an A in Driver Education. He drives his grandfather everywhere, and you know how nervous old people are about driving."

"I'm beginning to." Jill looked anxiously out the window.

"I can't go to school and tell my friends I missed the concert because my mommy wouldn't let me go out in the rain," Daisy declared. "You can't treat me like a baby."

Jill looked at the slender figure dressed in size-seven jeans, at the pale blue blouse demurely buttoned over a 34C, at the faint trace of blush on rounded cheeks and the hint of mascara on dark lashes, at the auburn hair that had been both curled and waved in a style copied, and copied well, from an issue of *Seventeen.*

You're right. I can't treat you like a baby. But, oh, God, I'd like to, Daisy. I'd like to watch over you, keep you safe every minute.

"Tell you what, Mom," Daisy said slowly. "If we start out and the weather's so terrible we think it's dangerous, we'll turn around and come back."

"You will?"

"Right away, Mom." Daisy smiled. "Promise."

"Are you humoring me, Daisy?" Jill asked suspiciously.

"I'd worry if you were going out tonight, Mom." Daisy was serious. "Not all your fears are neurotic."

"Well, thanks. I—"

The doorbell rang, and Daisy ran off, shouting "Lenny!"

Jill glanced in the mirror, hoping she looked presentable for the big moment, or if not presentable, at least like an anchor.

I wonder if Daisy would stay home if I fainted in the living room.

She looked at herself in horror. "My God, I'm becoming my mother!" She was still staring at herself when she heard Daisy call "Mother, I'd like you to meet Lenny."

In the soft peach glow of the Tiffany lamp Daisy was standing next to a tall, well-built boy with curly black hair and the blackest eyes Jill had ever seen.

"This is Lenny," Daisy said, with a look that begged Jill not to say anything "motherly."

"How do you do, Lenny," Jill said, shaking hands with the living image of Heathcliff. "Daisy's told me so much about you." Jill glanced at Daisy, who was frowning. "Well," she said quickly, "not that much. I mean, she's mentioned you. Once."

"I'm pleased to meet you." Lenny smiled. "Daisy talks about you, too."

"Hmmmm." Jill switched to fail-safe nonverbal communication.

"I know you must be concerned about the weather tonight," Lenny said. "I want to assure you that I'm a very careful driver. I got an A in Driver Education, and I chauffeur for my grandfather in all kinds of weather."

Jill nodded. "Your grandfather is nervous."

"He's seventy-one, and he says that the last thing that made him nervous was his heart attack twenty-seven years ago. Since then it's all been gravy."

"Remarkable attitude." Jill was impressed.

Lenny grinned. "Remarkable man. The tires on the car have been recently rotated, the brakes are in perfect order, my father has given me directions to the Forum that will keep us off the freeway, and I brought an umbrella. It's on the porch. I didn't want to drip on your rug."

"Oh, my." It was all Jill could say.

"Well, good night, Mom," Daisy said cheerily. "Don't wait up."

"I won't." Jill crossed her fingers behind her back.

She walked them to the door, wanting to hug Daisy good night, but, deciding that would be "motherly," settled instead for a friendly pat on the back. "Take care," she called as they stepped out the door. "Drive carefully. Call me if you have trouble. Have fun. Don't smoke anything."

"Mom!" Daisy's voice drifted back through the rain.

"Don't worry, Mrs. Kenyon," Lenny called out. "I belong to the Automobile Club. I have a spare in the trunk and flares. I don't smoke. Anything."

Jill waved, smiling a smile her heart didn't feel and watching as her responsible daughter disappeared into the rain with her responsible boyfriend.

She closed the door, leaned against it, and groaned, wondering why she felt as though she'd just watched the Babes in the Woods wander into the forest without even a basket of bread crumbs.

Is it possible all *mothers become Kate in the end?*

She scooped the mail off the hall table and walked into the bedroom.

"Act as if," she told herself. "Act as if you're not aching with worry. Act as if Daisy's growing up causes no ambivalence whatsoever. Act as if you believe all this bullshit coming out of your mouth."

She sat on her bed, leafed through her bills, threw the ads in the wastepaper basket, then reached for a small, square manila envelope. In lieu of letters Julie always sent cassettes which she recorded, with appalling efficiency, while doing something else. Her verbal chronicles always had as background music the sound of chopping, dicing, clanging pots, the washing machine, and on one memorable occasion Chicago rush-hour traffic as Julie drove home from work.

Jill slipped the cassette into the recorder next to her bed, then paused with her hand on the Play button. On an evening when she was struggling to act as if she didn't feel foolish, wasn't worried about Daisy, and understood the logic behind the people and procedures at UBC, she wasn't sure she needed to hear a tape from Julie extolling the ever-increasing marvels of her life. To hear the wonders of Fred would give her a headache. To hear about bliss on a schedule would

255

give her hives. To hear that Julie was juggling home, business, church, and community responsibilities without deodorant failure or hair-spray poop-out might well send her to the nearest locked ward.

I'll call Nick. She reached for the phone, her hand hovering over the receiver as it had over the Play button. She considered it.

Maybe I'll act as if being Nick's muse isn't the honor he thinks it is. I'll act as if I'm tired of being the whipping boy for writer's blocks and unrealized aspirations. I'll act as if his career is his problem, not mine. I'll act as if I don't want to call him. And I won't. Thank you, Dan.

Jill pushed the Play button and sat back, wishing all *acting as if* was that easy. It was somehow disheartening to realize that the only emotion she felt for Nick was a twinge of guilt at how easily she was giving him up. She wondered why. Perhaps the superficial relationships that seemed to bring out the best in Patti merely left her feeling . . . superficial.

Maybe I'm doing it wrong. Maybe Patti's better at it than I am.

Jill tried to concentrate on Julie's tape. Julie had been saying something about Kate, and Jill had missed it, caught up in her reverie. No matter. Julie's tapes were all the same. From year to year the only changes were the ages of Julie's children and the length of her list of accomplishments.

"So Fred is flying to Boston this weekend," Julie was saying, *"He's reading his paper at MIT. You can't imagine how proud I am, and of course Morgan and Kendrick are, too. I shall miss Fred desperately, but I try to look on the bright side, and the bright side is that I can put the time to good use. I'm usually a month ahead in my class lesson plans, but right now I'm a week behind in being a month ahead. That's not like me. Yesterday I forgot to put starch in Fred's shirts. That's so unlike me that Fred's suggested I have a physical. Isn't it like Fred to worry that I might be run-down? I think that when I was born, God gave me Fred as my guardian angel. Remember the holy pictures they gave us at school, the ones with the guardian angels? They were so beautiful, with wings like rainbows and faces Botticelli must have seen in his visions. Sister Mary Martha told us that when we're naughty, our guardian angel cries. I used to think about that. I didn't want to make my guardian angel cry. That's why I never licked the center out of the Oreo cookies, then stuck them together and put them back in the box like you did. I was tempted, but I never did. Not once. I don't buy Oreo cookies. I walk right past*

them in the supermarket. I should be ironing. Kendrick's school clothes are still in the basket. He's growing so fast. His clothes get bigger and bigger. I'm so proud of Kendrick. And of Morgan of course. And Fred. Did I tell you about Fred and the paper he's reading at MIT? Oh, wait, yes, I did, just a minute ago. Well, that's how proud I am. I can't stop talking about it. I wish he was reading it here. Boston is so far away from Chicago. At least it's only one hour away. When I wake up on Saturday morning and Fred isn't here, at least I'll know that ten o'clock for me will be only nine o'clock for Fred. Sometimes when I talk to you in Los Angeles, it strikes me as strange that you haven't had breakfast and I'm about to eat lunch. It's like you have more of your life ahead of you than I have, and if I don't hurry, I'll never catch up. I don't mean I feel that way often. Just once. Long ago. It doesn't matter. It was only a thought. That's not like me. I can't have a physical now. Father Norton and his youth group seem to be taking more of my time than I'd originally allotted. Father Norton is going through some crisis of faith or coming down with mono, it's hard to tell. He has swollen glands and lassitude. Of course, these symptoms can also be caused by internal conflict, and, God knows, poor Father Norton's conflicts are severe and not of his making. He was PUSHED into the seminary, Jill, PUSHED by his parents, the third son of nine children, destined to be a priest, THEIR priest, from his bassinet. Well, we are all Irish Catholics and know what can happen. It's a good thing that John was an only son or he would have gone into the seminary from eighth grade. Wouldn't he have made a wonderful priest?—so tall and he's always looked good in black. Jerry doesn't. He's too sallow. But if he'd get some sun, if he went camping . . . if he was happy . . ."

The tape ended abruptly. Jill stared at the cassette recorder.

Something's wrong. Julie sounds like me on one of my good days, but not like herself.

She glanced at the clock, fighting an irresistible urge to call Julie. She'd only wake her and frighten her as well.

Jill picked up the television remote control and pushed the UBC button. *Please stand by* came into focus. She shuddered and pushed another button.

All the King's Men was on. Jill settled back on her pillows, hoping that watching Broderick Crawford out-demagogue Huey Long would dull the sharpness of her concern about Julie.

Still, it nattered and poked at her mind, filling her with a sense of having missed Julie's forest in the wilderness of her trees. Worry about Julie and watching Brod fall in a hail of bullets on the state-house steps diverted her to the extent she was somewhat surprised when she heard the front door open and Daisy's voice yell "Mother, I'm home."

Jill rolled off her bed and hurried to see that Daisy had arrived safely, in possession of all of her fingers, all of her toes.

"How was the concert, honey?"

"I loved it, Mom. Why aren't you asleep?"

"I was . . . uh . . . watching television."

"You were waiting up for me, weren't you?"

"No. I was watching an old movie and . . . wait a minute! You're fifteen years old. I'm your mother. Why shouldn't I wait up for you?"

"I'm sure it'll turn out to be one of my golden childhood memories, Mom, but right now it's a pain in the neck. Night."

"Night, Daisy." Jill smiled after her.

Jill returned to her room, listening to the sound of Daisy singing in hers: *"Mem'ries, light the corners of my mind . . ."*

The phone rang, and Jill jumped for it, twitching with apprehension. Phone calls after midnight bring only news of death.

"Hello?" she quavered. There was no response. "Hello?"

Jill sat on the edge of her bed, repeating "Hello" to the sound of heavy breathing.

"Oh, thank you, thank you." Jill said into the phone. "An obscene phone call is just what I needed. The perfect end to a perfect day."

CHAPTER
18

On the evening of Steve's birthday Jill and Daisy puttered about the kitchen, preparing dinner and icing the cake. More than once Jill reminded herself to walk carefully through the emotional minefield of the evening ahead, both for Daisy's sake and because she had her own nostalgic yearnings for a return to former, more comfortable times.

"The roast is done," Daisy announced, "and I think I heard Dad at the door. This may be the start of something big."

"It's your father's birthday, Daisy, that's all," Jill called after her.

Steve seemed equally aware of the evening's emotional overlay and behaved as though he and Jill had made a pact to concentrate on Daisy without yielding to her transparent machinations. They danced around Daisy's repeated *remember whens* as prudently and gently as possible.

Steve laughed at Jill's UBC stories, blew out his candles, and grinned as Daisy sang "Happy Birthday" off key in his ear. He unwrapped the briefcase that was Jill's present, responding with appropriate oohs and ahs, and promptly donned the T-shirt from Daisy that read "If you tell me your sign, I'll throw up on your shoes." The evening ended pleasantly with Daisy and Jill walking Steve to his car. Jill had successfully resisted the urge to tell Steve about the disturbing tape from Julie. She was acting as if she didn't need his reassurance, especially accompanied by what she was certain would be his recommendation that she curb her imagination. She also resisted the impulse to tell him she was *acting as if*, just in case the community-property settlement had blessed him with the power to have her committed.

But in a note she told Dan.

Dear Dan, she wrote. *As usual, your good advice works, and the surprise is that as time goes on there's less and less "acting" involved, and the "if" is closer to what I actually feel. At first I was "acting as if" I was you, a difficult chore at best, as I've always considered you the substance and myself the able, but limited, shadow. Lately there's less of trying to be you and more of myself functioning well with the aid of what you've taught me. I've read that certain primitive tribes eat the hearts and brains of those they respect in the belief they will thus acquire their wisdom and strength. And, of course, psychologists have long held that the bereaved emulate desirable characteristics of the departed, integrating them into their own personalities. Both these ideas—and they are one and the same—must be true. God knows, I gobbled you up as fast as I could, and I thank you for being a feast. Love, Jill.*

She mailed the note with fingers crossed, hoping that Dan wouldn't borrow Steve's power to have her committed.

In the next weeks Jill successfully fought intermittent impulses to call Dan, but did send seven additional notes up the coast to the monastery in Santa Barbara.

Despite these impulses, life went on, consistent only in its inconsistency. In a week when Jill had thirty-seven meetings with people anxious to sell their ideas to UBC, there were also six programing meetings, the subject of which was dwindling network revenue. There would be no further ideas bought by UBC, at least until after the upcoming affiliates' convention, or the network might well be reduced to entertaining station owners and wives with an in-house amateur night at a banquet featuring tuna-fish sandwiches and Billy Bear. In the midst of all this Daisy had another menstrual period, which prompted a series of phone calls initiated by Jill and returned by an increasingly impatient Dr. Baker, who finally shouted, "Stop worrying, Jill! Time will take care of it!"

His words provided no light at the end of this particular tunnel, but they did generate sufficient heat to end Jill's twice daily calls. She considered taking Daisy to see another doctor, but Daisy opposed the idea on the grounds that waiting for her problem to stabilize made absolute sense to her.

"Waiting doesn't make you nervous?" Jill asked.

"No. Dr. Baker told me it isn't serious."

"Wouldn't you like another opinion?"

"Why? Is Dr. Baker a nerd?"

"No, he's a good doctor."

"Then why would I need another opinion?"

"For reassurance."

Daisy laughed. " 'Like mother, like daughter' is only a saying, Mom."

At work, Alex continued to remember the names of everyone in the television industry and often, in response to Jill's bewildered looks, passed surreptitious notes to her identifying the anonymous faces she was currently "taking a meeting" with. She would have preferred that he tell her the names of these moguls and mavens before they came into her office, but Alex enjoyed watching her vamp.

He always came to her rescue before she could totally disgrace herself and make him look bad in the process, but only at the last minute and always with a gleam in his eye. It was partially his penchant for cliff-hangers and the adrenaline they provided and partially the revenge of his masculine ego, because try as he might—and he did—the romantic interlude of the night of Dan's departure was not repeated. Jill offered no explanation, though Alex seemed to think one was in order.

However, brooding wasn't his style, and Alex took ample comfort in his ongoing tits-and-ass secretarial sweepstakes. His enthusiasm for this game remained undiminished, even on the day when an unreceptive applicant raised a lump on his head with his desk lamp. Alex shared the secret of his contented afternoons with Zippy, who promptly fired *his* secretary, an efficient but staid lady who held the unmellow opinion that sex is one thing you don't give at the office. So Zippy joined Alex in pursuit of the biggest tits and the tightest jeans, and they became best buddies, sharing ladies, political maneuvers, and dope-chip cookies as they plotted their hops up the corporate ladder.

One of Alex's maneuvers involved becoming as well-known as possible in the shortest period of time.

"It don't matter what the fuckers say about you," he told Jill. "The important thing is, they know who you are."

To that end he assembled a wardrobe which combined Gucci with Machismo, Pucci with Ah-Men. On alternate Tuesdays he wore his "Baby Mogul" T-shirt and sandals in fluorescent colors.

"They're all talking about me," he burbled happily to Jill. "The fuckers think I gotta be creative to go around looking like this."

Just to keep them guessing, he bought three Brooks Brothers suits.

261

Jill received another tape from Julie. She waited three days to play it, telling herself that she had too many scripts to read—clearly a coward's excuse. Finally, late one night she played it. When the machine clicked off, she picked up the phone and called Polly.

"I woke you up, didn't I?" she asked when Polly answered the phone yawning.

"It's all right. What's wrong?"

"Another tape from my sister. There was the usual ten minutes of raving about the wonders of Fred, two minutes on Morgan's accomplishments, and three on Kendrick's—"

"Who are they?"

"Her son and daughter. Morgan and Kendrick."

"Which is her son and which is the daughter?" Polly asked.

"When you're children are perfect, who cares?" Jill reached for a cigarette. "But following the paeans to Fred and the Munchkins, Julie began sounding like she was lost in a revolving door. She said she'd run out of her home-cooked flash-frozen dinners and hadn't had time to make more because of her involvement with Father Norton's youth group. Then she broke off in the middle of that to say she had exam papers to correct and would play a musical interlude while she was gone. I listened to both sides of 'Old Blue Eyes Is Back,' then Julie returned to say that the exam papers were finished, she hoped I enjoyed the music, the sweetest sounds she's ever heard are still inside her head, and when I'm feeling low, I should remember our heritage—'Give me your poor, your tired, your muddled asses longing to breathe free!' Then the tape ended. What the hell is going on, Polly?"

"I think she's feeling poor and tired," Polly said. "I think she's yearning to breathe free."

"Not for a second of her life has Julie ever felt like a muddled ass," Jill said emphatically. "I don't even know what her problem is."

"My instinct tells me that you're the only one who can help." Polly sounded eerily certain.

"Don't say that, Polly. Please," Jill begged. "It's bad enough that I drop my life and run off to Cleveland for calls from Intensive Care. I can't start flying off to Chicago, too. My life isn't as droppable as it was when Steve and I were married and I either had no job at all or one with few responsibilities."

"Is that the only reason you've dropped your life for family emergencies, Jill?" Polly asked. "Time to spare?"

262

Jill hesitated. "No. Dr. Kerry says it's the nature of black sheep to butt their heads against the fence looking for a way back into the fold."

"Dr. Kerry says?" Polly sounded surprised. "What do you say?"

"If I had insights of my very own, I wouldn't be spending fifty bucks an hour for the store-bought kind." Jill laughed. "The theory is that I'm trying to make up for being the one with the crazies, the divorce, the lapsed religion, and the profligate ways. I'm not proud of it, Polly, but there it is. I'm just another dog drooling at the sound of Pavlov's bell."

"It costs you fifty bucks an hour to feel like a reflex?" Polly asked scornfully.

"So far." Jill tried to laugh, but the sound rang hollow. "Makes me feel like a fool, I'll tell you." She paused. "Except sometimes, like this last trip home, when my being there seems to have made a difference, I don't feel like a fool. I feel like I did the right thing."

"Listen to that feeling, Jill," Polly advised. "Don't discount it because it comes from yourself."

"My feeling may be wishful thinking, Polly, and that's what I can't afford anymore. I've finally learned what I need to know about the best job I've ever had. UBC could be my future."

"It could," Polly agreed. "Or you might hear a different drummer."

"UBC is what I have, and there's nothing else I want more. Like my sister, the sweetest sounds I've ever heard are still inside my head, so if there's a different drummer skulking in the bushes, he can march on by."

"If you say so." Polly yawned.

"I'm blathering, and you're half asleep," Jill said apologetically. "I'll see you in the morning."

"Don't forget you have an interview with the reporter from *Fame* magazine who's doing the article on women executives."

"Rats. I'd forgotten. Good night."

On the following day Alex and Jill saw a rough-cut of the rock-and-roll movie. They were alone in the screening room, a circumstance that proved fortunate. If the producer had been there, he would have strangled them both. They laughed so uproariously that Jill felt as if she had been transported back in time to the days of Rialto Saturday matinees.

"How could this happen?" Alex demanded. "This was supposed to be a gutsy melodrama about two talented guys trying to make it in rock and roll?"

Jill laughed. "It's more like *Abbott and Costello Meet an Electric Guitar.*"

"I'm not going to take the heat for this piece of shit." Alex waved at the screen. "This fucker is Carmichael's responsibility."

"Dan would take the responsibility if he was here, but he's not. So, I'll take it," Jill said, one eye on the screen.

"You aren't going to see me get hung for someone else's mistakes," Alex said adamantly.

"I don't know why not." Jill lit a cigarette. "Eventually someone else will get hung for yours. Besides, it's not a mistake."

"It's a fucking disaster."

"It's a comedy," Jill said, "or will be if they'll recut it. All the crazy stuff could stay in, all the melodrama come out. With a new ending and additional music the promos can use words like *crazy* and *wild.*"

"A comedy?" Alex thought it over. "Hey, man, that's not a bad idea." He struggled out of the plush screening-room chair. "Excuse me a minute. I have to go to the men's room."

Jill reached up and clamped her hand around his wrist. "Stay where you are, Alex. It's too late to call Zippy and tell him that turning *Rock and Roll Love* into a comedy is your idea. I've already sent a memo saying it's mine. Relax. You can't win them all."

He sat down, but instead of relaxing, he jiggled and squirmed, refusing to respond to questions Jill directed at him.

When the lights came on, Jill got up, stretched, and grinned. "Don't pout, Alex. It's a repulsive habit in a big, strong man."

"Fuck you."

"Spoken like a big, strong man."

When Jill returned to her office, Polly was chatting with a young woman who'd obviously read *Dress for Success.* Her beige suit was accessorized with beige purse, shoes, and scarf. She looked like an oatmeal cookie.

"This is Marsha Lindley," Polly said by way of introduction. "She's the reporter from *Fame.*"

"Let's go into my office," Jill suggested.

"Fine," Marsha said agreeably, following Jill through the door. "Tell me, how does it feel to be a role model for so many other women?"

"I don't know. I'm not."

"You're a woman in an executive position. That makes you a role model."

"That makes me a woman in an executive position, that's all."

Marsha was nonplused. "Well, then, will you tell our readers how a woman today can best go about forging her way up the executive ladder?"

"I can only tell you what happened to me. Someone offered me a job, and I took it."

Marsha's eyes popped. "That's *it*?"

"I thought the job sounded interesting. I was right. It is."

"But your game plan?"

"I didn't have one. Still don't. Like Freud's cigar or Gertrude Stein's rose, sometimes a job is a job is a job."

"Hey, Jill!" Alex burst through the door. "You wanted to see this report and . . . whoops . . . I didn't know you had someone with you."

"Come in, Alex." It was an unnecessary invitation. "This is Marsha Lindley from *Fame.*"

"Talking about television, huh?" Alex asked. "Well, in my view all the hype about cable is just that—hype. It will be years before the pay-TV people can afford to produce the kind of shows the audiences want to see, for instance, our movies this season—"

"Ms. Lindley is interviewing me for an article on women executives, Alex," Jill said.

"Oh." Alex pulled his chair close to Marsha's. "That's not an easy assignment. I mean, it's been done."

"I know." Marsha sighed. "But the assignment editor thought it would be good for another go-around, so here I am."

"Just doing the best you can. A real pro. I admire that."

Marsha smiled. "I'm trying to work my way out of features geared for women into hard news."

"I knew that the minute I saw you. I said to myself, 'Alex, that woman's a Woodward, a Lawrence, a Pulitzer-prize winner someday.'"

"You think so?" she asked, delighted.

"I know so. I'm never wrong about those things. Ask Jill."

Jill laughed. "You want to hear about game plans? Ask Alex."

"Unfortunately this article's about women," Marsha said regretfully.

"If you'll wait ten minutes, Alex will run home and put on a dress."

Jill grinned. "Wait twenty, and he'll have a sex-change operation."

Alex glared at Jill. "Jill has a dynamite sense of humor. That's why I love working with her." His eyes lit up. "Hey, that gives me a wonderful idea, a fantastic twist to your story. Why not interview the men who work with the executive women? It's a whole new angle."

"I've never seen it done," Marsha said excitedly. "My editor will love it. I can start with you, Alex."

Jill reached for the papers Alex was holding. "Excuse me. I'll go dictate this to Polly."

As she walked out of the office she heard Alex's voice behind her. "I'm a liberated kind of guy, and I knew by the time I was twelve that television would be my life—"

Jill shut the door behind her.

Polly looked up from her typewriter. "The kid's really cooking, isn't he?"

Jill nodded. "The only thing better than having a game plan is pretending you had one after the fact."

It took nearly two hours to finish the report, and in that time Jill's door never opened.

"That's it." Jill looked up from her cross-legged position on the floor. "I'll proof it in the morning. Alex's part of the report was terrific, Polly. When he settles down to work, there's nobody better." She stretched, feeling creaky. "Well, as the poet said, we'll live to fight another day. Put the cover on your infernal machine. I'll walk you out to your car."

"Do you need anything from your office?" Polly gestured toward the closed door.

"I wouldn't open that door if Lawrence offered me Abelard."

"Afraid you'll catch Alex in the middle of something embarrassing?"

"Alex? He wouldn't be embarrassed if his mother, his wife, and eight rabbis arrived to sit shiva." Jill snorted. "But that poor girl would never recover."

"I can see the interview now." Polly laughed as they walked into the hall. "Under the headline 'What's New at UBC'—'Let me tell you about television, my dear, the young executive said with his hand on my milk-white thigh. . . .' "

Polly continued her sexy version of Alex's interview all the way to the parking lot, and Jill drove home laughing, relieved that the object of Alex's mercurial affections was Marsha Lindley and not her.

When she entered the house, the telephone was ringing. She

stopped long enough to scoop up the mail, including a note from Daisy, then dashed into the bedroom, flung herself across the bed, and reached for the phone.

"Hello."

"There's something wrong with your sister." It was Kate. "You've got to do something."

"Ma?"

"Who else? I've gotten three tapes in the mail and thought they were from you, they sounded so crazy."

"Is this the mother who's never going to speak to me again?" Jill asked, sitting on the edge of the bed.

"I have painters in the living room, plasterers in the hall, and a plumber coming in the morning, and today I got another tape."

"The mother who disowned me?"

"I haven't played it yet. What I don't know won't hurt me," Kate said. "Except I know what I know. What kind of names are Morgan and Kendrick? They sound like a couple of lawyers. What's wrong with Brian and Kathleen?"

"You're upset about Julie."

"Just because Julie was born with red hair doesn't mean she takes after me. You, either. Julie took after me until she started this . . . this . . . who knows what this is. There's never been any craziness in *my* family. Your sister sent me a tape of Sousa marches and a poem she wrote about Fred. It didn't even rhyme. What kind of a poem is that?"

"Free verse."

"What else? Who'd pay for it?" Kate yelled. "You have to come home, Jill. You're the only one in the family who's ever been crazy. You know what to do."

"It isn't like being a midwife, Ma." Jill smiled in spite of herself.

"What about that doctor who cured you?" Kate asked. "You can call him about Julie."

"Neil Kaiser? I'm supposed to call Dr. Kaiser from Los Angeles to tell him that my Cleveland mother is upset because my Chicago sister is sending her tapes of Sousa marches?"

"Yes," Kate said vehemently. "That's what you should do."

"He'll send out an army of men with white coats, Ma, only they'll be coming for me."

"If you don't come, you'll regret it the rest of your life," Kate warned. "I might have a heart attack. Already I've had leaping."

"Is Jim there?" Jill asked, hoping he was.

"At this hour of the night?" Kate was offended. "What kind of question is that to ask your mother?"

"You shouldn't be alone when you're upset, Ma."

"A woman whose children have left her is always alone." Kate sniffed. "Even in a crowd. Even Christmas shopping. Even at Easter Mass, and you know how damn crowded—"

"Say hello to Jim for me," Jill interrupted, adding quickly, "When you see him, that is."

"Say hello yourself," Kate said, then bellowed, "Jim, come here. You tell this girl to come home. She won't listen to her mother."

Jill sprawled on the bed, waiting. Within a minute Jim was on the line. "Come home. Your mother's worried about Julie."

"I'm worried about Julie, too. Maybe Ma should come here."

"That doesn't make sense." He sounded puzzled.

"Of course it doesn't. What good would it do for Mother to come here or me to go there? Julie's in Chicago."

"Oh." He hadn't thought of that. "Then you'll have to go to Chicago."

"I can't. I have a job. I have Daisy."

"Well, your mother can't," Jim grumbled. "She has painters and plumbers, she's afraid of flying, and she's never driven for longer than an hour without crashing into something."

"How is she, Jim? Has her heart been leaping?"

"Well . . ." He was slow to answer. "Maybe a little bounce now and then, but, Jill, I've got to admit, Dr. Keriakan's regime works. The vitamins, the walking, the diet. It's a miracle. Of course, I could have given her the same advice. It's all there in *Prevention* magazine. Just this month there was an article about dissolving gallstones with a mixture of— Kate, what are you doing?"

"Give me that phone, you fool!" Jill heard Kate say, then, "Jill, Jill, are you there?"

"I'm here, Ma," Jill said, wishing she wasn't.

"I just want you to know that a person who would put her mother in a home and let her sister be crazy in Chicago without so much as lifting a finger is not going to waltz into Heaven. There are things God doesn't forget."

"Not if He's made in your image and likeness, Ma," Jill said fervently.

"I'll never speak to you again!" Kate shouted, and hung up.

Jill hung up, feeling as she had as a child when Kate put her in charge of seeing that Julie and John crossed the street safely. She was no older than they, no larger, no taller, no more practiced in dodging the traffic across State Street, yet Kate had charged her with the care of their bones and being. For years Jill had suffered from nightmares in which an immense black sanitation truck scooped up John and Julie and carried them off, shrieking, in its teeth.

I am not my brother and sister's keeper. I'm having enough trouble keeping myself.

Jill read Daisy's note: *English exam tomorrow. At library with Lenny.*

Jill smiled at the note, thinking how fortunate she was in her choice of daughters. If Daisy said she was at the library, that's where she would be. If she'd gone to a teenage orgy, she would have written that, too.

Jill set her briefcase on the edge of the bed and pulled out a script: *Yodeling Cowboy.*

She'd read three pages, trying to picture a hero who wore lederhosen and a ten-gallon hat, when the phone rang again. She wasn't surprised. Kate's *never*'s usually lasted until she thought of something else she wanted to say.

She reached for the phone. "Hello, Ma."

Ten seconds later, she was still saying hello to the sound of heavy breathing. "Oh, shit," she said, and hung up, angry at whoever was making the phone calls, which had become an almost nightly nuisance.

She picked up the script, returning to the cowboy, whose predilection for yodeling seemed strongest when he was shooting a bad guy.

The words began to blur about the time the cowboy said howdy to the schoolmarm. Jill closed her eyes, and the script dropped from her hand.

A pounding at her front door woke her. Half-asleep, she struggled out of bed thinking, "Daisy's forgotten her key." As she stumbled to the door she heard the sound of Daisy's radio playing low.

"Let me in, for God's sake!" It was Patti Gerard on the porch, hopping about like someone in dire need of a rest room. "Jesus Christ, Jill! Jesus Christ!"

"Come in, come in." Jill stared as Patti bounced past, her Rodeo Drive haircut tousled and hanging in her eyes. She was dressed in shabby green pants, at least four sizes too large, and a sweat shirt with holes in the sleeves.

"Have you been raped?" Jill asked anxiously, following Patti into the den.

"No. If I had, I could handle it. I'd just get a gun and shoot the son of a bitch. I can't shoot Greg." She began to sob.

"Greg?"

"I told you. My accountant."

"Oh, yes, I remember. Look, Patti, sit down. I'll make some tea. Just excuse me for a moment while I check on Daisy."

She left Patti in the living room and hurried to Daisy's door. She opened it a crack and peeked in. Daisy was home, tucked in and sound asleep with her quilt pulled up to her chin. Jill smiled, then glanced at Daisy's clock. The glow-in-the-dark numerals registered a few minutes after four.

Oh, my God, Jill thought, closing the door softly. *Whatever's happened to Patti, it's more than not getting laid on a date.*

She returned to the living room to find Patti pacing the fringes of the rug. Her hands were locked behind her, and her eyes, devoid of makeup, continued to pour out tears.

"What happened?"

"Oh, Jill, it's too awful," Patti gasped between sobs. "We went out to dinner again and talked and talked and talked. I told you how much we talk. Talk, talk, talk, talk—"

"Sit down, Patti. You can tell me sitting down."

"I told him about the hospital!" Patti blurted out, and paced faster. "I told him that I'd had a nervous breakdown and tried to kill myself. I told him that I was locked up for three months. I told him that I've had twenty-one shock treatments. I told him that when I first came here from Cleveland I couldn't even go to the mailbox." Patti stopped her pacing long enough to pound her fist on the couch. "God help me, Jill. I even told him I used to be fat!"

"Oh, my God!" Jill sat on the couch, not knowing what to say. "He reacted badly?"

"He proposed to me!" Patti cried. "I told him *everything,* and he wants to marry me. He says he loves me—past, present, and future!"

"That's wonderful." Jill was astonished. "I'm happy for you, Patti. I mean, if you love him, I'm happy."

"I love him," Patti sobbed. "Until tonight I thought he was the best man I've ever met."

"Then I'm thrilled," Jill squealed. "I can do better than tea. I'll make breakfast, a big one. I can understand why you're so overwhelmed, honey. After all this time—"

270

Patti flashed across the room, gripped Jill by the shoulders, and shook her. "You're so stupid! You're stupid!"

"Patti, stop! What the hell's the matter with you?"

"You don't understand. I thought Greg was . . . He's never slept with me. . . . He knows everything. . . . He says he wants me to go away with him for a week, wants to make love to me in a house on the beach where we can fall asleep listening to the surf. . . . He wants me to meet his brother. . . ."

"You're right! I don't understand. This Greg sounds perfect."

"If he's so fucking perfect," Patti wailed, "why the hell does he love *me*?"

"Oh, shit. Now I understand." Jill watched Patti, who'd resumed pacing the carpet. "You're a terrific lady, Patti. You should know that."

"I'm not," Patti moaned.

"You're smart and—"

"Like *that* I'm terrific." Patti beat the front of her sweat shirt. "The lady who manages the boutique and has ambitions. *She's* terrific. The lady who had all the shock treatments. *She's* a mental case. He fell in love with the wrong one!"

"They're both you!" Jill shouted, exasperated. "This man is in love with all of Patti Gerard."

"He says he likes me without makeup. There's definitely something wrong."

"Patti—"

"I can't go to a beach house. Salt air makes my hair frizz. I know. I'll have Tai Ling whip up another dozen designs. I'll go to New York on a buying trip. . . . I'll . . . I'll . . . Some friend you are!" Patti said furiously. "Say something funny about Greg. Make a joke about him so we can both laugh."

"This time your love affair isn't funny, Patti. This one seems to be real."

"Some fucking friend!" Patti exploded. "I'm leaving!"

"Wait." Jill stepped between Patti and the door. "You're too upset to drive."

Patti tried to brush her aside. Jill held her ground. "Who put you in charge of my life? Who asked for your advice? Or your help?"

"You did!" Jill was as angry as Patti. "You arrived here in the middle of the night, hysterical and asking me what to do. What is that if not asking for help?"

"Forget it!" Patti shouted. "I've changed my mind."

"Bullshit!" Jill shouted louder. "You can't walk out of here half out of your mind and leave me to worry. I won't let that happen."

"I'm going for a drive." Patti whirled toward the door.

"Then I'm going with you," Jill decided. "I mean it. You're not leaving here without me."

"Suit yourself," Patti said through clenched teeth.

"Don't move until I get back. I'm going to wake Daisy."

There was no need to wake Daisy. She was sitting on the edge of her bed.

"We're going for a drive with Patti."

"I heard. The whole neighborhood heard."

"I'm sorry to haul you out in the middle of the night, honey, but Patti's my best friend."

"*My* friends have their traumas before midnight. Why can't I stay home?"

"Not alone. Not at night. C'mon, Daisy, I'll owe you one."

"You sure will. A real biggie." Daisy reached for her shoes. "Wait'll I tell Lenny about this."

A few minutes later Daisy was dressed in a sweat suit and they were on their way with Jill driving.

"Anywhere special?" Jill asked Patti.

"Just drive!" Patti ordered. "I've got to keep moving."

"Anybody want a granola bar?" Daisy asked from the back seat.

A half hour later they'd passed Thousand Oaks and were ascending the hill leading out of the San Fernando Valley.

"Men have been so simple for me," Patti was saying. "They're only for fun. Fuck 'em and forget 'em."

"Daisy, don't listen," Jill said quickly.

"I can't hear anything, Mom," Daisy assured her. "My ears are plugged up from this hill."

"Take Alex for instance," Patti continued. "He—"

"Don't tell me about Alex," Jill interrupted. "Tell me about anyone else."

"But Alex—"

"I mean it." Jill raised her voice. "I don't want to talk about someone we both know."

"You have to hear about Alex!" Patti outshouted Jill. "When I'm talking about Alex, I'm talking about me."

"I vote for hearing about Alex," Daisy said.

"Sometimes he calls me at midnight, says he's in the neighborhood and would like to drop in."

"He does?" Jill was surprised.

"And I let him," Patti said. "He never stays for more than an hour. Just wham, ba—"

"I know, I know," Jill interrupted. "Why do you let him?"

"Why do I let anyone? He makes me laugh. He tells me what I want to hear. He makes no promises, but he makes no demands either. He's what I can handle, Jill. Alex and the guys who want a six-week fling or a weekend in Palm Springs. I tell all of them that my work comes first, that I wouldn't trade my independence for the Peacock Throne. I tell them I'm Cinderella, that I'm only theirs at the ball."

Jill shrugged. "If that's all you want or expect . . ."

"I've learned the hard way," Patti said bitterly. "That's all *they* can handle—drop in and drop out of my life. They're just passing through. I feel like a filling station."

"It's not always that way, Patti," Jill said.

"When isn't it?" Patti demanded. "When's the last time a man didn't disappoint you?"

"Let's stick to you." Jill saw Daisy in the rearview mirror, sitting up straight, hanging on every word.

"I tell them they're all terrific in bed," Patti sniffed. "Even Alex, and he's the worst."

"I know," Jill sighed, then, quickly, "Then why did you tell me he's your first best. . . . Why did you say that?"

"Because you know him, and I know him, and I thought he might tell you about us. When I tell guys they're terrific, they fall all over themselves believing it, and then they think *I'm* terrific, too. I have to be terrific!" Patti wailed. "When that's all you have to offer, you work at it."

"That's *not* all you have to offer," Jill said firmly.

"Men! I hate the sons of bitches," Patti said grimly. "They're all assholes."

Jill glanced in the mirror. "C'mon, Patti. Men aren't the villains. They just aren't the heroes we thought they were."

"*They* think they are. They think we should be grateful for every — I don't even know if I like sex!" Patti twisted around, trying to find Daisy in the back seat. "Don't be in a hurry for sex, Daisy."

"Don't look at me," Daisy told her. "The closest I've come to sex was my pelvic."

They stopped at Loop's Restaurant in Ventura. The waitress set coffee cups before Jill and Patti and a plate in front of Daisy.

273

"Oh, boy, I've never had a cheeseburger at five A.M. before," Daisy said gleefully, reaching for the catsup.

"I told Greg about the men in my life. That was *after* he proposed. I thought he'd run away screaming."

"And he didn't."

"He said he was sorry I've been so lonely." Tears splashed into Patti's coffee. "He said he understood."

"What's so terrible about having a real person in your life? What's so frightening about having somebody of your own?"

"In order to *have* somebody, you have to *be* somebody. A person who makes a commitment deserves a commitment in return."

"Then make one, Patti," Jill said encouragingly. "You can. I know you can."

"Let's go!" Patti got up from the table and in one blurred motion ran out the door. "I've got to keep moving."

"Patti, wait!" Jill called after her, then turned to Daisy. "Wrap your cheeseburger in a napkin, honey, and I'll pay the bill. The way Patti feels, she could take off without us."

"Mom!" Daisy protested, but she grabbed two napkins and began wrapping. "This is the way it was, moving west," she said, sliding out of the booth.

Patti was behind the wheel when Daisy and Jill reached the car.

"I know where I want to go," Patti said. "I want to walk on the beach."

"Then we'll walk on the beach," Jill said. "But I'm driving."

A half hour later they were walking on the beach that fronts the Miramar Hotel in Santa Barbara.

At first Patti half-ran, pacing the shoreline as she had Jill's carpet. Gradually she slowed to a more relaxed stroll.

"Was Greg right?" Jill asked. "Are you lonely?"

"I didn't know I was lonely until he said it. Isn't it strange that sometimes someone will say something, and you realize you knew it all along? It's as if the words had to come from one special voice."

They sat on the beach watching the ocean ripple, rolling with gentle laps at the shore. In the distance Jill saw oil derricks with their warning lights still burning against a lightening sky.

"Dawn doesn't break," Jill mused. "It just sort of sneaks up on you. Would either of you mind if I left you for half an hour? The monastery Dan is in is about two miles from here. I don't know if they allow visitors, especially at dawn, but—"

"Go," Patti ordered. "We'll wait here. Daisy and I can talk."

"I've already told Daisy about sex," Jill warned.

"We'll talk about fashion," Patti said. "Daisy has fabulous cheekbones. She may have a career."

"She may have her education first, or her mother may murder her. I'll be back in less than an hour."

Jill left them on the beach and drove through streets that reminded her more of the eastern suburbs of Cleveland, of Pepper Pike and Chagrin Falls, than they did of Los Angeles. Trees shaded the lawns of homes that looked like they had a history, perhaps not as interesting to tourists as one owned by Charlie Chaplin's gatekeeper, but considerably more substantial.

She drove past the monastery gates, then through grounds reminiscent of the cemetery where her father was buried.

There was a sign that read "Visitors' Entrance," which led to a door with a sign that read "Visitors' Bell."

The signs make me feel like I'm carrying the plague, but at least they allow visitors.

The elderly monk who answered the door asked Jill to wait in the garden.

She walked through a gate and into a garden where a white wrought-iron bench circled a juniper tree. Mums and marigolds brightened trimmed flower beds, and a statue of Saint Anthony beckoned birds to a fountain where water danced and sparkled in the early-morning sun. Jill sat on the bench and looked around her, feeling she'd come to a place where time stood still. Outside, the twentieth century might be rushing toward a collision with the twenty-first, but inside, Jill sat in eternity's stillness, the ocean breeze touching her face and drops of sunshine splashing through leaves over her head.

"Jill!" It was Dan's voice and Dan coming toward her with long, even strides and a smile on his face.

She jumped up from the bench. "Dan! You're wearing clothes!"

He looked down at himself and grinned. "We have to be decently covered. It's a rule."

"I meant I thought you might be wearing . . . a . . . robe?"

"I'm not a monk, Jill. Not yet, anyway."

"I suppose not. Uh . . ." Now that he was there, close, a hand's reach away, the questions she'd been storing up to ask slipped from her mind. "How are you?"

275

"Fine."

"You look fine . . . uh . . . um . . . How's the food?"

Dan laughed. "You drove up from Los Angeles to check on my diet? I don't believe it. What's going on?"

Jill told him about Patti and her panic over Greg's proposal. Dan listened carefully.

"She sounds like a lady who's had her equilibrium upset. Remember that old saying about being careful what you pray for?"

"I'm not sure Patti was praying for a man."

"Maybe not *a* man, or even *this* man. But we all pray for someone who'll love us exactly the way we are. A lover. A child. A parent. Someone. How's your child? And your parent?"

Jill told him about Daisy and Lenny, Daisy and Steve, Daisy and her fantasies about a reconciliation, Daisy and her possible emotional problems.

"I don't believe it," Dan said stoutly. "Anything's possible, and I would believe it if Daisy believed it, but from what you tell me, she doesn't think of herself as a girl with emotional problems, so why should I? Mental institutions are full of people who bought the idea when someone said go."

"And what about monasteries, Dan? Why are you here?"

He smiled. "This is where I need to be, with my old life behind me."

"I envy you." Jill watched as birds swooped over the fountain, skittering wings through water and calling to one another. "At least once a day I'd like to give my life to a worthy charity, run somewhere, and hide."

Dan glanced at her sharply, the old cutaway. "When I left UBC, I threw you into the deep end of the pool with the sharks. But you're swimming."

"You're sure about that?" Jill was amused by his certainty. "Most days I'm not sure I'll make it through to lunch."

Dan nodded. "I'm an excellent judge of character. "You're a survivor, and survive you will."

They sat in silence for several minutes, then Jill sighed, feeling both relaxed and wistful. "I could sit in this garden for the rest of my life and feel my problems were locked outside the gate."

"What problems?"

Jill told him about Julie, the tapes, and her mother's demands.

"Go home," Dan said. "Go to your sister. Do what you can to help."

"But to just drop everything, Dan, to—" Jill shook her head help-lessly.

He placed a calming hand on her shoulder. "Did you see the stars last night? And the full moon?"

"The moon lit my path up the coast."

"How many full moons have there been, Jill?" Dan asked. "And how many dawns? When the moon looked down on tribes dressed in skins, huddling together around a fire, did it illuminate a world with less value than this one? When dawn announces another day, ten million sunrises from now, will the sun shine down on a better world or just a different one? What will families be huddling around if it isn't a fire or a television set?"

"It's hard to imagine."

"But huddle they will. That I do know." Dan smiled at her skepti-cal look. "Life only lasts for a second, Jill, maybe twenty-five thou-sand sunrises out of a billion gone and a billion yet to come. Our genes tell us that, and as busy as we make ourselves trying to forget that four score and ten is a blink in God's eye, we can't. So we huddle together for comfort, knowing that the nurturing of one another, and therefore of the human race, is the point of it all, not crumbling bridges and fallen monuments, or the civilizations that dissolve into other civilizations or nothing at all. We huddle, that is, if we haven't become so slick at forgetting our truest instincts that we remember only when it's too late."

"You're talking about Nancy?"

"Of course."

"Is this place helping you, Dan? Are you recovering from Nancy's . . ."

"Death, Jill." He moved restlessly, clasping both knees with his hands. "My life here is one thing, getting over Nancy another. At first I thought I could run away from the pain or bury it here in this garden. But I couldn't run far enough, fast enough, and what's still alive can't be buried. I've found that the best I can do is to simply stand still and hurt."

"And you're hurting," Jill whispered, wanting to hold him, want-ing, in truth, to be held.

"On the morning of the day Nancy died, I was halfway to the office when I remembered I hadn't kissed her good-bye. I almost went back, but I didn't. My meeting, screening, whatever, was more im-portant. I thought I'd make up for it later, bring her flowers, something. There wasn't any later. The next time I saw Nancy, the doctor had just closed her eyes." Dan lowered his head to his hands. "More than anything else I wish I'd gone back to her that morning. I wish I'd kissed Nancy good-bye."

"You couldn't have known, Dan." *Small comfort, no comfort.*

"I didn't *want* to know. I was too busy being slick." Dan reached for her hand and held it lightly. "Listen to what's inside you, your instincts, your heart. Go to your sister. When blood calls to blood, it demands an answer."

"But, Dan . . ."

"Promise you'll think about it."

"I will."

"I know you will." Dan smiled. "When I asked you how your life was going, you told me about family and friends. Alex would have talked about his career."

"I'll let you know what happens," Jill promised.

"Please do. And forgive me. I tell you to trust your instincts, and then I give advice."

A bell began tolling, and they looked up at the tower, where a glint of brass swung upward to meet the sun.

"Mass," Dan explained. "Time to go. I'm going to give you a hug."

He did, and she held him close. "Take care of yourself Dan, and say one for me. Please."

"I will." He walked her to the gate. "Don't stop sending your notes, Jill. They make me laugh, and I need that, even in a monastery."

"My pleasure." Jill squeezed his hand, then reluctantly walked away. She looked over her shoulder just once. Dan was standing motionless, half in and half out of the shadows.

Returning to the beach, she saw Daisy and Patti in the distance, running along the shore. She ran after them, starting out like Bill Rogers and ending up like Roy.

"I'm out of shape," Jill panted.

"Daisy's like a gazelle," Patti told her. "She outlasted me."

"I'm only fifteen," Daisy was quick to point out. "If I can't outlast someone more than twice my age—"

"Daisy!" Patti was wounded. "Do you have to remind me?"

"Would you like a teenage daughter, Patti? I have one for sale." Jill laughed. "We'd better go. If we don't hit major traffic, we'll be in L.A. in time for work. And school."

"Don't break any speed laws on my account." Daisy grinned.

Daisy started down the beach at a trot, followed closely by Patti.

Jill watched them for a moment, amused at Daisy's exuberance and Patti's spirit. She might be undone, but she wasn't done for.

Jill kicked off her shoes, bent over to pick them up, then straightened up sharply, a sensation that was something between an electric current and a shiver shooting up her spine. Behind her, farther down the beach and almost at the water's edge, was the gray clapboard house of her dreams. Whoever owned it had thrown the white shutters open to the sun.

More than anything Jill wanted to approach the house, wanted to see if there were white starched curtains on the windows and a pane of stained glass running the length of the door. But she was transfixed, immobile, and would have remained so if Daisy hadn't returned, laughing and not the least winded, to run gleeful circles around her.

Jill hurried, or rather stumbled along, following Daisy to the car.

As they drove, Patti regaled Daisy with stories of the fashion world and the men she'd encountered there. Jill tried to listen if only to interrupt Patti when she became too graphic. Once or twice it occurred to Jill that Patti had recovered too fully, too fast, but each time the thought shot through her mind, Dan, or Julie, or the shock of seeing the house on the beach pushed it away.

I must have seen that house before, or one like it. It's déjà vu.

"You don't read pornography, do you?" Patti was asking Daisy.

"Not unless you count Chaucer."

"Never read that one, but I'm telling you, kid, porn can ruin you. All those male things poking into female things, and heavy-breathing gymnastics and stuff spurting all over the place. Makes sex sound unappealing, like the Olympic trials with goo."

"Would anyone like to hear the news?" Quickly Jill turned on the radio.

Just as quickly Patti turned it down. "Why are you getting nervous, Jill? I'm telling Daisy to stay away from dirty books."

"Your motives are impeccable, Patti, but I don't think Daisy needs a warning about pornography."

"I wish someone had warned *me* at fifteen," Patti said fervently. "It could have saved me from a lot of false impressions. And expectations. I mean, have you ever had a man actually plunge at you like a stallion? Your whole pelvis could break!"

"Patti! Stop!"

"And trembling and sighing." Patti was not to be suppressed. "Trembling and sighing isn't my style, even when sex is great. But the guys have all read this stuff and they expect trembling and sighing, so I tremble and sigh. I should go on the stage."

"Patti." Jill turned the radio up. "Listen to Roger Mudd."

They listened to the early newscast with its usual compendium of disasters, followed by a local weather report that promised more rain.

"Time for the Anne Klein tweed ensemble with a bright yellow slicker to finish it off," Patti decided. "Go for eclectic, Daisy. It's more fun and you'll develop a style of your own." She tapped Jill on the shoulder. "And you need to get pulled together before you get canned for dressing funny. You haven't been at UBC long enough to be eccentric."

"Alex hasn't either, and you should see him." Jill laughed.

"Men!" Patti bit off the word. "They get away with it. Speaking of Alex, that's over."

"It is?" Jill wasn't surprised.

"He's too crazy, even for me. And the next time he makes one of his obscene phone calls—"

"*Alex!*" He makes *what!*"

"Obscene phone calls," Patti repeated. "At first it was just heavy breathing. Then he began to . . . well, talk about porn! You know, between dropping in at midnight and calling me even later than that, I've decided Alex must slip Nina a Mickey every night."

"Heavy breathing?" *Alex!*

"Yeah." Patti shrugged. "Juvenile, isn't it? Or weird. Or both. He reminds me of a guy I used to date who'd jump every lady he met, then call them up and breathe in their ears. He finally went into therapy and discovered the root of his problem."

"That's encouraging." Jill said brightly, thinking there might be hope for Alex.

"Yeah." Patti giggled. "My former friend is now living in Loma Linda with a male masseur who's massaging the root of his problem."

"Oh, my God!" Jill said. "Poor Nina!"

"I don't understand what you're saying," Daisy complained. "What kind of therapy cured this guy?"

They pulled up to the house, and Patti jumped out of the car. Jill got out, stretching and yawning, feeling like she'd already lived through a full day.

"I won't try to thank you for tonight, Jill." Patti hugged her. "Your being here saved my life."

"What are you going to do about Greg, Patti? Have you made any decision?"

"I'll date him," Patti said casually, "and other people as well. Why should I sell the cow when I can give the milk away free?"

"Greg sounds like a really nice guy, Patti. . . ."

"And we all know how they finish." Patti laughed. "Watch out for people you meet under nuthouse pianos, kid. Sooner or later they drag you out in the middle of the night."

"We haven't had such fun since the loony bin." Jill returned her hug. "Take care of yourself."

"That's what I'm best at."

"I mean it, Patti, no phony stiff upper lips. Call me."

"Will do." Patti waved from her car window. "Good night. Or good morning. Or something."

She drove off, leaving Jill and Daisy on the sidewalk.

"I like Patti, Mom." Daisy said. "She's got what they call pizzazz."

"Enough for us all, Daisy."

"Well, it's time for my May Company corduroy ensemble with a Jefferson High School warm-up jacket to finish it off. Okay if I shower first?"

"Sure, Daisy. Just make it quick. And, honey . . ."

"Yes, Mom."

"I hope you didn't get the wrong impression from Patti's continual dwelling on sex. There are other things in life. And in relationships, too."

"I know, Mom." Daisy was beginning to smile.

"I mean, someday you'll meet a man, and I'm not saying you have to be married, but it should be special."

"I know that too, Mom."

"You're still too young to deal with the feelings that should be a part of a physical relationship," Jill said, looking straight into Daisy's eyes. "I know you must be curious, but even Patti would tell you that it should happen at the right time. You don't have to experiment."

"I'm not ready for that yet, Mom. How can I know what kind of man I'll want until I know what kind of woman I'll be?" Daisy smiled, adding kindly, "I'll tell you when to worry."

"Oh." Jill was taken aback. "Well, thank you, Daisy, and I'll be here if you have any more questions."

"I didn't have any to begin with." Daisy's eyes sparkled. "I'm going to shower."

Daisy ran for the shower, and Jill walked into her room, wondering if Daisy's observation might apply to her as well. Perhaps her trouble with men stemmed from her uncertainty about what kind of woman she was. Or would be.

The phone rang. Jill reached for it, wondering if Alex had switched to obscene early-morning wake-up calls.

"Hello," Jill said.

"Jill!" Kate was sobbing. "Julie is in my living room, sitting under the scaffolding with paint dripping on her head. She won't move away from the television set, and I can't understand what she's saying. She doesn't sound like my Julie. She sounds like you the day you went crazy. Mother of God!" Kate wailed. "I called your brother, but he was in a meeting and his goddamned secretary wouldn't put me through. My heart is leaping! Your sister is crazy! Your father would kill me! What can I do?"

"Don't cry, Ma. I'm coming home."

CHAPTER 19

"Who came running when you were in trouble?" Daisy demanded, watching Jill pack. "I didn't see Grandma or Uncle John or Aunt Julie breaking down *our* door when you were cra— er, upset. Or when you and Dad got divorced. You could have used a shoulder to cry on, but *they* kept *their* shoulders at home. What about that, Mom?"

"Please hand me my bathrobe, Daisy. The warm one."

Daisy handed Jill the robe, then perched on the end of the bed, bouncing with youth and indignation. "It's like they have some strange hold over you, like Mrs. Danvers in *Rebecca* or Rochester in *Jane Eyre*."

"You forgot Daddy Warbucks in *Orphan Annie*." Jill closed her suitcase. "There's no strange hold, Daisy, at least not in the gothic sense. And I can't explain why I'm going."

"You can tell me," Daisy assured her. "I'm old enough to hear family secrets."

"If you were a wizened crone, I couldn't explain. My decision has nothing to do with logic."

"What did Dad say when you told him?" Daisy asked.

"He surprised me. He said he thought I should go, wished me a pleasant trip, and said he would look forward to spending time with his best girl." Jill glanced quickly at Daisy. "That's you."

"I'll keep an eye on Susan for you, Mom," Daisy promised. "I'll keep Dad so busy he won't have time for anyone else."

"You're the one who can do it. Let's go. I have to stop at the office before I go to the airport."

As they pulled up in front of school Daisy threw her arms around Jill in a deliberately rib-crunching hug.

"Take care of yourself, Daisy." Jill kissed her. "Look after your daddy. He could use some huddling together." Jill opened the car door. "I'll miss you. And honey, read *Profiles in Courage*. You've had enough exposure to people who exert strange holds over people. You need an introduction to people who've managed to take hold of themselves."

"I'll get it at the library, Mom."

"And good luck on your history exam," Jill called as Daisy ran up the steps.

Jill drove to the office, continuing to puzzle over Steve's reaction to her trip. She'd repeated Dan's phrase, "When blood calls to blood, it demands an answer." He'd been silent for several seconds, then said, "How can I help?" He hadn't told her what she *should* do, or *should* feel, or *should* think. He hadn't asked why. He hadn't advised her to "think it through."

Passing strange.

Polly was waiting at the door of Jill's office, holding a bundle tied with twine. "Here are the reports you wanted. And the scripts. And a list of your personal phone calls, including six from Dr. Neil Kaiser."

"Six? The fish must have died. Anything else?"

"A note from Dale Neiman," Polly pulled it from her pocket and read: " 'Lawrence and Abelard love the comedy angle on *Rock and Roll Love*. Have assigned round-the-clock editing for projected air date next week. Congratulations!' "

"I knew it was a good idea, Polly. I didn't know it was that good."

"The grapevine is that Abelard beeped his brains out when he heard it," Polly chuckled. "And Lawrence drank a quart of Tang."

Jill laughed. "I'm a success. Thanks for coming in so early this morning. You didn't seem surprised when I told you about my plans."

"I wasn't. And I agree with what you're doing. You won't be the same person when you return."

Jill grinned. "If I have my choice, can I be Barbra Streisand? I'm tempted to ask how this will all turn out, but as my mother says, what I don't know won't hurt me. Just tell me if the plane's going to crash."

"No!" Polly's response was immediate. "Though I do sense turbulence over Chicago."

"That's my sister. Or my stomach. I hate flying."

"Who's flying?" Alex walked into the office, natty in a gray Brooks Brothers suit with matching circles under his eyes.

"Family emergency," Jill told him. "I'm on my way to Cleveland."

"*Now!*" Alex was incredulous. "Just when we've had our greatest success! You're out of your fucking mind! The talk on the walk is that Lawrence thinks you're a genius, and Abelard's about to propose. You're going to blow it—"

"I think the talk where you walk is pure hype, Alex, and I don't expect you to understand." Jill took the bundle from Polly. "You and I march to different drummers."

"What the fuck are you talking about?" Alex raged.

"In fact, it's not just the drummer, it's the whole damn band." Jill frowned, thinking of Patti's revelation. "Please be reachable by phone, Alex. I'll call in regularly, and Polly will fill you in if we miss connections."

Alex scowled. "Hey, I've got better things to do than sit here dead on my ass waiting for you to call. I've got ideas, too, you know. And I won't take any fill-ins from any goddamned secretary, either."

"Sure you will, dear." Jill patted Alex on the cheek. "And don't dump your work on Polly. She isn't your personal servant."

"Polly can do whatever I tell her until I've hired my own girl. That's not something I'm rushing."

"And last but definitely not least, stop making obscene phone calls, Alex. They aren't entertaining enough to warrant the breath you're wasting." Jill smiled pleasantly.

"Holy shit!" Alex turned scarlet, then white. "How . . . I mean. . . . You couldn't believe . . . You don't think . . . I wouldn't . . . How low . . ."

Jill interrupted his sputtering. "Good-bye, Polly. Keep a light in the window. I'll be in touch."

"I'll be here, Jill. Good flight." Polly waved.

"Gimme that bundle." Alex yanked it out of Jill's hands. "I'll carry it for you."

He followed her down the hall to the elevator. They got in, and he threw himself at the button. "Let me. I'll do it."

"Thanks, Alex." Jill wasn't sure the elevator would contain him. He was jiggling in four directions at once.

"I swear to God, I won't make a fucking move without telling Polly," Alex raved. "If I have to go to the can, I'll tell her."

"That ought to brighten up her day." Jill stepped out of the elevator into the lobby.

Alex followed her through the lobby into the parking lot. "I've interviewed a dynamite secretary, Jill. I'll call her, hire her this afternoon! She's on the elderly side but has years of experience. Did you hear me, Jill?" He waved his arms wildly. "I said she's old! Experience! A real secretary!".

"That's wonderful, Alex." Jill smiled as they reached her car. "Maybe she'll let you sit on her lap and call her Mommy."

"That's kinky, Jill!" He hopped like one possessed. "I'm not a kinky person. I don't even talk to kinky people. If I meet somebody kinky, man, I run the other way." He clutched at her arm. "You haven't mentioned the phone calls to anyone, have you? Told anyone at UBC? I mean, those phone calls you're getting from some unknown kinky person!"

"I haven't said anything."

"Thank God," he said fervently. "Of course, I'm only concerned about *your* reputation, Jill. Sometimes women really dig obscene calls, and guys think—"

"You ought to know." Jill slid behind the wheel. "You've provided many a midnight thrill."

"I'm seeing a shrink," he blurted out. "I started this morning. This sucker's the best in town, Henry Sitzbach."

"Television's own Henry Sitzbach?" Jill laughed. "Trust you to go for a show-biz shrink. I can see you now, Alex, discussing telephone techniques on the *Six O'Clock See It Now News.*"

"It's helping, Jill!" Alex roared above the sound of the engine. "It's worth getting up at dawn for!"

Jill leaned out the window and waved. "I'm glad you're in therapy, Alex. You'll just love Loma Linda."

Drops of rain fell on Alex's new suit as he trotted alongside her moving car.

"This morning we delved into my childhood!" he shouted. "My mother used to lock me in the closet, Jill! I was scared, just a little boy alone in the dark, hugging his mother's mink!"

"Maybe there's a series in it!" Jill yelled. She stepped on the gas and swung to the right, out of the parking lot.

As Jill approached the airport the steady rain had formed puddles that stretched halfway across the street.

She locked the car and made a run for the terminal, carrying her bundle and one small bag. It wasn't optimism that had inspired her to travel light, but the experience of the last trip.

On the plane a pleasant stewardess handed Jill a pillow. "Is your trip business or pleasure?"

"Business," Jill replied, unwilling to explain about painters, plumbers, and a sister supposedly stricken with insanity.

The squat, hairy man in the seat next to her laughed, a sharp barking sound, like a dog. "No law says you can't have both on the same trip, honey."

Jill sighed, wondering if there was a target painted on her forehead. Even on trips she had taken with Steve, the fringies of the world had gone out of their way to cross her path. Hare Krishna assaulted her with books and flowers, righteous youth assailed her with petitions—*Save the Nukes! Nuke the Whales!*—unattached males sent up signals that were invitations to transient attachments —one night of bliss, breakfast, and a million cc's of penicillin, *stat.*

"Where are you staying in Cleveland, honey?" the bulldog man asked as they roared down the runway.

"The Sacred Heart Convent." Jill smiled. "I'm a nun."

"Oh, jeez." He was appalled. "I'm a Catholic myself. No offense intended, Sister."

"None taken," Jill said graciously.

"How's a man to know?" he mumbled as they ascended in pelting rain. "When the Pope told nuns to modernize, he couldn't have meant they should wear Vanderbilt jeans."

The plane jolted upward with engines straining as they lurched through clouds that surrounded them like an ominous, stormy tunnel. Jill realized that she hadn't exhaled since they'd left the ground. Since she'd so cleverly severed connections with her traveling companion, she'd have to find another distraction. She tugged at the twine on her bundle and reached in.

The script fate gave her was titled *Broken Promises.* As the plane dipped sharply sideways Jill gasped, seeing tomorrow's headline in *Variety: UBC Exec Ankles Web for Great Beyond.*

She ignored her seatmate, who was crossing himself frantically, noted the position of the emergency exits, kicked off her shoes, and began to read.

Four hours later she'd read the script three times. As the plane made a long, graceful circle, its final approach to Cleveland's Hopkins Airport, Jill tried to repair the makeup that her tears had washed away.

The eyes reflecting from her compact mirror were puffy beyond help, so she settled for a stroke of blush on each cheek and a dab of lip gloss.

"Hope everything's all right, Sister," her companion said as the plane taxied and slowed. "I didn't want to bother you while you were crying. Thought you might be having a religious experience."

Jill smiled at him. "No, I just read something sad."

She was swept along in the crush of deplaning passengers. The same crush propelled Jill to the lower level, where she went through the motions of claiming baggage and renting a car.

She drove away from the airport with the final scene of *Broken Promises* playing in her head: A mother and teenage daughter regarding one another coldly over the grave of their husband/father, the promises implicit in their relationship broken, their last hope for reconciliation vanished in missed connections.

Jill thought of Dan mourning his Nancy, despising himself for having built the shabby fantasy that there would always be time "later."

That could be Daisy and me if I'm blind enough to ignore those moments when her hand reaches for mine. . . .

She pulled up in front of Kate's and sat for a moment, contemplating the outside of the house. It seemed quiet enough, almost sleepy and certainly benign, but then, so had the house in *Psycho,* and mayhem had nestled beneath those eaves. She wondered why some houses look separate, apart, unattached to the landscape or the houses around them. Just another of life's mysteries, she supposed, like the way some of us feel like orphans with our parents in the room.

She got out of the car and walked briskly up the drive, *acting as if* she expected Kate's door to open on nothing but love, laughter, and a heroine's welcome. Though *acting as if* didn't still all the wobblies, it did keep her legs going forward. That would have to be enough for the moment.

She paused at the back door, uncertain as to the protocol involved in entering this house.

As children, John, Julie, and Jill had shoved one another on Friday afternoons in a ritual contest to determine who would be the first through this door, the first to hear Kate yell "I just scrubbed, don't walk on the floors," and the first to shout in return "I can't walk on the ceilings, Ma." As a virgin in white she'd walked out this door on the arm of her father and returned two hours later, still virginal and still in white, but on the arm of her husband while her father walked behind.

And it was out this door that a priest, a doctor, and his only son had carried him years later, wrapped in a sheet as white as Jill's gown and most certainly dead. Whatever the protocol, waiting outside only increased her apprehension, so she grasped the doorknob and burst in, yelling "Mother, I'm home."

I sound like Leave It to Beaver.

She tiptoed through the laundry room, feeling she'd shot her last bolt of bravery just getting through the door.

In the kitchen she found Kate removing a pie from the oven.

"Mince." Kate held up the pie. "Fresh from last Christmas. Want some?"

"Thanks, Ma. I ate on the plane." Jill wondered where the hysterical mother of the phone call had gone—and who was this pie-baker in her place?

"Airline food will kill you," Kate warned. "You could embalm an entire family with the preservatives they put in that crap. Ask Jim. He'll tell you." Kate carried the pie to the door that separated the kitchen from the living room. "Jim, come in here and tell Jill about airline food."

Kate set the pie on the table. "I'm cutting the pie, and you'll have some. You're too skinny for a woman your age."

"How fat should a thirty-five-year-old woman be, Ma?"

"Watch your mouth," Kate hissed. "I told Jim you're thirty-one. He thinks I'm fifty-five."

"*I* thought you were fifty-five. That's what you told me."

"And I am," Kate declared. "No matter what my driver's license says. The DMV made a mistake. Computers are only human, you know."

"Tell me about it." Jill took the pie from Kate, then watched silently as she poured coffee into blue china cups. "Uh . . . Ma, God knows your mince pie from last Christmas is reason enough for a trip from Los Angeles, but . . . uh . . . where is Julie?"

Kate handed a cup to Jill, whispering "Your sister is in the living room, watching a rerun of *Let's Make a Deal*."

"I'd certainly call that a crisis, Ma."

"John is still in his meeting," Kate continued. "Any company that has meetings all day is sooner or later going to catch hell from the stockholders. How can they build computers if all they do is talk?"

"John doesn't build them, Ma. He sells them."

"He can't sell something that nobody's building. Where's Jim? I called him five minutes ago. Fred will be here for dinner," she went

289

on distractedly. "He said he has to arrange for someone to stay with Morgan and Kendrick. He says this isn't something one drags one's children into. Pah!"

"Why is Fred coming from Chicago for dinner, Ma?" Jill handed Kate her empty plate, knowing that somehow, someday, she'd hear the whole story. Kate could never be pushed, only led, and, then, only as far as she'd go.

"Fred had to *arrange* for someone to take care of his kids," Kate said. "Well, if his family is too damn good to baby-sit for their own grandchildren . . . wait till the next time Fred asks me!"

"Ma, I know you're upset," Jill said gently. "If you weren't upset, you wouldn't give me pie before dinner. But I came a long way as fast as I could, and I just have to ask. Why is Julie in your living room watching *Let's Make a Deal?*"

"She ran away with a priest"—Kate threw up her hands—"last weekend!"

"Julie did *what!*"

"It was that Father Norton. You know, the one from St. Basil's— the parish has started bingo again, and a lot of people are upset, but I always say, What the hell? if people enjoy it, and the money goes to the church . . ."

"Julie did *what!*"

"She went to a youth-group meeting on Friday night, and never came home until Sunday. They might not have come home then except Father Norton had to perform a baptism, and—"

"Julie did *what!*"

"Of course Fred was beside himself. He'd even notified the police, which made it very embarrassing when he had to call them back and say his wife had come home. Serves him right! Jim told me about Fred sending that lawyer to the hospital. Where the hell is Jim?"

"Ma, you are making this up." Jill sank into one of Kate's polished chairs and buried her head in her arms.

"I am *not* making it up," Kate asserted. "Julie's admitted it. When Fred asked her where she'd been, she said, 'I went to Muncie, Indiana, with Father Norton. We had an affair.' Just like that. Can you imagine? At least you always lied to Steve."

"Oh, God." Jill's voice was muffled.

"Sit up straight, Jill. Do what you want in your own house, but in my house people don't put their heads on the table." Kate pulled her chair close to Jill's. "After Julie told Fred about the affair, she packed her suitcase and came home. That's why she's in the living room watching *Let's Make a Deal!*"

"Muncie, Indiana?" Jill wondered how many people go to Muncie to get laid.

"In a TraveLodge," Kate elaborated.

"Oh, Ma." Jill tried to picture Julie banging her brains out with a man of the cloth in Muncie, Indiana. She gave up. It would be easier to picture Alex becoming Pope.

"But I still don't understand why you called me, Ma. Isn't this a private matter between Julie and Fred?"

"Your sister is in the living room, sitting on a drop cloth. When I ask her a question, she babbles. I don't know what to do."

"What makes you think I do?"

"You've babbled. You've run off with men. You've even been locked up in one of those places. You must have been cured, Jill. They let you out." Kate shook her head. "*I* wouldn't have. A woman who divorces a man like Steve can't be all there, but at least you're not babbling. Just go in the living room and tell Julie whatever that doctor said that cured you."

"Now I understand," Jill said, and she did. She'd been summoned to perform magic, to provide the cure. *Jill Dunn Kenyon, black sheepess and part-time magician.* She should have cards printed. "It's not that simple, Ma."

"It must be," Kate said resolutely. "You went away crazy, and you came back . . . not so crazy. What did that doctor say that cured you?"

"We talked a lot, Ma. I can't precisely remember."

"You *must* remember what the doctor told you. You have to tell Julie so she'll be all better before Fred gets here. We'll have pot roast and gravy. They'll go home together." Kate looked woefully at Jill. "Why does everything happen to me?"

"I finally found it." Jim rushed into the kitchen carrying a magazine. "The article on airline food in *Fit as a Fiddle Now!* It says right here—"

"Hello, Jim," Jill greeted him.

"Carry fruit," Jim advised. "For the trip home your mother will give you a bag of peaches. Fruit with pits will protect you from preservatives."

"Peaches cost a fortune," Kate informed him. "I'll give her prunes. Or grapefruit. Grapefruit are in season."

"Grapefruit have seeds, Kate. Seeds are not pits. See, it says right here—"

"Forget it, Jim. Jill won't eat fruit. When she was a kid, she ate library paste. She'd come home from school with her lips stuck together. . . ."

Jill walked into the living room, the overpowering smell of fresh paint and turpentine used to clean brushes causing an instantaneous churning of her stomach. The furniture had been stacked against one wall and shrouded in tarpaulins, the rugs rolled in long, lumpy cylinders and propped up against the Everest of chairs and tables. Only the old console television set remained in its familiar position, solid, immovable, entrenched.

Julie sat on a drop cloth before it, her legs folded under her in the classic pose for meditation. Stone-silent and transfixed, Julie stared at the screen, where a woman dressed as a treehouse chose door number three.

"Julie? It's Jill."

Julie gave no sign that she'd heard. Jill moved closer. "May I sit down, Julie?"

There was no response, so Jill lowered herself to the drop cloth, tucked her legs under her, and waited.

On television the treehouse woman was bug-eyed as door number three slid open to reveal a shiny convertible and forty-nine feet of garden hose. Overcome, she squealed with delight and bounded straight into the air, landing with an impact that knocked off her branches. Undaunted, she hugged Monty.

Jill forced herself to sit quietly, to wait for Julie's response. In the hospital she'd seen patients whose superficial tranquillity was only a resting place, the last stop before the final, full flight into insanity. Jill had seen that flight precipitated by the good intentions and bad timing of someone who "just wanted to help."

"Will you talk to me, Julie?" Jill asked softly. "If you like, you can tell me what's troubling you."

"Okay," Julie said. Her voice was a shadow of the voice Jill knew. "I ran away to Muncie, Indiana, with Father Norton. We had an affair."

"Oh." Jill hadn't expected her to be so straightforward. "Well . . . uh . . . you must be very . . . upset."

Julie nodded automatically, her eyes riveted to the screen. "I did a terrible thing. Fred will be here for dinner. I hope Ma makes mashed potatoes. Fred loves mashed potatoes."

God help me. What do I say now?

"Uh . . . Julie, dear, if you want, but only if you want, you can tell me why you . . . uh . . . did what you did." Jill crossed her fingers, hoping she wasn't pushing.

"I got tired," Julie murmured, "so tired, like one of those dramas where you run and run and never get anywhere. Just tired. Not sick. I never get sick. Even when we had measles. You and John were sick, but I just had spots."

"I remember our measles, Julie." Jill did. Julie's fever had remained dangerously high for days. She'd been delirious, the only one of the triplets who'd been seriously ill.

"Perhaps you've been doing too much," Jill suggested. "Your schedule is rather demanding."

"It's not the schedule's fault." Julie's eyes grew round at the thought. "It's a good schedule. It's my fault I got behind."

"Sometimes that happens, honey. We can't always be perfect." Jill reached for her hand and held it.

"My lesson plans got shorter and shorter." Julie cocked her head to one side. "My students began talking in class. And they got louder and louder . . . like trains coming . . . and I forgot Kendrick's piano lesson. . . . He has a gift. . . . Fred loves Bach. . . . There's a precision in Bach, like physics. Did you know that on a Touch-Tone phone our number is discordant? I call home, and the number sounds like bang, bang, clang, dong. And the ironing . . . It grows in the basket. I burned my hand. See? The night I went to the youth-group meeting, I left dishes in the sink . . . didn't even scrape and rinse . . . Carrots all over. Morgan doesn't like carrots. She mashes them up and hides them under things. I never leave dishes in the sink. Dissolute women do that. Worthless women."

The definitions that kill us. Worthless. Worthy. Dissolute. Damned.

"So, that night you went to the youth-group meeting. Then what, Julie?" Jill said encouragingly.

"Father Norton asked me to stay and have coffee with him." Julie sounded pleased at the memory. "He has an espresso machine, a gift from his family. He told me about them. Or how he's suffered . . . the conflict . . . the existential despair. It's not cold and numb. Despair burns to the touch. . . . He has circles under his eyes . . . lassitude and swollen glands . . . a pain in his lower back . . . despair or too much espresso. . . . His touch burns. . . ." Julie's words drifted away, and she seemed to drift with them.

"Julie?" Jill tried to pull her back. "How did you get from coffee at church to Muncie, Indiana?"

"I'll be punished. It's only right that I am. I didn't wash my dishes. Oh. Oh." Julie was suddenly rigid, breathless. "Do you suppose Fred did the dishes? That would be awful! It isn't his job. . . . He works so hard. . . . He's so important. . . . It's all my fault!" Julie squeezed the tips of Jill's fingers. "I can't ask him that. You do it, Jill. Wait in the kitchen. Ask him. Come back and tell me. If Fred did the dishes, I'll have to be punished. I'll kill myself!"

"Uh . . . wait here, Julie." Jill scrambled to her feet, patted Julie's shoulder, and headed for the kitchen.

Jim was reading his magazine to Kate, who was peeling potatoes. "Don't ask Julie how her affair happened," Jill warned, "or why."

"Hear about an affair with a priest?" Kate was aghast. "I'd have to go to confession from hearing about that." She dumped the potatoes in a pot and clamped on the lid. "Is Julie better yet?"

Jill shook her head. "Not yet, Ma."

"Well, *do* something," Kate demanded. "Dinner's almost ready."

"I can't cure Julie, Ma. She needs professional help."

"Then call that doctor of yours, what's-his-name?"

"Neil Kaiser." Jill scrambled for a reason not to call Neil. "Julie should see a therapist in Chicago, Ma. That's where she lives. Therapy can take time."

"For you maybe," Kate snorted. "But your sister has always been sensible. For her, it should take ten minutes."

"But, Ma—"

Kate waved her potato-masher at Jim. "Have I ever told you how Jill used to stamp her foot and shout at me when she was no more than two years old? Julie never did that. Julie was my good girl. I can't imagine what's happened to her."

"Sugar, fat, artificial coloring, and sodium nitrate, that's what," Jim announced. "People have been losing their minds since the invention of lunch meat."

Kate removed the phone from its place on a small wicker table and placed it before Jill. "Call your Dr. Kaiser. Make an appointment for tomorrow."

Nervously Jill turned away form the phone. "He could be out of town."

"Nonsense. Doctors don't vacation in November. They might miss Thanksgiving dinner with their mothers. Call." Kate thrust the phone into Jill's hand.

Jill held the receiver for a moment, then slowly replaced it. She'd run out of excuses. The only remaining option was to tell Kate the truth—that until she could reconcile the Neil Kaiser of the past, that knight in shining armor, with the rusty, tarnished being he'd become, any contact with him was a trip across a minefield that could blow her to smithereens.

"Sometimes a person changes." Jill tried for a half-truth Kate might accept. "Time passes, and the person isn't what he was before, if indeed he ever was to begin with, and it may well be that he never was, or, to be fair, he may be again at some point in the future what he was—"

"Mother of God!" Kate burst into tears. "Now *she's* babbling!" Kate flung herself at Jim, who hugged her, while glaring over her shoulder at Jill. "I've been a good mother, Jim," Kate sobbed. "How can they do this to me?"

"I didn't mean to upset you, Ma." So much for half-truths. It had availed her nothing. "I do want to help."

"What do you know?" Kate glowered from the circle of Jim's arms. "You can't even remember how Dr. Kaiser cured you." Kate picked up the phone. "I'm calling your brother."

While Kate haggled with John's secretary Jill tiptoed into the living room. Julie was just as she'd been, motionless and transcendental before the television set.

Let's Make a Deal continued, with a man in a banana suit apoplectic over the loss of a trip to Tahiti. He brandished his peel at Monty, who backed away, looking nervous.

Jill returned to the kitchen just as Kate slammed down the phone. "The family's falling apart, and John's still in a meeting!"

Jill reached for the phone. "I'll give it a shot."

"You're calling John?" Kate was surprised.

"I know a man in a monastery who's more accessible than John." Jill dialed. "It's un-American to be unreachable by phone."

When John's secretary answered the phone, Jill dropped her voice an octave and said "To whom am I speaking?"

"Christy Fortman," the young woman replied. "Who is this?"

"Are you Mr. Dunn's secretary or his assistant?"

"His . . . uh . . . assistant." She hesitated only a second.

"I thought so." Jill smiled at the phone. "For an order this large I should speak to Mr. Dunn personally, but I'm sure I might just as well take the matter up with you."

"An order?" Miss Fortman was interested, very.

"What is she doing?" Jim whispered to Kate.

"Ask me something I know," Kate snapped. "Like God's middle name."

Jill lowered her voice another half-octave. "I represent Global International Telemetrics with subsidiaries in Europe, the Near East, the Far East, the Middle East, and Kalamazoo. Our board of directors has empowered me to purchase approximately four hundred personal home computers for our middle- to high-level executives. They're to be installed as individual terminals linked to our main computer in Zurich. When can we expect delivery?"

"Four hundred!" Miss Fortman gasped.

"Perhaps more."

"Um . . . just a moment, please." Miss Fortman put her on hold, and Jill waited, thinking that Alex at the peak of his form couldn't have done better.

"Mr. Dunn speaking." It was John. "How may I help you?"

"For openers, you can say 'Welcome home.' "

"Jill! Is that you?"

"It's me."

"But my secretary said—"

"Getting through to you is a problem, John. Some things can't wait until meetings are over. I'm at Mother's house."

"Is Ma in the hospital again?"

"Ma's fine," Jill assured him.

Kate leaned over the phone. "Don't listen to her. I could have a heart attack any minute!"

"What *is* going on?" John demanded. "They're holding the meeting for me. Most of our inventory is stuck in a boxcar on a siding in Buffalo—"

"Julie's here, Johnny. She came home to Ma with a problem."

"That's why you're in Cleveland? Your sister went home to her mother? No wonder Steve gave up. With you it's always a mountain, never a molehill."

"This is a mountain kind of problem, Johnny."

"I'm sure Fred and Julie can handle whatever tiff, whatever spat—"

"Fred's coming for dinner," Jill interrupted. "I doubt that handling it is what he has in mind."

"Fred's coming to Cleveland from Chicago for dinner?" John sounded thoughtful. "Something's not normal."

"Now you're catching on. We need a family conference."

"Why?" There was more apprehension than curiosity in his voice.

Jill glanced at Kate, who was chopping lettuce and listening intently. "Because we're a family, Johnny, that's why. And one of us has a problem."

"I'd like to help, Jill, honest I would," John said in his I'm-a-stranger-here-myself voice. "But I have to work late tonight. If I don't get those computers out of Buffalo . . . Candy isn't available either. She'll be downtown at a Fascinating Womanhood lecture."

"Johnny!" Jill was desperate. "If Pa was alive, he would be here. Pa would have a family conference!"

There was a long silence. "I'll be there as soon as I can."

"We'll keep your dinner warm," Jill promised, "and when you get here, I'll give you the hug you deserve."

"He's coming?" Kate asked in astonishment as Jill hung up the phone. "He answered the phone, and now he's coming? How did you do that?"

"Executive skills, Ma. That's why they pay me big bucks."

Kate shook her finger at Jill. "Lying! That's what it was. Calling a secretary and lying is not executive skills."

Jill grinned. "Wanna bet? They hold seminars to teach people how."

The doorbell rang.

"Fred's always on time," Kate said approvingly. "He's a son of a bitch, but he's punctual." She removed her apron. "Tell Julie, Fred is here. Maybe she'll stop babbling."

"I only hope he doesn't make her worse," Jill said uneasily.

"How could he make her worse?" Kate asked. "He's her husband." She handed the pie to Jill. "Reheat the mince."

While Kate answered the door Jill slipped the pie into the oven and thought about what she'd told John.

It was true. Pa would have had a family conference. During the time they were growing up family conferences were infrequent, but solemn, events. John Dunn, Sr., would gather them around the dining table and intone "We are about to have a discussion."

His use of the word *discussion* did not mean an exchange of ideas. It meant he would make pronouncements, and they would acquiesce. Jill came to think of these sessions as "getting our marching orders," and passed this on to John and Julie, who'd giggled and agreed. She'd never dared use it in the presence of Pa. It was an *if* phrase.

If Pa's mood was expansive "marching orders" might well have been received with a smile and a delighted "Right you are, Jilly, just like General Patton. And by the God that made us, this family could take on an army of huns!"

But *if* his mood was dark and brooding, "marching orders" might have been met with a thunderous "By God, I'll not have such disrespect!"

The thunder would be accompanied by a terrible swift throwing of handy objects or, on the worst days, Johnny, whom an importune fate invariably placed within his father's reach, if not his grasp.

There was no way of knowing, ever, which it would be, for Pa was the eye of the hurricane, deceptively tranquil, even sunny at times, but subject to sudden and cataclysmic change.

Even so, Jill would have taken her chances with thunder, would have welcomed the hurricane home, would have found refuge, as always, in his consistent unpredictability, if only, *if* only, Pa might appear, take his accustomed place at the head of the table, and tell them all what to do.

CHAPTER 20

"I am not a vindictive man, Mother Dunn." Fred accepted the coffee Kate offered him. "I simply do not understand Julie's behavior."

"She's not acting like the Julie we both know and love," Kate agreed. "We *do* love her, don't we Fred?"

"I expected to love Julie until death did us part." Fred's voice was cold. "It's Julie and her . . . liaison . . . that's torn us asunder."

"Don't forget 'in sickness and health,' Fred. Julie is sick." Kate turned to Jill. "Tell Fred your sister is sick."

Jill complied. "Julie's sick. She's also in the living room. That is, if you want to talk to her."

"That depends." Fred sipped his coffee. "Has she shown any signs of remorse?"

Kate clapped her hands together. "I've never seen such remorse, Fred. Such tears, such pleas for forgiveness."

"What's there to forgive?" Jill demanded. "Julie's having a nervous breakdown."

Fred scowled. "Before leaving Chicago, I consulted the head of the psychology department, presenting this as a hypothetical case, of course. He listed the symptoms of a nervous breakdown. They do not include spending a weekend with a priest in Muncie, Indiana."

Jill smiled sweetly. "Your colleague is an even bigger ass than you are, Fred."

"Jill!" Kate tugged her into a corner of the kitchen. "Finish your coffee, Fred, dear. Jill and I have to check on the pot roast."

"Ma, Fred *is* an ass," Jill whispered as Kate shoved an oven mitt into her hand.

"I know," Kate hissed, "but he's Julie's husband. She's his responsibility. That's why husbands and wives cleave to one another, so when they get sick, they don't have to go home to their mothers. *I* took care of your father—"

"You aren't a Prussian with a broom up your ass—"

"Jill! Where did you get such a mouth? It's a mystery to me how I could have raised—"

"Ma!" Jill broke in. "I'm just worried that Fred will make Julie worse. He doesn't even think she's sick."

Kate nodded wisely. "You're forgetting one thing. Julie loves Fred. Doesn't she love Fred?"

"Beyond all reason, Ma."

"And her children? Doesn't she love her children?"

"She's a wonderful mother," Jill agreed. "Better than me."

"Then, in her hour of need doesn't she deserve to be with the husband she loves? And the children who can comfort her?"

"I . . . suppose," Jill said reluctantly, knowing Kate wasn't wrong.

"So be nice to Fred, or I'll cut you out of my will!"

"I'll try, but I'm not sure the Drexel sofabed is worth it." Jill sighed and, just for form's sake, checked the pot roast.

"Dinner's ready." Kate danced to Fred's side. "I made mashed potatoes. Julie told me how much you love them. Isn't that just like Julie, always thinking of you?

"A woman who thinks of her husband does not commit adultery, Mother Dunn and . . . sacrilege. She does not abandon her children."

Kate nodded vigorously. "And never will again, Fred. I swear. *She* swears. Or would if she was here in the kitchen. Go into the living room. Julie will swear for you."

Jim walked into the kitchen, sniffing the air. "The pot roast smells wonderful. I can't stay in the living room. The paint fumes are eating my liver."

"Someone should be with Julie," Jill said. "What is she doing?"

"Ah, broccoli." Jim peered into a steaming pot. "Julie's watching Walter Cronkite."

"That doesn't sound like remorse to me," Fred said angrily. "We'll see about this."

Fred led the way, with Jill close behind and Kate on her heels. Like a scraggly mummers' parade they picked a path through the paint cans.

Julie sat motionless, her eyes fixed on Walter Cronkite. "Good evening, Julie," Fred said. There was no response from Julie. Fred cleared his throat. "I said, good evening."

"She hears you, Fred. Sit beside her," Jill suggested.

"On that dirty cloth? Please." Fred squatted in front of Julie. "Your mother and sister feel you're having a nerv— you're ill. Are you ill, Julie?"

Julie continued to stare at Walter Cronkite, who was explaining stagflation as though it made sense.

Fred waved his hand before Julie's eyes. "I'm a reasonable man, Julie. I'm willing to hear what you have to say. Why did you do it? Why did you run off with Father Norton?"

Julie stared at the screen. "I got behind in my schedule."

"Stop that," Fred ordered. "I insist on an answer. Why did you have an affair?"

Julie glanced briefly at Fred, then returned her gaze to the television screen. "I had an affair with Father Norton because that's what I wanted to do."

"That's willful! That's brazen!" Fred shouted at Kate. "Listen to her.

Kate tried to link her arm through Fred's. "Poor Julie is so overwhelmed with remorse, she doesn't know what she's saying. Let's all go in the kitchen and have a nice dinner, then you can take Julie home."

With considerable difficulty Fred disengaged himself from Kate. "I have no alternative. I am divorcing Julie."

"No!" Kate cried.

"Julie may retain an attorney, but under the circumstances I shall certainly retain custody of the children. I shall tell them something appropriate, but not the truth. It would be too traumatizing."

"Coming home without their mother will be worse," Kate insisted. "You must think this over, Fred. You're making a terrible mistake."

"I made my mistake years ago, Mother Dunn." Fred stormed off toward the kitchen. "God knows, my parents warned me."

"Warned you about what?" Kate's voice was edgy as she followed Fred to the kitchen.

Jill stayed with Julie. "How are you feeling, dear?"

Julie smiled. "Whatever would I do without Fred?"

"Oh, God," Jill sighed while on television Cronkite intoned "And that's the way it is. . . ."

The voices in the kitchen were louder, combative. Jill heard Kate yell "Jill, come here!"

She scrambled to her feet. "I'll be back in a minute, Julie."

In the kitchen Fred was saying, "The women in *my* family would never do such a thing."

"Well, no one in *my* family would do such a thing, either," Kate declared. "Except Jill, and we all know how she is. And even Jill has never run off with a priest. There you are, Jill. Have you ever run off with a priest?"

"No," Jill answered. "Not unless somebody lied."

"There!" Kate was triumphant. "It doesn't run in *my* family."

"Waiting until the wedding to meet Julie's family was clearly a mistake." Fred shook his head balefully. "How could I know? Julie seemed so sensible, so organized."

"She was. She is. She will be again." Kate smiled reassurance. "Stay. Have mashed potatoes."

"My parents said 'Blood will tell,' and they were right." Fred sighed. "Julie's blood told."

"Told what?" Kate demanded. "Are you saying there's something wrong with my family's blood."

Fred looked down his nose at Kate. "You're all so . . . uh . . . so . . ."

"What? Spit it out, Fred," Kate's eyes flashed.

"Irish!" Fred exclaimed. "Classically Irish! Emotionally over-wrought, with untidy minds and no perspective, always brawling in pubs and keening in bogs or whatever it is you people do—"

"Get out of my house, you stiff-necked Prussian!" The fire in Kate's eyes could have singed Fred's tie.

"Mother Dunn!" Fred backed toward the door with Kate's fist shaking wildly in his face.

"I wouldn't let Julie go home with you if the famine was upon us and you had all the potatoes! Out!"

"Gladly. I'll welcome a return to my own kind." He turned and fled, one step ahead of Kate, who bulldogged him down the hall.

"And tell your highfalutin family that their worries aren't over!" Kate bellowed at the door. "Your children are Irish, don't forget that. You can give them tight-assed names, but you can't make them Prussians. Their blood won't just tell, it'll howl you into the ground. You'll have keening aplenty! I'll light candles on that!"

Jill heard the door slam, then seconds later a red-faced Kate stormed into the kitchen. "Julie's crazy all right, but not now. She was daft the day she married that son of a bitch!" She glared at Jim. "Don't just stand there with your mouth hanging open like a guppy. Get the brandy. My heart will stop if I eat when I'm all riled up."

Jill smiled. "Sit down, Ma. After that, you deserve a rest."

Kate sat down, and Jim put a glass of brandy in her hand. "Drink it, Kate." He handed a glass to Jill. "You, too."

They sipped their brandy in silence, which Kate finally broke. "Julie's my daughter, and her being loony doesn't make her any less so." Kate nodded at Jill. "When you three were little, you used to ask me who I loved best. I always said I loved each of you equally, absolutely the same. I said that because you were children, and that's what children should hear. But I fibbed. The one I love most is the one who needs most love at the time."

Jill smiled. "I always knew that, Ma."

"You didn't know that," Kate scoffed. "How could you know that?"

"I watched. I listened."

Kate drank the last of her brandy. "What do you know? You don't even remember how the doctor cured you. Well, what are we sitting here for? The pot roast's dried out, the potatoes are cold. All that's warm is the lettuce, and it looks like dead weeds. . . ." Kate began bustling, scooping food into dishes. "Having Julie home will be nice. When the painting's done, we'll house-clean. We'll shop for new curtains. We'll go to the park. Julie loves squirrels. We'll go to the movies. Julie's always loved movies. Or was that Jill? On Christmas we'll have everyone to dinner. Julie can help me cook. Remember how cute she looked in my apron?"

"First, we have to find a doctor for Julie," Jill said quickly, hoping to set Kate back on the track before her return to times past could extend to braiding Julie's hair and enrolling her in Our Lady of Perpetual Dismay.

"Tomorrow morning after breakfast, we'll visit Pa in the cemetery." Kate handed the pie to Jill. "Reheat the mince."

"Finding a doctor takes time, Ma. I can't just go off—"

"How would you like it if you were dead, and Daisy never came to see you?" Kate demanded.

"I'd figure Daisy had common sense and less morbid things to do."

"Jim, go get Julie for dinner," Kate ordered. "Jill, you take this gravy boat."

As Jill reached for the gravy boat Kate gripped her arm—her small fingers incredibly strong. "Either you go with us in the morning, or I'll tell your father you tried to put me in a home. Think how angry he'll be."

Jill tried to pull the gravy boat loose. "I don't like cemeteries, Ma."

"We're not going for a picnic, Jill. We're going to show respect. And to edge." Kate tugged her side of the boat.

"Edge what?" Kate's grip loosened, and Jill won the gravy-boat tug of war. A few drops splashed on her blouse.

"Look what you've done!" Kate exclaimed. She opened a cupboard and yanked a can from a caddy. "Stand still." She aimed the can at Jill's blouse and sprayed.

"Ma, my chest's on fire!" Burning, Jill blew down the neck of her blouse.

"It was only a little spot-remover, and it's better than you deserve." Kate was banging pots and slamming pans. "When I die, no one will come to the cemetery, and my grave will be covered with weeds."

"They have maintenance people who take care of that, Ma."

"Maintenance people mow, but they don't edge. Maybe you want to spend eternity surrounded by crabgrass, but I don't." Kate scooped a mountain of mashed potatoes into a serving bowl. "Ten pounds of mashed potatoes, and where's Fred? On his way home to divorce my daughter, that's where." She set the bowl on the table, then turned to Jill with a stricken look. "And I told him to. I did a terrible thing." Kate sank into a chair and buried her head in her hands. "Julie's being divorced, and it's all my fault. . . ."

"Nonsense. Fred had his mind made up when he got here."

"You're right! That son of a bitch! Julie will be alone for the rest of her life, and that Prussian's to blame."

"Julie's young. Why should she spend her life alone?"

"She won't marry outside the church. I know my Julie. She's not you!"

"I haven't remarried."

"But you will, when you've finished flitting," Kate predicted. "It better be soon. You have crow's feet."

"I don't flit," Jill protested. "Stop telling people I flit."

Kate bounded to her feet. "Maybe there was an impediment to the marriage. Maybe they were never married at all!"

"What impediment? They aren't first cousins. Both of them were competent, at least at the time."

"Maybe he drugged her!"

"They were engaged for four years, Ma. You're trying to prove Julie's a junkie."

"Watch your mouth!" Kate warned, pacing the floor. "I know! I'll ask a Jesuit. They know loopholes no one has invented. That's it. After dinner Jim and I will go to St. Ignatius'. We'll see Father Monahan. Wait'll I tell him what Fred said about the Irish. He'll find a way to get that son of a bitch!"

"John will be here after dinner," Julie reminded her.

Kate shrugged. "So? When he was nine and had pneumonia, I sat up with him for three weeks. Tell him to wait."

Jim walked into the kitchen, leading Julie. "Where do you want us to sit, Kate?"

"What difference does it make? You can sit on the roof to eat a cold dinner. What took you so long?"

"We were watching *Buck Rogers*," Jim explained. "How can they have naked girls running around like that?"

Jill smiled. "They aren't naked, Jim. They're scantily clad. It's supposed to be the future."

"Was I ever born too soon," Jim sighed, then noticed Kate scowling at him. "I don't mean for naked girls. I mean for rocket ships . . . and robots. They had the cutest little robot."

"Sit down, you fool," Kate snapped at him. She took Julie by the arm. "Here, dear, sit at your old place. Would you like me to fix your plate?" There was no response, so Kate heaped a plate with pot roast. She handed it to Julie, who smiled.

"Did Fred bring Morgan and Kendrick? Where are my children?"

Kate gasped and nudged Jill. "Say something to her. You're good at lying."

Jill shook her head and whispered "I can't do that, Ma. Being emotionally ill is hard enough without having people lie to you." She turned to Julie. "Fred didn't bring the children, honey, and he's gone back to Chicago."

Julie's green eyes clouded over with a murky brownish film. "Fred's left me?"

Jill nodded with tears in her eyes. "I'm sorry."

Julie, head cocked to one side: "I got behind in my schedule. I got behind in my schedule. I got behind . . ." She went on repeating the phrase in the saddest of voices.

"See what you've done!" Kate's whisper was hoarse. "You had to tell her the truth!"

"The truth can't make you crazy, Ma, not unless you've been living a lie."

They ate dinner in near silence, Jill feeling the angry heat from

Kate's body as she chewed pot roast with quick snaps of her teeth. Kate urged Julie to eat, and when Julie responded "I got behind in my schedule," everyone reverted to conversationless chewing and watching Julie not eat.

"You clear the table," Kate ordered Jim. "Jill will do the dishes. I'm changing my dress before church. If Father Monahan is busy, we'll stay for the novena. The Little Flower owes me a favor."

"Say one for me, Ma." Jill wondered what kind of a favor a saint could owe Kate.

"Hah!" Kate brushed past her. "God will hear your name and say 'Jill who?'" She paused at the door. "I'll light a candle for you. Saint Monica prayed for thirteen years before her wayward son turned into Saint Augustine."

"Then you'll have to pray I have a sex-change first," Jill smiled.

"Don't talk dirty in my house." Kate shook her finger and disappeared through the door.

Jim removed Julie's plate from the table. Julie handed him her spoon and said, "I got behind in my schedule."

"I think she'd be happier in the living room," Jim suggested. "She babbles less when she's watching television."

They settled Julie on her drop cloth. "I'll be back in a few minutes," Jill promised.

Jim returned to the kitchen with Jill. "Your mother's quite a woman, isn't she?" Jim said.

"You're not just whistling 'Dixie.'" Jill grinned.

"I've never known anyone like her. My wife, Martha, God rest her soul, was a different kind of woman. If I said 'Jump,' she would ask 'How far?' There was nothing that woman wouldn't do for me. When the doctor told me my ulcers were so bad I had to retire, Martha puréed all my food, even used homemade baby-food recipes. She was careful I never got excited or did anything strenuous. Hovered over me night and day. Then one night Martha went to sleep and never woke up."

"You must have missed her terribly."

"I thought I'd starve to death. Then I met Kate. She invited me to dinner, and I gave her Martha's recipes. She told me I'd eat what she cooked or keep company with somebody else. I ate what she cooked. It was wonderful. No pain. No nausea. No feeling like a grinding machine working its way through my belly."

Jill was beginning to get twinges. "That *was* wonderful, Jim."

"After dinner Kate made me rearrange all the furniture in the living room. Then we sat on the front porch and had brandy-and-soda."

"Moving furniture and drinking brandy didn't make you sick?"

"Made me feel like a man. Martha, God rest her soul, made me feel like an invalid." He set a stack of dishes on the sink. "Martha kept saying we were in the twilight of our lives. Our house was like the waiting room in the morgue. Kate's not waiting to die. Fact is, I don't think she plans to." He tossed silverware on top of the dishes. "Looking back, I think it was living with morbid old Martha that gave me the ulcers."

"Time for church," Kate said from the doorway.

"I'll get the car." Jim was already on his way out the door.

"You look pretty, Ma." Kate did, in a beige dress and cherry-red coat. "Jim thinks the world of you."

"He'd better"—Kate worked her hands into her gloves—"or he can eat his meals elsewhere."

"I mean, he genuinely likes you. I guess some men don't mind being told what to do."

"What you mean is, I didn't behave that way with your father," Kate said evenly. "When Pa said 'Jump,' I asked 'How far?' "

"Yes, Ma. You did." Jill waited for Kate to answer the question that hung in the air, the why of the radical change.

"I'll be late for church." Kate turned on her heel. "I'll light a candle for Daisy, too. God knows the poor kid can use it."

"Thanks, Ma." Jill filled Kate's sink with warm, soapy water.

Between frequent trips to the living room to check on Julie, Jill finished the dishes.

She was putting the last cup on the shelf when she heard the back door slam and John yell "Mother, I'm home."

We all *sound like* Leave It to Beaver.

"John!" She hugged him tightly, her tall Johnny wearing Pa's coat. Gently he moved her aside. "Where's Ma?"

"She's at church with Jim. Coffee? Dinner?"

"Church? I left the office with a stack of work on my desk, broke all the speed limits, and Mother's at church!" Irritated, he ran his fingers through his hair. "This can't be an emergency."

"Ma is seeing Father Monahan about a church annulment for Julie."

"Annulment!? What for? Where's Fred? What's going on? I'll have

307

coffee." He sat in a chair, loosening his tie. "I don't want to hear about this. Shoot."

Jill poured the coffee. "There's no way to break this gently, so I won't try. Julie is in the living room, having a nervous breakdown. Fred went back to Chicago to divorce her because she had an affair with a priest."

The cup crashed to the floor. "Not Julie! That's not possible!"

"It happened, Johnny, and in my opinion it's the result, not the cause, of her nervous breakdown."

He looked thoroughly confused. "Are you sure it's not you who had the affair with the priest?"

"No." Jill blinked at him. "I said it was Julie."

"There must be some mistake. I mean, it could have been you who had . . . did that . . . and then maybe you told Julie about it and she got upset. Hearing about that would upset Julie. You know. Just hearing."

Jill stooped and began picking up the broken pieces. "Why is everyone so certain I could have had an affair with a priest?"

"It's something you would do, Jill, but for Julie it's not normal."

"For Julie it's not normal. For me it's business as usual." She moved his foot to retrieve a shard. "Bovary should have lived in this house. The arsenic would have flowed like pot roast."

"It's all wrong." John buttoned his father's coat to the neck. "Everything's out of kilter."

The telephone rang. Jill glanced at John, who was hunched in his coat, and ran to answer it.

"Hello."

"Hello, Jill." It was Candy. "Is my Johnny there?"

"Yes, he is. How are you, Candy?"

"Never better." Her voice was light and lilting. "My lecture was fantabulous, Jill. Fascinating Womanhood has opened my eyes. I expected John would be here when I got home, but I'm not complaining. A real woman understands her husband's priorities. Stand by your man, and he'll stand by you."

"You really did love your lecture, didn't you?" Jill smiled. "I'll call John to the phone."

"If it's too much trouble, don't bother."

"A real woman is considerate of others." Jill grinned.

"How did you know?" Candy was surprised.

"I was raised to be a 'wifey,' Candy. That's what Fascinating Womanhood was called before it became big business. I'll get John."

308

She laid the receiver on the table. "Johnny? It's Candy." John stared straight ahead, unhearing. "Johnny? Candy."

"Oh? Oh, yes." Slowly he got to his feet and picked up the receiver. "Hello?" He listened. "No, it's nothing important, Candy. You know how Jill overreacts. Ma's at church. Does that sound like an emergency?" He listened. "All right. I know you get nervous in the house alone at night. I'll ring the doorbell when I get home. Twenty minutes, no longer. Bye, honey." John hung up.

"Now you can talk to Julie," Jill told him.

"Uh . . ." He glanced nervously toward the living room. "Perhaps I should come back tomorrow after Julie's had a good night's sleep. Candy's waiting—"

Jill reached for John's hand. He pulled away. "Johnny, what's wrong? It's only Julie in there."

John stood his ground. "Something's not normal."

"I *know*. Julie's sick. We are her sister and brother. More than that, we're her triplets."

"I see no reason to make a point of it, Jill."

"Point! Your lying makes the point of it, Johnny. Being one of triplets doesn't make you a freak."

"It doesn't make me normal either. Especially with two of you female."

Jill was astonished. "You feel somehow . . . unmasculine?"

"It's not normal to conceive both sexes at once." Abruptly he walked away from her. "Candy's waiting. . . ."

Jill followed him. "Giving birth to two sexes happens all the time, Johnny—twins, other triplets, quads, quints . . ."

"Tell Ma to call me at the office," he called over his shoulder.

"What's normal, Johnny?" Jill was right behind him, determined to have her say. "And how would we cope with it even if we knew? We weren't raised that way."

He stopped as though frozen and, from the set of his shoulders, angry. "Don't include me in your misperceptions, Jill. Our upbringing was entirely normal."

"We weren't the Addams Family, but we weren't the Waltons either. In some ways everything was traditional, in others . . . How many fathers make their children stay in the yard the whole of summer vacation?"

John faced her, frowning. "I don't remember that."

"He fenced in the yard and we weren't allowed out of it, not until

309

high school. You *must* remember. You never played baseball or foot-
ball—"

"That was *my* choice, Jill. Sports didn't interest me."

"We weren't allowed friends—"

"We were allowed everything other children were allowed. We
just naturally played together." His brows knit together in a tense
black line, a duplication of Pa's warning of thunder to come.

Jill ignored the signal, for once unwilling to have her feelings
labeled as misperception. *If he is angry, so be it. If he is angry, I'll
die.* "I know what I know, Johnny. We were literally locked up."

"It's like you to confuse the choices you make, many of which are
. . . inappropriate, with the choices of others," he said angrily. "You
pretend to know something about psychology. Isn't that called projection?"

"We were locked in that yard from one summer to the next," Jill
said evenly. "You hated every minute of it. You climbed the fence,
and when Pa found out he flew into a rage, and—"

"Pa was never angry with me!" John shouted. *"Never!"*

"He was angry with you ninety percent of your life, no matter how
you tried to please him. He had rages and black moods—"

"My father had an even disposition!" John's voice was coldly dispas-
sionate, the final detachment of pure rage.

"He was unpredictable, mercurial, violent." Jill felt tears as hot as
her frustration. "Why can't you remember, Johnny? *Why?*"

She fell into a chair, weeping, expecting to hear a slamming door
announce John's angry departure. Instead she felt a hand on her
shoulder, a clasp at once firm and gentle.

"Jill?" John's voice was low, healing. "We've never talked about
what you've been through, but I haven't forgotten. I wasn't around
when you . . . had problems, but I was thinking of you. I called Steve
several times."

"I know." Jill patted the hand on her shoulder. "Steve told me."

"I just want you to know I understand more about you, and even
psychology, than you think. I know that it's easier to project, to feel
that our problems are caused by another or several others than to
admit to a basic personal flaw. Often it's the only way we can continue to cope, and, all things considered, you cope very well."

"I don't project, John, and if that's what you think—"

"Now, don't overreact, don't—"

"Ma, Ma, *Ma!*" It was Julie calling from the living room.

"You must see Julie. You must!" Jill grabbed John's arm, dragging him toward the sound of Julie's frantic "Ma, Ma, Ma . . ."

"I'm here, Julie. So's John. See?"

Julie smiled like a child presented with a present. "Johnny! I got behind in my schedule."

"Uh . . . you'll catch up." John kept his distance. "Try harder."

"Don't say that!" Jill whispered fiercely. "That schedule has her crazy. Talk about something else."

John nodded and leaned over Julie. "How are Morgan and Kendrick? How are your children?"

Julie moaned. There was a flicker of fire in the eyes that had gone murky. "I got behind in my schedule," she whimpered.

"That's it. Everything I say is wrong." John looked at Jill bleakly. "I'm going home."

"No, no." Jill stopped him. "She's happy to see you. You saw how her eyes lit up."

John glanced at Julie, who was staring at him. "Lit up is right. She looks like a pinball machine."

"Talk to her," Jill urged. "Talk about current events. Or movies you've seen. Anything bland and neutral. I know, tell her about your computers."

"Good idea." John's eyes gleamed. "We have some new models so innovative, they'll revolutionize the industry."

"Just the thing," Jill said encouragingly. "Sit in front of Julie where she can see you. Tell her about your computers."

John did just that. He sat cross-legged in front of his cross-legged sister and talked about his computers. At first he was somewhat disconcerted to have his glowing descriptions of technological miracles met with "I got behind in my schedule," but he rallied and soon was speaking animatedly while Julie listened, head cocked to one side.

Jill watched from a distance, content to witness the most intimate conversation her brother and sister had had in years. It made not a whit of difference that John's words were incomprehensible to Julie and Julie's responses wholly inappropriate. They were communicating.

John looked up at Jill. "Do you think Julie would get upset if I told her about the shipment stuck in Buffalo?"

Jill shook her head no, and John continued as enthusiastically as before. He was still talking when Kate and Jim returned from church.

Kate smiled at the scene in the living room. "How wonderful. All my children home at once! This calls for a celebration!"

"Hello, Ma." John said. "I have to be going. Candy is—"

"First you'll have something to eat," Kate decided. "Jill, reheat the mince."

"You told Father Monahan Julie's story?" Jill asked.

"Oh," Kate said airily, "I told him that my daughter's husband has taken a notion for divorce, God knows why, and my daughter was inquiring after an annulment. I told him what Fred said about the Irish. Monahan's family came here to escape the Troubles. He'll settle Fred's hash."

"You didn't tell him the whole story," Jill said warily.

Kate poked her chest with a small, pointed finger. "I'm supposed to tell a priest that my daughter was in Muncie, Indiana, with a . . . a . . . a . . ."

"Colleague?" Jill suggested.

"Father Monahan said she should come see him herself," Kate said. "There are questions only she can answer."

"Good luck to him, Ma. The only answer he'll get is 'I got behind in my schedule.'"

"Julie will talk to a priest. They have a way about them."

"Evidently," Jill said tartly. "I think that the priest in Muncie is all the religion Julie can handle right now. She needs a doctor."

"Jill has a good point," John agreed.

"I said she didn't?" Kate demanded. "Have I taken to speaking in tongues that my children don't understand me?" She sighed. "'Sharper than a serpent's ear is the ingratitude of your children.'"

"Tooth, Ma, tooth," Jill corrected.

"Tooth, ear, what's the difference?" Kate snorted. "Wait till you get to Heaven and God wants to know how you kept the Fourth Commandment. That'll keep you on the wrong side of the gate."

"I got behind in my schedule," Julie whimpered.

"Not you, sweetheart." Kate rushed to Julie and folded her in her arms. "I didn't mean Mother's own girl."

Julie smiled and hugged Kate, who rocked her back and forth like the small child she'd become.

In the kitchen the phone rang, and Jim called, "I'll get it, Kate."

Kate continued to rock Julie, rubbing her back and murmuring, "There, there, everything's going to be all right. Mother's own girl is safe."

Julie smiled. "I'm mother's own girl."

Gently Kate brushed wispy strands of hair from Julie's face. "I'll brush your hair like I used to. I'll find you a clean white nighty. I'll tuck you into your own little bed. Would you like that, Julie?"

Julie smiled beatifically, her face glowing like a Raphael angel. She touched Kate's face with fingers that barely brushed her cheek. "Funny Mommy. I'm not Julie. I'm Jill."

"Mother of God! Holy Jesus!" Kate stared aghast at Julie, then folded her in a fierce embrace. "Mother of God!"

John and Jill stared at one another, too stunned for words and too anguished for silence. "I'll find a doctor in the morning" was all Jill could say.

"You . . . uh . . . do that." John backed toward the kitchen, eyes wide. "When something's not normal . . . a doctor . . . that's wise. . . ."

"John, where are you going?" Jill went after him. "We need to talk about this."

In the kitchen Jim waved the phone at John. "It's your wife. I can't make it out."

"I told you Candy was waiting!" John shouted at Jill. "Look what you've done."

John snatched the receiver from Jim. "I'm on my way home, Candy." He listened, then, "I can't understand you! Calm down!" He listened. "Whatever possessed you?" He listened. "No, Charlie wasn't trying to take advantage of you. I borrowed his power saw. He had a right to come over and ask for it back." He listened, then thundered, "I don't give a damn what you were trying to do. That's the craziest, most insane—what do you mean it's a Fascinating Womanhood technique? Candy, stop crying. Please stop. No, I know you didn't mean . . . I'm on my way home. We'll talk." He hung up and turned furiously to Jill. "If I had been home, this wouldn't have happened!"

"Tell me! What happened?"

"The doorbell rang, and Candy thought it was me, so she answered it—stark naked and wrapped in cellophane! Christ! Now she's hysterical, and it's all your fault!"

"Mine? *Mine?* Do I hear projection going on?"

"Nothing's normal anymore!" John yelled and ran down the hallway. A moment later Jill heard the door slam.

"Your brother's got quite a temper," Jim observed. "Handsome though. And your father's old coat fits him like a glove."

CHAPTER 21

"See. What did I tell you? Crabgrass!" Kate was on her knees before a tombstone that resembled a submerged refrigerator decorated with angels. "Ugly, dirty weeds!" Kate's small hands attacked the crabgrass as though it had grown there purposely to affront her.

"Would you like to sit on the grass?" Jill held Julie's hand. "Or perhaps on this tomb— er . . . nice stone seat?"

Julie's eyes drifted aimlessly, like those of a sleepwalker who had been awakened prematurely. "Where's the TV?"

"There aren't any television sets here, honey. This is a . . . sort of park."

"No TV?" Julie's lip trembled.

"Not here, dear. You can watch TV when we get home."

"I got behind in my schedule," Julie mumbled, settling herself on the grass. "I'm mother's own girl."

The gates of Holy Ghost cemetery were flanked by tremendous stone angels who'd seemed to frown at Jill as they'd driven through. Once inside all was serene, a fitting final resting place for those who'd gone to rewards, as promised by pastors, or the fiery pit, as predicted by mothers they'd placed in homes.

As with most Catholic cemeteries, it was a subdivided community, each section having its own status and presided over by a sculptured saint, or manifestation of the Lord or a member of His immediate family. John Dunn, Sr., was buried on the crest of the high-rent district in the shadow of a crucifix upon which hung the body of Christ with face turned to Heaven and an expression that said "Why me?"

The solid middle class resided in the St. Peter and Paul section while somewhere in the lowlands the minority community gathered in a tight Hispanic circle around a granite misconception of the Pietà.

"Don't stand around mooning." Kate shoved a pair of clippers into Jill's hand. "Edge!"

They worked in a companionable silence that reminded Jill of her childhood. Her task had been to dust the undersides of tables, and she'd crawled from one mahogany cave to the other, usually so quietly that Kate, forgetting Jill was in the room, would talk out loud to herself, usually in furious debate with a plumber she felt overcharged or a butcher she was sure short-weighted.

Jill glanced at her watch. "We should get back to the house, Ma. I have to call the doctors suggested by the APA."

"Looking for a doctor in the phone book is stupid." Kate spat the words in Jill's direction. "I wouldn't look for a boy to shovel snow that way."

"I know you wouldn't, Ma." Jill almost wished *she* hadn't. She'd flipped the Yellow Pages looking for *Psychotherapists*, then came upon the word unexpectedly and read it in parts: *Psycho-the-rapists*. It had taken three cups of Kate's coffee before she'd stopped shivering. "It's standard procedure, Ma. You call the American Psychiatric Association, and they give you the names of three doctors."

"So, you think they give you the names of *good* doctors?" Kate challenged. "They give you the names of doctors who need work."

"They must be good doctors, Ma. They're all board-certified."

"I don't care if they've kissed the True Cross! If they're so good, why can't they get patients without the APA pushing? Did you ask how many people these strangers have cured?"

"I couldn't ask that, Ma."

"Some executive skills!" Kate yanked at a tuft of crabgrass that came up, roots and all.

"If you can do better, Ma." Jill sighed.

The silence that followed was less companionable, with Kate fuming as she clipped and pruned, creating a landscape that suited her better than God's. Finally she rested, leaned back on her haunches and examined her work. "It's an improvement, isn't it, Jill?"

"The Tivoli Gardens don't look this good, Ma."

Kate tossed her clippers into the grass. "What difference does it make? Your father isn't happy."

"Pa's not what?"

Kate sighed. "I never should have buried him."

Jill blanched. "You had to, Ma. He was dead."

"I should never have done it." Kate hoisted herself to her feet. "It's

315

dark and creepy underground. And only Pa knows if the mortician was lying when he said the vault was airtight. Even if it's dry as a bone, he's not happy."

"How do you know Pa's not happy?" Jill asked skeptically. "I've been here often, and I haven't seen a lot of tossing and turning."

"You can't be married to a man for thirty-four years without knowing how he feels," Kate declared, then smiled happily. "But Pa's in luck. The cemetery has just built a magnificent mausoleum in the Sacred Heart section. We'll move Pa there. He'll be happy."

"Move Pa? You mean, a disinterment?" Jill dropped her clippers.

"On our way out we'll stop at the office to make the arrangements."

"We?"

Jill groaned, knowing that what had begun as a gleam in Kate's eye would end with her explaining to some fish-faced cemetery mogul that they wanted to disinter a father who wasn't happy underground. It was absurd, so absurd that Jill had to resist an impulse to lean over Pa's tombstone and shout "Hold on, Pa, help is on the way." She giggled.

"Just what do you think is funny?" Kate demanded.

"I didn't know Pa was still so emotionally involved, that's all. Maybe we should do more than dig him up and schlepp him over the hill to a box in the wall. We should take him downtown to see the urban renewal, and Johnny's new house, and the interstate, and—"

"Watch your mouth!" Kate exclaimed. "That's sacrilege. Or blasphemy. Or slander. Or . . . Mother of God! Where's your sister?"

Jill bounded to her feet looking wildly around for Julie. She'd vanished.

"I'll go that way, toward Saint Michael," Kate directed. "You look over by Gabriel the Archangel."

Kate galloped off, hollering "Julie, Julie" while Jill obediently trotted in the direction designated by Kate.

She walked briskly, stepping around tombstones, her soft cries of "Julie" getting no response. She doubted Julie would have wandered the half-mile to the gates and beyond them onto Brookpark Road, but her agitation grew as she neared the statue of Gabriel, with Julie nowhere in sight.

She stood in the bell-shaped shadow of Gabriel's trumpet, calling, "Julie, Julie, where are you?" Then, struck by a sudden inspiration, she raised her voice and called, "Jill?"

"I got behind in my schedule." A small voice wafted from behind Gabriel's skirts.

Jill jumped at the disembodied voice and peered around the statue. Julie sat on the ground, her knees drawn up to her chin and eyes focused on a huge rectangular monument, dazzling white in the sunshine.

Julie smiled happily and pointed at the gleaming edifice. "TV."

Jill reached for Julie's arm and gently helped her to her feet. "We have a better TV at home, honey. Let's find Ma."

"I'm Mother's own girl," Julie said dreamily and fell into step beside Jill.

Jill retraced her steps, following the sound of Kate's frantic yoo-hoos. When they finally caught up with her, she was shouting at a gravedigger, who was frowning with incomprehension.

"We're here, Ma." Jill ran up to Kate. "Julie's okay."

"Thank God," Kate breathed fervently, then snapped, "Why did you let your sister wander away?"

"I didn't. I wasn't—"

"And this fool here"—Kate jerked an accusing thumb at the grave-digger—"was no help at all."

The man shrugged. *"No entiendo."*

"He doesn't speak English, Ma."

"Then he shouldn't be working in a public place."

"Ma, he digs graves. Who's there to talk to?"

"It's all your fault!" Kate placed a protective arm around Julie's shoulders and led her away.

Jill knew Kate would remain distraught until she'd recovered from the shock of losing Julie. Until then, and perhaps beyond, Julie's temporary disappearance would be Jill's fault, along with the grave-digger's failure to speak English.

Jill turned to the gravedigger, reading the question in his worried frown—what did I do wrong?

"It's all right. Really."

He spread puzzled arms, his eyes blinking like a railroad crossing light.

Oh dear, I've just made it worse.

She pointed at Kate, hustling Julie to the car, then to the side of her head. Her finger described a circle. "El goofy."

The man smiled broadly. *"Sí, Señora."* He returned to his digging and Jill followed Kate to the car.

Conversation on the ride home was dominated by Julie, who without a television set, real or imagined, tended to ramble.

"I've never been a conventional person," Julie was saying, "or cared what my family thinks. I love my job in Los Angeles. Television is my life. I'll have that tattooed on my ass, I think."

"Mother of God!" Kate exclaimed. "Will you listen to her? One daughter with a mouth is enough. God, what are you doing to me?"

"Listen to the radio, honey." Jill tried to distract her, but the Cleveland Symphony calmed Julie as little as Roger Mudd had Patti Gerard.

"I love all the men in Los Angeles," Julie continued. "I sleep with them. They sleep with me."

Kate clutched her heart. "It's leaping! I warn you, it's leaping!"

Desperate, Jill tried a game Julie had loved as a child. "The first one who sees a moo cow gets a piece of candy."

Julie wasn't interested in moo cows. "Not that it's always easy for me. I have to raise Daisy and work. But when I come home to Cleveland, my mother hugs me. All I do is play and play, and my mother gives me hugs and kisses the same way she does stuffy old John and prissy old Julie, who pay and pay with the prices going up. I don't even have a schedule. I don't need a schedule. I would tear up a schedule and stamp on it and set it on fire and I wouldn't let it near me or even look at it. I would run away from it and kill it and it would be dead. I'm free. I'm Jill."

Free—Julie sees me as free!

"I'm going to die," Kate moaned.

"You can't die now, Ma. Julie needs you."

"My children are killing me, and I can't even die. They might want to kill me again."

"What would we do without you, Ma?"

"Go to Hell in a handbasket, that's what." Kate's voice was drenched in despair, but her jaw thrust forward with the determination of a mother who's needed.

Jill swung into the driveway, then braked suddenly, having come within inches of a tall young man in black who was trudging up the middle of the driveway, suitcase in hand.

"Who's that?" Jill inquired.

"No relative of mine." Kate frowned. "Fuller Brush?"

"From the way he's dressed, more like Jehovah's Witness."

"Well, he can keep his tracts and his mealymouthed Bible-spout-

318

ing." New-found determination and undischarged anxiety had Kate spoiling for a fight. "And if he makes a sneering remark about the Pope, the only end that'll be near is his when I kick it."

Jill set the emergency brake. Kate bolted from the car.

"Ma, wait!" Jill tugged at Julie. "C'mon, honey. You don't want to miss the *O.K. Corral.*"

Jill dragged Julie across the lawn as speedily as conscience would allow, coming up behind Kate as she brandished a practiced forefinger under the startled man's nose. "The Pope's word is infallible, young man, and the Vatican is the seat of my church!"

"Mine, too." He smiled soulfully. "I'm Father Norton."

"You!" Kate clasped her hands to her chest. "It's not leaping! It's stopped! Feel Jill. It's not beating!"

Jill had no choice but to feel. "It's beating, Ma."

"It's not!" Kate's lips were white.

"If your heart had stopped beating, you wouldn't be alive to tell me about it, would you now, Ma?"

"I . . . guess not."

That resolved, Kate turned to Father Norton who was assiduously avoiding eye contact with Julie, unaware that eye contact was no longer part of Julie's schedule.

"I have come all the way from Los Angeles"—Father Norton made it sound like the dark side of the moon—"to beg Julie's forgiveness for a . . . disservice . . . I may have done her."

"So here she is." Jill gestured at Julie. "Beg."

Kate took charge. "Nobody's begging on my front lawn. What will the neighbors think?" She bustled behind them, shooing them into the house like vexatious chicks.

Once in the house Kate steered her little group into the kitchen. "Mr. Klein, the painter, is putting the second coat on the living room," she explained. "I'll put on the coffee. Jill, reheat the mince."

Father Norton shoved his suitcase under the table and leaned close to Julie. Somewhat nervously, he smiled. "Hello, Julie. May we speak privately?"

Julie smiled brightly, "I'm Jill. I play. Would you like to play with me?"

"Gee whiz!" Norton was dismayed. "What's wrong with Julie?"

"She's ill," Jill said.

"I'll say." He gawked. "She looks ten years older than she did . . . uh . . . in . . . uh . . ."

"It was dark in Muncie, Father Norton. Besides, Julie's life has fallen apart. I'm sure if she'd known you were coming, she'd have worn mascara."

"Then you know?" he asked weakly. "I thought this was something Julie would keep to herself. I should have known when her . . . hus— . . . Mr. Hildebrandt called my pastor. . . ."

"Fred spilled the beans!" Jill was shocked at Fred's insensitivity. The pastor he'd blabbed to was Julie's pastor, too.

"Why are you here, Father Norton?" Kate asked.

"I have been sent to ask for Julie's forgiveness—not that I wouldn't have done so without orders from my pastor. However, I would have chosen a more propitious time and place."

"Perhaps over an intimate dinner with a bottle of good Chablis?" Jill asked, knowing she would have hated him on sight even if he hadn't been Father Norton. He was lean but soft, with the eyes of a dissipated adolescent.

"This is not an easy confession to make." Father Norton squirmed in his chair. "I should think you'd have the same compassion I'm sure has been shown to you."

"He's right, Jill. You gave a few priests heartburn in the days when you still went to confession. None of them threw you out of the box." Kate smiled generously at Father Norton. "Eat your pie, Father, and tell us what's on your mind."

"I have come to ask Julie's forgiveness and to make amends if I can."

"That's good," Kate said approvingly, looking to Jill for confirmation. "Isn't that good?"

Jill wasn't impressed. "He should say three Hail Marys and jump off a bridge."

"Your mouth! Have some respect for the collar!" Kate smiled at Norton. "Go on with your confessing, Father."

"Er . . . yes." Norton looked far from pleased. "You must understand that, where celibacy is concerned, my spirit has always been willing to celibacy, but when an attractive woman like Julie . . . was . . . makes it clear she's interested, perhaps more than interested . . . Julie certainly came to church a lot. Not that her motives weren't beyond reproach, at least initially. But who knows what Satan might have whispered in her ear? If I am mortal flesh, then Julie has a right to be mortal flesh also, although what a married woman with a husband and a conjugal relationship is doing being mortal flesh with a priest who has no conjugal relationship to take comfort in . . ." He stared plaintively at Kate. "You can't imagine the loneliness of my life!"

Kate clucked sympathetically. "I'm a widow whose children left home, Father Norton. My life is crowded with loneliness."

"Then you *do* understand." Father Norton's voice was hopeful and sad. "Trust the kindness of a mother's heart. Well, *some* mothers' hearts. *My* mother's never been lonely. There are eight other children in the family."

Kate's eyes widened. "How many living at home?"

"Uh . . . four, maybe five." Norton seemed uncertain. "The last time I was there, breakfast was bedlam."

"Lucky woman." Kate sighed. "Your father, too. How proud they must be. They encouraged your vocation?"

"Encouraged! They pushed me into the seminary! They wanted a priest in the family, so they sent me away when I was only thirteen. Thirteen, Mrs. Dunn."

"A baby! I would never have done that to Johnny."

"Of course you wouldn't, Mrs. Dunn. You have a kind heart. Please call me Jerry."

Kate was delighted. "I've never called a priest by his first name before. We haven't been blessed with one in our family."

Jill snatched his plate from beneath his raised fork. "You've made your apology. Good-bye."

"I wasn't finished." Norton reached for the plate. "The crust is superb. You must have made it, Mrs. Dunn."

Kate glowed. "I did. Last Christmas."

"Christmas?" He stared at the near-empty plate in Jill's hand, then reached for the suitcase. "I think I'd better take one of my pills."

"Are you ill?" Kate asked, watching him rummage through his worldly possessions.

Norton came up with a vial of pills and popped one into his mouth. "Swollen glands. They used to be golf balls, now they're like Ping-Pong."

"Why have you brought a suitcase?" Jill asked warily.

"My pastor has ordered me into a retreat house in the upstate Michigan woods. It's incredibly primitive, Mrs. Dunn. No television. No beer. Just thirty days of silence, prayer, and meditation."

"Who do I have to know to get in?" Jill asked.

Norton didn't share her enthusiasm. "I've been there twice before!"

"Whatever for?" Jill asked innocently, glancing at Julie, who stared straight ahead, evidently transfixed by the refrigerator door.

"The silence is maddening." Norton shivered. "No human voices at all, unless you count monks sneezing. Would you count that as human voices, Mrs. Dunn?"

"Certainly not, Jerry." Kate warmed to his misery.

"I'd lie on my pallet and try to meditate, but the silence oppressed me, Mrs. Dunn. I can't meditate in utter silence."

"I'll bet you used to do your homework with the television on," Jill broke in.

"And the little animal feet, scampering and scurrying through the underbrush. I'm a child of the city, Mrs. Dunn. I found no solace in thoughts of hungry eyes and sharp-pointed teeth. I crawled the floor of my cell, checking the walls for cracks large enough for small furry bodies to fit through."

"You poor boy!" Kate cried sympathetically. "How frightened you must have been!"

"I shall collapse completely if I'm forced to return. Therefore, I have no alternative but to leave the priesthood."

"But your vows!" Kate was agog. "You promised God."

"God does not require self-destruction!" Norton stood up, raising one arm like an evangelist winding up for the pitch. "Would God require me to work in a shipyard and breathe asbestos?"

Kate thought about it. "I've never heard of a vocation like that."

Norton nodded, encouraged. "Or work in a coal mine and risk black lung? Or disseminate pesticides? Crop-dust defoliants?"

"Father Damien got leprosy," Kate pointed out.

"The Lord hasn't called me to Molokai, Mrs. Dunn. Nor, I believe, to a godforsaken wilderness retreat house overrun with rabid creatures. Rabies shots are hideous. They jab a long needle straight through your stomach."

"Mother of God!" Kate automatically clutched her belly. "What'll you do? Are you going home?"

"My parents won't have me if I leave the priesthood." He sank into a chair looking fairly undone.

"A mother who won't have her own son isn't a good mother!" Kate said sternly. "Of course with that many children she can afford to be picky."

322

Norton moaned. "I have disobeyed the injunction of my pastor. I am an outcast, a pariah, a man without a country, a family, a home, gainful employment . . ."

"There, there," Kate said soothingly. "Once a priest, always a priest. You can hear confessions, give last rites . . ."

"Those are not marketable skills, Mrs. Dunn. With the unemployment rate what it is and rising inflation—" He licked two fingers, then pressed them to his brow. "I'm feverish."

"Let me feel." Kate bounded at his forehead, her mother's hand outstretched. "Oh, my, you are warm."

"Your hand is so soothing, so cool." His brown eyes went limpid, like those of a Labrador retriever. "Your children are blessed."

"Tell *them,*" Kate snorted. "You must rest, Father Norton. While you're sleeping, I'll make you some soup."

Alarmed, Jill said quickly, "Ma, the seats on Scenic Cruisers recline. He can sleep all the way home. When he gets there, he can open a can of Campbell's."

"Shame on you, Jill," Kate admonished. "You're forgetting the Good Samaritan."

"The Good Samaritan didn't have a sister who babbled because the Wayfarer screwed her!"

"Watch your mouth!" Kate deserted Norton's side for Jill's. "He's consecrated, Jill. Catholics don't throw priests out of the house. It would bring bad luck on the family."

"God forbid! Our luck's been so good up till now." Jill lowered her voice to match Kate's. "He'll upset Julie."

"I'll ask." Kate leaned over Julie, an affectionate arm around her shoulder. "Dear, would you mind if Father Norton rests here awhile?"

"I'm mother's own girl." Julie smiled.

Kate smiled triumphantly. "See?"

"She'd say the same about Attila the Hun." Jill cast about for an additional argument, but there was none.

"Come along, Father Norton." Kate helped him to his feet. "It's my house. I'll do as I please."

Jill turned her back as Kate led Norton into the living room. "Just a short flight of stairs, Father. Nothing too taxing."

"Call me Jerry," Jill heard him say. "May I call you Mom?"

Jill lit a cigarette, then threw her lighter on the sinkboard next to the coffee pot. "Shit! Double shit! Goddammit shit! Son-of-a-bitch

323

shit!" She was totally involved in her swearing and rather enjoying it when a voice behind her said, "Begging your pardon, the second coat's finished."

"Oh!" Jill flushed crimson and reluctantly turned to Mr. Klein, a hulk in white overalls splashed with even whiter spots.

"Don't mean to bother ya, ma'am. Just wanted to tell ya I'm done."

"Thank you, Mr. Klein. I'll tell my mother."

"I'll clean my brushes in the garage and be gone." He paused at the door. "You the divorcee?"

"Why, yes, I am."

"Thought so." He lumbered through the door.

Rats, I'm a dissolute woman.

Jill decided to call Keriakan and request a psychiatric referral for Julie. Perhaps Kate would feel less anxious about dealing with a doctor once removed. She picked up the phone, hearing Kate's voice on the line. ". . . So, as you can see, my daughter's in a terrible state—"

Jill hung up quickly. She had no wish to eavesdrop on Kate's conversation, most likely with Jim.

"Ma, ma, ma," Julie whimpered. *"Ma!"*

"What honey?" Jill bent over Julie. "Ma's busy right now. What do you need?"

Julie pointed at the refrigerator door. "Please change the channel."

"Oh, Julie." Tears blurred Jill's eyes. She longed to breach the walls of Julie's insanity, to rescue her from the bleak, barren wasteland to which she'd fled. Jill well knew that wasteland, had paced its desolate perimeter, had stumbled through its rubble and fallen, shrieking with pain and rage. From time to time there'd been travelers who'd glanced at her as she crouched in her hole, her mouth full of sand. But they'd passed quickly by, perceiving not a supplicant lost in a wasteland, but a mute and self-absorbed woman curled in a fetal ball beneath the piano in the best nuthouse in Cleveland.

"Come back, Julie," Jill whispered. "Don't be frightened. I'll help you. I understand."

"I'm Jill." Julie smiled. "I'm free. Please change the channel."

"Oh, God." Jill knew it would take more than empathy and the sharing of a similar experience to get through to Julie.

"Change the channel. Change the channel," Julie whimpered. "TV? TV?"

"All right, Julie. TV."

Julie allowed herself to be led to the living room, where Jill placed her gently on the drop cloth. Julie's restless discontent dissolved into approbation as Jill switched on the television set.

"Here, Julie. Watch *Lucy.*"

"*Lucy!*" Julie was delighted. "Is Pa home from work yet? Is Johnny home from school?"

"Oh, dear." Jill returned to the kitchen, wondering how anyone can know what decade it is with *Lucy* running three times a day.

Intent on calling a doctor, she reached for the phone just as it rang.

"Hello."

"Hello." It was Polly. "Is this Jill?"

"I'm not sure. There are two of us here."

"Your sister's no better," Polly said sympathetically.

"I'm trying to find a doctor, Polly, and it's not easy. Kaiser is out of the question, and my mother doesn't want strangers. Is something wrong there?"

Polly chuckled. "What? Here in Oz where the flying monkeys have everything under control? M. B. Smythe Jones circulated a petition requesting that *Freak People* be yanked off the air. Of course, everyone was afraid to sign it except a janitor who speaks only Italian and thought it had to do with deporting homosexuals. Neiman told Jones it's too late for petitions anyway. Not only is *Freak People* a hit, but Lawrence and Abelard are planning a spin-off called *That's Disgusting.* Lawrence would have gone nuts about Jones's petition if he hadn't already gone nuts about something else—Carolyn McCaffery quit."

"She *did?* When?"

"Yesterday morning, right after you left. Lawrence called McCaffery's husband, offering him big bucks to divorce her. Of course, Carolyn's husband called her immediately, and Carolyn whisked Donny off Lawrence's lap and never stopped running till she and Donny were safely locked in her car and on the way home."

"Good for her! But it's too bad it had to happen. I know how much she liked her job."

Polly laughed. "Don't go gray over it. This morning, Carolyn signed a contract with CBS—vice-president, Programs."

"Oh, my." Jill was impressed. "Well, she'll be good at it. Send her a plant for me, will you, Polly?"

"A profusion of bird of paradise is nesting in her office, bearing your name. Anything else?

"You're terrific, Polly. I hope Alex isn't giving you problems."

Polly giggled. "Right now he's down the hall emptying my wastepaper basket."

"You're kidding?"

"And his new secretary is a sweet old lady, looks like Mary Worth. She calls Alex 'sonny.' Wait, Jill, here he is now. Hang on."

Jill hung on and was rewarded with "Hey, man, how's the hometown?"

"Fine, Alex. How are you?"

"Dynamite! Great! Nose to the grindstone! Work all day and straight home to the wife."

"That sounds . . . uh . . . normal. Alex, will you do something for me?"

"You got it. Just tell me. It's done."

Jill could feel Alex's jiggling through the phone. "There's a script I'd like you to read—*Broken Promises*."

"Hey, man, you got it. It's as good as read. That all you want, a script read?"

"With your other work, that's enough."

"Your house doesn't need painting, your garage cleaning out?"

"No, Alex. Calm down."

"Have you . . . uh . . . talked to anyone here, Jill?" Alex's voice was riddled with apprehension. "Any conversations with the brass? Mention my name?"

"I haven't talked to anyone other than Polly, and I haven't mentioned your name."

"Hey, man," he boomed with relief. "I didn't think you had. My therapy's coming along great. I told Sitzbach about the way I was battered. My mother battered me . . . my father battered me. On weekends my Uncle Harry came in from The Bronx to batter me. My sister battered—"

"Alex! Alex!" Jill shouted. "I don't mean to cut you off, but—"

"Go ahead. Cut me off. I don't mind. Bye."

The phone crashed in Jill's ear. She hung up, uncertain as to which Alex she liked best—the unabashed hustler who viewed the acquisition of corporate power as life's highest goal or the obsequious Son of Uriah Heep he'd become, willing to eat her dust and his ego—at least until he devised a better strategy. Jill was torn between letting Alex off the hook entirely and making him paste-wax her car.

She was reaching for the phone when Kate walked into the kitchen.

"Don't touch that phone," Kate commanded. "I'm waiting for the cemetery to call. Julie's wandering off gave me such conniptions I forgot to stop at the office. Pa will love the mausoleum. It's expensive, but who cares?"

Jill chuckled. "Wait'll I tell Alex that death's not the end of upward mobility."

Kate scowled. "Is Alex one of your boyfriends?"

"No. We work together, Ma. He'd love the idea of Pa's coming-out party."

"Don't make fun, Jill. Burying the dead's no joke."

"Evidently it's not permanent either."

The doorbell rang. Kate looked up from scrubbing the coffee pot. "Please."

"Sure, Ma."

Jill opened the front door for a potted plant the size of the porch.

"Florist delivery," a voice announced through the billowing green.

"Christ! Where are you? What is this?"

"Biggest plant old man Resnik ever grew. A mutant really. Resnik won't say what he grafted together. He hated to part with it, but the guy who bought it didn't want anything else. Anyway it was taking over the store. Sign here."

"How?" Jill couldn't see through the Brazilian rain forest.

"Well . . . uh . . ." A hand with nail-bitten fingers holding a pen and receipt book worked its way through the branches. "You gotta sign, lady."

"Help me inside with this, and I'll sign."

"Geez, lady, I already got a hernia getting it up the steps."

Jill was firm. "You don't help, I don't sign. You'll have to take it back."

"Geez, lady . . . geez . . ."

They bumped their way down the hall, Jill pulling the pot and brushing branches out of her eyes while the delivery boy pushed, mumbling "Geez . . ."

"Mother of God!" Kate exclaimed. "What is that?"

"The forest primeval. Birnam Wood come to get Macbeth," Jill panted.

"Sign here." The delivery boy emerged from his camouflage, a pleasant-faced, sandy-haired youth.

Jill signed, then reached for her purse and a tip.

"Hey, thanks, lady. Enjoy your plant. It likes indirect sunlight, nitrogen, phosphorus—"

"—puppies and small children," Jill finished. "Thanks."

The delivery boy let himself out while Jill and Kate searched the greenery for a card.

"Here it is." Kate ripped it open. "It's from John to Julie. It says: 'Hope this finds your health improved.' " Kate glared at Jill. "Whatever possessed John? Look. The branches stretch from one wall to the other. How will I open the refrigerator? The oven? What am I going to do with this thing?"

"It can live in the guest room with Father Norton. He'll think he's in the upstate Michigan woods and won't feel so guilty."

"I don't understand John." Kate flattened herself against the wall, trying to wiggle past the plant without disturbing its branches. "You send plants to people who have pneumonia, not a sister who thinks she's someone else. I'm going to call him."

"If you talk to John, thank him for the plant, Ma."

"Why?" Kate demanded. "He should be here helping us cope, not sending trees."

"Knowing what someone *should* do is easy," Jill snapped, then winced. She sounded like Steve at his worst. "A plant may not be what you want, Ma, but it may be the best he can do."

"I'll thank him for the thought," Kate decided. "And tell him to be here for dinner. After all, on the day Pa died he made John the head of the family."

"What a wonderful legacy, like being made head zookeeper." Curious, Jill poked a branch, then jumped three inches. She could have sworn it poked back. "Don't water it, Ma. Maybe it'll move away."

But Kate was already on the phone, involved in the intricacies of getting through to John. Jill only half-listened to Kate's mounting frustration. She was contemplating the bristling plant, wondering what would happen if she gave it a solid right hook.

The doorbell rang. Kate made an impatient gesture in Jill's direction.

Jill nodded. "I'll answer the door. It's probably the delivery boy with the plant's dish and toys."

Jill went to the door, thinking that Kate wasn't the only Dunn whose frustration was mounting. Hers was a volcano about to erupt. On a day when her only goal had been to find a doctor for Julie, she'd visited Pa, become involved in plans for improving his plot in life, and witnessed the return of the Prodigal Son. That he wasn't Kate's son was only a technicality; Norton was somebody's son, and that was good enough for Kate.

She opened the door.

"Well." A familiar voice rumbled surprise. "From what your mother said, I'm amazed you're up and answering the door."

"Come in," Jill said automatically. Her voice, Kate-trained, was polite. She stepped backward, heart thumping, as her mother's hall was invaded by the substantial bulk and portentous presence of Neil Kaiser, M.D.

CHAPTER 22

"I came as quickly as I could." Neil twisted around, trying to glimpse Jill's face as he preceded her down the hall.

Jill bobbed and weaved behind him, dodging his backward glances.

Is this the Neil Kaiser of "Come here, beloved" or the Neil Kaiser of "Go away, you pest," the Neil of ultimate fantasy or the Neil who's "divorcing, not divorced"?

"So, this is your Dr. Kaiser." Kate extended her hand, beaming as though Jill had finally brought home an acceptable beau.

"Mrs. Dunn." Neil covered Kate's small hand with both of his. "Jill's told me so much about you."

"I know," Kate sighed. "I've tried to forgive her for that."

"And Jill." Neil was professionally proper, objectively concerned. "I must say you seem fairly composed and extremely alert."

"I should hope so. I'm not the patient."

"You're not? But your mother said—" His poise unraveled. Bafflement gleamed through.

"Ask my mother." Despite *acting as if* Jill's knees were wobbly. Quickly she moved to the kitchen table, where she sat down, half-hidden behind the plant.

"I've never seen a houseplant that size." Neil eyed it warily.

"You know how it is when you have only one," Jill chirped. "It gets all the watering, the fertilizer, the best schools, ballet lessons—"

"I have two daughters, Dr. Kaiser," Kate interrupted. "I know you can do for my Julie what you did for my Jill."

Father Norton already has, and look how well it's worked out.

"What seems to be your . . . uh . . . Julie's problem?" Neil circled Kate, finally backing her up against the plant and positioning himself so that he could catch quick peeks at Jill through the branches.

Kate quickly gave Neil the same expurgated version she'd given Father Monahan, omitting Father Norton and the winking, blinking TraveLodge bear.

"Tell him about Muncie, Ma."

"Jill!" Kate was shocked. "We've just met! What will Dr. Kaiser think?"

"Shrinks don't make judgments, Ma. They're accustomed to the extremes of human behavior, sometimes from personal experience."

"True, Jill. So true." Neil searched the shrubbery for an opening that would provide an unobstructed view of Jill. "Sometimes even we professionals experience transitory difficulty when confronted with crises of a traumatic nature. We may exhibit signs of disorientation, even *mildly erratic behavior.*"

"Mildly!" Jill propped one foot against the pot. "I'd hate to see moderate. I can't imagine severe."

"We may even require the assistance of a sympathetic colleague with whom we can work through our transitory crises to underlying conflicts, thereby effecting resolutions which in turn thrust us to *new pinnacles of self-actualization!*"

"Is this how you talk when you cure people? No wonder Jill can't remember," Kate groused. "You don't have to shout, doctor, and get off my foot."

"Oh, excuse me." Neil hopped to one side. "I was merely emphasizing that therapy is beneficial, *in a variety of situations.*"

"We don't have a variety, thank God. One daughter at a time breaking her mother's heart is enough. How soon can you cure Julie?"

Neil smiled at her naïveté. "That all depends, Mrs. Dunn."

"On what?" Kate was puzzled. "Julie's in the living room. Just go in and say whatever you said that cured Jill."

"But Jill and I talked for months!"

"Months!" Kate's face crumpled beneath the weight of unacceptable disappointment. "Months! But Julie's not nearly as crazy as Jill was, and she's been this way for only a week or two. If you count the first tape, maybe a month."

"Tape?" Neil asked.

"Julie sends tapes instead of letters. So, maybe on one or two she was a little confused. Don't you get confused when you're tired, Dr. Kaiser?"

"We all do, Mrs. Dunn, but—"

"See? So Julie's just tired. Being pooped isn't a disease."

Jill parted the branches, fixing her gaze on Kate's red ringlets as though by staring at her hair she could read the twists of the mind underneath. "Those tapes upset you so much, you asked me to fly to Chicago, Ma. You asked me to call Dr. Kaiser."

"So?" Kate folded her arms defiantly. "Maybe *I* was pooped, what with painters and plumbers. Have you ever walked through the living room and had plaster fall on your head? You think you've been shot by a sniper in the chimney. My heart leaped—"

"The tapes upset you," Neil interrupted.

Jill detected the Kaiser of old through the screen of familiar technique.

And between the coming and the going, Neil Kaiser cured me.

"Upset me? My son-in-law divorcing my daughter upset me, but my Julie, never!" Kate said, looking distinctly upset. "I'll admit, at first the Sousa marches bothered me a little, but does liking Sousa marches mean a person's crazy?"

"In most contexts, no, Mrs. Dunn, but—"

"You won't find a crazy person in *my* living room, Dr. Kaiser, just a girl who's exhausted and likes Sousa marches. So she rambles a bit. They say Albert Einstein hardly ever made sense when he talked, just on paper with numbers."

Neil took Kate's hand and patted it gently. "There, there, Mrs. Dunn, I can see why you're upset."

"You can?" Kate's eyes glowed in the reflection of his warmth.

"Of course. And I can understand why your Julie might be upset, too. Going through a divorce is a most traumatic experience. *Most traumatic!*"

"I'm not deaf." Kate winced and stepped back. "My heart is leaping, but my ears aren't plugged."

"Excuse me, Mrs. Dunn. I'm just eager to reassure you that I'll do anything in my power to assist *any member of Jill's family.*"

"Have you had your hearing checked?" Kate frowned. "My poor aunt Kitty had ringing in her ears and you could hear her private conversations from the fish market on the corner."

"I'm fine, Mrs. Dunn. It's *you* I'm worried about."

"Me?" Kate quivered, the overwhelmed recipient of a doctor's spontaneous concern.

"We must alleviate your anxiety about Julie. Anxiety can cause insomnia, loss of appetite, palpitations—"

"You hit the nail on the nose, doctor," Kate said delightedly. "If you only knew what I've been through."

"I can imagine." He smiled compassionately. "So, let's get to the heart of your anxiety. Where's Julie?"

"But you said it might take months."

"Sometimes, yes, sometimes less."

"How much less?"

"That depends."

"On what?"

Jill's head spun with the effort of tracking Kate's circles. "Ma, for God's sake, let him talk to Julie!"

Kate whirled, stooped, and stuck her head through the bush. "That's easy enough for you to say. You don't have daughters on psychiatrists' couches blaming their problems on you!"

Neil tugged gently at Kate's arm. "Mrs. Dunn, Mrs. Dunn!"

Kate continued to shout while a quaking Jill shrank away from the venom that poured like a scalding waterfall into her haven of leaves. "You'll be sorry you divorced and gave up your church! You'll be sorry you flitted when Daisy starts babbling!"

Neil tugged at Kate's shoulder. "Mrs. Dunn. Jill's not the problem."

Kate popped out of the bush and turned on him angrily. "Keep your hands to yourself! I know what goes on in psychiatrists' offices!"

"Jill told you!" Neil went green.

"Lying on couches complaining about mothers, that's what!"

"Oh, that." Neil exhaled with the sound of a whale pumping air, then straightened, professional poise restored. "Mrs. Dunn, you are suffering from a common, tenacious, fallacious assumption."

"You know that without X rays?" Kate was wide-eyed.

"I'm not talking about a disease, Mrs. Dunn. Allow me to assure you that even Jill's less coherent verbalizations were liberally laced with positive references to you."

"Her verb— She spoke well of me?"

"Repeatedly. Sincerely. Besides, blaming mothers is passé, as antediluvian theory-wise as the notion that mental illness is caused by the curse of an evil eye."

"My aunt Elsie believed that. She hung scapulars over her bed." Kate eyed Neil shrewdly. "So, then, what causes it?"

"Uh ... there are a multiplicity of factors, Mrs. Dunn, any combination of which—"

"But not fathers. My husband was a saint."

Neil glanced through the leaves at Jill. "From what Jill's told me, her father was a major influence in her life."

"For a change, Jill's right, Dr. Kaiser. In this house the sun rose and set on that man."

"Have I relieved your anxiety, Mrs. Dunn?"

"Well . . ." Kate was not wholly convinced.

Neil smiled encouragement. "Genuinely devoted mothers disregard personal anxiety when a crisis threatens their children. Nurturing mothers. Selfless mothers."

"That's me all over." Kate's head rose proudly. "All right, Dr. Kaiser. You may see Julie."

"Wise mother, wise decision." Neil lavished approval on her. "I think it best you prepare Julie. Please tell her I'm the doctor who once treated Jill and I'm here to see her."

"Telling her won't do any good. She's watching *Days of Our Lives.* She won't even hear me."

"Perhaps not. But preparing her is the fair thing to do."

"You're right," Kate decided. "I'd hate to have a psychiatrist sneak up on me."

She bustled into the living room, leaving Neil in the kitchen with a suddenly wary Jill.

"Come out," Neil rasped in Jill's direction. "I can't see you."

"You didn't come here to see me. Go look at your patient."

"I thought *you* were the patient, or I wouldn't be here." Neil's voice was gruff with exasperation.

"Oh? Is there any particular reason you thought I might have had a relapse? Are you disappointed that I'm not a dissembling wreck?"

"Of course not. Though I'd have no objection to caring for you again. Actually this is better. If you were psychotic, we couldn't have dinner. Have dinner with me, Jill."

"What a wonderful idea! Tell your wife to set an extra place."

"I don't have a wife! She's gone for good! She ran off. . . . Goddammit, I can't talk to you like this!" He stomped around the plant and stood before her, trembling with frustration. "Look at me!"

Jill focused firmly on his kneecaps, avoiding the piercing, perceptive eyes experience had proven could read any emotion, including ambivalence, through her most solidly constructed façade. *Acting as if* wouldn't save her.

"My divorce is going through. Do you know what that means?"

"You have to iron your own shirts?"

"For the moment I'll ignore your defenses," he said severely. "There's something I want to say." He leaned over, bringing his eyes level with hers. "I'm in love with you, Jill."

"Don't expect me to fall into your arms, Neil. You said you loved me before, and then you went fishing. You wished me good luck and went off to catch carp."

"Pike," he corrected automatically, then added softly, "I knew I was hurting you then."

"And you didn't care."

"You know better than that." He cupped her chin in his hand and kissed her, his mouth barely brushing her lips. The regret in his eyes was undeniable, his sincerity an irresistible force battering at her defenses. Jill felt them crumbling within her.

Too late to dissemble, assemble a bastion.

Try. Try.

"Why would I know better, Neil? I'm not psychic or mystic. I can't read your mind, and I have no affinity for riddles. I believe what I hear, what I see. What I heard was good-bye. What I saw was you gone."

I'm trying. I'm trying.

"You didn't look beyond that? I don't believe it." Neil eased himself to the floor and sat down close to her chair. "I remember a girl under a piano, refusing all help, even mine. A girl with green eyes unable to trust for fear of rejection. That girl would know better. Do you remember the afternoon I joined you?"

"Yes," Jill whispered. "I do."

He'd crawled in to sit beside her, and she, nerve endings vibrating to his presence, had stared stolidly ahead into unfocused space.

"I couldn't push you into reality or coerce you into trusting, Jill. But you needed affirmation, assurance I would be there at the moment you were ready. You intuited that, didn't you?"

Her "Yes" was a whispered admission.

I tried.

"I thought as much," Neil sighed. "We're alike, you and I. We gather our griefs around us and run. Do you understand why I ran from you?"

"Dr. Kaiser, Dr. Kaiser," Kate clamored from the doorway. "The commercial is on. Julie will talk to you now."

Neil hesitated. "I haven't finished speaking with Jill."

335

"You've already cured that daughter." Kate rapped testily on the doorjamb. "Come give this one a shot."

Slowly and with poorly disguised reluctance Neil regained his feet.

He stood for a moment, silent, looking not quite at Jill but at the space around her. "I'm better these days, but not yet entirely whole. In one or two areas I remain . . . fragile. Only a woman with perception and empathy could understand. Only a woman . . . like . . ."

"Hurry, Dr. Kaiser," Kate urged. "*All My Children* comes back after the New Blue Cheer."

Jill watched Neil as he followed Kate through the door. She reached for her cigarettes and removed one from the pack, but her thoughts drifted off before she could light it.

The man who'd been savior, omniscient, a rod and a staff if only for one hour a week, had said he was fragile, had said they were alike. He'd been right. He fled with his grief to solitary riverbanks, she to shared, lonely beds.

Understand you? I am you.

Neil's the opposite that always attracts and a mirror of myself simultaneously. For this there is no defense.

Flee? Fight?

Flee where?

Fight what? Neil?

Shadowboxing . . . on the ropes . . . down for the count . . . seven . . . eight . . . nine . . .

"Yoo-hoo!" It was Candy, yodeling in the hall.

Saved by the dingaling!

"I'm here in the garden," Jill called.

"Hello, Jill," Candy trilled, then gasped at the sight of the plant. "My goodness! Where did *that* come from?"

"I traded the cow for a handful of beans." Jill ducked under the branches as Neil had done. "My goodness yourself, Candy!"

Candy was dressed in an ankle-length rosebud-print creation with leg o' mutton sleeves and a Peter Pan collar. "You look like *Little House on the Prairie*."

"Like it?" Candy smiled. "I made it myself. It's Simplicity."

Jill grinned. "How appropriate. What's in your basket?"

Candy lifted a large wicker hamper onto Kate's immaculate counter. "Let's see. There's custard in this container and in this one my homemade vegetable soup. And in this, sweet butter I bought at the Westside Market, in case Julie's tummy is on the fritz." In seconds

Kate's counter was buried beneath every shape container Tupperware ever devised, including some still in experimental stages. "I wanted to make the butter myself, but John won't buy me a churn."

"Even the realest woman can't do everything, Candy." Jill smiled at her good intentions.

"But a real woman *tries*. We're wives and mothers, friends and lovers, ladies in the parlor and you-know-whats in bed. We find our joy in giving."

"To those who find their joy in taking," Jill agreed. "It's a wonderfully balanced system, isn't it, Candy?"

"God-given." Candy smiled. "How's Julie? Any better?"

"Not yet, Candy, but I'm sure she will be," Jill said, unwilling to worry Candy. "Ma and the psychiatrist who helped me are with her now."

"Why would Julie need a psychiatrist? John says she's just overworked."

"Chronic overwork can exhaust a mind, Candy. Sometimes recovery requires more than a few nights' sound sleep."

"That's why I worry so about John." Candy frowned. "He works such long hours. All those computers to deal with, and now there's a shipment stuck in Buffalo. I don't know how he does it. Ah, well, my mother always said that men think thoughts women will never understand. I know how important his work is."

"I'm sure you do, Candy," Jill said, thinking of how completely Nancy had understood Dan.

"I have John's dinner in the car," Candy continued. "There's chicken and dumplings, homemade rolls, celery sticks, brownies, olives, pickles—"

"Then John won't be available if we need help with Julie?" Jill was beginning to understand.

"How can he help?" Candy's eyes were round as Nerf Balls. "There's that shipment stuck in Buffalo—"

"I heard. I heard," Jill interrupted impatiently. "That shipment isn't all that's being shuffled off to Buffalo. When you deliver John's dinner, tell him I'll be calling. Regardless of his work we may need his help."

"I'll try, but I may not get to see him. Yesterday when I dropped in with my fresh blueberry muffins, his secretary just whisked them away. She said John couldn't be disturbed."

"That's what I need," Jill decided, "a secretary out front to tell the

337

world I can't be disturbed—preferably one with a gun in her hand."

"I could never deal with computers." Candy giggled at the thought. "They're always breaking down or getting stuck in cities where they don't belong. People don't do that."

"You could have fooled me, Candy."

The phone rang, and Jill answered it.

Please, God, let it be Johnny.

"Hello?"

"Jill Kenyon?" It was Dr. Kerry, sounding definitely grumpy.

"What is it?" Jill asked apprehensively. A psychiatrist calling a patient long distance is not a good omen.

"Where in hell are you?"

"You're calling me. You should know." Jill wished he wouldn't shout.

"You've missed three appointments in a row," he complained. "Do you think I like sitting in my office waiting for a patient who doesn't even call?"

Jill winced at the picture of him sitting alone, waiting for her, her hives, mother, and men. "I'm sorry. I apologize. Every time I make an appointment to tell you what's happened, something else happens. Life's going so fast, I barely have time to live it, never mind drive across town to explain it to you. I know. I'll write you a letter. Maybe send you a tape."

"Right now you can tell me what you're doing in Cleveland. Your secretary said something about a family emergency."

Quickly Jill explained Julie's problem, omitting Neil Kaiser's involvement.

"I see. Your sister needs professional help."

"I'm . . . uh . . . working on that."

"Just stay away from Neil Kaiser," Kerry warned. "You've never resolved your feelings for him, and now that he's become erratic . . . I'll bet you never broke appointments with *him*."

"Well . . . uh . . . ." Jill hedged. She'd kept every appointment with Neil, even on days when she couldn't remember her name.

"See what I'm up against? Unresolved transference! No wonder I can't make progress with you. I'm trying to build a mansion on a cracked foundation."

Jill hesitated, tempted to hang up on his long-distance kvetching. "Just consider me hopeless, doctor."

"Never say hopeless." He said quickly. "But we certainly have our work cut out for us. Make an appointment the second you get back. I'll bill you for the appointments you missed. Oh, and take your pills. A positive attitude and Valium, that's all you need."

"I don't take Valium, Dr. Kerry. You have me confused with some-one . . ." She was protesting to a dead line.

"Maybe you should take Valium." Candy ventured an opinion. "A lot of my girl friends do. It's easy to get. Just go to a doctor and tell him you're nervous. He won't even ask why."

"Of course not. Why inquire about trivial women-type problems when you can hand her a pill?"

"Women think too much, Jill. Thinking too much is unfeminine. If we'd just learn to put our loved ones first . . ."

"Kate. Oh, Kate!" The door slammed. Jim huffed into the kitchen, bent beneath the weight of a huge shopping bag. "I've brought— Where's Kate? My God, what's that?"

"Ma's in the living room with Julie and her doctor, and the plant's a gift from John," Jill explained.

"Kate shouldn't have called the doctor yet. I have just what Julie needs."

"The doctor is a psychiatrist," Candy told him. "What did you bring?"

Jim snorted. "Psychiatrist! Witch doctor, you mean! Psychiatrists are like fairies. They exist because enough people clap!"

"A psychiatrist helped me when I needed it," Jill felt compelled to say.

"Years ago," Jim grumped. "And you're still going. Kate told me."

"Jill's high-strung." Candy peered curiously into Jim's bag. "She should take Valium."

"Drugs! Pah! Poison! She should take Stresstabs, kelp, B com-plex. . . ." He fished a tiny white vial from the bag and bran-dished it at Jill. "These! I'm giving Julie two right away."

"What is that?" Candy pointed at the bottle.

"Gerovital. It comes from Rumania. It's illegal here."

Jill nodded. "Reason enough to buy it. Does it do anything besides make you a criminal?"

"It's rejuvenation I'm holding in my hand! A youth pill!" Jim tapped the side of his head. "Brain cells die every minute, but only a few at a time and scattered all over the brain. Either Julie's brain cells are dying too fast, or the ones that are going are all in a clump. Gerovital will rejuvenate her brain!"

339

"Does it work for bodies too?" Candy was interested.

"Certainly. Certainly. It perks everything up."

"Perks? Bosoms?"

Jim was embarrassed. "I don't know much about . . . womanly things . . . but . . ."

There was a noise in the hall, like someone bouncing off walls. Father Norton stumbled into the kitchen. "I heard voices. It woke me. I think my fever's gone up. My glands are like beach balls." He noticed the plant and gawked. "What in God's name is that?"

"It's been here for years, Father Norton." Jill gave him a pseudo-concerned look. "You don't remember seeing it before?"

"Oh, God, I'm not well." Norton sank into a chair, head in hands.

"Who's he?" Candy whispered to Jill.

"He's Father Norton . . . uh . . . a visiting priest." Jill was certain John hadn't confided Julie's religious experience, coming as it did under the heading of "not normal."

"*He's* the one," Jim blurted out. He knew.

"Is Julie so sick she needs a priest?" Candy was alarmed.

"No, Candy," Jill assured her. "He just dropped in. Being Catholic's like cleaning fish in the sink. Sooner or later cats show up at your door."

Candy remained unconvinced. "I'm Catholic. I don't have priests in my kitchen."

"Join the youth group, Candy," Jill advised. "Maybe you'll get lucky."

Norton lifted his head from his arms, moaning. "I'm far too ill to travel. May I stay the night?"

"It's my mother's house, Norton. I'm sure her answer will be different from mine. Wait until she's finished with Julie and the doctor."

"A doctor?" Norton's eyes clouded. "Julie's no better?"

"She might be worse," Candy said.

"Oh, no." Norton sagged, pale and anguished. "This is terrible. Julie's a good woman." He leaped to his feet. "I can't live with this on my soul. I must have Julie's forgiveness!"

"What's he talking about?" a baffled Candy whispered to Jim. "Is he delirious? Is it fever?"

Jim scowled. "He's overheated, for sure."

Norton reached for Jill's hand. Jill snatched it away, and he stood groping at the air like a blind man. "You must believe that I meant no harm. I know there's a weakness in me, and I pray constantly that

340

it be removed. But my life is so lonely, Jill. A life chosen by my parents, not me. You don't know how difficult it is to have parents who insist you be what you're not."

"Don't I? I'm Jill Hyde, raised by a family named Jekyll."

"Then you *do* understand." His eyes lit up with hope.

"I do indeed."

"Then you'll forgive me for what I've done?"

"For your part in what's happening to Julie?"

He nodded eagerly.

"No." Jill walked away from him.

"But you have to!" He shot ahead of her and wheeled around blocking her way. "I've confessed my fault, begged your forgiveness—"

"Beg forgiveness elsewhere, Father. God's often recommended in cases like these."

"But you said you understand my loneliness, my life—"

"I understand your reasons better than anyone you'll ever know. But I won't forgive your behavior. You're right about Julie. She *is* a good woman. Too good to be damaged by a man who's used his position to become part of her life, then used her as a distraction from the debacle of his. Go away, Father Norton. You disgust me."

He flushed. Beads of sweat lined his upper lip. "I must speak to Julie. She'll forgive me."

"Wait!" Jill commanded. "Julie's talking to the psychiatrist."

"Psychiatrist!" Norton's flushed face went pale. "You said she was with a doctor. You didn't say a psychiatrist! We can't let a psychiatrist treat Julie."

Jill stared. "*We,* Father Norton?"

"See?" Jim came alive. "Even priests who aren't good at it know psychiatrists are quacks. Listen to the man, Jill." He gave Father Norton his friendliest smile. "I think I might have something to cure those glands. I was going to give them to Julie, but—" He dove into his bag.

"If you could see what comes into my pastoral office!" Norton fumed. "The cases mishandled by psychiatrists! Poor souls foundering in a sea of rationalization, houses divided against themselves. People need guidelines, not the moral ambiguity of psychiatric theory. They need spiritual counseling . . . spiritual direction . . ."

"Acupressure shoes." Jim thrust a shoebox at Norton. "Put these on, Father. They'll massage your pressure points."

341

"Thank you." Norton tried to brush the shoebox away. "I don't think my pressure points need massaging."

"But pressure points are connected to vital organs, Father. These shoes will stimulate your glands."

"Christ!" Jill exclaimed. "That's like giving gin to a drunk!"

"Mother of God! I can't bear it!" Kate came flying across the kitchen and threw herself on Jill's neck, sobbing. "Your Dr. Kaiser wants to take my baby away! He wants to lock my Julie up in one of those awful places!"

"Oh, Ma." Jill held Kate, staring over her head at Neil, who stood in the doorway, his eyes soft with sympathy for them all.

"I'm sorry, Jill," he said gently. "If there was another way, I would take it. Julie needs hospitalization."

"I was afraid of that, Neil." Jill bit the inside of her mouth, willing the tears away. Kate was too frightened, too overwhelmed, to cope with tears other than her own.

I'm *frightened. For Julie. For myself. When the strong crumble, the fragile beware. The fragile return to pianos.*

"See here," Norton broke in. "I can't allow this hospitalization."

"I beg your pardon?" Neil was startled. "Who are you?"

"He's a priest," Candy was eager to explain. "He does marriage counseling."

"Did Julie's husband send you?" Neil asked.

"Uh . . . indirectly. The real point here is that Julie's a practicing Catholic. She should be counseled by someone who understands her complete frame of reference. You cannot treat the mind without considering the soul, doctor."

"I'll take care of her mind, Father." Neil was curt. "You may pray over her later."

"I'm not talking about praying over her. I'm talking about therapy with a moral base. This area of counseling is my particular area of specialization. I have degrees in both psychology and sociology."

"From the Holy Roller School of Voodoo?" Neil was furious. "Where they teach you to dump such guilt on people, they crack under the load?"

"Guilt isn't always harmful, doctor. It can reinforce positive behavior by making negative behavior emotionally stressful. And I took my degrees at Fordham!" Norton folded his arms.

"Congratulations! Too bad Fordham neglected to teach you about

constructive reinforcement for positive behavior. Beating people
with guilt is like amputating for a hangnail."

"That's better than— Wait!" Norton was suddenly calm. "Did Julie
request a psychiatrist?"

"I was called in by the patient's mother," Neil said levelly.

"But not by the patient?" Norton smiled.

"No," Neil admitted.

Norton approached Kate, who continued to tremble in Jill's arms.
"I know you're distraught, Mother Dunn, but you must reconsider
. . . this . . . this . . . psychiatrist."

"I only want what's best for Julie," Kate sobbed. "It will break my
heart to see her in one of those awful places, Father Norton."

"*You're* Father Norton." Neil's voice was a low and ominous rumble. "*You're* going to tell me how to treat the woman you . . . I'll make
the arrangements for Julie's hospitalization."

He started toward the door, with Norton on his heels shouting,
"No, you won't!"

"Wait!" Kate shrieked, and both men froze as though turned to
salt. Kate's tear-streaked face swiveled slowly from one to the other.
"Julie's my daughter. I must have the final word."

"You have that right," Neil said equably.

Norton smiled ingratiatingly. "You know what's best for Julie.
You're her mother, her Catholic mother."

Kate clasped Jill's hand, holding it as though it was her last link
with life. "Dr. Kaiser cured Jill when we thought she was hopeless.
On the other hand, priests work among the . . . disturbed . . . and do
miracles. If Dr. Kaiser looks after Julie, she'll have to go to the . . .
hos— that place. If Father Norton counsels, he can work miracles
right here, without leaving the house. I've made my decision." She
squared her jaw bravely. "Jill will decide."

"What?" Jill tried to shake loose, but Kate held her hand in a death
grip. "Ma, it's not my decision to make!"

"You have to! I can't!"

"But, if I make the wrong decision—"

Kate flung Jill's hand back at her. "If Julie gets worse, it'll be your
fault."

"It can't be!"

"It will be, if you don't decide." Kate ran sobbing to the open circle
of Jim's arms. "Just wait till it's Daisy who's sick, and see if *you* can
lock *her* up."

343

"*Daisy!* Don't say that, Ma!" Jill pleaded.

"Mark my words!"

Daisy's mother flits. Daisy's mother works. Daisy's mother . . .

Their faces swirled around her, a murky, boiling cloud. From its center barbed and sharpened expectations hurled lethal silver at her throat.

If Julie doesn't get well . . .

If Daisy ends up in a nuthouse . . .

It will be your *fault.*

"No!" Jill screamed, a blind and frantic animal, bolting at first touch of the trap.

Unseeing, Jill ran through the kitchen, down the hallway, and onto the porch, slamming the door behind her.

CHAPTER 23

"Here we are!" Peter glowed with anticipation as he unlocked the motel room door. "Welcome to Cleveland's answer to Eden, the Brookpark Ramada Inn!" He bounced across the threshold, waving his arms like a cheerleader.

Jill faltered behind him, her movements the graceless reflexes of a carelessly carved marionette. She felt drained, incapable of anything beyond resolute concentration on the business immediately at hand.

Earlier, in the phone booth, she'd pressed her forehead against the cold, grimy glass, head spinning with cause and effect. She'd fled guilt, only to find she'd exchanged a future "It will be your fault" for an immediate "You ran away."

She shadowed Peter's footsteps over the threshold, focusing determined attention on his broad-shouldered back and the soft, fine hair curling over his collar.

Peter opened eager arms. "Close the door and give me a kiss."

Obediently Jill closed the door, shutting them in and shutting out any expectations that might have followed, like Norton's rabid animals, vicious and intent on tearing her to shreds.

If you don't make a decision, you're guilty.

"What a pleasant surprise, Jill. I'm so glad you're here."

Make the wrong decision, you're guiltier yet.

His kiss was warm and wet and probing. She opened her mouth against his, greedy for sensations to replace emotions too painful to feel.

Damned if you do. More damned if you don't.

"You're still the best kisser." Jill smiled up at him, wondering if he'd noticed her agitation.

"You're the lady I most like kissing," he murmured, nuzzling her neck.

Peter hadn't noticed. His expectation was blissfully simple—that Jill would be, as advertised by phone, a cheerfully horny lady ready for an uncomplicated roll. No fear that Peter would read beyond her façade. It was the façade he wanted, the face painted on.

Smiling, Peter gestured toward the bed. "After you, madam."

"You promised to tell me about Crazy Camille." Jill stood still, wondering at her obvious stall.

Jump into bed, fool, get what you came for.

What did I come for?

Distraction, diversion, a detour around pain.

Not Peter? Specifically Peter? The body and mind named Peter?

"Oh, that Camille." Peter shook his head. "You won't believe this Jill, but in only six months that woman had me stone-stupid and pussy-whipped. *Me.*"

"What happened?" Jill threw her shoes on the floor next to Peter's and began unbuttoning her blouse. "What did she do?"

"Fucked me over, that's what. She was sneaking around, seeing some other guy on the side. I should have dumped her the first time I suspected." He unbuckled his belt with one hand, then snapped it, whipping through belt loops. "A man can't have his wife slutting around."

Jill's fingers froze on her buttons. "I was married to Steve when we began our affair. You used to congratulate me on being liberated."

"That was different, Jill." He patted the bed. "C'mere."

Jill remained standing. "Not until you explain the difference between me, the liberated, and Camille, the slut."

Peter smiled, prepared to humor her. "Camille is flat-out round-heeled, honey. You do what you do with some class."

"Interesting." Jill stiffened, feeling suddenly cold and exhausted. "A woman who sleeps with you is free-spirited, a woman who sleeps elsewhere is easy."

Peter reached for her. "I've never seen you so tense, Jill. What you need is a good fuck."

"I had one once, Peter. It didn't change my life." She bent to retrieve her shoes.

Distraction, diversion.

"You're not leaving?" Peter watched her, dismayed.

Someone to hold me when I'm hurting.

"You don't care why I'm here, do you?" Jill found her purse half-hidden under the bedspread.

346

"We both know why we're here, Jill." Peter blocked her path to the door. "Don't play games with me."

"But isn't that what you want, Peter? A nice fast game of 'Let's pretend we're all liberated and fuck'?"

"What's wrong with that?" Peter smiled, bending to kiss her. "We always have fun."

Valium's easy to get.

Jill ducked his kiss. "It makes no difference that it's me here with you. Any woman will do."

What do you do when you're hurting?

"That's not true, Jill," Peter insisted. "You've always been special to me. I didn't come here just to get laid."

Simply stand still and hurt.

Jill stared for a moment at her fine, feckless Peter, then smiled ruefully. "But I did, Peter. I came here just to get laid. That's why I'm leaving."

"Catholic girls!" Peter snapped furiously. "Live like a nun, then. It won't last. You were born to have lovers."

"I was born a romantic, Peter. I was born believing in a love so profound it could bind one soul to another forever. In this best of all cynic's world that made me a fool, so I stopped. But I've missed believing in love. I've missed it passionately."

Peter rubbed the back of his neck, clearly uncomfortable with the mention of love and passion in a conversation he thought was about sex. "Look, Jill, I don't know what's bugging you, but I've got some really good grass in my car. I'll get—"

"Stop! We're all users using users, and all I'm getting is used up." Jill was angry, more at herself than at him.

"All right. All right." Peter opened the door. "Go home. The next time you want to get fucked, call someone else."

"The next time?" Jill thought about the next time, the way it could be if she'd learned to stand still with herself. "The next time a call won't be necessary. The next time whoever he is will be there with me because we belong together. And we won't be fucking, we'll be making love."

She closed the door on his "Catholic girls!"

Jill drove home, wondering when "the next time" would be, hoping for soon, but willing to wait. She suspected it would take some time to discover if she had a self to stand still with.

She walked into the kitchen, where Kate and Jim were drinking coffee.

"I hope you're proud of yourself," Kate said bleakly.

"Thanks, Ma. I'd love a cup of coffee." Jill poured Kate's excellent coffee into a Stoneware cup. "Where did everyone go?"

"They all got in a donkey cart and went to the Pocono Mountains," Kate snapped. "What do you care? You ran away."

"I needed cigarettes."

"You need a good shaking, and that's what you'd get if your father was here," Kate said with conviction. "Why isn't your father here?"

Jim slipped a soothing arm around Kate's shoulders. "I'm sure that even in Heaven John is thinking of you."

"He'd better be," Kate said grimly. "With all I'm going through, the least he can do is look down and feel terrible."

Jill gulped the remainder of her coffee and refilled her cup. "Have you reached a decision about Julie, Ma?"

"I can't." Kate turned her head away. "You know I can't, Jill. She's my own little . . ."

Damned I may be. I won't damn Julie, too.

"I've made a decision, Ma. Julie's going to the hospital."

"Naaa." The sound from Kate was a strangled "No" edged with anger. "That's easy for you to say. She's not your daughter."

"Julie's my sister and more than my sister—she's part of myself. Deciding to put her in the hospital is many things to me, and not one bears the slightest resemblance to easy."

"But Father Norton said—"

"Father Norton is part of the problem. He can't also be the solution."

"Are you sure it's the right thing?" Kate picked up Jill's cigarettes, twisting the pack in her hand.

"If it turns out well, you'll say you knew it would. If it doesn't, you'll hate me. It's the best decision I can make, Ma."

"It had better be." Kate lit a cigarette.

"What are you doing, Kate!" Jim blew at the burning tip. "Cigarettes are bad for your heart!"

"So what? My heart's broken. If you shot me in the chest, you couldn't make it worse." Kate puffed furiously. "So I may as well smoke. And eat fatty foods. Stay for dinner. I'll fix Polish sausage."

"Kate, you don't mean it—"

"For dessert, devil's-food cake with real whipped cream and licorice whips, the ones with red dye. Tomorrow for breakfast, bacon and eggs. . . ."

"Bacon and eggs are slow suicide, Kate." Jim looked ready to cry.

"Then I'll also have ham. It'll go faster." Kate coughed, a ripping hack. "Get the brandy. I'm dying from this cigarette."

Jill leaned over Kate, gently stroking the side of her cheek. "I know how upset you are, Ma. Believe me, Julie will get well."

"Are you sure?" Kate looked at her with eyes red-rimmed from unaccustomed smoke and familiar tears.

"I'm sure, Ma."

No "broken promises."

"Then Julie may go to the hospital," Kate decided, "and you'd better be right." Kate wiped her eyes with the back of her hand and blew her nose in a napkin. "Well, that's done. Jim and I are going to evening Mass."

"Here's your brandy, Kate." Jim was beside her, bottle in hand.

"You think I'd drink brandy and then go to church? Well, if that's the kind of woman you want, go see Maggie McCaron. She tipples all day and falls asleep in confession."

"But you said—" Jim protested.

"I'll get my own coat." Kate bustled toward the hallway. "How do I stay so cheerful with all this aggravation?"

They departed for church, Kate unintentionally dashing in her cherry-red coat and hat of unspecified fur and Jim cocooned against chill and viruses in muffler, mittens, and a fuzzy gray hat with ear flaps.

Obeying the omnipresent Kate-voice, Jill rinsed the coffeepot and set it on the draining board, where it nudged Jim's bottles and Candy's containers. Though they hadn't held the disparate cures for Julie that Jim and Candy obviously had envisioned, they overflowed with good intentions. Compassion was packaged in Tupperware, and tenderness, however specious, rattled in small white bottles.

Jill reached for the phone, hoping that Neil and his hospital would prove more effective than Jim's rejuvenation, or at least as harmless as Candy's vegetable soup.

"Dr. Kaiser's office." It was the tinkling trill of Mrs. Silverstone.

"It's Jill Kenyon."

"Oh, my dear. It's always good to hear from you, even though I've heard your family's little ship has hit a snag in the water."

"There's good news and bad news, Mrs. Silverstone. The ship is sinking, but I've been elected captain. That's why I'm calling. Has Dr. Kaiser mentioned the possibility of arranging hospitalization for my sister?"

"Oh, yes, indeed, and your sister's in luck. There happen to be several vacancies, and you know how crowded the psychiatric ward can be this time of year."

Jill nodded. "During November in Cleveland depression blows in off the lake with the snowstorms."

"Perhaps your sister will be home for Christmas, Jill. Wouldn't that be a nice present for your family?"

"Christmas!" Jill groaned. "I can't stay for Christmas. I can't stay here until next week. What was I thinking of?"

"The longest journey begins with a single step," Mrs. Silverstone encouraged. "Have your sister here at nine o'clock in the morning."

"I'll have to leave Julie in the hospital and go back to L.A." Jill was appalled. "My mother will kill me."

"Come now. How could your momma ever get angry at a nice girl like you? Dearie me, I almost forgot. Dr. Kaiser wanted me to buzz him when you called. Hold, please."

She exiled Jill into the land of hold without waiting for her response. Jill waited, wondering what she'd say to Neil, the healer who needed healing. And to Kate about Christmas. And Steve about "thinking it through." And Daisy. And . . .

Mrs. Silverstone returned to the line, laughing. "Dearie me, he's not answering his buzzer."

"Must be busy," Jill mumbled, involved with her thoughts.

"Who *says* Dr. Kaiser is dizzy?" Mrs. Silverstone asked indignantly. "Some people have nothing better to do than gossip and spread rumors."

"I said *busy*."

"Oh. Mea culpa. Well, as you know, the morning was lost in the situation at your house. He hasn't had time to catch up."

"It was nice of him to come to the house. I appreciate that, Mrs. Silverstone."

"That's him all over. He's sending me to Mexico, you know, for a Christmas vacation."

"I'm sure you'll have a wonderful time."

"Margaritas olé," Mrs. Silverstone sang. "And those sweet little burritos with their big brown eyes. Maybe this time I'll catch an eligible sombrero."

"First go back to Berlitz," Jill advised. "You may need a brush-up."

"Good idea," she agreed. "Will you be home later? Dr. Kaiser may want to call."

"I'll be here. Good-bye."

Jill decided to pack Julie's suitcase before Kate arrived home to supervise, or Julie might arrive at the hospital with a full wardrobe, including après ski. But where was the suitcase?

Jill found Julie huddled on Kate's new white sofa, surrounded by equally pristine chairs. There were still finishing touches to be added, but the ambience Kate had sought was established; with white walls and white high-tech furniture, glass oblong tables and high Tensor lamps, the living room resembled nothing so much as the Intensive Care Unit at Pres Gen. All it lacked was beeping monitors, and knowing Kate, she'd soon have those, too.

"Julie?" Jill said softly. "Do you know where Ma put your suitcase?"

"I'm Jill." Julie frowned. "I have to go home and spank Daisy."

"Why, honey. Why would you want to spank Daisy?"

"So my little girl won't grow up like me," Julie whimpered. "I'm bad."

"You're not bad, sweetheart," Jill said soothingly, then realized Julie was talking about her. "What makes you think Jill's bad?"

"Everybody loves Julie. Julie's so perfect, such a good mother. She never does anything wrong. God blesses Julie. So does Mommy. It's nice to be blessed all the time."

Jill sighed. "I wouldn't know."

"But I'm so bad. I do everything wrong." Julie was whimpering again. "I divorced my husband. I sleep with men. Isn't sleeping with men a sin?"

"Only when they're good at it," Jill assured her. "Most of the time it's just exercise."

"I'm going to Hell!" Tears trickled through the fingers Julie held to her face.

"No, you're not." Jill pried Julie's fingers away. "Look at me, honey. You're not going to Hell. Jill's not going to Hell."

"But sometimes I'm bad."

"Don't you love Mor— er, Daisy . . . when she's naughty?"

"Daisy's my own little girl."

"I know. And you love her. Well, you're God's own little girl." Jill sat next to Julie. "God's a wonderful Father. He doesn't stop loving His children when they make mistakes."

351

"I got behind in my schedule."

"God doesn't care."

"He *doesn't*?" Julie's eyes were huge.

"Not a bit. So don't worry, honey. You don't need a schedule or have to be perfect. You just need to be you, God's own little girl."

"Oh." Julie smiled, hugging herself, as pleased as any child being told she's loved. She suddenly frowned. "Then why is there Hell?"

"Oh, dear." Jill wished Julie had quit while Jill was ahead. "I don't know, honey. The reason for Hell is a mystery. But, if God wanted us to know all the answers He'd take us to breakfast and tell us. We'd have eggs over easy and revelations. But I do know God loves you."

"Are you sure?"

"I promise."

"Turn on *Lucy*."

Jill flipped the switch on the old Sylvania console, now as out of date in Kate's new décor as a pterodactyl would be in the aviary at the Cleveland Zoo. She clicked the dial past local stations and stopped at UBC, staring at the screen. The image she saw was more than familiar. It was the opening credits of *Rock and Roll Love*.

"My God, it's on already." Jill was astonished. "They really rushed it to air." She turned to Julie. "Watch this honey. It's as funny as *Lucy*."

"Okay." Julie was instantly absorbed, but not, Jill thought, ready to laugh.

Jill decided to start dinner while waiting for Kate, who by now had probably lit every candle in the church and been hauled off to jail for arson. She started toward the kitchen.

"Good Lord!" She ran into Father Norton, who was standing like a shadow in the doorway. "I didn't see you!"

"It's the black clothes. Priests and burglars get run over at night." He followed her into the kitchen. "I heard what you said to Julie, about God's love I mean. That was beautiful."

Jill opened the refrigerator. "I'm a beautiful person."

"I think you are," Norton said sincerely. "Your remarks about God's love were comforting."

"They were meant to be comforting." Jill removed lettuce, tomatoes, an onion, and celery and closed the door.

"And I liked what you said about Hell being a mystery. . . ."

"Just like the Loch Ness Monster." Jill slammed the salad bowl on the counter. "Don't you have anything to do?"

He moved closer. "With your beliefs I'm surprised you don't practice your religion."

"With your vows I'm astonished you don't practice yours." Jill chopped lettuce into the bowl.

Norton shrugged. "I'm only human. And, as you pointed out, God doesn't expect His children to be perfect, even His priests."

Jill stabbed a stalk of celery. "I have no idea of what God expects and neither do you. Besides, I've never understood the concept of a God with human emotions. They say God is angry or sad, pleased or displeased, righteous or saving up for a toaster. That's not a supreme being, Father Norton. That's my mother." Jill chopped a tomato, smashing it in the process. "Go away."

"If you are confused as to the nature of God, the Church teaches—"

"I know what the Church teaches. I spent my formative years at Our Lady of Perpetual Recriminations. In second grade Sister Lucille taught us 'Thou shalt not kill' and 'The Blessed Mother cries when little girls chew gum'—both being equally deadly sins."

"Come now, Jill. We can't take the little peculiarities of nuns seriously—"

"We can't?" Jill glared. "I thought that's what we were there for."

"But surely you must have realized that chewing gum couldn't be a sin."

"*Must* have? How? I was seven years old, and in that classroom Sister Lucille was the voice of God. I believed every word she said, every word *anyone* said—nuns, priests, parents. I bent my head around all manner of rubbish, superstition, old Pope's tales . . ."

"As we get older we learn to discriminate."

"You, maybe." Jill slashed at the onion. "I just lost interest in picking gold out of the garbage. I wrapped it all up and threw it away."

"So now you believe nothing of what the Church taught you?" Norton frowned at her.

"There's a dogma or two I'm fond of, a dictum or two I've retained," Jill said. "For instance, I believe that our souls are spiritual and eternal. . . ."

"Basic theology," he approved.

"Glad you agree." Jill smiled pleasantly. "Therefore, you'll agree our souls are sexless."

"Well." He seemed puzzled, not by her question so much as by what she might be leading up to. "The spiritual is asexual."

Jill hacked at the onion. "Would you say that God prizes the asexual souls of His sons above the asexual souls of His daughters?"

"Uh . . . er . . . of course not."

"The Church does, Father." Bits of onion flew everywhere. "Its sons are full members, its daughters junk mail."

"That's a contemporary point of view I find difficult to accept," Norton stated.

"That's because you're standing there in your cute little priest suit with your vested interests hanging out of your pockets." Jill sneered at him. "If I were you, I wouldn't accept it, either. Why franchise women when you can control them?"

"I simply do not understand you, Jill."

"Ask me if I care." Jill picked at the onion skin she'd inadvertently tossed in the bowl. "Go somewhere and meditate, Father. Cooking and theology don't mix."

"All right. I'll go talk to Julie."

Jill caught up with him at the door. "If you bother my sister, I'll cut your heart out."

"My God," he quivered, "there's no need to get violent. Did you know your eyes flash when you're angry?" He was breathless. "I've never met anyone like you."

"Go say a prayer of thanksgiving, Father." She turned her back on him.

"We'll talk after dinner," he promised, and disappeared into the hall.

"That's what you think," Jill mumbled, and returned to the salad. She made a face at the bowl. Her tossed salad looked like it had been tossed from the Golden Gate Bridge. "Maybe if I grate cheese on top," she speculated.

While she was heading for the refrigerator the phone rang. She reached for it, still eyeing the salad. "Hello."

"Mom?" It was Daisy.

"Daisy!" Jill was delighted. "I was going to call you after dinner."

"I was just wondering how you are." Daisy sounded tentative, un-Daisy-like. "It's raining here."

"Still?" Jill's inclination was to shout "Daisy, what's wrong?" but she waited, afraid that such a question would provoke an "Oh, mom."

"The streets are flooded. Cars are floating away. The canyons are closed and flood warnings out."

"Oh, God. Is your dad's house all right? Is ours?"

"Dad's roof has a leak here and there, but so far we're holding. Dad says he'll drive me over to our house every day until the storm ends. Just to make sure everything's tight."

"That's nice of him. How's school?"

"Lenny's moving away," Daisy blurted out. "His father is opening a veterinary hospital in Goleta. He wants to be closer to horses."

"Oh, honey, I'm so sorry." Jill ached with the pain in Daisy's voice.

"They're taking Lenny's grandfather with them. Lenny says it'll be nice to be out of the smog."

"Lenny will miss you, Daisy. Terribly."

"He says he will." Daisy sounded forlorn. "He says that leaving me is the bad part."

"And you'll miss him. Oh, I wish I was there, honey. I wish I was there to hold you and help."

"It's okay," Daisy said quickly. "It isn't so bad. Goleta's not far from where we went with Patti Gerard. Lenny says he'll drive down to see me whenever he can. We'll still go to concerts and stuff. Not so often, but sometimes. When I get my driver's license, I can drive up the coast and see him."

"Of course you can. I'll teach you to drive the minute I get home."

"They do that in school, Mom, so we don't pick up our parents' bad driving habits."

"Oh."

"But it was nice of you to offer." Daisy's voice was soft. "So that's all that's going on in school."

"I know how upset you must feel. Lenny's your best friend."

"He's not going to Bulgaria, Mom." Daisy sounded less tentative. "He'll be less than two hours away."

"But you'll miss seeing him every day, at lunchtime." Jill winced, picturing a solitary Daisy eating endless lunches alone. "I'm sorry this happened."

"Well, yeah, but I guess that's life." Daisy sighed, then added quickly, "How's Aunt Julie?"

"She's being taken care of, Daisy. She'll be just fine."

"Then you'll be home soon?" Daisy asked. "I mean, I know how busy you are at work."

"I'll be home as soon as I can, Daisy. And it's not work I'm anxious to get back to. It's you."

"Well, I just called to make sure you didn't get lost on your way to Cleveland." Daisy's forlorn tone had taken on a cheerful veneer.

"Dad says that he expects someday he'll get a call that you've taken the wrong plane and are wandering around downtown Istanbul looking for Lake Erie."

"Anything's possible." Jill wondered what made Steve think that if she was lost, she'd call him. "But so far I've muddled through. I've never taken the wrong plane, Daisy."

"That's right." Daisy sounded surprised. "You never have."

"I'll always find my way home, honey. So will you."

"I know, Mom. Well, I have to go now. Lenny's picking me up for the movies. We're going to enjoy ourselves while we can."

"Have fun, Daisy. And say hello to Lenny for me. I'll call you tomorrow. Bye." Jill hung up, riding crests of conflicting emotions —sorrow for Daisy and her impending loss of Lenny, satisfaction that Daisy had called her for comforting, and bemusement at Daisy's method of dealing with loss. Daisy's distress had been apparent, yet when Jill had gone to the specifics of her loss, Daisy had backed off and began sounding like Steve. But not quite. Daisy hadn't shown her feelings the door when they'd proven cantankerous. She'd allowed them to remain without giving them the run of her house.

Interesting. My penchant for overreaction has combined with Steve's denial to produce Daisy, who expresses negative feelings but looks on the bright side.

She wondered if the balance that seemed to be Daisy's was the result of exposure to both parents, a felicitous accident, harmonious rising- and sun-signs, or a triumph of the gene pool.

Most likely a triumph of Daisy.

Jill foraged in Kate's freezer, emerging with stinging fingers and a block of turkey tetrazzini undoubtedly created from the leftovers of some Thanksgiving or Christmas dinner. If so, it was a bona fide second-, perhaps third-generation, meal. Jill slipped the frozen brick into a pan, thinking that only in Kate's house would the furniture be new and the food heirloom.

By the time Kate and Jim returned from church, dinner was steaming, the table set, and a fresh pot of coffee, Jill's anemic version of Kate's black plasma, hiccuping in a percolator accustomed to better stuff.

"If God had wanted us to speak English, he would have made us Protestants," Kate declared, huffing into the kitchen.

"Personally I like speaking English," Jim said. "What's the use of praying when you can't understand a word coming out of your mouth?"

"You're not praying to yourself," Kate reminded him. "The priests used to tell us that the prayers of Catholics from all over the world rose in Latin to God in one voice. Now everyone's speaking a different language, and God's sitting in Heaven with His hands over His ears."

"Mass upset you," Jill guessed.

"If I'd had any sense I would have left before the announcements," Kate said.

"Your mother's upset because Father Monahan announced plans for an ecumenical dinner," Jim explained.

"Sounds like a nice idea, Ma," said Jill.

"Nice?" Kate groaned. "It was nice when the rules didn't change every week. I wasn't raised to eat potluck with Presbyterians. Or hamburgers on Friday. Or sit in church next to nuns with permanent waves."

Jill smiled, understanding that Kate's complaint was not so much about specific changes as about the inevitability of change. "We're supposed to accept change and adapt, Ma."

"Who says I'm supposed to?" Kate demanded. "And who says I haven't? When I got married, I expected to have two children, and those two years apart. Instead I had triplets. I adapted. Just when I was used to having three underfoot, you all started school on the same day. I adapted. Just when I expected to have my grandchildren around me, my children moved to strange cities. I adapted. Just when your father and I were planning his retirement, he . . . Instead of buying a cute little house in a warm climate, I was buying a plot at Holy Ghost. It damned near killed me, but I adapted. Now Julie, who's always been so sensible, is sitting in my living room babbling, and you're making arrangements to have her locked up. Well, I've adapted enough. If anything else changes, don't tell me. To hell with it all." Kate's tears slid down her face. "I'm tired of changes."

"I know how you feel, Ma. So from now on the changes will have to be for the better." Jill glanced at Kate, hoping that modest optimism would lead her from a history of changes that came with loss as firmly attached as a Siamese twin to some mythic future of change where the sick would get well instead of dead, loved ones would live within the same area code, and the number announced in Dublin

357

would be the same as the ticket in her hand. "The change for the better will begin with Julie."

"When?" Kate asked, trembling.

"Tomorrow, Ma. Nine o'clock," Jill replied. "A change for the better, I promise."

Later that night, when the only discernible sound was the half-groan of Kate's restless sleep, Jill switched on the lamp next to her bed, sat up, and stared at Julie.

Julie slept as she had as a child, one hand cradling her cheek and the blankets wrapped close around her body in a cuddling, comforting swaddle.

Sleeping, she looked like the Julie of their coloring-book days and of the tea parties where John and Jill, dressed in their parents' clothes, had eaten vanilla wafers and drunk milk from Julie's Christmas-gift teacups. Julie had always conducted these soirées with the utmost seriousness, becoming angry, then tearful, when, inevitably, Johnny roistered, tumbling and spilling his "tea" to gleeful laughter from Jill.

"I'm sorry I laughed," Jill whispered in Julie's direction. "I'm sorry I didn't take what was important to you more seriously. I should have loved you better and envied you less."

Jill knew that sleep was out of the question. The prospect of taking Julie to the hospital left her with nerve endings jumping. She stared at the ceiling, wishing she could believe her only concern was for Julie.

It isn't taking Julie that frightens you. It's taking yourself.

Frightens? Attracts?

I was a good mental patient. Everyone said so. There's a knack to being crazy well.

They say you never get over it. They say you're a mended vessel, just waiting to crack. They say . . . Better believe them. They lie better than you live.

Lock up—prison.

Lock out—cold.

Lock in—safe.

Prison, punishment, haven, home.

When the strong crumble, the fragile beware. The fragile return to pianos.

Enough! Enough! Enough!

Quietly Jill slipped out of bed, picked up her briefcase, and padded down to the living room. She selected a chair designed to fit the contours of the human body and sat down, twisting uncomfortably, wondering what human body had been used as the model.

She leafed through her scripts, glanced at *Broken Promises,* then firmly set it aside.

In an hour she'd finished her update and sealed it in a large manila envelope Polly had preaddressed and stamped RUSH.

She reached for her notepad and an unread script, but her hand had a life of its own. It drifted to *Broken Promises,* hovered, and fell.

She reread the script, expecting the story of a failed mother-daughter relationship to provoke tears as it had before. It moved her as it had at first reading, but instead of tears that might have proved catharic, she felt a disquieting opposition, a rejection of the story's point of view.

She thought of mothers and daughters—of Julie and Kate, Daisy and herself, herself and Kate; and sisters, Julie and herself; grandmothers and granddaughters, Daisy and Kate. She thought of the promises implicit in relationships, the bargains that must be kept, the imperative call of blood to blood—to refuse it was to orphan oneself.

Jill tapped her pen against her notebook, thinking of the final scene of *Broken Promises,* the mutual indifference of mother and daughter at opposite sides of a dead father's grave.

"That's not the story I'd tell," she murmured. Her pen tapped a faster staccato against the notebook's green, shiny surface.

She pictured herself with Daisy, Kate, and Julie—doing what?

She flipped the notebook open, closed her eyes, searched for the picture slowly forming in her mind, smiled, opened her eyes, and scribbled *Act One.*

CHAPTER 24

"I don't like yucky lumps." Julie scowled at the steaming bowl before her, then smiled and pushed it away. "I'm Jill. I'm free. I don't have to eat oatmeal."

At the counter Jill paused in pouring coffee and smiled. Obviously Julie was finding the fringe benefits in being "bad Jill."

She set a cup in front of Julie, grateful for Kate's departure for early Mass. Kate had gone, brimming with tears and "Poor Julie"s, her candle money clutched in her hand. Her prayers would do more for Julie, she said, than waiting in the kitchen for the unbearable moment when Jill would hoist Julie's suitcase and lead her out the door.

Jill had been surprised at Kate's unusually pragmatic decision. Occasionally during the long night she'd spent in the spinally deformed contour chair, Jill had envisioned the moment of parting, with herself attempting to detach a hysterical Kate from a relatively tranquil Julie or, worse yet, arriving at the hospital with both of them in tow and then trying to convince the staff that the calmly smiling young woman was the patient and the shrieking wreck a relative who'd come along for support.

She sat at the table, wanting to prepare Julie for what lay ahead, but uncertain how she would go about it. She felt much as she had the day she'd swerved to the side of the road, feeling ill-equipped but determined to describe the details of a pelvic examination to Daisy.

Jill glanced at the clock. The minutes ticked by on little lead feet, but they ticked. Jill knew she couldn't wait, couldn't repeat her performance with Daisy. If she swerved to the side of Brookpark Road, they'd either disappear, fenders akimbo, into a pothole forever or be smashed flat by a tailgating trucker with one hand on the wheel, the other on his CB, and both eyes on the sky, alert for a bear in the air.

It had to be now, and it had to be straight.

"Julie?" Jill said softly. "Julie?"

Julie looked up and smiled sweetly. "I'm Jill, Mother's own girl."

"I know," Jill said gently. "I have something important to tell you, honey, so try to pay attention. You haven't been well, and you aren't getting better." Jill paused. Julie's face was an undisturbed blank. "Do you remember the man who came to see you yesterday, the portly person who asked questions and made notes?"

Julie nodded. "Mother told me he's family. She said I should call him Uncle Neil."

"Calling him Dr. Kaiser would be more appropriate," Jill said, thinking Kate's efforts to be helpful were often as lumpy as her oatmeal. "He's a doctor, honey. When I was sick, he helped me."

"Uncle Neil is a doctor?"

"No. I mean yes. I mean, he's a doctor, but he's not Uncle Neil."

Julie beamed with sudden comprehension. "I wondered why he shined a flashlight in my eyes. Uncles don't do that."

"In this family it could happen. The point is that Dr. Kaiser is going to help you in the way he helped me."

"What is he going to do to me?" Julie's sea-green eyes darkened.

"He's going to take care of you in a hospital for people with problems like yours. I'm going to take you there now." Jill tensed, expecting protest that could range from whimpering babble to flight out the door.

Julie pushed her chair away from the table and rose heavily, as though she were being dragged by invisible weights. "Can we go now?"

"You want to go?" Jill was amazed.

"I don't want to." Julie's face was washed in sadness. "But I think I'd better."

"Why, honey?" Jill asked. She'd been so certain Julie would resist, would at the very least retreat into glassy stares and "I'm Mother's own girl." "Why do you think you should go to the hospital?"

Julie's lips trembled. "I can't remember my middle name—I try and try, but I can't. Sometimes when I'm watching television I almost remember, but then it slips away. I've been thinking that a person who can't remember her middle name must be sick."

"You've been worried." Jill said flatly, feeling extraordinarily stupid. How could she have forgotten? She'd never met anyone in the hospital so crazy he didn't know he was crazy. They'd all known they

361

were sick, even when they didn't know anything else. "Why didn't you say something, honey, to me or to Ma?"

"You all seemed so happy," Julie quavered. "I didn't want to worry you."

"Oh, Julie." Jill blinked back sudden tears. They'd all clustered in the kitchen, hiding their worry from Julie, who'd huddled in the living room, hiding her worry from them. "Let's Pretend" had struck again, slapping a coat of whitewash on a rotting fence.

"Can we go now?" Julie asked.

"Yes." Jill stacked their cups in the sink, knowing Kate's anxiety would turn to the relief of housework the second she returned from Mass.

Jill fetched their coats from the closet, making certain Julie's was buttoned to the neck. She slung her purse over her shoulder, picked up Julie's suitcase, and said, "Let's go, honey."

Julie took a long look around the kitchen, a full circuit that encompassed the room. Jill watched her, wondering what she was thinking. Or seeing. Or remembering.

"Good-bye, plant," Julie said, and walked out the door.

Jill locked the door behind them, understanding Julie's need to take leave of someone or, for want of someone, of something. Her own good-byes to Daisy had been the first step in each journey home.

Once in the car, Julie said nothing, just stared out the window, wrapped in a silence that could have been an understandable self-absorption or merely a fascination with the passing Cleveland scenery, which had become as unpredictable as Cleveland weather. Nearly everything they had grown up with had changed—seemingly immortal gray granite landmarks had vanished, new interstate highways gave the look of a foreign land to once familiar neighborhoods, parks where they'd played as children were the sites of new shopping malls, the old mall where Kate had taken them to buy their first bras was now a park of functional, sterile design, and at every turn wrecking crews worked beside construction crews, giving the surrealistic impression that they were simultaneously putting up and tearing down the same building, the ultimate in urban renewal.

Jill left the contemplation of progress to Julie, and let her mind wander to a theme that had played its leitmotif in her head all morning—her play.

The words she'd written the night before had virtually tumbled onto the paper. It was as though she'd poked a stick in the ground, then watched with amazement as a spring gushed up.

Hour after hour she'd scribbled tirelessly, seeming to draw energy from some current flowing between her mind and her pen, so absorbed that she'd felt rather than saw the coming of dawn in the thinning of the darkness around her. She'd glanced at the window, noted the lightening sky with surprise, then returned to her notebook, feverishly scrawling, compelled by an urgency she hadn't understood.

She'd had an idea. That part was simple. She had to write it down. That part was as complex as falling in love, an act of pure emotion defying logic and having nothing to do with will.

When the pitty-pat of Kate's slippers on the stairs had announced the beginning of Real Day, Jill had looked up in genuine annoyance. Being interrupted in the middle of the line she was writing was similar to being yanked out of a vivid dream.

"Are you writing one of your television reports?" Kate asked, bouncing by with morning coffee on her mind.

"No, I'm writing a play," Jill replied, choosing foolish truth over the wisdom of pretending her notebook was full of legitimate business.

"Mother of God! Her sister's on the way to the nuthouse, and she's writing a play! Daft!" Kate shook her head vigorously. "That's what happened to Rome, you know."

"Rome?"

"It burned. Nero fiddled. He was daft, too."

Jill had shut her notebook with a sigh that was more of a growl and followed Kate to the kitchen.

The Kate standing beside her in the kitchen had seemed a pale reflection of the Kate taking form in her notebook. She'd cocked her head, listening for the Kate-voice within, measuring it against the Kate-voice rattling on about Julie, and did Jill think any of them would ever see John again in this lifetime. In Heaven, Kate had vowed, she'd have a secretary to tell John she was busy.

Jill had known she must be tired. Staying up all night and not being tired was a symptom of being twenty, or crazy, or of myasthenia gravis.

But she hadn't felt tired. She'd felt . . . what?

Exhilarated.

That was it. She'd paused, egg in midair.

363

Four times in her life she'd known what Walt Whitman had meant by "the body electric"—for the first time when she'd smacked a solid line drive that had whipped over the pitcher's mound, and she ran, flying 'round the bases, to accept congratulations from a team that hadn't wanted her because she was a girl; on the occasion of her first orgasm marked not with the usual throaty moans but with a yelp of delight, and laughter so wild and protracted that Steve had thought her demented, not knowing that her whoops howled congratulations to a body that worked, a triumph of instinct over upbringing; on the delivery table when, exhausted but ecstatic, she'd looked between her legs and whispered, "My God, look what I've done!"; and last night, writing.

Kate had interrupted her reverie with a sharp jiggle to her elbow and a finger pointing at the egg. "Crack it or hatch it."

Words to live by, Jill had thought, wondering what Kate would do if she opted for hatching.

As complex as falling in love, she mused, turning left onto Erie Street. *As simple as writing it down.*

She followed a short jog to the right and brought the car to a rolling stop in front of the massive brick edifice that dominated Ontario Street.

"Here we are," she said, trying to sound as casual as though they were dropping by McDonald's for a quick Egg McMuffin.

She got out of the car, then leaned in again, reaching for Julie's suitcase. "It's all right, honey. I'll be with you. Don't be afraid."

"Wait!" Julie exclaimed. It was an order edged with panic.

"What's wrong?" Jill asked gently, well aware of what was wrong.

Julie frowned in the November sunlight. "Do they have TV?"

"There's a color TV in the parlor, a big one. Watching it is considered therapeutic, like keeping yourself clean."

"Okay." Julie smiled. Her eyes went glassy. "I'm Jill. I'm free." She was ready.

Jill shepherded Julie up the steps, resisting a natural impulse to place a guiding hand under her elbow. She'd arrived in the hospital lobby that way, with Steve's hand cupping her elbow in a gesture that looked like support but felt like coercion.

Jill looked upward at the hospital building she hadn't seen in years and was astonished to see they'd added a new wing. She felt as betrayed as she would if Kate had gone off to have a face-lift without telling her. Who needs to come home looking for Ma and find Zsa Zsa reheating the mince?

The wing was no face-lift. It was more of a transplant, a third arm
hastily grafted on. It was constructed of gray block concrete, low-
slung, and surly-looking, as though aware that its utilitarian ugliness
contrasted unfavorably with the traditional elegance of the original
building to which it had been unharmoniously attached.

Jill knew from experience that the rather lovely and certainly
impressive original brick structure contained wards afflicted with
windows that stuck open in the winter and shut in the summer,
echo-chamber plumbing, and cracks in the walls that made one shud-
der, thinking of scurrying rats. She was absolutely certain that the
new wing must contain the latest in technological marvels, climate
control, and electronic filtering devices. If there were rats, they
would be white, specially bred, and kept in sterilized cages for research purposes.

Still, Jill preferred the old building, a preference she recognized
as being more than the nostalgia-mongering of early middle age;
something good had happened to her in that building. Her favorite
swimming pool was still the one where she'd learned to swim.

As she led Julie through the darkened lobby she decided that the
mental hospital she was going to build someday would be castle-
shaped with the wards placed high in honestly gloomy towers and
presided over by orderlies named Igor. That way patients could
enter with their worst suspicions confirmed and relax, knowing that
the only way it could get was better.

Jill and Julie waited for the elevator alongside two nurses, one old,
one young, and a man carrying a bouquet of what appeared to be
weeds.

The elevator arrived, and they got in. The doors creaked shut
behind them. Jill glanced at Julie, who seemed as unconcerned as a
woman on her way to Fourth Floor Lingerie, while Jill shivered
beside her, growing dry-mouthed with panic.

For Jill the elevator was a time machine. All her vertical journeys
in it had been as a mental patient. Even on the day she'd been
released, she'd retained patient status until she carried her pink
discharge paper off the elevator and through the lobby to the cash-
ier's office. The lobby had seen her a solid citizen, but the elevator
never had, and she felt more the mental patient with each separate
jolt as the musty box creaked and jerked upward.

Their precarious progress didn't seem to upset anyone else.

"Did you enjoy your walk, Ralph?" the older nurse asked the man
with the bouquet.

"Am I screaming or crying?" Apparently Ralph considered it a dumb question.

"What pretty flowers," the young nurse enthused in a patronizing tone. "They'll brighten up your room."

"Not my room they won't." He was adamant. "This ragweed's for stoking ol' Dalmeyer's allergies. In three seconds flat her face will look like a water balloon, and she'll be sneezing her fool head off. That'll teach the ol' crow not to nag Ralph McGee."

Jill turned her head, hiding a smile. The nurse had been willing to accept McGee's "flowers" so long as he was willing to play the game. McGee had blown what sounded like an excellent plan by confiding in the Nightingales.

"I'm sorry you perceive the head nurse's concern as nagging." The older nurse frowned. "And we'll dump those weeds in the trash before we go into the ward."

"He's acting out his hostility," the young nurse decided.

McGee bristled. "You keep yer mitts off my weeds. A man's got rights."

"Mr. McGee." The older nurse sighed. "You've got to be reasonable about this."

"At two hundred bucks a day I don't got to be nothing." McGee moved closer to Jill and whispered, "Know any politicians?"

"No." Jill moved closer to Julie.

"Good," he said approvingly. "They're all controlled by a man in a cave in North Dakota. He has a machine that makes them do things."

Jill nodded, not knowing what to say.

"Republicans *and* Democrats," he added. "All the tax money goes to the man in the cave."

"In North Dakota." Jill tried to be agreeable.

McGee's face lit up. "You know 'im?"

"No!"

His eyes narrowed. "Then how'd you know about North Dakota?"

"You told me!"

"Wild horses couldn't drag it out of me!" he shouted, waving his weeds.

Jill stood on tiptoe, looking to the older nurse for help.

"Mr. McGee is . . . uh . . ." She rolled her eyes in a grotesque rendition of *harmless.*

"Harmless?" McGee read the pantomime faster than Jill, probably because he'd seen it before. "I've killed in my time!"

The elevator doors creaked open. "Out McGee," the older nurse ordered.

"Ol' crow! Bitch! Caveman minion!" McGee thundered, but he backed off the elevator as ordered.

The nurses followed quickly, with Jill and Julie bringing up a cautious rear. Jill placed a guiding hand under Julie's elbow.

The room they stepped into was a hall or antechamber, with a door leading to a seldom-used stairwell on one end and a locked door to the ward on the other. It was smaller than Jill remembered. And shabbier. A pay phone hung on the specked and spotted once-beige wall, so placed that a person using it was forced to stand. Beneath it were two worn chairs, vinyl-covered, like those found in dentists' offices in the poorer sections of town. An equally dismal sofa stood along the wall opposite the elevator. It sagged in the middle as though affected by the depression of patients who'd sat on it.

The nurses marched up behind McGee, who stood at the locked door, lethal bouquet in hand, salivating in his eagerness to enter the ward.

McGee pushed a button next to the door and bounced on the balls of his feet.

"McGee!" the older nurse addressed him imperiously. "McGee!"

He watched her out of the corner of his eye, said nothing, and pressed the button again.

"McGee!" she repeated, extending her dowager empress's hand. "Give me the weeds."

"No," he said, avoiding her eyes. He was looking less and less like a man who had killed in his time.

"Thorazine," the nurse said, her voice silky. "Thorazine, McGee. Thor-a-zine."

McGee hung his head and slowly, ever so slowly, handed over the weeds.

"Thank you, Mr. McGee." The nurse tossed the bouquet into a large institutional trash can.

The nurse signaled to someone on the other side of the locked door, an open sesame that resulted in an immediate discordant buzzing. McGee grabbed the door and yanked it open, anxious to escape from the nurses. He turned and waved at Jill. "Vote Abolitionist!" he called. "The cave machine doesn't have an Abolitionist lever." He darted through the door with the older nurse close on his heels.

The younger nurse held the door open for Jill and Julie. "Mr. McGee likes you." She smiled at Jill.

"Wonderful." Jill led Julie into the ward. "Maybe later we'll go dancing."

"I don't think Mr. McGee will have off-floor privileges for a while," young Nightingale said earnestly, then blushed at the look on Jill's face. "Oh. You're making a joke. I've been here only a month, and I've forgotten people make jokes. I'm so sorry."

"That's all right." Jill wished the young nurse would go away. She looked so sad.

"No, it isn't all right," she continued. "I shouldn't forget people make jokes. It's just that I've had such a hard time getting used to patients who say things that sound like jokes and aren't that I'm overcompensating. The first week I was here I wanted to laugh all the time. I mean, someone would say something weird like he was in love with a bus, and I'd smile. I got reprimanded for smiling. I almost got transferred for laughing. So I had to remind myself that things that sound funny aren't."

"It's all right. Really."

"No, it isn't," she continued. "My boyfriend says I'm getting to be a drag."

"That is a problem," Jill agreed.

She nodded. "He says that pretty soon I'll be fit company only for lunatics." Her eyes brimmed. "Maybe I should go into pediatrics. But, you know, there's something about psychiatric patients. They can be so darned *interesting*." She smiled at Jill. "I'm Miss Shermann. Betsy. If you need anything, I'm here."

Jill watched her walk away, head lowered and hands clasped behind her back. Miss Shermann, Betsy, appeared to be extremely pigeon-toed until Jill noticed that she was carefully stepping on only the black squares of the black-and-white linoleum floor.

"May I help you?" The sleepy voice belonged to a young man with a sallow complexion and dark circles under his eyes who was dressed in a burgundy-colored jogging suit. "You look rather lost."

"I'm fine." Jill eyed his casual resort clothes, pegging him as a patient. "I need to talk to someone on the staff."

"You got it." He smiled and yawned simultaneously.

Jill eyed him skeptically. "Maybe a nurse."

"I am a nurse." He was seized by a yawn larger than the first. His front teeth were white, the back teeth yellow, the pattern of a perfunctory brusher. "Bob Elliot, St. John's Hospital School of Nursing, Class of '78."

368

"Maybe the head nurse," Jill suggested, glancing at Julie, who stared straight ahead, her face devoid of personality.

"I know. It's these clothes. You think I'm a patient." He grinned. "Wearing whites is optional. We new-breed psych-techs think the uniform inhibits communication with the patient, creates resistance, like police uniforms. I don't know about you, but when I see a cop in blue, I'm automatically pissed."

"Yeah, well . . ." Jill looked around quickly. There seemed to be movement behind the desk at the nurse's station. Taking Julie by the arm, she began to move in that direction, sideways.

Bob followed her. "Here. I'll prove it. Look at my ring."

He thrust his hand under Jill's nose. On his ring finger was a thick silver circle, with a dull red stone. Around it were tiny letters: *St. John's Hospital Class of '78.*

"So, how do you like nursing?" Jill asked, as though she'd believed him all along.

"Love it," he gushed. "I'm helping alleviate the suffering of our most hopeless humanity, and I get laid like you wouldn't believe."

Jill's eyebrows hit her hairline.

"Not patients!" he exclaimed, looking appalled. "Oh, geez, no. I took an oath. I meant nurses. Horniest women you'd ever want. . . . I'll get the head nurse."

He all but dragged Jill and Julie to the nurse's station.

"Miss Dalmeyer," he called. There was a rustling sound from behind a file cabinet. "Dalmeyer."

"Coming, coming," a high, pleasant voice wafted out.

Jill tensed, about to confront the dreaded Dalmeyer, bane of her days in the nuthouse, the Dalmeyer of "Go take a hot bath and you'll forget all about suicide." That Dalmeyer.

The voice wafted, but Dalmeyer didn't. The person who emerged from behind the file cabinets was dressed in optional whites and looked like Moby Nurse. She was huge. Jill stared, trying to find the familiar, dreaded Dalmeyer face behind three chins and droopy jowls. The eyes that had once reminded her of an eagle, preying not soaring, were piggy slits folded in fat. Only the nose was the same, a craggy beak worthy of Rushmore. If it hadn't been for the nose, Jill would have passed her on the street without a blink of recognition.

"And what have we here?" Dalmeyer asked pleasantly. She glanced from Julie to Jill and settled her attention on Jill. It had been years since she'd mistaken the admitting relative for a patient, years and, from the looks of her, about eighty pounds. "May I help you?"

"My sister . . . uh. . . . She's here." Jill was suddenly tongue-tied, feeling as though she was there under false pretenses, conducting business considered to be the province of normal people in a place where she hadn't been normal—and with a woman with whom she'd never spoken as an equal, and wasn't sure she knew how.

"Name?" Dalmeyer hadn't seemed to notice that the "relative" before her was trembling. Or more likely she had and was using her efficient-nurse persona to help them get through the necessary formalities.

"Jill Dunn Kenyon," Jill replied automatically, then blushed the color of Bob's jogging suit. "I mean, the patient's name is Julie Dunn Hildebrandt."

Dalmeyer looked up from the form before her, her face thoughtful. Her eyes moved from left to right, as though she was reading Jill's face. "Don't I know you?"

"I was a patient here." Jill tripped over her words. "You were here, too." She paused, breathless, then quickly added, "But you were a nurse."

"I think I remember." Dalmeyer closed her eyes for a second. "Ahhhh. Got it. Kenyon, Jill. Attempted suicide, '71." She opened one eye. "Winter or summer?"

"Winter. Christmas."

"Suicide season. Except for Jews. They tip over in February." Dalmeyer's smile was perfunctory. "How's it been? Any further . . . ?" She left it hanging.

"No, no," Jill replied, thinking that if the missing word was *suicide*, then no was the right answer. If the word was *problems*, she didn't know where to begin. "I've been fine."

"Good." Dalmeyer's leonine head bent over the form. "Patient's name?"

"Julie Dunn Hildebrandt."

"Relationship?" She glanced up at Jill. "You're looking very well."

"Thank you. Julie's my sister."

"Admitting physician?"

"Neil Kaiser."

"You look younger than you did when you were a patient here." Dalmeyer filled in the form as she spoke.

"I was . . . uh . . . ill then," Jill said, "but thank you."

"That happens, you know. People get better, they look better.

Except schizophrenics. Sometimes the better they get, the worse they look. Birth date? Hers." She pointed at Julie.

"Same as mine." Jill tried a smile. "September 12, 1945."

"Hiroshima," Dalmeyer remarked. "Nagasaki."

"Not on *our* birthday." Jill was repulsed.

"Close enough," Dalmeyer said. "I quit smoking."

"You what?"

"Two years ago. Put on a few pounds." Dalmeyer's piggy slits challenged Jill. "Quitting took enormous self-discipline. Cigarettes are harder to kick than heroin, you know."

"Yes," Jill replied, understanding what Dalmeyer wanted. "I've tried many times, but I haven't been able to quit. I don't know how you did it."

"Will," Dalmeyer asserted. "Sheer guts and will."

"Beyond what I have, God knows." Jill smiled her admiration.

"Probably." Dalmeyer radiated satisfaction. "Is your sister allergic to anything? Food? Medication?"

"No."

"Done." Dalmeyer pulled the carbon from the original. "We'll take good care of Mrs. Hildebrandt." Her smile was crisp, professionally starched.

"I know you will." Jill's smile mirrored Dalmeyer's. The conversation had become a ritual of "correct" verbalizations that reminded Jill of UBC meetings, where pleasant exchanges were commonplace between executives who secretly would like to see one another's heads served on plates.

"Before you know it, your sister will be looking as good as you do. And functioning." Dalmeyer reached for a paper clip. "Still a housewife, Jill?"

"I'm . . . uh . . . in television." An instinct warned Jill that though functioning might be high on Dalmeyer's list of activities to encourage, appearing to function better than Dalmeyer might be considered an infraction of taste. "I read stories and tell people what I think of them."

"Sounds like something you could do." Dalmeyer was pleased. "Imagine getting paid to read stories."

"Imagine."

"All right. I've taken care of . . . uh"—Dalmeyer consulted the form—"Julie. Please wait in the parlor. Dr. Kaiser wants to speak to you."

371

"He's here?"

"Of course." Dalmeyer looked superior—she knew something Jill didn't. "Just wait in the parlor. Someone will come and get you."

Dalmeyer's hand replaced Jill's on Julie's elbow, and the nurse led Julie away quickly, SOP for the moment of parting, when relatives often become guilt-stricken and rival the patients in emotional displays.

Jill watched as Julie walked down the hall next to Dalmeyer, whose forward progress was marked by a series of ripples and rolls. Julie seemed undisturbed, her posture the familiar parochial "Don't slouch" with overtones of teacher.

Jill turned toward the parlor, identifiable from the sound of a television set blaring. The patients were watching a game show.

She walked down the hall as she had so many times before, knowing, in the same instinctual way she smelled snow and felt dawn, that she'd walk through this parlor archway, her own personal looking glass, tumble backward into herself, discover the wellspring—insanity—and crawl under the piano. Quickly.

She knew that, and was doing it anyway for no other reason than that she'd been instructed to "wait in the parlor."

Jill's head lowered as she concentrated on the tiles Nurse Betsy had defined as a talisman. She failed to hear a door bang open and someone dashing at her until she collided with a tall, masculine form. There was a crunch, the literal seeing of stars, and a mutual "Ooof!"

"Excuse me." His hand reached to steady her. It was Neil. "I'm sorry, I didn't see— Jill!"

"Neil?" Her head swam, then cleared.

"Do forgive me. I was looking over the notes I made on your sister. Are you all right?"

"I'm fine."

"I'll talk to Julie." He gestured toward the room. "And then I want to talk to you. I've been so rushed that the specifics of the plans we made for dinner have escaped me. . . ."

"What plans?" She thought her head had cleared.

"On the phone. Last night." He squinted, looking puzzled.

"We talked last night?" Jill's mind scrambled over the night before: dinner, trying to calm Kate, lying sleepless with childhood regrets, writing the update, reading *Broken Promises*, writing, writing, writing . . . Could she have forgotten a call from Neil? "I don't think you called me, Neil. At least, I don't remember . . . but my memory is

sometimes . . . I'm sure I would have remembered a call from you."
But she wasn't sure at all.

His face was so blank, it seemed his features had melted together.
For a moment he hung in space. Then he threw back his head and
laughed, a full, free sound, incongruous in this place of restrictions.
"That's one on me." He chortled. "I was so anxious to talk to you all
day . . . kept talking to you in my head . . . telling you I understood
why you ran out of your mother's kitchen the way you did." He
smiled and raised his hand in a no-need-to-explain gesture. "But,
then, I've always understood the why of what you do." He paused,
just a breath in time. "Haven't I?"

"You have."

"Better than anyone?" His was a who's-daddy's-little-girl? tone,
accompanied by a charming, self-mocking grin.

"Absotively." Jill smiled. "Also posilutely."

"So, by the time I fell into bed last night, I must have thought that
at least *one* of the conversations I'd had with you had been a dialogue
on the phone instead of a monologue in my head." He shook his head
as though he was amused. "No matter. I'll see Julie, and then we'll
talk."

"Fine."

"You're making me a believer in fate." He beamed down at her.
"Know that?"

"No," Jill responded, wondering how she could bring faith of any
kind to the faithless of any description. You can only give what you've
got.

"I feel alive again. It's your fault." He pretended to scowl. "What
do you plan to do about it?"

Jill said nothing. A Neil who teased was not a Neil she knew.

He laughed. "I have some ideas about that. Dinner-table talk.
Tonight."

Jill thought of Kate, of how devastated she would be if she was left
alone in the house to brood about Julie. "I'll have to see what my
mother—"

Neil overrode her. "*I'll* handle your mother. I'll tell her it's doctor's orders, me to you—a therapeutic dinner for two." He waved a
cheerful "Later," turned, and tracked Dalmeyer's route down the
hall.

Jill paused at the door of the parlor and peeped in. Like the entry
hall, it was smaller than she remembered. And shabbier. Considera-

bly. The furniture, kin to the stuff in the hall, had the same thrift-store look about it and was similarly covered with vinyl in colors of blood and bile.

Besides being smaller and shabbier than Jill remembered, the parlor also felt cold. It had no warmth of its own, and the patients sitting, or curled or sprawled on various pieces of furniture, generated no body heat. It was as if the engines that fueled them had stopped. *The parlor seemed warm when I was here.*

"Come in. Come in." It was Bob Elliot waving and shouting to make himself heard above the television's noise. He sat at a table with three stony-looking patients, dealing cards with a careless flip of his wrist. Some of the cards landed face up. No one protested. "Don't be nervous. Come in. Sit down."

Jill walked slowly past patients who never flickered, either purposely ignoring her intrusion or wholly absorbed in *Wheel of Fortune.* She sat stiffly in a chair next to the card table.

Bob grinned. "I raised your consciousness, didn't I?"

"Beg pardon?"

"You know. Being a male nurse. Heterosexual. Dressed in civvies. New-breed techniques. Kind of blew you away, didn't it?" Gleefully he continued to flip cards. "I really banged on your stereotypes."

"Is that your mission in life?" Jill looked around for an ashtray.

"You just don't like admitting you think in stereotypes." He tilted his chair, balancing on two legs. "Bet you got all your notions of mental patients from *Snake Pit* and *Cuckoo's Nest.* Admit it."

Jill lit a cigarette. She'd worry about the ashtray later. "I got my notions of mental patients from the four months I spent as a patient in this hospital, this ward, and this attractively decorated parlor."

"You were a patient here?" His eyes popped. "Geez."

"Don't I look like a typical former mental patient?" The edge in her voice had nothing to do with Bob. Her two minutes in the parlor had been a studious avoidance of the piano that was waiting at the far end of the room, waiting for her return. She tried to concentrate on Bob's crestfallen face, but the piano intruded, stalking the edges of her peripheral vision. "Well, don't I, Bob?"

"No. I mean, I don't have any idea *fixe* about former mental patients. We're all human. Right?"

"Occasionally."

The piano is dusty.

"So, when were you here?"

"Seventy-one. Winter."
The piano is smaller. Much.
"Mind if I ask what the problem was?"
"Depression. Suicidal."
"Heavy."
A person under that piano would be very uncomfortable—prisoner of the Cong in a bamboo cage.
"So you're fine now."
"Fine."
A person under that piano would be safe from the world.
"We do one hell of a job in this hospital."
"They said I was a good patient. I let them cure me, they said."
Jill watched herself crawl under the piano, watched herself curl into a ball. She felt the piano around her.
"Dalmeyer was here then, wasn't she?"
"She was here."
The piano doesn't feel like a hidey-hole, an escape hatch, a haven from life.
"Dalmeyer pisses me off. Runs this place like Ma Barker. Knows what she's doing, though. You're proof of that."
"I've never had so much approval as I got for getting well. They thought they were wonderful."
"Who was your doctor?"
"Kaiser."
The piano doesn't feel like a punishment either, or a closet for keeping black sheep.
"Strange duck, Kaiser. Talks a good game. Knows all the tricks. Sure used them on you."
"I thought he was a sorcerer."
The piano feels like a piano.
"He must have been. Suicidal patients are the hardest. Sooner or later they tip over. A shoestring breaks, *bam, bam, bam . . .*"
Jill watched herself crawl from beneath the piano that was only a piano. She watched herself set herself free.
"When we cure them, they stay cured."
"Nobody dragged me from beneath that piano. I came out on my own."
"What?" Bob blinked.
"When I was ready to get well, I did. It was something *I* decided." Jill was suddenly warmer. "I did it. I got well."

"Sure you did." His tone was that of the young nurse admiring the "flowers." "The staff provided you with a therapeutic environment, insight into your condition—"

"Rubbish," Jill interrupted without rancor. "My environment was the space under that piano. There was nothing therapeutic about it."

"Come on." Bob was piqued. "You know what I mean. The therapy here—"

"I don't remember any of it, not a word anyone said outside of 'Go take a hot bath.' I remember being sick and not wanting to be well, then being sick and wanting to be well. I remember crawling under that piano and then crawling out. That's what I remember."

"You're not trying to tell me that your sessions with Kaiser had nothing to do with it, your interactions with the staff . . ."

"I'm sure that whatever Kaiser and the staff said made sense. It was supposed to. I'm sure I heard that life was worth living and suicide not the answer, that depression was surmountable, and I could be well. I'm sure I agreed. I'm even sure I took hot baths."

"You know you were helped here—"

"Helped, yes. Cured, no." Jill looked at the piano. "Once I decided to get well, nothing on earth could have stopped me. Not the absence of therapy, not therapy itself." She shook her head. "Why didn't I know that?"

"Have you always had this . . . uh . . . sense of power?" Bob smiled slyly.

"Power!" Jill laughed, a sound that turned the heads of a few mute patients. "When I left here I thanked everyone for using their power to help poor, powerless me. Then I dragged myself out the door feeling like a thousand pounds of lead had been grafted onto my heels."

"Come now." Bob was prepared to humor her. "Why?"

"Because when I went out that door, I was dragging a mental patient with me. *And* a goddamned out-of-tune, dusty piano. I've been dragging her ever since, a lead shadow, afraid of *her* shadow—" Jill jumped to her feet. "Well, no more. This time I'm leaving her here."

Bob glanced around the room. "Now, don't get excited."

"But I am excited." Jill laughed. "*I* made myself well. I. Me. My sanity is inside me, it's mine. I can say anything, do anything. The worst I can be is wrong, and that's not the end of the world. And, who knows? I may even be right. I may surprise myself after all."

"Would you like to sit down?" Bob was getting anxious. "Maybe have a glass of water?"

Jill walked halfway across the room and swept an ugly ashtray off a scuffed coffee table. "Tell them." She waved the ashtray to include all the patients. "When they leave here, tell them the cure was theirs. It was hard, goddamned hard, they did it. Tell them the ruby slippers aren't borrowed, and no one can take them away. Tell them, you ninny, and stop congratulating yourself."

"You're upset—"

"*Stop!* I won't let you do that."

"Do what?" Bob tilted his chair farther, this time backing away.

"Don't tell me I'm upset just because my opinion is different from yours. Don't imply that I'm crazy."

"I wasn't!"

"You were. People like you do that. People like you think you can do that to people like me."

"I wasn't trying to do anything—"

"Bullshit!"

"Lower your voice. You're upsetting the . . . oooh . . . oooh . . ." Bob's arms flailed wildly in an attempt to recapture his balance as both feet left the floor and his chair teetered, hanging in space.

As Jill lunged across the room to grab him a sturdy male card player kicked a leg of Bob's chair.

"Aaaaargggh." Bob went down with a wail and a crash that shook the room.

The card player/patient leaned over the table. "Shut up and deal, sucker."

Bob lay tangled in arms and legs, his and the chair's.

"Oh, shit." He moaned. "The paperwork on this . . ."

Jill reached for his hand. Behind her, a woman patient shrilled, "Don't look at me like that!"

"Like what?" another woman responded. "Who wants to look at you. You're no ZaSu Pitts."

"This isn't good for my nerves," a female voice complained.

"*Shut up!*" a man bellowed. "I can't hear the TV."

"Who cares about your goddamned TV?" another man yelled. "I hate *Wheel of Fortune*. All they do is buy vowels."

Jill braced herself and yanked. Bob came to his feet, moaning. Behind them the din increased as patients, frightened or stimulated or both by the accident, continued to howl.

"My nerves! My nerves! I'm having another thousand-dollar break-down!"

"I hate the food! Why isn't lunch here?"

"I want to watch *Donahue!*"

"What are vowels?"

"Our Bob is dead! We need a new Bob!"

"See what you've done," Bob said accusingly.

"Go to it, new-breed Miracle Worker." Jill grinned, walking away. "You do one hell of a job here."

She walked into the hall with a free-rolling saunter, feeling like her hip joints had finally come unstuck.

She found Dalmeyer at the desk, unscrewing the caps of medication bottles.

"I want to see my sister."

"Dr. Kaiser just finished talking to her." Dalmeyer tossed pills of various colors into small paper cups. She gestured toward the parlor. "This'll quiet them down."

"Which room is Julie's?"

"823. But Dr. Kaiser wants—"

Jill sped down the hall, not caring what Neil wanted.

Julie sat on the edge of a high hospital bed, like a doll that had been placed on a shelf. She stared straight ahead, her face vacant of Julie.

Jill ignored the pity of it, abandoned her usual hesitant "Julie?" She clasped Julie's shoulders, pulling her into an embrace that was also a shake.

"Listen," Jill said hoarsely. "Your middle name is Katherine, same as mine. I was baptized Jill Katherine Dunn, you, Julie Katherine Dunn. Our brother is John Aloysius Dunn, after our father. We're both Katherine because Ma couldn't make up her mind which of us to name after herself, so she did neither and both. You're sick be-cause you've been trying to be someone you're not. That someone's not me. It's the someone you pretended to be for Fred, for Mother, and, a long time ago, for Pa. Listen." She shook Julie again. "The person you are is better, in every respect, than the person you've tried to be. You hear? Better. Someday you'll know that. And if you learn that because someone else says it, it won't be because that person is magic or possesses that one special voice. It'll be because you're ready to hear, ready to cure yourself. *You.*" Jill folded Julie in a rib-crunching, Daisy-type hug, kissed her on the cheek, and tucked her into bed.

At the door Jill stopped to look back at Julie, lying like Ophelia, hair spread out on the pillow. "You'll be well, Julie Katherine Dunn, and it'll be your own doing. Don't take any bullshit. Not from anyone. Ever."

Jill ran up the hall, arriving at the nurses' station breathless. "You take care of my sister," she said fiercely.

"Why, of course," Dalmeyer said blandly. She held her tray of pill cups, like a hostess about to serve mints. "We care for all of our patients."

"I remember," Jill said. "If hot baths were the cure, only the dirty would be nuts."

Dalmeyer sniffed. "Dr. Kaiser said you should—"

"Tell him I couldn't wait," Jill said truthfully. She couldn't. "Tell him I'll call him later."

"But he specifically said—"

"I don't belong here. I'm leaving."

"If you're uncomfortable—"

"I'm comfortable." Jill was already at the door. "Please buzz me out. I have to see my brother."

"Mrs. Kenyon—"

"Now."

Dalmeyer hit the buzzer. Jill opened the door to the sound of discordant buzzing. She ducked through, then glanced back.

"Good-bye, crazy lady," Jill whispered to the self who remained locked on the ward side of the door.

She walked away feeling eager, weightless, impatient. For the first time in years only one Jill lived in Jill's skin.

CHAPTER
25

John looked up from the scale-model computer he was assembling, on his face the look of a man unexpectedly confronted with the armed and dangerous. "What are you doing here?"

"I've just come from the hospital, Johnny. Julie's in the psychiatric ward."

"I'm sorry to hear that." Carefully he attached one tiny module to another, snapping them together with a twist of his wrist. "Sit down."

In the course of her journey from the hospital elevator to the lobby of John's office Jill had discovered the difference between determination and anger. They both carried a sense of action begun and moving inexorably forward, but the energy produced by determination felt like a controllable flow. She could feel the solid strength of it, like two sturdy legs set squarely beneath her.

Jill sat in the uncomfortable state-your-business-and-leave chair opposite John. This was appropriate. It was business she'd come to state, business left too long unfinished.

Reluctantly John moved the model to one side. "What hospital? I'll send flowers. Julie likes roses." His pen was quick, his notepad at hand, a businessman writing up an order.

"A roomful of roses won't help Julie. They'd be as useless as your plant."

John frowned. "I sent the plant because I care about Julie."

"You sent it because you need to pretend Julie's illness is 'normal' —a few days' rest, perhaps penicillin, then forget it, as though nothing of consequence had happened." Jill said evenly. "Your plant is a lie."

John's face was stony. "I'm sorry you don't like it."

"Not like it? It couldn't be more perfect. Your plant represents the quintessential Dunn-family dilemma, to be solved in our highest tradition." Jill leaned forward, her elbows on his desk. "The plant didn't fit the kitchen, so we simply rearranged the kitchen to fit the plant. We eat meals crammed into one corner, Johnny. We bend double to duck under branches. We dip and dive around it, like dancers in a limbo contest." Jill leaned farther forward to demonstrate, her elbow brushing the model.

"Be careful," John warned. "That's more fragile than it looks. And I'm sorry if the plant is causing any inconvenience."

"That's just the point, Johnny. It isn't. Everyone acts as though Ma's kitchen has always been blessed with a redwood. Our family always makes our lies fit, even when it means bending and twisting, crippling ourselves to do it."

John stiffened, bracing himself. "I know you're upset about Julie, and I wish we had time to talk—"

"Julie will be fine" Jill said with conviction. "Now that the lies are over for her, she can rebuild on the truth. No thanks to me. I lied to her, too."

John shook his head impatiently. "Julie just overdid it, Jill."

"No. Julie's schedule was always insane. From the time she was a child and Pa said, 'Keep busy and you won't be so nervous.' Nervous! Pa's definition! Just because she laughed easily, cried easily, was moved by what was around her. Remember the Christmas she cried in church because the Mass was so beautiful?"

"I don't remember that," he said quickly.

"You do." Jill insisted. "And you remember Pa being angry because a child bursting into tears at Christmas Mass didn't fit his definition of 'normal.' According to Pa, emotions weren't normal. So to replace Julie's emotions, he gave her a schedule, and Julie got busy, until not a moment of her day wasn't scheduled. Then Pa relaxed and Ma called her 'our own good little girl.' Buried beneath that good little girl was Julie, who'd been taught that the person she naturally was, was wrong."

John's fingers drummed on the model. "I'm short on time, Jill. Perhaps if we talk later—"

"We're fresh out of laters, Johnny. We can't dip and dive around this one." Jill wanted to pull the model from his hands, but didn't, knowing he needed it. "I could have told Julie the truth, given her schedule its proper name—obsession. But I didn't. I told myself that it made no difference. She wouldn't listen anyway. Truth was, I was afraid Julie would think I was crazy and everyone would agree. I've never minded 'wrong,' Johnny, but 'crazy' made a coward of me. The truth might not have saved Julie, but my pretense helped build her obsession. I'll carry that guilt, but I'll be damned if I'll repeat it. Not with Julie. And not with you."

"You and Julie have had your problems, that's true." John twisted the model from side to side. It suddenly snapped in his hands. "Christ! I broke it." He dropped the pieces on the table "I'm busy now, Jill. I'll visit Julie as soon as I can."

"That's a lie," Jill said quickly. "You won't go near that hospital or Julie while she's in it. You're too terrified of discovering something abnormal, but not in Julie. In yourself."

"Jill!" He swiveled in his chair, facing away from her.

"We're triplets, Johnny. Twins is a lie. You can change yourself to fit Pa's definition of *normal*, but you can't change the truth. Listen to me, Johnny! Look at me!" Jill's fist slammed the top of his desk.

John jumped, whirled, then folded his arms. "You're so excitable, Jill. You always overreact."

"Thank God! At some point, when I was too young to know it, I must have chosen between feeling too much and feeling nothing at all. Now I know I made the right choice. Much as I love you, Johnny, I wouldn't want to be like you. You don't even know who you are."

"Christ!" John made a display of looking at his watch. "I'm late for a meeting downtown!"

Determination drove Jill to ignore him. "I watched as a child, Johnny. I listened. I saw what you tried to do. Pa hated your music, so you gave up your music. Pa wanted a son who excelled as a student, so you were first in your class. What Pa disapproved of, you turned away from. What Pa approved of, you were. You turned yourself inside out to please him, and none of it helped. It just made him angrier."

John's face was a twist of pain. "Pa was never . . . angry . . ."

"He abused you, Johnny, and none of us knew why. Now Pa's gone, and it's too late for explanations. But it was Pa with the problem, not you, not Julie, not me. Pa wasn't always rational, Johnny, and somehow you thought it was your fault."

"No!" John bolted from his chair, sprinting past Jill to a door at the far end of the office. He tugged at the doorknob, flung open the door, and disappeared inside.

Jill sat quietly, resting easy with her determination. She'd said what she'd come to say, said it despite John's rejection and her own dis-

tress, said it because there are promises implicit in relationships—
where you truly love, you don't lie.

John reappeared, his father's coattails flapping behind him. Ignoring Jill, he stuffed random papers into an already bulging briefcase.

"I'll walk you to your car," he said briskly, a businessman being
polite at the end of a meeting.

"That coat is only a coat, Johnny," Jill said softly. "It isn't Pa, and
it isn't you."

John pulled the coat tighter around him. "Pa gave me this coat."

"Pa gave you his fear and his fury. Take off that coat, Johnny, and
take back your life."

"You have no right! Pa was a good man, a *good* man!" It was a cry
to splinter his soul.

It splintered Jill's also, and her arms were around him before she
was aware she'd moved. She held him as close as she had before birth,
her arms locked around the Johnny of long ago, the little boy with
arms flung over his face, flimsy defense against incomprehensible
rage. Her hand found the hair at the back of his neck, and she stroked
him—the little boy who'd followed Pa like a second shadow, imitat-
ing his walk, the timbre of his voice; the little boy who'd adored him,
who'd never felt loved in return.

The spasm that shook Johnny trembled through Jill. She pressed
him closer. "He was a good man, a father worth loving. I loved him.
I love you, too."

"Let me go, Jill." It was a mumble, a murmur, a cry of mourning
for fantasy.

"Hear me out, Johnny. The truth can't be told in pieces, with
pieces left over. It's those pieces we build our fantasies from." She
reached to kiss him, but he turned his head. "It wasn't his abuse that
terrified you. You were afraid that Pa didn't love you. Didn't and
couldn't and never, ever would. You were so desperate for his love,
his approval, that when he died without giving you either one, you
did the only thing you could. You became him, without the rages you
can't face remembering."

"No!" He pushed her, breaking her grip. "I'm going!" He snatched
his briefcase from the top of his desk. The latch sprung and papers
drifted to the floor. "Damn!" He bent to retrieve them, shoving them
into the briefcase, crumpling them with one shaking hand.

"He loved you, Johnny. He loved you and never knew he was sick.
You don't have to deny he was sick to love him." Jill reached for his

shoulder. He twisted away. "Pa was a good man who struggled with an emotional sickness he didn't know was a sickness. We can respect him for that. Only the truly good struggle. Only the brave don't lose heart. We can remember him with love for the good times, and with compassion for the struggle he never won. But only if we remember him fully. Otherwise, our only memory is fantasy. Our only alternative is hate."

John slammed the door with a fury that rattled the walls. He would deny what he'd heard, but he'd heard it, and the truth he'd heard would hang in the air, an irrevocable challenge to fantasy. It would hurt him only if he continued to deny it.

Jill rubbed her arm where he'd gripped her, wondering why the truth should have been so long in coming, so hard in the telling, wondering if in the end it would matter, if perhaps it had come too late.

Her arms would show bruises. Johnny hadn't meant to hurt her, any more than Pa had meant to hurt John. She shivered, wondering.

She closed the door of John's office behind her, for one moment longing to turn back the clock, to play "Let's Pretend." She ached for a hug from Johnny, but only the Johnny who pretended had ever wanted to hug her.

Too late for pretending. Too late for hugs.

She ignored the elevator and instead pounded down the steps, feeling the need of physical movement to match the racing in her head.

I'll love Daisy and make no mystery of it, no ritual requiring guilt and impossible demands.

I'll finish my play because it's complex and simple, because finishing is a commitment, as great an imperative as blood calling to blood.

I'll say what I think at UBC, then wait and see. It may be my destination or a stopping place on the way. Something will happen. I'll know. Enough for now to deal with perpetual ambivalence and the layer-by-layer discarding of guilt. I'll find right and wrong in my own way, my path in my own time. The choices I make won't always be right but in the end they'll be mine.

Jill arrived at Kate's house, determined to stop looking back.

I've wasted too much time living in the past. Or perhaps just enough. It takes what it takes.

In Ma's bedroom Jill found Pa's old typewriter, neatly covered and stored on the bottom shelf of the bookcase. Gasping, she wrestled it into her room and placed it on the table next to the window.

She uncovered it, gently touching keys so worn that some of the letters had all but disappeared. She remembered hearing Pa type late at night, hour after hour, a steady rhythm that pounded through her dreams. What he'd written, one knew. What he'd thought, no one knew. What he'd suffered, Jill could only imagine.

Her notebook lay on her bed where she'd left it. She read what she'd written, pausing often to squint at words illegibly scrawled. What she'd written pleased her, not in the sense that her writing was admirable but in the sense that what she'd written was true.

She rolled paper into the typewriter, thinking it entirely appropriate that truth-telling had begun with herself.

She deciphered and typed what she'd written, then continued, trying to conjure up the words for the scene playing in her head, when a voice behind her intruded: "Guess we're the only ones home." It was Father Norton, yawning as usual, but unclerically cozy in a blue velour bathrobe with tassels.

At the sound of his voice Jill's scene cracked in the middle and shattered. She turned on him, furious not merely at his interruption but that he should be there at all. "Speak of making lies fit and up you pop."

"I just took a shower."

"Wonderful. Now that you've mastered cleanliness, would you care to give godliness a shot?"

He stepped into the room, a blue, fuzzy moth attracted to the flame of her anger. "Your mother is at the cemetery. She said something about making arrangements."

"Thank you for the message. Go away, Father Norton."

"Dr. Kaiser called. He said you should call the minute you come in. He said it's crucial."

"Thank you. Go away, Father Norton."

"Someone named Polly called from Los Angeles. She said she'd call back. She didn't say it was crucial, but sounded excited."

"Thank you. Are there any further bulletins, messages from various fronts?"

"No."

"Good. Go away, Father Norton."

She swiveled her chair back to the typewriter and closed her eyes, annoyed at how swiftly her concentration had dissolved in an urge to slap him—once for Julie, once for herself, and once because frauds should be struck regularly lest anyone forget just how hollow they sound. She felt the hair on the back of her neck prickle. He hadn't gone away. He was behind her. Blowing on her neck?

"Writing something?"

Jill swiveled to face him. "How strange, Father Norton. Every time I tell you to go away, you move closer. Am I mumbling? Using big words? Or maybe Mommy never meant what she said." She glared at him over the flame of her lighter as she lit a cigarette.

"Aren't you going to call Dr. Kaiser?"

"Later."

"He must be calling about Julie. Don't you want to know about Julie?"

"I already know about Julie."

"But I don't!" he bleated. "And you know how terrible I feel about her."

"Bullshit, Norton. You're still eating and sleeping. Tell me you feel terrible when you have insomnia and rickets."

"You're a hard woman, Jill."

"Oh, God." Jill longed to kick him for the pest he was. Instead she reached for an ashtray. "Go away, Norton. Now."

"That's not what you tell other men." His voice was sly.

"What?" Jill dropped the cigarette into the ashtray and stared at him. The expression on his face was repulsive; venal. Venality slimed his eyes and puffed his lips into a pout. "What the hell do you want, Norton?"

"I heard what Julie said to you." His was the petulant whine of a born snitch. "When you were talking about God, I heard the rest. You've slept with a number of men."

Jill burned with anger. "This conversation is over."

"Your men must be in Los Angeles," he said softly. "You must miss them, a fiery woman like you. You pretend to be angry but it's another, more primitive urge you're displacing." He stepped toward her, eyes glowing.

"One step closer, and you'll get a swift kick in your blue velour tassels," Jill warned him.

"You've tempted me beyond my strength!" he bellowed, flinging himself at her. Before she could move he had one hand clamped over her wrist, the other twisted in her hair. "Jezebel!" he panted. His lips descended on hers with all the finesse of a kamikaze attack. Jill squirmed, trying to turn her head, but he was firmly attached and evidently intent on sucking her lips off her face. Her free arm flailed behind her, finally making contact with what her wriggling fingers identified as an ashtray. She grasped it firmly, raised it over their heads, and brought it crashing down on the back of his neck.

"Oohhh," he groaned, and slid to his knees. "Oooohhh." He weaved back and forth, as though uncertain which way to fall. "Oohhh, you've broken something."

"Only the ashtray." Jill tossed the piece in her hand on the desk. She wondered if she'd actually hurt him. She didn't know whether to sit on the floor and monitor him for signs of concussion or hit him again. Maybe both.

"Oohhh," he continued to moan. "Why did you hit me?"

"It's a new thing women are doing these days. It's called defending yourself against rape."

"Ohhh, God. I wouldn't rape anyone!" He struggled to open his eyes. They were crossed. "What's the big deal? You sleep around. What's one more man, more or less?"

His eyes uncrossed, then whipped to opposite sides of his face in a Ping-Pong wall-eyed flip that made Jill a trifle nervous. She'd wanted to dampen his ardor, not dent his head.

Jill bent over him, studying his eyes intently. "That's an interesting theory, Norton. The Madonna or Whore School of Philosophy, right? One you worship, the other you jump. Learn that in the seminary?"

"Ohhh, the seminary," he moaned, swaying like a confused cobra. "They shouldn't have ordained me."

"But they did, and you let them." Jill glanced away from his face, dizzy from tracking eyes doing loop-de-loops. "Either be a priest or don't, Father Norton. Chase the vocation you've chosen, or women —one or the other. Only you can decide, and, frankly, only you care. Become Pope or a paperboy, the world won't stop turning."

"Mine will," he whined. "My parents will disown me. From my earliest childhood—"

"Screw your parents and your asinine childhood. And stop whining at me. I'm not one of the gullible Catholic ladies you specialize in. Go ahead. Whisper *childhood trauma* in my ear. Then watch while I find another ashtray."

"But it was!" His whining was a fingernail on a blackboard, and his eyes tumbled like dice rattling over a craps table. "My childhood was traumatic."

387

"Everyone's childhood was traumatic, you dolt! No one received perfect love, perfect understanding. Not you, not me, not our parents, not theirs. We've all had empty bellies and sopping diapers in the middle of the night, but that's no license to whine. We've all had our toys stolen and broken. But that's not permission to take what we want and break what we will. We've all had our hearts broken, been deceived, discarded, abandoned, abused. That's not a mandate to go and do likewise. We're all human beings and none of us perfect, but we can recognize right when we've done it and wrong when we've done it and call it by those names. Don't mewl to me about the moral ambiguity of psychiatry, then think you can play the same dodger's game. You've taken your case to exactly the wrong court. I'll hang you, Norton, and smile."

"Ooohh." He covered his face with his hands. "I'm nauseous."

"Damn." Jill stood up. She'd have to call a doctor. She hesitated, nauseous herself. Could a concussion be catching? She sniffed, suddenly aware of a faint but pervasive, acrid odor—a short-circuited wire perhaps or . . . She saw it. The cigarette she'd thrown in the ashtray was burning a hole in the rug.

"Oh, shit!" Jill ground the cigarettes out with her heel. "Ma will have a conniption!"

"You're not going to tell your mother!" Norton struggled to his feet.

"I'll have to." She fell to her knees and scraped the scorched fibers with her fingernail. "Damn."

"I'll tell her first!" Norton's voice skirted the range of a dog whistle. "She knows you're a loose woman. I'll tell her you used your womanly wiles."

"What womanly wiles? It was a Kool Filter King! I didn't burn the carpet with witchery."

"You weren't going to tell her about us? About me?" He shook his head spastically, which set him groaning, but miraculously his eyes snapped and locked, at last, properly in place. "Thank God for that."

Jill sat back on her heels, regarding him as she would a spider in a fruit salad. "You thought I'd tell my mother about . . . what happened?"

Now that his eyes had stopped bouncing, he looked chagrined. "I thought you might be resentful enough for revenge."

"I am. I'd love it. Revenge is the cure for resentment. But not at the cost of upsetting my mother. She's got enough on her mind."

"I . . . probably . . . wouldn't have mentioned it, either." His head dropped in a drama student's exaggeration of "abashed."

"Get dressed. Then get packed and get out. Ten minutes."

"You can't make me leave."

"I can, and I am. Either go, or I'll call *your* mother and daddy. They'd love to hear the story I'd tell."

"You wouldn't!"

"Stick around. You can be disowned before dinner."

"Your mother will miss me."

"I'll buy her a dog."

"If I promise never to come near you again?" He was tentative, hopeful.

"I am walking to the phone." She did. "I am picking it up." The receiver was in her hand.

"I'm going. I'm going." He wobbled toward the door. "You're a hard woman, Jill."

"And loose. Don't forget loose."

"Well, you are," he said bitterly. "And I'm only human."

Jill waved the phone at him. "Want to say hello to the folks?"

"I'm going, I'm going." He doddered through the door.

Jill replaced the receiver and sighed.

Norton's head appeared again, stuck through the door like a free-floating muskmelon. "My glands are still swollen."

"I'll mention it to Mommy." She reached for the phone.

"I'm going, I'm going." The head and the whine withdrew.

The phone rang in Jill's hand, startling her with its noise. She snatched at it, juggling it up to her ear.

"Hello."

"Is Jill Kenyon in for Dale Neiman?" a chirpy long-distance voice inquired.

"Uh." One thought trampled through her mind. She was about to be fired. Neiman had finally noticed that her update was arriving by mail, her chair at the conference table empty, and her leg unavailable for attempted footsie. She'd heard rumors of how he fired people, eyes brimming, mouthing commiseration, with solicitous pats on the shoulder and "Gee, fella, it's a damn shame," and "Don't know how this could happen," as though the lopped executive was being axed by whimsical decree of some cosmic committee having nothing to do with him. More than one firee had ended up comforting Neiman, then gone off somewhere alone to ponder and throw up.

"Hello. . . . Are you still there?" The bird-girl of UBC twittered.

"I'm here."

"Hold, please," she chirped.

Jill held, various reactions and attitudes skittering through her mind. She could be angry, wounded, distraught—as whiny as Norton, as persecuted as Nixon, as stalwart as Nathan Hale on the gallows, as . . . She glanced at the typewriter. If Neiman didn't insist on a long-winded firing, she could finish Act Two before dinner.

"Hello, my dear. Hello." Neiman sounded like he'd swallowed a whoopee cushion. "How's our rising star?"

"Your who?" Jill frowned at the phone. "Have you been eating cookies with Zippy de Franco?"

"De Franco?" Neiman shouted. "He's got potential, along with a lousy haircut and a faggy giggle. But he's not a genius like you."

"Who?" Even with Neiman projecting like a coked Vegas comic, it was difficult to hear him above the noise in the background. Voices were clamoring, horns tooting, and a band, mostly brass, was blaring a song Jill didn't recognize.

"You, you, UBC's star," Neiman shrieked. "The woman of the hour, the best and the brightest, the girl with the golden . . . no, that's Silverman." He hiccuped. " 'Scuse me, I'm so excited. It's New Year's Eve here. The network that loves all America loves you best of all. Listen to this, star, it's for you."

The din increased, and Jill could hear separate voices shouting "Hip, hip, hooray."

Neiman returned to the phone. "Whaddya think of that?"

"It's . . . uh . . . very interesting, Dale. Is it a new show?"

"No, no." He laughed, a sound that amazed Jill. She'd thought "laugh like a hyena" was only an expression. "It's the best party UBC ever had."

"UBC's always been a fun network, Dale." Jill still didn't know what spirit had moved him to call. If his hiccups indicated anything, maybe he'd had a few and been inspired to go for long-distance footsie. "Thank you for sharing the party with me."

"Share, share," he cackled gleefully. "We've never had such a share, not to mention a rating. It's a miracle, thanks to you."

"What's a miracle?" Jill was suddenly certain that the bird-girl had called the wrong number. "What did I do?"

"Modest, too. Listen to this, folks!" he bellowed. Jill winced and held the phone away from her ear. "She asks what did she do?"

There were general shrieks that suggested merriment or a lion
loose in the building.

"Hear that?" Dale returned. "They love you. They adore you."

"Thank you." Jill decided to try bellowing. *"Why?"*

"You didn't get the telegram?" Neiman was shocked.

"What telegram?"

"I'm the first to tell you?" His enthusiasm bounded through the
phone. "That's great! That's terrific! A pleasure, an honor!"

"Tell me what?" Jill screamed. Either UBC's method of firing people was as weird as their methods for everything else, or she'd just
been elected Miss Personality, Programing Division.

"Rock and Roll Love got a twenty-eight rating, a forty-six share!"

"You're kidding!" Jill was stunned.

"We've never had a forty-six share," Neiman bubbled. "We've
never had a thirty-six share. Once, a few years ago, we had a twenty-
six share, and the board of directors voted themselves a raise. We get
sevens, nines, elevens. It's like shooting craps. Evangelists on cable
do better."

"What about the other networks?" Jill asked, excitement rising.
"How did they compare?"

"We took the night," Neiman hiccuped. "First time in our history.
ABC is screaming, CBS reeling, and NBC plucking the peacock,
they're so mad."

"That's fantastic." Jill laughed. "It's terrific when something works
out." It was more than terrific. In one pinnacle-straddling instant Jill
was taller, thinner, smarter, prettier, younger—meaning more vital
—and older—meaning wiser. She had accomplished something. In a
spontaneous fit of self-indulgence she decided to act as if she deserved it.

"America knows what it wants to tune into," Neiman chortled.
"And you're tuned into what America wants."

"Thank you, Dale." Jill repressed a giggle. She'd known *Rock and
Roll Love* had made her laugh, but she hadn't known nearly half of
America would sit down to chuckle along with her. The thought gave
her a cozy feeling, as though she'd shared a good joke at a family
reunion.

"You have the spark, the genius, the talent," Neiman enthused.
"Don't take any calls. Don't listen to people. This business is lousy
with liars."

"What? Dale, are you still talking to me?" Jill asked, certain he was

391

delivering an aside to a minion, none of whom he ever addressed by name.

"Of course, I'm talking to you. Listen to me. Other networks will call, studios, those bastards in cable, those pirates in pay. They'll offer you plenty, lie to you, sweetheart, say they have lawyers who can break your contract. But I know our star won't listen to bullshit. I know our star knows who made her a star. The network that loves you, sweetie, UBC."

"Nobody's called me, Dale." Jill smiled. She could hear the thirty-weight oil oozing, lubing the joints of Neiman's mania. "If someone from another network should call, I'll tell them the truth. Dan Carmichael hired me, and I don't have a contract."

"So Carmichael hired you. Big fucking deal. UBC promoted you after he left, and you owe UBC— *You don't have a contract?*" he screamed.

Jill held the phone away from her ear. She'd heard more restraint from patients on their way to the shock-treatment room. "I've never signed a contract," she said in the softest, most rational voice she could manage, a technique known to work with shrieking hysterics and children with boo-boos. "I've never been offered a contract."

"Who never offered you a contract? What son of a bitch? Give me his name." The glass-shattering owner of the corporate ax was itching to wield it.

"Uh . . . Dale." Jill was reluctant to set him shrieking again. He could self-destruct, and she wouldn't shed a tear, but her eardrums were beginning to ache. "Aren't contracts part of your job?" She turned the phone in the direction of the door.

"Christ Almighty!" he shrieked on cue. "My job! My life! My Mercedes-Benz! They'd fire my ass if they knew. I'm too old to start over. My prostate is going. You've got to sign a contract, Jill."

"I'll be happy to consider it," Jill said pleasantly, and indeed, outside of her next hug from Daisy, it was the stellar consideration of an ecliptical day. She waited as Neiman fought to control his breathing, downshifting from labored to heavy to something approximating normal.

As she listened to his wheezing dissipate she became aware of a low, whirring noise. It was her typewriter, left to hum through the interlude with Norton and his offer of wormy, forbidden fruit. She carried the phone to the desk and flipped the switch, then sat in the old swivel chair, her eyes traveling the page she'd typed. A line caught her eye and she frowned, momentarily puzzled, then picked up a pen and crossed out a word. Better.

"Well, Jill." Neiman was brusque, getting down to it. "We'll soon rectify our little . . . oversight." He chuckled to indicate ease and mutual agreement. "UBC is prepared to offer a thirty-percent immediate increase, stock options, bonuses, additional increases negotiable annually over a twelve-year period." He chuckled again, throaty affirmation of her anticipated acquiescence. "But we needn't bore ourselves with details. Have your people call my people."

"I don't have any people."

"You don't?" Neiman was nonplused. "How do you function?"

"I do have the informal services of a lawyer." Jill smiled, wondering how Steve would handle a call from Neiman's "people" to discuss raises, bonuses, and stock options. Would he accuse UBC of overreacting?

"Fine. Have him call. We'll have a contract for your signature in twenty-four hours."

"This is very flattering, Dale." Jill nodded down the holes of the mouthpiece. "But I can't sign the contract you've outlined."

"You must," Neiman wheezed. "I have two sons at Harvard, a yacht with dry rot. You can't do this to me."

"This has been very sudden, Dale."

"More money, that's it." Neiman charged forward. Jill imagined buckskin crackling as he donned his horse-trader's suit. "All right then, forty percent."

"It's not the money," Jill told him. "I just feel—"

"You're in Cleveland, right?" He pounced, refusing to hear an answer that sounded like no. "You like Cleveland? Your strokes of genius happen better there? Great. Terrific. We'll rent you an office in Cleveland. We'll buy you a house. Better yet. We—"

"Dale, Dale." Jill leaped in to catch him. "I can't stay in Cleveland. I have a daughter in Los Angeles."

"You have a daughter. You're a mother? I didn't know. I'm overwhelmed. You're an inspiration, a New Woman, a television mogul . . . moguless . . . who's also experienced the ultimate mystery of life. Who but you could brainstorm *Rock and Roll Love* and also give birth?"

Jill laughed. "I didn't do both simultaneously, Dale."

"Who cares when you did it?" Neiman hiccuped undiminished enthusiasm. "You're concerned about your daughter? Bring her to work. We have everything she'll need in the nursery built for that damn McCaffery kid, curse the day Lawrence ever laid eyes on him."

"My daughter's fifteen, Dale. She'd be bored in a playpen."

"Then what do you want, woman?" Neiman shouted the mercantile version of Freud's famous query. "What's wrong with the contract I'm offering?"

"The length," Jill replied, relieved he'd finally asked. She thought he'd planned to go on offering sugarplums forever. "I cannot sign away twelve years of my life."

"People would kill for a twelve-year contract!" Neiman barked. "What the hell else have you got to do with your life?"

"That's just the point. I don't know yet." Jill smiled, pleased at the thought of surprises ahead, the changes for the better she'd predicted to Kate. "I can't commit that much of my life until I know it's the work that's meant to be mine."

"I'm talking big bucks here, you're talking gobbledegook—"

"The work I spend my life doing has to have value for me. That's not gobbledegook—"

"You think you'd be better off at another network." His teeth ground the ax of his words.

"It never entered my mind."

A valise, hurled from the doorway, struck Jill's leg. "Not true! Not true!" Norton broad-jumped across the room, shouting, "It's always on her mind. She's a promiscuous woman!"

"Go away," Jill hissed.

"I won't go away." Neiman was peeved. "Not until you agree to the contract. You want me out on the street? That's it. You hate me."

Father Norton reached for the phone. "I'm going to tell my parents *my* side of the story. They'll know who seduced who."

"This isn't your parents," Jill rasped. "It's business, you creep."

"Creep?" Neiman's voice trembled. "Why do you hate me, Jill?"

Norton grabbed at the phone. Jill snatched it away. "I'll have to call you back."

"You ruined my party," Neiman wheezed.

Jill pictured a little boy with prostate trouble holding a busted balloon. "It's not personal. Honest. My lawyer will call your lawyer."

"Lawyer?" Norton froze. "You can't sue. I only kissed you. It wasn't rape." He lunged at the phone and shouted, "It wasn't rape."

"What wasn't rape?" Neiman was befuddled. "Jill, are you having a party, too?"

"Later, Dale." Jill hung up.

"Dale? That wasn't my parents? Oh, my." His grin was an idiot's delight. "I hope I didn't interrupt anything."

"Oh, no." Jill beamed at him and swept to her feet. "I can't thank you enough for inspiring a fantastic idea."

"Me?"

"I've just talked to UBC about doing a *Freak People* segment on philandering priests. They went wild. They think I'm a genius. You sure goosed the muse, Father Norton."

"They *wouldn't*—"

"Picture the promo—*woman driven mad by passionate priest*. You do remember my sister, the currently crazy?"

"They wouldn't—"

"*Freak People* is the *National Enquirer* of the airwaves. They'd kill for a story like that. Think of it, Norton. You'll have women following you in the streets. Off with the black suit, on with the love affairs. You'll never be sent to a retreat house again. Excommunicated priests can live where they like."

"The Church doesn't excommunicate priests for fooling around." He was stronger there, certain of territory he'd already covered.

"It will if it's embarrassed enough. Private sins gone public demand reform. Your name will be written into Catholic Church history, just like Martin Luther's."

"You're nuts." He shuddered. "I'm getting out of this house. Only crazy women live here." He snatched up his valise and headed for the door.

"You can't leave now," Jill called after him. "The video truck is coming. With a Minicam."

He fled down the steps with Jill clumping after him, hoping she could shove him out the door before the laughter bubbling in her throat burst out and betrayed her.

"You'll be sorry for this," he shouted over his shoulder. "Scandal is a sin."

"You mean a hot commodity," Jill shouted back. "Sensational sinning in prime-time. The ratings will go through the roof."

"Let me outa here." He flung the door open and leaped onto the porch, an Olympian maneuver that sent him crashing into Kate.

"*Aaaaaarrrgggghhhh!*" The house keys in Kate's hand flipped backward over her head. She reeled into Norton, who clutched her, whirling them both like a top.

395

Jill lunged first at one, then at the other as they spun in a frenzied tango, circling the tiny porch. Finally Kate seized the banister and with one frantic yank stopped herself dead. Norton whipped off her arm at terrific velocity and, like a man shot from a cannon, went hurtling over the steps and into the hedges.

"Mother of God!" Kate gasped, pale hand clasped to cherry-red bosom. "Mother of God! Jill! How many times have I told you you're too old to run through the house?"

"But I wasn't— Are you all right, Ma?" Jill put her arm around Kate. "Let me help you into the house."

"I'm alive, or I will be when my heart starts beating again. See if Jerry's hurt himself."

Jill peeped over the banister. "Nah, he's whining. He's all right."

"Get down there," Kate ordered. "See how he is."

Jill did as she was told, wondering where miracles are when you need them. A nice burning bush would get Norton on his feet.

"Hi," Jill said to the prostrate form draped over the greenery. "Come here often?"

"My back. My ribs. My whiplash. Ruptured spleen," he groaned.

Oh, no, you don't. The Man Who Came to Dinner isn't coming to dinner at my mother's house. If any parts are broken, I'll give you a Baggie to carry them home.

"Don't move," Jill cautioned.

"You're calling a doctor?" he asked, pleased as any man about to be pampered.

"Right after the Minicam comes," Jill whispered. "Just lie there, Father. They'll get a shot that suggests fooling around in the bushes. Dynamite promo!"

"Get me up!" He flopped, a flounder on the hook. "I'm going."

"No!" Jill protested. "You'll wreck my television career. Lie down. I'll join you."

"Christ!" He leaped to his feet as Kate walked toward them across the grass.

"You all right, Father Norton?" she called.

"Fine. Fine. Chipper. Shipshape."

Jill smiled at Kate. "Spunky, isn't he?"

"I'm so relieved. Come in the house. Jill will make coffee. It's the least she can do after half-killing us." Kate turned to go.

"Is that the truck?" Jill whispered to Norton.

"Where?" He whirled around.

396

"It's only a postal delivery." Jill sounded very disappointed. "Where *are* those Minicam people?"

"Are you coming?" Kate called.

"Uh . . . no . . . I'm not," Norton said.

Kate, startled, returned. "Why not?" She frowned. "Something wrong?" She glared suspiciously at Jill.

"Oh . . . uh . . ." Father Norton's fleet foot was, as usual, stuck in his open mouth.

"Father Norton's got wonderful news!" Jill broke in enthusiastically. "He was racing out the door to tell you. He's had a spiritual experience."

"In my house?" Kate glowed. "Mother of God!"

"Yes, well," Jill continued, "we all know how fervently he's been praying, and today God gave him an answer."

Kate nodded wisely. "God always does."

"He's returning to the priesthood. Isn't that marvelous?"

"I knew it!" Kate rejoiced. "I lit a candle!"

"So, kiss him good-bye, Ma. Here, Father Norton, kiss my mother good-bye." She wrenched Norton's elbow, thrusting him toward Kate, who folded him in her most motherly embrace.

"Take care, Father Norton," Kate said, with tears in her eyes. "Remember us in your prayers." She gave him the smile copied from Bette Davis in *Dark Victory* and held in reserve for just such occasions, then turned and walked slowly away while Jill imagined violins.

"I'll remember you, Mother Dunn," Norton called, then turned to Jill with a bewilderment beyond ashtrays bounced off heads and tumbles down steps. "I thought you wanted me to stay? Your television career? Your Minicam truck?"

"You were right after all, Father Norton. The bottom line is I'm Catholic, and I cannot render unto Caesar what rightfully belongs to Mammon. It's a far, far—"

"Uh . . . I think you've got that wrong." He frowned. "It's render—"

"Oh, shit." She gripped his arm, squinting into the sun. "Is that the truck? Quick, Father, duck down the alley. I'll cover for you."

He threw a hasty, harried glance over his shoulder and took off, loping like a wolf. He vaulted the hedge and hit the gravel, a man accustomed to ducking down alleys.

Jill waved cheerily as he sped around the corner without looking back. "Good riddance, you knot-headed proponent of laissez-faire lust."

Jill stood in the kitchen doorway, peering through plant leaves at Kate, who was at the counter, weeping genteelly into the percolator.

"Don't become overly fond of people," Kate sniffed. "The minute you do, they leave."

Words to live by, Jill thought, understanding her sadness. Kate had been thrilled to have a priest in the house, even one who whined and never made his bed.

"He'll pray for you, Ma," Jill gently reminded her.

"I'll light candles for him. *Somebody* has to. The Church will never canonize that one. But at least he's back in the fold." She sighed. "How's my Julie?"

"When I left her, she was resting."

"Resting! Ha! In a place like that. I'd rest better in a crashing airplane."

"It's not a bad place, Ma. It has value for her right now."

"What value?" Kate was dubious. "What can strangers in a hospital do for her that her mother couldn't do better at home?"

"It's too easy to pretend here, Ma." Instantly Jill regretted having said it. She hadn't meant to open that door.

"Pretend?" Kate was sharp.

Jill smiled to soften what hadn't been meant as the accusation Kate would take it to be. For Kate, the stating of a problem had to be accompanied by the immediate assignment of blame. "What I mean is, being in the hospital will help Julie concentrate on getting well. It's harder to deny you're sick when you're in a place for sick people. A man with a backpack and rifle knows he's in a war."

"Like hell!" Kate chose indignation as the antidote to despair. "We could have taken care of her. Everyone in this house knew she was sick."

"Knew!" Blame was overshadowed by sheer visceral reaction. "We always *know*. And then we pretend what we know isn't true."

"That's not so!" Kate's indignation erupted into anger. "You're always disparaging this family."

"Another pretense!" Jill's anger matched Kate's. "Like all the rest. Like pretending that when we were kids, we stayed in the yard because that's what we wanted. Lie! We were locked in, all summer, every summer! Pa locked us in!"

Kate's tears dried on her cheeks. She folded her arms, an instinctive defense, and dug in her heels. "You think you have to know everything! Okay. You're right. That was a lie. Your father did lock you in."

"Why?" Jill whispered, shocked. She'd expected anything from Kate but blunt truth.

"He was terrified of polio."

"Polio?" Mystified, Jill sank into a chair. "Polio?"

"You're too young to remember, but polio killed children then. Or trapped them in iron lungs forever. Or in braces or on crutches." Kate shuddered. "When summertime came, your father would go cra— get worried. There were health warnings to stay away from crowds, public places, beaches, parks, pools. It spread there, they said. So your father locked you up. He wanted you safe."

"Why didn't he ever explain? Why didn't you?"

"We didn't want you children to worry. Childhood is a carefree time."

Oh, God, for what children, where, since time began?

"Ma, when no explanations are given, children make up their own. I thought Pa . . . well . . ." Now that she knew, her own explanations were just history, and the only power they had was to hurt Kate. "But still, Ma, we had friends, schoolmates, cousins. Everyone's parents must have been afraid of polio, but no one except us was confined to the yard. And no one we knew got polio. Why was Pa so frightened?"

"He just was," Kate said obstinately. "Every day when he came home from work, he'd jump out of the car, run to the yard, check you for coughs, sore throat, fever. Then he'd come in the house and go straight to the newspaper to see how many cases had been reported that day. They used to print the number in a box on the front page, like a score. Even before you were born, he was afraid of polio, but then he was afraid for himself. Adults got it too, you know. He couldn't even listen to President Roosevelt on the radio. He said all he could see was the wheelchair. He couldn't abide the thought of anyone being helpless. Not himself, certainly not his kids."

"He had a phobia, Ma." It was a low-pitched truth, meant for herself.

"He had a worry," Kate insisted. "To have children is to worry every day of your life. You should thank God you've never had to worry about Daisy and polio."

"You're right. I should," Jill agreed, thinking about Daisy and her normally abnormal periods. "I've never had that particular worry.

But I guess any worry can be built into a phobia when you're the worrying kind."

"Your father was." Kate poured coffee. "He worshipped you kids."

"Why did Pa . . . hit Johnny?" Jill held her breath at the audacity of it. She'd flung it out of herself, torn it out, ripped it out. Out.

Kate stiffened, her back to Jill. "The mischief Johnny got into!" Kate choked on a dry, forced laugh. "Do you remember the time he dug up my roses . . . ?"

"*Why, Ma?*" With the unaskable finally asked, Jill demanded an answer. There couldn't be pieces left over for future fantasy-building.

The stiffness remained in Kate's spine, but her voice quavered. "Johnny got on Pa's nerves. I tried to keep John away as much as I could, but . . . Johnny got on his nerves."

"Pa was sick, Ma."

"He went to work every day."

"It wasn't that kind of sick. He had . . . emotional problems."

"There are things you don't know." Kate faced Jill, her chin trembling. "Don't understand."

"Then tell me, Ma," Jill pleaded tearfully. "I want to understand. God help me, I've got to understand. *Now*."

Kate scrutinized Jill's face, searching for something, perhaps an indication that Jill was looking for someone to blame.

"I loved Pa," Jill gently assured her. "I still love Pa."

"You should love Pa." It was an order, a plea. "No one ever tried harder than he did!" Kate sat down in a chair opposite Jill. Their knees almost touched. "Your father had moods and a temper. . . . He worried about both of them. Oh, God, how he worried."

"Why didn't he ever seek help?"

"Help!" Kate exploded. "His brother got help. He saw what help did to him!"

"What brother?" Jill gasped. She'd never heard of a brother.

"I'll tell you," Kate offered reluctantly, "but you must swear you'll never tell your brother and sister."

"Why, Ma?"

"I don't want them to worry."

"Please, Ma." Jill half-laughed, half-sobbed. "It's too late to worry about forty-year-old skeletons. We're busy becoming our own."

"All right. I'll tell you. Your father had a twin brother, Joseph—"

"Joseph!" Jill exclaimed. "The man in the picture!"

"What picture?" Kate was startled. "You've seen a picture of Joseph?"

"Johnny found it in the pocket of Pa's coat after his funeral. We all thought it was a picture of Pa, but when I turned it over, I saw the name Joseph and I wondered and wondered. . . . Tell me, Ma!" Jill leaned forward.

"Just promise you won't interrupt," Kate pleaded. "This will be hard enough."

"I promise."

Kate sighed, a sound heavy with remembered sorrow and, perhaps, anticipated relief. "Your father and Joseph were identical twins, but Joseph was a gambler, a wastrel, a devil with the ladies. He's gone now. I shouldn't speak ill. It's enough to say he was always in trouble and Pa was always pulling him out. Pa used to say it was only high spirits and Joseph would settle down. But he didn't. The scrapes he got into got crazier and crazier. At times he couldn't control himself. Then one day, he just went . . . He was running naked . . . but that's not important. The police took Joseph to Wilbur State Hospital, that horrible dungeon, that awful place. When your father went there to get him, the doctors said Joseph was sick. Joseph wouldn't listen to reason, they said. He needed treatment, but he wanted to go home. They warned Pa that if Joseph left, he'd hurt himself or somebody else. Pa was his only family, so . . . He loved his brother, wanted him well, so . . . He didn't want him to hurt himself, so . . . He . . . he . . ."

"He had him committed." Jill said what Kate couldn't.

"And he signed for the treatments."

"Shock treatments?"

"The doctors said Joseph would kill himself!"

"Poor Pa," Jill breathed.

"He could only do what he thought was right. What else could he do?" Kate asked plaintively.

"Nothing, Ma," Jill said quickly. "No one ever argued with doctors back then, even now too few do. I understand why he did what he did. Maybe it was for the best."

Kate shook her head. "Joseph never got well. If he had, your father wouldn't have suffered so. He didn't tell me about Joseph while we were courting. He asked me to marry him first. I said yes, then he told me. After we were married, Pa visited Joseph every Sunday. He wouldn't let me go with him." Kate stroked one hand with the other, like a woman who's arthritis is hurting. "Pa said we'd wait to have children. He never said why, but I knew. We would never have had children at all if I hadn't disobeyed." Kate's look warned against questions. "You came as a surprise to your father."

"Having three at once must have been a terrible shock to him."

"It was." Kate stiffened, gathering herself for the rest of her story. "He thought it was a sign, an omen, and after what had happened to Joseph, he couldn't take the omen as good. He tried, how he tried, just as he'd tried to believe Joseph would get better. For almost a year he'd come home every Sunday and say, 'Kate, Joseph was better today.' "

"Then what happened?"

"You can only hold on to false hope for so long. For a while Pa told me Joseph's progress was slowing down, then he admitted there wasn't any, then finally he told me that the shock treatments had taken his brother away. What was left, just a body, wasn't Joseph at all. Then one day when Pa went to visit, Joseph didn't know who he was. Pa got . . . upset. He started pounding on the walls and screaming. They sent for the head doctor, who gave him a shot, then sat him down and told him straight out that he'd better be careful, learn to control himself, because Joseph's disease runs in families and he might be next."

"What a horrible thing to tell Pa." Jill shook with anger. "What gave that doctor the right? Even if it was true about the disease being hereditary, he couldn't know Pa would get it!"

"He was the doctor, Jill," Kate said, as though that explained everything.

"If I'd been Pa and Joseph had been Johnny, I would have pounded the walls. So would you. So would anyone whose heart is breaking because he can't help someone he loves. Pa had reason for anger, reason for fear. There was a reason for it all."

Kate covered Jill's shaking hand with her own. "The doctor wasn't wrong, Jill. Pa started having headaches like Joseph, and his temper got worse. The harder he tried to control it . . . You know the rest."

"The awful thing is, Pa may not have been sick to begin with. It may have been an idea the doctor planted in his mind." Tears trickled down Jill's cheeks. "What a price Pa paid for getting upset in the wrong place. We'll never know." She wiped her tears on the back of her hand. "What happened to Joseph?"

"Eventually Joseph died of pneumonia. They didn't take care of

402

people in those places in those days." Kate handed Jill a cup. "Drink your coffee."

"And Johnny?" Jill asked, already knowing the answer.

"He was the spit of Joseph," Kate replied. "That terrified Pa. He thought he and Joseph had been taken by the devil, and he tried to beat the same devil out of John."

"I thought so," Jill said. "I always thought it was something like that." Jill took the cup. "Thank you for telling me, Ma. As ghastly as it is, what I'd imagined was worse."

"You thought he did it on purpose?" Kate was ready for "Yes."

"No." Jill shook her head. "I haven't thought that for years, not since before I had my own problems. But I thought something could have been done about it and wasn't."

"You thought I should have done something." Kate nodded, knowing the answer. She waited, defenseless.

"There was *nothing* you could have done. Nothing. I'm amazed you survived."

"What else would I do?"

"But it must have been so difficult for you. Pa was so hard to live with—"

"Your pa was a good man," Kate said firmly. "He had his moods and his tempers, but he wasn't Joseph. He didn't gamble or chase women. He loved me, and I loved him."

"But there was no companionship between you. Young as I was, I saw that. He didn't give you much of a life—"

"He gave me the best life he could," Kate shot back at her, "and you children, too. He gave everything he had in him to give. More. Don't you ever forget that."

Jill slipped both arms around Kate. "You've always said Pa was a saint."

"I'll say that on my deathbed. He suffered so."

Kate sniffed against Jill's shoulder, and Jill held her, grateful for the gift Kate had given—truth that reversed judgments previously rendered. There were no pieces left over, they were all in place, the puzzle complete with the addition of compassion for Pa and admiration for the lady Jill held in her arms.

Kate sat up, pulling her Kateness around her like the blouse Jill watched her tuck in. "The whole day is gone, and this house is a mess. Don't just sit there. Get the vacuum."

403

Jill scanned the spotless kitchen, warned herself not to laugh, and got the vacuum.

They started in the living room, dusting dust-free tables side by side.

"Remember how Pa used to take us out of school every time there was a new exhibit at the Art or Natural Science?" Jill smiled at the memory.

"He loved showing you kids what he called 'Inspirations.' He was never inside a museum himself until he was twenty-three. He said his life might have been different if he'd known as a boy there were such wonders in the world. He wanted you kids to know wonders."

"We did, because Pa showed us," Jill said. "I can remember staring up awestruck at the dinosaur while Pa read us the story. And art. Pa was so prudish, except in the art museum. We could gawk at Rubens and Rodin as much as we liked."

"Your father wasn't prudish. He had morals."

"Yeah, Ma."

They tore clean sheets off perfectly made beds and replaced them with cleaner sheets.

"Remember when Pa took us to see *The Crucible* and muttered the lines under his breath? I loved the play and was so embarrassed. People just glared at us."

"Your father did that at plays. Once I nudged him. He didn't know he'd been saying the lines out loud."

"I know." Jill laughed. "Imagine seven-year-olds seeing Arthur Miller."

They mopped the spotless kitchen floor and vacuumed the lint-free rug.

"Remember the butter pecan?" Jill asked.

"From Memorial Day to Labor Day, ice cream for everyone, every night after dinner. Your father loved butter pecan." Kate smiled.

"And I loved everything else." Jill laughed. "So did John. So did Julie. We'd wait after dinner for Pa to yell 'Treat!' "

"He looked like the Pied Piper walking up the street to the store. He loved to look over his shoulder and see the three of you bouncing behind. On the way home he'd carry whoever got tired on his shoulders."

"I remember sitting up there, pretending to be asleep and just enjoying the ride."

"There were plenty of nights I'd see your pa staggering up the

404

drive with one of you on his shoulders and one under each arm. 'The fresh air got 'em.' He'd grin and help me put you to bed."

"We had some good times, Ma," Jill said softly. Another gift of the truth—all memories thrown open to discussion, even the good ones.

"Of course we did," Kate said matter-of-factly. "Why would you think we didn't?"

"Ma." It was a laugh, and there was a hug that went with it.

They shoved the broom, vacuum, and mop into the closet and the rags under the sink.

"I've got some work to do, Ma. Would you mind if I didn't help with dinner?"

"No," Kate said amenably. "I'm defrosting potpie from the foundrymen's picnic."

"The who?"

"Jim's old union. Last summer. Lakewood Park. We played horseshoes."

"How was it?"

"I beat the old goat."

"I'm not surprised." Jill laughed. "He was probably afraid to win."

"He's not afraid of me," Kate said quickly. "He just likes a woman with grit. Turns out I have grit."

"I knew that."

"I didn't. Sometimes a woman doesn't know what she is till her father is gone and her husband is gone and there's no one left to tell her what to do. Then, for a while, she's lost." Kate sighed. "When you've always gone down someone else's road, you don't know you have a road of your own. But you stumble along, and you find it."

Jill smiled. "Not every woman does."

"Of course they do," Kate said blithely. "If they didn't, they'd just sit down and cry. The street out there isn't full of crying women."

"I'm not so sure about that, Ma. There aren't many with as much grit as you."

"Ah, get along now." Kate waved her away. "Go do your work. I'll call when dinner is ready."

"Okay. Thanks, Ma." Jill was halfway up the steps when she heard Kate call "Jill."

"Yes?"

Kate walked slowly to the foot of the steps, wiping her hands on her apron. "I've made the arrangements for your father's mausoleum," she said slowly. "The cemetery people will take care of every-

405

thing. They said I could have a nice quiet ceremony the day he's
. . . uh . . ."

"Disinterred?"

"That's it. All I could think of was *unburied,* and that sounds like
a horror movie. But, well, I thought Father Norton would be here to
say the prayer, and other than that, just family. Now Jerry's gone
. . . and I don't suppose you . . ." Kate waited.

"When is it, Ma?"

"A few days, maybe a week."

"Ma, I'm so sorry," Jill began, and it wasn't an excuse. She was
sorry. "I don't think I can wait—"

Kate's raised hand stopped her. "I know. I know. You have a job,
too."

"I'm sorry."

Kate looked at Jill, a very long moment, shrugged her shoulders,
and said, "Pa would understand."

"Would he?"

"Pa thought work was important."

"I know. Do you understand, Ma?"

"Since when does anyone worry about what I understand? Why
are you standing there with your mouth running off, keeping me
from dinner? Mother of God!" Kate wiped her clean hands briskly.
"When you kids come home to visit, I don't have a minute's peace."

Kate turned and marched toward the kitchen, a woman with more
than her fair share of grit.

Five minutes later Jill was lost in her story. Even the odors drifting
up the stairs from the kitchen failed to distract her, except for a
fleeting thought that she hadn't eaten all day.

She was interrupted once, by the phone ringing, but before she
could reach to answer it, Kate had picked it up in the kitchen.

Finally Kate called up to her, an old, familiar, piercing "Ji-ll."

"Coming, Ma." Jill flipped the switch on the typewriter and pulled
the page. Done with Act Two before dinner, her goal for the day.

Kate waved Jill to her seat. It occurred to Jill that Kate might enjoy
hearing about the shenanigans at UBC and the folks who thought her
a genius because of one good idea that had worked out.

"Eat your string beans," Kate ordered.

"You know I hate string beans."

"A daughter who can't be here for her father's . . . disimburial can
eat her mother's string beans," Kate said, with perfect Kate-logic.

"Ma." Jill took a bite of the potpie, then gaped at Kate, wondering where she could spit it out. No food had ever tasted like that. Maybe at foundrymen's picnics they throw the potpie and boil the horseshoes.

"Good, isn't it?" Kate chewed heartily.

Jill's head bobbed up and down, her face as red as a Hallowe'en apple.

"You'd better eat fast," Kate advised, dabbing her mouth with her napkin.

"Why do I have to eat fast, Ma?" Jill inquired pleasantly, then gulped her coffee. There was a taste that would linger until Judgment Day, and the skin seemed to be rolling off the roof of her mouth.

"I told Dr. Kaiser you'd be at his house in an hour." Kate resumed chewing.

"You *what*?"

"In an hour," Kate repeated. "He gave me the address. And directions."

"Why?"

"It must be about Julie." Kate stabbed at her potpie. "It must be important."

"But, Ma—"

"A daughter who can't be at her father's dismemberment—"

"I can't go to Neil Kaiser's *house,* for God's sake."

"For Julie."

"I can't—"

An hour and ten minutes later Jill drove up a sharp incline that led to Neil's house. She would have been on time had she not been forced to stop several times to reread the directions. Kate's jottings were mysterious, the squiggly lines even more so, and instead of proper street names, she'd written *Turn left at the Fazio's market, Turn right at Olenik's Sohio.* Jill couldn't fault Kate for that. She'd only written what Neil obviously had dictated—a guide to food and fuel stops on the way to his house.

Neil's house was set well back from the street in what, during the daytime, would have been a lush and lovely grove of trees. The drive circled to the rear of the house, and Jill followed it, pulling up beside a car that had to be Neil's, a long, low Chrysler or Cadillac, painted Panzer gray.

Jill stood in the driveway, gawking at Neil's house; a Hansel-and-Gretel cottage with dormers and eaves, multitudinous gingerbread

407

thingamabobs and a thatched roof that dipped over sugarspun windows almost to the driveway. It was a haven for elves, a nook in search of a cranny . . . a . . . She checked Kate's directions again. Yup, it was Neil's house.

Timidly she tapped on the door, hoping the witch hadn't arrived before her and stuck poor Neil in the oven.

She tapped louder, then noticed a doorbell. She pressed it. There was a disconcerting *tinkle, tinkle,* followed by the sound of a door being unlatched, followed by the door opening, followed by Neil's beaming face.

"Come in, come in."

She walked past him into a hallway furnished from Disney, featuring a table and bench where seven dwarfs might have supped, and beyond that, through an archway, a living room where Gepetto's easy chair faced the Wicked Witch's oval mirror.

"Like it?" Neil asked as he led the way to the living room.

"It's . . . uh . . . unusual," Jill replied.

"Yeah." He shrugged. "Actually the wife picked it out. You know, the one with all the kids. The one I divorced. Remember, the one who ran off—"

"I remember. You told me." Jill stared at a triple-bed-sized purple divan at one end of the room. The Wicked Witch again? Or had Beauty slept there? Behind it stood a monolith of a cabinet, solid oak from floor to ceiling with double doors and heavy brass hardware. She was sure if she opened it, *Fantasia* would fly out.

"The wife picked this place and then furnished it. Course, the kids thought it was . . . hip . . . hep . . . groovy . . . whatever kids think. I got it in the divorce settlement."

"Why?" Jill had to ask.

"That's the way divorce settlements are," he said darkly. "I'll find a more suitable place as soon as I can unload this. Know anyone who'd like to buy it?"

"Uh . . . not offhand." Jill was suddenly shy. "May I ask a question, Neil?"

"Ask away. I'll pour us a drink." From a long plank hewn by Robin in Sherwood, Neil fetched a tray with martini-shaker and glasses. He placed them on the floor before the godawful grape settee. "Sit here with me." He patted the plush.

But Jill had already thrown herself into Gepetto's chair, preferring a conversation that spanned the length of the room to perching next to Neil on a . . . mattress? She blushed. Obviously *her* thought. Neil seemed untroubled, unaware of lascivious vibes that hung from the beams along with the gingerbread. "Thank you," Jill said politely. "I'm quite comfortable here."

"Your question?" He poured a quintuple martini into a beaker-shaped glass.

"Is manic depression hereditary?"

"Tendencies sometimes. Environment or heredity . . . there are diverse schools of thought. Whether it's some chemistry that gets passed on to the child, or he or she unconsciously mimics parental behavior, who knows?" He waved the glass at her. "Drink?"

"No, thanks. I'm rather tired, and I have to drive home."

"If you get sleepy, I'll put you up for the night," he offered casually.

"I won't drink, and I won't get sleepy." Jill smiled, thinking that in this house besides getting sleepy, she could also get Dopey and Sneezy and Doc.

"Bottoms up." Neil chuckled, then, while Jill watched in disbelief, he drained the glass in one gulp.

Jill gasped. "Are you in some kind of contest?"

"So, though tendencies can be inherited, manic depression isn't, not in the strictest sense. At least not like green eyes and auburn hair, which, may I say, is my favorite combination."

"Thank you. You say there can be an unconscious adoption of parental behavior—"

"Let's not talk mental illness. It depresses me." He shivered his distaste. "Want another martini?"

"I haven't had one."

"Thanks. Don't mind if I do." He refilled the beaker. Faster than Jill could have said "Hi-ho, hi-ho," he gurgled it down.

"My mother said you wanted to talk about Julie," Jill probed.

"Your sister will be fine. Don't worry."

"I'm glad to hear that, Neil." Jill smiled. "I know she's in good hands."

"Her problem isn't that complicated. Not that much of a challenge. I get cases like hers all the time. . . . all the time . . . double time . . . hup. Want another martini?"

"No."

"Maybe one for the road." He refilled his glass and surprised Jill by sipping.

"I have to ask. . . . You're not considering shock treatments, are you? I mean, you didn't prescribe them for me. I don't want shock treatments for Julie."

"I agree. Don't like 'em either. Never did a damn thing for me."

"*You!*" Jill choked. "*You* had shock treatments?"

"When?" He leaped to his feet.

"What?" Jill bounded from Gepetto's chair.

Neil dabbed at the martini that had sloshed on his shirt. "What the hell are we talking about?"

"I'm not sure." Jill was torn between helping Neil mop, or making a break for the gingerbread door. "I thought we were talking about Julie, then you said you had shock treatments, then . . ."

"This isn't working out." He subtitled the obvious.

"Perhaps we should talk tomorrow, at the hospital," Jill suggested. "Or I can come to your office. I'm very tired and you're . . . you're . . ."

"Drinking?" His gaze was steady, something of a triumph as the rest of him wobbled.

"Perhaps I've caught you at a difficult time," Jill said with the diplomacy of one who's been caught at less than her best. The day you go crazy is the day all your neighbors drop in to borrow sugar.

"This *is* a difficult time. That's why I wanted to talk to you." With exaggerated care Neil set the beaker on the tray and walked toward her. "We have so much in common, Jill. Sensitivity, intelligence, finely tuned sensibilities . . ."

Jill hoped Neil wouldn't come any closer. Her finely tuned sensibilities were twanging like a Javanese xylophone. "Neil, I—"

"You care about me," he interrupted. "Admit it."

They met in the center of the room and faced one another, standing exactly one foot apart.

"Well?" he said expectantly. "Admit it."

"I do care." Jill admitted it, as directed.

"Good. That's a start." He smiled. "Look, we can't stand here like a textbook illustration of the moment before flight or fight."

He laughed, and Jill laughed with him.

"We can't shout across this stupid room. Sit with me, please."

Jill sat next to Neil, feeling stiff, self-conscious, and very, very wrong. She didn't want to hear about his current life crisis, and she thought that was brattish, selfish of her. She didn't want to hear about his divorce or his children or—yet again and she knew it was coming —about what he'd done for her. She'd admitted she cared, and she did, but now that she was there with his thigh touching hers, she cared about other things more. Most of all she didn't want to sleep with him, and, confused, she searched for the reasons within her. That he was lousy at it didn't really count. So, there had to be other, more complex . . . She listened for a voice whispering reasons, motivations, compulsions, reaction formations . . .

Goddammit, I don't want to!

Startled, she backed away from herself, thinking *Okay, okay, don't shout.*

It was as shocking as a handful of ice down her back, this simple "I don't want to!" *Is that reason enough,* she wondered? *Will it hold up in court?*

"Penny for your thoughts?"

"Just sort of drifting along."

"I'm going to see to it that you get some rest, young lady," Neil said firmly. "All this traipsing cross-country is exhausting."

"It's not that bad, Neil. I'm not too decrepit yet. Still have my own teeth." Jill braced herself. She could hear something, destiny or doom, approaching like a runaway train.

"You're beautiful. And far from decrepit. That's not what I mean. You always return to Cleveland, Jill. There's a reason for that, you know."

"My family's here, Neil."

"It's more than that. Your future is here. Your future with me. Have we discussed marriage?"

"Uh . . ." They had, or rather Neil had, and then denied he had, and then . . . *shit!* "Whose marriage?"

"Ours." Neil laughed. "What a little goosey you are."

"Goosey?"

"I wish it was spring! I wish it was June. Even May would be marvelous," Neil rhapsodized. "But November will have to do. We'll get married next weekend."

"Weekend! We can't."

Neil reached for her hand. "There comes a time in a man's life when he has to claim what's his."

"Neil, listen." Jill squeezed his hand, looking straight into his eyes. "I don't know you. You don't know me."

"We're alike, you and I. . . ."

"Neil! We don't know that! I've known you only as my doctor. You

411

know me solely as a patient. We've never known one another as people. I met you in 1971 and up till a month ago I've never seen you without a white coat."

"What's my coat got to do with it?" He was angry.

"A doctor-patient relationship is not a basis for marriage, Neil. First we'd have to know one another as a man named Neil and a woman named Jill. That takes time."

"Time?" he said bitterly. "I have nothing but time, and loneliness, and depression. I need you now."

"I know what you're going through, Neil. I've gone through it, too. Divorce hurts, hurts like hell."

"You don't care about me." He turned away from her.

"I do. I always have. What little I know of you, I care about very much."

"Then we'll get married." He patted her hand, smiling as though it was settled.

"I . . . uh . . . er . . . Neil?"

He nuzzled at her neck. "Hhhmmmmmm?"

"I don't want to marry you." She held her breath, expecting to be struck by lightning. Or Neil.

I want. I don't want. Dangerous words.

Words to live by, finally, finally.

"You don't want to?" he echoed, looking at her as though he *might* have heard wrong. "You don't want to?"

"I can't marry someone I don't know! I don't *want* to marry someone I don't know!"

"You don't want to?" Neil shouted. "Since when have you known what you wanted? The first time I met you, all you wanted was to kill yourself. Christ! You've never known what you wanted unless I was there to tell you."

"I think I'd better go." Jill stood up, with Neil wobbling to his feet behind her.

"I never walked out on you, Jill. I was there when you needed me, for as long as you needed me."

"I paid you, Neil." She hadn't meant to say that, but there it was, solid as concrete and undeniable.

"What?" His face was the color of her concrete truth.

"I paid you fifty dollars an hour, Neil. I needed a good psychiatrist, and that's what you were. I hired you to help me."

"You can't put a price on the care that I gave you."

"*You* did," Jill said quietly, hoping her controllable flow of determination would carry her down the road she'd chosen. "Besides, I don't think it's me you fell in love with at all. You fell in love with your cure."

"You think, you think!" His voice was a furious singsong. "For two goddamned years you didn't know what you thought unless you asked me first."

"I'm leaving, Neil."

"You do and I'll kill myself!" he roared behind her. He ran the barricade of the divan and flung open the door of the monolith cupboard.

Jill gasped. "What's that?"

There were three tiers of gun racks holding guns of every description.

"My gun collection!" he shouted. "The only fucking thing in this whole fucking house that belongs to me!"

"Tell me about your guns, Neil." As frightened as she was, Jill tried to soothe him. "They aren't loaded, are they?"

"Loaded and ready." He looked back over his shoulder. His face was bloodless. "I . . . love . . . to . . . shoot."

"Come away from there, Neil." Jill edged toward him. "You've had too much to drink. I'll help you lie down. In the morning you'll have a better perspective."

"No! You don't know how I'm hurting! Too much! Too long!" He snatched a rifle from the rack, waving it, trying to position it, butt over barrel, aimed at his head.

"Stop!" Jill made a flying leap that took her headfirst over the divan and into his belly. As they crashed to the floor the gun went off with a shattering crack. The bullet whined, pinging against brass hardware, then ricocheted, whistling until it struck and killed the Wicked Witch's oval mirror.

"Oh, God," Jill moaned, half-buried in Neil. "Oh, God."

She struggled to regain her feet. Removing herself from Neil was like climbing out of a soft, lumpy bed. "Oh, God."

Finally she was on her feet, gazing down at him. His eyes were closed and his breathing, while not exactly normal, was not that of a man in extremis. It was more of a snore.

"Oh, God." Jill checked the back of his head. No lumps, no cuts. She tried to remember if an abrasion was the same as a cut. Whatever it was, he hadn't struck his head.

"He's passed out," Jill breathed. "Oh, God."

What to do? she pondered. She could call an ambulance, but that would mean police, and that would mean a story in the paper. Neil would not forgive her. Neither would Kate.

"Who am I kidding?" she said out loud. "That's not something I need either."

She'd told Neil she was going home, and that's what she would do. *I'm a woman of my word.*

She considered covering him with a blanket, but that would mean a trip to the bedroom, and, all things considered, Neil's bedroom was a place she didn't want to see. He probably slept in a coffin.

She snapped the automatic lock on the inside of the door, then closed it behind her. Neil would be safe from intruders. More to the point, intruders would be safe from Neil.

She started the car engine, thinking that someday she'd laugh about this, perhaps when her mind was gone.

"So," she intoned as she pulled into the street, "as we bid fond farewell to the enchanted cottage . . ."

Neil would feel like a horse's ass in the morning, she knew. Jill wondered if she'd ever be able to face him again. She shivered, more with embarrassment than anger. Her father had often said that you can't hold a man accountable for the fool he makes of himself drunk, but then Pa was Irish, and defense of unregenerate boozers was written into his genetic code.

Still, there was some truth to it.

That's tomorrow's problem, and when tomorrow comes, I'll do whatever seems best. To me.

She drove toward Kate's, reflecting on the mystery of how a terrible day can also be a wonderful day. Terrible and wonderful. Bridges burned. Bridges crossed.

The best of times and the worst of times. Perhaps it's always like that. The best and the worst together. In every time, every age.

Like childhood. Every one traumatic. Pain, grief, loss, misunderstanding. And wonder. "Inspirations." Ice cream. Rides home on shoulders. Being tucked into bed. Hugs. Hits. Fear. Comfort. Nightmares. Morning.

The best of times and the worst of times. The only childhood we have.

I want to call Daisy.

She opened the door, hoping Kate had gone to bed but planning to tell her a soothing "Julie's fine" story if she hadn't.

414

She smiled in the semidarkness as she realized that with the beginning of her play, she'd ceased regarding herself as a liar and begun seeing herself as a storyteller. If nothing else, she'd revised one of her self-imposed labels to one she liked better.

Kate was waiting in the kitchen, coffee cup in hand.

"Daisy called," Kate said. "Call her back."

Jill's heart stopped. "Something's wrong with Daisy."

"Daisy's fine. Just call." Kate sipped her coffee. She didn't say "How's Dr. Kaiser? What's wrong with Julie?"

Jill called. There was only one ring. "Hello." A very small Daisy-voice answered.

With no fear of "Oh, Mom!" Jill asked, "Daisy, what's wrong?"

"You've got to come home, Mom," Daisy sobbed. "Patti Gerard is dead!"

CHAPTER 26

Patti's life had been a Mardi Gras of men; her funeral was attended by women.

Outside, an empathetic sky loosed torrents, stranding disgruntled tourists in crayon-painted Budget cars.

Inside, the chapel seemed like a set dressed for a funeral scene with extravagant, waxy floral arrangements, elegant tapers flickering discreetly, soft lights with a discreet spot on the coffin, and the coffin itself, Silver Cloud Rolls in color with baroque fittings, an overgrown jewelry box that would have set Patti hooting had she been in the pew with Jill.

Sitting next to Daisy, Jill listened to a rented minister intone scripted comfort as the organist struck reverent, nondenominational chords.

How Patti would have laughed at this, howled, shrieked, made manic fun, but only of course if it had been some hapless acquaintance. For herself, she would have despised it. On Patti's behalf Jill despised it, too.

Where are the men? Jill wondered, the men Patti had cherished, though cherished wasn't the word. Jill hoped that wherever they were, they were thinking of Patti. She doubted it. By now they had other Pattis, women who would also mime cherishing, who would pretend cherishing was the only word.

Then, too, the men would be leery of attending the funeral of a woman who'd died of her own volition. To appear on such an occasion would invite speculation, whispers of "Did she do it because of him?" What these men had in common, besides Patti, was prudence. Prudence and suicide notes.

Patti had scattered suicide notes like May baskets, leaving them in mailboxes all over town. She'd forgotten no one—friends, business associates, customers, lovers, the panoply of her life as she went about closing that bankrupt business down. They were chipper little notes, the kind written on the bottom of Christmas cards. For customers, there was thanks for their support and advice on their best colors, for business associates, more thanks and tips on fashion trends, and for lovers, who knew? The lovers weren't talking.

The L.A. *Times* ran a feature obituary about up-and-coming Patti Gerard who up and went after writing cheerful bread-and-butter letters full of pragmatic advice, messages far removed from suicide notes, had they not all begun "By the time you read this, I'll be dead. . . ."

Daisy had found Patti's note fluttering under the doormat, read it, and wordlessly handed it to Steve, who'd skimmed it, then dashed into Jill's house to call the Encino police. In his haste he'd left Daisy on the doorstep, rain and tears mingling on her face as she struggled with her first wholeheartedly unwelcome rite of passage—Patti was the first person she'd known who died.

The police informed Steve that he was the eighth call they'd received that morning. They'd acted promptly, they'd said, and had sped off, sirens blaring.

They'd found Patti dead, in her hand an empty bottle of pills prescribed to alleviate depression. Her body had been claimed by her business manager.

Steve had met Jill's plane, a thoughtful gesture she'd appreciated, and taken her for a dinner she could only stare at. He'd waited until coffee arrived to hand her the note. Jill read it, refolded it, and tucked it into her purse while Steve sat silent, prepared to dry tears Jill was too angry to shed.

Patti had written:

By the time you read this, I'll be dead, but promise no tears, or I'll come back to haunt you. It's been fun, kid, but you know me. I gotta keep moving. If the myths are true, there's a life beyond this, and maybe in that one commitments come easy. But what the hell? Can you picture me married to an accountant anyway? Playing wifey in the suburbs just ain't my style. Who needs him? Who the fuck needs him? Leastways that's what I told him. Whistling Christ, how men carry on! I called to tell you about this terrific one-nighter I had— a hitchhiker, can you believe it? Dangerous, huh? Just added more spice. Since you were out of town and you're the only one I share these stories with—I'll have to take this one with me.

Read Dress for Success. *NOW. I'm the only one who'll ever tell you —you dress like an uptight Gypsy. Best friend stuff, strictly. Sorry we never had our shopping spree. Busy, busy, both of us.*

If the Prince arrives at your door, slam it quick. The slipper in his hand is booby-trapped. Don't fall in love, kid. It's a killer. Love, Patti.

Called . . . best friend . . . out of town . . . killer . . . okay. That's what she was supposed to feel. Jill knew that. She knew it because Patti had woven the accusation like a malignant threat through her letter. She also knew it because, once upon a suicidal morning, she'd woven her own dark thread around Steve. "If you had come through for me . . ." she'd accused, veins spurting. "It's your fault."

Oh, Patti. I know the pain you went through. But Steve's wasn't the hand that reached for my razor, and mine wasn't the hand that reached for your pills. I know how angry you must have been, and I'm sorry, but I'm also angry at you. You can't be replaced. I'll miss you. I'll hold on to my anger for now. It's easier to bear than the grief. The anger will pass. The grief will go on forever.

The service finally ended with a burst of platitudes rocketing over their heads like a fireworks display. Jill reached for Daisy's hand. It was icy.

"You okay?" Jill asked.

Daisy nodded yes. "You?"

"Fine." Jill returned that polite lie, then winced as Julie, John, Kate and "Let's Pretend" ripped through her mind. "No, Daisy, I'm not fine," she whispered. "My best friend is dead, and I'm hurting. I feel lousy that I wasn't here when she needed me. And I'm angry because she did what she did."

"So am I!" Daisy whispered, round-eyed with surprise. "And I was feeling guilty about it. It's awful to be angry at someone who's dead."

"No. It's normal, Daisy. Everyone gets angry when someone they love leaves them. Death makes the loss final, and suicide makes it deliberate. There's reason for anger and nothing to feel guilty about."

"I'll miss her." Daisy sighed. "She treated me like a grown-up." Tears trickled down Daisy's cheeks, but she looked relieved at not having to be "fine."

Hand in hand, they joined the procession of women in the aisle. *Where are the men?*

Some of the women had been Patti's customers, identifiable by the designer labels they wore, along with a faint impatience as though socially prescribed attendance at the funeral service had screwed up their lunch plans. The exquisite Oriental lady sitting alone in a pew had to be Tai Ling, weeping genuine tears for her mentor. There were others, crisp business associates dressed for success stealing overt glances at dainty watches, late for dog-eat-dog lives. There were several girls who looked like models, either made up as though for the cover of *Vogue* or scrubbed clean and astonishingly drab, their professional faces left home to rest on the makeup table.

As they entered what in a Catholic church would be called the vestibule but in this fabricated place was most likely the wings, Jill felt a tug at her elbow. She turned, startled to see a face she recognized.

The picture that Alex carried in his wallet did scant justice to Nina Friedman. She was stunning, as simply and naturally flawless as a perfect rose.

"I'm Nina Friedman." Her voice was a zephyr. "I recognized you from the picture in *Variety*. Alex pointed you out."

"I'm happy to meet you." Jill remembered the picture, which had appeared following Dan's departure. Alex had been miffed that *Variety* hadn't requested his.

"I'm happy to meet you," Jill said. "I'm sorry it has to be here. This is my daughter, Daisy."

"How do you do," Daisy said, and shook hands with Nina as if shaking hands came naturally to her.

Nina smiled, and Jill felt her sweetness in the way she smelled her perfume. It enveloped her.

"I'd love to have a daughter someday," Nina said wistfully. "Alex said maybe in a few years. . . ." She smiled, a professional watch-the-birdie smile. "He's guiding my career, you know. He thinks I can be another Farrah . . . or a Suzanne . . . or a somebody. He's setting up meetings for me. He says he's getting me launched. I feel like a ship, a dinghy." She giggled self-consciously, then looked around quickly as though she'd made an unforgivable gaffe. "Oh dear, I didn't mean to laugh. I'll really miss Patti. She was so funny, so full of life. Oh." Her hand covered her mouth, and her eyes filled with tears. "I'm sorry. I always say the wrong thing. Alex says I'm to look at, not listen to. I should never open my mouth."

"You're right about Patti," Jill said quickly. "She was funny, and the part of her that was healthy was very full of life. Remember her that way. Okay?"

"Okay." Nina sighed. "Well, I should go now. Alex signed me up for acting classes, and today's my fourth one."

"Do you like it?" Jill asked.

"I throw up. Alex said I'll get over it." She sighed deeply, then added brightly, "and I'm sure I will. Who in their right mind would pass up an opportunity to be an actress, maybe a star? I'm lucky to have Alex behind me."

"Lucky," Jill said, thinking she'd use another word, like *doomed*.

"He wants what's best for me," Nina said with conviction. "He says I'll be a natural once my stomach settles down." She tapped her purse. "I carry Compozine. Well, nice to have met you. Gotta run."

And run she did, literally, dashing through pelting rain, down chapel steps with her purse held aloft, negligible protection against elements beyond her control.

"She's gorgeous, isn't she, Mom?" Daisy's awe was apparent.

"She is," Jill agreed, and Kate's words echoed in her head—*Sometimes a woman doesn't know she has a road of her own.* "I hope she'll be safe on the road Alex has chosen for her."

"What?" Daisy asked.

"The rain's letting up," Jill observed. "We'd better make a run for it."

They did, dodging the raindrops and jumping the puddles. They were dripping when they reached the car. Jill started the engine while Daisy shook herself like a wet poodle.

"It doesn't seem right that I should go to school this morning," Daisy said. "Patti just died, and I'll walk into English class as though it was just another day."

"You'll know it isn't," Jill consoled her. "That's what they mean when they say life goes on." She glanced at Daisy's face, her expression of angry distaste. "I know. I hate it, too. When someone close to me dies, I feel the world should stop, pay attention. Well, we're paying attention, Daisy. We have, and we will. Patti was part of our world, and she was worth it."

"It's too bad Patti didn't have a real family," Daisy said thoughtfully. "You know you won't be forgotten when you leave a family behind."

"True." Jill had to smile. "For the next twenty years at least there's someone at the Thanksgiving table saying 'Remember how Harriet loved sweet potatoes?' or 'What's that old joke Frank used to tell?' A family makes a difference, both before and after you're gone."

"Does your family make a difference?" Daisy asked, averting her face so carefully that Jill knew the question was important.

"Of course," Jill assured her, "particularly you."

"I mean . . . with a family you're not so likely to get . . . bent again . . . like Patti." Daisy's voice was low. "Are you?"

"You mean depressed?" Jill flipped the light signaling left. "Everyone gets depressed sometimes." She turned left, intending to say a few comforting words about the transient nature of most depression, then suddenly realized exactly what it was her daughter was asking. She swerved to the curb, cut the engine, and said, "Daisy, look at me."

Daisy stared out the windshield, head lowered, fists jammed into pockets. Jill reached out, gently tipping Daisy's face toward her.

"You're asking if I'm going to get depressed and kill myself, aren't you?"

"I didn't mean—" Daisy tried to wriggle away.

"You think that because Patti did, I might," Jill went on, determined to pull Daisy's fantasy from the shadows, with no pieces left over.

"Patti wasn't supposed to kill herself!" It was a wail of betrayal. "She was supposed to be well."

"Oh, honey." Jill put her arms around Daisy, who remained still, fearful of a further and even more profound betrayal. "Patti used to tell me she'd transformed herself, but she hadn't. The Patti you knew was a role that she played. I think she was beginning to play it when I met her in the hospital—put-together Patti, jokes for all occasions. She warned me to never let anyone know I was hurting. They'd go for my throat, she said. She never let anyone know she was hurting, and in the end she went for her own throat. Patti never got well, Daisy. She didn't have a second nervous breakdown. She never got over the first."

"What about you?" Daisy faltered. "How do I know—"

Jill guided Daisy's fingers to her cheek. "Feel. No paint. And I'm hurting, honey. A lot. I don't need to hide that from you."

Jill searched Daisy's troubled face, knowing that her first confrontation with life's brutal unpredictability would require some time for recovery, time and as much reassurance as Jill could give.

"Listen, honey. There's an old definition of an emotionally healthy person. It goes: 'An emotionally healthy person is one with a capacity for work and love.' Simple, isn't it? No magic. No jargon. I've always liked it, even though it gives me the responsibility. I'm the one who has to work. I'm the one who has to love. And I do. I have work I'm good at, even new work I might explore, and people I love. You. My family. Your dad as a friend. You are obviously in the company of an emotionally healthy person. You don't have to worry about me."

"You're not just saying that?"

"I promise you," Jill said firmly. "I promise you I won't do what Patti did. I'm not Patti, honey. Believe me."

"I believe you," Daisy said and, to Jill's relief, sounded sure.

Jill started the car and eased into traffic, knowing that for a while Daisy's optimism would be fragile, her faith in the certainties she'd taken for granted easily shaken.

This is the time to stay close, Jill decided, not to intrude but to be there.

They drove toward school in a heavy silence Daisy was the first to break. "None of your boyfriends have called, Mom." Her matter-of-factness betrayed her curiosity.

Jill smiled. "I'm not surprised. I have no boyfriends right now. There are no men in my life."

"Why not?" an astonished Daisy demanded.

Jill laughed. Daisy's question sounded as though she had carelessly lost them somewhere. "I didn't plan it, honey. It happened. And I'm not unhappy about it. Sometimes it's good to be alone for a while. Then there's no doubt about whose road you're traveling."

"So Suave and Sexy turned out to be nerds, huh?" Daisy reached her conclusion.

"They are what they are. It's more that the game wasn't worth the candle. Know that expression?"

"No."

"In the days before electricity, candles were expensive and precious. Families had to choose between going to bed at dusk or staying up for recreation that required lighting a candle. They only played games that were worth the candle."

"I like that," Daisy decided. "I'll remember that the next time I have a decision to make. If it isn't worth the candle . . ." She smiled and rolled her eyes, a welcome return to Daisy. "You aren't going to sit home every night and worry about me, are you?"

"I doubt it." Jill grinned assurance. "You don't give me much to worry about, and besides, I'm not renouncing romance, Daisy, just taking some time for myself."

"That's wise," Daisy said solemnly as Jill tried not to laugh. "I didn't think too much of old Suave and Sexy, but I wouldn't want you dried up and cranky, either."

"No chance of that." And this time she did laugh. "While I'm resting and stockpiling candles, I'll try not to get underfoot."

"I think I can manage until your next boyfriend. Maybe he'll even be Dad. Here we are."

Jill rolled to a stop, smiling at Daisy's tenacity. "I'll see you tonight, honey."

She reached to hug Daisy, intensely aware of the feeling of love, its unchangeable, limitless quality, and the unwavering nature of absolute commitment. And the joy. If only Patti had known that there could also be joy.

"You and I won't forget Patti," she whispered to Daisy. "We'll be the family who remembers."

"I'll remember her pizzazz." Daisy smiled through misty tears. "I'll remember the drive up the coast and the talk we had on the beach."

"And we'll go shopping. You'll help me pick out one beige dress. I'll wear it and think of Patti. Okay?"

"Okay."

"Now, go. You're late for English, and I'm late for whatever comes next. And, honey, ask Lenny to dinner tonight if you'd like."

"Are you cooking?" Daisy asked quickly.

"Don't panic, I was thinking of pizza."

"Good deal. See you tonight."

Another quick hug and Daisy was gone, her invitation to Lenny in mind, her life going on.

Jill turned the car toward UBC, wondering about her own life's direction. She could feel change around her, as definite as the first Winesap-crisp air that always heralded the beginning of autumn. It was something beyond her dissolution of the great boyfriend cartel, her resolution to save candles for a relationship that offered something more substantial than a surfeit of sex and a starvation of passion. In a sense, Patti had starved herself to death.

But what of the change she was feeling? She turned into the UBC parking lot, her mind spinning possibilities.

423

Perhaps Neiman was about to have her crowned Queen of UBC, with a velvet-draped throne installed in her office. Or, more likely, seeing as she hadn't returned his phone call, he was about to hire assassins for a discreet mid-day garroting, nothing fancy, just *aaaarrrggghhh* and out.

At the elevator, Jill ran into the young program executive, Kenny, who was attempting to carry one huge box while kicking another before him.

"It looks like you're carrying your entire office," Jill told him. "Where are you going?"

"Home. I just got fired." Kenny shook his head in disgust. "They gave me five minutes to get out."

"Why?" Jill was astounded. Kenny had seemed such a buttoned-down sort.

"I got fired because of *That's Disgusting,*" he said bitterly. "The people who produce that show have found a guy who's willing to stick his arm in a tank of piranhas."

"That's sick!"

"That's what I said, and that's what I told the producer. So he called Neiman, screaming that it was his show, he'd do what he liked, and, incidentally, who the fuck was I? You know Neiman." Kenny shrugged. "He folded in the middle, apologized, and offered my head as appeasement."

"I'm sorry."

"*You're* sorry. *I* just bought a house," Kenny sputtered. "Know what they should put on *That's Disgusting?* Neiman. Old ladies would puke."

"Most old ladies I know have seen worse. . . . Need some help with those boxes?"

"I'll do it. I'd better work off some of this mad before I get home. If I kick the dog, he'll just kick me back." Knees buckling, Kenny headed for the door. "I wish you luck, Jill. You'll need it. You're staying."

Jill stepped into the elevator, wondering why Kenny's "Good luck" should feel like a curse.

Her outer office was empty. No Polly, and the phone ringing off the hook.

"Hello?"

"Polly?" an elegant voice inquired.

"No, she's not here. May I take a message?"

There was an abrupt click, and the phone went dead. Jill hung up, puzzled. Why was Angela Kent calling Polly?

A few moments later the phone rang, and this time the mellifluous tones of Syco Fontaine purred a "Hello" in Jill's ear. His tones dimmed to dumpy when Jill identified herself. Then he too hung up.

"What the hell's going on?" Jill demanded of Polly's empty chair. "And where in the world are you?"

She settled herself at her desk, rehearsing the speech she'd planned for her inevitable moment with Neiman. The answer he wanted was *yes*. A *no* could cause mouth-frothing and other unseemly disorders, but how he'd react to *maybe* was anyone's guess.

Yet *maybe* was the answer she'd given to Steve when he volunteered, with an amusement that was only slightly patronizing, to act as her "people." Jill had told him she wanted time to think, mull the whole thing over. She hadn't confided her intuition about the change she felt coming. Had she done so, Steve's patronizing might be more than slight, perhaps including a return to that old dependable "crazy." She'd wait until the change arrived. Steve might regard intuition in the same light as little green men, but he was a consummate respecter of reality.

The phone rang again. Jill answered it quickly. "Polly's office, hired hand speaking."

There was a gasp and another abrupt click, this time no surprise.

Jill emptied her briefcase of scripts, notes, and notations Polly would transform into memos, if indeed she ever saw Polly again. Her unfinished play was the last out of the case. With no more than a cursory glance she slipped it into a drawer, which she closed, then opened again. The play had a life of its own. It would not be stuck in a drawer and forgotten.

Jill read through it quickly, her mind bouncing between the words she'd written and images of the people who were the source of those words—Kate, Julie, herself. The best of times and the worst of times, unburnable bridges.

Jill was beginning to wonder if Polly might be ill when she steamed through the door, hair flying, notebook in hand, and breathless. "I didn't think I'd be gone that long." She threw her notebook into a chair and collapsed on it. "I'm drained, totally drained." She sighed, then smiled sympathetically at Jill. "And you look exhausted. No wonder. Your friend's funeral on top of your trip. How is your sister?"

"She'll be fine." Jill looked at Polly curiously.

"I feel she will. But I sense another upset coming her way."

"Please don't tell me," Jill begged. "I can only deal with today's problems today. If I look any farther, I'll be buried under an avalanche of karma."

"I wish everyone around here felt that way." Polly sighed. "This bunch is crazy for karma."

Jill nodded. "That's why everyone's calling you. Predictions by Polly."

"Even Neiman," Polly said. "He wants to know if you'll sign your contract."

"What did you tell him?"

"I told him I see a change coming for you. Might be a new contract, might not."

"Bet that made him happy."

"You know that greenish tinge he gets sometimes? When I left his office he was the color of Key lime pie."

"Ugh." Jill shuddered. "Even dimpled and rosy, the man is a toad."

"Your contract is only one of his concerns," Polly confided. "Neiman's been a basket-case since Lawrence went into his slump."

"What slump? Neiman didn't mention a slump on the phone."

"Does the pilot tell the passengers the plane is going down?" Polly asked rhetorically. "Ever since Carolyn McCaffery took Donny away, Lawrence's been in the conference room, pushing computer buttons and sighing. Just sighing."

"The sighing is new, but the button-pushing isn't. Lawrence uses Abelard to program."

"Not anymore," Polly explained. "That's why Neiman's so crazed. Lawrence locks himself in the conference room, playing Abelard like an organist gone mad. Lights flash, thunderbooms rock, and lasers shoot holes in the ceiling, but when Neiman asks Lawrence what Abelard is saying, Lawrence just sighs."

"Lawrence won't interpret Abelard!" Jill was astonished. It was as though Moses had come down from Sinai with the tablets under his arm only to tell the expectant multitudes they could damn well guess the Commandments. No wonder Neiman was crazed, deprived of his *shalts* and *shalt nots.*

"And, of course, no one else can interpret Abelard, so . . ."

"Who wouldn't want to sign a twelve-year contract with UBC, Polly? Everyone is so sane here, I should work for free, just for the joy of it." Jill frowned as random twos suddenly added up to a logical four. "Polly, who's programing this network?"

"Well . . ." Polly was suddenly engrossed in her cuticles.

"Polly, look at me," Jill commanded. Polly did, sheepishly, but with what Kate would have called "the devil's own gleam" in her eye. Jill exploded with laughter. *"You are!"*

"I didn't say that."

"You didn't have to." Jill whooped as Polly's valiant attempt at restraint dissolved into helpless mirth.

"Oh, well," Polly said modestly.

"You're running the whole goddamned network!" Jill howled, eyes beginning to tear.

Polly giggled. "It's a filthy job, but someone must do it."

"Oh, Polly, I love it!" Jill sat back, helpless with laughter and thinking it made perfect sense. Any business improves when run on the advice of someone who's usually right.

"Why are you still typing my memos? I should think they'd have you in an office somewhere with a secretary of your own."

"Are you kidding?" Polly's laughter quit cold. "Do you actually think any of these people would admit they consult a psychic? Not on your life. They call me furtively, as nervous and whispery as though they were arranging a drug connection. And it's always a matter of life and death. Once I get there, it's 'What do you think about this, Polly?' and 'What should I do about that?' Ten minutes later when we pass in the hall, they don't know me. And if anyone asks if they've spoken to me, they deny it flat out or else say, 'Who? That kook?' "

"That's not fair."

"That's life. Mine anyway."

"Why don't you quit this job and go into the psychic business?" Jill asked. "Make them pay for what you do."

"I've thought about it," Polly admitted. "But when you're a psychic, half the people you meet think you're some kind of nut and the other half just want what you can do. Then, too, when someone consults me and I sense something terrible about to happen, I get sick. If I'm not honest about what I sense, I'm letting the person down. If I am . . . You can see what I mean."

"You're right, Polly. It's a very complicated business. Very hard," Jill said sympathetically.

"Sometimes people even blame you for the bad news you give them, thinking you're making it happen."

"That's ridiculous! Only a moron would do that."

"Neiman threatened to fire me if you don't sign your contract."

"Oh, Polly!"

"I'm not going to get fired," Polly said placidly.

"You're not?"

"No, but that doesn't mean I like being threatened, especially by chartreuse toads."

"How do you know you won't—" Jill grinned and then laughed. "Excuse me for asking."

"I knew you would," Polly said straight-faced, and that set them off into giggles again.

"Hey, man," Alex said from the doorway. "I'm glad Superwoman has time to yuk it up. We mortals are too fucking busy working our asses off."

"Hello, Alex. Come in. What happened to your face?"

"Fucking nothin' happened to my fucking face. I want to see you alone." He glared at Polly as though expecting her to vaporize.

"It looks like someone took a blowtorch to it. Why are you peeling?" Jill wondered if Alex had been washing his face in Kate's pot-pies.

"A tanning salon just opened down the street," Polly explained. "Alex is into *Los Angeles* image. Hustle twelve hours a day, and look like you spend your life on the beach."

"Who asked you?"

"Nobody," Polly said pleasantly. "Sometimes I speak even when I haven't been spoken to."

"I don't like Polly's attitude," Alex complained to Jill.

"Oh, dear, and I thought you did." Polly smiled. "Excuse me while I water the plants and change my personality."

Polly scooped Jill's papers off her desk and handed her a note she'd just scribbled.

"If you need me," Polly glanced at Alex, "I'll be outside typing and filing as God intended me to do."

"Thanks." Jill nodded, and read Polly's note. *Neil Kaiser calls every hour on the hour. If you want to avoid him, don't answer the phone. I'll handle. P.*

"Polly," Jill called, and Polly reappeared. "Thanks again. Please pick up my calls."

Polly made the okay sign and closed the door after her.

"Now"—Jill returned her attention to Alex—"why are you angry with me?"

Alex seemed uncomfortable, even subdued. His feet scuffed the

428

carpet. "You know how it is. I came in here all fired up, wanting to congratulate you . . . a forty-six share! Shit, this place went fucking bananas! The party Neiman threw . . . Too bad you missed it. It would still be going on if some sucker hadn't complained about naked people running around on the roof. The cops showed up, and we had to flush the cookies, pronto . . . Anyway, I've been bursting to see you, and then I came in and you and that . . . Polly . . . are laughing together . . . and . . . it . . ."

"Took the wind out of your sails?" Jill suggested, thinking it typical of Alex to be miffed at laughter not initiated by him. "Laughter is good, Alex, even when it's someone else's joke."

"Yeah . . . uh. . . ." Alex's scorched faced twisted with irritation. They'd moved far afield from the conversation he'd rehearsed. "Uh . . . Jill. I know you talked to Neiman from Cleveland. You didn't by any chance mention—"

"—the heavy breathing, et cetera. . . ." The room's drawn drapes made Jill feel claustrophobic. She rose from her chair, wanting light. "I didn't mention it, Alex. I won't mention it, ever. You're off the hook."

"Why?" His eyes glinted suspicion.

Jill yanked the cord, opening the drapes on a view of the deluge. "I don't tattle, simple as that."

Jill waited with her back to him, hoping he'd thank her quickly and go.

"My shrink says you're trying to castrate me!" Alex blurted out.

"You're welcome," Jill said automatically. "What?"

"He says you're after my balls!"

Jill peered down into the street, half-expecting to see an ark and half-wishing that she cared about Alex's shrink's opinion or, for that matter, Alex. "I've never been a collector, Alex, but if I ever am, I'll collect something more interesting than your . . . anatomy."

"You're not taking me seriously."

"Say something serious, and I will." Jill tried to remember if Daisy had been wearing her boots.

"You've been holding this phone-call business over my head—"

"There's nothing over your head, Alex."

"Well, you were!" he insisted. "And you never gave me the credit I deserved for *Rock and Roll Love*."

"What credit?" Jill asked.

"*I* was in the room when you screened that movie!" His voice was loud, his face contorted. Sunburnt skin flaked snakelike from his forehead and drifted onto his Brooks Brothers vest. "*I* laughed at the funny parts."

"So?"

"So, in another minute I would have had the idea first! I was sitting right next to you."

"I sat next to Milton Berle once, but that doesn't make me a stand-up comic."

"You're trying to rob me of my masculinity!" Alex waved his arm in a blizzard of skin.

Jill decided to remain calm. "Petty theft doesn't interest me, Alex."

"I'll show you!" Alex said bitterly. "Neiman put me in charge of *That's Disgusting.* I won't let you anywhere near that fucking show."

"Hark"—Jill tilted her head—"do I hear my life improving?"

"I'll turn that fucking turkey into a fifty-two share. A *sixty-two* share!" Alex's eyes glittered. "I'll get that fucking lunatic to stick *both* arms in a tank of piranhas!"

"Alex, you can't!" Jill exclaimed. "It's immoral. And it won't do you any good. The FCC won't let UBC air it."

"I've thought of that," Alex said, eyes wild. "If we can't air the show, we'll make a news item of it, with bulletins at every station break. *Ex-cabdriver Gets Arms Chewed Off On* That's Disgusting! *Film at Eleven!* We'll make film of the tragedy available to all networks, and *bang* . . . we've got a dynamite promo airing on all channels for free. The audience will eat it up. Brilliant, huh?"

"More like disgusting."

"Neiman told me to think of another title," Alex fretted. *"That's Disgusting* is too honest."

"How about *Bread and Circuses*?" Jill suggested.

"I'll think of something," Alex vowed. "Something catchy. How about *Sex and Violence*?"

"How about getting out of here?" Jill picked up her phone. "I'm calling my mother."

His eyes flashed at the summary dismissal. "I'm warning you, Jill. Stay out of my way."

"Hello, Ma," Jill said into the phone. "How's the weather in Cleveland?"

"Oh, fuck," Alex said disgustedly.

"It's raining here, Ma. Is it raining there?"

"Fucking women!" Alex exclaimed, and half-ran, half-slunk out the door.

Jill hung up quietly, watching her door close on a man who'd found his métier. If Alex was a man whose time had come and *That's Disgusting* what he brought with him, then these were hard times indeed, hard and confusing.

"Armageddon is coming, and I haven't a thing to wear."

Polly reappeared with a handful of papers for Jill to sign.

"I heard Alex shouting. You okay?"

"Fine." Jill watched the rain run rivers down her window. "He doesn't bother me anymore, Polly, and I have no idea why. *That* bothers me. I've always insisted on knowing the whys of the changes I go through."

"Perhaps in some way Alex has become a part of the past. We don't give much thought to the bus passing through, but we do to the one taking us home."

"Perhaps"—Jill paused to consider for a moment—"I don't have hives anymore, not since . . . I can't remember. I don't know the why of that, either."

"Alex doesn't bother you, and you don't have hives." Polly laughed. "What miracles can be next?"

"Last night it occurred to me that I should call Dr. Kerry and tell him about this—Alex and hives and . . . other things. But it was a 'should,' not a 'want,' so I didn't."

Watching rain fall had always made Jill feel cozy inside, the reverse of the chill most people felt. She'd watch and remember the rainy nights when Pa laid a fire, then invited the three of them to bring pillows and lie in front of the hearth. They'd cuddled together, growing dreamy with warmth while imagination created dancers in the flames. "Ah," Pa would eventually say, "isn't this nice?"

Pa was a good man.

Reluctantly Jill turned her gaze from the window. "I'd like to send a letter to Dr. Kerry."

"Shoot." Polly flipped the cover on her omnipresent notebook.

"Dear Dr. Kerry," Jill dictated. "You were right when you said we have hard work ahead. You have yours, and I know I have mine. However, it's not the same work. I know you'll have no difficulty in filling my time. This town is one huge nervous breakdown. Best wishes, Jill Kenyon."

Polly beamed. "That's it?"

431

"Sayonara, shrink world." Jill smiled. "Farewell to the land of the speckled ego and the duck-billed superego, where Valium melts like lemon drops and patients spin like tranquil tops. . . . Stop me before I burst into song."

Polly obliged. *"Stop!"*

"And one more favor, please." Jill handed her unfinished play to Polly. "This is an impulse, so you'll have to be quick before I change my mind. Will you copy this and send it by whatever means is fastest to Dan Carmichael in Santa Barbara?"

"It's done, and it's gone."

"Wait," Jill called.

"Too late, the script is halfway up the coast."

"I can see that." Jill smiled. "I just wanted to say that, psychic or not, you're a very smart lady. Maybe *wise* is a better word. I may not want a view of my future, but I appreciate your advice."

Polly smiled. "Thank you."

"If you ever go into the psychic business, I'll put you on retainer. Five bucks a week *not* to tell me what's going to happen. If I'd known what was ahead in '71, I wouldn't have crawled from beneath the piano."

"You have a point there," Polly said, closing the door behind her.

Jill dialed Kate several times before she finally reached her.

"Ma, how are you?"

"Tired, exhausted, half-dead," Kate said energetically. "Between arranging your father's funeral and running to see Julie . . . ."

"You've been to the hospital?" Jill was surprised, knowing Kate's aversion for such places.

"Are you here to visit your sister?" Kate snorted. "When haven't the burdens fallen on me?"

"What about Johnny?"

"John's in his office."

"But in the evenings . . . ?"

"He hasn't come home from the office since the day Julie went to the hospital," Kate said angrily.

"How can that be?"

"Ask me something I know, like how far is up. Candy calls me ten times a day, crying. It's not enough that she brought all John's meals to the office. He's also had her bring his clothes, his razor, towels, pillows, blankets, and the portable TV.

"Oh, God, he's barricading himself."

432

"I just hung up with Candy. John wants the electric toothbrush, the *family* toothbrush. She was hysterical. She thinks it's her fault."

"It isn't. Did you tell her it isn't?"

"Who knows?" Kate said grimly. "John was fine before he got married."

"He wasn't fine! He was never fine!" Jill tried to calm herself. "Ma, listen, John in his office is no different from Julie in the nuthouse. Tell Candy that John needs help. Are you listening, Ma?" The silence that followed lasted so long, Jill thought they'd been disconnected.

"I have to call the caterer about your father's funeral lunch," Kate said finally. "Do you think little sandwiches and cakes are enough?"

"Ma, talk to Candy about Johnny. Please."

"I am not the mother of three crazy children!" Kate shouted, and hung up.

For a very long while Jill gazed out at the rain. She stood still, hurting.

Later that day, when the inevitable moment with Neiman arrived, Jill's well-rehearsed speech proved useless.

"Sign here." He threw the contract on her desk.

"I need time—"

"You hate me. Lawrence hates me. That goddamn computer hates me. I've given my life to a business that hates me."

"Has my lawyer called . . . ?"

"I've worked my ass off for UBC. To an imbecile astronaut with a berserk machine they give a million a year. To me they give grief. Why didn't the government send Lawrence to Mars? The government hates me." He paced the carpet in front of Jill's desk. "The board of directors says, 'Get Kenyon to sign her contract. Find out what the computer is saying. Make UBC number one in the ratings.' Ha! PBS is running *I, Claudius* again. We'll be lucky to finish fifth!" He whirled, shaking his fist at Jill. "Do you know the chairman of the board is senile?"

"No," Jill shook her head, thinking *but if you'll hum a few bars*. She edged toward the buzzer that would summon Polly.

"He is! He is!" Neiman ranted, shaking his fist at the ceiling. "Do you hear that, you doddering old son of a bitch? You couldn't run a Tonka truck, never mind a network! You belong in a home, you—"

"Dale, calm yourself," Jill pleaded, pressing the button for Polly. Where *was* she? "Is there anything I can do?"

"Sign here," he said quickly, and smiled.

433

Jill abandoned her frantic buzzer-pressing. "Dale, I know my law-yer has called you, and you're aware I need a few weeks—"

"Weeks!" he screeched. "You listen to me. In less than two weeks I have to face a convention of affiliates with a senile chairman of the board and a president who's getting big bucks to play with a com-puter and sigh. That forty-six share is the only good news I've got. That and possibly *That's Disgusting.* Of course *Freak People* is doing fairly well and—" He caught himself cheering up and quit cold. "I need your signature, Jill. I want to tell the good folks at the affiliates' banquet that the gal who brought us the forty-six share is staying."

"I think you're exaggerating the importance of one idea, Dale, and—"

"Sign!"

"I'll let you know after the affiliates' convention, and please stop shouting at me. I don't like it."

"Sorry," he said in an elaborate whisper. "Why do you hate me?"

"It's not personal. I just want to feel solid about the commitments I make, certain I'm going to keep them. You understand that, don't you?"

"This morning my dog peed on my leg!" Neiman bellowed. "The whole fucking world hates me!"

He slammed the door on his way out of the office.

Several days later, having ignored twenty-one phone calls from Neil and spoken to Kate six times, Jill received a call from Steve, asking her to dinner. "Now that we're in business," he said.

Tactful as always, he chose a restaurant they had never tried while they were married.

"I hope this is all right. I would have taken you to Scandia, but when they see us coming, they prepare for two orders of veal piccata and a fight."

"This is charming," Jill said, and it was—an opulent Indian estab-lishment, redolent with spices and featuring food that blistered Jill's alimentary canal.

"How's Julie?" he asked, spooning soup made from fire and twigs.

"She'll be fine," Jill replied, drinking a quart of water.

"I'm surprised to hear you say that, Jill."

"I'm surprised you didn't say it first, Steve."

"Perhaps you've learned not to overreact," he said approvingly.

"Don't get too excited, dear. This morning I broke a fingernail and fainted dead away."

"You're kidding." Steve smiled. "Aren't you?"

"Guess." But she smiled in return.

"You haven't asked my advice about your contract." Steve forked up heart-of-palm-and-brimstone salad.

"No, Steve, I haven't."

"You should, you know. I'm acting as your attorney in this. Forget we were married."

"Not easy to do. I just kissed your daughter good night."

"She's quite a girl, Daisy. I'm very proud of her, Jill."

"So am I." Jill laughed. "At last, a subject on which we agree."

Steve set his fork to one side and fixed Jill with a look she remembered—his moment of deliberate composure preceding a pronouncement that usually concerned behavior he felt Jill should modify. "You're a good mother, Jill."

She stared at him, speechless.

"I thought it was time I said that." He continued, almost shyly, "You've done a very nice job with her."

"My goodness" was all Jill could say.

"I believe in paying deserved compliments." He resumed forking up his flammable salad.

"I remember. You gave me one in '69 and again in '73. Both had to do with my breasts, I believe."

"Uh . . . about your contract, Jill. As you've instructed I've promised UBC an answer on the first of the month."

"Fine."

"Is there a reason for your hesitation?"

"Yes." With her spoon Jill dug a crater in her vegetable vindaloo. Lava bubbled from its center. "I'm not certain UBC is what I want. Part of me backs away."

"I don't understand."

"Neither do I. But I will."

"When? How?"

"When it's time for the answer, I'll know."

"Have you joined an Eastern religion?" This with wrinkled brow.

"Something happened to my family, Steve. I changed for the better, and they fell like dominoes."

"We need yogurt. Where's the waiter?" He peered into the opulence, searching for a passing turban.

"Do you suppose there's a balance in families, a delicate tension as precise as finely tuned strings?"

"You're not eating," he pointed out. "Would you like something else?"

"Do you suppose that a change in one can cause reactive change in the others?"

"It's time to give some thought to the terms of your contract, Jill. We have to prepare—"

"Is that what happened to us, Steve? When I changed for the better, started to grow up, the father in you feared losing his child?"

"I'll need to familiarize myself with UBC's stock-option plan." Steve scribbled a note on the back of a napkin.

"There will always be a child in me, Steve, a child who needs comforting, but now there's a woman who can love as an equal and even comfort the little boy in a man."

"You must take this job!" he said loudly, turning heads and startling himself.

"Why?" Jill's smile promised a return to shallower conversational waters. Steve would learn to swim in his own time, like everyone else.

"It's a very good job"—he radiated relief—"especially for a woman."

"Especially for a 'wifey.' " She laughed and was pleasantly surprised when Steve laughed, too.

"Will you have dinner with me once in a while?" He stared at the tablecloth, protecting his shyness.

"To discuss terms?"

"To get reacquainted."

"I thought you were seeing someone." This gently, a reasonable question.

"Susan's only a friend, a very nice woman, very . . . uh . . . efficient."

"Why do you want to get reacquainted, Steve?"

"You've never bored me, Jill." He looked embarrassed at the admission. "Where the hell is that waiter?"

He had her fed, driven home, walked to the door, respectably kissed, and wished good night, all by eleven thirty.

Jill stretched out on her bed fully clothed, staring blankly at the television set while the *Tonight* show rolled through her room. Music and jokes floated by. Nothing landed. Nothing connected.

Carl Sagan appeared, catching her eye, a second later, her mind.

"We carry the seeds of our own destruction," he was saying. "We live in dangerous times."

Armageddon, Jill thought, and shivered.

"But our species is young and brave and curious." His face was lit from within. "There's reason for optimism."

Jill sighed and believed him, his light as much as his words. Truth carries its own illumination, a beacon from teller to told.

She undressed, carefully hanging her new beige dress in the closet, then tucked herself gently into her own warm bed.

She fell asleep peacefully, feeling young and brave and curious, feeling the seeds she carried were not of destruction but reason for optimism.

Several nights later Jill waited up for Daisy, a half-written letter to Kate keeping her mind off the clock. "Try not to become discouraged because there's no discernible change in Julie," she was writing, when she heard the front door open and shut, slowly.

"Daisy." Jill met her in the hallway.

"It was a terrific concert, Mom, and we had a wonderful time. Lenny insisted we stop to eat, even though he has to be up early tomorrow." Daisy's face flushed with the effort she was making. "Their moving van is arriving at seven. Why do they come so early, Mom? It isn't cross-country, just a drive up the coast. Lenny says he'll be back to visit me in only a couple of weeks. Do you think he could stay over, Mom? In the guest room, I mean. You can be chaperon."

"Lenny's welcome to stay over, honey."

"It'll be fun, Mom. We'll go to a movie, see some of the kids. . . . *Oh, Mom!*" Daisy wailed as her dam gave way. "I'll miss Lenny so. He's my best friend!"

"I know, honey, I know." Jill pulled Daisy into her arms, feeling her own dam burst. They stood in the hallway holding each other and weeping for lost best friends.

CHAPTER 27

On the evening of the affiliates' banquet Neiman instructed Jill to sit at a table with station-owning strangers.

"Be charming," he ordered. "We don't want them to dump UBC."

"Might they?"

"With ABC just down the street, wouldn't you?" Neiman sighed. "Just keep repeating that UBC will be number one."

"How?" Jill inquired. "Just in case somebody asks."

"Tell them we're bidding for the '96 Olympics," Neiman replied, sweating into his cummerbund.

"1996!?"

"Tell them, tell them!"

"All right," Jill agreed. "But news that exciting could cause cardiac arrest."

"Go," Neiman commanded, with a gentle push to the small of her back. "Smile at the people. Make nice. Maybe they won't notice that the food is crummy."

"They've already noticed that the cocktails were watered."

"That's too fucking bad!" Droplets dripped off his brow. "All they have to do is eat, drink, and complain, while I have to drag Lawrence away from his computer and keep the chairman from wandering into the street. Go."

Then Neiman was off, weaving his soppy way through the crowd. Jill looked after him with an approximation of sympathy. Only an evil man deserved the night ahead, and Neiman wasn't evil. To be evil requires a point of view, and Neiman had only the fear of losing his job. To forestall that eventuality, he might do evil deeds, but only the minimum necessary and those with considerable angst.

Jill moved toward her assignment, stopping at a nearby table, where Nina Friedman, gowned in green and looking like a goddess rising from sea foam, sat between Alex and Zippy de Franco.

"How they hanging, Jill?" Zippy giggled.

Jill ignored him. "How are you, Nina?"

"I'm fine." Nina smiled, but the barely discernible shadows beneath her lovely eyes said otherwise.

"You two know each other?" Alex frowned, as though suspecting a conspiracy.

"We met at Patti Gerard's funeral," Jill explained.

"Oh, yeah," Alex remembered. "Fucking bummer, that. Well, some people aren't meant to survive. Lots of talent but no killer instinct." He nodded solemnly. "It's a fucking jungle out there."

"Out there?" Jill said mockingly. "Tarzan would feel at home in this room."

"For business you need balls." Zippy seemed to hover three inches above his chair. "Women don't have 'em."

"Balls is a state of mind," Jill said pleasantly, then smiled at Nina. "Enjoying your acting class?"

Nina glanced quickly at Alex. "Oh, yes. Very much."

"Fucking right she does," Alex asserted, wrapping one arm around Nina. "This little lady's going to be a fucking star. We'll have *two* stars in the family, right, honey?" He smiled brilliantly, his arm squeezing her shoulders. "Isn't that right, honey?"

"Right," Nina said obediently. "Right. Right."

"Cookie?" Zippy gestured at a small plastic bag half-hidden under the centerpiece. "Help yourself."

"Put them away, Zippy." Jill smiled. "We're here to be nice to the people. Have fun on your own time."

"You go be nice to them." Alex snorted. "The whole fucking bunch belongs on *Freak People.*"

"There's an empty seat here next to me," Nina said hopefully.

"That seat's saved for M.B. Jones," Alex said quickly. "He said he'd be late, has something to do."

"He makes cookie runs for me." Zippy giggled. "Good man, M.B. Always knows how much change he has in his pocket."

"I'll see you after the banquet, Nina," Jill promised. "Perhaps you and I can have lunch."

Nina brightened. "I'd like that. I don't know many women in Los Angeles."

"She'll let you know when her time frees up," Alex said quickly. "Lots of modeling dates coming up, her classes, interviews—"

"We'll talk later," Jill said to Nina, then walked away from the table without saying good-bye.

439

"Woman's got a burr up her ass," she heard Zippy remark to Alex. She couldn't hear Alex's reply, but their laughter chased her, a nuisance nipping at her heels.

Most of the crowd had seated themselves and were staring with distaste at limp-looking salads. Jill approached a table, which like the others was plywood covered with rose damask cloth. It was set with caterer's china and rent-a-silver, eight settings in all around a centerpiece of roses, candles, and ferns.

The flowers and soft candlelight imparted an aura of elegance to the cavernous room, remarkable considering that a mere twenty-four hours earlier it had been the UBC first-floor employees' cafeteria. Stagecraft had transformed the drearily utilitarian into "A Night on the Champs-Élysées." In reality it could have been a night in Peoria had it not been for the replica of the Eiffel Tower, also plywood, which dominated the center of the room. Whoever was responsible for the tower's construction had thrown in a hint of Pisa. It leaned to the left, not dangerously so, just enough to provide an ice-breaking topic for affiliates introducing themselves to one another.

"Well, well." A jovial gray-haired man greeted Jill as she sat down at the table. "I see by your badge you're with UBC."

Jill introduced herself.

"I'm Howard Beamer, and this is my wife Clara." He smiled. "The gentleman on my left is Harry Simpson from Tuscaloosa."

"How do you do?" Jill smiled at Harry, who emerged from his wineglass long enough to nod.

"And this here's Web Schaffer from Danville and his missus, Cathy, no, Katie." He struck his forehead with exaggerated regret. "How could I mess that up? Pretty little lady, pretty little name."

Howard continued around the table, making introductions, adding personal comments to each. Jill said a brief prayer of thanks for Howard, who by appointing himself master of ceremonies had removed that burden from her.

"So," Howard said, "what do you do at UBC?"

"Movies," Jill replied. "I'm with the movie department."

"In what capacity?" Howard's smile was affable, his eyes shrewd. Jill told him.

"Hear that?" he boomed at Clara. "A woman executive. Wait till you tell your consciousness-raising group back home."

"Why aren't we having the banquet at a hotel?" Clara asked pointedly. "The other networks throw gala events at the Century Plaza."

"The other networks have advertisers who want to sponsor their shows," Howard said with no loss of affability. "I'm not sorry to see UBC tightening its belt. Prudent. Fiscally prudent."

Clara wrinkled her sharp nose. "This room smells of cabbage."

"I think of the UBC station I own as being a long-term investment," Howard confided to Jill. "Don't you, Harry?"

Harry nodded, his nose in his wineglass.

"The walls are cinder block, Howard," Clara said sulkily. "This looks like a place labor leaders come to be assassinated."

"Where is home?" Jill asked.

"Xenia, Ohio," Howard said proudly. "Bet you've never heard of it."

Jill smiled. "My ex-husband proposed to me at the Red Lantern Inn on Route 21. I'm from Cleveland."

"Geez, Louise, an Ohio gal!" Howard beamed. "Hear that, Clara? This lady executive's from just down the road."

Clara sniffed. "Wish I'd gone on that Jaycee Auxiliary tour to Nova Scotia."

"So do I, Clara, darlin'. So do I." He noticed Jill eyeing him sympathetically. "I'm president of the Junior Chamber back home."

Jill smiled. She'd already guessed that.

Dinner arrived, gray roast beef served by aspiring actors waiting tables till their first big break. They projected personality, flashing star quality across serving dishes heaped with broccoli.

Clara scowled at Jill. "Are the waiters on dope?"

"Not the waiters," Jill answered. "The waiters are fine."

Halfway through dinner a tall, thirtyish man slid into the chair next to Jill's.

"Hey, what have we here?" He grinned at her with the confidence of one who's been told he looks like Clint Eastwood.

"I'm Jill Kenyon."

"You certainly are." His eyes made a slow survey. "You attached?"

"I work for UBC."

"That's good news, honey." He leered. "You're getting paid to be nice to me." He poked her arm as though he'd just made a joke. "I'm Doug Hiller, upstate New York."

"How do you do?" Jill sighed. There would be no prayer of thanksgiving for Doug Hiller.

"Pass the rolls, honey." Doug was set to dig in.

Jill complied. He tossed four on his plate, then handed her the basket. "Haven't eaten all day. Had meetings round town, some big deals going down."

"That's nice."

He hacked at his beef. "I worked my way through college running a whorehouse in Albany."

"You're a pimp?!" It popped out.

"Not a pimp." He was insulted. "Ran the damn place. There's a difference, honey. I never touched the girls myself. Put that damn place in the black, I did. Barely nineteen at the time."

"That's . . . uh . . . remarkable," Jill said, thinking that *remarkable* was the safest of several words that came to mind.

"What say you and me get outa here?" Doug nudged her leg under the table. "Soon's I eat."

"Sorry, I can't do that," Jill tried to infuse her voice with regret, but only icky-poo-yuck came through.

"Sure you can." He was determined, a man with big deals going down. "Who's your boss? I'll talk to him."

"He's . . . uh . . ." Jill scanned the room. "I don't see Dale Neiman anywhere."

"This is Dale Neiman," a voice boomed above them, "and welcome to UBC."

Dale stood on the "constructed for the event" stage, mike in hand, blinking out at the audience, while a too-hot spotlight made a gleaming egg of his head.

"There he is." Doug waved his fork in Neiman's direction. "I'll talk to him later. We'll work out a deal."

"Oh, shit," Jill said, under her breath.

"You good folks keep right on eating," Dale boomed, and everyone winced as feedback whined through the room. "I'm not here to spoil your fun, just to tell you about UBC's plans for the future and introduce you to some of the folks who are part of the UBC family." He waved at the band behind him, seven men in red-sequined tuxedos who looked like they'd played their last gig during the heyday of swing. They jumped for their instruments and struck up a disco rendition of "What I Did For Love."

"Yes," Dale boomed. *"Kiss today good-bye, and point us toward tomorrow. . . .* That's the theme here at UBC. Of course, we don't want to kiss *everything* good-bye, especially the *stars* who've made

UBC *great!* Ladies and gentlemen, some familiar faces would like to say hello to you." He made an elaborate bow toward the back of the stage. "May I present the UBC *Parade of Stars!*"

Behind Neiman a curtain opened, and a blinding spotlight outlined an old lady, a dog, and a kid.

"We have bigger parades than that in Xenia," Clara said scornfully.

"*Yes!*" Neiman shouted. "These stars who have brought you so much entertainment will continue to be seen weekly in their own UBC series." He paused, waiting for applause that wasn't forthcoming. So, like any good cheerleader, he began it himself.

The affiliates followed and the sound of polite clapping rolled through the ballroom as the old lady waved, the kid smirked, and the dog wagged its tail.

"Thank you, thank you, thank you," Dale enthused. "Our stars will join you at your table while we continue our program."

A moment later the kid, Jamie Laser, glared down at Jill. "This seat empty?"

"Sit down."

He pulled out the chair and sat down. "Do I have to talk to these jerks?" he whispered to Jill.

"May I have your autograph?" Clara was suddenly interested.

"Certainly, ma'am." Jamie replied, flashing six dozen perfectly-capped teeth.

"And now for a special treat," Neiman boomed from the stage. "Tonight we unveil the new UBC *logo!*" He waved at the band, who struck up a rock version of "What I Did For Love." "*Yes!*" Neiman bellowed. "*Point us toward tomorrow!* Ladies and gentlemen, I give you *tomorrow!*"

Suddenly the room was plunged into darkness. Then, just as suddenly, a blue spotlight focused laserlike light on the ceiling as a massive banner unfurled slowly over their heads.

"What the hell is that?" Clara demanded.

As if in answer to Clara's question, Neiman intoned, "Yes, folks, it's UBC's new symbol of greatness, a wombat rampant on a field of laurel, surrounded by the slogan that will soon be on all America's lips —*UBC, warm as a wombat, the network that loves you!*"

"Wombat, my ass," Clara groused. "If I saw a critter like that in *my* house, I'd call the exterminator."

"Let's hear it for the wombat, folks!" Neiman shouted. While the band played wildly and Neiman led the cheering, Jill shifted uneasily in her chair. There seemed to be a hand working its way from her knee upward in the general direction of her . . .

"Stop that!" she hissed at Doug, who was shoveling Jell-O chocolate pudding into his mouth.

"What say, honey?" he asked. "Can't hear you."

Doug continued to gobble and the hand continued to move. Jill stiffened. The hand was on her left leg, far removed from the whorehouse Baruch. It belonged to the kid.

"Stop that!" she hissed in his rosy ear.

"Beg pardon, ma'am. You talking to me?" He flashed the innocent smile beloved by millions.

"I ought to smack you," Jill told him.

"Don't try," he said without moving his lips. "It'll cost you your job."

"And *now*," Neiman shouted, "it's my *great* and *particular* pleasure to introduce the man responsible for our new logo, our all-American *hero*, former astronaut and the new president of UBC, *our fearless and dynamic leader, Mr. Theodore Lawrence!*"

The band played madly, a mazurka version of "What I Did For Love."

"Mr. Theodore Lawrence," Neiman repeated, looking frantically toward the curtain. "Captain Lawrence? Astronaut Lawrence? President Lawrence? *Te-deeeee!*"

Lawrence appeared onstage, staggering as though someone had pushed him. For a moment he stood in the spotlight, looking thoroughly lost. Neiman leaped at him, grabbed him by the arm, and dragged him toward the mike.

"Ladies and gentlemen!" Neiman bellowed ecstatically. *"Mr. Theodore Lawrence!"*

The audience roared a welcome, at least half rising to their feet in a spontaneous standing ovation, Howard and Clara among them.

"I hear he's a genius!" Clara yelled at Howard.

"Our best shot at the future!" Howard yelled back.

Gradually the crowd quieted down and resumed their seats. Every eye turned to Lawrence, and the silence was that of a crowd holding its collective breath.

Lawrence gazed over the sea of expectant heads, his eyes wide, unfocused, staring like a blind man's into the spotlight's glare. A minute passed, then two, until the room hummed with silence, the low vibration of unbearable suspense. Still Lawrence stared, and the room grew restive, with an undercurrent of nerves stretched too far. Finally Lawrence's mouth opened, provoking a mass exhalation. The genius was about to speak.

"Doooonnnsssyyy!" It was the soul-seared wail of a man past all sensation but pain. "Where are you, Doooonnnsssyyy?"

Horrified, Neiman plucked at Lawrence's arm and pulled him toward the wings, waving wildly at the band, who, befuddled by an event not part of the program, straggled into a halting rendition of "What I Did For Love."

"Abelard?" Lawrence asked Neiman as Neiman waved at the band to play louder. *"Abelard?"*

"Abelard's waiting for you," Neiman said. With that, he shoved Lawrence into the wings, then pressed both hands to his head with the look of a man whose brain has just thrown itself on a grenade.

Finally he looked up, confronting the crowd. Jill could hear him thinking *My job, my job.*

Neiman stepped to the mike, a hideous smile spread across his face. "How *about* that folks?" he boomed. "As you can see our *fearless dynamic leader has only one thing on his mind*! That's making UBC, you and me, *number one!*" He began to clap in a rhythm that demanded participation and soon, most of the affiliates joined in.

"What's wrong with Lawrence?" Clara asked Howard.

"Nothing, sweetheart," Howard replied. "The man is so brilliant we can't understand him, that's all."

Neiman picked up the pace of the clapping. His instincts were good. The crowd responded like Buckeyes at an Ohio State homecoming game. Cheers and whistles were added to the clapping and a chant of *Lawrence! Lawrence!* began as a rumble and rose to a roar. In the back of her mind, Jill understood what had happened in beer halls over bratwurst and beer.

She shifted, uneasily aware of a hand on her knee, this time her right knee. She glared furiously at Doug.

She was opening her mouth to tell him to stop when she felt a hand on her left knee. Her head swiveled sharply, her nose grazing the kid's boyish grin. He leered at her. "I dig older women."

"That's enough." As Jill rose abruptly, two hands slithered down her legs and fell off her kneecaps. "Clara, Howard." Jill smiled pleasantly at the Beamers. "It was nice to meet you. Give my regards to Xenia."

She turned and fled the table with Doug's "Honey, hey honey" ringing in her ears.

Jill made her way through tables of affiliates caught up in a frenzy of cheering and chanting. She sat down next to Nina, with *Lawrence! Lawrence!* pounding in her ears.

"Is it always like this?" Nina's eyes were wide and alarmed. "I wish they'd stop." She trembled violently. "I don't like this at all!"

Alex leaned toward Nina. "Open up, babe."

Nina obediently opened her mouth, and Alex popped in a cookie.

"Alex!" Jill protested. "What are you doing?"

"Relaxing my wife. Any objections?" By the glittering look in his eyes, Alex had had several cookies.

"I'll take one of those." Smythe (MB) Jones leaned out of the shadows he seemed to carry with him. "Kenyon, pass 'em down."

Jill ignored him.

Alex reached across her and shoved the plastic bag down the table toward Jones. "Here, buddy, fall in."

"Jill's got a burr up her ass." Zippy giggled. "A burrrr. It's an icicle."

"Thank you, thank you!" Neiman was shouting, trying to quiet the din. "You have the *spirit,* the UBC *spirit,* but let's get on with the business part of our dinner so we can get to the drinking and dancing."

Another roar followed this suggestion, and Neiman glowed like a lighthouse. He had the crowd hogtied.

"A few words about our schedule," Neiman continued, to a quieter crowd. "You've all been thrilled and excited by the dynamite ratings generated by *Rock and Roll Love. . . .*"

"Fuck. Gimme another cookie." Alex grabbed the bag and stuffed two into his mouth.

". . . well, you're going to be even more excited when I tell you that in the upcoming season, *Rock and Roll Love* will be expanded to a thirty-seven-part miniseries to air twice a week *plus*"—he held up his hand to still the rising cheer— "we are also announcing a half-hour sitcom *All in the Rock and Roll Family,* scheduled for Thursdays eight-to-nine *plus* a dynamic hour-long drama series titled *Rock and Roll Urban Cowboy* to air Sundays nine-to-ten *plus* a hard-hitting look at the contemporary scene, *Rock and Roll Social Worker,* a show designed for across-the-board impact and maximum viewer response." Neiman stepped forward, smiling with the sincerity of an incumbent about to kiss a gooey brat. "As we all know, television has a responsibility to enlighten and inform as well as entertain. To that end, we are pleased to announce that next season UBC will be offering two full hours of informative programing, *of* the people, *by* the people, and *for* the people—one, a show formerly known as *That's Disgusting,* now more appropriately titled *Speak Out, Incredible American People* and the other, a show you all love, UBC's hottest new hit, *Freak People.*"

The roar that greeted this announcement rattled the silverware.

"That does it!" M.B. Jones threw his napkin on the table and leaped from his chair. "I told them to cancel that show. I warned them. Why didn't they listen? Now the piper will be paid." His face—what could be seen of it behind his fogged glasses—was white. He pivoted on one heel and took off at a dead run.

"That's one fucking weird cat," Alex said fondly.

"Pushes the best dope in town." Zippy giggled. "Nothing weird about that."

"I'm going to the ladies' room," Nina said, smiling serenely at Jill. "Your daughter is so beautiful. I know my baby would have been a girl."

"I'll go with you," Jill offered, thinking Nina shouldn't be alone.

"Stay here," Nina said sadly. "When I look at you, I see your daughter. Do I look like I'm crying?"

"No," Jill said, hurting for her.

"Well I am." Nina smiled angelically and wafted away.

Furious, Jill turned on Alex. "You're really a shit, you know that?"

"Stuff it," Alex said, and popped another cookie into his mouth.

"And now, folks." Neiman was rolling. "The moment you have been waiting for—may I present our venerable and venerated *chairman of the board, Mr. Henry Gregg!*"

The cheer was deafening as a frail but erect figure doddered onto the stage. The crowd rose as one, roaring an ovation while the band played a Sousa version of the only song they knew and Alex, overwhelmed by company loyalty and cookies, stood on his chair, cheering louder than anyone.

Neiman waved for silence, a maneuver he was forced to repeat before the thrilled affiliates returned to their seats.

"Please take your seats," Neiman begged. "Quickly now. When Mr. Gregg is on his feet for more than five minutes, he tends to keel over. So, if you'll all settle down . . ."

They did, and with Neiman's assistance Gregg doddered to the microphone.

"Hello, hello," he crackled, in a voice like an ancient parrot's. "Don't you all look nice. I love parties. Hello. Hello."

"UBC," Neiman hinted. "Say a few words about UBC."

"Hello, hello," Gregg cackled. "In 1936, when I was but a lad of fifty, television was in its first stages of birth . . . . It was in labor . . . so was my wife . . . hello, hello . . . my second wife, Matilda . . . or was it Hilda?" He looked at Neiman questioningly.

"Sir?" Neiman urged. "Television? UBC?"

"You're not Hilda." Gregg pushed Neiman away, then continued. "On May 25, 1936, I purchased a company originally founded by Australian criminals, then sold to an American merchant who manufactured the worst crackers I ever tasted. And his pretzels were worse. They tasted like pig shit."

"Mr. Gregg." Neiman nudged him. "Television? UBC?"

"Hello, hello," Gregg cackled. "Founding UBC made me hungry, so I went across the street to Horn and Hardart, where I met Jonathan Frebault who once dated my wife Matilda . . . or was it Hilda . . . ? Hello, hello . . . and we talked about television, which in those days we called . . . uh . . . television . . . hello, hello. . . ."

Gregg continued to drone on in what soon became apparent might be a verbal diary of his life, day-to-day, from May 25, 1936, to the present.

"Oh, fuck," Alex moaned to Zippy. "Let's get out of here."

"Yeah." Zippy giggled. "Let's go cruisin'."

"Where?" Alex was interested.

"We'll cruise Sunset. Pick up some stuff."

"Hey, man, that's dynamite!" Alex liked it. "You ever cruise Santa Monica?"

"You?" Zippy made no attempt to focus his eyes. They flopped as they would, jus' ramblin'.

"Just once." Alex giggled. "I picked up this blonde, stacked like a pile of grapefruit. Took her to one of those sleazy motels on Sunset . . . you know . . . feeelthy pictures . . . got her undressed, and, hey, man, you'll never guess. . . ."

"*She* was a *he*." Zippy laughed.

"Shit man, how'd you know?" Alex was disappointed.

"That's what you get on Santa Monica." Zippy poked Alex's ribs. "So tell me, whaddya do?"

"I'd already paid 'im." Alex shrugged. "So I fucked 'im."

"Oh, God!" Jill groaned.

"It was my obligatory homosexual experience." Alex grinned. "C'mon, Zip, let's get out of here."

"But Nina!" Jill protested.

Alex threw a ten on the table. "Tell her to take a cab."

"Then, on the evening of May 25, I went home to my wife, Matilda . . . hello, hello . . . Hilda . . . and she said to me, she said, 'Henry. . . .' "

VAROOM!

A deafening explosion rocked the room, sending candlesticks flying and china shattering to the floor. Cries of *"Bomb! Terrorist! Bomb!"* were heard, along with terrified shrieks as the room plunged into darkness.

VAROOM!

A second prodigious explosion followed, rattling the walls and setting those who had restrained themselves at the first shock screaming along with the rest.

After the first frozen moment, instinct propelled Jill under the table, where she bumped heads with Alex.

"What the fuck? What the fuck?" Alex moaned, bewildered.

Chunks of something, possibly plaster, rained down on the tables with a sound like boulders hitting cement.

Sirens could be heard overhead, screaming as Neiman shouted "Be calm, folks, be calm!"

VAROOM!

With the third explosion the floor rippled and rolled like a waterbed. The Eiffel Tower creaked, groaned, and toppled, creating a mushroom cloud of balsa dust and glitter. Panic became pandemonium as shrieking affiliates scrambled for exits they couldn't see.

From the remnants of the stage Neiman bleated, "We're doomed, *doomed!*"

"Mommy," Alex whispered, and fainted with his head in Jill's lap. Jill's own panicked cry was lost in the fourth *VAROOM!*

In the weeks to follow UBC enjoyed the highest ratings in its history. Audiences couldn't get enough of the real-life story of a network blown up by a madman.

For all the noise and chaos most of UBC remained standing. Only the north wing had been completely demolished, though damage elsewhere would run into the millions.

There were those of snide and petty mind who carped, saying UBC had gained more than it lost in its partial apocalypse. Using the burnt-out north wing as a set, *Freak People* broadcast live, garnering a 72 share.

There had been two casualties. Because they'd been star-stuff, not ordinary people, their deaths only added to the legend. Though people spoke of their deaths in appropriately hushed tones, it was with muted excitement, not grief.

Smythe (MB) Jones had been blown to kingdom come in the final explosion. Some said he would have survived had he not been indulging in drugs before setting his charges. His timing was off, and he'd lingered too long, enjoying the spectacle. Just as well. The legend would grow, unhampered by reality. Already there was talk of a miniseries.

Lawrence was dead. They found bits and pieces of him mingled with bits and pieces of Abelard.

The conference room had been hit by the final explosion. With the first three as warning Lawrence could have escaped, but he'd chosen to stay with his computer. Perhaps *chosen* wasn't the word. Whether to abandon one's heart and one's head is not a choice humans make. There's no living without them.

Though the official casualty-count was two, those who'd sat agog in the conference room counted three—there were even a few who genuinely mourned the passing of Abelard.

Following a brief but thorough examination by a hospital intern, Jill had been driven home by a policeman.

She'd gotten out of the squad car, thanked the officer politely, then looked up at the sky, wondering if the souls of those who belong there go to Mars.

450

CHAPTER 28

"Is Daisy with you?" Dan asked.

"Of course. It would have been heartless to leave her at home," Jill answered, wondering why Dan's was the only face etched in her memory in complete detail. Most faces, even of those she loved, drifted mysteriously away, taking their noses, mouths, and eye colors with them. "Her best friend, Lenny, lives three miles from here. I left them on the beach, chasing one another like puppies. He's taking us to dinner before we drive back tonight."

"Ah, a wise young man." Dan smiled. "They way to a girl's heart is through her mother's approval."

"Usually the opposite"—Jill grinned—"but I've been blessed with Daisy. My opinion seems to matter to her."

Dan nodded. "And hers to you. It's the best of both worlds when children and parents can also be friends."

"Daisy's the best of my world right now, Dan. I try to remember that one day she'll be gone, that she's only mine for a while, and that's as it should be. But that's tomorrow's bridge. I'll cross it tomorrow." Jill smiled, feeling peaceful with the premonition of a loss that wasn't a loss but a natural completion. "You've heard about UBC? About Lawrence?

"I heard," Dan said. "Truth is, I heard, then went out and bought *Variety*. Read it cover to cover. It seemed to affect me like the famous firehouse bell on the fabled farmhouse dog."

"You miss television?" Jill was surprised.

"Something is stirring through these old bones, Jill. Missing television may be part of it." He sighed. "I think what I'm missing is life."

"Involvement?"

"*Hhhhmmmm.* Some of us are meant to live in the world. You and I, for instance. Our feet are wedded to earth, our spirits to the people we love."

"There's nothing wrong with time away from the world, Dan, time to stand still and hurt."

"You're right. Sabbatical can be a time for regaining perspective, but a sabbatical gone on too long is withdrawal."

"You're over it, then? Nancy's death, I mean?"

"There are more sweet memories, Jill. Less self-recrimination. Or perhaps I've just grown less self-indulgent about it." Dan smiled. "But you didn't come here to test my devotion to the monastic life. You want to know what I think of your play."

"I'm not certain I'm ready to hear what you think." Jill's mouth was dry.

"What did you feel while you were writing it, Jill?"

"It engaged me heart and soul."

"I thought so. Does UBC engage you that way?"

Jill laughed. "No. For a time I was very comfortable. At first I thought it was you, the encouragement you gave me. When you left I lost the encouragement, but not the compelling sense of familiarity. That remained, even when UBC got crazy. And it really got crazy, Dan."

"I heard."

"Then, when I went to Cleveland, I discovered the source of the familiar feeling. I took my sister to the same mental institution I'd been in, and there it was, Dan, UBC with nurses."

"You're kidding." His eyes sparkled with amusement.

"It's true," Jill insisted. "There are only two differences between UBC and the nuthouse. At UBC they dress better, and in the nuthouse they know they're crazy."

Dan laughed with all the free, hearty warmth she remembered. "UBC could get better, Jill. It depends on the next president. If he's thoughtful, rational, and cares about television, it could work."

"I thought you hated television," Jill said, thinking that Dan was full of surprises today.

"Hate? I hated everything the day I said that, most particularly myself. I dislike much of what television does, but . . . do you remember *Omnibus*?"

"Of course."

"And Olivier in *Hamlet* and *Twelve Angry Men*, and Miller's *The Price* and *Victory at Sea* and Sid and Imogene, the moon landing, the '68 Democratic convention, all the Olympics and war—the reality, not the John Wayne movies?"

"You're talking about the way I grew up and the major events of my life."

"Mine, too. All of ours."

For a time they sat in silence, thinking of all the events of their lives they'd seen on a television screen.

"Would you like to come back to television, Dan?"

"I don't know," he replied. "If I return to the world, it has to be to work I take pride in. Pride and a reasonable amount of joy. Life's too short to settle for less."

"*If* you return . . ."

"More likely when," Dan admitted. "Have you decided about signing your contract?"

"Have you decided what you think of my play?"

Dan smiled at her anxious face. "You haven't come here to hear a review. It's a different question you're asking."

"Should I finish it?" Jill asked hesitantly.

"Can you walk away and leave it unfinished?"

"Never!"

"You've answered your own question." He grinned. "See? You didn't need me."

Giving way to an impulse she refused to restrain, Jill threw her arms around Dan's neck. "Thank you for being in my life, Dan. I'm richer for knowing you."

The bell in the monastery tower tolled, stately and serene.

"Vespers," Dan said. "I'm saying a litany for Nancy."

"I'll come see you again," Jill promised.

"I may come see you first." Dan smiled, his eyes bittersweet. "I'll miss the simplicity here, Jill."

"Take it with you, then."

"If I can. Send me the last act of your play."

"You'll be the first to read it."

Jill watched Dan disappear through the massive monastery doors, thinking that men needn't always be lovers. Perhaps some could be loved even more deeply as friends.

On the beach Jill found Daisy and Lenny sitting together, voices low in best-friend conversation.

"Hi, Mom," Daisy greeted her. "We're starved."

They walked the beach toward Jill's car, taking their time, picking up shells, skipping flat stones over ocean ripples.

"Look, Mom, there's that house you like." Daisy pointed at the

453

gray clapboard set in the sand just steps from the ocean. The windows had been flung open, white curtains fluttered, and someone had added stained glass to the expanse of the bay. To one side, in a scrub of grass, someone, perhaps the same someone, had placed a "For Sale" sign.

Something will happen. This?

They ate in a restaurant that featured fresh fish along with equally fresh vegetables. The bread was coarse, of many grains, reminding Jill of her childhood when Pa had bought everything fresh as tomorrow, home from the Westside Market. She ate hugely, then waited patiently as Daisy and Lenny said a long good night. That, too, she remembered from the days of her youth—the need for lingering farewells.

Eventually Daisy was in the seat next to Jill's, and they began the journey home. Though neither spoke, they rode easily with one another, and finally their mutual silence made them closer companions than any conversation could have done.

They arrived home, pleasantly tired from their peaceful ride, ready for bath and bed.

"You first," Daisy was generous. "I'll do some homework while I'm waiting. Call me when you're done."

"Thanks." Jill kissed Daisy's pug nose. "I'll make cocoa while you take your bath."

Jill ran the tub, sprinkling bath salts into the water. The phone rang, and she ran to answer it, throwing herself over the bed. "Hello?"

"Jill!" Kate was sobbing. "That son of a bitch Neil Kaiser put Julie in Wilbur State Hospital! Your brother won't come out of his office, and your sister is in the place where Joseph died!"

"Ma, stop crying," Jill tried to make herself heard over Kate's sobs. "Hold on till I get there. I'm coming home."

"You are?" Surprise stopped Kate in midsob. "But I haven't even said you have to. I'm not making you come home this time."

"You've never had to make me, Ma. I've always come home because that's what I wanted to do. Didn't you know that?"

"No, I didn't." Kate's voice was low. "I thought you'd never come unless I . . . Well, if you're coming, hurry. Everything's terrible, and with your father's funeral . . ."

"I'll be there, Ma."

"I'll light a candle to Saint Christopher for you. I don't care that the Church says he doesn't exist. He's watching over you, Jill."

"Somebody is," Jill replied. "I'll see you as soon as I can get on a plane, and, Ma, please light two candles. I won't be alone."

She hung up the phone, then ran into Daisy's room, her bathrobe flapping behind her. Daisy looked up, startled. "What's wrong, Mom? What's up?"

"Pack your bags, Daisy. We're both going to Cleveland. It's time you knew where you came from."

CHAPTER 29

"I remember! I remember!" Daisy shouted as Jill turned the corner of Kate's street. "This is where Grandma lives! I remember my formative years!"

Jill smiled. "I knew you would."

They pulled into the driveway with Daisy hanging out the window, trolling for memories. "Grandma's house looks smaller, Mom."

"You're bigger, Daisy. That's all."

Daisy danced up the porch steps. "Here's where I used to play with my doll, and here's—"

The front door flew open. Kate bounded onto the porch, her arms wide in a swooping embrace. "Daisy! Come to Granny!"

They hugged one another, squealing with happiness. Daisy spun joyfully as Kate whirled her in a sprightly jig that carried them both through the door.

Jill stood alone on the porch, looking after them and smiling. "Hello, Ma. I'm thrilled to see you, too." She followed them down the hall and into the kitchen.

"You're so big, such a young lady." Kate was crooning over Daisy's head. "You're the image of me when I was your age. I have pictures. I'll show you."

"I thought Daisy looked like me, Ma." Jill wondered how Daisy could already be seated at Kate's table, a cookie in one hand and a glass of milk in the other.

"Grandma remembered my favorite." Daisy's eyes shone. "Oatmeal and raisin, see?"

"They were probably baked before we moved to Los Angeles." Jill grinned.

"That's not all I remembered," Kate announced, pulling a doll from beneath her apron.

"My Raggedy Ann!" Daisy shouted. "You saved it!"

"And wait'll you see your room." Kate implied wonders to come. "Remember the patchwork quilt?"

"My cuddle quilt!" Daisy glowed. "I'd say, 'Now I Lay Me Down to Sleep,' and you'd pull the quilt up to my nose. I loved sleeping at your house, Grandma."

"Everything's just the way it was before your mother took you away. Ah, Daisy, I'm so glad to see you!" Kate flung her arms around Daisy, who returned her zealous embrace. "The pictures, Daisy. I'll get the pictures."

Kate zipped off in the direction of the hallway with Jill grinning after her. "Hello, Ma. I'm home"

Behind her, Daisy bubbled with glee. "Oh, Mom, isn't it nice to know that some things don't change. Grandma still gets carried away."

"Ebullience. It's part of her charm."

Daisy nodded. "When I told Lenny about my real Irish grandma, he told me about his real Jewish grandma. They sound like the same person, Mom."

"There's a Grannys' School somewhere, Daisy, and yours graduated with top honors." Jill smiled. "So, you don't think Grandma has changed, maybe aged a little?"

"*Shh,*" Daisy cautioned. "Grandma might overhear. Grandmas *hate* hearing they look older."

"And how have you suddenly become so wise in the ways of grandmas?"

"Lenny told me. He said that once he told his grandma her hair was getting grayer, and she rapped him on the head with her knuckles until he took it back."

"Old granny trick. Works every time."

"I used to *love* the way Grandma tucked me under that quilt." Daisy smiled. "But I can't say I loved that prayer. Why do they make kids say, 'If I should die before I wake'? That prayer could make a kid nervous." Daisy surveyed the kitchen. "Everything looks the same, except for the tree. Why does Grandma have a tree in her kitchen?"

"At first it was a way of avoiding the forest, Daisy. Now the tree is only a tree."

"Here we are." Kate breezed into the kitchen, bearing an album, cordovan leather embossed with gold. "Now I'll show you pictures of a little girl who looked just like you."

Jill tried again. "Hello, Ma."

"This is me when I was five." Kate opened the album to the first page. "Here on this pony."

"Where did the pony come from?" Daisy asked, immediately engrossed in her roots.

"Every summer a man with a pony went door to door taking pictures," Kate explained. "My mother said he was a Bolshevik, but he took wonderful pictures."

"The pony looks thin," warm-hearted Daisy observed.

Kate sniffed. "That's the Bolsheviks for you. In the summer they starve their ponies. In the winter they eat them."

"Grandma!" Daisy was shocked.

Kate shrugged. "That's what my mother told me. It must have been true. Every summer the Bolshevik had a different pony."

"Ma," Jill interrupted, "I don't want to intrude on the handing-down of family folklore, but we need to talk about Julie."

"Shh," Kate said quickly, then smiled at Daisy. "Look at the pictures, precious. Grandma has to talk to your mother."

Kate scooted Jill into the hallway. "I don't want Daisy to hear about Julie. She's too young to know about such things."

"I've already told her, Ma," Jill said. "What's happened here is a family problem, not some shameful secret to be hidden away. I won't have Daisy growing up confused and wondering. Now, tell me what happened."

"All right." The happy mask Kate had worn for Daisy dissolved into the stark anxiety beneath. "Yesterday, when I went to see Julie, the nurse told me that Dr. Kaiser had transferred her to Wilbur State Hospital. I didn't understand how that could happen. I started to get . . . upset." Kate's chin trembled. "I remembered what happened to Pa when he got upset in a hospital, and I . . . got . . . scared."

Jill bit the inside of her mouth. She was angry, furious at Neil. "You had reason to be upset, Ma."

"I'm Julie's mother." Kate sniffled. "I should have thought of her first. But I got . . . scared."

"I could kill Neil Kaiser and never feel guilty." Jill's face was pale, her jaw set. "What he's done is outrageous and awful."

"Maybe he had reasons—"

"We all have reasons for the evil we do, Ma. Reasons don't make it less wrong."

"You'll go see Julie at Wilbur State?" Kate asked, trembling. "Forgive me, I can't. . . ."

"I'll get Julie out of there, Ma."

"But she's still . . . There's no change. . . ."

"There are other doctors, other hospitals. Don't worry. I'll take
care of Julie."

The look on Kate's face deepened from anxiety to fear. "Please, Jill,
don't do anything crazy."

"I won't, Ma," Jill promised, slipping her arm around Kate. "There
are some things I know how to do, and leaving a mental institution
is one of them."

"I'm so confused," Kate moaned against Jill's sheltering arm. "Neil
Kaiser cured you. How could he have become a bad doctor?"

"The same way twenty-game winners end up in the minors. Neil
lost his fastball." Jill smiled at Kate. "You've earned a rest. Go and
enjoy Daisy. I'll handle the problems."

"If you say so." Kate visibly relaxed, then suddenly, lithe as a
schoolgirl, bubbled her way to the kitchen.

"Daisy!" Jill heard Kate say. "Remember the park where we
used to feed squirrels? I'll take you. And this evening we'll go to
novena."

"That sounds nice, Grandma," Daisy said politely. "What's a
novena?"

"Mother of God! My granddaughter's being raised a heathen!"

Jill smiled and climbed the steps to the bedroom, grateful that
Kate's herd of worries had found another pasture to graze in.

Jill dialed Neil's office and, as expected, was greeted by Silver-
tongue Silverstone. "Dr. Kaiser's office."

"Hello. It's Jill Kenyon. May I speak to—"

"Oh, my dear, it's so nice to hear you." Sleighbells rang through
the phone. "Have you finished your Christmas shopping?"

"I'm in a bit of a rush, Mrs. Silverstone. Is Dr. Kaiser—"

"I had to shop early, what with my trip to Mexico and all. I took
your advice, went to Berlitz. My instructor's so nice, says I speak
Spanish just like a gringo. Isn't that sweet?"

"I'll be there in twenty minutes," Jill said, stopping what she'd
finally recognized as a vamp.

"Oh, my dear, please don't do that. You'll be so disappointed. Dr.
Kaiser's gone fishing."

"Fishing!"

"A few days to recoup and refresh. You know the pressures—"

"Neil stuck my sister in a state institution and went fishing?" Jill's voice was low.

"You should have returned his calls, my dear. He wanted to tell you himself. Your sister wasn't responding to treatment, so . . ." Mrs. Silverstone sounded rational, reasonable, and just a bit nervous. "Sometimes a long-term-care facility is the only answer."

"He did it for revenge," Jill said simply. "I wouldn't do what he wanted me to do, so he did something to hurt me. That's immoral, tacky, unprofessional, and disgusting."

"Oh, I know." Mrs. Silverstone sighed. "But you must understand his problems."

"For fifty bucks an hour I'll understand his problems. For free I don't give a shit. Now tell me where I can reach him."

"Oh, deary me, all this lying has me worn out." Mrs. Silverstone sighed. "I give up. He's in Willoughby Sanitarium."

"Drying out?" It came as a shock, but not a surprise.

"When he gets depressed, he drinks. Then he gets more depressed. Then he drinks more. Then he gets more depressed. Then he—"

"I don't care, Mrs. Silverstone. He'll have to interrupt his cure long enough to sign my sister's discharge papers. Please call him for me."

"I can't!" Mrs. Silverstone started to cry. "He won't talk to me! I do everything he asks, but it's never enough. When he's drinking, I tell the hospital he's home with the flu and his patients he's tied up at the hospital. I'm sitting here lying to crazy people while he's off getting B-12 and sympathy."

"Why do you do it, Mrs. Silverstone? You said you'd retired. Why did you come back?"

"Oh, deary me, what else can I do?" Her sigh whistled through the phone. "I'm his mother."

"His mother?" Jill was astonished. "Mother, like in you gave birth?"

"If I wasn't Neil's mother, do you think I'd put up with his bullshit for two-fifty a week and no lunch hour?" Mrs. Silverstone asked bitterly. "But he's my son, and I hurt him. I married five times, and poor little Neil just couldn't cope with all those papas. Not that I purposely tried to hurt Neil. I'm just lucky at love and rotten at marriage. And I didn't even know Neil was hurt until he grew up and became a psychiatrist. When he explained that his drinking was all my fault—"

"I need to talk to him."

460

"Impossible this week dear, but maybe next—"

"Next week's too late. I'll have to find another way. Good luck, Mrs. Silverstone. You'll need it." Jill hung up.

Rats.

Without Neil's cooperation, getting Julie out of Wilbur State Hospital could take days, maybe weeks. Between the red tape and the red tapers . . . and what about Julie? She might well regress in the meantime.

Jill reached for the phone, praying that a miracle had occurred, that John had come out of hiding.

"Hello."

"Candy. It's Jill. How are you?"

"Surviving, Jill. Women are born survivors. We give birth by the side of the road, then drive the cattle to California."

"Not anymore, Candy. They don't allow cows on the freeway." Jill frowned at the phone. Candy sounded strange, even for Candy.

"I'd like to rap, but I'm late for my class." Candy was brisk.

"Sewing?"

"Karate."

"Women's lib?" Jill was surprised.

"No. I'm already liberated, even if it wasn't my idea. I've joined the Survivalists' Movement. A woman alone has no other choice. Right now I'm learning martial arts. I want to know I can take care of myself."

"What happened to Fascinating Womanhood?" Jill asked.

"It's impossible to be submissive and subservient when you're the only one home," Candy explained. "I loved Fascinating Womanhood, but unfortunately being a fascinating woman requires a fascinated man. These days I have only myself to defer to."

"Are you thinking of divorce?" Jill asked, selfishly hoping for John's sake the answer would be no.

"I don't believe in divorce," Candy said firmly. "I don't like my marriage the way it is, but I can't change my convictions every time something goes wrong."

"Don't move to L.A., Candy. You'll have no one to talk to."

"I've got to run, Jill, but I'll look forward to seeing you tomorrow."

"Tomorrow?"

"Your father's disinterment. I told your mother I'd come."

"It's *tomorrow*. Ma didn't tell . . ." Jill sighed. "Ma's been very

461

upset. I'll see you tomorrow, Candy. I'll be the one with the banner that says 'Welcome Home, Pa.' "

Candy laughed. "I've always liked you. You aren't afraid of life like Johnny is. Bye."

Jill hung up, thinking that life is a series of shocks that come as no surprise. How could she not have guessed the reason behind Neil's erratic behavior? Or that someone had been covering for his boozing? And who would cover for long, without deep emotional ties?

Jill wondered how the systems she'd lived by could have failed so spectacularly, one after another in mournful progression—a parade of dull, gray feet trampling long-held beliefs and formerly solid assumptions. Those who'd once supplied the answers were now busy asking questions, mostly directed to their navels, or, like Neil, were vacillating between the roles of doctor and patient, or, like Norton, publicly championing disciplined institutions while privately disporting themselves as libertines.

A fine mess we've gotten ourselves into, my expectations and me.
You're not a crazy lady.
There's reason for optimism.

"We were just talking about you, Mom," Daisy said as Jill entered the kitchen.

"I told Daisy how you used to stamp your foot at me and how you never cleaned your side of the bedroom." Kate turned to Daisy. "Your Aunt Julie was neat as a pin. Paddy's pigs would have been at home with your mother."

"Our house is always neat," Daisy volunteered.

"Of course it is, dear. You must be a good little housekeeper."

"Mom and I do most of the housework," Daisy said. "There's a lady who comes in once a week."

"I never had a lady come in," Kate scoffed. "I wouldn't hire a stranger to do my work."

"Well, Mom works, and I go to school, so the lady scrubs floors and stuff. We do everything else."

"The waxing?" Kate asked.

"What waxing?" Daisy frowned.

"The pigs, honey." Jill lit a cigarette. "Grandma and Paddy like their pigs polished."

"The floors, what else?" Kate scowled at Jill.

"We don't wax the floors," Daisy replied.

"You don't wax the floors!" Kate was shocked.

"Lenny's mother waxes floors. She asked me if we do. I thought it was a Jewish thing."

"Jewish? Who's Jewish?" Kate wanted to know.

"Lenny. He's my best friend."

"Your best friend is Jewish?" Kate turned to Jill. "Her boyfriend is Jewish?"

"*Best* friend, Ma. That means of either sex. Lenny's her best all-round buddy."

"Does your father know about Lenny?" Kate asked Daisy.

"About Lenny? Sure." Daisy grinned. "Dad likes Lenny a lot."

"The daughters of divorced Catholic women go out with Jewish boys." Kate sighed.

"Is that a Gypsy curse, Ma, or is it supposed to mean something?" Jill asked. "Can we go back to discussing my pigs?"

"Is he a nice boy?" Kate asked Daisy.

"Lenny's the nicest *person* I know."

"Good. He'll convert."

"Gosh, Grandma." Daisy was surprised. "That's what Lenny's mother says about me."

"Mother of God!" Kate exclaimed. "Help me get dinner on the table, Jill. I have candles to light."

The meal was on the table so quickly, Kate didn't have time to provide her usual historical background. The second Daisy finished, Kate had their coats out of the closet and Daisy halfway out the door.

"Good dinner, Grandma," Daisy said. "What were those crunchy things in the meatloaf?"

"Fossilized onions"—Jill laughed—"1976 was a vintage year for meatloaf. It was subtle, yet provocative, full-bodied, yet—"

"I'll light an extra candle for you," Kate interrupted. "Though for all the good it's doing, the bees could keep their wax. C'mon, Daisy, I have a special intention to make."

"Oh, boy, a novena!" Daisy enthused. "Wait'll I tell Lenny!"

"Mother of God!"

And they were gone with a slam of the door, leaving Jill alone with the dishes.

Where are the pigs when you need them? Jill wondered, scraping garbage into the sink.

Suddenly she laughed, picturing Kate in church, lighting candle after candle and fervently nagging God to convert Lenny. On the other side of her mind was a picture of Lenny's mother in temple, equally fervent about the conversion of Daisy. Superimposed over all this was the translucent figure of God, holding his head and groaning "Ladies, ladies, gimme a break!"

Jill wondered what would happen if God grew weary of the candlelight cacophony and granted each lady her wish. Hocus-pocus, Daisy would become Jewish and Lenny would become Catholic and . . .

The phone rang, and Jill ran to answer it, hoping, for no reason other than optimism, that John would be on the line. "Hello."

"Hello," a very soft voice whispered. "Jill?"

"Julie, how are you, what are you—"

"I can't talk long," Julie interrupted. "I had to sneak out of the ward. They unlock the doors at mealtimes, but . . ."

"I'm making arrangements to get you out, Julie. Just try to relax. . . ."

"You don't know what this place is like, Jill." There was panic in Julie's voice. "The other hospital was fine, but this! People here are incoherent, violent, incontinent. Kaiser had me put in a back ward!"

"That son of a bitch!"

"Jill," Julie whispered, "this crazy I'm not. Please come and get me."

"First thing tomorrow," Jill promised. "Can you sleep there tonight?"

"I'll try." She sounded frightened. "But I haven't slept for days. Some of the patients should be in restraints and aren't. The staff doesn't care if the patients beat each oth—"

"I'm on my way, *now,*" Jill told her. "Sit tight. I'll get you out."

"If you could, if you would," Julie whispered. "Oh, dammit, someone is coming—"

There was a click, and Julie was gone. Jill stood with the phone in her hand, warning herself to stand still and think.

At this hour the hospital office would be closed, the keepers of official forms home kissing their wives in triplicate. The machinery required for leaving the hospital AMA (against medical advice) or, in patient parlance, AOT (ass over teakettle), would be locked in limbo. If she went now, she would only be asked to return in the morning when the head doctor or nurse or Grand Wazoo would be available for futile consultation. And even then she'd be told that Julie's release would require the signature of Neil Kaiser, who himself at this very moment was likely skulking along the corridors of Willoughby Sanitarium in search of an orderly who'd slip him a bottle.

Without a plan Jill would be stymied and Julie would remain locked . . .

Jill smiled. She had a plan, one that could only occur to a born storyteller who had also been born a triplet.

The first step—call Mrs. Silverstone.

A half-hour later Jill was turning into a long, winding drive that led from the street to a building set among trees. Like most structures built before 1900 in Cleveland, it had a Victorian Gothic quality, as though the architect had been asked to design a country estate for a spooky queen. Its gray stone façade, ironwork gates, and stone lions with gargoyle faces hinted at high tea served by social inferiors while liveried fiddlers played Mozart to drown out the wails of the wretches consigned to the dungeons.

Jill parked her car, then walked quickly across the lush oval of grass leading to the stone steps of the building, where she paused, overcome by nerves. The plan that had seemed so feasible in the bright light of Kate's kitchen seemed in this formidable darkness to be a bomb about to go off in her pocket.

At first Mrs. Silverstone had refused to cooperate, but the single word *malpractice* had magically altered her perspective. She'd agreed to make the call Jill had requested in return for Jill's promise that she, along with poor little Neil, would never again hear from a Dunn.

That accomplished, it had taken Jill only a moment to find Kate's ancient, voluminous carpetbag and the other items she needed. She'd driven the distance from Kate's humming with optimism and a plan for survival.

Now her throat was dry with a nervousness that undercut optimism but not determination. True, her plan showed little respect for the system it was about to abuse, but, then, it was a system that lately had deserved no respect and had freely showered abuse.

Jill sidled up the intimidating steps, steeling herself with the thoughts that had buoyed her across town (one) when "normal channels" become clogged drains, the system has failed, (two) waiting until morning would result in a well-rested bureaucracy, one even more energetically crossing *i*'s and dotting *t*'s, and (three) when your shrink is in the loony bin himself, all bets are off.

Jill foraged in Kate's carpetbag for her sunglasses. She put them on, feeling she was stumbling through midnight fog.

Thus armed, she opened the massive front door and stepped into the foyer, expecting to be met by Vincent Price carrying a lighted taper and a severed head.

A large, gloomy hall painted institutional green and lined with gouged wooden benches opened at both ends into narrow corridors. Acting on Mrs. Silverstone's reluctant instructions, Jill took the corridor to her immediate left.

She approached the nurses' station, noticing that, unlike the open space of the private psychiatric floor, it was an enclosed cage with a wire-mesh-lined window and securely bolted door.

Jill pressed the wall buzzer. From inside the cage she heard a television set turned low and a tap, tap, tapping, but nothing else. She pressed the buzzer again, then nervously glanced over her shoulder, surprised to see that shadows do indeed dance and, further, actually assume strange shapes in surroundings intrinsically uneasy.

The door opened slowly, and a pleasant-faced young man appeared. "Sorry. Didn't mean to keep you waiting. Sometimes I get lost in my work."

"Work?" Jill knew she would have to tiptoe into his personality. Would he respond best to imperious commands, the friendly approach, or a let's-get-on-with-business attitude?

"I'm a writer." He gestured into the cage. "The TV is just for background. Helps me think."

"Are you the night orderly?"

"Until my book's published. Kesey wrote *Cuckoo's Nest* while he was working in a mental hospital. Took LSD there, too. They used to leave it laying around. Them was the days." He looked at her, hopeful.

"Fresh out," Jill said.

"Thought maybe with dark glasses and all, you was into something," he said casually.

"I take it Mrs. Silverstone called you?"

"Yeah, and I gotta tell ya, I don't see the rush. Kaiser's got substitutes running in and out, covering his ass six ways from Sunday. None of 'em hardly come in at night and never to see a patient that's been schitzy so long."

"Dr. Kaiser expects an imminent breakthrough with Mrs. Hofstetter," Jill explained.

"Aw, c'mon," he was dubious. "The woman hasn't spoken since the Beatles broke up."

"Regardless, I am here to examine her," Jill said firmly. She'd moved from "friendly" to "business."

"It's your wasted ten minutes." He shrugged. "Orders is orders, Dr. . . . uh . . ."

"Kenyon." Jill smiled crisply.

From a peg on the inside of the door he retrieved what looked like jailer's keys. He nodded toward a door at the end of the hall. "Just through that door, bear to the right. When you're done, push the buzzer, I'll let you out."

"Thanks." Jill made a show of looking at her watch. "Running late. I have to see another patient cross town at Dedham."

"Kaiser's?"

"Yes."

"Shit." He laughed. "That's some asshole. Has every shrink in town dancing to his tune."

He unlocked the door and stood aside. "Don't know what Hofstetter would do if she did have a breakthrough. No family. No money. Been three presidents since she came here."

"That's her problem," Jill said callously, in her best imitation of a bureaucrat.

"Yeah. Buzz me when you're done." He waved her through. "Back to work. I'm writing a sex scene that'll knock your socks off."

The door shut behind her with a solid thud and a click that jabbed Jill's nerves. She started down the hall with purposeful strides that soon slowed to a nightmare crawl. In this hall the shadows didn't dance. They sat where they were, waiting for her.

Jill removed her sunglasses, peering into the darkness of a ward to her right. She could see the outlines of patients in beds, rows of beds arranged barracks-style with only inches between. Jill moved on.

She'd asked Silverstone to give the orderly the name of a patient in the same ward with Julie. If Hofstetter's bed was on the right, so was Julie's.

She continued down the hall, feeling the insanity that emanated equally from the pores of drugged patients and the unfathomable intentions of those who'd created this hellish boot camp.

"Julie?" she whispered. "Julie?"

In the ward to her right Jill saw the outline of someone sitting bolt upright in bed. "Julie?"

"Jill! Jill!" The figure leaped off the bed and ran toward her. "I didn't think they'd let you in."

"Shhh," Jill cautioned. "They think I'm a doctor. I'll explain later, just do as I say."

467

Jill opened the carpetbag, removing several items of clothing. "Here. Put these on."

"Why?" Julie looked frightened.

"I'm getting you out of here, honey. Kaiser only put you here to get even with me. If I try to get you released the ordinary way, it could take days."

Julie clutched at Jill's arm. "This is a terrible place!"

"I know. That's why I'm here. Change your clothes."

Julie pulled off the sweat shirt she was wearing. "This isn't like the other hospital, Jill. Nobody cares. Nobody helps. They lead patients to shower, to eat, to the bathroom, just moving bodies around. This isn't a place where people get well."

Jill thrust the sunglasses into Julie's hand. "Put these on. Tie my scarf over your head. When you get to the door, push the buzzer. A young man will let you out. Do you know him?"

"We *never* see anyone after lights out. Sometimes patients wander around, getting upset, getting angry . . . crying . . . hitting—"

Jill interrupted Julie's nightmare recital. "This will be easy. You'll be me. We look just enough alike to pull it off."

"We should." Julie giggled, surprising Jill.

"Now, when the orderly lets you out, just say, 'You were right. Mrs. Hofstetter's a vegetable. Kaiser's an asshole.' Sound disgusted."

"That won't be difficult."

"I've already told him I'm late for another appointment. He'll expect you to be in a hurry. My car's parked at the end of the drive. Get in and wait for me."

"How are you going to get out?"

"Don't worry about it." Truth was, Jill hadn't planned that part. "If I'm not out in ten minutes, go to Ma's without me. The keys are under the seat."

"I can't do that!"

"You must! The worst that can happen is, I'll spend the night here and they'll feel like jerks in the morning. If you don't go now . . . maybe weeks."

"But . . ."

"Go!" Jill eased Julie into the hall and gave her a gentle push.

For a moment she listened to Julie's footsteps recede, then sat on the floor, resting her head on her knees.

I'll give it ten minutes. Julie will be safe in the car by then.

She searched her mind for a plan. She could pretend to the orderly that he was so involved in his sock-knocking sex scene he'd only *imagined* he'd let her out. No. He wasn't that bright, but he wasn't that stupid, either. She could wait till he opened the door and yell "Fire!"

Shame on you. Bite your tongue.

Jill wished she'd developed the knack of going for the soft spots in people, or even of discovering where those soft spots might be. Unlike those whose careers seemed to be one long search-and-destroy mission, the UBC group, for example, with Neiman as . . . *Neiman!*

That's it! Eureka and also whoopee!

The button that always pushed Neiman would push anyone whose job had become too important, in this case, a job which allows a writer to write.

Jill checked her watch, got to her feet, and walked up the hall, carefully avoiding the sticky, webbed shadows.

At the door she pressed the buzzer, then waited, untroubled by nerves. The bottom line was simple—it would work or it wouldn't. If it worked, she'd go home with Julie. If it didn't, she'd die.

She pressed again, then a third time.

Finally the door opened slowly, revealing the orderly's irritated face. "Goddammit, you know patients aren't allowed to . . . Christ!" He stared, struck dumber.

"You're fired!" Jill pushed the door open with an imperious sweep of her arm. "No use arguing with me. Where's the phone?"

"But I just let you out!" he bleated. "How can you . . . What do you mean . . . ? I just let you . . . *Fired!*"

Briskly Jill walked toward the nurses' station, thrilled she'd been right about his knee-jerk reaction to *fired*. "Abominable security . . . malfeasance," she mumbled, then whirled on him. "Besides being fired, you should also be shot!"

"Fired!" He trembled. *"Fired? What is this?"*

Jill squinted maliciously at him. "This is a test. The hospital runs periodic checks on staff efficiency. You flunk. Where's the phone?"

"What test . . . how . . . where . . . I just let you out." He stopped, mouth hanging open.

"When you let me out, I merely slipped a piece of cardboard between the door and the jamb. You never even noticed. Then I waited till I heard your typewriter and walked free as a bird through a door that was no longer locked. *Your* door. *Your* responsibility. *Shame!*" Jill folded her arms, fixing him with Sister Mary Martha's turned-to-stone stare. "Any patient could have done the same thing. *Our* patients. *Your* responsibility."

"Geez, no wonder people go crazy, with everybody pulling tricks on everybody else—"

"You are not being paid to write novels," Jill said sternly.

"Me and my big mouth!" He slapped his forehead. "And I thought you were a nice lady. Say, are you sure I just let you out? You look—"

"Fired! Fired!" Jill shouted.

"Fired! Christ! Gimme another chance," he pleaded. "I got five, maybe six chapters to go—"

"You have abdicated your responsibility."

"Never again. I swear. I'll pay attention. By the time they throw the next test, my book'll be done, and I'll be long gone. Hey, please, this job pays shit, but right now I need it. You must know what it's like to need a job."

"Well . . ." Jill appeared to vacillate.

"Look, what's the worst that could have happened? If the patients got out, they'd only mill around until someone came to lead them somewhere. Maybe a little nookie under the trees . . ."

"You have a point there." Jill edged toward the door. "No harm done. Write your book."

"You won't report this?" he quavered.

"I'll report hunky-doryness here. Send me a copy of your book." Jill reached for the doorknob.

"I knew you were a nice lady," he called as Jill turned and dashed out the door.

She jumped down the steps, flew over the grass, and flung herself into the car next to Julie.

"Hi." Jill gave Julie a hug, noting her pale, anxious face, the trembling that shook her slight frame. "Let's get out of here."

Rubber burned concrete as Jill sped down the long, dark driveway, slowing down as they reached the street.

"Relax, Julie." Jill reached for Julie's hand. "The hounds aren't after us.

"But . . . what . . . what's going to happen when they find out I'm gone?" Julie fretted.

"Nothing," Jill assured her. "You weren't committed. There's nothing they can legally do. Believe me, honey, they'll be so embarrassed, there's nothing they'll *want* to do. The hospital will notify Kaiser, and, cured or not, he'll have to deal with them."

"Cured? Has Dr. Kaiser been ill?" Julie asked.

"You could say that." Jill sighed and told Julie about Neil.

"Oh, my," Julie said finally. "Who would have thought . . . ? But that explains . . . it might explain . . ."

"What, honey?" Jill said encouragingly.

"The day he transferred me, we talked. I told him I was beginning to understand . . . to see. . . . I remembered my middle name. . . . I knew who I was. . . . I even understood some . . . Oh, I'm so tired." Julie fell silent, exhausted.

"You mean that Neil knew you were getting better the day he transferred you?" Jill asked, feeling cold to her toes.

"He must have," Julie answered. "We talked, and I told him so."

"Interesting," Jill remarked, vowing that someday she'd return to the enchanted cottage and break both Neil Kaiser's knees. "Well, Julie, Dr. Kaiser's in the past for us both. How are you feeling?"

"Tired and disoriented in the strangest way, as though I just woke up from a long, bad dream. But better—I'm better, Jill." Julie's words came with effort, but without hesitation.

"You sound better," Jill agreed. "The disorientation is normal. Believe me, I felt the same way. It's reentry. The world seems slightly unreal."

"Even riding in this car feels . . . different, as though it's been years, maybe another life."

"That will pass," Jill assured her. "As will the fatigue. You need time to rest, to be kind to yourself. I'll help you find another doctor."

"Perhaps I'll want another doctor, perhaps not," Julie said softly. "Someone to talk to might be a good idea. . . . I think I know what happened. . . . I think I know why. . . . Even so, there are other problems . . . Fred . . . the children . . ."

Jill patted her hand. "You don't have to think about everything now. Just take one step at a time. If you're better, and you are, and you have some understanding, then you've already taken the most important step. Everything else will fall into place."

"I hope so . . . I . . ." Julie faltered.

"What, honey?"

"You aren't going to like this, but I think . . . Neil Kaiser helped."

"How?"

"In one of our sessions . . . I still wasn't talking . . . but I heard . . . everything. . . . You, too . . . what you said . . . he told me that I'd identified with my schedule. When it fell apart . . . and it had to . . . I disintegrated with it." Julie was silent for a moment. "Then he said, 'You are not your schedule. You are Julie, not a collection of activities. The Julie inside you is alive and healthy.' He said it over and over until I began to connect with his words."

"You were ready to hear," Jill nodded. "As for Neil, his words have never lacked merit. I just wish he'd listen to them."

"Oh, Jill." Julie sighed deeply. "Why didn't I see it? Every time I got . . . nervous . . . I'd add something new to the schedule. I even scheduled hours to sleep."

"I'm not surprised."

"I thought if I just kept busy . . . So now I'll have to find another way." Julie's voice sounded stronger. "Dr. Kaiser was right. The schedule was the sick part of me. But there's a healthy part, too, or I wouldn't be sitting here telling you this. I'll just have to work on it."

"You'll do that. And you'll have all the help you need," Jill promised.

"Is Father Norton . . . still . . . ?" Julie asked timidly.

"Forget about him," Jill said quickly. "He's gone."

"I'm so ashamed. . . ."

"Don't be," Jill said firmly. "He was only your way of saying 'Enough is enough, I'm angry.' It was the best you could do at the time."

"How did you know I was angry?" Julie was surprised. "I never told . . . Oh, you *do* know. Attempted suicide is anger."

Jill nodded. "The ultimate 'Enough is enough.' "

"Did you know Ma came to see me, Jill?"

"She told me." Jill smiled. "I think it was brave of her."

"So do I. She'd sit next to my bed, talking in a bright, cheery voice, pretending she wasn't terrified. She talked a lot, nerves I suppose. She even told me about Pa and Uncle Joseph."

"I'm glad she did," Jill said approvingly. "That's a story we should have heard years ago. It could have made such a difference."

"And she told me about John, the retreat to his office," Julie continued. "Jill . . . if you wouldn't mind . . . before we go home . . . I'd like to see John."

"You would?"

"He should know Uncle Joseph."

"You're right, Julie. It's time." Jill turned the car toward John's office and reached for Julie's hand.

CHAPTER 30

"So, when Uncle Joseph died, Pa tried to bury his fears along with his brother." Julie leaned forward, her elbows on John's desk. "He couldn't, Johnny. He carried such a burden . . . his illness . . . his worries . . . his terrible fear."

John leaned back in his chair, instinctively moving away from Julie. "I find it difficult to believe Pa wouldn't mention having a brother, particularly a twin. Would either of you like coffee?"

They both declined.

"I'll have a cup." John took a cup from a desk drawer and went to a corner of his office that resembled a small appliance department. Coffee-maker, toaster, hot plate, and electric toothbrush shared space on a crowded table, beneath which was a large cardboard carton of foodstuffs. He turned, gesturing with his cup. "Sure you don't want . . . ?"

"No, thanks," Jill answered. "Johnny, what Julie told you is true. Pa didn't want us to know, and he made Ma swear not to tell us."

John poured coffee, his back turned to them. "Why dig it up, then? Why not respect Pa's wishes and Ma's."

"We can't live that way, not anymore!" Jill heard her voice trembling. "Johnny, I have a friend who died from pretending. Died! Like Ma and Pa, she lived in a world of 'Don't talk about it and it'll go away.' Pa created a secret where there shouldn't have been any secret and then spent his life protecting it."

"Would either of you care for an English muffin?" John asked. "I have raspberry jam and peach marmalade."

"Johnny! You must listen to us," Jill insisted. "Pa's need to guard his secret made him vulnerable, defensive, angry, and withdrawn. We thought it was our fault, that we'd done something wrong. We lived with the effect without knowing the cause."

"You look quite well, Julie." John smiled at her. "I'm delighted you feel better. You needed a rest. You were just overdoing it."

"I was *not* overdoing it," Julie said intensely. "I wasn't doing it at all. I was pretending to do it. Every morning I wound myself up like a cuckoo clock and went ticking out in the world."

"You needed a rest," John said stubbornly. "Now you'll be fine."

"I will . . . in time," Julie agreed. "In fact, I may be better than I've ever been. The thing I feared most has happened to me, and I'm still here, alive, on my feet. That makes me feel strong."

"I'm pleased to hear that." John didn't look pleased. "Well, it's always good to see you girls, and any time you'd like to drop in . . ."

"Why are your clothes in the office?" Julie asked. "And blankets and pillows? And that television set?"

"It's temporary, just till I get caught up—"

"How is this different from Wilbur State Hospital?" Julie looked straight at him. "How are you different from me?"

Quickly John turned away from her probe. "It's paperwork, Julie, that's all. Nothing significant or anything else. . . ."

"When are you going home?" Jill asked.

"When the inventory is . . ." He squared his chin defiantly. "I've just been promoted. This company appreciates me."

"Why wouldn't it?" Jill was suddenly angry. "The company will love you until the day you drop dead at your desk. Then it'll send flowers to your widow and hire another workaholic whose neuroses can be fed with promotions."

"That's enough, Jill," John said icily. "I've no intention of arguing about our differing points of view. I'm conscientious about my work. If you choose to read something into that . . ."

He's not ready to hear, not ready.

Jill backed off. "You're right. I didn't come here to argue, especially on a night that should be a celebration for Julie."

"Ma must be thrilled that you're home." John smiled at Julie.

"She doesn't know yet." Jill glanced at her watch. "We'd better go. Ma will be wondering where I am."

John was already on his feet, preparing to herd them to the door. "Bring Daisy by sometime. She must be quite a young lady."

"She is," Jill agreed. "By the way, I spoke to Candy this evening. The children are fine, and she seems very involved with her life."

"She hasn't called lately." John frowned. "I've been meaning to call her but—"

"Don't worry, Johnny. Candy sounds like she has everything she needs. I'll tell her you said hello when I see her tomorrow."

"Tomorrow?"

"Pa's coming-out . . . disinterment. Or funeral. Whatever. Two o'clock. Holy Ghost."

"Christ!" John exclaimed. "Is Ma going through with this? It's such a craz— Why?"

"I think I know," Julie said softly. "Ma wants to be buried in the mausoleum herself. She can't bring herself to admit it, so she tells us that's what Pa wants."

"Two o'clock," Jill repeated.

"I . . . uh . . ." John shuffled through some papers on his desk. "There's an order coming in tomorrow. I couldn't possibly . . ."

"I'm not surprised." Jill hugged him, the brother who wasn't ready to hear. "Take care of yourself, Johnny. Call us if you'd like. Whenever you have time."

"I'll be staying with Ma for a while," Julie told him. "I'll have to make plans . . . no more schedules . . . just some idea of what to do next. I'd like to call, ask your advice."

"Anytime, honey." John slipped an arm around each sister, enfolding them in a simultaneous embrace. "My favorite redheads."

"That's what Pa used to call us," Julie remembered and smiled.

John walked them to the door. "I'll call a security guard and ask him to see you to your car."

Jill opened her mouth to tell him that wouldn't be necessary, then noticed the look on his face. He looked exactly like Pa had the day he'd taken them to the door of the kindergarten room—fierce protectiveness for their welfare and sadness at their loss played in Johnny's face. And loneliness. In a moment a closed door would separate them. A door closed purposely is still a closed door, and the person closing it no less lonely for having been the one to make the decision.

"Give Ma a kiss for me," John said, kissing them in turn on the cheek. "Drive carefully."

Julie and Jill stepped into the hall. "Take care, Johnny," Julie said.

Halfway to the elevator Jill looked back. John stood in the doorway, a solitary figure silhouetted against the harsh and barren light of his office.

"We love you," Jill called to him. "You know that, don't you? We love you, Johnny."

John waved, then, slowly but very firmly, closed his office door.
Once in the car Julie sighed. "We tried, didn't we Jill?"

"We did," Jill reassured her. "And, I think, so did he."

"I don't understand it." Julie sighed. "Why does our family have
so many secrets?"

"I think most families have secrets," Jill replied. "I'm sure Adam
and Eve told the neighbors that Abel dropped dead tilling the fields
and Cain relocated to Nod for his health. If all the skeletons fell out
of everyone's closet, we'd be up to our clavicles in rattling bones."

Julie stretched, yawning. "I'll rest for a while before I make plans,
though I'm not sure how good I'll be at just doing nothing."

"Better than you've been." Jill smiled.

"When I'm rested, I'll go to Chicago, see the children . . ."

"Fred?"

"Fred will never understand what happened to me. If I go back
to him, he'll make me feel like a fallen woman for the rest of my life.
If I don't, I'll miss him. He's loved me, looked after me for years. I
can understand why he's hurt. . . . I don't know."

"Don't decide now, Julie. Rest first," Jill advised. "Give Ma a
chance to fatten you up."

"And she will." Julie smiled, too.

They drove on in the kind of companionable silence Jill loved
sharing with Daisy. Julie relaxed, finally dozing. From time to time
Jill glanced at her, hoping Julie wouldn't forget what she'd learned
—one step at a time and realistic expectations.

"Home, sweet home." Jill stopped the car in the driveway.

"I've been thinking—" they both said at once, and laughed.

Jill nodded. "Ma."

"Just in case."

"I'll go first, tell her I've brought you home."

"Good idea. I wouldn't want her to faint."

"Neither would I. One hospital a day is the quota, even in our
family."

Jill entered the house, searching for a way to tell Kate that Julie was
home without startling her. She knew that good news can shock
cardiovascular systems as severely as bad and with equally disastrous
results. Hearts seldom care what stimulus has set them leaping. They
simply take umbrage at inconsiderate owners and, wreaking revenge, stop. A simple "Julie's home" might precipitate chest-clutch-
ing and fainting. A more measured "I have something to tell you"

476

might sound like an announcement of death, resulting in even more severe trauma. Good news can be a bitch.

As Jill stood in the hallway, trying to think of the most innocuous form her announcement could take, she heard Daisy and Kate in the kitchen.

"This is just like your mother," an agitated Kate was saying. "Running off, worrying me sick."

"Mom must have a reason," Daisy said calmly. "She'll tell us when she gets home."

"What good reason could she have for doing this to me?" Kate stormed. "I don't know how you've turned out so well, Daisy. It must be your father's influence."

"My dad's a good guy and really smart, but I listen to Mom's advice, too."

"How can you?" Kate scoffed. "Your father's got both feet on the ground, while your mother—"

"My mother does what my father does, Grandma. They just do it in different ways."

Kate's voice softened. "I'm not one to speak ill, Daisy. But I wish your mother hadn't divorced. A girl needs her father."

Daisy laughed. "I have my father. They divorced each other, not me."

"Well, your parents are very different, Daisy, and what with running back and forth between them, I think you'd get confused."

"My parents don't confuse me," Daisy told her. "They love me and show it. They listen to my problems and sometimes even know when to leave me alone. Not always, but parents are like that. Best of all, they tell me I'm terrific and I shouldn't be afraid to make mistakes. I have girl friends who think they're failures because their parents never talk about the good stuff they do. They just yell about what they do wrong. I feel like a terrific person who's allowed to make mistakes. Don't you think that's important, Grandma, to hear how terrific you are?"

"Only when it's warranted, Daisy. Actions speak louder than words."

"People who feel terrific act terrific more often than people who feel like failures," Daisy said seriously. "What if I said you're a terrible grandma?"

"I'm no such thing!" Kate defended herself instantly.

"You're a wonderful grandma," Daisy agreed. "But if all you heard was how terrible you are, after a while you'd wonder. You might even get grumpy."

"Me? Never! Where do you get all these notions?"

"From my mother."

Kate clucked. "I've always wondered if you'd turn out like your mother, Daisy."

"I think I'll turn out like myself, Grandma, but if I ever have a daughter, I'll treat her the way Mom treats me."

"*Hmmm.* Well, just don't get divorced," Kate responded. "Mother of God, where's your mother? Such inconsideration!"

Jill heard coffee cups rattle and knew Kate had ended the conversation in a classic Kate way—washing dishes. She felt a tap on her shoulder and heard Julie's whisper. "What are you doing? I counted to forty-nine."

"I'm eavesdropping, and I'm so glad I did," Jill whispered with tears in her eyes. "I just found out I'm a good mother."

"Just now? How could you not know?" Julie was incredulous. "I just escaped from a mental institution, and I know I'm a good mother."

"I take after my daughter." Jill smiled. "I need to be told I'm terrific."

"Then I'm happy you heard. . . . My God . . . Ma!" Julie shrieked.

Kate stood in the doorway with a cast-iron frying pan held in both hands raised high over her head. "Mother of God! I almost whopped you! Julie! Julie! You're home!"

Kate folded Julie in a wrap-around hug and rocked her, crooning "My own Julie, my own little girl is home. Oh, sweetheart."

Jill stood to one side as Kate's cherishing arms enveloped Julie and Julie snuggled in the warm embrace. She felt the warmth reflected to her and was glad in her heart for them both.

"Let me look at you." Kate held Julie at arms' length. "Skinny. We'll soon fix that."

"Aren't you surprised to see me home, Ma?" Julie asked.

"Where else would you be?" Kate smiled. "I lit candles."

Now that they'd said hello, Jill couldn't restrain her curiosity. "What were you doing with that frying pan, Ma?"

"I heard voices. I thought you were burglars. So I sent Daisy upstairs and picked up the frying pan."

"Don't ever do that," Jill pleaded. "You hear a strange noise, you call the police. Killers break into houses, Ma, not people afraid of frying pans."

"Good thing for you I didn't. By now nine policemen would be taking my daughters away," Kate declared.

"Mom! I thought I heard you." Daisy bounced into the kitchen. "Here's the sweater you wanted, Grandma."

"You're Daisy." Julie smiled. "Other than growing, you haven't changed."

"Hello, Aunt Julie. Mom's told me all about you." Daisy's eyes sparkled with pleasure at the addition to her roots.

Kate beamed at Julie. "I'm so glad Dr. Kaiser released you from that horrible Wilbur State."

"He didn't release me, Ma," Julie told her. "Jill came right into the hospital and took me out."

"Took you . . . ?"

"Just like *The Great Escape.*" Julie grinned.

"You didn't!" Kate gasped.

"I did." Jill made an elaborate bow.

Kate regarded her steadily for what seemed like an interminable time, then opened her arms in invitation. "Come get a hug, Jill. You're terrific."

CHAPTER 31

"Good news, girls." Kate walked into the kitchen, her furry hat cradled under her arm like a pet raccoon. "Dr. Keriakan is going to meet us at the cemetery."

"Is a doctor required at a disinterment?" Julie asked.

"No," Kate replied. "I just thought it would be nice to ask him. He's practically a member of the family, what with curing me and pronouncing Pa dead."

"Why would a doctor go to a funeral?" Jill asked. "Do public defenders go to hangings?"

"He's not really coming to see Pa . . . uh . . . dislodged," Kate said. "He's coming to see me. He says he needs the inspiration of a patient who does what she's told. Then he said something about being driven crazy by Norman Cousins. Who's Norman Cousins?"

"A writer," Jill answered, puzzled.

Kate understood immediately. "Ah, one of those gotrocks who expect housecalls. What can be keeping Jim? I told him one o'clock sharp or we won't have time to trim around gloomy old Martha. Jill, call Daisy. She's upstairs with the scrapbooks."

"I'll get her," Jill volunteered, heading for the steps.

Kate indicated the bowl on the table before Julie. "More oatmeal?"

"No thanks, Ma." Julie smiled. "Three bowls in one day is enough."

"See, it's working already. You look so much better than you did last night."

"It was my first real night's sleep in over a week," Julie said, adding quickly, "Of course your oatmeal helped."

"It's just what you need. Rest. Vitamins. Wait! I have a wonderful idea. I'll ask Keriakan to prescribe a regime for you. That's what you need, not your sister's goofy psychiatrist stuff. You've always been the sensible one, Julie. Now Jill, she's something else."

"You're right, Ma," Julie agreed. "Jill isn't a sensible woman. A sensible woman wouldn't drop her life when one of us has a problem. She'd tell us she has problems of her own. A sensible woman would have left me in that snake pit overnight. A sensible woman doesn't wear her heart on her sleeve. If Jill was a sensible woman, I wouldn't be sitting here, would I?"

"Don't forget it was Jill who wanted to put me in a home!" Kate's eyes flashed. "I can't forgive that."

"Are you in a home, Ma?"

"Mother of God, no!" Kate said angrily. "The minute she said those horrible words, I got out of bed and came home!"

"What else would have gotten you out of that bed?"

"Well . . . uh . . ."

"Case closed." Julie grinned.

"You mean it was a trick?" Kate was dumbfounded. "Jill lied to her mother?"

"Jill always told the best stories, Ma, even when we were kids. I think it's her gift." Julie smiled with admiration. "I never would have thought to do that. Then, too, I was in a hurry to get back to Chicago, my children, and my job. *I* am a sensible woman."

"Still, Jill should be ashamed of her— She does wear her heart on her sleeve, doesn't she?" Kate mused. "How did I ever get a daughter like Jill?"

"You must have lit candles."

A few minutes later Daisy and Jill walked into the kitchen to the sound of laughter.

"I saw Mom's old report card," Daisy announced. "Boy, she used to be smart."

"Ah, the good old days before old age set in to addle me brain." It was the best brogue Jill could muster. "It's good to hear you laughing, Julie."

"Yoo-hoo." It was Jim, dressed in what had to be his very best suit and carrying a large wreath of gold-and-amber chrysanthemums. "Like it?"

"You wasted your money, Jim," Kate told him. "They don't allow wreaths in mausoleums.

"The wreath is for Martha," Jim said sheepishly. "I never bring her anything, and I'm not even putting her in the mausoleum, so—"

"But you can!" Kate said excitedly. "Martha could be right next to John. She'd love it!"

"But, Kate, if I did that, I'd have to spend the money I'm saving for a new car."

"Jim, I'm surprised at you! Thinking of money where Martha's concerned."

"Do you want to take our New England foliage tour next autumn in my old clunker?" Jim asked.

"On the other hand, rest in peace, I always say. Well, time to go." Kate hugged Daisy. "I'm so glad you're here, sweetheart. Your grandpa won't believe how much you've grown. We'll go in one car. A family should be together at a time like this."

Kate swept out the door with Jim and his chrysanthemums, leaving Jill, Julie, and Daisy shaking their heads and laughing.

"Promise to poke me if I laugh at the cemetery," Jill asked Julie.

Julie smiled. "I'll break your ribs if I have to. It's the least I can do after what you've done for me."

"Oh, boy," Daisy enthused. "We're going to Grandpa's funeral, and he's been dead for years. Wait'll I tell Lenny. And his family thought it was a big deal when his aunt ran off with a wetback."

"Small potatoes," Jill said.

"Hardly worth mentioning," Julie agreed.

The phone rang.

"I'll get it," Jill offered. "You and Daisy keep Ma from going into orbit."

Jill reached for the phone as Julie and Daisy followed Kate out the door.

"Hello."

"I got your message." It was Polly.

"I didn't call."

"I know. But I got your message."

"Polly." Jill smiled wistfully. "Whatever will I do without my pragmatic mystic?"

"I am available for luncheons, dinners, long chats, and other fringe benefits of friendship."

"My pleasure, Polly. Though I'm not certain I'll recognize you without your God-given typing. Which reminds me, there's something I'd like you to type for me."

"It's on your desk, Jill. Some vibrations are so strong and so right, they come through like a trumpet. I typed your resignation this morning."

482

"Oh, Polly, what can I say, except thank you? When I get back to Los Angeles, we'll dine in style."

"I'll be the lady at Chasen's with the glassy eyes." Polly laughed. "Neiman was at my apartment until one o'clock this morning waving executive résumés under my nose. He wants me to pick UBC's next president, and he doesn't care who'd be right for the job. He just wants someone who won't fire him."

"Situation normal," Jill proclaimed. "I'm leaving the network in good hands, Polly. Yours."

"I try, oh, God, I try." Polly chuckled. "Take care, Jill."

Jill hung up and fairly skipped out the door.

At the cemetery they tumbled out of the car like clowns out of a Volkswagen.

"Mother of God! My coat's covered with mum petals." Kate brushed herself vigorously. "Your wreath's shedding, you ninny."

"I'm sorry, Kate," Jim said apologetically. "It's winter. Flowers get brittle."

"Now, don't stand there with a long face. It's only flowers, not tar." Kate pointed toward a hilly section. "Go give Martha her wreath. If you're late, we'll start without you."

"Where are we going?" Daisy whispered to Jill.

"The mausoleum, I think," Jill said. "Just follow Grandma."

Julie and Daisy started after Kate.

"Jill," Jim called her softly. "Don't be offended, but I'm going to stay with Martha until your Pa is . . . This is for family."

"You're part of the family, Jim."

"Your Pa wouldn't think so," Jim said. "Maybe Kate won't notice."

"I doubt that, but I understand. See you later." Jill waved at him and ran to catch up with Julie and Daisy, who hadn't yet caught up with Kate. "Where is Ma going?" Jill asked Julie. "The mausoleum is in the other direction."

"Grandma walks fast for an older lady," Daisy panted.

"Ma does everything fast," Julie agreed. "Shoots first and never asks questions. Saves a lot of energy that way."

"I think Ma's going to Pa's old grave," Jill said. "I'll catch her and ask."

Jill ran after Kate, who was scooting along at an awesome pace.

"Ma, Ma, *Ma*!" Jill called.

"Don't hoot in the cemetery," Kate called back over her shoulder. "Where's your respect?"

Jill caught up with Kate as she crested a shallow slope. "Ma, this is the way to Pa's grave."

"You think I don't know where I'm going?" Kate was insulted. "I told Mr. Peters, the mortuary man, I want to see Pa's casket raised."

"Ma, why?" Jill asked. "I thought we would gather in the mausoleum, and Pa would . . . uh . . . already be there."

"Three years ago I spent a fortune for what Mr. Peters guaranteed was an airtight vault. I want to see for myself that I got what I paid for. No one's going to switch caskets on me!"

"Nobody would switch caskets, Ma."

"Oh, no?" Kate snorted. "What about Lee Harvey Oswald? I heard on the news he's not even in his grave."

"Ma, that's just an old rumor. And it's got nothing to do with caskets."

Kate shook a finger under Jill's nose. "Your father used to say 'Cravats emperor,' let the buyer be there."

"Ma." Jill groaned and huffed after Kate, who'd resumed scooting. "Seeing Pa's casket raised will only upset you."

Kate stopped in mid-scoot, hand poised on bosom. "Are you telling me you don't want to see your own father's casket raised?"

"Of course I do, Ma, but . . . no! I don't want to see it. That's last on the list of things I want to see, ever!"

"What's going on?" Julie asked as she and Daisy finally caught up.

"Your sister thinks I'm upsetting myself, and I'm not. I'm a bereaved widow who paid for an airtight vault with her deceased husband's hard-earned money. I owe it to Pa to see he didn't spring a leak."

"Ma!" Julie blanched.

"If Mr. Peters didn't bury Pa properly the first time, I won't give him a second shot."

"Oh boy," Daisy enthused. "Grandma sounds like an irate consumer."

"I only tilt at windmills," Jill sighed. "Ma builds them."

"Grandma's right," Daisy decided. "If Grandpa isn't airtight, she should write to Ralph Nader."

"Thank you, Daisy." Kate smiled smugly and scooted off, hopping tombstones set flush in the ground.

"There's Keriakan." Julie pointed at a burly figure lumbering toward them from the opposite direction.

Ahead lay Pa's gravesite, now a yawning hole with dirt piled on all sides. Behind it, three bored-looking workmen in coveralls leaned on shovels. To the left, a short, bald man eyed Kate apprehensively as she approached him full steam. To the right was a lady who resembled, and was, a streamlined Candy. Gone was the Tammy Wynette hair, flounces, and Barbie-Doll pout, replaced by short curls framing her face, moss-green corduroy suit, and a lively expression. The total effect was vibrantly feminine.

"That's your Aunt Candy," Jill told Daisy.

"I don't remember Aunt Candy. She looks like Jane Fonda," Daisy noted with admiration.

"I don't remember that Aunt Candy, either." Julie was wide-eyed. "What's happened to her?"

Jill smiled. "She's surviving."

They approached the grave, where Mr. Peters was rubbing hands and frowning at Kate. "This is most unusual, Mrs. Dunn. I do wish you'd wait in the mausoleum."

"Hoist," Kate ordered.

Mr. Peters signaled the workmen, who moved toward the pit.

"I feel a rite of passage coming on," Jill said to Daisy. "My first leaping heart."

"If this is going to bother you, Mom, don't look," Daisy advised.

"Good idea." Jill turned her back, noting with some amusement that Daisy and Julie did likewise.

"This must be Daisy." Candy approached them, smiling. "You're the image of your mother, honey."

"Different noses, see?" Daisy turned profile to demonstrate.

"It was nice of you to come, Candy," Jill greeted her.

Candy smiled. "I think I'm the consort standing in for the king."

"We've all been that," Julie remarked.

"Well, well, well." Keriakan joined them. "Here's the whole family. The whole healthy family. Doesn't your mother look wonderful, like a red-haired Helen Hayes? *Spry*'s the word. Spry and healthy." He waved at Kate, who ignored him, preoccupied as she was with staring into the hole.

"What's that noise?" Jill asked Daisy.

"A winch, mom. They're using a block-and-tackle thing."

"Oh, God." Jill shuddered.

"If I'd developed my regime earlier, your father would be here instead of *here*," Keriakan said regretfully. "Have you people read *Anatomy of an Illness*?"

485

"Norman Cousins wrote it!" Jill exclaimed. "I knew I'd recognized the name."

"That bastard is ruining my practice," Keriakan moaned. "A book on how to get well by laughing! Laughing! None of my patients want to try the regime. They want to check into hotels and watch Marx Brothers movies. *Pah!*"

"Are they getting well?" Jill asked.

"Who cares? I'm going to talk to your mother. Now, *she's* what I call a patient!"

Keriakan deserted them, moving toward the sound of the ghastly grinding.

Candy smiled warmly at Julie. "I'm so glad to see you, Julie. For all you've been through, you look so much better than I've ever seen you."

"I am better, Candy, and I know I'll be better yet." Julie seemed to glow from within. "For the first time in years I'm looking forward to tomorrow."

Watching her, Jill felt a rush of gratitude, a free release of delight. Julie's smile was the shining quicksilver lost since their childhood, the smile of an eager, curious child with her whole life ahead.

"Jill! Julie! Daisy! Come here!" Kate shouted.

"Oh, God," Jill breathed, bracing herself.

Reluctantly Jill walked over to where Kate was standing, looking at everything, everyone, except *it*.

"Look." Kate gestured at the coffin. Jill looked at the trees.

"It's somewhat scuffed, I know, Mrs. Dunn," Mr. Peters said anxiously, his hands clasped together. "But, after all—"

Kate cut him short. "Why shouldn't it be scuffed? It's been buried."

"Then it's all right, Ma?" Jill asked hesitantly.

"Of course it's all right. I wanted my money's worth, not a miracle. This is a . . . uh . . . dismissal . . . not the Resurrection. If only my house was that airtight, my gas bills wouldn't be . . . Now, what's keeping Jim? He never has two words for Martha. If he's edging without me . . ."

"May we proceed, Mrs. Dunn?" Mr. Peters unclasped, greatly relieved.

"Proceed away." Kate waved her hand imperiously, like the off-with-their-heads! queen. "We'll start without Jim."

Jill continued to avoid the casket as the workmen loaded it onto a dolly. The women and Keriakan waited, gathered close to Kate's cherry-red coat as though to a warming fire.

"Mrs. Dunn." Keriakan smiled his pudding-faced version of "friendly." "I know how highly you regard my regime. Therefore I have no hesitation in asking you to provide a testimonial . . . just a few paragraphs in your own words, saying something simple like . . . oh . . . um . . . it saved your life."

"Maybe it did, maybe it didn't." Kate's eyes narrowed. "What kind of testimonial is 'maybe'?"

"Better than none. Enough to convince those bozos that laughing—"

"Is that why you came here?" Kate demanded. "To ask for a testimonial?"

"Well . . ."

"Go home. Vamoose," Kate ordered. "This is a family occasion."

"But . . ."

"Scat." Kate stamped her foot.

Keriakan took a step backward. "You've developed a mercurial temperament, Mrs. Dunn. Perhaps a checkup is in order."

"I am a rock," Kate snorted. "Good-bye."

They watched as Keriakan shambled off, mumbling to himself.

Kate humphed in her throat. "The next time I invite a stranger to a family occasion, remind me of this. Who needs a doctor in sheep's clothing?"

"Ma." Jill pointed at Mr. Peters, who looked impatient but professionally solemn. "They're ready." She glanced to one side, looking for Daisy, then shivered, her heart turned to ice. Quite inadvertently her gaze had fallen and focused on the dull bronze rectangle lashed to the dolly.

Pa. Oh, Pa.

"Please follow me." Mr. Peters walked well ahead of them, leading the workmen, while the women followed, walking slowly behind.

As they walked they drifted closer together, until at the crest of the slope they were elbow to elbow, each moving in step with the other's rhythm, a blending of bodies and memories.

Julie broke the silence. "Remember the winter when Pa was in bed with pneumonia, and Mr. Perkins next door had a stroke? He got right out of bed and went over."

"I remember," Jill said. "Poor old Mrs. Perkins was so upset. Pa handled everything, doctors, ambulance, hospitals."

Kate nodded. "Pa was so good with elderly people. So patient, so gentle, so kind."

"Sick people, too," Jill added. "I can still see Pa sitting on the edge of my bed when I had the flu, cool cloth in one hand and a dish of rhubarb in the other."

"Pa thought rhubarb was all sick kids should eat." Julie laughed softly. "How sour it was!"

"Pa stewed it himself." Kate smiled. "Cut in pieces exactly three inches long and boiled in six quarts of water. I'll never know where he got that recipe. It tasted like boiled tin cans."

"When I married Johnny, Pa took me aside," Candy remembered. "He gave me a bear hug and a kiss, then asked me how John had managed to snag such a beauty. He made me believe it. On my wedding day I felt beautiful."

"Gallant." Jill smiled. "Pa was old-fashioned gallant."

"I wish I'd known Grandpa," Daisy said wistfully.

"You should have known him, Daisy." There were tears in Jill's eyes. "It's not fair that you didn't. But none of us did. Pa died too soon."

"I never kissed him good-bye," Julie said regretfully. "The last time I saw him I just waved and ran out the doors. If I'd known it would be the last time . . . Oh, Ma, I wish Pa was here so I could kiss him good-bye!"

"Such a lonely man." Kate had started to cry. "So much he held inside."

"I miss him," Jill whispered. "I miss the pa who loved us."

"Aw, girls." Kate sighed through her tears. "Your pa knew you loved him for the love he gave you, but I wish from my heart he could hear you say so now. Pa died thinking he hadn't been a very good father."

"But he was!" Jill cried. "If only he'd lived long enough to . . . Ma, look!"

Jill pointed in the direction of the mausoleum. In the shadow of the marble archway a tall man stood with his back to them.

"Johnny!" Jill called.

He swung quickly and saw them, an entourage of women walking like wraiths behind a scuffed bronze casket. He ran toward them, his father's long black coat flapping behind him.

Together they watched John approach, each woman in separate contemplation of son, husband, and brother—the man who carried his father within him, his essence and memory.

As do we all, essence and memory, and, finally, the truth that will keep us from repeating the past.

"Thank God you're here." John was breathless, his face pale with exhaustion and relief. "I arrived at the mausoleum, and no one was there. I thought I'd come too late."

"We're so glad you came, Johnny." Jill smiled at him.

"Hello, John," Candy said softly.

"Jill told me you'd be here," John said, almost shyly. "When I thought I'd missed you . . . May we talk later?"

"In your office?" Candy asked hesitantly, her caution born of hard-won survival.

"At home. I'd like to come home."

"It's your home, Johnny. We'll talk."

"Thank you." John turned to Kate, whose face was buried in trembling hands. "Why are you crying, Ma? Tell me."

"You look so much like your pa, and you're so much like him inside. Only the best of him, Johnny, only the best. Pa would be so proud of you." Kate was a blur as she threw herself into Johnny's arms. "I should have known you'd be here."

John's tall form bent over Kate, his arms wrapping her in a protective cocoon. His eyes were closed, his hand stroking her back as he whispered to her in a voice they all heard. "Pa was a good man who loved me. His love was confused, but it was love nonetheless. Pa gave us his best, Ma, and then some. That's all anyone can do."

As John and Kate stood motionless Jill instinctively reached out, needing to touch Johnny and through him the father they'd both loved.

Johnny looked up, then opened his arms to include her, to include all of them.

They moved into his arms, Julie, Daisy, Candy, and Jill, forming an embracing circle with Kate as its center. Arms interlocked and heads bowed, they swayed with a gentle motion, sharing their comfort, sharing their tears.

Detached from the world and oblivious to it, the Dunn family huddled together, mourning not mystery or myth, tyrant or saint, but a man, a brave, lonely man who'd loved his family and done the best he could.

EPILOGUE

I bought the house on the beach for Daisy and me.

We moved in on a day when the world looked as God must have intended on the day of Creation.

We spent half a morning unpacking boxes while casting longing looks at the beach and ocean just outside our thrown-open windows.

Finally Daisy asked, "Will the police come and take us away if we don't finish unpacking today?"

"I don't think so, Daisy," I replied. "But the men in white coats should if we do."

So we adjourned to the beach, where we walked, then ran (with Daisy thoughtfully setting a slow pace), then sat watching the ocean and talking.

"I didn't know there could be so many shades of blue," Daisy remarked.

"And purple and gray and green. We'll see the ocean change with the seasons, Daisy."

"I'm glad we moved to a place with seasons, Mom. The same weather all the time can be boring, like all work and no play."

We watched the sunset that day, as I have every day since. Later we cooked our first meal together, then laid a fire in the fireplace, and sat watching it, feeling the new house around us slowly transformed into our home.

We moved to a different rhythm here, or rather two different rhythms, Daisy's and mine. When Daisy isn't busy with activities at the new school she loves, or in town, shopping with girl friends, or off with Lenny at some ranch visiting the horses his father moved to be close to, she joins me for sunsets.

"I'm glad we moved here, Mom. I feel like I'm living my life."

"Strange you should say that, Daisy. I was just thinking that, too."

Connection. The best of all worlds. A parent and child who can also be friends.

I spend my days in the room with the stained-glass windows, rolling sheets of blank paper into a typewriter, then rolling them out covered with words, and most often straight into the wastepaper basket. Perhaps that should bother me, but it doesn't. The work I do now is the only work that for me is home run and birth and passion. The pages that go into the box kept on my desk for that purpose please me more than any forty-six share.

"Are you going to sit there in your bathrobe and type forever?" Daisy's query of a late afternoon.

"Not forever, Daisy. I promise I won't miss your wedding."

"There's a bicycle-rental place near the marina, Mom. People rent bikes and ride along the ocean."

"I haven't ridden a bike in years."

"They say you never forget."

"I haven't forgotten, Daisy. When I was a kid, I fell off more than I rode."

"We'll get a bike built for two, Mom. I'll balance. You pump."

"An arrangement like that could save marriages, Daisy. Let's go."

Julie calls from time to time. At first she called twice weekly from Ma's, full of anxiety one time, bursting with hope the next. Whichever emotion compelled her to call, my message was much the same: "It takes time, Julie. Be kind to yourself."

"I won't forget," she'd say. "Realistic expectations and one step at a time."

Julie's calls are no longer "emergency hotline!" Her anxieties have been alleviated by the progress she's made and her hopes, still high, generate energy she turns to the task of rebuilding her life.

She's gone back to Chicago, but not to Fred, who continues to mourn his "old Julie" while developing a fledgling fascination for the new one. His interest is as obvious to Julie as is his need to deny it, particularly to himself.

"For the first time in his life, Fred is confused," Julie laughed to me over the phone.

"Confused and pompous is an unusual combination, Julie." I said, substituting *dreadful* for *unusual* in my head.

"Somehow I find it endearing, Jill. I've never thought of Fred as a man who might need some looking after, himself."

"Realistic expectations," I cautioned.

"I know. I'll wait and see."

While Julie's waiting and seeing she's resumed teaching the classes she loves while dropping everything else, the self-imposed punishments of her schedule. She sees her children daily and on weekends takes them home to the apartment she's grown to cherish as her own special place. She told me she's surprised at how much fun Morgan and Kendrick are now. I suspect it's Julie who's grown more adept at funmaking.

Johnny calls on special occasions, meaning the proper ones—birthdays and holidays, both national and religious, and, peculiarly, his wedding anniversary. But call he does, and when he does, he puts business on hold and actually chats.

"What's the weather like?" John's standard opening question.

"Beautiful. Come out for a vacation sometime. Both you and Candy would love Santa Barbara, and the kids would adore the ocean."

"If I can ever get away for that long." John paused, evidently thinking. "You know, Jill, that's not a bad idea. I've promised Candy a family vacation, and California would be interesting for us all."

"When?"

"In six months," he said quickly. "That's a promise."

"I love you, Johnny."

"I love you, too, Jill. You're one of my favorite redheads."

Candy tells me John's already worried that vacation-getaway day will dawn with shipments stuck in Buffalo and orders unfilled. Yet he remains resolute, grimly determined to take this vacation and, by God, enjoy it.

"Men have marched to their executions with more enthusiasm," Candy giggled on the phone.

"Once he's here, he'll enjoy himself, Candy."

"We'll see. He's stockpiling paperwork to bring with him and already has a footlocker full. But it's an improvement, Jill. We haven't gone on vacation in six years."

"One step at a time and realistic expectations, Candy."

"I'll say. Well, got to run. I'm putting in a patio, and if I don't watch the kids every minute, they'll write their names in the wet cement."

Often Daisy and I have visitors. I'd like to think it's my charisma that brings them up the coast, but I suspect they're attracted at least equally by Santa Barbara's beauty and peace. And why not? That's why I moved here.

Dan usually arrives before sunset, which we watch together before going to dinner at the small restaurant I discovered with Daisy and Lenny. Though it lacks the status of L.A.'s "in" restaurants, it's Dan's favorite, too, and perhaps for that reason. The new president of UBC remains unimpressed by status.

"Were you surprised when I returned to UBC?" he asked at our first dinner.

"No. Television is your home run."

"Neiman was flabbergasted," Dan chuckled. "When he heard that the executive board hired me without consulting him, he fainted dead away in the halls."

"Are you going to fire Neiman, Dan?"

"No. Every company has its Neiman. They do nothing good but little that's actually harmful, and their jobs are their lives. I'll put him in charge of something ambiguous and try not to scream when he yesses me to death."

"Are you happy now, Dan?"

"I have part of what I need, Jill. I like the work I'm doing even more now that I have some perspective. As for my personal life . . . all in time. And you?"

"Work and love, Dan. I have both. The love part is Daisy, in case you're wondering."

"I was. If you ever want a job with me . . . "

"I'll ask. Asking you for what I need has never been a problem for me."

"Nor for me, Jill. That makes you very special in my life."

Polly kept her promise of friendship. The first time she visited, Daisy was instantly charmed, and the three of us laughed and chatted so far into the night that Polly slept over, making it a slumber party.

"Where is your God-given typing, Polly?"

"I had it surgically removed before I drove up the coast."

"You look radiant without it."

"That's not the sole reason for my glowing good looks. Dan Carmichael has asked me to be his secretary, and Alex is gone with the wind."

"Dan fired him?"

"No. Alex quit. He said it was because of 'creative differences,' but truth is, Dan wouldn't respond to his rantings, and Alex can stand anything except being ignored."

"You're telling me? Alex thinks brilliance is having six tricks and a good hustle. What will happen to him, Polly?"

"Weep not. Alex won't wander the cold, mean streets. He's . . . Let's see how he announced it. . . . Oh, yes . . . 'giving up my own pursuits to manage my wife's career.'"

"Nina?"

"She's going to be a superstar, Jill. I know that psychically. And it's already happening. She's been offered the lead in a movie that's going to be a major success."

"But she hate's acting!"

"Acting is giving her ulcers, but Alex takes care of that. When Nina's too sick to act, he pops cookies down her throat, and, by God, she acts."

Jill shook her head. "I'm sure Alex tells her it's for her own good."

"I'm sure he even believes it."

"Not entirely, Polly, not deep in his heart. For some reason I believe Alex's story about being a little boy alone in the dark, hugging his mother's mink. He still is."

Steve all but abandoned Daisy's weekends with him in favor of weekends with us, a situation that could have been strained had he not been so straightforward.

"I'd like to spend time with you both, Jill, but I don't want to intrude."

"I wouldn't let you intrude on me, Steve."

"I'll stay in a hotel when I'm here."

"That would be wise, Steve. We don't want Daisy spinning fantasies from nothing."

"Perhaps she's not the only one spinning lately. We did have some good times, didn't we, Jill?"

"The best of times and the worst of times, Steve. The most important parts of life are somehow always both."

"Important. That it was. Maybe . . ."

Ma and Jim have been talking about marriage. Rather, Jim's been proposing, and Ma's been refusing.

"Why would I want to marry the old goat?" Ma asked me on the phone.

"Companionship, Ma. Someone to share your life."

"Ha! He's here for breakfast. He's here for dinner. I do his laundry. What's left to share?"

"Ma, there are certain comforting intimacies between husband and wife—"

494

"Mother of God! Watch your mouth!"

"Jim finds you attractive, Ma, and he's rather attractive himself."

"The day I give up my independence for a pair of cold feet in my bed . . ."

"You can still think it over, Ma."

"Jim is a wonderful person, Jill, and I love him like a friend, but if I ever get married again, it'll be to someone I love as madly as I did your father."

"Ma! You're a romantic!"

"Ah, sure I am, Jill." Kate laughed like a girl. "And why wouldn't I be? It's the gift of my Irish blood!"

Often Daisy reads over my shoulder in the room with the stained-glass windows.

"Not bad, Mom. The lady in your story sounds just like Grandma. I wonder what she'll say about that?" Daisy waits, something else on her mind. "Lenny says I'm getting to be more like you every day."

Ah, Daisy's worried.

"I'm sure he means only superficially, honey, red hair and . . ."

"Don't get all tweaked, Mom." This with a laugh. "I could do worse."

Sometimes when I'm walking the beach I think of a line from Robert Frost: "Home is the place where, when you go there, they have to take you in."

And I ponder.

From the cave-dwellers to now, only one human link has sustained —the imperative call of blood to blood and the need to huddle together in families.

So it has been and will always be, to futures beyond imagining.

There's reason for optimism.